Arundel Haven

book one-Mordecai and Raven

Arundel Haven

book one-Mordecai and Raven

Jeffrey Jacobs

ARPress
45 Dan Road Suite 5
Canton MA 02021

Hotline: 1(888) 821-0229
Fax: 1(508) 545-7580

Ordering Information:
Quantity sales. Special discounts are available on quantity purchases by corporations, associations, and others. For details, contact the publisher at the address above.

Printed in the United States of America.

ISBN-13:   Paperback   979-8-89389-551-3
                  eBook   979-8-89389-553-7
                  Hardback   979-8-89389-552-0

Library of Congress Control Number: 2024920619

Table Contents

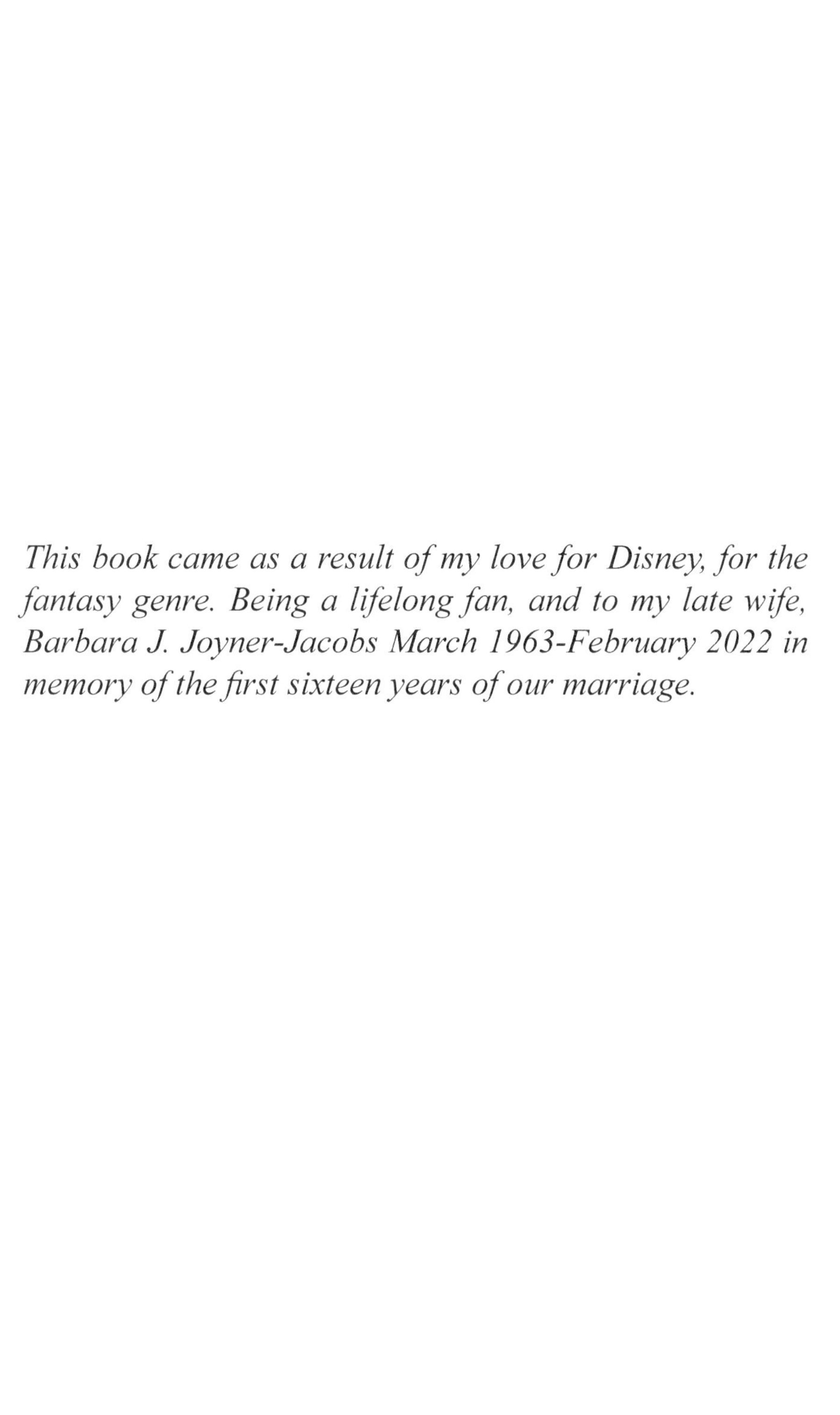

This book came as a result of my love for Disney, for the fantasy genre. Being a lifelong fan, and to my late wife, Barbara J. Joyner-Jacobs March 1963-February 2022 in memory of the first sixteen years of our marriage.

Chapter One

Arundel Haven.

Those words had been on the mind of world-renowned geneticist, Dr. Haman Von Braun, for most of his life. Ever since he found a book dealing with the existence of fairies and their secret kingdom during his days at Oxford, before he had graduated in 1971 at 24 years old. He had read about the kingdom and the secret people and was convinced they really existed. Wisely, he kept it much to himself, save when he felt they knew something about fairies. He had spent many years finding evidence of their existence. He was more convinced when, one day, on a camping trip in England, he caught a glimpse of a fairy in the woods. He tried to follow but the fairy had taken to the air and disappeared. He was angry with himself for not having a camera to take a picture. So, he kept on with his secret obsession.

Now, at 63 years old, he was exceedingly rich, and one of the top geneticists in the world, well respected in his field. He had moved from his base of operations in London to the most lavish communities in the Orlando, Florida area. He was invited to different universities to speak and was granted a job at the University of Central Florida where he taught genetics. He had heard the rumor years before of sightings of fairies in a heavily wooded area in the Orlando area and wanted to check out the lead. He was healthy for his age, had grey hair, green eyes, stood just over six feet tall, slim and fit. His 205-pound frame was covered with a light grey suit and pants, a white shirt and a black tie, which was his favorite outfit. Whatever rumors he had heard about fairies, he was eager to follow it up. He had hoped to find a fairy and find out the location of the hidden kingdom, Arundel Haven.

He was very close to the President of the United States, Ahmad Farouk, who had been elected in 2008 and re-elected the past year. He was in his second term now. It was felt he was elected for the color of his skin (he was black) than the key issues. He was 50 years old, had short black hair, with a short moustache on his face. He wore a black suit over a white shirt and black tie. He did all he could to push his policies around the Constitution, pushing the agendas he espouses, even if a lot of Americans disagreed with him. He was charismatic, an eloquent speaker. He knew about Dr. Von Braun's interest in proving the existence of fairies and of Arundel Haven. They talked and became fast friends. Von Braun and President Farouk would meet as often as their schedules would allow. Von Braun had shown the President the book he had found and kept from his days at Oxford.

'They are theories only, most of them,' he told the President, 'I had seen a fairy with my own eyes before, but unfortunately, did not have a camera at the time. It would be foolish for me to reveal this without empiric proof of their existence.'

'You investigate each rumor you hear?' President Farouk asked. 'Most of them, yes,' Dr. Von Braun answered, 'but most of them are just rumors, unfortunately. I have every intention of finding their hidden kingdom of Arundel Haven. What secrets could be found there?'

'Indeed,' President Farouk answered. 'I once heard of such a rumor, but I had dismissed it at first, but now that I hear you are investigating this, it began to pique my interest. I had discovered something that I cannot reveal to you at this point in time because it is unrelated to your quest of finding the mythical fairy kingdom. If such a place exists, what a find it would be.'

Dr. Von Braun nodded. He drank another round of vodka. President Farouk had a small glass of whiskey. 'Where are you living now, Haman?' he asked.

'Right now, I am living in Orlando,' Dr. Von Braun answered, 'I am teaching classes at the local university. There had been two sightings of fairies in a heavily wooded area. True, it is only a rumor, but if there is a possibility that it could be true, then I think it's worth investigating. I may find evidence yet.'

'And you have kept this fascination a secret all these years?'

Dr. Von Braun nodded. 'It doesn't make sense revealing it without proof,' he told his friend, 'I had seen one myself, but I prefer to have proof, ere I make it known.' He raised his glass. 'The American people are wise to re-elect you, Mr. President,' he smiled.

'My enemies are many,' President Farouk said, 'but I have the media on my side and groups that would do anything to defend me. I have been very good to them, and they have been very good to me. How many people know of your secret obsession?'

'Very few,' Dr. Von Braun answered, 'but once I gather evidence, maybe capture a real, live fairy, then secrets are no longer a concern. People would think me a madman if I had made it public, especially without sufficient evidence, without proof.'

President Farouk drank his whiskey. 'Nothing like a good shot of your favorite poison to make the day,' he said.

'I am disappointed you do not have any scotch,' he frowned. 'Vodka is fine, and I like vodka, but I am more partial to scotch. I'm not complaining, mind you.'

President Farouk laughed. 'Understood,' he nodded. 'I never was a scotch man myself. I do like tequila and a good beer as well.'

'Depends on the beer,' Dr. Von Braun replied, 'A beer is especially good when it's ice cold. Who likes a warm beer, anyhow? Does sound ridiculous.'

'And how are things going at your job there?'

'Quite well, actually,' Dr. Von Braun answered. 'It serves me well as a cover to my real intentions, though I must do my searching on my own personal time as to not arouse any suspicions. From time to time, there are some young ladies who do believe the old stories. Separating fact from the myth is a trying job in itself.'

'More vodka?' the president asked, rising up from his desk. Dr. Von Braun nodded. 'Don't mind if I do,' he nodded.

President Farouk poured the doctor another drink. 'As of now,' Dr. Von Braun said as he took the glass, 'there has been no significant progress in finding any leads to Arundel Haven.'

'Any ideas where it could be?' asked the president.

'No leads as yet to even the possible general area of where it could be,' answered Dr. Von Braun. 'I have heard of a report of possible remains of what some believed to be a fairy somewhere deep in the woods. I will not know until I look at the remains myself. If it is, I can take DNA samples from the remains and study them. It will give me some idea of what they are like. From the fairy I'd seen, they are human-like in appearance except for having wings. I will know more as I come across the evidence.'

'I am curious to know myself,' President Farouk replied, pouring himself another glass of whiskey. 'I will see about getting you some scotch when you come here to the White House on your next visit,' he continued. 'You will keep me up-to-date on your search for fairies and Arundel Haven?'

'As they become available,' answered Dr. Von Braun. 'I can only hope something will break for me soon on this. All this searching has been exasperating, to say the least. I am anxious to find more proof, any clues to the existence of Arundel Haven.'

The president nodded. 'I look forward to hearing the reports,' he said.

After he was done teaching for the day, Dr. Von Braun packed up his materials, placed them inside his briefcase, and prepared to leave for the day. At that moment, his cell phone rang. He pulled it out of his pocket and spoke. 'Hello?'

'Doctor, it's Seymour,' the voice said.

'Have you followed up on the lead?'

'That I did, sir,' came the voice of Seymour. 'I'm afraid it's just another dead end. I am keeping my ear to the ground to see if I hear anything else.'

'Keep at it, Seymour,' ordered Dr. Von Braun. 'I know there are fairies out there somewhere, there must be someone who knows and has encountered a fairy.'

'I don't think there would be anyone who knows, Doctor.'

'There must be!' the doctor replied sharply. 'I feel it this time! I believe the rumors are true. Unlike the other times, I feel I am getting closer to finding a fairy.'

'That doesn't seem to be the case, Doctor, with all due respect.'

'I pay you and Wilfred, and I pay you both well to find out, to listen to any rumor of possible fairy sightings, do I not?'

After a pause, Seymour with a sigh said, 'Yes you do.'

'Keep up the search, Seymour, you and Wilfred,' he told the caller. 'Sooner or later, we will find what we're looking for. Keep your eyes and ears open, both of you.'

'As you wish, sir,' Seymour replied as Dr. Von Braun hung up the cell phone and placed it back in his pocket.

Chapter Two

Mordecai sighed.

He tossed his books down on the bed. The dirty, blonde-haired white youth sat down at his desktop and hung his head low. The seventeen-year-old sighed as he sat there, his blue eyes vacant and full of pain. He felt alone in the world. He was six feet tall and was a slim 185-pounds, wore dark blue pants and a white shirt. His hair was short and neatly trimmed and combed. He rubbed his head, it was throbbing. He'd had a bad encounter with three football players at school who had been teasing and harassing him ever since he'd known them. He was still hurting from the beating he had received from the men. He painfully rose to his feet. His legs were hurting, his body was hurting, as well as his shoulders. He winced in pain as he headed into the bathroom, grabbed a towel, and took a hot bath to see if it would help.

Thirty minutes later, he was lying down on his bed. He was listening to a song on his laptop and reading the Bible. He was dressed in black slacks and a black shirt. He was still hurting as he lay upon the bed.

He heard a knock on the door. Staring at it, he asked, 'Who is it?"

The door opened. A red-haired girl, 15 years old, walked through the door. She was slim, stood five feet, eight inches tall and wore black slacks and a pink blouse. She had a golden necklace of a fairy hanging around her neck. Around each wrist was a charm bracelet, the left bracelet had the letters of her name, Cece. Mordecai sighed as he looked at her. 'At least you knocked,' he said as he painfully stood up. 'I thought you would be spending time with Oscar.'

Cece shook her head, sighing. 'I don't know what's going on,' she sighed. 'For the past week, Oscar's been avoiding me for some reason. I called and left messages. When I had seen him, he said, "I'm sorry, Cece, but I've been busy." He wouldn't tell me why he was busy. He's been giving me the run-around.'

Mordecai groaned as he stood there. 'Why has he been avoiding you?' he asked. 'You think he may be seeing someone else?'

Cece sighed. 'I don't know,' she answered. 'Whenever I see him and confront him, he avoids answering the question. I don't understand.' She watched as Mordecai moved around slowly. 'What happened to you?'

'Three things: Frank McCoy, Stu Hatfield, and Chuck Jones,' he winced in pain, 'Up to their old tricks again. They roughed me up today.'

'Say what?' exclaimed Cece. 'Why are they allowed to do this? Why do they love to pick on you?'

Mordecai sighed. 'It seems they get preferential treatment because they are the stars of the football team,' the young man groaned 'I told one of my teachers, but they refused to believe me.'

Cece shook her head. 'I don't understand that,' she exclaimed, 'Why won't the teachers do anything? Just because they're star football players doesn't give them the right to do what they are doing to you and to others like you. To me, that sounds like favoritism.'

'I know,' groaned Mordecai. 'It's frustrating! It's been like that since I was a freshman.' He moved toward the door. 'I got to go downstairs and get something to drink.'

Cece saw the way her older brother moved. 'Judas Priest, looks like they did a number on you,' she exclaimed. 'How can the teachers allow this to go on? I wonder how many others they've been bullying?'

'I'm sure there are others, but as far as I know, just me,' said Mordecai, moving slowly out the door. 'It's as if those teachers have become a part of what McCoy, Hatfield and Jones are doing. This should not be happening!'

'Are you sure you're okay, Mordy?' Cece asked.

'I'll have to be,' Mordecai groaned. 'Got to go to school tomorrow.'

'Have you spoken to Mom and Dad about it?'

'I tried, but they're too busy,' Mordecai answered. 'It seems they're always too busy for me. Not for you, Cece, or Randall, though.'

'That's not true, Mordy,' Cece disagreed. 'Mom and Dad love you, too.'

Mordecai shook his head. 'I don't feel it,' he frowned as they walked down the stairs, 'I honestly don't feel that. I feel more left in the shadows a lot.'

They reached the end of the stairs. 'Why do you say that?' Cece asked.

Mordecai stopped in front of the stairs. 'Randall started driving when he was your age,' he told his sister. 'How long has Dad been teaching you to drive?'

'A few weeks,' Cece answered.

'I am 17 years old, and I am still riding a bike to school, not been offered to be taught how to drive by Mom or Dad,' he said, frustration in his voice. 'What's wrong with that picture? It just doesn't seem fair, Cece, because you're being taught to drive while I'm not. Can you tell me why I am not being taught? Can you tell me why I'm not allowed to drive?'

Cece shook her head. 'No.'

Mordecai made his way to the kitchen and grabbed a soda. 'They won't even allow me to have a job,' he continued. 'I don't understand that!'

'Maybe it's because you suffer from depression,' Cece stated.

Mordecai stared at his sister. He felt the frustration building inside. 'Does it warrant them treating me like… like…' He struggled to find the right words. 'What they're doing to me is just making my problem worse!' he said sharply. 'I'm frustrated! I feel like I'm nothing to them; a loser and a nobody like the voices had been telling me!' He turned away. 'Why was I even born to begin with?' He sat down at the table.

'Did you take your antidepressants this morning?' Cece asked.

'I've been taking them, but they haven't been helping,' frowned Mordecai, frustration in his voice. 'People seem to think all I need are therapy and antidepressants, that's it! No love, moral or emotional support from loved ones to help me beat this devil! I'm forced to face it alone, all alone in the world with no help! I'm in a hopeless losing battle being all alone!' He paused as he stared at Cece. 'Do you know what it's like to have no friends at all, nobody to help deal with the hurt, the pain inside? I am ostracized in part because of the depression, not just for my faith!' He burst into tears. 'Cece, I wish you could understand my pain! The things I need to beat this depression have been denied to me!'

'And that is moral and emotional support?' Cece asked.

Mordecai nodded. 'Good friends whom I know will stand by me, to love and encourage me, basically a shoulder to lean on, to cry on. I've been denied that for so long. Do you know what that's like?'

Cece sighed. 'No,' she softly answered. 'I had no idea. You mean you have nobody at all? Not even in church?'

Mordecai shook his head. 'It seems they're too busy doing "the work of the Lord" to deal with the hurting and the broken hearted.'

'That's not right,' Cece exclaimed. 'Didn't Jesus Himself love and care for the broken hearted?'

Mordecai nodded, drinking his soda. He wept softly as he drank. Cece bowed her head sadly. She sighed as she stared at her brother. She wished she knew what she could do for him, what words she could say to make him feel better. She found she had nothing to say.

Cece turned and walked away sadly as Mordecai sat alone, weeping.

Mordecai rose from the table minutes later and headed to the backyard. He stared out into the sky as the sun was setting. From time to time, he would see birds passing through the air, heard the cries of different birds. He drank the can of soda he had gotten from the refrigerator before he stepped outside. As the skies grew darker, he continued to stare at the sky. He then caught a brief glimpse of something in the air he thought was human shaped. He blinked. The shape was gone as quickly as it had appeared. What was it? Was his mind playing tricks on him? He rubbed his eyes. 'Maybe I just imagined it,' he sighed. Still, he couldn't help thinking what it was. He drank his soda. He couldn't quite explain in his mind what it was. He wondered who else saw it? Was it just him? 'Maybe my eyes are just playing tricks on me,' he sighed. After a while, he entered inside. He didn't see the shape again that day.

He painfully returned to his room. He laid back down on his bed and looked out the window. The sun had gone down, and the moon was beginning to rise in the night sky. Scattered about were stars shining in the night. He sighed. He felt discouraged and all alone in the world. He felt the pain growing stronger inside. He took out his Bible and started reading a little. Tears filled his eyes as he tried to read. He closed the book after a few minutes.

He knelt and prayed, not speaking an audible word, weeping as he remained there, unmoving. He remained there for so long he fell asleep in that position.

The next morning, Mordecai rode his bike to school, not wanting to take the bus. He'd had enough of the people on the bus teasing him and making fun of him taking his Bible to school. His books were bound and secured on the back of his ten-speed as he rode down the busy highway. It was over a five-mile bike ride from his home in the Southwood subdivision to Oak Ridge High, where he was now in his senior year. He felt he was the only senior in the whole school who was not driving a car. He had decided to take his bike instead of taking the bus after the first week of the new semester. He kept as close to the curve as possible as not to slow down traffic.

At that moment, a bus passed by. As it passed, a carton of orange juice flew his way and struck him on the head. He growled but pedaled on. He barely heard the brief laughter as the bus passed. He wiped the excess juice out of his hair. He knew he would have to go to the bathroom and wash the stickiness out of his hair and off his clothes. He sighed again. He wondered how much longer this would go on. He was so weary of the treatment, of the ridicule, of being bullied by fellow students, particularly by three of the star football players. He pedaled on. When he reached the school grounds, he chained his bike to the bike station, wrapping the chains around the wheels and the body. He secured the locks, took his books, and walked on campus.

After he washed the stickiness from his hair and clothes, he headed to his first class. He headed to his locker and grabbed his books. He was approached by Cece, who was in a cheerleader's outfit. The outfit was green and gold and had the school nickname "Pioneers" on it. He stared at her. 'You got cheerleading practice again?'

'What happened to you?' Cece asked.

'Some jege threw their carton of orange juice at me while I was cycling to school,' answered Mordecai. 'A school bus passed by, and somebody threw it at me as it passed. I had to go to the bathroom to wash off the stickiness.'

'Why didn't you take the bus like you used to?'

'Have you been on board that bus with the kids in there?' Mordecai asked in frustration, 'I refuse to take the bus again, no matter what! I have a poncho secured to the back for when it rains. I have no intentions of riding the bus again the way they are!'

'Come on, Mordy,' Cece replied, 'It can't be that bad.'

'Believe me, sis, it is,' Mordecai groaned, 'I've been ridiculed, picked on, even tripped a few times as I passed by. I got sick of it, so I started taking my bike to school.'

'What about the bus monitor?' his sister asked him.

'Wouldn't do anything,' Mordecai sighed. 'Seems she turns a blind eye to all that is going on to me.'

'You're not serious, are you?'

'As serious as death,' answered Mordecai. 'I had to start riding a bike to school. You're fortunate not to take the bus since you catch rides with your good friends, Sharon and Tiffany. You don't have to worry about cruel people on that bus!'

'I can't believe you would even take your bike when it's raining,' Cece said.

Mordecai sighed. 'I do what I have to do,' he replied, grabbing his books, and closing his locker. 'I've got to get to class before the bell rings.' Cece sighed as she watched her brother walk away. She was joined by two other cheerleaders as they headed to their first class.

At lunchtime, Mordecai sat down alone at one of the small tables outside the lunchroom eating his lunch. His sister, Cece, ate with Sharon and Tiffany. Tiffany was shorter than Cece and had blonde hair. Sharon had black hair and was about Cece's height. All three wore the same-colored outfits as Cece: the green and gold of the school.

'What do you think of the new album by the Stupid Things?' Tiffany asked the others.

Cece shook her head. 'I can't get into their music,' she said. 'For some reason, I can't stand the songs they sing. I've heard so many bad things about their lead vocalist, Butch Morrison.'

'Yeah, he's different levels of crazy all right,' Sharon replied. 'Mjolnir knows how to rock, though. I prefer them over the Stupid Things.'

'What about Ivory Godiva or Iron Axe, Cece,' Tiffany asked, 'Do you like any of them?'

Cece shook her head. 'Not particularly,' she answered. 'Not my cup of tea, really. For one thing, my parents don't like any of them. Frankly, I'm forced to agree with them. I tried to listen but couldn't get into their stuff.'

'Come on, Cece,' Sharon said, 'We're talking about the hottest bands in America.'

'I don't care if they are,' Cece frowned. 'I just don't like them.'

'I think they're the best,' came a voice from behind Cece. Three men wearing green football jerseys appeared behind them. One of them was six foot three, 245-pounds, had black hair, and wore blue jeans. His jersey had the number 66. The teenager wearing the number 12 was six-three and weighed 225-pounds. He had blonde hair and green eyes. The other teenagers wore a number 32. He had dirty blonde hair, stood six-three, and weighed 240-pounds. 'And what's wrong with the Stupid Things, Cece?' the youth with the number 66 asked her.

'I don't know if I should answer your question, Frank McCoy,' Cece sternly said, 'especially the way you, Stu Hatfield and Chuck Jones think you guys are so bad!'

'We are,' said the boy with the number 12 on his jersey, 'We are all-state players, the best in the country as well! Stu here is the best fullback in the state, Frank here is the best pass rusher, and I, of course, am the best quarterback. Who cannot love us?'

'Why are you so upset, Cece?' Tiffany asked her. 'We've got the best here at Oak Ridge High, and they will take us all the way to the state championship!'

Cece stared hard at Tiffany, a sour look upon her face. 'I am upset because of what you do to people like my brother Mordy,' she told the boys with the same hard look, 'What has he ever done to you that warrants how you treat him?'

'We ain't done nothing to the jege,' Frank insisted.

'That's not what Mordy had told me,' Cece retorted. 'What have you got against him, anyway?'

The others laughed. Cece frowned at them. 'I can't believe you happen to be his sister, Cece,' scoffed Stu.

'And why do you think that, Hatfield?' Cece snapped.

Frank just shook his head. 'Look, let's just drop it, okay?' he said. 'It's nothing, really.'

'Not to my brother, or me,' Cece snapped. 'Yesterday, he came home and was hurting all over. What did you jeges do to him?'

They shook their heads. 'Nothing, nothing at all,' Stu insisted.

'Somebody else must have done it to him, not us,' Chuck stated.

Cece rose from her seat, an angry look upon her face. 'Spare me the lies, jock breaths,' she said. 'Why don't you fess up and admit it? Why do you love to pick on people smaller than you? What have people like Mordy ever done to you that you would push them around so?'

'Come on, Cece,' Stu said. 'You can't believe everything you hear.'

'Yeah,' Chuck said, 'You can't believe rumors.'

'You hate my brother,' Cece insisted, 'and those like him. What you love to do is to pick on them and use them as your personal punching bags!'

The three football players laughed. 'No, we don't,' Frank said. 'That's not true.'

Cece growled. 'You are terrible liars,' she cried. 'I don't know why I bother wasting my time on you. Go away!'

Tiffany looked at Cece. 'I mean it,' Cece continued.

The three boys shrugged and then walked away. Both Tiffany and Sharon gave Cece a sour look. 'Not another word,' Cece warned, 'I don't take kindly to bullies.'

'But these are the stars of our football team,' protested Sharon.

'I don't care,' Cece frowned. 'Bullies are bullies, and I don't like bullies!' She sat down and went back to her lunch. She did not speak any more at that time to her friends.

It was raining by the time school was out. Mordecai sighed. He knew it would be rough out on the road given the conditions as well as the problems of how crazy people on the road could be. He did his best to keep the books he carried with him from getting wet, covering them with the spare poncho he had packed on the back of his bike. He covered and secured them, then unlocked the chains that bound his bike and wrapped it around his seat. After locking it, he did his best to dry the seat before he sat down and made his way back home, waiting for the traffic to pass before he made his way onto the road.

He made the left turn from Hoffner Ave. onto Oak Ridge Rd. being as quick and careful as possible to make the turn. One of the drivers, who happened to be a student, honked him impatiently and said some things he couldn't hear and probably didn't want to hear. He drove past Mordecai and stepped on the gas and sped down the road. Mordecai shook his head as he pedaled. The traffic sped past him, some going at dangerous speeds. Mordecai managed to keep at a speed near 20 miles per hour while trying to keep out of traffic.

The rain got worse. Mordecai pedaled on. He waited in the pouring rain for the light to change to green at the intersection of Oak Ridge Rd and Orange Blossom Tr. When it turned green, he pedaled along, keeping out of the way of traffic.

The rain began to ease up by the time he crossed John Young Parkway. At the entrance of a nearby apartment complex, he saw the same car that had honked at him being pulled over by an Orange County sheriff, the lights of the vehicle flashing. *Serves him right*, he thought, *flying like a bat out of hell*. He continued to pedal his way home as the rain began to fall harder again.

By the time he got home, he was exhausted. He placed his bike in the garage and headed to the bathroom to freshen up. He had draped his poncho over his bike to dry. He was glad to be home, away from the bullies: Stu, Chuck, and Frank. He was thankful he had not run into them today but was still sore after the previous day of dealing with the jocks. He put on another set of black pants and black shirts, for he had started to wear nothing but black in his junior year and was criticized, even by his parents, but they agreed to get him, at his request, only black shirts and pants. 'If they only knew the real reason I choose to dress in black,' he said to himself. He remembered hearing a song that One Bad Pig had done with the late Johnny Cash Man in Black two years earlier and got the idea in part from that song, but he wore black because he felt he was in mourning. He longed to be loved, to have that someone special in his life. He often dreamed about being in love again but began to feel it was only a pipe dream. He felt like a loser in love. He prayed God would send that special someone his way. The pain of his loneliness was becoming more and more unbearable, and he felt nobody, not even his sister, Cece, understood what it was like to be alone. He remembered hearing a blues song *Train of Love* some years back. Like in the line of the song, he felt like he was at Loneliness Station, fated to be there for life. He felt discouraged and all alone.

Outside, the rain continued to fall harder. He took out his portable keyboard and started to play a little. He wasn't as good at playing as he would like to be, but he felt music was the only true and faithful friend on Earth he had, how it seemed to understand his pain and loneliness. But *music cannot love you back*, he thought, and it was true. 'It may understand my pain, but it cannot love me back, cannot show affection or stand by me when things are bad. God, I need somebody in my life!' He prayed to God to bring that someone in his life, weeping as he prayed. He needed a good friend, a best friend, to help him through the difficult, emotional periods in his life.

About thirty minutes later, he heard the door open and shut. He got up from the bed and slowly moved out of his bedroom. He made his way downstairs as he heard voices. 'I hope it's not raining tomorrow when it's gametime,' the voice of Tiffany said.

'Me too,' came the voice of Sharon, 'I hate being out in the rain.

It causes havoc with my hair. I wish it would stop now!'

Mordecai saw that his sister and her friends were sitting down. 'I'm glad we had our practices in the gym,' he heard Cece say. 'My brother has to ride the bike in the rain.'

'What's wrong with taking the bus?' asked Sharon.

'He says there are people who pick on him, doing bad things to him,' Cece answered. 'He refuses to take the bus now.'

'He rides home in the rain?' Tiffany asked. 'Why doesn't he drive a car?'

'He told me Mom and Dad won't let him drive for some reason,' Cece answered. 'He doesn't know why, though. Dad's been teaching me how to drive, but not Mordy.'

'Man, that sounds grossly unfair to your brother,' Tiffany replied. Cece nodded sadly. She grabbed the controller and turned on the TV while Mordecai went in and grabbed a soda from the refrigerator and slowly returned upstairs.

'Have you heard about that geneticist, Dr. Haman Von Braun? The one who teaches a genetics class at UCF?' Sharon asked Cece.

Cece shook her head. 'Not too familiar with him,' she answered.

'I read somewhere that he believes in the existence of fairies,' Sharon said.

Cece laughed. 'Are you kidding?' she exclaimed, 'Where on earth did you read that?'

'From *Mockingbird* magazine,' Sharon answered, 'My mom loves that magazine. She's a regular subscriber.'

Cece shook her head. 'Sharon, that's a gossip magazine,' she frowned, 'You can't believe everything you read from that rag! We're talking about a magazine that says and claims a woman married a space alien that looks like Elvis Presley! Judas Priest, Sharon, you've got to stop reading that trash!'

'Do you believe fairies exist?' Tiffany asked her.

Cece laughed. 'Do I believe fairies exist?' she repeated. 'I may be fascinated with fairies, but I'm afraid they don't exist. It would be nice if they did, though. I can remember when I was young being fascinated with fairies, and I still am, in a way.'

'It sure seems like you believe they exist,' Sharon chuckled, 'Your room is so full of pictures and figurines of fairies. Heck, you even have a fairy screensaver and wallpaper on your personal computer and laptop.'

'I know, I know,' Cece nodded. 'I would like to believe they do exist. I would love to see one if they do.'

The other girls laughed. 'Who knows?' said Tiffany, 'Perhaps they do. You just have to know where to find them.'

'Do you believe fairies exist, Tiffany? Sharon?' Cece asked her friends/

Both girls shook their heads, laughing. 'Me? Of course not,' Tiffany answered. 'I grew out of that phase years ago. It's ancient history, though.'

'Same here,' Sharon added. 'I'm surprised you are still fascinated with them.' After a pause, she continued, 'I know they don't exist. If what I heard is true about Dr. Von Braun, I'd say he's gone off the deep end indeed.'

'Like I said,' Cece said, 'Don't believe what you read in gossip magazines.' She frowned. 'I like to think they exist, but I don't let it get in the way of reality, though. There are more important things in life, like school, finding the right boy. I am sure more and more each day that Oscar is not the one. I haven't heard from him in over a week! I don't know what's going on, but I'm not going to continue to play his game! I think he is seeing someone else behind my back!'

'You tried calling him?' Tiffany asked.

'I called him, I texted him,' said Cece in frustration. 'I've heard nothing at all from him. If it's over between us, then he needs to tell me! Otherwise, I will end it and move on! I'm not going to wait for his ugly can all day and night without knowing what's going down.'

Cece headed to the kitchen and grabbed a soda for her and her friends. She gave one can to Tiffany and one to Sharon, then sat down. They continued to talk as they drank their sodas.

That evening, Mordecai and Cece were at the table with their parents. Their mother was like Cece but had shorter hair that wasn't as red as her daughter's. She wore red slacks and a white blouse. She was slightly taller than Cece. Her husband had short blonde hair, a moustache upon his face, blue eyes, wore blue slacks and a white shirt. Both were in their early 40s. They ate as they talked.

'What time is the game tomorrow, Cece?' her father asked.

'At seven,' Cece answered, 'We play Colonial at home. I hope it doesn't rain. The forecasts say it might rain tomorrow night.'

'I don't like the fact you'll be out on the field in the pouring rain,' he frowned, 'It's bad enough Mordy rides home in the rain. I could tell from the poncho on his back he rode home in the rain.'

'Why won't you take the bus?' his mother asked Mordecai.

Mordecai sighed. 'I've told you already,' he answered. 'I have to! I'm sick and tired of being bullied on the bus, having some students trip me or throw things at me. The monitor refused to do anything about it! It's bad enough that three members of the football team push me around and harass me! Yesterday, they roughed me up! It was a miracle I managed to ride home in spite of the pain!'

'What do the teachers say?'

'I told them, but they dismiss it because they are star football players,' Mordecai sighed, 'They refuse to listen to me! This has been ongoing since I had started attending Oak Ridge. They refused to believe me! It seems they allow them to get away with anything they want to do!'

'That can't be right,' Cece exclaimed, 'I couldn't believe it myself until I saw some time ago! I can't believe the teachers won't do anything about it! Of course, the three boys deny it. Perhaps we need to talk to the principal!'

'Have you?' Mordecai's mother asked him.

Mordecai nodded. 'They would not believe me,' he sighed. 'I don't know what to do anymore! They didn't believe me any more than the teachers when I had told them!'

His father shook his head. 'I find that hard to believe,' he said. 'Why won't they do anything? Could you be imagining all this?'

Mordecai stared in pain at his father. 'You don't believe me, do you?' he asked.

He shook his head. 'I don't know,' he shook his head, 'What have you done to them?'

'Nothing,' he immediately answered. He began to feel that his father did not believe him. He sighed, finished his drink, and left the table. Cece stared after her brother. Her mother turned toward her and said, 'If it's going to rain at the game tomorrow, you better take some dry clothes to change into. I don't want you to come home in a wet uniform.'

Cece jumped and turned toward her mother. 'Oh, yes, yes, Mom, sure,' she replied. 'Bring dry clothes with me. Got it.'

'Are you okay?' her father asked.

Cece sighed. 'Yes, I'm okay,' she answered. 'I am worried about Mordy, though. It's frustrating how—'

'I'm sure he'll be all right,' her father replied. 'It's just a phase he's going through. I haven't seen you and that Oscar boy around. How is he doing?'

'I've been trying to find out for the past week,' Cece answered, frustration telling in her voice. 'I've called him, texted him, but he doesn't return my calls or texts. I don't know what's going on with him. I'm not going to wait forever, though. There're plenty of other guys out there. He's not the only fish in the sea.'

'It's a shame,' her mother shook her head, 'That Oscar boy seemed so nice. I'm sure it's nothing.'

'I disagree,' Cece replied, 'I don't know what's going on, but I will find out one way or another, and he better have a good explanation why he has hasn't returned my calls or texts.'

Her mother shook her head. 'Doesn't sound like him,' she said.

'It still bothers me,' Cece frowned. 'If he continues, it is definitely over between the two of us! I don't like what he's doing to me, and I told him so in my last message, whether he received it or not! Right now, I don't feel like talking about it! I've got to get ready for school tomorrow. I still got a little bit of homework to do.' She finished her drink and left the table.

In his room, Mordecai was seated near the window. He watched with tear filled eyes as the rain continued to fall. It wasn't as heavy as it was when he was riding home from school, but it was still falling at a steady pace. The sun had set, and it was close to eight in the evening. He remained there, motionless, just staring out into the starless night as the rain steadily fell. There was a soft knock at the door. Mordecai seemed to disregard it, making no motion. The knock came again but he made no move. Slowly and softly, the door opened. Cece stepped inside and saw her brother at the window. She called his name. 'Mordy? Mordecai?'

When he didn't respond, she walked toward him and stopped beside him, touching him gently on the shoulder. He gave a startled jump, then stared at his sister. 'Cece? I'm… I'm sorry,' he said. 'I didn't hear you come in.'

Cece sighed. 'I'm sorry,' she told him, 'I don't understand why Mom and Dad won't listen to you. Couldn't they see what you are going through? When I come to think about it, I can understand why you feel the way you do. I hope you're not mad at me.'

Mordecai stared at Cece. 'Mad at you? For what?' he asked softly.

'I don't want you to be mad at me.'

Mordecai slowly rose to his feet. 'Why would I be mad at you, sis? I don't understand.'

'I'm being taught how to drive and you're not,' Cece answered. 'Being given the privileges that should have been given when you were my age but weren't. It does seem they love me more than you, but I don't want you to be mad at me for—'

Mordecai shook his head, tears flowing down his eyes. 'It's not your fault, Cece,' he sighed. 'No, I am not mad at you. This is not your fault. In fact, you give me more of a listening ear than Mom and Dad have. Yes, we have our disagreements, we've had moments when it's seemed we can't stand each other.'

Cece gave out a little laugh. 'Yeah, I remember,' she replied, 'Typical brother-sister stuff. I remember you would ridicule me for being a believer in fairies when I was young.'

Mordecai gave out a little laugh. 'I know,' he nodded. 'I can remember Randall would chide me for teasing you so.' His face turned grave again. 'I feel bad about it now. Time has a way of changing one's perspective. I see you're still a fan of fairies.'

Cece smiled. 'Yeah, I guess you could say that,' she nodded. 'I still have quite of lot of fairy posters and figurines in my room.'

Mordecai nodded. 'Yeah, I kind of noticed that,' he told her, 'but the time of ridiculing you for that is long gone. I won't do it anymore; you'll be happy to know.' He glanced at her hand. 'What is that?'

Cece showed Mordecai the small figurine of a fairy with red hair much like Cece's. 'I had found it when I was at the mall,' she said.

'Kind of looks like you,' he told her.

Cece nodded. 'That's why I had bought it,' she replied. 'It does look like me. It's one of my favorites.'

'I can understand why.' Mordecai smiled. 'I know we've had our differences in the past, Cece,' he continued, his face turning grave again, 'but lately, you've been there when I've needed someone to talk to, and unlike Mom and Dad, you listened. I was jealous of you before, having the advantages that were not granted to me, but I know it's not your fault. How could I be mad at you for something that's not your fault?'

Cece gently wiped the tears from his eyes. 'It means a lot to me to hear you say that,' she said, 'I know there are times we can't stand each other, but please know, deep down I do care about you and do love you.' Tears started filling her eyes.

Mordecai nodded and leaned his face toward hers. 'I promise I won't forget it,' he replied as tears continued to stream down his face. 'If you promise you'll remember the same thing.'

'I promise,' she said. They embraced as tears flowed freely from their eyes as they wept on each other's shoulders. They remained there for long moments. When they stared at each other, Cece said, 'Please don't hesitate to come talk to me when you need someone to talk to, when the pain becomes too great.'

'I promise,' Mordecai nodded. Cece wiped the tears from his eyes. 'I am glad to have you as my sister.'

Cece sighed. 'I am glad as well, that you are my brother,' she smiled. They released each other and looked out the window. The rain continued to fall. Cece groaned. 'Please don't let there be rain tomorrow,' she said. 'I know the field will be muddy enough as it is. Are you coming to the game?'

'I don't know,' Mordecai answered. 'Are you going to ride with your friends, Tiffany and Sharon?'

Cece nodded. 'I plan to,' she answered. 'Mom and Dad said they might go to the game, but I don't know if they will.' She stared at the fairy figurine. 'Do you think there could be fairies out there somewhere?'

Mordecai thought for a moment. 'I don't know,' he said. He then thought of what he had seen the other day. 'When you were young, I thought you were crazy to think fairies did exist, but who knows? There could be.'

Cece stared at Mordecai, a queer look on her face. 'You're not teasing me, are you?'

'No,' he answered simply and with sadness in his voice.

Cece saw he was serious. 'Have you seen one?' she asked.

Mordecai thought for a moment. He sighed. 'I saw something yesterday,' he told her, 'It looked like a human in the air, but maybe I was just seeing things, I don't know. I was out in the backyard at the time. I didn't get a real good look at it, though. It was a brief glance. I'm still not sure what I saw was real. I was very depressed at the time. If it was real, it was gone just as quickly as it appeared. I wasn't sure what it was.'

'You pulling my leg?' Cece asked.

Mordecai sighed. 'Maybe I should not have mentioned it,' he frowned.

Cece sighed. 'I'm sorry,' she said. 'My fault. I should not have asked. Maybe I'm crazy to believe that fairies do exist.'

'It may have explained what I saw yesterday, but I can't be sure,' he said softly. 'I won't lie to you, but like I said, it was a brief glance, and I couldn't tell what it was. I wish I could be certain.'

They both stared out the window as the rain came down. 'Who knows?' Cece ventured to say. 'You could have seen a fairy. Maybe there are fairies out there.'

'We may never know,' Mordecai said.

Mordecai found himself in a valley. It was very dark, a black starless sky. There was no light coming from the moon on account of the clouds covering it. In the distance, there was a group of mountains, black and foreboding. He saw no living thing in sight. He was all alone. 'What is this place?' he asked himself. 'Where am I?'

He continued to look around. He could feel despair and hopelessness around him, how it permeated the atmosphere. What was it about this place that he felt fear and death all around? Every breath he took, he could sense and smell evil. He walked onward.

'How did I get here and how do I get out of here?' he asked himself.

As he walked, he heard a mighty roar, the sound of a hideous beast. He looked around. At that moment, a large black lizard with outstretched wings appeared before him. Nearly thirty meters tall and forty-five meters long, his bat-like wings spread nearly thirty meters from tip to tip. Its scales were jet-black, black as coal. When Mordecai first saw the monster, he fled. With a mighty leap, the dragon sprang and landed directly in the young man's path. The beast gave him a hard stare. 'Who are you?' it asked. Its voice was deep, sending chills of fear down Mordecai's spine.

Mordecai backed away as it spoke. 'Who are you, human?' it asked again.

Mordecai fell to the ground. 'N-nobody really,' he stuttered.

He heard the dragon give out a laugh that seemed to shake the earth around him. 'Exactly, human,' it boomed. 'A worthless nobody! I don't know why I should be afraid of you, but I have learned appearances can be deceiving. You think you can destroy me? Ha! What a joke!'

Mordecai was scared and confused. 'I don't-I don't know what you're talking about!' he proclaimed.

'Of course not, human,' the dragon replied. 'But sooner or later, you will.'

'I don't understand.'

'If you had any sense whatsoever, you would stay in the human world and don't become involved with anything that is not your business, that is too big for you to understand. Sooner or later, I will find you and I will know who you are.'

'What have you got against me?' Mordecai asked.

'So many questions,' laughed the dragon, 'but no answers at all will I give you! I will find you and I will keep the prophecy from being fulfilled!'

'Prophecy? What prophecy?'

The dragon only opened its mouth and spewed fire at Mordecai. Mordecai woke with a cry. He was alone in his bed. He shook his head. 'What a nightmare,' he said to himself. He sighed. 'It seemed so real! Why did I dream about that? What-what does it mean?' He laid down again and tried to go back to sleep.

The next morning, he got dressed for school. He began to think about the nightmare he'd had. For some reason, he could not get the dream out of his head. As he got on his bike, he placed the poncho over his body and his books beneath the poncho, secured to his bike. He looked out into the sky. Rain clouds were gathering again. He sighed. He got onto his bike and started pedaling, heading away from his home.

Inside the house, Cece came out of her bedroom wearing her cheerleader's uniform. She knocked on Mordecai's bedroom door and opened it. She saw that he was gone. She then ran downstairs and headed toward the kitchen.

She found her parents sitting down at the table. She looked around. 'Have you seen Mordy?' she asked them.

'He already left for school,' her mother answered, 'He was insistent upon not taking the bus.'

'I was hoping he would still be here,' Cece frowned. 'I was going to ask him if he wanted to ride with me and my friends. What time did he leave?'

'He left just before your father and I woke up,' her mother answered, 'He should have stuck to taking the bus. Is it really that bad for him?'

Cece nodded. 'He feels it is,' she answered, drinking her milk. 'He feels all alone in the world because he is getting no help from being bullied and constantly picked on at school and on the bus. None of the teachers believe him because the three all-star football players are highly recruited by major colleges. He feels worthless and a nobody because of it. He needs our support!'

'He suffers from depression,' her father said. 'He needs to continue to go to therapy and take his antidepressants. Once his antidepressants kick in, he'll be fine.'

Cece sighed. 'I don't think so,' she shook her head, 'I still worry about him.' A honking noise came from outside. 'My ride is here,' she said, finishing her milk. 'I've got to go!' She grabbed her books and headed out the door. She got into the car, sitting in the back seat. Tiffany was driving, and Sharon was in the front seat on the passenger's side. Cece buckled herself in while Tiffany backed out of the driveway and drove off.

'Heard it's going to rain all day today,' Tiffany said. 'I hate going out in the rain!'

'My parents told me to bring dry clothes,' Cece said. 'I need to return home and pick them up before the game. I already have them laid out on the bed and ready to take with me just in case.'

'Good call,' Sharon nodded. 'I wish I would have thought of that.'

'We'll head back and pick up dry clothes if the rain continues,' Tiffany said.

When they turned onto Oak Ridge Rd, Tiffany picked up speed. Sharon looked at Tiffany. 'You may want to cool it, Tiffany,' she told her as the rain fell slowly and lightly. 'There may be cops in the area. I'm sure your father will have a fit if you got a ticket or got into an accident.'

'I'm fine,' Tiffany insisted. 'Besides, I've been driving long enough to know that cops don't always hang around here.'

'I wouldn't be sure of that if I was you,' Sharon warned. 'Rhonda got a ticket last week for exceeding the speed limit around the Westridge Middle School area. They will crack down on drivers!'

'Let me worry about that,' Tiffany retorted. 'We'll be fine!'

As the rain fell a little harder, they passed Mordecai as he pedaled down the road heading past Sadler Elementary and Westridge Middle School. Cece looked back at her brother until she could not see him anymore. She then turned back around. On the radio was the song What Can I Do (To Win Your Love) by a band called Foxtrot. Tiffany's face turned sour. 'I don't like this song,' she said. 'I wish they would play something by the *Rolling Stones.*'

'The *Rolling Stones?*' Cece laughed. 'Why them? They've got to be in their 70s or something.'

'They've been around for 50 years,' Tiffany replied. 'They were the ones who discovered the Stupid Things.'

Cece's face turned sour. 'I hate the Stupid Things,' she frowned, 'I could never stand them. You know that!'

Sharon shook her head. 'So sad,' she replied.

'And what do you mean by that?' Cece asked, giving her a queer look.

'The Stupid Things are a great band,' Sharon stated. 'They have great songs; Butch Morrison is so cute.'

'He is also a devil,' Cece said. 'I heard a lot of bad things about him and his band.'

'Who do you like, Cece?' Tiffany asked.

'Rosangela Ferreira, for one. Her husband's band, Sonic Riptide, is pretty good too.'

'If you like 70s classic rock,' quipped Sharon. 'Jesse Clemmons and his band plays music that belongs in the 70s or early 80s! It's archaic!'

'Didn't he used to be with Mjolnir when they were Red Alert?' Tiffany asked.

'Yeah,' Cece answered, 'They had some good stuff when they were Red Alert, but ever since they had dismissed Jesse Clemmons from the band and renamed their band Mjolnir, I stopped listening to them. Their stuff now sucks dirt.'

'Why did they dismiss him anyway?' Sharon asked. 'It seemed to help their career by leaps and bounds when they got rid of him. It was a good move for them. What has he done besides marrying Rosangela Ferreira?'

'He had produced his wife's albums for one,' Cece said. 'He also wrote songs for Rebecca Alabama, Daphne Felicity Lockhart, produced albums for Octave Blues and Seventh Sojourn as well as his band, Sonic Riptide. He even produced albums for Vivica Black and Vivian Jackson.'

'He wrote songs for Daphne Felicity Lockhart?' Tiffany asked. 'Man, that girl knows how to rock! She is one of my favorites!'

'Yeah, she is great,' Sharon agreed. 'I loved her show when she came to Orlando. She can rock as hard as her male counterparts. Looking at her, I can't believe she performs hard rock, being black and all.'

'I wouldn't mind meeting her myself,' Cece said.

At that moment, Sharon looked ahead and noticed the light at Orange Blossom Trail had changed and the traffic was slowing down. She looked at Tiffany and cried, 'Tiff, light change up ahead!'

Tiffany looked up and cried, 'Oh, snap!' and slammed on her brakes. The car skidded and hit the stopped car ahead. Tiffany groaned. 'Oh, man, Dad is going to kill me!'

'You okay back there, Cece?' Sharon asked.

'Yeah, just shaken up,' Cece answered, 'What happened?'

Sharon looked at Tiffany and said, 'I hate to say, "I told you so", but…'

'Don't!' Tiffany snapped back. She then sighed. 'I am in deep trouble!' she groaned.

The driver up ahead stepped out of the car and walked over to the three girls. He stared at the damage done and then stared at the girls. He walked back to the car, turned off his motor, and grabbed his umbrella. He then walked back over to the girls. As he reached Tiffany's side, she rolled down the window and said, 'I am so sorry, sir, I feel so bad about what happened.'

The man just shook his head and said nothing, giving her a sour look. He dialed numbers on his cell phone and spoke into the phone. Minutes later, two police cars arrived at the scene. They instructed both drivers to move to the side to allow traffic to continue. Both cars moved toward the entrance to Krystal's and pulled over while they were joined by the police vehicles. One car pulled behind Tiffany's car and the other in front of the man's car. While the officers spoke to both drivers, Cece and Sharon stepped out, grabbing their umbrellas. They stood by Tiffany while the officer asked her questions.

Soon, Mordecai caught up to them. He saw Cece, Tiffany and Sharon standing with an officer. He immediately rode toward them to check on his sister. One of the officers walked over to him and said, 'There's nothing to see here, son! Move along!'

'I came to check on my sister,' Mordecai said, 'My sister, Cece, was in the car.'

'Which one?'

Cece walked over to Mordecai. 'It's okay,' she said. 'He's my brother.' To Mordecai she said, 'I'm okay. I'm not hurt.'

'What happened?' Mordecai asked.

'Tiffany rear-ended a man,' she answered. 'She's talking to the cops right now.'

'I'll have to ask you to move on, son,' the officer said. 'This does not concern you.'

'I just wanted to check up on my sister,' Mordecai told the officer, getting ready to turn around.

At that moment, the officer stopped him. 'Wait!' he cried. 'If I may ask, why are you riding a bicycle in the rain?'

'Because I have to,' Mordecai answered. 'I don't want to take the bus to school.'

'Why not?'

'I'm being bullied on the bus and at school,' Mordecai answered, 'I tried to tell the teachers and the monitor on the bus but they will not listen to me.'

The officer sighed. 'I'm sorry to hear,' he said. 'Do you wish to talk to somebody?'

Mordecai sadly nodded. 'The only one I have now is my sister Cece,' he sighed, 'My parents won't listen to me. The teachers won't do anything since the ones bullying me are football stars and very popular in the state and in recruiting.'

The officer pulled out a card and handed it to Mordecai. 'If you need to talk, here is my number,' he said. 'Please feel free to call. Leave a message if you can't reach me. Perhaps I can help you.'

Mordecai nodded, placing it in his pocket. 'Thank you,' he said, 'I have to get going so I won't be late for school.' He turned around and pedaled away, riding down the road and across Orange Blossom Trail before the light turned red.

Cece watched as her brother rode away.

Mordecai rode his bike, making a turn onto Hoffner Ave. As he was about to turn up the driveway leading into the school, there was a honk behind him as a car nearly struck him, causing him to fall into a nearby puddle. He stared angrily at the car. He recognized the car as belonging to one of the football players who bullied him, Chuck Jones. He rose from the puddle, picked up his bike, and ran over to chain his bike up. He then took his books and headed to his locker.

He opened his locker and grabbed his books. He shook the excess water from his poncho, shaking it as much as he could to get as much of the water off as possible before he hung it up. He then folded it up and grabbing his books, closed his locker and headed to his first class.

At lunchtime, Mordecai had a seat all by himself. He sat alone and ate while others around him purchased their food, sat down, and talked while Mordecai read the Bible as he ate. At another table, the three jocks sat together with a group of cheerleaders, laughing as they talked. 'I'm going to pass for over 300 yards tonight, rain or no rain,' Chuck said. 'We are going to kick Colonial's butt tonight! Stu's going to run through their defense as if they were made of paper, and Frank is going to flatten the ball carrier, whoever it may be. Nothing's going to get past him.'

'Where do you hope you will go, Chuck?' one of the cheerleaders asked.

'To the University of Miami,' Chuck answered. 'Gators and Noles suck dirt! Been a big Canes fan since I heard The Rock had attended Miami.'

'I like Georgia myself,' Stu replied. 'Love them Dawgs!'

'I'm hoping Notre Dame gives me a scholarship,' said Frank, 'Such a rich tradition there. My mother hopes I go either there, Stanford or Boston College since she had been brought up Catholic. I prefer Notre Dame, though. I'm certain I'd wind up there and be a star.'

'But first, we've got to lead Oak Ridge to the state title,' Chuck stated, 'I'm so looking forward to the game tonight. I'm going to listen to the Stupid Things to get fired up.'

'What about Mjolnir?' Stu asked.

'I kind of like the Stupid Things better,' Chuck answered.

At that moment, they were approached by a young man who was the same build as Frank. He was joined by two other boys. They each wore a green and gold jacket with the letters "OR" and the school mascot in the midst of it. The larger of the boys pulled Chuck from his seat. Chuck gave him an angry look. 'What is your problem, Sam, besides the obvious?' he growled.

'You're the one with the problem, Jones, you and your jege buddies,' Sam growled, 'I don't like what you did to my brother, James or Alan's brother, Benny! You think you jerks are so big being football stars that it gives you the right to pick on anybody weaker than you! Only cowards do that!'

Stu and Frank rose from their seats. 'You calling us cowards, Collins?' Frank growled.

'If the shoe fits, McCoy,' one of the other boys snapped. 'I am sick and tired of you Neanderthals picking on people, like my brother Peter or even Mordecai Jefferson! I've seen his sister Cece confront you about the matter! It's a sin that the teachers turn a blind eye to all this just because you're such big football stars! Even if we happen to get in trouble, we're not going to tolerate your bullying and you getting away scot free all the time!'

'You want to do something about it, jege?' growled Stu, pushing the young man to the ground. Sam and Alan charged Stu and Frank and knocked them down as the other young man quickly leapt to his feet and knocked Chuck to the floor. The students scattered when Alan knocked Frank into a nearby table, while Stu knocked Sam into a table opposite. Chuck knocked the other boy into a nearby wall and proceeded to punch him in the stomach.

Mordecai saw the commotion. He shook his head as he hurriedly finished his lunch and left as quickly as possible, leaving his tray on the table, unwilling to go near the commotion. He exited the lunchroom and headed to his next class, not wanting anything to do with the incident.

He was met by Cece, who had followed him out. She called out her brother's name. Mordecai stopped and allowed her to catch up. 'I can't stand them,' she cried. 'I'm glad somebody had the nerve to stand up to those bullies!'

Mordecai sighed. 'More likely, Jones, Hatfield and McCoy will get away scot free as they usually do,' he frowned, 'Could you tell who was standing up to them?'

'Sam Collins, Alan White, and Jon Palmer,' Cece answered. 'They've had younger brothers who like you are victims of their bullying. They got tired of the teachers and the principal not doing anything about it. You're right, Mordy, they will be punished, and the terrible trio will get away with murder again.'

'It seems like here it's "damn the underdogs,"' he sighed. 'It seems like they favor the bullies and people like me can go to hell, in their opinion. It's not right!'

Cece placed her hands upon her brother's arm. 'I know, Mordecai,' she sighed. 'I know nobody said life was fair. It grieves me, too, the way things are. The guilty are treated like the innocent while the innocent are treated like the guilty. What class do you have next?'

'I've got history next,' Mordecai answered. 'Not my strongest subject.'

'I have trouble with algebra,' Cece said, 'I've got that next. Fortunately, it's not too far from your next class. We still have time to talk while we wait.'

Mordecai looked out at the sky. 'Looks like the sky is trying to clear up,' he stated.

Cece nodded. 'For how long, I wonder?' she asked. 'We both know Florida weather, so unpredictable at times. The field will be muddy enough as it is without more rain.'

'Yeah, I can imagine,' he nodded.

'I wanted to see this morning if you wanted to ride with me and my friends,' Cece said, 'but you had left already. How on earth could you stand riding in the rain?'

'I stand it because I have to,' Mordecai answered, 'It's better than fighting bullies and people who have nothing better to do than to harass and torture people like me.' He paused. 'I bet Tiffany's father is going to be mad that she got into an accident. What happened?'

Cece shook her head. 'I'm not sure,' she said. 'Maybe she got distracted by something for a moment. I don't know how it's going to affect her situation. I can only hope Tiffany will be able to continue to drive.'

'No telling,' Mordecai said.

At that moment, they were joined by Tiffany and Sharon. They had been searching for their friend ever since the fight had broken out in the lunchroom. 'I was wondering where you went,' Sharon said.

'Just talking to my brother,' Cece replied. 'He had the common sense to get out of there when the fight broke out. Honestly, I wish Hatfield, McCoy, and Jones would get in trouble for once! It's not fair, the way they're allowed to keep up their antics!'

'I told my father what happened earlier this morning,' she told her. 'To say the least, he wasn't happy. He said he's going to have a long talk with me when he returns home.'

'Oh, boy, that usually means you're in deep trouble,' Cece said.

'We may all have to wind up riding with somebody else, or what's worse, the bus,' Sharon said.

'Let us hope it doesn't come down to that,' Cece replied. 'I'm beginning to agree with Mordecai about the bus. It must be bad if he tolerates the rain to go to school over a bunch of unruly kids who don't have a brain.'

'I can ask Jennifer if we could ride with her if worse comes to worst,' Tiffany suggested. 'I'll have to ask her the next time I see her. I'm sure she won't mind taking the three of us.'

Cece glanced at Mordecai. 'That would leave no place for my brother, though,' she said. 'I don't want him to be left out.'

Mordecai sighed. 'It's okay, Cece,' he said. 'I still have my bike if those jeges don't decide to do anything to it. This morning they intentionally tried to run me over.'

'Say what?' the three girls exclaimed.

'Are you sure it was them?' Tiffany asked.

'I'm sure,' Mordecai answered. 'I fell in the muddy puddle as a result. I recognized Jones's car. Fortunately, I wasn't hurt. It did make me angry, however.'

'Remember the card the officer gave you?' Cece asked. 'Maybe you should talk to him. Maybe he could help. Do you still have it?'

Mordecai pulled out the card from his back pocket. 'I got it,' he said. 'I will call him once I get home from school.' He turned toward Tiffany. 'How bad was the damage?'

'Only cosmetic to both cars, but thankfully nothing serious,' answered Tiffany. She sighed. 'I don't know how much it's going to cost to get the damage fixed. The other driver wasn't happy either, but he was more reserved. All he told me was to be careful next time.'

'I'm just glad it wasn't some nutcase you hit,' Mordecai said, 'I've heard so much about road rage. No telling what would have happened if you had hit a loony toon.'

'I know,' Tiffany said. 'I'm still in deep trouble with my father.'

By the end of the school day, the sun was starting to peek through the ominous black clouds. Mordecai unlocked the locks on his bike and wrapped it around his seat. He secured the lock and got on his bike, securing the extra poncho to the back. He made his way onto Hoffner Ave. and eventually onto Oak Ridge Rd. The light had turned green before he reached the intersection and he managed to get through before it turned yellow. He rode down the road.

By the time he crossed Orange Blossom Trail, the sky had darkened again. He held off putting on his poncho as he rode on. He started to get thirsty. He finally stopped at the nearest convenience store to get something to drink. He parked his bike, secured it, and headed into the store.

He headed to the assortment of soft drinks and tried to decide on what he wanted. As he looked, three men, two in their late 40s and a man in his mid-60s with white hair were looking over the alcoholic drinks. Mordecai took a quick glance at them. It happened the white-haired man was the world-famous geneticist, Dr. Haman Von Braun. He was speaking to his two associates. Mordecai managed to overhear them.

'This one is supposed to be good,' one of the men told Dr. Von Braun.

'Hardly,' he said in an English accent, 'I go with the standards.' After a pause he asked, 'Did you find out anything?'

'Not so far, Doctor,' answered the other. 'We asked around the young people here. All dead ends so far.'

'What about at the local high school, what is it called?'

'I think it's Oak Ridge, Doctor,' the first one answered. 'We have yet to try it.'

'Sooner or later, we've got to find somebody,' Dr. Von Braun said. 'Somebody must know about the existence of fairies.'

Fairies? Mordecai overheard as he searched for something he wanted to drink. He continued to search. *Then the magazine Sharon read was right? Why would he want to find out about the existence of fairies?* He then thought of the figure he had seen in the air earlier that week. *Could what I had seen before had been a fairy? Why would Dr. Von Braun want to search for fairies?* He quickly decided on a drink, paid, unlocked his bike, and headed toward home.

Mordecai made his way back to the main road and crossed John Young Parkway. As he rode, a black Cadillac followed behind him, moving at the same speed as him. He noticed the car after he had passed Westridge Middle School. He sped up to hopefully allow the car to pass, but it stayed on his tail. Mordecai wondered what was going on. The car did not pass but remained behind him. He glanced in the other lane to see if he could get into the next lane, but traffic kept passing by and kept him from moving. He finally decided to turn onto Brookgreen Ave. in the Camellia Gardens subdivision and decided to cross to the other side to the Southwood subdivision via the light on Harcourt Ave. He turned onto Brookgreen and rode down the side street. The Cadillac kept following him. *What is going on? Why are they following me?* He tried to pedal faster, but his muscles were tired, and he could not.

By the time he reached the light on Harcourt, it had turned green. He crossed via the light and headed down the other side street. Suddenly, the Cadillac passed him and stopped in front of him. He moved past the car, which pursued him again. The second time it passed him and forced him to stop before he had reached Fairlawn Dr. Mordecai tried to take off again, but the driver stepped out and stopped him, grabbing the handlebars. Mordecai looked angry. 'What's the meaning of this?' he cried. 'What is your problem?'

From the back of the car, Dr. Von Braun stepped out and approached him, a lit cigarette in his mouth. He took the cigarette out and walked over to the young man. 'What's going on?' Mordecai demanded.

'I took it you overheard our little conversation at the convenience store, did you not?' Dr. Von Braun asked.

'Why? All I went in there for was to get a drink,' he said, showing him the bottle. 'Why are you bothering me?'

'You had overheard us while you were purchasing a soda,' insisted Dr. Von Braun. 'I'm certain of it. You should ditch the soda. A beer would be better for you.'

'Not in this lifetime,' Mordecai disagreed. 'I choose not to drink, if it's all the same to you.'

Dr. Von Braun laughed. 'You don't know what you're missing, boy,' he replied. He puffed on his cigarette. 'On to business, however. We know you overheard our conversation at the convenience store. Do not deny it, boy!'

'Why? What's it to you?' asked Mordecai.

'You know what we seek from the conversation,' stated Dr. Von Braun, taking another puff on his cigarette. 'Tell me what you know about fairies.'

'They are mythological creatures,' Mordecai told him, 'Why do you believe they are real?'

'That is none of your concern, boy,' retorted Dr. Von Braun. He stared harder at him. 'You've seen one before, I can tell,' he continued, 'I have a feeling you have.'

Mordecai shook his head. 'No, not to my memory,' he said.

Dr. Von Braun stared harder at the young man. 'I have a feeling you have seen one,' he repeated. 'Tell me the truth and do not lie to me.'

Mordecai sighed. 'I may have seen something days ago, but I am not sure,' he said, 'Flying briefly amid the trees where I live, but I'm not sure what it was. It was the only time I've seen it. Why is that such a big deal?'

Dr. Von Braun smiled. 'My dear boy, that was a fairy you saw,' he said, 'That would be the only explanation.' He paused. 'You must think me a madman to be obsessed with seeking out and proving the existence of fairies.'

'Would there be any other conclusion?'

'Have you ever heard rumors of a fairy kingdom called Arundel Haven?' asked the geneticist.

Mordecai shook his head. 'Never heard of it,' he answered. 'I've heard absolutely nothing about it.'

'Back in my days of Oxford,' Dr. Von Braun told the young man, 'I had come across a book, an old book, talking about a kingdom where fairies lived called Arundel Haven. This was back in 1968. Some years back, I had seen a fairy in the woods but was unable to photograph it. I had recently found the remains of a fairy and had taken DNA samples of it.

'They are real, I assure you. I heard rumors of fairy sightings here in the Orlando area where I had found the remains of one. I know they exist.'

'Like I said, I don't know what I saw that night,' Mordecai replied.

'What is your name?' the old man asked him.

'Mordecai Jefferson,' he answered. 'Why are you so obsessed with finding fairies and this Arundel Haven?'

'Merely scientific curiosity, of course,' Dr. Von Braun answered, 'I've been researching this for many years. I have not made it public for the fact there is not much empirical evidence. Once I obtain the needed evidence, I will make it public.'

Mordecai felt an uneasiness at his words. Could he have another motive for finding Arundel Haven? Somehow, he found himself not believing his words. He felt there was more to this than what Dr. Von Braun had told him. He then remembered his talk with Cece about fairies and wondered if they really existed. It was clear to him that Dr. Von Braun *believed* they existed. Something inside told him not to trust him. He kept it inside.

Dr. Von Braun gave him a card. As Mordecai looked at the card, he heard Dr. Von Braun say, 'I expect you to tell me, Mordy Jefferson, when you encounter a fairy. I will be in touch.' He and his men climbed back into the car. Before he entered, he said, 'You will call me the moment you encounter a fairy.' He got into the car and closed the door. The car roared to life. Mordecai watched it drive away as it started to rain. Mordecai took the spare poncho and put it on as he started pedaling again, turning onto Fairlawn Dr.

Inside the car, Dr. Von Braun finished smoking his cigarette and placed the butt in the ashtray. He took a beer and started to drink it. 'I want you men to keep an eye on Mordy Jefferson,' he told them. 'I have a feeling about this boy. He may be the one.'

'The one, sir?' the passenger asked.

'Yes, Seymour, the one,' answered Dr. Von Braun. 'If he hasn't had a personal encounter with a fairy already, he will. Something inside tells me he will, more than he even realizes.'

'What's so special about him, anyhow?' the driver asked. 'He's just a nobody.'

'Maybe so, Wilfred,' Dr. Von Braun replied. 'I have a gut feeling about this kid. I have never had this feeling before until now. He is the connection I've been looking for. Until further notice, keep an eye on this Mordy Jefferson kid. Keep close tabs on him. Sooner or later, he will lead us to a fairy.'

'As you wish, Doctor,' nodded Seymour.

Dr. Von Braun continued to drink his beer. 'I expect you gentlemen to keep me abreast of the situation. He will obviously be riding a bike to school on Monday, apparently in the rain as well. Follow him when he rides to school, but make sure he doesn't see you. Follow him when he returns to his home. All my years of research will finally be rewarded, and soon, I will find the hidden kingdom of Arundel Haven.'

'You're the boss,' Wilfred said. The rain began to fall harder as they drove down the road. Dr. Von Braun took out another cigarette and started smoking.

Mordecai reached home as the rain fell down harder. He took off his poncho and draped it over his bike. He looked out of the garage doorway as the rain continued. He took out the card given to him by Dr. Von Braun, stared at it, and threw it in the garbage pail that stood by the door, shaking his head. 'He is insane like Hussein,' he said to himself. 'Fairies? How ridiculous is that? As rich as he is, he needs to find another hobby.' He closed the garage door, unlocked the door to the house, and went inside.

He took a hot bath and after getting dressed, grabbed a can of soda from the kitchen. He sat down at the table and looked at the card the officer had given him. He was debating whether to call him or not. *What could he do?* he thought. *Technically, bullying is not illegal, at least to my knowledge. It may be morally wrong, but not illegal.*

He sat down at the table in deep thought. He thought more about the words that Dr. Von Braun had spoken, how he honestly believed that fairies existed. He shook his head. He didn't know what to think on the matter. Why was he obsessed with finding a fairy and their dwelling place, which Von Braun had referred to as Arundel Haven? He had questions he had no answers to.

He looked out the glass sliding door leading to the backyard porch. The rain fell down harder. He continued to look out, standing unmoving as he watched the rain. The wind blew gently as it caressed the trees and the branches, each leaf dancing with the gentle breeze. Rain clouds continued to gather and moved slowly across the dark sky. Mordecai sighed. He remained motionless. Cece entered through the front door and saw Mordecai staring out into the rain-filled sky. She walked over to him and gently asked, 'Are you okay, Mordy?'

Mordecai gently turned to his sister and said, 'I'm okay, Cece. Looks like what you feared earlier would come to pass. Rain's really coming down hard.'

Cece sighed. 'Tiffany's father is waiting for her at home,' she said, 'She has to drop off Sharon before she can head home. I have a feeling it's not going to be good for her.'

Cece grabbed a soda from the refrigerator. She drank it as she joined her brother. 'Something happened I thought was weird when I was on my way home,' he told her.

'What happened?' Cece asked.

Mordecai sighed. 'I don't read gossip magazines at all,' he said, 'but what happened seemed worthy of one of those magazines.'

'What?'

'I couldn't believe it myself,' he continued. 'However, this, I can show you.' He walked away from the window and opened the garage door. He went into the garbage and retrieved the card he had thrown away. He gave it to Cece. 'What's that?' she asked.

She looked at the card. '"Dr. Haman Von Braun?"' she said.

Mordecai nodded. 'I was followed by him and two of his men after I left the convenience store after buying a soda,' he told her, 'I was stopped on the side road just before I reached home and he questioned me.'

'About what?'

'Fairies,' Mordecai answered.

Cece laughed. 'You have got to be kidding me, Mordy,' she exclaimed, 'Dr. Von Braun asked you about fairies?'

'I'm not kidding, Cece,' replied Mordecai. 'He stopped me and asked if I had ever seen a fairy. It sounded something like—'

'What a minute,' Cece exclaimed. 'I remember Sharon was telling me that she heard about it in one of the gossip magazines. Are you telling me that it is true that he's searching for fairies?'

'I know it's hard to believe,' Mordecai said to her, 'I don't blame you if you don't believe me.'

Cece sighed. 'It does sound far-fetched,' she said, 'but I haven't known you to lie or exaggerate ever since you got saved. I trust you in this. But why?'

Mordecai shook his head. 'I don't know,' he answered. 'It sounds to me that his elevator doesn't go all the way up. But somehow, I'm beginning to wonder if he could be right? Yet, I have a bad feeling about this, that his intentions may not be pure.'

'What do you mean?'

'I don't trust Von Braun,' Mordecai stated, 'Something in my spirit tells me not to trust him. If there are fairies, he must not be allowed to know of their existence. He has something else planned, I'm sure, that he has not told me.'

'I guess we better hope if there are fairies, we don't meet one for their sake,' said Cece.

Mordecai nodded. 'I have a bad feeling I haven't seen the last of Dr. Von Braun.'

They watched as the rain continued to fall. They wondered if what Dr. Von Braun believed about the existence of fairies was true? They wondered what the geneticist's plans were if he ever found one?

Mordecai felt he wouldn't want to know the answer to that question.

The rain continued to fall.

Chapter Three

Arundel Haven.

Raven looked down as she flew through the sky, looking ahead at the buildings of the city and the large castle in the midst of the city standing tall and erect. She enjoyed the way the wind blew through her long black hair as she soared. Her wings were about four feet long and about eight inches wide, but they managed to support her and allowed her as well as the fairies that lived in Arundel Haven, to enjoy flight into the sky. A blue dress covered her five-nine frame. Her skin was a deep mahogany color, her black eyes were keen, sharp, and beautiful. Light began to shine from her angelic face as the sun went down. She was nearly two months short of her 22nd birthday. As she lowered down to the ground, fairies of different sizes, ages, and colors flew past her.

She finally landed near a small cottage where she stayed. She had lived alone ever since her parents were killed by the dragon, Shadowfire, nearly a year before. Before she could enter, she was approached by two fairy women, both about 20 years old and light-skinned, who landed behind her. One fairy maiden had long, reddish hair, wore a pink dress that ran down to her knees, green eyes and wore a necklace of gold with an emerald in the middle of it. The green-eyed fairy was named Laurelin. She stood slightly shorter than Raven, about an inch shorter. Her friend, Lavender, was about Laurelin's height and age, had white hair and blue eyes, wore a light purple dress upon her slim frame and around her neck wore a gold necklace with a diamond. Raven turned around. 'So sorry you missed the picnic earlier today, Raven,' Lavender said, 'Too bad you had to babysit for your sister. How old is Starla's daughter?'

'Twila?' Raven said, 'She's two now. She is quite a handful, I tell you. She's started flying now since her wings have gotten stronger.' She sighed. 'I know I have to expect that when I have children of my own.' She opened the door. 'I'm about to fix supper. You care to join me?'

'Ha! Need you ask?' Laurelin replied.

They entered the dwelling. Raven lit the candles around the room as to give out light. She then lit a fire in a black stove and lit some logs for warmth. Raven poured some water in a five-quart black pot, cut up some vegetables, and placed it on the stove. She stirred the mixture with a wooden spoon, waiting for it to come to a boil. It was minutes before the mixture started boiling. 'It's still going to be a while,' Raven stated, 'I hadn't time to get any kind of meat today since I was babysitting. Some chicken would have been nice in the soup, but it'd be too much for just one person. Who did you go with?'

'Jax and Derreck,' Lavender answered.

Raven sighed. 'I bet that must be wonderful, having someone special to share the good times with. Someone who will always fly side-by-side with you. You girls are so lucky to have them in your lives.'

'Yes, Jax is a wonderful fairyman,' Laurelin replied, 'So polite, so gentle. I am so much in love with him.'

'So is Derreck,' Lavender said. 'That's what you need, Raven, a good fairyman in your life. I'm surprised you don't have that. I wonder what gives?'

'You tell me, I think ever since Abin had broken up with me over two years ago, he's been spreading rumors about me. It seems like the young single fairymen have bought whatever lies he had said about me. I don't understand how he could do that to me!'

'Come on, Raven,' Lavender said. 'Don't let it get you down. It just shows you how much of a jerk Abin is. He's not worth fretting about, especially how he did you wrong the way he did. You'll find a great fairyman someday.'

Raven sighed. 'I hope so,' she replied. 'Sometimes it seems like all the good fairymen are taken. There must be someone out there for me.' The water continued to boil as Raven stirred it now and then.

She set the table for Lavender and Laurelin. 'What's not to like about you, Raven?' Laurelin asked. 'You're a great cook, you got a great personality. To me, it's their loss.'

'Then how come I feel like the loser in love?' Raven cried out of frustration. She took a deep breath. 'I'm sorry, guys, I didn't mean to snap at you like that.'

'We know, Raven,' Lavender nodded, 'but hold on! You'll find that fairyman someday. Who knows? He could be looking for you right now.'

It was about a half hour before Raven served the stew to her friends. They sat at the table as the evening sky began to set in. They continued to talk as they ate. 'You still miss your parents a lot, don't you?' Laurelin asked.

Raven sadly nodded. 'There's not a day goes by that I don't think about them,' she answered. 'I was devastated when I first heard they had been seized and no doubt killed by Shadowfire.'

'He's been a menace to our people for about 150 years,' Lavender frowned, 'There's no telling when that dragon will attack and assail us! We haven't been bothered by him as of late, but there's always no telling when he might appear and attack. I'm only sorry it was your parents who had fallen victim to him. I wish there was a way to destroy him once and for all! I hate that dragon!'

'Every fairy of Arundel Haven feels the way you do about Shadowfire, Lavender,' said Laurelin, 'We have lived under his shadow ever since the last king of Arundel Haven, King Zebulon, had left to try and rescue his queen, Beulah, and gave the crown to his daughter Hephzibah, who became Queen. Ever since then, the dragon has afflicted us whenever he felt the need to do so! No fairy would dare venture to the Mountains of Shadow where the dragon lives!'

'Something needs to be done about Shadowfire,' sighed Raven. 'How long will our rulers tolerate the terror of the dragon?'

'There is no known way of destroying him,' Lavender stated, 'He is practically immortal thanks to the sorcerous powers he wields.'

Raven shook her head. 'No, I can't believe that,' she said, 'Queen Cymbaline is wise. Surely, she must know of a way.'

'If she did, she and Prince Avondale would have acted by now,' sighed Laurelin, 'If there is a way, no fairy in Arundel Haven knows what it is and how to destroy him.'

They continued to eat, drinking a sweet drink that was made from the fruits that grew in Arundel Haven. Raven drank and thought for a moment. 'I think there is a way, but it's just a matter of finding what it is. I pray the Lord will reveal it to Queen Cymbaline.'

Lavender and Laurelin shook their heads. 'You still believe in God?' Lavender asked incredulously, 'It's a human religion, Raven! It's bad enough Queen Cymbaline and Prince Avondale believe in the Father and the Son, but what fairywoman or fairyman would share such an outdated belief?'

'I do believe it, and I'm not ashamed to believe it,' Raven retorted, 'Like the Scriptures say, I am not ashamed of the gospel of Christ. You know how bad humans are, how wicked they are, selfish, violent, unnatural in affection. Yet, not all humans are like that. Those who follow Jesus Christ, for one, who *truly* follow Him are not bad. Not the ones who falsely claim to know Him and who don't do what He commands. In His words are warnings about wolves in sheep's clothing, false Christians if you will. They may fool men, but they can never fool God.'

Lavender shook her head. 'So you say, Raven,' she frowned, 'A lot of fairies don't believe what you or our Queen believes.'

'But she never forces her faith upon us, nor does Prince Avondale,' Raven stated, 'They allow us a choice to serve Him or not, to accept Him or not. Not like a lot of rulers in the human world who force you to convert or die. Like I said, there must be a way to destroy the dragon!'

'I can only hope you're right,' Laurelin sighed, eating her soup.

The next morning, Raven rose up early and flew away from Arundel Haven, avoiding the Mountains of Shadow where the sorcerer-dragon Shadowfire lived. She soared high into the sky and disappeared in the clouds. After she left, Lavender and Laurelin dropped by her place and knocked on the door of the cottage. They waited for a response. 'Raven? Raven?' Laurelin called, 'Are you awake?' There was no answer.

'Try again,' Lavender told her.

Laurelin knocked again. Again, there was no answer. 'Raven, are you in there?' Laurelin cried.

'Where is she?' Lavender asked.

'This is not the first time Raven has done this,' Laurelin stated. 'She's been gone off and on for the past two weeks. Where could she have gone to?'

'We'll just have to ask her the next time we see her,' Laurelin said, 'I would like to know myself. I would love to hear her explanation.'

They took to the air again.

In the air, they were met by two fairymen. One of them was about six-one, had black hair, grey eyes, wore green pants and a green shirt, the other was six-two, had brownish hair, grey eyes, wore a white shirt and blue pants. Lavender hovered in front of the brown-haired fairyman and asked, 'Did you or Jax happen to see Raven, Derreck?'

Jax hovered in front of Laurelin. 'Is she gone again?'

'Yeah,' answered Laurelin. She then stared at him again. 'What do you mean "again?"'

'Did he say again?' Jax asked.

Laurelin gave the boys a hard look. 'What are you not telling us? You're hiding something from us! Where is Raven?'

'I don't know,' Jax answered.

'Where is Raven?' repeated Lavender, 'And don't lie to us! Tell us the truth!'

'Honestly, we don't know,' Derreck answered.

'And what do you mean when you said, "Is she gone again?" Tell us, where did Raven go before?'

'She didn't say,' Derreck answered. 'She didn't tell us, even when we asked her. Honest!'

'Do you have any ideas where?' asked Lavender.

'I think past the Mountains of Shadow, but not there actually,' Jax answered, 'She is smart enough to avoid it, rising above the clouds. I'm not sure where.'

Lavender and Laurelin stared at each other. 'You don't think…' Lavender said, shaking her head.

'No, she couldn't,' Laurelin exclaimed, 'I'm sure she's smart enough not to go there.'

'Go where?' Jax asked.

'To the human world,' Laurelin answered, 'I sure hope that's not where she's been and where she's going.'

'Did you see her today?' Lavender asked, 'This is very important!'

Jax and Derreck shook their heads. 'Honestly, no,' Derreck answered. 'You really think she's been flying to the human world?'

'I hope not,' Laurelin answered, 'Queen Cymbaline would be mad for sure if that was the case.'

'For Raven's sake,' Lavender said, 'it better not be where she's been flying to. Queen Cymbaline would be angry for sure!'

Raven returned that evening. She landed in front of her door and opened it. Entering, she lit the candles that were closest to the door and proceeded to light the rest. She heated up the rest of the leftover soup she had stored and began to eat. After she took the first bite, there was a knock on the door. She rose, headed to the door and opened it. Lavender and Laurelin stood in the doorway.

'Raven, where have you been?' Laurelin asked.

'I'll answer your questions after I am done eating,' Raven said, 'I haven't eaten anything practically all day.'

She allowed her friends to enter as she sat back down at the table and continued to eat. Lavender and Laurelin sat down on the chairs and stared hard at her. 'We've been worried about you, Raven,' Laurelin stated, 'We had dropped by this morning to see if you wanted to go on a picnic with us, but you weren't there.'

Raven continued to eat while they watched.

'Will you talk to us, Raven?' Lavender insisted.

'What is it you want to know?' asked Raven.

'You know well, Raven,' Laurelin frowned, 'Where were you today?'

'No place special,' Raven told them.

Laurelin shook her head. 'That's not a good enough answer, Raven, tell us, where were you today?'

'I was out,' Raven answered, taking another bite of her soup.

Lavender scoffed. 'Obviously,' she frowned, 'but that's not a good enough answer.'

Raven gave Lavender a hard look. 'Then what do you want?' she asked irritably.

'A straight answer,' demanded Laurelin. 'Don't try and evade the question!'

'I did not go anywhere special, Laurelin,' replied an irritated Raven. 'I just needed some "me" time, that's all.'

'Where at?'

'That is none of your concern,' Raven frowned, 'That is all you need to know.'

'You didn't go anywhere near humans, did you?' Lavender asked.

'Near humans? Of course not,' Raven retorted, 'I know better than that—to go near humans! I went nowhere near where the humans live, I can assure you! Now, will you please allow me to finish my soup?'

Both fairies stared at Raven hard. 'You sure about that?' they asked her.

Raven gave them a look. 'Yes, I'm sure,' she answered irritably, 'I went nowhere near any humans.'

'Then where did you go?' Lavender asked.

'It's my private place, and that is all I will say about it,' snapped Raven. 'Now, if you please, I would like to finish eating!'

Both Lavender and Laurelin rose from their chairs, not too pleased with Raven's answer and the tone of her voice. Without another word, they headed out the door. Raven immediately stood up and cried out, 'Wait!'

Lavender and Laurelin merely stared at Raven with sour looks upon their faces. 'Look,' Raven said, 'I'm sorry I snapped at you. I know you are my friends. I know you're concerned about me, but there are times I need to get away from Arundel Haven. I like it here, yes, this is my home, but there are times I do need a change of scenery, but rest assured it is nowhere near humans.'

'Where is it, then?' Laurelin asked.

'It's a secret place for me and me alone,' Raven answered.

'I see,' Lavender frowned. Both fairies turned away and walked out the door, taking to the air as Raven sighed and closed the door.

The next day, Raven's sister, Starla, dropped off her daughter, Twila, at Raven's house. Raven agreed to look after Twila while Starla helped out her husband, Roosevelt, in the fields—Roosevelt was a farmer who grew crops and raised livestock just outside of the main city. There were numerous farms outside, in lands that were fertile enough to grow food.

Twila had a homemade doll in her hands that she clutched. Her skin was almost as dark as Raven's. Twila could walk but she enjoyed flying from the first time she started. The clothes she wore were of bright yellow with seams that allowed use of her wings. Raven flew to a spot near a wide river, which they called the Silverstreams. Raven watched as Twila played and laughed. She sat down. 'Stay close to your aunt Raven, Twila,' she told the toddler.

Twila flittered and landed on Raven's lap, who was sitting down at the time. Raven felt the impact of the drop, wincing a little in pain. 'Not so hard, sweetie.'

Twila wrapped her arms around Raven as she rose, sitting down again on her lap. The water of the Silverstreams flowed at a steady pace, reflecting the light from the sun as it shone in the sky. Raven felt a cool breeze blowing.

'Too bad it won't stay like this for long,' she said to herself. 'I hate it when it's wintertime. I guess I better think about getting some winter clothes before the snows come.'

Twila started playing with Raven's hair, running her small hands through it. Once, she accidently pulled too hard and she let out a cry. 'Careful, Twila.'

'Sorry,' Twila managed to say. 'Twila sorry.'

Raven smiled, holding her young niece close. 'I know you didn't mean it, dear,' she said, kissing her. 'Just be careful, okay?'

'Okay, Aunt Raven,' Twila said. She then flittered her wings and rose into the air. Raven immediately grabbed her. 'And just where do you think you're flying off to, little girl?' she asked.

'Where Mommy?' Twila asked.

'With your daddy, working in the fields,' Raven answered, 'Didn't your Mommy tell you?'

'I want to fly,' Twila said, struggling to break free.

'Oh, no you don't, little girl,' Raven said, 'You're not going anywhere. I know you're excited because you learned to fly, but you just can't go flying off like that!'

They were joined by Lavender and Laurelin, who had happened to be flying in the area. They hovered in front of Raven and Twila, who broke free and flew into Lavender's arms.

'Hello, little Twila,' she said.

Twila tried to say Lavender's name but somehow couldn't.

Laurelin looked at Twila. 'Can you say my name, Twila?' she asked.

Twila merely covered her face and giggled.

Raven took to the air and hovered in front of them. She stared at them. 'I hope you're not still mad at me,' she told them.

Lavender stared at Raven and sighed. 'I don't know what to think really, Raven,' she said. 'You've been acting unusual as of late, and Laurelin and I don't understand that.'

Raven sighed. 'Is it really causing a strain in our friendship? I don't mean it to be. It's just… It's just sometimes I need to get away for a time, just to see different things. I assure you, it's nowhere near any humans.'

'Are you sure about that?' Laurelin asked, concern telling in her voice. 'Can't you tell us where exactly it is?'

Raven shook her head. 'No, I can't,' she answered, 'At least not now. Can we drop it, please?'

'I don't know, Raven,' Lavender frowned. 'Something doesn't feel right for some reason, and it's bugging me. I don't feel comfortable with your response on the matter. Raven, wherever you've been going for the past three weeks, I can't get this feeling of some kind of danger out of my head.'

'There is no danger, I can assure you,' Raven insisted.

Suddenly, Twila broke free from Lavender and flew away from the river. Raven gasped as she flew after her young niece. Giggling, Twila flew in a way that made it difficult for Raven to catch her. Lavender and Laurelin heard Raven crying out Twila's name.

'I think we should help her,' Laurelin told Lavender. 'We are still her friends.'

Lavender nodded, not saying a word. They flew after Raven and Twila.

Twila flew erratically but not as fast as Raven, but Raven still had a difficult time trying to catch the lively toddler. She kept calling out

Twila's name as she continued her flight. Raven groaned. *Oh, I'm going to be in trouble with Starla and Roosevelt for sure if anything happens to Twila!*

'Twila, stop!' she cried.

Twila did not heed Raven's call. She flew into the town area, flying past the other fairies in the square. Some laughed when they saw the trouble Raven was having. Raven groaned. *Now I wonder if I really want children?* Twila was a handful to her.

Twila giggled as she flew inside the castle. Raven gasped. *No, no, no, Twila, you're going to get me in trouble with Queen Cymbaline for sure!* Lavender and Laurelin stopped and did not enter the castle after Raven and Twila. The guards were about to stop Raven but when they saw she was after her niece, they stayed where they were and laughed softly. They saw Lavender and Laurelin and approached them.

'Is the child always like this?' one of the guards asked.

Lavender and Laurelin laughed. 'I guess so,' Laurelin answered, 'Raven did say Twila was a handful.'

'Her daughter?' the second asked.

Lavender shook her head. 'Her sister's daughter,' she answered, 'She's babysitting for her sister and husband. Boy, are they going to be upset when they hear about this!'

Inside, Twila giggled as she flew around the castle, avoiding Raven's grasp as she tried to catch her. Raven called out to Twila. 'No, Twila,' she cried. 'We're already in trouble for entering the castle! Come here, Twila!'

Twila flew around the corner and into the arms of a fairyman in royal clothing. The six-three fairyman had a small crown set upon his head. He had long blonde hair, blue eyes and wore a sky-blue robe of satin upon his body. On his finger was a ring with a small emerald embedded within it. Instinctively, he caught the toddler and with a laugh he said, 'Whoa, what is this? Who are you?'

Raven stopped in front of him and bowed. 'Prince Avondale, your highness! Forgive me!' she said nervously. 'I… I was just looking after my niece and… and she got away from me!'

Prince Avondale smiled. 'Little ones are a handful I heard,' he smiled. To Twila he asked, 'What is your name, little one?'

'Twila,' she answered, touching his long blonde hair.

'I did not mean to intrude,' Raven said apologetically. 'I'm sorry. I tried to catch my niece but…'

'Who is there, Avondale?' came a feminine voice. Raven looked up and beheld a fairy maiden, very fair and slim, with a golden bejeweled crown upon her head. Her black hair flowed down past her shoulders. Her scarlet and gold dress ran down to her feet and she wore a robe of purple satin upon her shoulders. She was slightly shorter than her brother, but she was three years older—she was 35 and Prince Avondale was 32. She stared at Prince Avondale and the toddler while Raven bowed. 'Your majesty, Queen Cymbaline, forgive my intrusion,' she said.

'And who do we have here, brother dear?' Queen Cymbaline asked her brother.

Prince Avondale laughed. 'This little one,' he answered.

'Forgive me, your majesties,' Raven said apologetically.

Queen Cymbaline bade Raven to rise, though the Fairy Queen laughed a little. 'Your child?' she asked.

'No, your majesty,' Raven answered, 'My sister Starla's daughter, Twila. I was babysitting her and she kind of flew away.'

'Me like flying,' Twila told the Queen.

'What is your name, little one?' smiled Queen Cymbaline.

'Twila,' she answered, hiding her face.

'And your name?' Prince Avondale asked Raven.

'I am Raven,' she answered.

Queen Cymbaline's face turned grave. 'I remember you now, Raven,' she said. 'You had lost your parents almost a year ago when Shadowfire had seized and killed them. How are you doing?'

Raven sighed. 'I still miss them, your majesty,' she answered. 'I've been living alone ever since. Not even close to getting married. I sometimes babysit for my sister, Starla, from time to time when she helps out her husband, which is kind of the case here.'

Queen Cymbaline took Twila from Prince Avondale's hands. She looked at Twila as she touched the Fairy Queen's long black hair. 'It is good to hear you are okay, Raven,' she said, handing Twila back to Raven, 'But you do need to keep a tighter watch over your niece since she discovered she can fly.' She laughed softly as she said this.

'I'm only sorry for the intrusion, your majesty,' Raven said.

'Do not worry, Raven,' smiled Queen Cymbaline. 'Your intrusion was not an inconvenience in the very least. Toddlers can be a handful. Do be careful with her, though, especially whenever the dragon should show himself again and attack.'

Raven sighed, thinking about her parents, how much she missed them. She then turned to the Queen. 'Isn't there a way that the dragon could be destroyed once and for all?' she asked. 'There must be!'

Queen Cymbaline sighed. 'If only,' she said sadly. 'If there is a way, I know not of it. I would love nothing more than to get rid of the threat of Shadowfire once and for all. Sadly, none of us knows of such a way unless the Lord of Sabaoth reveals it to us.'

Raven nodded sadly.

Queen Cymbaline and Prince Avondale escorted Raven out of the castle to the surprise of Lavender and Laurelin, who thought they would be angry at Raven's intrusion. They saw the expressions on the faces of the Queen and her brother but they were not expressions of displeasure or anger. They flew toward Raven and bowed before the Queen.

'Your majesties,' Lavender and Laurelin said in unison.

'Your friends, Raven?' Queen Cymbaline asked.

Raven sighed. 'I hope so.'

'Raven, we are,' protested Lavender and Laurelin.

'These are my friends, Lavender and Laurelin,' Raven told the Queen. 'They are my best friends.'

Queen Cymbaline bade both Lavender and Laurelin to rise. 'It is a pleasure to meet the both of you, Lavender, Laurelin,' she said.

'And you too, your highnesses,' they both said.

'Were you looking after young Twila as well?' Prince Avondale asked.

'Not really,' Laurelin answered. 'Not at the time. We found Raven and Twila by the Silverstreams when we flew by.'

'It is one of my favorite spots to go to in Arundel Haven,' Raven said. 'Nice and peaceful, hearing the sounds of the water flowing down the river.'

'Will you be returning to the Silverstreams now that you have your flyaway niece back, Raven?' asked Prince Avondale.

'I think I will just go home and look after Twila there,' Raven sighed. 'I am still winded from flying after her. She's becoming more and more of a handful as of late.'

'We'll help you look after Twila, Raven,' Lavender told Raven. 'For one thing, it'll be good training for me when I have one of my own.'

Laurelin nodded.

'Thank you, girls,' Raven smiled.

'Provided we have a picnic at Rosemont Meadows,' Laurelin continued, 'There, Twila will have plenty of room to fly or run around if she chooses. It's more of an ideal place to have her play.'

Raven agreed.

Queen Cymbaline and Prince Avondale nodded and returned to the castle.

An hour later, they were having a picnic at Rosemont Meadows. Twila chased a butterfly while Raven kept an eye on her as they chatted. Raven had stuff for sandwiches and tea, which was brewed the night before by Raven after her friends had left. They drank the tea from glasses made by Raven's mother years before the dragon had taken Raven's parents. After a while, Twila returned to Raven's side and whined, 'I'm hungry, Aunt Raven.'

Raven gave Twila a slice of bread with homemade grape jam on it, which Twila took and ate. Raven poured tea in a small cup for Twila to drink. Twila drank a little bit before spilling some on the blanket that Raven had brought. 'Twila,' Raven chided the little girl.

Lavender and Laurelin giggled.

They ate and drank tea while the wind gently blew. The temperature had dropped a little and it was slightly cooler than before. 'You make that jam yourself?' Laurelin asked.

'No, Starla had made it,' Raven answered. 'She's better at making jams. I still don't know the secret to making jams as good as her. I'm better at making soups and stuff like that.'

'I guess I have to learn how to cook before Jax asks me to marry him,' Laurelin said, 'Learn how to make homemade jam and stuff.'

'My sister can show you how to make jams,' Raven said to her, 'I can help you with the rest.'

'Good deal,' Lavender nodded.

Raven wiped the jam off Twila's face after she had finished. Raven sighed. 'You sure know how to make a mess, don't you, Twila?' she told the toddler.

Twila giggled.

Lavender stared up at the clouds. 'We may be getting some rain very soon,' she said. 'I think we better cut our picnic short. I hate getting wet.'

'Do you think it'll hold up until we get home?' Laurelin asked.

'I hope so,' Raven said, sniffing the air. 'Smells like rain, all right, and… something else.'

'Like what?' Lavender asked.

There was a boom in the sky. They looked up and saw the clouds becoming dark. They felt a hot, bitter breeze blow through. Raven gasped.

'Shadowfire! Shadowfire's coming!' She grabbed Twila. 'Fly, fly!'

Laurelin looked up and saw a dark, ominous figure descending from the sky. Lavender grabbed her hand. 'Come on, Laurelin! Forget about the stuff!'

The fairies took to the air and scattered. The dragon started after Raven, who turned around and saw the black figure approaching. She managed to evade the outstretched claws as she flew low, dodging every swipe the dragon made. She cried out, 'Help, help!'

The dragon laughed as he continued to pursue Raven. She held on to Twila tighter as the toddler cried in fright. 'Don't worry, Twila,' Raven cried, frightened as she was.

As the dragon continued his pursuit, he laughed. 'Who are you trying to fool, fairy?' he asked. 'I can smell your fear, hear it in your voice. You and your young one are mine!'

'Leave me alone!' Raven cried.

Raven made it into the woods, but that did not stop Shadowfire. He belched forth fire from his mouth as he rose above the trees. Raven landed in the middle of the woods and saw that Shadowfire was surrounding the trees around her with flames to trap her. He circled the area where he had trapped the black fairy and her niece, waiting for them to emerge. Raven breathed heavily, her face an expression of terror. She could already feel the heat coming from the flames, closing in around her.

'Come out, come out, little fairy,' mocked the dragon. 'The flames are magical, and I have commanded them to close in around you. You can either die by my hands or by incineration. Your choice!'

Raven cried out. 'Father God, deliver me I pray, in the name of Your Son Jesus Christ,' she prayed. 'Spare me and my niece by Your grace and mercy!'

The enchanted flames closed in around her. She breathed a deep sigh as sweat flowed from her body. She tensed herself and shot out from among the trees before the flames could reach her.

Shadowfire was waiting. He made a grab for Raven but missed. Raven cried out to God to deliver her as she flew as fast as she could away from the dragon, but the dragon did not relent. He continued after her, reaching out to her but missing witheach attempt. Raven headed down the Silverstreams, flying low and close to the water.

Shadowfire belched forth flames in Raven's direction, but Raven dodged.

Raven whispered a silent prayer as the chase continued. 'I will catch you, fairy,' the dragon boomed. 'It is inevitable! You are doomed!'

Raven continued down the flowing river. She heard her niece crying, 'I scared, Aunt Raven!'

'I know, honey,' she cried. 'As the Lord lives, I will not let Shadowfire have you! Not while there is breath in me!'

Shadowfire caught Raven with a swipe, knocking the ebony fairy to the shore. Raven landed hard, crying out in pain but keeping a tight hold on the weeping Twila. As the dragon laughed, he hovered over her.

'No place to fly, fairy,' he mocked. 'You would make an excellent sacrifice to my master.'

'Raven, fly!' she heard Lavender and Laurelin cry. 'Get Twila to safety!'

'What about you?' Raven cried.

'I will have all of you,' the dragon shouted, seizing Lavender as she flew by. Laurelin flew around him to try and confuse him.

'Let her go,' Laurelin cried. To Raven she cried, 'Raven, fly! Get Twila to safety! We'll distract the dragon as long as we can!'

'I can't move,' Raven cried. 'I think I broke my leg!'

'Can you fly?'

'I can't stand up,' cried Raven.

'Let me go,' Lavender cried.

'No hope, no escape for you,' Shadowfire replied as he caught Laurelin. He secured her with his tail and proceeded to grab Raven. Before he could grab her, there was a mighty roar in front of him. A mighty wave approached, growing as it drew closer. The surprised dragon was caught, releasing Lavender and Laurelin in the process. They immediately flew toward Raven, grabbed her arms as she held Twila, and flew away.

Shadowfire was carried down the river for nearly a kilometer before he was able to break free. By the time he was free, he looked around for the fairies, but he could not find them. He cursed and after a final, unsuccessful sweep, flew back to the Mountains of Shadow.

When they flew into town, a few of the Queen's soldiers flew toward them, having heard the rumor of the dragon's presence. Raven was wincing in pain.

'Let me take Twila,' Laurelin told her. Raven gave Twila to Laurelin.

'Raven's hurt,' Lavender told the soldiers. 'Shadowfire was after her, but we escaped. I'm not quite sure how, but I am thankful to be alive.' Her voice was shaky, frightened by the incident.

'We can take her to the royal healers,' the leader said. 'We'll tend to her.' Raven was taken to the healers. As it turned out, she had severely strained muscles in her leg, but it was not broken. As she was being tended to, Queen Cymbaline entered the room. She stared at Raven and asked, 'Are you okay? We heard of Shadowfire's apperance.'

Raven could not speak. She was overcome with fear. 'Take your time, Raven,' the Queen gently said. 'Try and relax first.'

One of the nurses gave her a cup of water to drink. Raven drank it and took deep breaths to try and calm down. 'I was at a picnic with Lavender and Laurelin at Rosemont Meadows,' she said. 'I felt a hot breeze and a foul scent in the air before he attacked. He flew after me and Twila. She was so scared, as was I.'

'Easy, Raven,' Queen Cymbaline said softly. 'You are safe now.

Where is your niece?'

'I gave her to Laurelin to return to my sister,' Raven answered, 'I first hid in the woods, but he sent enchanted flames my way to flush me out into the open. I made my flight to the Silverstreams where he knocked me to the shore, where it felt like I had broken my leg.'

'Your muscles were merely strained, but nothing broken,' the doctor told her, 'I will give you a drink to help ease the pain.'

'Thank you,' Raven said.

'What happened after that?' asked Queen Cymbaline.

'God answered my prayers, He must have,' Raven asked, 'He sent a mighty wave to deliver Lavender, Laurelin, and me from his grasp.' She shuddered. 'I have never been so frightened in all my life!'

Queen Cymbaline nodded sadly. 'I believe you are right, Raven,' she said softly. 'There must be a way to stop Shadowfire once and for all. Unfortunately, no fairy, or human for that matter, would know how to destroy him. For as long as it has been going on, we've not had the power to do anything about it.'

'There's got to be a way,' Raven proclaimed.

Queen Cymbaline bowed her head sadly. 'Stay the night here, Raven, and let the healers continue to tend to you,' she said. 'Then you can return to your home or stay with your sister if you prefer.'

'Thank you, your majesty,' Raven said.

Raven stayed overnight and was released the next afternoon. Raven still found walking painful, but she was able to fly. The moment she was released, she was met by Lavender, Laurelin, and a fairy who was in her late 20s. She looked almost like Raven but was slightly taller, had shorter hair, and wore a pink dress. In her arms was Twila, who looked at Raven.

'Boo-boo all better, Aunt Raven?' the toddler asked.

'Boo-boo still hurts, Twila,' Raven answered.

The fairy embraced Raven and wept, then looked into her eyes. 'When I heard Shadowfire had come after you, I thought you would end up like Mom and Dad!'

'I was very scared, Starla,' Raven replied, tears filling her eyes. 'I thought for a time I wouldn't make it! I was determined not to let Shadowfire have Twila.'

'Lavender and Laurelin told me everything,' Starla said. 'I am so thankful you were spared.'

'Lavender and Laurelin helped,' Raven said, releasing her older sister. 'God delivered us by sending a mighty wave to wash Shadowfire into the river long enough to escape.'

Starla sighed, shaking her head. 'You stayed at the castle all night?' she asked.

Raven nodded. 'She had the royal physicians take care of me overnight,' she answered. 'They gave me an elixir to help with the pain. I shouldn't be on my feet too much, so I'll have to keep winging it until my leg gets better.'

Starla sighed. 'I'm just thankful you survived an encounter with Shadowfire,' she said, 'It's a rarity to have a fairy escape the dragon's grasp once he sets his sights on one of us. I feared the worst when I first heard. Will you come stay with me and Roosevelt until you're better?'

Raven shook her head. 'No, I'll be fine,' she insisted. 'I can still cook and move around. I just have to not use my leg so much. I'll be okay.'

'I don't feel good about you being by yourself, Raven,' Starla protested, 'At least have your friends, Lavender and Laurelin, stay with you until you're better.'

'I'll be fine, sis, don't worry,' Raven insisted. 'I can have Lavender and Laurelin drop by and check on me until I'm better. I'll be okay, Starla, trust me!'

Starla shook her head. 'I still don't feel right about this, Raven,' she told her sister, 'You need someone to stay with you until you're better.'

'I'm a grown fairywoman now, Starla,' Raven protested. 'I've been living alone now for almost a year now. I've been just fine taking care of myself.'

'What you need, Raven, is a husband,' Starla stated, 'You need to find yourself a good fairyman and settle down.'

'You think I haven't been trying, Starla?' Raven shot back, 'I've been searching for years ever since Abin and I broke up, I've been looking *unsuccessfully*. Of course, it didn't help when he had started spreading vicious rumors about me! It's not from lack of trying, I assure you! It's just a matter of finding the right fairyman. It's so hard to find somebody trustworthy, true, faithful, and supportive.'

'Okay, okay, I get the picture,' Starla sighed, 'I'm so sorry, Raven. Who knows? Maybe that fairyman will find you when you least expect it, even when you're not looking. It was like that when I found Roosevelt.'

'He happened to be looking for you?'

'Something like that,' Starla answered, 'He was doing something for Dad when I first met him. We kind of hit it off and the rest is history. Sometimes, it's just a matter of being patient. Love will come when it's time.'

Raven sighed. 'I hope you're right,' she said sadly, 'Sometimes, it seems like love has been avoiding me altogether. I wonder if I will ever find that fairyman.'

Raven turned around and headed for home. Lavender and Laurelin followed her. Twila watched and turned to her mother. 'Aunt Raven go bye-bye,' she said.

Starla nodded. 'Yes, Twila,' she nodded, 'Your aunt Raven is going to her home.'

'Hungry, Mommy,' the toddler said.

'Okay, okay,' Starla said, 'We'll go home and feed you, Twila.' Starla turned around and flew back to her home.

Queen Cymbaline stared out the window of her chambers. Her thoughts were on what had happened to Raven the day before, how Shadowfire came after her and nearly caught her. Her heart was troubled dealing with the dragon. She wondered if there was a way to rid their lands of it and how it could be found. She fell to her knees by her bed and prayed silently, inaudible as her lips moved. She continued to pray for guidance and for God's direction. She was more troubled than when Shadowfire had killed Raven's parents the year before.

Prince Avondale found her older sister kneeling by her bed. He felt in his spirit that her heart was troubled, and he guessed it was from dealing with Shadowfire. He entered the room and knelt by her, clasping his hand in hers. When she looked at him, she had tears in her eyes.

'I fear for our people, Avondale,' she told him. 'How long must this go on? How long must our people suffer at the claws of Shadowfire?'

Prince Avondale sighed. 'I wish I had the answers, Cymbaline,' he sadly answered. 'I wish I did. I am just as grieved as you are, unsure of what to do.'

'I pray to God with all my heart for the answer,' Queen Cymbaline wept, 'for a way, for a sign.'

Prince Avondale sighed again. 'Perhaps now is not the right time for the answer, I know it is of no comfort, dear sister, but God allows things to happen for a reason. He will reveal the way when the time is right. I find it difficult as well, but we must trust God in this, no matter how hard it is.' He gently kissed his sister on the forehead and held her close, weeping with her as they continued to pray silently. They wondered if the matter with the dragon would be dealt with in their lifetime. 'Perhaps soon, God will have mercy on us and hear our prayers,' he said.

After nearly a half hour, they headed to the cottage where Raven was staying. They knocked on the door. At first there was no answer. 'Either Raven is gone or is asleep,' Prince Avondale said.

Queen Cymbaline knocked again. After a few seconds, Raven opened the door. She tried to bow, but she winced in pain when she tried. 'I'm sorry, your majesty,' she said, favoring her hurt leg.

'I wanted to check up on you, Raven,' Queen Cymbaline said, 'It's all right. Your leg is still sore, I see.'

Raven invited them inside. 'I am honored to welcome you to my home,' she said, 'Would you like some tea?'

'Thank you, Raven, we would,' Queen Cymbaline nodded as they sat down at the table. Raven grabbed a cup for each and placed them on the table. She poured hot tea in the cups and grabbed a cup for herself. She poured tea in her own cup and sat down as carefully as she could. 'I'm afraid I'm still in pain,' she said. 'I'm trying not to move it so much.'

'It would have made sense for you to have stayed with your sister, would it not?' Prince Avondale told her, taking a sip of his tea. He nodded and took another sip.

'Is it to your liking?' Raven asked.

'Speaking for myself, Raven, it is,' Queen Cymbaline answered, 'Avondale is right. Why won't you stay with your sister, Starla? Your leg needs as much rest as possible if it is to heal properly.'

'I know, your majesty,' Raven replied, 'I just don't want to be a burden to them. They have their hands full with Twila as it is, seeing firsthand how lively she is.'

'Indeed,' Prince Avondale said, 'but you are hurt. It will be hard for you to take care of yourself alone.'

'I know, it is difficult, but I am fine. I can hover without putting weight on my leg. Just so as long as I don't bump my leg on anything.'

'Sometimes it is hard to ask for help when you need it,' Queen Cymbaline said, 'Most of the time we think we can do things by ourselves but later find out that we are wrong. Please do not feel you are a burden to your sister. She loves and cares about you. Please don't harden your heart to help when you need it, especially to those who are willing to help.'

Raven nodded. 'I know, but I feel I can manage enough without help. I just don't like depending on anybody.'

'That is understandable,' Prince Avondale said, 'but there are times we must humble ourselves when the situation becomes too much for us to bear. It's good to be independent, but even the strongest of us need help when it's time.'

Raven sat down quietly as she drank her tea. After a long moment she asked, 'Do you think we will ever be rid of the dragon Shadowfire? I had nightmares last night about what had happened yesterday. I couldn't get the thoughts or the dream out of my head.'

'Prince Avondale and I have been praying about it and wondering the same thing,' said the Fairy Queen, 'It has been a burden on my heart and on my brother's.'

'I was very scared when the dragon attacked,' Raven said, 'It doesn't seem right that Twila has to grow up with the threat of Shadowfire attacking our people. I hope that if I have children, they will not grow up fearing the dragon may attack at any time.'

'As do I,' Queen Cymbaline sighed, 'Indeed, the times are evil. So much evil in the world, especially the ways of the humans.'

'Surely there must be some good humans out there,' Raven responded.

'They cannot be trusted,' Queen Cymbaline reiterated, 'The Word says that evil things proceed out of the heart of man, lies, deception, lust, unnatural affections. I forbid the fairies from making contact with humans for any reason.'

'But Jesus died for the humans as well, did He not? There are some good humans out there who, I feel, love the Lord as we do.'

Queen Cymbaline nodded. 'I am forced to agree with you there, Raven, but there are also those who pretend to be good but are wicked inside. They pretend to know the Lord but show they are of the devil.'

'Only God knows the heart of a person,' stated Raven.

'Still, contact with humans is forbidden, Raven, remember that,' Prince Avondale quipped. 'The humans are too wicked to ever live in peace with fairies, given their nature.'

'But we are no better than the humans, surely, does the Word not say, *Whosoever shall call upon the name of the Lord shall be saved?*'

'You give a compelling argument, Raven,' Queen Cymbaline said, 'But my decree must stand for the good of all fairies of Arundel Haven. If any human found out about Arundel Haven, who knows what wickedness would befall us? For our protection, we must remain hidden from human eyes. They must not set foot in Arundel Haven!'

Raven nodded. 'I understand, your majesty, *The heart is deceitful above all things, and is desperately wicked.* I know it is for our protection, but what if it is God's will that a human would meet one of us?'

'Just what are you suggesting, Raven?' Prince Avondale asked.

'What if God allows a human who knows Christ to know of our existence? It could happen.'

'It *must not* happen,' insisted Queen Cymbaline sharply. After a pause, she sighed. 'I am trying to do what is best for our people, maybe there are humans who can be trusted, but dare we take that chance? There are those who claim to be of Christ but are not, who even kill for their religion, praying to other gods and the goddess Ashtaroth as it were instead of the true and living God. We cannot afford to be exposed to their poison.'

Raven remained silent. Could Queen Cymbaline be right in isolating Arundel Haven from the human world? She found herself longing to meet a human for herself, someone who knew Christ like she did, who loved the Lord and His Word. *Would it be possible, she thought, that despite what Queen Cymbaline believed, that fairies and humans could live together in peace?* She knew it would be difficult to find honest and God-fearing humans, but she knew they were out there. She spoke nothing to the Queen and the Prince. 'You seem deep in thought, Raven,' said Prince Avondale in observation.

'It's nothing, really, I'm just thankful God delivered me from the claws of Shadowfire.'

Both Queen Cymbaline and Prince Avondale nodded when she said that. Raven poured some more tea for them.

The next day, Raven was visited by Starla along with Twila. She spent most of the day resting her sore leg. The pain was easing up but the physicians in the castle had told her to get as much rest as she could. She hated to stay in bed. Starla cooked a mixture of rice, chicken, and okra, which Raven loved. Try as she might, she could not make it as well as her older sister. Twila sat at the table and ate while Raven sat at the table with her foot propped up on a chair with a pillow on top. 'I'll be glad when this leg is better,' Raven said. 'I am sick of lying in bed and not moving! I think I'm starting to go stir crazy here!'

'You're beginning to act like Twila, Raven,' replied Starla, 'I declare, you can be such a baby!'

'You try having to remain in one place for a long time not being able to move without pain,' groaned Raven. 'Would you like to switch places with me, then?'

Starla scoffed. 'No thanks, Raven,' she answered, 'Being chased by a dragon flying for my life is not my idea of fun.'

Raven ate the bowl of rice mix. 'What is your secret to making this?' she asked. 'I can never get it right.'

'It all depends on the spices you use; I'll have to show you what spices you need to get.'

'Want more, Mommy,' Twila told her mother, holding her bowl.

'My, my, Twila,' Starla chuckled, staring at her daughter, 'You must be one hungry little girl!'

She took her daughter's plate and gave her a little more and gave it back to her. 'It's hot, Twila,' she warned her.

'More juice, Mommy?'

'What do you say, Twila?'

'Please?'

Starla nodded and poured her some more juice. 'Thank you, Mommy,' Twila said sweetly.

Starla poured Raven some more juice as well. 'Thank you, Starla,' she said.

'How long did the physicians say you have to rest it?' Starla asked.

'A few more days, I'm sick of just sitting here.'

'If you want your leg to heal up properly, Raven, you'd better do what the physicians say. You don't want your leg to get any worse, do you?'

Raven sighed. 'No, I suppose not.'

Outside, they heard the pitter-patter of rain falling. Starla sighed. She'd suspected it would rain, having seen the rainclouds on her way to Raven's place. 'Looks like we're going to be here for a while, Twila,' she said.

'Is it raining, Mommy?' Twila asked.

Starla nodded. 'It's not good for our wings, we can't fly well in the rain.' She laughed. 'I remember when you were younger, Raven, when it was raining.'

Raven frowned. 'Don't remind me, I wound up coming home all muddy, which did not please Mom and Dad. I wasn't allowed to come inside until the mud was washed off me.'

Starla laughed. 'Mom and Dad would warn us not to fly in the rain, but you had to learn the hard way. In fact, I see a little bit of you in Twila.'

Raven merely drank her juice and ate some rice. 'I'd rather forget about it, if that's all the same to you, I didn't know any better, okay? I was younger then.'

'You were always stubborn and had to do things your way,' said Starla. 'You insisted you knew better but you found out the hard way that you didn't. You were also adventurous, trying new things.'

'I am older and wiser now, thank you very much,' retorted Raven sternly. All the while, Twila giggled at the exchange between her mother and aunt. Raven stared in mock anger at Twila.

'You think it's funny, little girl?' she asked, placing her hands upon her shoulders, 'Does Twila think it's funny?'

Twila giggled and hid her face. Raven couldn't help but burst into laughter. She couldn't stay mad at Twila, even mock mad. Twila was so cute and had a certain charm to her.

'She is definitely another you, Raven,' Starla laughed.

Raven's face turned grave, looking at Twila. She sighed. 'I wish Mom and Dad could see Twila now,' she said softly. 'They had barely known her when the dragon had taken them away.'

Starla nodded sadly. 'I know, Raven, I miss them too.'

'I honestly hope and pray I find a wonderful fairyman as you found Roosevelt,' sighed Raven.

'He will come to you in time,' said Starla reassuringly.

Raven flew from her seat and opened the door, watching the rain fall from the sky. She looked up into the clouds. Rain clouds had covered the sky, blocking out the sun. In the distance, outside the town, she saw a patch of light shoot through the black clouds, a rainbow appearing. Raven felt a touch of encouragement in her heart. She continued to stare at the rainbow. Starla and Twila joined her and looked out the door. Twila saw the rainbow and pointed it out to her mother. 'Twila like rainbows, Mommy,' she said.

Starla smiled. 'I know you do, isn't it pretty?'

'Yes,' the toddler answered.

'I think so, too,' Raven smiled.

They watched as the rain continued to fall, staring at the patch of light and the rainbow. For the moment, Raven forgot about the pain of her injury.

Her thoughts went to a place where she had been before, but she had told nobody about, what she called her private place. She thought more and more about it, and she decided as soon as her leg was well enough, she would return.

She was determined to return there again.

Starla and Twila flew back home after the rain had stopped. She stored the leftover rice her sister had cooked. It was about sunset. Raven lit her candles in her home before the sun fully settled beyond the horizon.

She sat down again at the table and propped her leg upon the chair with the pillow. Her thoughts returned to the secret place she had been, which she did not tell Lavender, Laurelin, or any other fairy of. It was a wooded area in the human world, secluded and cut off from the human population, which no human really went to. She also felt something else, what was it? She wasn't quite sure what. She had a feeling that what she desired, what she sought, was out there, out in those woods. But what? She wasn't quite sure herself.

The desire was stronger than ever, to find out what it was. She knew what she wanted, but was what she really wanted out there? She made up her mind to find out as soon as she was better. No, tomorrow, tomorrow—if it was not raining. It was decided, then. She would return tomorrow. Perhaps whatever it was she was looking for was out there.

She heard a knock on the door. She rose from her seat and fluttered toward the door. When she opened it, Lavender, and Laurelin along with their boyfriends Jax and Derreck appeared. Laurelin had a plate of food and Lavender had a container of tea. 'Come in,' Raven said as she made her way back to her seat.

'How's your leg feeling?' Laurelin asked.

'Still sore, but getting better,' Raven answered. 'I don't like being so inactive, not being able to walk or fly.'

'I still can't believe you had encountered Shadowfire and survived,' Jax said in awe, 'I thought that would be it for you when I first heard. Do you know you're the first fairy to ever successfully escape Shadowfire?'

'Hey, don't forget us,' protested Lavender, giving Jax a queer look.

'Yeah, but Shadowfire mainly flew after Raven and Twila,' Derreck stated.

'*We, Lavender, Laurelin and I,* are the first fairies to ever escape Shadowfire,' Raven corrected them. 'We wouldn't have escaped had the Lord not intervened.'

'It's a miracle we survived,' Lavender said, 'but why do you credit the God of the humans?'

'God created *all* living things,' Raven stated, '*all* of us! He rescued us and delivered us from Shadowfire. How do you explain the wave that appeared and crashed into Shadowfire? Can you explain that?' Lavender and Laurelin shook their heads.

'When Shadowfire pursued me, I prayed for Him to deliver us, He guided me to the Silverstreams then sent a mighty wave to wash Shadowfire away and allowed us to escape.'

'Why would the God of the humans have anything to do with us fairies?' Derreck asked.

'I believe that whosoever shall call upon the name of the Lord Jesus Christ shall be saved' Raven explained, 'Yes, humans are wicked and evil, natural born sinners, ever since Adam and Eve disobeyed God for partaking of the forbidden fruit, the fruit of the knowledge of good and evil. Many humans reject our Creator and serve false gods or goddesses, worship the creature and not the Creator. Do you think anybody deserves to go to heaven, anybody?'

'Queen Cymbaline,' Jax answered.

'Why?'

'Because she is a good queen, wise and benevolent. Prince Avondale as well.'

'They would tell you they *don't* deserve to go to heaven,' Raven told them, 'Yet, they are going because of not for what they'd done, but what Jesus has done.'

The other fairies laughed. 'You've got to be kidding, Raven,' Laurelin scoffed, refusing to believe Raven's words.

'None of us deserve heaven, and both Queen Cymbaline and Prince Avondale will tell you likewise. They believe, like I do: Jesus died on the cross for our sins, we are sinners bound for hell, and in need of repentance. We put our faith and trust in Jesus Christ to forgive us of our sins and we commit our lives to Him, trust in His finished work and in His finished work *only* for our salvation. Queen Cymbaline has committed her rule to the King of Kings and Lord of Lords, to the Lamb of God, the Holy One of Israel, Emmanuel, who reigns forever and ever.'

'You are crazy, Raven,' Laurelin frowned, 'That's the one thing I disagree on with Queen Cymbaline. I don't trust in the God of the humans. Do you know how bad humans are?'

'Yes,' Raven nodded, 'They do not know God, they do not know the Saviour who can deliver them from hell. All of us are like sheep and have gone astray, we have gone our own ways, and that is where we and the humans have gone wrong.'

Raven sat down. Laurelin sat the plate down and Lavender grabbed a cup and utensils and placed them upon the table. 'You are one crazy fairy, Raven,' Lavender responded, 'but I guess that's what we love about you.'

Raven said nothing as she drank some tea. 'I love you guys too, but heaven is real, and hell is real. I don't want any of you to go to hell.'

The others shook their heads. 'It's good your leg is getting better,' Jax said, 'but I don't want to hear any more of the human religion.'

Raven shook her head. 'If only you knew.' She then changed the subject and continued eating.

'Did your sister stop by today?' asked Laurelin.

'She and Twila,' Raven answered. 'Twila is better and has maybe even forgotten about the dragon. She shouldn't have to live in the darkness of the threat of Shadowfire.'

'I wish none of us did,' Derreck frowned, 'There are times I step out the door and worry about the dragon appearing out of nowhere to swoop down and destroy me.'

Raven did not speak immediately. She sat deep in thought. 'There must be something we can do to rid ourselves of the dragon,' Jax groaned.

'Even Queen Cymbaline doesn't know how to destroy the dragon,' Derreck retorted, 'as wise as she is.'

'If there is, how do we find out what it is?' Jax asked.

Raven shook her head and said nothing.

'How are you emotionally?' Lavender asked Raven.

'Scared and angry,' Raven answered, 'The worst thing is the helpless feeling and not knowing what to do about it. I know it's the same old story, but I just hate not knowing what to do about it!'

'I'd hate to have to move from Arundel Haven,' Lavender said, 'but where else can we go? This is our home, and I don't want to leave here, the only home we fairies have ever known.'

'There is a way,' Raven said, 'It's just a matter of finding out what it is.'

Something inside her told her the answer would be revealed soon, and the death of the dragon would be drawing nigh. She kept silent about it, and silently prayed that it would be so. She finished her meal and sat back in the chair. She poured herself another glass of tea as Laurelin took the plate away and washed it.

'Thank you for bringing me the food, Laurelin,' she said.

'Thank my mother,' Laurelin replied, 'She cooked the meal. She's beginning to teach me how to cook. I hope you can show me how to cook as well.'

'I will do my best once I am able to,' said Raven.

A short time later, they left for their homes, leaving Raven all alone. She flittered toward her bed and laid down, getting settled on her pillow. The candles continued to burn as she laid there, staring up at the ceiling. She felt a touching in her spirit again, deep inside. She felt led to go to her usual place tomorrow, to her secret place.

'What else is out there?' she asked herself aloud. 'Is there anything special about that place?'

She remained silent as she felt the touch again. 'And the dragon?' she asked, 'What about the dragon? I'm sure Queen Cymbaline and Prince Avondale have been praying to You to provide a way as well. Why speak to me? I'm not that prevalent. I'm not anything special. I was grateful when the Queen and Prince had visited me yesterday. I am grateful they were concerned about me, but I am nothing special at all, just a regular fairy woman.'

She laid there, silent, as she closed her eyes. 'I have so many questions, but I know you already knew that,' she sighed, 'but I can't help but wonder. My knowledge and abilities are very finite. I was very scared when the dragon came after me, but I thank You that You delivered me from Shadowfire. I know if it wasn't for You, I wouldn't be here at all.'

After almost a half hour, Raven fell asleep as the candles continued to burn and eventually burned out.

She awoke the next morning. The pain in her leg was almost gone. She slowly rose from the bed and tried walking on her bad leg. She still felt pain, but it was much less than before. She looked at the candles.

'I should have put the candles out before I went to sleep,' she frowned. She went into one of the drawers and grabbed a handful of candles and replaced them. She tossed the used candles in the small garbage can in the kitchen. She opened the door and stared outside. She felt the moving in her spirit to go. 'What would Queen Cymbaline say if she found out?' she wondered, 'I hope she won't be too mad, but if this is from You, Lord, I will go. Just protect me from the dragon!'

She sighed, closed the door, and took to the air, flying away from her cottage, and as she left the village, she rose further into the air and into the clouds.

An hour later, Starla arrived at Raven's house, holding Twila in her arms. She knocked on the door but there was no answer.

'Raven? Raven, are you home?' she cried, knocking again.

She stepped inside. She again called out her sister's name. She headed into the bedroom and found it empty. 'Where Aunt Raven, Mommy?' Twila asked.

Starla shook her head. 'Mommy doesn't know, sweetheart, Mommy wants to know that too.'

'Aunt Raven went bye-bye?'

'Yes, it looks like your aunt Raven did go bye-bye, sweetie,' answered Starla, 'but where did she go? When did she leave and when will she come back?'

'That's what we would like to know,' came the voice of Lavender. She entered the house with Laurelin beside her. 'Did you come here looking for Raven, too?'

Starla nodded. 'I wanted her to look after Twila again since Roosevelt needs help,' she told them, 'I just got here and wondered if she might have overslept, but I found her gone. Any idea where she could have gone to?'

'No idea,' Lavender answered. 'Unless…'

Starla stared at her. 'Unless what?'

'Raven mentioned something about a secret place,' Laurelin said, 'She refused to tell us anything more than that. She says it's a private place, but we're concerned it may be too close to humans.'

'Humans?' Starla exclaimed, startled.

'This is not the first time she has done it,' Lavender said, 'She has gone to this place other times before, four or five, I'm not sure.'

'What? Is she crazy?' Starla exclaimed, 'She knows we're not supposed to be anywhere near humans! Sooner or later, she's going to get into a lot of trouble!'

'What's worse, what if the Queen finds out?' Laurelin asked, 'Something's going on, and Raven is not telling us what! What if she's been going to a place too close to humans? She could very well risk revealing the knowledge of our existence!'

'Indeed, she could be putting all of us in danger,' Lavender added. 'As if Shadowfire wasn't bad enough!'

'Should we tell Queen Cymbaline?' Laurelin asked.

Starla shook her head. 'I don't know,' she groaned in frustration, 'It could be nothing, but then again, it could very well put all of us in danger. We'll give Raven a chance to explain herself when she gets back.'

'If Shadowfire hasn't found her and taken her,' Lavender said. 'You'd think that after her encounter with Shadowfire that she would not leave Arundel Haven.'

'Apparently that's not the case,' Starla frowned, 'I'm worried about Raven, though.'

'Where Aunt Raven?' Twila asked.

'I don't know, sweetie,' Starla answered, 'That's we're trying to find out. We hope she comes back.'

'And when she does,' Laurelin stated, 'she better have a good explanation. This time, we won't take no for an answer.'

'And if she won't answer us,' Lavender added, 'she'll have to tell Queen Cymbaline.'

'I just want my sister home safely,' Starla said.

Chapter Four

Mordecai awoke with a startled look upon his face.

He found himself in his bed, his body shaking. It was the same dream he had been having the past four nights, about being in a valley and confronting a dragon who seemed to know about him, though he did not know his name or what prophecy the dragon was talking about. He couldn't stop thinking about the dream. *Why the same dream over and over? he asked himself, What does it mean? Dragons couldn't be real, could they?* The only dragon he knew was real was the devil, who was called the dragon in Revelation 20. He was still shaking from the dream. He stepped out of bed and walked downstairs.

He entered the kitchen, grabbed a soda, and sat down. He did his best to try and forget the dream. He didn't understand why he was having that particular dream. 'LORD, what does it mean?' he asked, 'It's gotten me frightened and confused. I don't know why I keep having this dream.'

As he sat, Cece headed downstairs, seeing the light on. She saw Mordecai sitting at the table. She walked over to him and said, 'Mordy, it's three in the morning. What are you doing up? You need to get some more rest before school.'

Mordecai turned around. 'I've had a bad dream; the same one I've been having the past four nights.'

'Dream?' Cece tentatively asked. 'What kind of dream?'

Mordecai drank his soda while Cece sat down. He shook his head. 'I can't get it out of my head for some reason, and it scares me,' he told her.

'What was it about?' Cece asked.

'I was in a valley, a dark valley,' Mordecai said, 'I could feel the darkness, the despair and hopelessness, of death. I could see no one else there. I was all alone. As I journeyed through the valley trying to find a way out, there appeared before me a dragon, a large dragon, maybe forty feet tall, something like that. He was totally in black, pitch black all over him from scale to scale. He gazed at me and asked me, "Who are you, human?"

'I did not tell him my name. He continued to question me and asked me who I was. I then said, "A nobody. Just a nobody."

'I heard him laugh. "Indeed you are," he replied, "And yet, I know you are a threat to me. I know this now beyond a shadow of a doubt."

' "Why do you consider me a threat?" I asked.

' "I sense you are the one the old prophecy speaks of," he answered me, "the one who will destroy me. By all that's unholy, I will not allow that to happen!"

' "Prophecy? What prophecy?" I asked him.

' "You do not know now, but soon you will, human," he insisted, "Tell me your name."

' "Who are you?" I asked, "Why do you believe I am the one that some prophecy had spoken of? What threat could I be to you?"

' "As long as you live, human," the dragon answered, "I can never be at peace. Sooner or later, I will find out who you are and where you live! You seek answers that will not be given to you, but I will deal with you when I find you. I will not allow the prophecy to come true!" He roared and belched forth fire in my direction. I was surrounded by the flames, and then I woke up. I've had dreams like that for the past four nights, and it's weighing heavily on me.'

'Wow, must have been some dream,' Cece replied, 'But, Mordy, you know dreams are not real.'

'Yet I've been having this same dream night after night and I don't know why,' groaned Mordecai. 'It's gotten me on pins and needles, not knowing what it means or why I've been having them.'

'Could it be some things you've eaten the past four nights?' Cece asked.

Mordecai shook his head. 'I ate nothing unusual or bad,' he answered, 'I've eaten what the whole family ate. Nothing more than that.'

'And you say you've had the same dream the past four nights?'

Mordecai nodded. 'More or less,' he answered.

'And he spoke of some kind of prophecy in the dream?'

Mordecai nodded. 'I don't know what he meant by that. He refused to give me any answers, but he claims I will know.'

Cece sighed. 'It was all a bad dream, Mordy. Let it go. A bad dream, nothing more. But it is puzzling why you have the same dream every night.'

'That's what troubles me, sis,' said Mordecai in frustration, 'I'm afraid I may have that dream again. Why do I keep having that dream? What does it mean? I don't understand.'

Cece could not answer. 'I'm going back to bed,' she said, yawning. 'Maybe the dreams will stop after a while. I don't know what to tell you.'

Mordecai sighed. 'Nothing to say, I'm afraid, I just want the dreams to stop, even find out why I'm having them.'

Cece returned upstairs. Mordecai finished his soda and made his way back upstairs and back to bed.

Mordecai was unable to get back to sleep, disturbed by the dream. He laid there, tossing, and turning, until the alarm went off before sunrise. He sighed and got up, a bit tired and disturbed. He had to shake it off. It was time for school. He got dressed and headed out of the bedroom door with books in his hands. Instead of heading for the kitchen, he entered the garage and grabbed his bike, securing the books on the back. He looked out the door as he wheeled his bike out. He prepared his poncho just in case. It was still a bit dark and was hard to tell if there were rainclouds or not. He had heard reports that it may rain again, but it was best to be prepared, he thought. He sighed. He closed the garage door, got on his bike, and pedaled away.

Cece yawned as she exited her room. She saw that her brother was already gone, as was his wont. She sighed. She was happy that her friend Tiffany was still allowed to drive to school though she would have to pay for the damages out of the money she earned part-time. She was hoping Mordecai would still be home and allow her to ask him if he wanted to ride with her and her friends to school. She shook her head. She hated to see her brother having to go through what he was going through, his battle with depression, dealing with the bullies.

She wondered why their parents wouldn't teach Mordecai how to drive? She felt it was unfair to him and felt bad that she was being taught and Mordecai wasn't. She grabbed some cereal from the cabinet and a bowl of milk from the refrigerator and ate. She continued to think about her brother, unable to forget. She ate silently as she waited for Tiffany and Sharon to arrive. By the time she finished her cereal, she heard a knock on the door. She put the bowl in the sink, the cereal in the cabinet, the milk in the refrigerator, grabbed her books, and headed toward the door.

Sharon was stood waiting. 'Ready?' she asked.

Cece nodded. She looked out into the sky. 'So far so good, at least for now. I just hope the rain clouds will stay away today.'

She followed Sharon to the car. She got in the back seat while Sharon sat in the front. Tiffany sighed. 'I'm fortunate to still be allowed to drive,' she said, 'but only to school and work.'

'You were fortunate,' Cece said, 'Be glad you can still drive to school.'

'I do have to pay for the damages, pay to have the body fixed,' frowned Tiffany, 'It'll take a month for me to work it off.'

'No going to the mall or anything like that?' Cece asked.

'He was explicit. Only to work and school, that's it. Kind of bummed out about it. I hope to have it worked off soon.'

'Wouldn't the insurance pay for the repairs?' Sharon asked.

'It will,' Tiffany answered, 'but my father said I have to pay for the damage in full. His way of punishing me. He says it's for my careless driving.'

As they reached Oak Ridge Rd, Tiffany turned right. As she sped up, Sharon said, 'I hope you've learned your lesson.'

'Oh, pipe down,' Tiffany retorted.

As Tiffany drove down the road, she saw a limousine going about 20 miles per hour. She slowed down as traffic passed by. She honked her horn. 'Come on, snails, speed up,' she cried.

'Take it easy, Tiff,' Sharon said softly.

'"Take it easy?" Take it easy my foot,' she growled, 'This is a 45 mile an hour zone and this nut's doing 20! He needs to speed it up!' She glanced in the other lane and saw cars passing by, preventing her from changing lanes. 'What is this guy's problem?' she cried, 'If he's having car problems, he needs to put on his emergency lights.'

'Maybe he's following Mordy,' Cece suggested. 'He is riding down the road.'

'Well, he better be,' Tiffany frowned.

'I don't see Mordy up there,' Sharon stated. 'I think I see him further ahead, about close to a half mile in front.'

'Then why is this jege going so slow?' growled Tiffany.

Tiffany continued to glance at the other lane, hoping for the break to pass the slow limo. When she saw a break, she quickly shifted to the other lane. As she did, the other car behind her switched at the same time and nearly hit her, speeding up and passing her using the medium lane as the horn was honked, nearly hitting Tiffany as she merged to the other lane. Tiffany honked back. 'Jackass!' she cried, 'Stinking jege!'

'Is that guy crazy?' Sharon cried.

'Idiot!' Tiffany added.

'Got to be careful, Tiffany,' Cece said. 'There's so much road rage going on. You don't want to get into it with someone who is completely insane and demented.'

Tiffany said nothing but growled. She went back into the right lane a few hundred yards in front of the limo. Up ahead, she saw a few cars passing by Mordecai. She heard the same driver that had passed her honk at Mordecai and speed past him. She then carefully passed Mordecai and drove down the road.

'Poor Mordy,' Tiffany said, 'He has to put up with a lot of junk from these insane jeges.'

Cece looked behind at Mordecai but said nothing.

'I hope it's not raining when we play Jones,' Sharon said. 'I hate having mud on me or my uniform.'

'It shouldn't be raining on Friday,' Cece replied, turning back around. 'At least, it better not. The forecasts say it should be clear.'

'They're not always right, though,' Tiffany frowned. 'Sometimes they say it'll rain but it doesn't, and they say it won't rain but it winds up raining.'

'Go figure,' scoffed Sharon. She turned to Cece, 'Heard anything from Oscar yet?'

Cece shook her head. 'Nothing,' she sighed. 'I don't know what's going on with him. I'm not going to wait forever. I told him unless he contacts me, it's over. I'm just sick and tired of having to play his sick game. I don't appreciate being treated like that.'

'He's given you no explanation at all?' Sharon asked.

'Nothing,' Cece answered. 'Still no reply of any kind at all. I think he's seeing somebody else, but I don't know exactly who, though.'

'If he is seeing somebody else,' Tiffany said.

'He's got to be seeing somebody else,' Cece frowned. 'I can't think of anything else at this point. Got to be the only explanation. If it isn't, then why would he refuse to talk to me? This doesn't make any sense at all!'

'Give him a little more time, Cece,' Sharon calmly said. 'Give him a chance to explain himself.'

'I have, and I'm sick of waiting,' Cece replied irritably, 'Any boy that plays games like that is not worth having, no matter how good he looks! I have feelings, too! I don't mind being there for him, but he's got to be willing to do the same for me! A relationship ought to be 100% on both sides, not one way all the time.'

'I hear you, Cece,' Tiffany said. 'I wouldn't want any boy treating me like that. Personally, I wouldn't tolerate it.'

'That's how I feel right now,' Cece groaned.

Tiffany pulled into the parking lot and parked the car. She waited for the other girls to get out before she locked it. They walked together as they made their way on campus.

As they walked, they found Frank, Stu, and Chuck surrounded by five of the other cheerleaders. They were standing near the lunchroom entrance. A few other students listened as they talked. 'Did we not say that we would kick Colonial's butt, rain or no rain?'

Chuck said. 'Their defense had no answer to my passing or Stu's running and Frank just stopped their runners cold as well as gaining some sacks. I told you I would pass for over 300 yards!'

'You did say so, Chuck,' one of the cheerleaders replied.

Cece shook her head. 'Judas Priest, do we have to listen to his garbage all day?' she groaned.

'They did say they were going to come out and do what they were going to do, and they did,' Sharon said. 'We won and we won big.'

'I'm not debating that, I have no problems,' Cece said, 'but these guys are so high on themselves they have enough hot air to fill all the balloons in the world for a century to come at least. I don't like people who are so full of themselves.'

'Did you see the way I had flattened their quarterback?' Frank told them. 'Dick Butkus, eat your heart out! When I get to the pros, I'm going to show them I'm the best ever!'

'So will I,' Chuck replied, 'My career will be pure hall of fame, baby!'

Cece scoffed. 'If you ever get to the pros.'

One of the cheerleaders turned around and said, 'Everybody's a critic. You're jealous because you don't have a boyfriend who's as good as Frank, Chuck, or Stu.'

'Or as full of themselves. There's no question you guys have skill and athletic abilities, but your attitude sucks dirt!'

'What do you know, Cece Jefferson?' another cheerleader asked, 'You must have been asleep during last Friday's game when they kicked butt.'

'Sometimes, I wish I was.'

'Cece, how can you say that?' Sharon asked. 'Come on! We're 5-0, we beat Edgewater the week before, supposedly the best team in the state, and practically handed their butts to them on a silver platter. The terrific trio has led us to a certain #1 ranking in the state and will lead us to the state championship. What's not to love about them?'

'I don't like bullies, whether it's picking on Mordy or anybody else,' frowned Cece, 'Bullies are no good, no matter what they do on the athletic field! I remember what Mordy had told me one time: *The Word says that pride comes before destruction and a haughty spirit before a fall,* and by the way it looks, you three are setting yourselves up for a fall.'

'What your loser brother believes is irrelevant and full of bull junk,' Chuck retorted, 'Who is he that he would say such things?'

Cece was mad. She scowled at Chuck and said angrily, 'Don't you dare call my brother a loser! He may not be as smart, strong, and popular as any of you jeges, but Mordecai is a wonderful person and has a good heart, and he doesn't deserve the way you and your gorilla buddies have been treating him! He has more dignity in his smallest toenail than you three combined! I say that not because I am his sister, but because it's true!'

'You are entitled to your own opinion, Jefferson,' another cheerleader said, 'I wouldn't want to date that loser for a billion dollars!'

'And I'm sure he wouldn't want to date you either, Tess McElroy,' shot back Cece. 'given the kind of person you are. You seem to have a problem staying with just one boy.'

'Watch it, Jefferson,' warned Tess. 'I wouldn't talk if I were you! Your boyfriend, Oscar, or should I say, your ex-boyfriend, has just started going with that new girl, Carol Rogers, who had transferred from New Orleans. He's been spending a lot of time with her. Heck, I even saw them hugging and kissing at Rossi's when Tommy took me there.'

Cece placed her hands upon her mouth, shocked by the news.

She then thought of when he avoided her and did not return her calls. Tears started welling up in her eyes. Sharon and Tiffany turned to comfort her. 'I'm sorry, Cece,' Sharon told her softly.

Cece wept as Tiffany turned and saw the smile upon Tess's face. 'Are you telling the truth, McElroy?' she asked.

'Tommy and I were there,' Tess replied. 'We were on a date when we saw them. The way I see it, Oscar traded up.'

'Now you're going too far, McElroy,' snapped Sharon. 'You are clearly taking pleasure in Cece's pain! How would you like it if Tommy did the same thing to you, huh? Would you like it if Tommy started seeing another girl behind your back the way Oscar was seeing someone else behind Cece's back? You're a real piece of work, McElroy!' Tess charged toward Sharon, knocking her down. The students around them started cheering and urging them on. Both rolled around on the ground, trying to get the advantage over the other. Tess managed to throw a couple of punches at Sharon, who did her best to break free. She landed a couple of punches of her own before Tiffany pulled Tess off Sharon. 'Stop it,' she cried. 'Stop it this instant!'

Tess threw Tiffany off her.

'Let go of me, witch,' she cried.

Sharon got up and charged at Tess as they both hit the wall. Some of the students were cheering while others cried, 'Cat fight! Cat fight!'

Two of the cheerleaders grabbed Sharon while another two held Tess back to keep her from retaliating. Tess tried to break free to lunge at Sharon again, crying, 'Let me go!'

'Come on, Maleficent,' cried Sharon. 'Come on! I'll kick your sorry can back to whatever hole you crawled out of!'

'I want to see you try, Skiles,' spat Tess.

The cheerleaders who held both women back continued to pull them away. In the midst of her tears, Cece said to Sharon, 'Don't,

Sharon, she's not worth it!'

'No, no,' Stu laughed. 'Let them fight!'

'You shut that beer hole of yours right now, Hatfield,' Tiffany shot back, 'Not another word out of you! I don't know what man in his right mind wants to see two girls fight, but then again, you don't have a mind, do you?'

'Save it, Tiff,' sighed Cece. 'They're not worth it. None of them are. They love to cause trouble wherever they go.' She turned around and left, weeping. Both Tiffany and Sharon glanced back briefly, then left to join Cece.

It wasn't long until Mordecai arrived, having locked up his bike and walked onto campus. He stopped by his locker and put the spare poncho inside, folding it and storing it. Before he grabbed his books, Cece, Sharon, and Tiffany approached him. Mordecai noticed Cece was crying and Sharon a bit of a mess. Cece leaned her head upon her brother's shoulder as she wept. 'What happened?' he asked, holding her.

'We found out about Oscar, for one,' Tiffany answered. 'We were told by Tess McElroy. She said she and her boyfriend, Tommy, saw him with that new girl, Carol, who just moved here from New Orleans while they were at *Rossi's.*'

Mordecai shook his head, stroking the back of Cece's head. 'That probably explains why he's been avoiding her and not returned her calls or texts. If he wanted to date her in the first place, he needed to be straight up with her and not give her the run around like that!' He stared at Sharon. 'What happened to you?' he asked her.

'I got into a fight with Tess,' Sharon answered. 'Tess claimed Oscar had traded up. I told her how she kept dating different boys, and that's when she went at it with me. The jocks encouraged the fight as well as those around her.'

Mordecai shook his head. 'Bunch of barbarians. Makes me wonder what's wrong with them besides the obvious, what their major malfunction is. Would they feel the same if it happened to them?'

'Fortunately, as far as I know, the principal hasn't heard about it,' Sharon said, 'but somebody needed to put that witch in her place! She even put you down.'

'I am not worried about what Tess thinks of me,' replied Mordecai, 'She's not my type anyhow. I personally don't find her attractive, especially after hearing how she keeps seemingly changing boyfriends. I'm looking for a steady commitment, a virtuous woman.'

'Good luck with that,' laughed Tiffany.

Cece stared angrily at Tiffany. She didn't like the response her friend had made toward Mordecai.

'Whoa, Cece, claws in,' Tiffany said. 'I didn't mean any harm.'

'My brother is a wonderful person,' Cece cried, fighting the tears in her eyes. 'People look down on him for the wrong reasons. He has depression, sure, but abandoning him is the worst thing to do to a person with depression. What if it was you who suffered from depression? Would you want people to isolate and ostracize you because they think you're a psychopath or a psychotic killer? By the way, Mordecai is neither of those things; he is picked on by people like McCoy, Hatfield, and Jones who look down on him! Any girl in their right mind would see how wonderful he is and would want a man like him, and it hurts me to see him suffer as he has been, not even getting support from our parents!

'I was afraid he would hate me for being given advantages that he hasn't been given, but I'm glad that was not the case! We had our differences before, but deep inside as brother and sister, we do love each other, and I am hurt by the lack of support he has been given. Right now, I'm the only one in the world that he has!'

Mordecai kissed his sister on the forehead in response. 'Thank you, sis,' he smiled briefly, 'I just hate hearing what Oscar did to you.'

'Do you have a crush on a certain girl?' Tiffany asked.

Mordecai shook his head. 'It's like they're saying to me, "I wouldn't touch you with a forty foot pole",' he sighed, 'That seems to be their attitude. I am trying not to worry about it, but it's not easy.'

Cece released him, drying her eyes. He was about to say something but decided not to at the last second. 'I just have to put it out of my mind,' he continued. 'Nothing else to do.' To Cece he asked, 'Will you be okay, Cece?'

Cece nodded her head, fighting back the tears. 'Eventually I will,' she answered. 'It's still kind of a shock to me, though. I am angry at him, angry at the way he gave me the runaround, seeing this other girl behind my back!'

'You don't deserve to be treated like that, no girl does,' sighed Mordecai. 'For his sake, he better not come around me and ask for you. Right now, I'm so angry at the way he hurt you—I am ready to read him the riot act big time!'

'He deserves it,' Sharon stated, flatly.

They turned to head to their first class while Mordecai watched them leave. He then turned around, grabbed his books, and headed to his first class.

On the way, he caught a glimpse of the two men he had seen before when he had been stopped by Dr. Von Braun. *They are Von Braun's two men, all right, but what were they doing here?* he thought. He felt the urge to keep out of sight, which he did. He then thought of the conversation he'd had with Dr. Von Braun about the existence of fairies. *Von Braun must be desperate to find out about the existence of fairies, why, I don't know. Why would he waste his time on finding out? Why does he feel I have anything to do with it?* The two men continued to look around. *Where are the cops when you need them? They have no right to be here!* When they had passed, he hurried to his first class, making sure he wasn't spotted by Von Braun's men.

After his first class was over, he made his way to his second class. He headed to his locker to grab another book for the class he was heading to. He then looked around. He only saw other students—

Von Braun's two men were nowhere to be seen. He opened the locker, grabbed a book while putting the book for his first class away, then closed his locker.

As he closed it, he was bumped hard by Frank. His head struck the metal surface of the locker. He turned around and saw Frank staring hard at him. 'You!' Mordecai exclaimed.

Frank immediately grabbed Mordecai by the collar and slammed him against the lockers. 'You should have been more careful, Jefferson,' he said as his friends Stu and Chuck flanked him. 'You're just begging for trouble here.'

'It was *you* who bumped into *me*,' claimed Mordecai. 'You are always looking for some kind of excuse to bully me or those weaker than you. Why do you love to pick on people?'

'Correction, fool, *you* bumped into *me*, and I have two witnesses who will back me up!'

'Vultures of a feather flock together,' Mordecai grimly replied, 'Even when you're in the wrong, you back each other up. I don't find that surprising. I pity you, though.'

'What do you mean by that, Jefferson?' Stu asked.

'Obviously you guys are talented, all-state players, but you turn out, all three of you, to be bullies and jerks. One of these days you will fall if you don't change your ways, repent of being bullies. There is a God in heaven, and He is watching.'

'That's all bull,' Chuck scoffed, 'Only a fool believes in such fairy tales! It's nothing but old legends and myths. There is no heaven or hell.'

'Can you be certain of that? *The fool hath said in his heart, there is no God.* Of course, you have the right to reject God's loving gift to you, even though people like you seek to violate the rights of those who love God to serve Him. If you hate me for that, then go ahead! You may get away with a lot of the junk you guys pull in the eyes of the principal, but your sins will sooner or later catch up with you and bite you in the butt with the teeth of a great white shark—and bite you big time!'

Frank slammed him hard against the lockers again. 'Who do you think you are to talk to us like that, Jefferson? Get it through your head that you are a worthless nobody, a total loser, lower on the evolutionary scale than an amoeba—and they are low!'

'There's a problem with that, McCoy,' Mordecai replied, 'We were created by God, not evolved from apes. The way I see it, evolution is basically scientists who make monkeys out of themselves. If evolution is true, by the way, you would be gorillas.'

Frank delivered a hard punch to Mordecai's stomach, causing him to cry out in pain. Around them, students had gathered, some cheering them on. Mordecai, wincing in pain, looked disdainfully at the students. Stu stared at Frank and said, 'We have to get to our next class. Let's wait until after school to deal with him, teach him a lesson for disrespecting us.'

Frank tossed Mordecai against the lockers one more time before releasing him. He nodded at his friends. 'Yeah, teach him a lesson later,' he said. He turned to Mordecai and said, 'Punishment is only delayed, Jefferson! After school, we continue this! See you then, loser!'

Mordecai painfully got up as he heard the other students laugh at him while walking away. He frowned, painfully picked up his books and headed to his next class.

Out of nowhere, Cece appeared, approaching him. She stared and recognized the forms of Stu, Frank, and Chuck walking away with the crowd and the dying laughter. 'Not them again,' she said, 'What happened?'

'McCoy intentionally bumped into me looking for a reason to rough me up,' Mordecai answered, 'They said they would meet me after school to do a number on me then. I got punched in the stomach and thrown into the lockers thrice. The back of my head hurts.'

'Do you need to see a nurse?'

'Not much they will do,' Mordecai sighed, 'They allow McCoy, Hatfield, and Jones to get away with practically anything they want because of they're all-state players, including bullying. That is so not fair!'

'I can imagine,' Cece replied, 'I am starting to hate them.'

'No. Don't hate them. Hate only what they do. God wants us to love people but hate their sins. I am so tempted to do the same, but hating people is of the devil. It is said hatred darkens and damns the soul. I have to remember not to hate—even them.'

Cece shook her head. 'I'm sorry, but I find it hard not to hate them, especially after what they have done. I can't understand why you don't hate them.'

'If you knew the Lord, you would understand. Loving them does not mean giving the stamp of approval on what they do. I will continue to pray for them.'

'Why?' asked Cece.

'Jesus said in His Word: *Love your enemies, bless them that curse you, do good unto them that hate you, and pray for them which despitefully use you, and persecute you.* Looking at the three bullies, it reminds me of how I must seem in the eyes of God, how we all must seem in God's eyes: wicked, violent, cruel. We are all sinners born into sin. I am still learning to love them as Jesus loved me, since in God's eyes, I am like unto them, no better than them.'

'There is still much I don't understand, but I wish they would stop being bullies.'

'Me too,' sighed Mordecai, 'I better head to my next class.'

'Are you sure you don't want to see a nurse?' asked Cece.

'They won't believe me when I tell them they've been bullying me,' sighed Mordecai, 'It's not fair, but nobody said life was fair. I only wish it wasn't like this.'

'So do I. I hate what those Neanderthals have been doing to you and others like you!'

'I know,' sighed Mordecai as they walked to their next class.

At lunchtime, Cece sat with Sharon and Tiffany. Cece looked around to try and find her brother but could not see him. Sharon looked around occasionally. 'Tess better not show her ugly witch self.'

'Will you let it go?' Cece told her, 'She is so not worth it! Try and forget about this morning. I am forgetting the bad things she said about me.'

'Why?'

'Mordy told me we should forgive others,' Cece answered, 'He told me once it was for our own benefit. We should hate what people do to us, not them. We don't have to give our stamp of approval on what they do.'

'How could he say that?' Tiffany exclaimed. 'Especially when it comes to being bullied, how could he say such a thing?'

'Because of his convictions,' Cece answered, 'He tells me he is still learning that, though.'

'I now see why he still believes that Frank, Stu, and Chuck are as bad as he says they are,' Tiffany replied, 'I can't believe they urged on the fight between Sharon and that witch Tess!'

'They were bullying him earlier this morning,' Cece stated, 'He says they plan to get him after school today. Do you still believe they are all that?'

'Yes, they're all-state quality football players, guaranteed to get scholarships to major colleges,' Tiffany answered, 'but now I'm beginning to doubt the kind of people they are. I'm glad I'm not interested in any one of them.'

'They are bullies, total jerks who think they can get away with anything,' Cece frowned, 'The way Mordecai is being treated is testimony to that. The problem is nobody, whether it be at school or home, will listen to him, to stand by him. And Mordy is not the only one he bullies. I'm appalled that Sam Johnson, Alan White, and Jon Palmer got suspended for standing up to them. They had younger brothers who had been bullied by Jones, Hatfield, and McCoy and neither the principal nor teachers were doing anything about the bullying! Tell me, how is that fair? It's not! Would any of you like it if three of our girls' basketball players were all-state players and started bullying you and got away with it? How fair would that be? It wouldn't! I hate bullies and hate the way they get away with anything and everything.'

'I sure wouldn't,' Sharon said.

'Nor would I,' Tiffany added.

'What kind of example are those boys setting?' continued Cece. 'By getting away with bullying and those in charge allowing them to get away with it, they give their stamp of approval to bullying, and the principal and teachers become just as guilty as those actually doing the bullying. Would you want somebody close to you to be a victim of bullying, or worse, when you have children, one of your children a victim? It wouldn't feel too good, would it?'

At that moment, they heard a commotion across the room. They stood up and saw Frank beating up an unidentified black student while the students who stood around them cheered and urged him on. Stu and Chuck kept the student from escaping, pushing him back toward Frank, who slammed him against the wall and started beating him again. Cece slammed down her silverware and quickly rose to her feet.

'Where are you going?' asked Tiffany.

'Somebody's got to stand up to these bullies,' cried Cece, angrily. She raced toward the scene and pushed away some of the students, making her way to the middle of the group. She grabbed Frank's arm to try and stop him. Frank turned angrily toward Cece and said, 'Let go, Jefferson!' To Stu and Chuck, he cried, 'Why didn't you hold the witch back?'

'Look who's talking,' snapped Cece. 'What a big man you are: picking on people who are smaller and weaker than you. It clearly shows your true colors: you are yellow, all yellow, all three of you!'

Stu and Chuck tried to grab her, but she kicked each of them in the shins with a series of hard kicks. They backed off, wincing in pain.

'Doesn't feel good when you're on the receiving end for a change, does it?' she told them.

'What in the blazes are you doing?' Stu cried.

'Standing up to you bullies,' Cece shouted. 'It's a sin that you can get away with anything and everything! Why were you beating up on this boy, eh? Because he's black? Because he's just like my brother? You are nothing but a coward, Frank McCoy, you, and your cronies! Nothing but mud-sucking devil-loving cowards!'

'You better watch it, Jefferson,' warned Frank.

'Or what, McCoy, you'll beat me up, too?' snapped Cece. 'How will it look on you if you beat up a girl, eh? You would stoop to a new low, lower than you are right now, and you are lower than a snake's belly as it is! Mordy had told me what you had done to him earlier today and what you and your orcs are going to do to him after school today! If you so much as touch him, I will make sure you'll be in bigger trouble than you are in right now, and you'll be in so deep that neither you, nor your thug friends, will be able to dig yourselves out of the hole you dug!'

'I said, let go!' Frank growled, pushing Cece hard to the floor. 'Thank you for reminding me what we have to do with that loser brother of yours! Now stay out of the way!'

Cece rose quickly, and as Stu and Chuck tried to grab her, she kicked them hard in the shins again, in roughly the same place. 'Son of a vulture!' she cried as she delivered a hard kick into Frank's shin. He cried out as he raised his hurt leg.

At that moment, five teachers entered and broke up the ring. They saw the black student sitting in the corner, his face bruised and bleeding. Two of the teachers helped him to the nurse's office.

'What happened here?' one teacher asked.

'These three have been beating up that student,' Cece answered, 'I was having lunch with my two friends when we heard the commotion and saw that McCoy was beating up that student. My older brother, Mordecai, is a victim as well, having been harassed and physically assaulted by them earlier this morning, even threatening to do more after school! This is a travesty this has been allowed to happen here!'

'Is this true?' asked a second teacher.

'No, no,' lied Frank.

'Then how did he get beaten and bloodied then?' shot back Cece, 'and no more lies!'

'That's enough, Miss Jefferson,' the third teacher said.

'Surely you're not going to let him get away with beating up another student again?' cried Cece, 'How long are you going to turn a deaf ear to all this bullying, allow students like my brother to be beaten up by these monsters?'

'We will take care of it,' the second teacher said.

'Like you did the times Mordecai was bullied by them?' Cece replied angrily. 'This has been happening to him ever since he started attending Oak Ridge, but you all turned a blind eye to all this while he suffers psychological and physical harm at the hands of people like McCoy, Hatfield, and Jones! He had started riding a bike to school after being bullied, even on the bus, but the monitor wouldn't do anything about it! Why not? There's no excuse for all of this! Why are people like my brother allowed to continue to be bullied, while people like those three can get away with anything they please? This is wrong on all fronts!'

'If you don't want to be given detention, Miss Jefferson,' the first teacher warned, 'then you better go back to your seat now and wait for your next class!'

'I want her suspended,' Frank sneered. 'That wench kicked me and my friends in the shins!'

'To keep you from beating up that student any further,' Cece interrupted, 'Yes, I did it, no lie, but they were about to lay their hands on me! McCoy pushed me hard to the ground!'

'I think we should all go talk to the principal,' the first teacher said, 'He needs to hear the story behind this. Come with us!'

Cece sighed. 'Let me get my books,' she said. She had a bad feeling the result would not turn out well. She knew she faced the possibility of being suspended and figured that the three bullies would escape scot-free like they had done before.

Cece went over and grabbed her books. Tiffany and Sharon stared at her and the teacher escorting her. 'What happened?' Tiffany asked.

'I'll have to tell you later,' she told them. 'I'm being sent to the office.'

'For what?'

'Let's just say I have a bad feeling about this,' Cece frowned, following the teacher as they walked out the door.

Mordecai arrived just after Cece and the three bullies were being taken to the office. As he headed in line to buy his lunch, Sharon saw him and called out his name. As he stopped, he saw her approaching him. 'Cece got sent to the office,' she told him.

'What happened?' Mordecai asked.

'McCoy, Hatfield, and Jones were beating up some black kid,' Sharon answered, 'Cece went over to stop him. There was too much of a crowd to see any more. Some teachers came in afterwards and took the kid to the nurses, I'm sure. I'm beginning to believe that Cece was right about them.'

'What I have known all along,' Mordecai frowned, 'but I have a feeling they will get away with it again as they always do.'

'Cece told us you said that they plan to beat you up after school,' Sharon said softly.

Mordecai nodded. 'Frank intentionally slammed into me to give him an excuse to harass me,' he replied, 'He punched me while throwing me into the locker three times. Before they left, they said they were going to meet me after school.'

'What will you do?' asked Sharon.

'I have to be very careful, for one,' answered Mordecai, 'Try and get to my bike when they're not around. That will be hard, unless they are serving detention, which I doubt will happen. How long must this go on with them, why are they allowed to keep bullying those weaker than them like me?'

'Too long,' Tiffany frowned, 'I saw the face of that kid who was taken to the nurse, and I realize you have been right all along. We want to help you.'

'What can you do?' Mordecai asked.

'You can start riding to school with us from now on,' Tiffany answered, 'It must be terrible having to ride your bike to school, especially when it's raining.'

Mordecai nodded. 'I will take you up on your offer, but I'll need to come back for my bike. I will still need it to get around.'

'I will have a while to pay for the damages done to the car last week in the accident,' Tiffany sighed, thinking about the accident the day before.

'I'm just glad none of you were seriously hurt,' said Mordecai, 'Better damage to the car than to any of you.'

Tiffany sighed. 'I guess you're right. My father was still upset about the accident. He says I've got to learn to take responsibility for the consequences of my actions. Why doesn't your father teach you how to drive?'

Mordecai shook his head. 'I'm sure Cece told you that I don't know. I wish I knew.'

'That is so not fair to you,' Sharon exclaimed, 'You're older than Cece, and yet she's the one being taught to drive. Cece told me she'd fear you'd despise her for that.'

'No. It's not Cece's fault,' replied Mordecai, 'We patched up our differences last week, and I'm glad. Yes, it is unfair, but that's not something she can control. In fact, Cece was the only one who has been there when I needed to talk to somebody.' He sighed. 'I hope she'll be okay. Did she tell you why she's being sent to the office?'

'No,' Sharon answered, 'but I know it had something to do with our star football players.'

Mordecai only shook his head. 'I'm afraid I can only guess the outcome,' he frowned, 'Par for the course with them.'

After talking to Sharon and Tiffany, Mordecai was on his way to his locker. As he passed an empty classroom, he was grabbed by two men and dragged inside. He struggled to break free but couldn't. He then heard a familiar voice say, 'Let him go, boys. No force is needed. We just need to chat.'

'Dr. Von Braun?' he said in surprise as he recognized the voice of the geneticist before facing him, 'What are you doing here? What business do you have here?'

Dr. Von Braun stared at the young man. 'I've been invited today to be a guest speaker at the request of the principal,' he answered, 'I will speak to the students of the last two periods in science, specifically in genetics. I will have some of them, I'm sure, as future students in my class should they attend UCF.'

'Then what do you want with me, as if I didn't know?'

'Oh, you know all right,' replied Dr. Von Braun, 'We both know, but that matter I do not discuss in the classroom, not officially, of course.' He then stared hard at him. 'Have you had any unusual dreams?' he then asked.

'What do you mean?' frowned Mordecai.

'Any strange dreams, any recurring dreams?' repeated the geneticist.

Mordecai did not answer.

'Tell me,' the geneticist insisted.

Mordecai sighed.

'I'm waiting,' Dr. Von Braun continued.

After a pause, Mordecai spoke. 'I did have a recurring dream of a dragon—a black dragon,' he said. 'But what does that have to do with anything?'

'Oh, it could mean more than you know,' replied Dr. Von Braun, 'What can you tell me about this dragon?'

Against his will, Mordecai spoke. 'I was in a valley, barren, lifeless. I was walking through the valley and then came upon this dragon.'

'What did he look like?' asked Dr. Von Braun.

'Must have been over thirty meters tall, jet black in appearance,' answered Mordecai, 'He had a wingspan almost as long as his body, almost bat-like wings. He seemed to know me but not my name. He kept asking me my name, but I refused to tell him.'

'Did he reveal his name to you in the dream?' asked Dr. Von Braun.

'No,' Mordecai answered. 'He never did. I never found out his name. It's strange, because it's the same dream I've had the past four nights, and it bothers me.'

'Interesting,' nodded the geneticist.

'Why do you ask about the dream?' asked Mordecai.

'Oh, no particular reason.'

'Come on, Dr. Von Braun,' frowned the young man, 'There must be a logical reason for asking me such a question.'

'My reasons are my own, and that is all you will know.'

'I thought you were going to ask me about fairies,' Mordecai frowned, 'Now you ask me about what unusual dreams I had.'

Dr. Von Braun slid a vanilla envelope toward the young man. Mordecai instinctively took the envelope and stared at it. 'Open it,' the geneticist said.

Mordecai opened the envelope and pulled out the picture. He stared at it closely. 'Remains?' he exclaimed, 'What is this?'

'These are remains of a fairy that had died perhaps a year ago,' answered Dr. Von Braun. 'It looked like it was a female, perhaps in her 30s, cause of death: unknown. No broken bones, though. You can tell the shape of the wings on the back.'

'Why show me this?' Mordecai asked, 'Who took them?'

'I have my sources,' replied the geneticist, 'I will not tell you. Rest assured those are remains of a real fairy. That is not satisfactory evidence to make their existence public. More proof is needed. I have studied the DNA and found it strangely similar to our own. How they got wings, how they came to be, is still a mystery, a mystery I intend to solve.'

Mordecai shook his head. 'I still don't know why it has anything to do with me,' he frowned.

'I feel there is a connection between you and the existence of fairies,' the geneticist said, 'The recurring dreams of the dragon has convinced me of that.'

'How?' asked Mordecai skeptically.

'My reasons are my own,' replied Dr. Von Braun. 'Perhaps you have not yet encountered a fairy, but you will. When you do, I am planning to offer you six million dollars for proof of their existence.'

'Why would you do this?' Mordecai asked.

'I have only partial proof, though I feel not empiric enough, on the existence of fairies,' said Dr. Von Braun, 'I need to find one, capture one if necessary, to prove their existence.'

'What would you do with the fairy if you captured one?'

'Study it,' answered the geneticist, 'see how similar they are to humans. I wonder how they evolved wings and have the ability to fly?'

'I still find it hard to believe that they do exist,' Mordecai said, 'The thing is, I don't believe in evolution. I believe we were created, all of us, in the image of God.'

'Then how do you explain the wings?' Dr. Von Braun asked.

'I have no explanation,' replied Mordecai. 'But I still doubt their existence.'

'Talking about believing in fairy tales,' scoffed Dr. Von Braun, 'What about the myth that God would choose to come down in the form of man and die and then rise again in three days?'

'I am not good at debating,' Mordecai replied, 'but the wickedness of man has caused us separation from God.'

'Yes, yes, I've heard it all before,' interrupted Dr. Von Braun, 'but I cannot believe that God would send His only Son to shed His blood for our sins and to save our souls from hell.'

'And this is coming from a man who believes in fairies?' retorted Mordecai.

Dr. Von Braun picked up the picture that Mordecai had laid down and slammed it upon the desk again. '*This* is proof, boy!' he shot back. 'I have seen a fairy for myself! I know they exist! The remains of a fairy proves they exist, and I *will* find one, rest assured!'

He then walked over to the youth. 'Just think of it,' he told him. 'If you find one, you would no longer be a nobody. You would be famous, as well as rich! Find a fairy, and I will personally give you six million dollars, cash!'

Mordecai did not respond immediately. He thought about the money, thought about the fact that he had no job, nobody special in his life. As he thought, he then felt a wrongness about all of this. *Why would he think I still know anything about fairies? Could they truly exist? What do my dreams about a black dragon have to do with the existence of fairies and why does Von Braun think it does? What is his true purpose toward fairies?* He shook his head. 'I still can't bring myself to believe fairies exist,' he said softly.

'And this is coming from someone who believes in a God who would die for him to save him from hell?' scoffed Dr. Von Braun, 'Sooner or later, you *will* encounter a fairy, and you *will* let me know once that happens. The world must know of their existence.'

He pulled out a card and placed it in his front pocket. 'In case you lost my number the first time. I expect you to contact me once you meet a fairy.'

He motioned to his men. 'Come, Seymour, Wilfred,' he told them. 'I must speak to Mr. Richards before classes start, go over some things with him.' He grabbed the photo and placed them back in the envelope and headed out the door, followed by Seymour and Wilfred.

Mordecai stood there, thinking about Dr. Von Braun and his words, thinking about the picture. He found himself refusing to believe his words, but what if he was right? He felt that whatever his intentions were concerning fairies, it did not feel right to him. If fairies did exist, he felt Dr. Von Braun must not know. He determined to tell him nothing, money or no money, if he ever found one, but he doubted in his heart he would ever meet one, which would be a good thing for them, if they were indeed real as Dr. Von Braun insisted.

He tried to dismiss it from his mind as he picked up his books and exited the empty classroom, but he could neither forget it nor the dragon in his dreams. He couldn't explain why he kept having dreams of the dragon as hard as he tried to forget it. He stopped by his locker, exchanged books, and headed to his next class.

After the fourth period, Cece joined her friends between classes since they had a science class together. She had an unhappy look upon her face. 'I should have known,' she said angrily.

'What happened?' Sharon asked.

'I still can't believe how they can get away with murder,' Cece said angrily, 'If I hadn't seen it for myself, I wouldn't believe how right my brother was!'

'I'm sorry, Cece,' Tiffany replied, 'What about you?'

'I got detention today after school,' growled Cece, 'Now I know how Mordy feels! It does seem like that McCoy, Hatfield, and Jones can get away with anything they want! This is blatant favoritism! How can this go on in this school?'

'We believe you now,' Sharon told her, 'We spoke to Mordy earlier, just after you and the beast boys were being taken to the office. We can wait up for you.'

'All three of us,' Tiffany added.

'Who's riding with us?' Cece asked.

'We asked your brother if he would like to ride with us, Tiffany said, 'He agreed.'

Cece sighed. 'That's great to hear. I get so worried when he rides his bike to school and back, especially in the rain. It just doesn't feel right to me.'

'I suppose I could find a way to put his bike in the trunk,' Tiffany said. 'Too bad I don't have any rope in the back to secure it. I can see if I can get some after school.'

'Thanks, Tiff,' Cece said, 'That means a lot to Mordy, and to me as well.'

At that moment, Mordecai appeared from around the corner, trying to reach his locker. He saw his sister and immediately forgot about heading to his locker. The way she looked had told him enough. 'I should have known,' he said sadly. 'They got away with beating that kid up, didn't they?'

'They sure did,' grunted Cece. 'They said somebody else beat him up. They claimed Jimmy Russo beat him up, but that was a lie. I hear they're going to suspend him.'

'What a liar McCoy is,' exclaimed Mordecai, 'Did they ask the kid who beat him up?'

'The boys must have threatened him because he said that Russo did it,' Cece answered. 'This is disgusting! How blind can they be?

Russo has lunch first period, not second period! He couldn't have done it! Why couldn't he just tell them that McCoy beat him up? Is he really afraid of retaliation from them?'

'It would seem. I can talk to him if I ever see him and get him to reconsider his story and tell the truth,' said Mordecai, 'This cannot continue like this!'

'Where do you have to go next, Mordy?' asked Sharon.

'I've got astronomy class next,' Mordecai answered, 'Somehow, it's one of my strongest subjects. I do pretty well in it, surprisingly. I hate the references to evolution, though.'

'Obviously,' Cece replied.

'Other than that, it's okay.'

'Do you believe in life on other planets?' Sharon asked.

'That's like asking: "Do you believe in fairies?",' replied Mordecai, 'I don't think there is.'

'In fairies or life on other planets?' Tiffany asked.

'Answering Sharon's question, nothing more,' answered Mordecai. 'Talking about life on other planets, I seriously doubt it.'

'What about fairies?' Tiffany asked.

Mordecai paused for a moment. 'That's strange,' he said. 'Dr. Von Braun was here and was asking me about it. He believes there are fairies.'

'Say what?' Tiffany, Sharon, and Cece said together.

'When was this?' Cece asked.

'During lunchtime,' Mordecai answered, 'He said he was here to lecture in Mr. Richard's last two science classes. That's why I'd seen two of his men.'

'Whoa, wait a minute,' Sharon exclaimed. 'Are you saying that *Mockingbird* magazine was right about Dr. Von Braun's obsessions with finding fairies, and you know him?'

Mordecai nodded. 'It was not my first meeting with him. He followed me after I had bought a soda from the store when I was thirsty on Friday after school. I did hear him talking about fairies, and he followed me until I reached the Southwood subdivision. He stopped me and inquired about what I had overheard and insisted I knew something about the existence of fairies.'

'Say what?' Tiffany exclaimed. 'Are you kidding?'

'I wish I was,' replied Mordecai, 'He pulled me aside and first inquired of any peculiar recurring dreams I had. I told him, Cece, about what I told you about the black dragon.'

'Why would he ask you something like that?' Cece asked.

'He would not give me a reason,' the young man frowned, 'He said the reasons were his own.'

'Why did you tell him about the dreams, and what were they about?' asked Sharon.

'He told me this morning,' Cece broke in, 'He had woken up two hours before sunset disturbed about the dream. He said he had been

having it for the past four nights but he doesn't know why.'

'This sounds disturbing,' Tiffany replied.

'It is,' Mordecai nodded, 'and I don't know why I've been having them. I dreamed I was in a valley, a dark dead valley. As I searched for a way out, I met a black dragon, about thirty meters, I think. He asked me my name and seemed to know some things about me. He mentioned something of a prophecy.'

'Prophecy?' Sharon asked. 'What prophecy?'

'I don't know, he didn't say,' Mordecai answered. 'He considered me a threat somehow, though I have no idea how. I know it was only a dream, but I've been having the same dream for the past four nights, and I don't know why. Dr. Von Braun did not give me a reason why he had asked me, but I believe he thought it was important somehow. He then showed me something I still couldn't believe.'

'What?' asked Tiffany and Sharon.

'He showed me the picture of the remains of what he considered to be a fairy,' Mordecai answered, 'Just bones and what looked like the outline of wings, but I couldn't be sure. He insisted it was a fairy and he claimed to have seen one flying some time ago, but had no camera to photograph it.'

'Was it a fairy?' Sharon asked.

Mordecai shook his head. 'I'm not sure, really,' he said, 'It did look like it could be, but I won't say for sure. He seems obsessed with finding fairies.'

'What about the picture?' Cece asked.

'Dr. Von Braun took it back,' Mordecai answered. 'He also claims the recurring dream I've been having about the black dragon has convinced him somehow of my connection with fairies, but I don't see how. He insists I will encounter a fairy sooner or later. He was adamant about it.'

'Boy, is that man insane like Hussein,' Tiffany laughed. 'Why would he think that of you?'

'He did not tell me much,' answered Mordecai, 'I agree with you, Tiffany, he is insane like Hussein. I don't know about the picture he showed me. A part of me believes it was real, but I'm not sure. I won't say any more about the matter, but he seems hell bent that I could have a possible connection to fairies.' He shook his head. 'He told me to call him if I ever come across one, and he insists that I will see one and that I will call him.'

'That sounds so hard to believe,' Tiffany scoffed.

Mordecai sighed. 'I tend to agree, but those were the words he had spoken to me. I wish I didn't go to the store for a soda on that day and that I'd never met him. If he ever finds one, I sense his intentions are for evil and not good. I could sense it.'

'You're joking, Mordy,' Sharon laughed.

Cece shook her head. 'I trust Mordy not to exaggerate or lie,' she stated. 'I know him too well. I still can't understand how Von Braun could believe you know anything about fairies, if they existed.'

'Nor do I,' Mordecai replied, 'but he believes it so, especially since I told him of the dream. He seems obsessed to me. I better get off the subject. We have one more class to go to. We can talk more after school.'

'After I spend time in detention,' sighed Cece. 'I still can't believe I'm forced to do detention, especially with the ghastly trio getting away with murder again! This is so unfair!'

'I know,' Mordecai sighed, 'I hate it, too! A grave injustice indeed! I hope somewhere down the line that it will turn around and they will finally pay for their sins.'

They broke up and each headed to their next class.

After class, Mordecai headed to his locker to put his books inside and wait for his sister to do her time in detention. He decided to try and find her friends while he waited. He walked from his locker and suddenly caught a glimpse of Frank, Stu, and Chuck, who he figured were searching for him. He quickly turned the other way and tried to keep out of sight until he could find Tiffany and Sharon.

The three jocks reached the bike area where Mordecai had chained his bike. When they found he was not there, Frank turned to the others and said, 'One of us must wait here until we find Jefferson. It was his fault we almost got into trouble earlier today, make him pay for what his sister did.'

'I can wait here,' Chuck said, 'You two can go look for him.'

'We'll call you when we find him,' Stu said, 'Have the car ready for when we catch him. It's time we teach him a lesson once and for all. All losers and nobodies like him need to learn their place!'

They turned back toward the campus to search for Mordecai.

Mordecai headed into the 400 building, looking around. He searched for a good place to hide. He thought he must make his way back to his bike and hope he could get out before they noticed he was gone. He whispered a silent prayer that God would deliver him from his enemies. He wished he was a fighter and able to defend himself against bullies like McCoy, Hatfield, and Jones. He made up his mind to try and make his way back to his bike and explain things to Tiffany later. He focused on trying to evade his antagonists and try to escape his antagonists on his bike.

He bumped into one of his teachers, who was startled by his sudden appearance. He gazed hard at the young man and asked, 'Mr. Jefferson, what are you still doing here?'

'McCoy, Hatfield, and Jones are after me,' Mordecai gasped, 'They want to beat me up again like they did to Malik Johnson earlier today!'

'But he said that Jimmy Russo did it,' the teacher said.

'He said that out of fear of retaliation, I'm sure,' said Mordecai amid deep breaths, 'Jimmy Russo has lunch in the first period, not the second period when the attack happened! Russo is innocent! Malik is also a victim of bullying from the three, just like me!'

The teacher shook his head. 'I find that hard to believe. I don't believe McCoy, Hatfield, and Jones are capable of—'

'I've no time for this,' grunted Mordecai as he headed out the door, trying to find a way to evade the bullies. He headed into an adjacent building. He knew he couldn't count on any of the teachers to listen since he felt they believed the jocks were model students instead of the bullies that they were. Why won't they listen? They never seemed to listen to him for reasons he wasn't so clear on. He sighed. He had to find a way to evade the bullies, get on his bike, and pedal as fast as he could home before he was caught. He prayed he would find help from somewhere, but he knew he was on his own. He dialed his sister's cell phone number and hoped at least to leave a message. When the phone went to voice mail, he left a message after the beep. 'Cece, this is Mordecai. McCoy, Hatfield, and Jones are hunting for me right now! I'm trying to make my way to my bike and get out of here before they catch me. The teachers won't listen to me so I'm on my own! Relay the message to your friends that I—'

He heard a shout of 'There he is!' and saw Frank and Stu racing toward him. He hung up his phone and started running as fast as he could, trying to find a place to hide and somehow elude the bullies. He saw little hope of escape, but he prayed that God would help him and deliver him from his enemies.

Stu pulled out his cell phone and dialed the number for his comrade, Chuck. As he ran, he said, 'Chuck, we found him! We're running after him now!'

'I see him now,' replied Chuck. 'I'm going to try and stop him!'

When Mordecai saw Chuck, he headed back toward the buildings. He entered the 200 buildings and then exited out through the entrance nearest the cafeteria. He raced inside the cafeteria and searched for a place to hide. He entered into the line area and made his way into the kitchen area, where he was met by one of the custodians. 'What's going on here?' the lady asked.

'Chuck Jones,' Mordecai gasped. 'He and his friends are after me!'

'Say what? That can't be true!'

Mordecai had no time to argue. He raced toward the back exit while the custodian stared in disgust at him. She then heard the door to the cafeteria open and close. She saw the three athletes looking around. 'Where are you, Jefferson?' called out Frank between breaths.

'This is one game we hate to play, jege,' shouted Stu. 'Come on out and take your medicine like a man, and we may go easy on you.'

'Should I go back to his bike and make sure he doesn't leave?' Chuck asked.

Frank shook his head. 'He won't have time to unlock the locks he's put on his bike,' he stated. 'One good thing about this, it's that he's giving us a great workout and will give us a better workout when we teach him a lesson.'

'It's only a matter of time before we catch him,' Stu said. 'Did you find a rope, Frank?'

'Sure did,' Frank answered, 'Had to take one from the shed on campus, but they won't miss it. They hardly use it.'

The custodian had heard enough. Mordecai was right, she realized. They were bullies. She shook her head and turned to check to see if Mordecai was still there.

But he had gone. He had made his way out the back door before they knew he was gone. He stopped to catch his breath, looking around to see if they were coming. He tried to conserve as much energy as he could. He decided to try and make his way back to his bike and hoped they wouldn't have noticed him until he was gone.

He made his way back down the corridors of the 100-building, hoping he could reach his bike. He looked back from time to time to see if they were coming. His heart was racing. He hid behind a hallway to catch his breath and hoped he was not spotted.

He was spotted, but it was neither of his adversaries. Tiffany and Sharon found him breathing heavily. 'Mordy?' Tiffany said.

'Hatfield, McCoy, and Jones,' he gasped. 'They're coming after me!'

'If you're heading for your bike, it won't do you any good,' Tiffany told him, 'It'll take you some time to get it loose, but that's time you can't afford!'

'Tell me about it,' Mordecai groaned between breaths. 'I know of no other way. I've got to keep moving, lest they find me!'

'Then what?' Tiffany asked.

Mordecai shook his head. 'I don't know.'

At that moment, Sharon caught a glimpse of the boys heading her way. She ducked behind the corridor and said softly to Mordecai, 'Run, run!'

Mordecai leaped to his feet and immediately raced down the hallway. Stu caught a glimpse of Mordecai disappearing around a corner and called to the other guys. 'There he goes. Follow me!'

'Leave him alone,' the two girls cried.

'Go to hell!' shot back Frank.

Mordecai raced back toward the office area, which was on the other side of the campus, running as fast as he could down the corridor, but they were beginning to gain on him. He felt fatigued, his strength failing as he raced for his life. He then began to slow down as he rounded a corner and headed inside the 400 building again.

He headed inside a classroom where he hid under a desk, breathing heavily. He tried to quiet his heavy breathing and hoped they wouldn't hear him. He remained still, not daring to move a muscle.

Two of the antagonists, Stu, and Frank, entered the classroom, looking around. 'He's got to be in one of the rooms,' Frank said. 'He couldn't have gotten far. He's tiring. We've got him now.'

'The sooner the better,' Stu gasped, 'I'm getting tired of this cat and mouse game, as much as I like it.'

'Check the storage room,' Frank told him, 'See if he's hiding in there.'

Mordecai knew they would check behind the desk before they left. He knew he had to get out of there, lest they find him. Gathering up what strength he could, he silently moved from behind the desk and prepared to run. He looked as they were in the far side of the room. He then sprang to his feet and raced out the door.

Only to run into the waiting form of Chuck Jones, who caught him and held him fast. He called for the others, saying, 'I got him! I got him!'

Stu and Frank walked out and saw him. Frank scowled at him and said disdainfully, 'You gave us quite a chase, Jefferson. You gave us a good workout to be sure.' Chuck and Stu held him as Frank grabbed him by the collar and threw him against the wall. He delivered two hard punches to the stomach. 'You had crossed us too many times, loser,' continued the bully, 'This is what happens when you do! We don't tolerate inferior dogs like you.'

Stu and Chuck grabbed Mordecai while Frank went into his enemy's pockets and took out his wallet and cell phone. It was there the card that Dr. Von Braun had given him fell out of his pocket. Frank put Mordecai's wallet and cell phone in his pocket and picked up the card, taking a glance at it. 'Dr. Haman Von Braun?' he said. 'Where'd you get that?'

Mordecai did not say a word.

'Answer me!' snapped Frank, punching him hard in the stomach again.

Mordecai refused to answer.

'Take him to Chuck's car,' Frank said, 'Time to use the ropes!' To Mordecai he said, 'Time to teach you a lesson you will never forget!'

They took Mordecai to Chuck's black Cadillac. Chuck unlocked it, opened the hood, and brought the rope out. While Mordecai struggled, Frank beat him more in response to their victim's resistance. Before they could tie him up, Mordecai's cell phone rang. Frank felt the vibration and thought it was his cell phone but found out it was not. He stared at the number.

'Look at this,' he said, 'Little sister trying to call big brother. How sweet is that? Isn't she supposed to be in detention?'

'No thanks to you, McCoy,' gasped Mordecai defiantly. 'It's you and your goons that should have been in detention, or better yet, suspension!'

'Shut up, jege!' snapped Stu, throwing him to the ground and kicking him. Mordecai tried to get away, but Chuck dropped an elbow on top of his head, incapacitating him. Stu began to tie up Mordecai's arms and then his legs. Frank pushed the call button on the phone but spoke not a word.

After a pause, there came Cece's voice. 'Hello? Mordy? Mordecai? Are you there? Hello? Are you okay?'

Frank pushed the button to end the call. He put the cell phone back in his pocket and kept it in there even after the phone had started ringing again. 'Make sure you secure him good,' he told them. 'Put him in the trunk!'

Mordecai was placed in the trunk and the door closed. As Frank and the others prepared to climb into the car, Tiffany and Sharon found them and caught up to them. 'Stop right there!' cried Tiffany.

Frank stared disdainfully at the girls. 'If you witches had any brains,' he said, 'You would mind your own business!'

'Or else what, you'll beat us up, too?' Sharon cried, 'Where's Mordy Jefferson?'

'Say what?' Stu laughed. 'Why do you care about that loser?'

'We saw what you three are really like,' Tiffany snapped, 'Especially after what you did to that kid in the lunchroom today, how you somehow must have forced him to lie and blame it on Jimmy Russo, who wasn't even on our lunch period! He was in class when that boy was beaten up! You got someone else to take the fall for your crimes and you get away with murder practically!'

'We did not murder anyone, wench,' snapped Chuck, 'You don't know what you're talking about!'

'I managed to get a phone call from Cece, and she told me her brother had called her and told her you were after him,' Tiffany cried, 'Now, where is Mordy? What did you do to him?'

'Nothing,' laughed Frank. 'We didn't find him.'

'Cece told me she had tried calling him, but he did not answer the phone for some reason,' Sharon cried, 'We know you did something to him. We know you were chasing him. What did you do to him?'

'We did not catch him,' Stu lied, 'He got away. He was too fast for us.'

'Liar!' Tiffany shot back. 'You are athletes and in superior shape! He is not in as good a shape as you! He could not outrun even the slowest of you three, and you know it! Don't presume to lie to us! We know the truth!'

'Now for the last time, where is he?' Sharon demanded.

'Why do you care?' Chuck asked.

'We care because he is the brother of our best friend and a good guy,' Tiffany snapped, 'We thought you guys were the greatest, but lately we have seen for ourselves that you are nothing more than lowlife bullies, classless and despicable!'

'Watch your tongue, witch,' snapped Frank. 'We are all-state players going on to big colleges and eventually the pros! You two are only cheerleaders, who are only good for firing up the crowd and cheering us on to victory!'

'Keep such names to yourself, McCoy!' snapped Sharon. 'Now for the last time, where is Mordy Jefferson?'

Suddenly, they saw the car shake and a thumping sound in the back, barely hearing a cry for help. Sharon and Tiffany stared at the three jocks, 'What did you do to him?' snapped Sharon. 'Why do you have him in the back of your trunk?'

Frank and Stu got into the car while Chuck proceeded to get into the driver's seat. 'If you were wise, I'd suggest you keep your traps shut about this!' He got in, started the engine, and drove off, forcing the girls to move out of the way as he backed out. Sharon and Tiffany only watched as the car disappeared, turning onto Hoffner Ave., and disappearing.

At that moment, Cece appeared, running and out of breath. One of the teachers appeared and caught her, trying to catch her breath. Cece managed to say, 'Where's Mordy? Where's my brother?'

'They took him,' Sharon cried in a panic. 'Hatfield, McCoy, and Jones put your brother in the trunk and drove away! They denied it, but we saw the car move and barely heard your brother's cry for help!'

'Are you kidding me?' the teacher asked.

'Open your eyes, Miss Jameson,' Tiffany cried. 'They've been doing this ever since they started attending Oak Ridge! Cece's brother is one of their main victims! They locked him in the trunk and took him away!'

'I'm afraid it's true, Miss Jameson,' came the custodian woman's voice, who approached them, 'I saw a kid come in, scared and tired, and then saw and heard the boys in question searching for him. He managed to slip out the back door before they caught him in the cafeteria, but unfortunately, they caught him. I saw them dragging him away, but I don't know where they had taken him till I saw her running out of detention with you after her.'

'I'm sorry, Miss Jameson,' gasped Cece, 'but they're going to do something terrible to my brother! I saw them on a few occasions bullying other students, including the kid they beat up today in the lunchroom and they forced the boy—I'm sure—to lie and to say that it was Jimmy Russo when he was in class at the time!'

To her friends she asked, 'Did they say where they were going?'

'No,' Sharon answered, 'They just warned us to keep our mouths shut! We know they have him in the trunk, but I don't know where they've taken him.'

Cece began to weep. Sharon and Tiffany stood by her to comfort her. 'They're going to do something terrible to my brother, I know it!' She wept, 'Why have the administration allowed them to run amok on people like my brother for so long? This is so wrong!'

Miss Jameson grabbed Cece gently by the arm. 'Tell me about it while we walk back to detention,' she said softly, 'I want to hear what you have to say, every word. I'm only sorry we refused to listen to you or others—like your brother. Tell me what you know, and maybe we can get Principal Spooney to see what's really going on.'

Cece followed the teacher as the custodian followed after them. Tiffany and Sharon joined them as they headed back onto campus. They wondered if the other teachers and the principal would open their eyes and see the atrocities that were being caused at the hands of the three jocks.

Cece continued to weep, thinking about what would happen to her brother, Mordecai.

Tiffany and Sharon caught up to them and decided to stand by Cece. Miss Jameson agreed and allowed them to join their good friend. The teacher found herself hoping Mordecai would be all right.

Cece feared the worst.

Chapter Five

Mordecai struggled to free himself from the ropes. He was stillhurting from the beating he had received from Frank and his friends. He wasn't sure where they were taking him or why they'd tied him up, but then again, it seemed to him the only reason they needed was because they hated him, hated people like him. To bullies, there was no rhyme or reason. He began to wonder if they were going to kill him.

Would they really go as far as to kill him? Where were they taking him? He laid back and whispered a silent prayer.

He felt the car stop and the engine shut off. He heard the car doors opening and then shutting. He heard them conversing and laughing. 'You think this would be an ideal spot?' came the voice of Stu.

'It'll be okay,' Frank said, 'Let's get rid of this excess baggage.'

The car trunk was opened. Mordecai blinked as the light hit his eyes. He was pulled out of the trunk by Stu and Chuck. They slammed him into a nearby tree. Mordecai felt the pain shooting through his back. He felt a pair of punches to the face as Frank laughed. 'Free shot, Stu,' he told his comrade.

Stu rammed his shoulder into the chest of the tied-up Mordecai. He cried out in pain from the impact. Chuck gave Mordecai a punch to the face and the stomach. Blood started flowing from Mordecai's mouth as Stu delivered a kick to his stomach. Mordecai slumped to the ground, moaning in pain. The three laughed as they saw him fall on his side. 'Let that be a lesson to you, Jefferson,' Frank told him. 'You cross us, you pay the price! It's simple! If you do it again, we'll do the same thing to you again! You keep in line, you'll be fine. Give us flack, we'll pay you back. You think about it a while!'

'Untie me!' cried Mordecai.

'You do it, jege,' laughed Frank as Stu and Chuck got into the car. 'You're going to learn that you are worthless, and you are a nobody! This is the fate of any nobody like you who gets out of line! Learn your place, or even worse things will happen to you!'

He got into the car as the engine was started. Chuck had *Highway to Hell* by AC/DC playing over the speakers as loud as he could play it as the car drove away.

Mordecai groaned. Painfully, he tried to free himself, working the best he could to try and get himself loose, but was limited to the injuries he had suffered at the hands of the bullies. As he struggled, he thought of calling Cece but remembered that Frank had stolen his wallet and cell phone. He groaned. He wasn't quite sure where he was, just near some wooded area surrounded by trees. He figured he'd have to follow the general direction the car had gone to at least find out where he was, and then it was a matter of walking home.

He managed to get one arm free. He first wiped the blood from his face and then worked to get his other arm free. He then managed to untie the ropes and remove them from his body. It took long minutes to get the ropes off, though he had to stop for a moment from the pain he felt in his body. He sighed. He threw the ropes to one side, sat down, and wept. He knew no teacher would believe him when he told them what the three jocks had done. They had them in their back pocket, given the fact they were all-state athletes and felt they could get away with anything they wanted, even bullying others weaker than they were. He felt in deep despair.

From nearby in the trees, Raven watched him and saw what had happened. The black fairy had been in the woods, spending time alone, when she heard the car coming and had seen what had happened to Mordecai. She was moved when she saw what had happened to him, heard his silent weeping. Something moved within her heart to move in closer. She gently flittered from the trees, landing on the ground. She moved in closer, slowly toward the weeping form of Mordecai, sighing sympathetically as she approached. *How could humans be so cruel to each other like that? I hope he's okay. Poor dear.* Her heart was moved with compassion toward him.

Mordecai looked up at that moment and saw the black fairy approaching him. When he saw her, she gasped and ran toward the trees, hiding herself behind a wide oak tree. 'Please don't go,' Mordecai cried.

He slowly rose from the ground, groaning in pain. Raven peered from behind a tree. He stared with tears still flowing from his eyes, looking her way. 'Please come back,' he whispered softly.

As if she heard him, Raven, trembling, moved slowly toward him. Mordecai saw her wings and gasped, staring in amazement, forgetting the pain of the beating he had received for a moment. 'You…' he gasped. 'You have wings? You're a fairy?'

Raven nodded, compelled to draw closer to him. She managed to say, 'Are you okay?'

Mordecai sighed. 'I'm still in a lot of pain from the beating I had received,' he groaned, 'It's kind of hard to move. I'll have to manage the best I can. I can't contact anybody to help me.' He then thought of his encounters with Dr. Von Braun. *So, Dr. Von Braun was right. I can't believe that fairies do exist. She is so beautiful!* He did his best to retain his balance as he rose to his feet. 'I am Mordecai, Mordecai Jefferson,' he told her. 'Do you have a name?'

'Why did those people treat you so badly?' Raven asked, 'Why do they hurt you?'

'They take pleasure in hurting people like me,' Mordecai sighed, 'They are bullies who take pleasure in inflicting pain and misery on others weaker than they are. I feel like I'm their favorite whipping boy.'

'"Whipping boy?"' Raven repeated, 'What is that?'

Mordecai sighed. 'How can I describe it?' He thought deeply for a moment. 'They love to pick on me more than anybody in school, it seems. I am kind of an outcast, a nobody, a pariah, a misfit.'

'Why are you considered a nobody?' Raven asked.

Mordecai sighed. 'I am picked on for not being like them, for being different from them,' he said sadly, 'Even for my faith in Christ.'

'So you know the Saviour?' Raven asked.

'Yes,' Mordecai answered, 'and often put down and ostracized for it.'

Raven bowed her head sadly. 'Jesus did say we would be hated for His name's sake. There are some of my people, including Queen Cymbaline and her brother, Prince Avondale, who rule my home of Arundel Haven, who share my beliefs, but many do not believe in the Saviour. Queen Cymbaline has forbidden us from contact with other humans.'

'Why?' Mordecai asked.

'The heart of humans is wicked and deceitful,' Raven said.

'The Word of God confirms her beliefs,' sighed Mordecai, 'I have to agree with her.'

'But I know there are some good humans in the world,' Raven said.

'Too few and far between it seems,' Mordecai said, 'There are some of us who are good, but too many wicked hearted of us, it would seem. I have been ostracized, treated like I'm a leper or an infectious disease.' He sighed. 'I'm sorry.' He turned away. 'I have been hurt a lot. My parents don't understand the pain I'm going through.' He sat down and wept. 'I just feel so alone in the world!'

Raven sat down by him as he wept. The fear she had felt was gone. She found her heart aching as a result of the pain Mordecai was feeling. 'No, you're not alone, Mordecai,' she said softly, 'You have me now. I am here.'

'Why would you want anything to do with me?' he asked her. 'I am a nobody.'

Raven wiped the tears from his eyes, took his hand, and kissed it. 'You are not a nobody, Mordecai,' she said soothingly, 'Not to me, and certainly not to God.' She wiped more tears from his eyes as she stared at him. 'Raven.'

Mordecai stared at her. 'Who?'

Raven smiled. 'My name is Raven, and I'm very happy to meet you, Mordecai.' She rose, and took his hand, helping him to his feet.

'I am very happy to meet you too, Raven,' Mordecai smiled, 'You are so beautiful.'

Raven smiled. 'Thank you.'

'Am I still bleeding in the mouth?' Mordecai asked.

Raven wiped what little blood that was there from his mouth. 'A little. Your mouth seems to be a little swollen.'

Mordecai sighed. 'I know I'm not the only one in school they've been picking on, but it feels like it,' he said, 'It seems I'm their favorite person to harass, to bully.'

'That is terrible. Why are they so cruel to you? I see why Queen Cymbaline believes all humans are evil and wicked.'

'Sometimes it does seem like it is, but I know it's not,' Mordecai sighed.

Raven stared at Mordecai, taking his hands. 'The good thing about those bad men taking you here, is that I met you.'

Mordecai smiled. 'I agree,' he replied softly, 'I really hope I can see you again.'

Raven nodded. 'I would like that too, Mordecai,' she smiled.

Mordecai sighed. 'I have to try and get home before it gets dark, I want to know more about you, Raven.'

'I will be here tomorrow,' Raven said, 'I will be more than happy to see you again.'

Mordecai released Raven's hands and turned to go, moving as carefully as he could. 'I wish there was something I could do to help you get home,' she said.

'I'm afraid there is nothing,' he replied, 'I don't want your existence to be known, especially since there is a madman investigating the existence of your people.' He stopped.

Raven flittered toward him. 'Somebody has heard about the existence of Arundel Haven and the remains of a fairy found somewhere in these parts,' Mordecai continued. 'His name is Dr. Haman Von Braun. I sense his intentions are evil.' He sighed. 'I still can't believe that what he believes is true.'

'He is a bad man?' Raven asked.

'I have a feeling deep inside he is, or at least his intentions toward fairies,' Mordecai answered. 'He believes I have a connection with the existence of your people.' He sighed. 'Now that I know of your existence, Raven, I must work very hard to keep it a secret. Von Braun must not know. I promise to do all I can to keep the existence of your people a secret.'

'Perhaps there is somebody you can trust?' Raven asked.

'I don't believe so,' Mordecai sighed, placing his hand upon Raven's face. 'I swear as the Lord lives to keep your existence a secret from people like Dr. Von Braun.'

Raven smiled, placing her hand upon his. 'I believe you, Mordecai,' she said.

Mordecai turned around to go. 'I wish I could stay with you longer, Raven, but I better head back home before it gets dark.'

'I wish you would stay too, Mordecai,' Raven replied, 'I look forward to seeing you again.'

Mordecai smiled. He turned to go. Raven smiled as she watched him leave. 'Be safe, sweet Mordecai,' she whispered, 'Until tomorrow.'

Mordecai followed the path he guessed Chuck's car had taken. He managed to find the main road and walked beside it. He watched the traffic go by as he made his way slowly toward home. He wondered how long it would take for him to walk home.

At that moment, a green car honked as it passed by and pulled over twenty meters in front of him. He then recognized the car as belonging to Cece's friend, Tiffany. He saw Cece stepping out of the car and running to him, embracing him as she wept. He wept with her.

'Thank God you're alive,' she said amid her tears. 'I feared they would have killed you! I tried to call you, but you didn't answer.'

'McCoy stole my wallet and cell phone,' replied Mordecai, 'He took all the money I had, which was not much.'

Cece looked at his face, her expression turning to anger. 'They've gone too far this time,' she growled, 'What did they do to you?'

'They tied me up, used me as a tackling dummy and a punching bag, usual bully stuff,' he answered, 'My jaw hurts, my body hurts.'

'We're going to take care of this once and for all. There is no excuse for what they've been doing to you, for the teachers and the principal to do nothing about this!' She sighed, releasing him. 'Let's get you home.'

Mordecai nodded. Cece led him to the car. Mordecai opened the door and slid inside, allowing room for Cece to sit down. Sharon and Tiffany stared at Mordecai with worried looks upon their faces. 'Are you okay, Mordy?' Tiffany asked.

'What happened?' Sharon asked as Cece got inside.

'They tied me up and locked me in the trunk,' Mordecai answered, 'They took me to the woods and beat me up. They left me tied up in the woods.'

'How did you get untied?' Cece asked.

'Fortunately, I managed to get my hands free and untied myself,' Mordecai answered, 'It was fortunate that I did. They threatened to do more if I don't stay in line.'

'Are you going to tell your parents?' Sharon asked.

Mordecai shook his head sadly. 'It won't do any good,' he frowned, 'I doubt they will listen to me. Seems like nobody listens.'

'We have to try, Mordy,' Cece replied, 'We both have to try!' She burst into tears as she leaned upon Mordecai's shoulder. 'I was so worried about you!'

Mordecai nodded sadly, wrapping his arms around her, weeping, not saying a word.

The first thing Mordecai did was take a hot bath to try and ease the pain. There were times his thoughts went to Raven, the fairy he had just met, and he smiled. He looked forward to seeing Raven again the next day, but he had to get his bike from school. He decided not to tell Cece about Raven, at least not yet. He then thought about Dr. Von Braun. He thought about how he had offered him six million dollars for the proof that fairies existed. It would help to have that kind of money, but he then thought about the promise he had made to Raven. He firmly decided he would keep the promise he made, which he felt was more important than money. He began to have feelings for Raven but wasn't sure about it. He decided to let it go. Would it work out between a human and a fairy? Had there ever been such a relationship before? Would it even be possible? He decided to keep it to himself.

He painfully made his way downstairs where Cece, Sharon, and Tiffany were sitting down. He was about to go for a soda when Cece said, 'I already got one for you, Mordy.'

Mordecai headed toward the couch and sat down on one of the easy chairs, wincing from the pain. 'What time do your parents come home?' Tiffany asked.

'Not for another hour,' Cece answered, rising up and giving Mordecai an unopened can of soda. 'I should have come and gotten it from you, Cece,' Mordecai winced. 'I'm sorry.'

'Don't worry about it,' Cece said, 'How are you feeling?'

'I'm still in pain,' Mordecai said, 'I tried taking some pain relievers before I took a bath. I don't know if that's going to help.'

'Maybe it takes some time to kick in,' suggested Sharon. 'Were there any bruises on you besides your face?'

'Two on my body,' answered Mordecai, 'It's painful in those places. I'm kind of waiting for the pain to die down. My legs hurt too, but I don't think they're bruised.' He drank his soda as he, Cece, and her friends talked.

Raven returned to her home about two hours after sunset. She opened the door to her cottage and managed to light one of the candles. She then proceeded to find and light the other candles in the other rooms. She then noticed her bad leg was starting to hurt again as a result of her encounter with Shadowfire. She grabbed some bread and cheese and some juice and sat down at the table. As she ate, she thought about the human she had just met, Mordecai. As she did, she felt a strong feeling toward him, a feeling of love. Was she falling in love with Mordecai? Would it be even possible for a fairy and a human to fall in love? Does Mordecai feel the same way about her as she does about him? She admitted to herself that she had fallen in love with Mordecai, and she knew Queen Cymbaline would not approve of such a relationship for sure, but she did not want to be without Mordecai now that she had found him. It would be no good, she thought, to tell them of her meeting with Mordecai. She knew they would not approve of such a relationship. She had never heard before of a relationship between a fairy and a human and doubted such a union had never happened before. She looked forward to her meeting with Mordecai the next day. At that moment, there was a knock on the door. She stood up and headed to the door. As she opened it, Starla, with Twila in her arms, stood in the doorway along with Lavender and Laurelin. 'Hi,' Raven said.

'Don't you "hi" us, young fairy woman,' Laurelin said sternly, 'Where have you been all day? We were all worried sick!'

Raven heard Twila giggle when she said that. She tickled the toddler and said, 'Hey, Twila.'

Twila laughed as she was tickled.

Starla gave her sister a queer look. 'Raven, where were you all day?' she asked.

'I was flying around,' Raven answered. 'Stretching my wings. I just love to fly.'

'That's kind of Twila's line, don't you think?' Lavender said coldly.

'Look, why are you making a big deal out of this?' Raven asked irritably. 'I was out flying around, okay?'

'To your secret place?' Laurelin asked.

'I was there too,' Raven nodded, 'but I was mainly flying around. I wasn't flying where humans lived, if that's what you're worried about. Is it wrong for a fairy to go out flying from time to time?'

'Not where there are humans,' Lavender retorted. 'If you keep this up, it's sure to draw attention from Queen Cymbaline and Prince Avondale, and no matter what rapport you have with them, they will not look kindly toward you flying to the human world.'

Raven let out a sigh. 'You all are worrying for nothing,' she insisted.

'Are we?' Starla responded sternly. 'It's a serious matter for a fairy to venture into the human world. You know that full well, Raven! You could have been captured, and the location of Arundel Haven and our existence would be compromised! It would be the end of all fairies as we know it!'

'You think I don't know that?' cried Raven. 'I have gone nowhere near the human world if you must know. You are all worrying for nothing! What would it take to put your minds at ease in this matter?'

'You are telling us the truth, are you?' Starla asked, 'You haven't been flying to the human world?'

'Nowhere near any humans,' answered Raven. 'I swear!'

'How is your leg?' Lavender asked.

'Still sore,' Raven answered, 'but it's getting there. I'll be glad when it's completely better. I hate being immobile and in one place for a long period.'

'You sure didn't rest your leg while you were out,' Starla frowned. 'I think we may have to chain you down to your bed until that leg is healed up.'

'Boo-boo still hurt, Aunt Raven?' Twila asked.

Raven nodded. 'A little, Twila,' she answered, tickling her young niece. Twila let out a series of laughs. 'No tickle, Aunt Raven,' the toddler giggled.

'Now, are you going to rest your leg tomorrow?' Starla asked.

'Yes, I will rest it,' answered Raven. 'I will be fine.'

'Twila and I will drop by tomorrow to check up on you,' Starla said. 'Roosevelt won't need me to help out. We will drop by early in the morning.'

Raven nodded. 'I will be here. I may be asleep, but I will be here.'

'If you're asleep, we will come in anyway,' Starla added.

Mordecai looked out into the night sky. His thoughts remained on Raven, the fairy he had met. The injuries he had suffered still bothered him. He hoped he would be able to sleep tonight despite the pain. He looked out the window, his thoughts reaching out to Raven, wherever she was.

There was a knock on the door. He glanced toward the door and saw Cece. 'Come in,' he told her.

'I just came to check up on you before I turn in for the night.'

'You okay, Cece?' Mordecai asked. Cece sighed. 'You're thinking about what Tess told you earlier this morning?'

Cece nodded, leaning on Mordecai's shoulder and weeping. 'I guess it all makes sense when I come to think about it,' she wept. 'How he had been avoiding me, not returning my texts or calls.'

Mordecai held her close as she wept. 'I had been too busy worrying what those jerky jocks were doing to you to think of Oscar at the time. I am so glad you are okay!'

'I know,' Mordecai nodded gravely, kissing her on the forehead. 'I was scared, too. I was afraid I wasn't going to make it.'

'I can't understand why Mom and Dad dismiss it as a harmless prank.' Cece shook her head. 'Maybe you should have shown them your bruises.'

Mordecai sighed, shaking his head. 'Why are they blinding themselves to the obvious when it comes to me? I don't understand.'

'It's just not fair to you, Mordecai,' she wept. 'I had the fear before of you hating me because of what they've been doing you.'

'I don't hate you, Cece,' he insisted as tears welled up in his eyes. 'We established that last week. I will never hate you. You are my sister, and I love you. None of this is your fault.'

Cece wept as she held on.

'I will always love you, little sister,' continued Mordecai. 'No matter what!'

Cece continued to weep. 'Thank you, Mordecai, that means a lot to me.'

'I'm here for you as well when you need me,' he told his sister, 'You're going to find a young man who's better than Oscar, who's going to treat you better and respect you. Know that I got your back, Cece.'

Cece nodded as she wept.

'Things are going to get better for the both of us, I can feel it,' Mordecai continued, 'but I feel they will get worse first. No matter what, Cece, I will always be here for you.'

'And I you,' Cece replied amid her tears.

That night, Mordecai found himself in the valley again, the same valley where he had met the dragon before. Why was he here again? What's the significance of all this? He tried to search for a way out, to get away. He didn't know what direction to go or how to get out. Everything seemed darker than before. He continued to walk.

He suddenly heard a loud roar from up in the sky ahead of him. He saw the familiar shape of the dragon, fire spewing out of his mouth as the shadow of the dragon revealed its hideous form. He laughed mockingly as he landed in front of the young man. 'There is no escape for you, human,' he said. 'I know you are the one the prophecy had spoken of, that much is clear to me.'

'What are you talking about?' Mordecai asked, 'What prophecy? Who are you?'

'So many questions,' mocked the dragon, 'but no answers will you find. What answers you seek I know, but I refuse to give them to you. All I know is that as long as you live, you are a danger to me, a mortal danger.'

'Why? Why am I a threat to you?'

'Ask if you must, human,' continued the dragon, 'but no answers will I give. I know you have already had contact with a fairy, that much I know.'

'How do you know?' Mordecai asked.

'I have my ways,' boasted the dragon, 'Ask if you must, but don't expect any answers. My reasons shall remain my own, the answers hidden from you. Now, your name. Who are you, human?'

Mordecai frowned. 'Since you choose to leave me in the dark, I shall do the same to you. I don't know of this prophecy you speak about or why you think I am the one to destroy you according to this prophecy, or what threat I could possibly be to you. I am a nobody, nothing special at all.'

The dragon laughed. 'That, I agree with you. Worthless and insignificant. If I did not honestly consider you a threat, I would laugh at you to scorn. But the danger to me is real, the threat you pose to me is real, and I take the danger seriously. Wherever you are, I will find you and I will end the threat you pose to me once and for all.'

'If you think I will tell you where I live and my name,' cried the young man, 'you are mistaken as well. I will tell you nothing.'

'I shall find out all about you sooner or later,' the dragon boomed, 'who you are, where you live. I can invade your dreams, but I cannot divine who you are and where you live. By Ashtaroth and all the powers of hell, I will not allow the prophecy to be fulfilled!'

The dragon then roared and spewed fire in the direction of Mordecai.

Mordecai awoke with a jump. He shuddered as he shook his head, placing his hands up to his face. He then raised his head, his lips whispering the name that came to his thoughts.

Shadowfire.

The dragon's name is Shadowfire.

He found himself downstairs minutes later, his body still aching from the beating he had received the day before. He had a can of soda in his hands, thinking about the dream. Why was he having the same dream? Is the dragon's name in the dream really Shadowfire? He somehow guessed it was. He then thought of Raven. How did Shadowfire know that he had met a fairy, though he didn't know who he was or who the fairy was that he had met? He had so many unanswered questions concerning the dream.

Cece walked downstairs in a purple robe and saw Mordecai sitting down at the table. She sighed and shook her head. 'Not again,' she whispered.

She walked toward him. 'Same dream again?'

'Same dream,' sighed Mordecai, 'Still with the dragon and being in the valley. He continued to speak about the prophecy, whatever that is, that foretold I would be the one to destroy him. He can't be real; he couldn't be real.'

'That is strange. Five nights in a row now?'

Mordecai nodded.

'What else could you tell me about the dream?' Cece asked.

'Not much that I haven't told you already,' answered Mordecai. He did not tell Cece that the dragon had mentioned he had met a fairy. 'A name came to me when I woke up: *Shadowfire.*'

'Shadowfire?'

'I think that name is appropriate for the dragon' the young man said, 'I call him Shadowfire. Whether it is his correct name or not I do not know.'

Cece sat down. 'I don't know what to say. I don't know what to tell you, why you keep having this dream.'

'What explanation could be given?' replied Mordecai, 'I just want these dreams to stop. He also claims he has the ability to invade my dreams, if that was possible.'

'Invade your dreams?' Cece repeated.

'I wish I had another explanation for having those dreams,' said Mordecai, 'I wish they would stop!'

Cece wished she knew what to say. It was hard to understand why the dreams had kept occurring with Mordecai. She knew nothing about dreams, but she wished she did, if it would help her brother.

'Having it one night is one thing,' Mordecai continued, 'but *five nights in a row?* Something must be going on, but what? Why do I have the feeling this dragon is real and that somehow, he has the ability to invade my dreams as he said?'

'Then fairies must be real as well,' laughed Cece.

Mordecai smiled. His thoughts went to the black fairy, Raven, whom he had met yesterday. He looked forward to seeing her after school as soon as he retrieved his bike. He figured that Tiffany could put his bike in her trunk and when he got home, wash up, change, and head for the woods where he had first met Raven.

'Hey, you okay?' she asked.

Mordecai shook his head as if he was snapping out of a trance.

'Oh, I'll be fine,' he told her, 'I'll be okay.' He stood up and finished his soda. 'I'll have to try and get some more sleep.' He sighed. 'I only hope I can get back to sleep. Last night, I wasn't able to after waking up from the dream.'

'I hope the dreams do stop,' Cece replied sympathetically.

Mordecai nodded as he started up the stairs. 'So do I.'

That afternoon, after school, Mordecai headed to the woods on his bike where the three jocks had taken him, beaten him up, and left him before he had met Raven. He saw the familiar form of the black fairy appearing from the woods as he parked his bike. They embraced and looked into each other's eyes. 'I am happy to see you, Raven,' Mordecai said.

'As am I,' Raven smiled, taking his hand.

Mordecai stared at her legs, noticing she had her left leg slightly off the ground. 'What happened to you?' he asked.

'I hurt my leg escaping from an evil dragon that lives in the mountains near Arundel Haven,' she answered, 'He was after me and my niece, Twila.'

'A dragon?' Mordecai exclaimed as Raven nodded.

Mordecai thought about the dream he had about the dragon for the past five nights. He stared at Raven and said, 'This is strange, I have had dreams the past five nights about a dragon. He said I was a threat to him, citing some kind of prophecy, though he did not tell me anything more than that.'

'Prophecy? What prophecy?' Raven asked.

'He did not clarify' the young man told her, 'It's been happening, having the similar dream for the past five nights.'

'Did he tell you his name?' asked the black fairy maiden.

'No,' answered Mordecai, 'I did not tell him mine either. He considered me a threat for some reason. That's when you mentioned you got hurt escaping from a dragon.'

'What did the dragon look like in your dream?' asked Raven.

Mordecai sighed. 'He was a large dragon, all in black. Over thirty meters high and over forty in length, its wingspan very wide.'

Raven gasped.

'I did not know its name,' Mordecai continued, 'and he would not reveal it, nor how he knew about me. When I woke up, a name came to my mind: Shadowfire.'

Raven gasped. 'That's his name,' she exclaimed 'He was the one that tried to capture me. He has been afflicting the fairies of Arundel Haven for 150 years. He was the one that had killed my parents.'

'Then that is his name, Shadowfire?' gasped Mordecai, 'Shadowfire is real?'

Raven sadly nodded.

'I'm sorry about your parents, Raven,' he whispered as Raven fell into his arms. She started to weep.

'I was nearly taken by Shadowfire as well, along with my young niece, Twila,' she wept. 'I was scared for my life!'

Mordecai held Raven close, careful of her wings. He caressed the back of her head gently, anxious to comfort her. 'Since he is real,' he said, 'I wonder what this prophecy is. He keeps insisting that I am the one to destroy him?'

'I know of no prophecy,' replied Raven, 'I wonder if Queen Cymbaline would know? I could ask her about it.'

'But how would she react if she found out you were interacting with a human?' Mordecai asked, 'She would disapprove of our meeting, I am sure, since I am a human, and she would be angry with you for venturing here to the human world.'

As he held her, he heard a sound like a cell phone coming from the black fairy's pocket. They jumped; Raven more startled than Mordecai. 'A cell phone?' the young man exclaimed. 'It sounded like a cell phone.'

Raven pulled out the cell phone as it continued ringing, then stopped. 'Is that what this is, a cell phone?' she asked Mordecai. 'What does it do?'

'It's how humans communicate with each other,' Mordecai answered, 'talk to each other over long distances.' He stared at the phone as Raven handed it to him. 'Where did you find it?'

'I found it earlier today while I was exploring these woods,' Raven answered.

'I'd never thought I would get my cell phone back,' Mordecai said, putting it in his pocket. 'McCoy must have thrown the cell phone out while he was leaving. I wonder if he had thrown out my wallet?'

'This?' Raven asked, pulling out a black wallet.

'Bless you, Raven,' he exclaimed, taking his wallet. He looked inside. 'Figures he would take all the money from my wallet.' He sighed. 'Not surprising of him.'

'How cruel this McCoy person is,' Raven exclaimed.

'His first name is Frank,' replied Mordecai, 'His friends are bullies as well: Stu Hatfield and Chuck Jones. They are the ones who keep bullying me and others like me.'

'That is terrible,' exclaimed Raven. 'I've known humans can be cruel.'

'It's in the nature of man to sin, I'm afraid,' replied Mordecai, 'It is easier to do evil than it is to do good.'

'Same with fairies as well, I imagine,' said Raven, 'though not as bad as you humans, but still bad enough. We all need Jesus Christ.'

'That's why He came down and suffered himself to be crucified,' replied Mordecai, 'for us, but we don't deserve it. He did it because He loved us.'

'I, personally, am glad I have met you, Mordecai,' smiled Raven, 'You are not like the other humans.'

'I am not perfect, Raven, but I know what it's like to need a true friend and to be a true friend. I am glad I have met you too, Raven.' He took her hand.

Raven smiled.

Mordecai smiled as well.

The next day, Raven was having a little picnic with her niece, Twila, in an area near where the Silverstreams flowed. Raven had been watching Twila while her sister, Starla, was running an errand for her husband.

Raven's thoughts constantly dwelt on Mordecai, feeling more of a connection than before with the young human. She smiled as she thought of him. She knew she was definitely falling in love with Mordecai, and she felt, somehow, he felt the same way. She made sure she kept her head clear in case Twila tried to fly away again.

But Twila did not feel like flying. She ate the jam and bread Raven had given her. She started yawning to the relief of the young fairy. She crawled up onto Raven's lap and snuggled close to her aunt. Raven smiled, gently kissing her. 'Twila tired?' she asked.

Twila merely yawned.

Lavender and Laurelin appeared, a basket in Laurelin's hands. They sat down beside her and saw the toddler on her lap. 'Twila's finally getting sleepy?' Lavender asked.

'Fortunately,' Raven answered, 'She's unusually quiet today.'

'Is she feeling sick?' Laurelin asked.

'She feels fine,' Raven answered, 'She's not sick or anything. I guess she must have burned out some of her energy before Starla brought her to me. She said she will be here as soon as she's finished.'

'Your leg any better?' Lavender asked.

'Steadily getting better,' Raven answered, 'I try not to walk on it too much still. I usually flitter to keep from putting weight on it.'

'Brewed any more of your tea before you left?' Lavender asked.

Raven shook her head. 'Sorry, Lavender,' she answered, 'I forgot to brew some last night.' They felt a gentle breeze, a little cooler than before. Raven sighed. 'It's almost time to break out the winter clothes. I wish I would have brought an extra blanket.'

'Maybe you should wait until the spring to have another picnic, Raven,' Laurelin suggested, 'Just saying, though. I wonder if the snows will come early this year?'

'I hope not,' they heard the voice of Starla say. The black fairy appeared, exhaling air. She was a little fatigued. She looked at Twila, who had fallen asleep on Raven's lap. 'I am so happy Twila is finally asleep.' She smiled, sitting down. 'What do you have?'

'I brought some cheeses, a little bit of chicken, bread that my grandmother baked,' Laurelin answered, 'She's teaching me how to bake bread.'

Starla slowly sat down.

'Are you okay, Starla?' Raven asked.

Starla nodded. 'Just a bit winded, a bit tired,' she answered, 'Nothing serious.'

Laurelin pulled out the food in her basket. 'Twila really wore you out this morning?' Lavender asked.

'You know Twila,' Starla replied, 'She is so much like Raven when we were growing up. I see a lot of her in Twila.'

Raven gave a queer star at her sister, displeased by her words.

'Admit it, Raven,' Starla told her. 'You were like that when you were Starla's age. I remember!'

Raven sighed. 'I was young then,' she replied.

'Admit that you see a lot of yourself in Twila,' insisted Starla.

'Perhaps,' replied Raven softly.

Lavender and Laurelin laughed. 'So you're saying that Twila is another you?' Laurelin asked Raven.

'Just wait until you each have a child of your own,' Raven said. 'And you,' Laurelin said, laughing.

Raven simply nodded. She said nothing. *I wonder how you would feel if I told you I had fallen in love with a human?* Her thoughts then went to Mordecai. *I know you would not approve of him because he is a human,* she sighed as she thought.

'You okay, Raven?' Starla asked.

'She hasn't found her fairyman yet, Starla,' Lavender replied, 'She'll find him sooner or later.'

Raven did not speak. She looked down at Twila, who was asleep on her lap. She smiled. 'She looks so cute when she's asleep,' she said.

Starla smiled. 'I am proud of her; despite the trouble she gets herself in. I can't believe she flew into the castle and into the arms of Prince Avondale!' She laughed. 'How on earth could she have eluded you, Raven?'

'She's a toddler,' Raven said, 'I was fortunate neither Queen Cymbaline nor the prince were sore with me. I was afraid they would be.'

'You should have seen the chase, Starla,' laughed Laurelin. 'She somehow dodged every attempt Raven made to catch her. I can't believe how well Twila can fly now!'

Starla sighed. 'It's going to be tougher for Roosevelt and me very soon,' she said, 'I may not be able to keep up with Twila in the coming months.'

'What do you mean?' Lavender asked.

'I haven't told Roosevelt yet.'

'About what?' asked Laurelin.

Raven gasped. 'You're pregnant again?' she exclaimed.

Starla nodded.

Raven got close enough to embrace her sister. Lavender and Laurelin did the same. 'That is so great to hear, Starla,' Lavender exclaimed, 'I'm sure Roosevelt will be happy. Twila is going to have a little brother or sister!'

'That is so great to hear, Starla,' Raven said, smiling, 'When are you going to tell Roosevelt?'

'When the time is right,' Starla answered, 'I know he will be very happy with the news.'

When they had finished eating, Lavender and Laurelin gathered up the food and put it all back in the basket. Starla picked up the napping Twila from Raven's arms and turned to go. As Lavender and Laurelin turned to go, Laurelin asked, 'You coming?'

'I'm just going to sit here for a while before I go home,' Raven told her.

'You are coming directly to your home?' Lavender asked.

'Of course,' Raven answered.

Without another word, Lavender and Laurelin took to the air and flew back toward town. Raven remained on the ground for a few minutes and, when she was sure, took to the air and flew away from Arundel Haven, anxious to see Mordecai again.

Dr. Von Braun stared at Seymour and Wilfred from behind his desk. They were in his office on the campus of UCF. He had a look that told the men he was not pleased. He put down his glass of scotch and frowned. 'What do you mean you couldn't find Mordy Jefferson?'

'We looked for him on his bike, but it was still locked up at the school when it ended Friday,' Seymour answered, 'We didn't see him come out.'

'What happened to him?' asked Dr. Von Braun.

'He must have gotten a ride with somebody else,' Wilfred said, 'It's the only explanation.'

'He may have started taking the bus again,' Seymour suggested, 'We can check for him on the buses that pull up when they arrive at the school in the morning.'

'We can check the students who gather to wait for the bus to come to his subdivision,' Wilfred added.

'Not too close,' Dr. Von Braun warned. 'I don't want him to see you. If he should see the car that you drive, he could become suspicious. I do not want him to know you have been watching him. Keep a low profile. Keep a watch on the school and follow the bus that goes into the subdivision.'

'You're the boss,' Seymour said, 'but I don't understand how you could think he would encounter a fairy.'

'Just keep a watch on him tomorrow,' Dr. Von Braun said. He saw Seymour pour himself a glass of tequila. He shook his head. 'There's nothing more that can be done this day. I still have one more class to teach ere calling it a night. I need to buy more scotch and whisky.' To Seymour he said, 'Tequila is your preference?'

Seymour drained his cup. 'Yes, indeed,' he nodded.

'Just not too much, unless you want Wilfred to drive,' Dr. Von Braun warned, 'Law enforcement tends not to take kindly to those who drink and drive.'

'Of course,' Seymour nodded.

'Would you want us to pick up your favorite beer while we're out?' Wilfred asked.

Dr. Von Braun laughed. 'You know me,' he replied, 'I need to watch what I drink as well. I think two glasses of scotch will be more than enough for now. Being intoxicated would not make me look good. I need to be sober and clear-minded when I teach classes.'

'Anybody else we should keep our eyes on?' Wilfred asked.

'Anybody associated with Mordy Jefferson, but mainly him alone,' answered Dr. Von Braun, picking up his books, 'Get some rest. You will need it for tomorrow. Keep a close eye on him! Follow him everywhere he may go. Sooner or later, he will lead us to a fairy.'

They escorted him out of his office and left the campus while Dr. Von Braun headed to the classroom he was teaching in.

Mordecai laid on his bed. He thought of his meeting with Raven earlier that day, the third day he had visited the black fairy. He smiled as his thoughts remained on her. He put the Bible on his nightstand and closed his eyes, thinking about Raven.

As he thought about Raven, his thoughts against his bidding came to Dr. Von Braun, the geneticist who had sought information from him about fairies. He knew now that fairies were real, ever since he met Raven and thought about the picture of the remains of the fairy Dr. Von Braun had shown him before meeting the ebony fairy, causing him to accept the possibility that indeed there could be fairies. He knew now he must keep Raven's existence a secret. He knew now, from what Raven had told him about Arundel Haven and the dragon in the dreams he had been having the past six nights now. He hoped and prayed the dreams of the dragon, Shadowfire, would stop. He remembered the dragon had told him that he had been invading his dreams. How did he come to figure he was the one to destroy him? He didn't seem to know his name or where he lived, which was good. If he was the one to destroy him—as some prophecy said, which he was still unclear about—how would he do it? Why him? He was a nobody, or so he thought, but he remembered Raven did not think so, nor did Cece. *Should I tell Cece about Raven? Should I tell Cece that fairies do exist? I want to, but with Dr. Von Braun eager to find fairies, I don't think it would be a good idea. He could go after Cece in his quest to find fairies.* He did not want to put Raven in any kind of danger.

Raven laid on her bed. Her thoughts were on Mordecai. She wanted to tell him when she saw him earlier that she had fallen in love with him but was somehow afraid to. How would a romance work out between a fairy and a human? She told nobody in Arundel Haven about Mordecai and her feelings toward him, for she knew they would disapprove wholeheartedly and rebuke her for even meeting a human. She was determined to see him again and find a way so that they could be together always, spend their lives together. She then thought of the children she would bear. Would it be possible for a fairy to conceive and bear children by a human? To her knowledge, it had never been done before, but she began to welcome it, tried to imagine having children by Mordecai. Would they have wings and be able to fly like their mother? What would they look like? She knew they would have both parents, a human father and a fairy mother, who loved them so much as well as each other. They would be together, she determined, someway, somehow. She then felt a touch in her heart. She felt that Mordecai was the one God had chosen for her. She smiled and whispered Mordecai's name.

It was at that exact moment, Mordecai, on his bed in his room, whispered Raven's name. It seemed that their very thoughts touched from the distance that separated the lovers. Mordecai then knew in his heart, and the touch on his heart confirmed, that Raven was his and he was Raven's. Both were still unsure if the other felt the same way. Could he risk rejection to tell Raven how he felt about her? How could he tell Raven how he felt?

Raven wondered the same thing. How could she tell Mordecai the way how she felt? She knew he was the one for her, but could she tell him?

Could Mordecai tell Raven she was the one for him?

Both lovers pondered this in their hearts as they laid in their respective beds.

Mordecai awoke a few hours before sunrise.

He moaned, 'Not again! The same dreams? Who is this Shadowfire and why does he believe I will be the one to destroy him?'

He rose from his bed. 'Isn't seven nights in a row enough?' he groaned.

He met Cece as she headed out of the bathroom. She saw the look on his face. 'Not again,' she said, eyes wide.

Mordecai nodded as he sighed. 'This is insane like Hussein,' he groaned. 'I don't understand!'

'Do you think you need to talk to somebody about this?' asked Cece.

'Who do I talk to?' retorted Mordecai. 'Who do I tell, "For the past seven nights, I've had a dream about a dragon called Shadowfire who insists that I am the one some cotton-picking prophecy says will destroy him?" They would think I was out of my mind.'

Cece sighed. 'It does sound farfetched,' she nodded. 'One or two nights is one thing, but *seven nights in a row?* I don't know what to think.'

They headed downstairs to the kitchen and sat down at the table, Mordecai grabbing a soda for both Cece and himself. 'This is crazy,' Mordecai said. 'I don't know what to think or do about it.'

'I can't believe seven nights in a row,' replied Cece, 'and this Shadowfire did not tell you anything still about this prophecy?'

'Nothing,' Mordecai answered, 'He still doesn't know who I am or where I live. I have a feeling he may be real. If he has been invading my dreams, then he must be real.'

Cece laughed. 'How can you be sure?'

'I have this feeling.' He did not reveal anything about Raven's existence and that she had told him the dragon was real. As much as he wanted to tell Cece about Raven and his feelings for her, he did not want to put Raven in danger.

'Next thing I know, you're going to tell me that fairies are real,' laughed Cece.

Mordecai only smiled.

'You're joshing me? You think fairies could be real?' exclaimed Cece.

'Who can say?' replied Mordecai, determined to keep Raven's existence a secret. His face turned grave again. 'I can't understand why I keep having these dreams, why they keep happening.'

'Is there anything different in the dream you just had?' Cece asked.

Mordecai thought for a moment. 'Shadowfire insisted that I had met a fairy,' he said, 'Kind of makes me think of Dr. Von Braun.'

'I still can't believe what I had heard about him, what you had told me about him.'

'Shadowfire insisted that I had come into contact and wanted to know about the fairy,' continued Mordecai, 'I told him nothing, which enraged him. "You have come into contact with a fairy," he insisted, "and I will know who it is, sooner or later!"

' "You are insane like Hussein," I told him, "What makes you think so?"

'The dragon only grew angrier. "I swear by all that is unholy by Ashtaroth," he cried, "I will know all that I need to know and not let this prophecy come to pass! I will find you, human, whoever you are, wherever you are!"

'He asked for my name again, but I did not tell him. He was infuriated and spewed out more flames at me.'

'And you woke up after that?' Cece asked.

Mordecai nodded. 'I have a strange feeling this Shadowfire could very well be real.'

Cece laughed. 'You can't be serious about that.'

'I feel it,' the young man said, 'How else could I be having these dreams for seven nights in a row? I know it's crazy, but I believe that he could very well be real.'

'Like fairies?' Cece said, laughing, 'I'm surprised at you for believing all that.'

Mordecai sighed. 'I wish I had a better explanation.'

At that moment, their mother came downstairs, having seen the lights on in the kitchen. She found her children talking at the table. 'What are the two of you doing up?' she asked. 'Aren't you supposed to be asleep?'

'I had a bad dream,' Mordecai answered, 'It kind of bothers me, but nothing serious.'

'We just came down here to talk,' Cece assured her mother.

'It's good to see you two getting along. It's hard to believe it.'

'We had our differences in the past,' Mordecai replied gravely, 'but we kind of came to terms with each other last week. She's still upset about the way Oscar had treated her.'

'I thought he would hate me because Dad is teaching me to drive and not Mordy, afraid he would resent me,' continued Cece. 'but he told me it was not my fault. I still don't understand why Mordy has not been taught to drive. He's been hurting and right now I'm the only one he has to turn to since cousin Amy had left for Gainesville.'

Their mother laughed. 'You're kidding, aren't you?' she asked, 'about the two of you getting along?'

Mordecai nodded gravely. 'It is true.'

Their mother shook her head in disbelief. 'Well, at least you haven't been arguing and fighting lately,' she said, 'How long will it last?'

'Get used to it.' Cece smiled.

Mordecai smiled. His smile faded as he said, 'She's the only one who has listened to me and given me support after Amelia had started attending college in Gainesville. I can't and won't despise Cece for something that is not her fault. I do feel thankful for her.'

Their mother laughed as she turned to go. 'I'll have to see it to believe it. You two need to get back to sleep.'

'Fair enough,' they both said. They burst into soft laughter together. As their mother left, Cece stared at Mordecai and said, 'Talking about strange dreams. I've been having a dream about you for the past three nights.'

'What about?' Mordecai asked.

'It just came to my mind,' said Cece, 'I dreamed that you had met a fairy, a fairy wearing a blue dress with dark skin, or black skin, if you will. The first dream I had, you and her were dancing.'

'What was her name?' asked Mordecai.

'I don't know,' answered Cece, 'I never found out, but her voice was beautiful and angelic. She was singing a beautiful song, a song of love, I think. In the second dream, you were holding her in your arms and kissing her as you two were singing to each other.'

Raven. His thoughts immediately went to the young fairy.

'In the dream about an hour before I woke up, you and her were in front of us, along with what seemed to be other fairies and the both of you were in wedding attire and were getting married.' Cece laughed.

'Sounds funny, doesn't it?'

'Sounds beautiful to me,' sighed Mordecai. 'I wish I had those dreams and not about Shadowfire, the dragon.'

'Well,' laughed Cece, 'Better I had the dream I had than the ones about Shadowfire.' She stopped laughing. 'If fairies do exist, do you think such a union would be possible?'

'Who knows?' Mordecai replied as he finished his soda, 'It could very well be possible.'

Cece pondered the question and her brother's answer as they both stood to their feet and headed upstairs to go to bed. They stopped in the middle of the stairs as Mordecai stared at Cece. 'Thank you for being there for me, sis. It means a heaven of a lot to me.'

'I love and care about you, big brother,' she smiled. 'You are special to me. I will always be there for you whenever you need me.'

'And I will gladly do the same for you, Cece.' Both siblings embraced. Mordecai kissed her gently on the forehead. 'You will find that man you're looking for, Cece. He will be better to you than Oscar was.'

'With all due respect to our father.' Cece smiled. 'I hope he's as wonderful as my dear brother Mordecai. You will find your woman, wherever she is.'

Mordecai smiled. His thoughts went to Raven, *I believe I already have.*

Mordecai and Cece got into the back of the car Tiffany was driving. Sharon was in the front seat as the siblings buckled themselves up. 'Another day at the mosh pits,' Sharon said.

'That's new,' Cece replied.

Mordecai sighed. 'Another day to have to deal with those barbarians,' he groaned, 'I can't believe they got away with what they'd done to me!'

'That is so asinine the way they get away with junk like that,' Tiffany agreed, 'I wonder what it's going to take to get the school to do something about them? They need to forget that they're all-state quality players and see how much wickedness they've been doing before it gets worse!'

'What's it going to take to get them to act against those jeges?' Sharon frowned, 'I thought they were going to kill you on Monday!'

'I was scared for my life,' Mordecai said sadly, 'That's exactly what I thought when I was in the back of the trunk tied up.'

'I can't believe your parents won't do a thing about it,' Tiffany said, 'How could they be so apathetic to you? I bet if it was you, Cece, they would definitely do something about it. That is so unfair to your brother. It seems they love her more than you, Mordy!'

Mordecai nodded.

'I'm still surprised your brother doesn't hate you for that,' Tiffany told Cece.

'I was afraid of that too,' replied Cece, 'Didn't turn out to be the case, though.'

'She thought I would say it was her fault,' Mordecai said, 'but Cece is the only one who has been on my side. We have become closer than we thought we would be. She is not to blame for something that wasn't her fault.'

'But that leaves us back on square one with Hatfield, McCoy, and Jones,' Cece said. 'They're still free to do whatever they want. They're not about to stop what they've been doing.'

'In my eyes and in the eyes of a lot of the people,' frowned Mordecai, 'The administration has become partakers of the sins of Hatfield, McCoy, and Jones's bullying of people like me!'

'I tend to agree,' Cece said, 'Why won't they do anything to stop the bullying?'

When they arrived at school, Mordecai headed to his locker as was his custom, grabbing the book he needed for his first class. As he grabbed his book, he suddenly had the feeling he was being watched. He looked around. He saw only other students. As he went back to his locker, he had that feeling again. Again, he looked around. He shook his head. *Am I going crazy?* he thought. He closed his locker and headed to his first class.

When he left the 100-building area, he thought he caught a glimpse of Dr. Von Braun walking down the corridors. The geneticist did not appear to see him, but Mordecai was bothered that he was on campus. *Isn't he supposed to be at UCF teaching classes, and not here at Oak Ridge obsessing with finding fairies?* He sighed. *Now that I know fairies like Raven exist, I have to be very careful as to not reveal to him the fact that I had met Raven.* He thought of Raven, how much he had fallen in love with her. He knew he had to keep his head clear and be careful to avoid any contact with Dr. Von Braun. *I swear, Von Braun, as the LORD lives, I will never tell you about Raven or my involvements with her!*

He fell to the ground. He heard the laughter of three familiar voices. He looked up and saw his adversaries: Frank, Stu, and Chuck.

'Look how clumsy that jege is, guys,' he quipped, quickly pulling back his leg.

Mordecai already knew who had tripped him.

'You never will learn, will you?' Frank continued.

'Funny,' Mordecai frowned, 'I was thinking the same thing about you sons of a vulture.'

'And what do you mean by that?' growled Stu.

'You three think you're great just because you are great football players,' he retorted, rising to his feet. 'I'll give you that, you are. Nobody here can deny that. But you've become so full of yourselves, full of pride, that you think it makes you better than anybody else!'

'We are, jege,' snapped Chuck.

'You are nothing, all three of you,' snapped Mordecai. 'You use your notoriety to get away with anything you can think of, and that includes bullying! One of these days, each of you will have a great fall. Prides goes before destruction and a haughty spirit before a fall!'

'How dare you quote the Bible here,' growled Frank, grabbing him by the collar. 'You know you could get suspended for even carrying a Bible here. We need to punish you just for that!'

'Better to be suspended for bringing a Bible to school than be suspended for fighting,' Mordecai retorted, 'If so, so be it! You three keep going the way you're going, sooner or later, your sins will catch up to you! You can take that to the bank!'

Frank threw him hard against a nearby wall. Students started to gather around him as Frank moved in. Before Frank could throw a punch, Dr. Von Braun appeared, standing between Mordecai and the bully. 'Is there a problem, boys?' he asked.

Mordecai could only mouth the name of the geneticist.

'Oh, no problem, no problem at all,' answered Frank, backing off. To Mordecai he mouthed, 'This isn't over, jege!'

The geneticist lifted the young man to his feet. 'I suppose I should thank you for intervening on my behalf,' Mordecai said as the bullies walked away, 'I am grateful, though.'

Dr. Von Braun nodded. 'I suppose you wonder what I am doing here?' he asked.

'The thought had crossed my mind,' said Mordecai.

'It's business outside of the business I have with you,'said Dr. Von Braun, 'and you know what our personal matter is. However, this is neither the time nor the place to speak of it. Rest assured before the end of the day; we shall discuss the matter.'

Mordecai sighed as he picked up his books. All he could say is, 'I've got to get to my next class.'

Dr. Von Braun nodded. 'Of course. You mustn't be late.'

Mordecai headed for his next class as Dr. Von Braun smiled. 'Later,' he said.

It had started raining during third period and was coming down hard by the time Mordecai was at lunch. He sat alone as he ate his lunch and drank his drink. He was feeling nervous because of the presence of Dr. Von Braun, especially now that he had met Raven. He began to fear revealing Raven's existence to the geneticist. He still didn't trust him, even though he did save his neck from the bullies earlier in the morning. He knew Dr. Von Braun would grill him and push him into revealing Raven's existence. He was more determined than ever to keep her existence a secret from Von Braun.

He felt something wet being poured upon his head, running down his clothes. He quickly turned around and saw Frank, Stu, and Chuck laughing. He growled when he saw them. 'We would have poured beer on you,' Stu said, 'but unfortunately, they don't have beer here in school, so we had to make do.'

'You're pushing it, jeges,' growled Mordecai.

'Oh yeah, nobody? What are you going to do about it?' Frank sneered.

'I can do nothing because vengeance is not mine,' Mordecai said.

'You can't because you're a wimp, a loser, a moron,' declared Chuck.

'Keep such names to yourselves,' Mordecai scoffed, picking up his books. 'Vengeance is mine, I will repay, saith the LORD. It is Him you should fear.'

Frank grabbed Mordecai and slammed him against the wall. Stu and Chuck immediately grabbed Mordecai and held him fast, preventing him from moving. 'Forget the fear of the Lord, loser,' Frank said. 'You better learn to fear me!'

'I don't fear you,' Mordecai replied defiantly.

'I wouldn't do that if I were you,' came the voice of Cece. She, Sharon, and Tiffany stood facing them. 'Tiffany and Sharon have taken pictures of you pouring soda on Mordecai and throwing him against the wall. You wouldn't want us to show these pictures to the principal or post them on the school website, would you?'

'You wouldn't dare!' Chuck shouted.

'Lay another hand on my brother, and we will!' Cece warned, 'One way or another, your bullying will come to an end! Too long have people like my brother suffered at your hands just because you believe they are inferior to you! Wherever you go, any person you bully, we will be there photographing you and catching you in the act! You will face dismissal from the football team should these photos come to light, and you continue to bully and to harass my brother and others like him!'

Mordecai picked up his books and tried to leave. As he did, Frank grabbed him again and said, 'Get your butt over here! We're not through with you yet!'

'Thanks for the new photo,' Sharon proclaimed.

The three stared at them in shock. 'You didn't just—'

'Yes, I did,' Sharon replied coldly, 'I am prepared to show it to teachers and the principal, and I will take it to the school paper and website!'

'Get away from my brother and get away from him NOW!' warned Cece.

Frank, Stu, and Chuck turned their attention from Mordecai to the girls. Cece, Sharon, and Tiffany stepped backward. 'Give me the pictures,' Frank demanded.

'Stick it where the sun don't shine, Frankenstein,' Cece cried, 'Lay a hand on anyone of us, and we will have you charged with assault.'

'Empty threat,' Stu sneered.

'Is it?' Cece retorted, 'I had just dialed 911 when you had started picking on Mordy and told them where I was calling from. They are on their way here now. If I were you, I would go back to your own business and leave my brother and us alone!'

'Give me those pictures,' Frank cried angrily.

He grabbed Cece and gripped her arm hard. She cried out in pain. 'Let her go,' Sharon and Tiffany cried.

Mordecai grabbed Frank's hand and squeezed it hard. Immediately, he let go of Cece's hand and broke the grip that Mordecai had on his arm. 'Leave… my… sister… ALONE!' growled Mordecai.

'Look what worm grew a backbone,' mocked Frank, throwing a punch into Mordecai's face. The blow knocked the young man down. 'Bad move on your part!'

'You can pick on me if you wish, Nimrod,' Mordecai growled, 'but you DON'T lay a hand on my sister!'

'Or else… what? You'll beat us up?' laughed Frank. 'Yeah, that'll be the day!' He grabbed Mordecai by the collar and again slammed him against the wall. Before he could lay another blow, he heard a voice say, 'Cut, and print!'

Frank and the others turned around. They saw the young black man who had been beaten up days before by the trio using a video camera and pointing it at them. 'Malik Johnson?' Mordecai exclaimed, surprised.

'I got everything, McCoy,' Malik said, 'I had started filming you orcs just before you had poured soda on Mordy. I felt bad about being forced to lie and having Jimmy Russo suspended. I decided to do the right thing and undo what I had done. Once the principal sees this, he'll have to reinstate Jimmy Russo and suspend the three of you! I am willing to take any punishment for lying and getting an innocent person suspended!'

Frank, Stu, and Chuck turned their attention toward Malik. Cece and her friends helped Mordecai up as he grabbed his books and headed out of the cafeteria.

'Give us that camera, Johnson,' warned Chuck.

Malik, when he saw that Mordecai, Cece, Sharon, and Tiffany were out the door, made a dash toward the door, leading the bullies away. Some of the nearby students tripped them up, causing them to stumble to the floor.

While all this was going on, Mordecai headed away from the cafeteria, joined by Cece, Tiffany, and Sharon. He sighed. He felt the soreness in his jaw. 'And just when it was starting to get better,' he grumbled, 'I almost lost it when he had laid a hand on you, Cece.'

'We are fortunate to have gotten pictures of the incident,' Tiffany said.

'You mean you weren't joking?' Mordecai asked.

'Not when it comes to the brother I love,' proclaimed Cece, placing a hand on his shoulder. She then took it off.

'It's still sticky,' sighed Mordecai. 'I've got to go to the bathroom to try and wash it off.'

'I wasn't playing games with them about the photos,' Cece said, 'We're going to have them printed and sent to the administration and to the school newspaper, and they better take notice. If all else fails, I will take it to the police. They're on their way here now. One way or another, their bullying will stop!'

'And the video taken by Malik will surely be damning,' Tiffany said, 'He had gone directly to Jimmy and his parents and formally apologized to them. I heard Jimmy had forgiven him. In fact, the camera was Jimmy's, and he gave it to Malik for the purpose of catching them in the act. The principal will have to do something about it now.'

'If the orcs don't catch him first,' Mordecai replied, 'Malik needs help.'

'And it looks like it arrived in the nick of time,' Tiffany said, seeing three cops with Malik and the bullies.

'Don't wash up yet, Mordy,' Cece told him, 'We need to show them what they have done to you first.'

Mordecai, Tiffany, Cece, and Sharon waited as the cops approached them.

The rain began to ease up and turned to a drizzle.

After classes, Mordecai met with Cece, Sharon and Tiffany met at Mordecai's locker. He put the books for the last period away and headed for home. 'I hope that closes the chapter on bullying at Oak Ridge High School,' Mordecai sighed. 'I will be very disappointed if somehow, someway, they get away with this even with such evidence against them.'

'I wonder what their parents are going to say when they find out about the people they've been bullying?' Cece said, 'I'm sure the parents of the victims, save ours, were outraged by the bullying. I don't understand why our parents wouldn't stand by you, Mordy! I'm angry about it!'

'They'll be outraged when they hear how they had laid a hand upon you,' Mordecai replied, 'I nearly lost it myself. It was fortunate for him that I am not a fighter, or else I would have gone gung-ho on his rear end! These are the times I wish I was a fighter, though.'

'Now *that's* what a brother is all about,' boasted Cece, kissing him on the cheeks, 'Instead of running, he stood by in my defense.'

'We are family, Cece,' Mordecai said, 'I couldn't let him get away with what he had done to you.'

At that moment, they were approached by Dr. Von Braun and his two men, Seymour and Wilfred. Mordecai groaned. 'Mr. Jefferson, we would like a word with you,' Von Braun proclaimed.

'Why?' Cece asked.

'It's a private matter,' said Mordecai.

'This will only take a moment,' stated Dr. Von Braun. 'It's a matter that concerns Mr. Jefferson and me.'

Mordecai was about to say something when Dr. Von Braun grabbed his arm and said, 'I insist. I did save you from the bullies earlier this morning.'

Mordecai sighed, nodding his head. 'I know what this is about,' he told the girls, 'I'll be right back.'

Tiffany groaned as Dr. Von Braun escorted Mordecai into an empty classroom. She turned to Cece and asked, 'What is this all about? Why is Dr. Von Braun…' She trailed off as she remembered what Mordecai had told them.

'Fairies,' they said together.

Cece shook her head. 'He came all the way from UCF to continually ask about mythological creatures?'

Sharon shook her head. 'This is insane!'

'Mordy will tell us when he returns,' Cece said.

'I hope it won't be too long,' Tiffany said, 'I have to be home before five.'

Seymour shut the door behind him after the four had entered the classroom. Dr. Von Braun stared at Mordecai and said, 'This will take as long as it has to until I get what I need to know. The six million dollars is still on the table for you. Have you met a fairy yet?'

'Where would I meet a fairy?' he asked, exasperated.

'What about the woods just across the bridge on the other side of the Florida Turnpike?' suggested Dr. Von Braun.

'Why would I go there?' Mordecai responded, 'I have schoolwork, homework. There are times I have to rest up from being used as a tackling dummy by the three Neanderthals on steroids!'

Dr. Von Braun stared hard at Mordecai. The young man stoodd uncomfortable by his stare. 'There's something you are not telling me. You found one, didn't you?'

'That's ridiculous,' scoffed Mordecai.

'Do not presume to lie to me, boy,' said Dr. Von Braun sternly. 'You met a fairy, did you not? You had an encounter with a fairy, did you not?'

'Why would I want to go into the woods?' insisted Mordecai, determined to hide Raven's existence, I had gone there once when the bullies had tied me up and left me there. I untied myself eventually and found the main road and walked home.'

'You were untied by a fairy,' accused Dr. Von Braun.

'I had untied myself,' Mordecai shot back, 'Fortunately, they weren't very good at tying knots. I managed, all by myself, to untie the ropes and went home. That is all there is to tell.'

'You untied yourself,' he repeated skeptically, 'All by yourself, you had untied yourself. Are you sure it wasn't a fairy that untied you?'

'Now you're being ridiculous,' Mordecai shot back, 'Of course not! I did untie myself. They did not tie it good enough. That is why I had managed to free myself.'

Dr. Von Braun stared at him hard. 'You're lying,' he frowned, 'You're lying to me. You *were* untied by a fairy. That's the only explanation there is. You had met a fairy, and you are not telling me for some reason.'

'I told you already,' snapped Mordecai, 'I was taken to the woods, tied up, escaped all by myself, and left for home and that is all there is to tell.'

'Did you ever return to the woods?' the geneticist asked.

Mordecai frowned. 'Why would I?'

Dr. Von Braun gave Mordecai an angry look. 'I am not in the mood for games, Mordy Jefferson,' he growled, 'I have a feeling you *have* met a fairy. It would be the only explanation for how you got untied. Who was it? What was the fairy's name? Male or female?'

Mordecai refused to talk.

'Six million dollars is a lot of money,' snapped Dr. Von Braun, 'For some reason, you indeed have met a fairy and for some reason, you are not telling me. You know you could use the money. Do you have a job?'

Mordecai shook his head. 'My parents won't let me drive or get a job.'

'And why is that?' the geneticist asked.

Mordecai shook his head. 'I wish I knew,' he sighed.

'All you have to do is to show me the fairy, take a picture and show me where you found it, and the six million dollars is yours! You know you need the money.'

'I do,' nodded Mordecai.

'Then tell me about the bloody fairy that you had found.'

'I told you it was just me,' Mordecai shot back, 'There was nobody else there! The bullies had left me in the woods. I managed to free myself from the ropes and that's all there is to tell! There's nothing else, no fairy, nothing!'

Dr. Von Braun stared hard at him. 'You want to play games with me, boy?' he said in a low voice, 'Fine. We'll play it your way. I *know* you saw a fairy in the woods that day. Somehow, someway, I *will* find out. I *will* find that fairy you saw. One way or another, I promise you, *I will find that fairy!*'

Mordecai was allowed to leave, happy to be away from the geneticist. As he left, Dr. Von Braun turned toward his men and asked, 'Have you found out which bus he rides on?'

Both men shook their heads. 'He wasn't in any of the gatherings of students we'd seen in the Southwood subdivision,' Wilfred answered, 'Perhaps he's riding with another student?'

'That could be a possibility, boss,' said Seymour. 'It's the only explanation to why we haven't seen his bike at school or riding down the road.'

'I think he was riding with the girls who were with him,' said Dr. Von Braun, 'Perhaps they may know something about fairies as well. Question them, but discreetly, mind you. Do not do anything to draw attention to yourselves. Question them in private. Find out who they are, all three of them. I want to know what they may know about fairies.'

'As you wish,' Wilfred said, 'We'll keep an eye on them.'

'They should be out there still,' Dr. Von Braun said as they headed to the door. When he looked, they were gone. He ran down the corridor and looked around. He saw only gatherings of students. He did not see either Mordecai or the girls he was with.

Inside Tiffany's car, they hurried inside at the bidding of Mordecai. As they got inside, Tiffany turned to Mordecai and asked, 'Now, Mordy, will you tell me what the heck is going on? Why you have us running like crazy to my car?'

'I didn't want Dr. Von Braun to see any of us,' Mordecai answered.

'This is insane,' Sharon replied, catching her breath.

'It is,' Mordecai said. 'He's so obsessed with finding fairies, and he thinks I've seen one.'

'When you were taken into the woods on Monday?' Cece asked.

'I told him I had untied myself after McCoy, Hatfield, and Jones left me there and took my wallet and cell phone. Fortunately, I found them the next day. They had thrown them away, but McCoy took all the money from my wallet.'

'They always seem to stoop to new lows,' Cece said quietly, 'Hopefully after today, we will have no more problems with them. No more bullying.'

'I fear Dr. Von Braun will be a new problem, for me at any rate,' Mordecai frowned, 'He insists that I had been untied by a fairy.'

'Well, were you?' Tiffany asked. 'Were you untied by a fairy?'

'Tiffany, I thought you said you grew out of believing in fairies,' Cece told her friend.

'If Dr. Von Braun says they're real, then they could be.'

'Well, did you?' Sharon asked Mordecai. Mordecai did not answer. He remained silent.

Tiffany continued to drive. 'You *did* meet one, didn't you?' she asked in surprise.

Mordecai did not say.

'Come on, Mordy,' insisted Tiffany. 'How else did you get untied?'

'I'm telling you the truth about untying myself,' insisted Mordecai.

'Is it true—you *did* see a fairy like Dr. Von Braun claims?' exclaimed Cece.

Mordecai sighed. 'Let's say I did see one,' he started, 'Let's say I did. With that madman Dr. Von Braun hounding me about fairies, would you want *him* to find them? I don't trust him at all. There is no telling what kind of cruel experiments he would do on a fairy. I personally shudder to think. If fairies do exist, he would be one of the last people who should be told. If you found one, would you want to put that fairy in mortal danger to people like him? I personally would not. Perhaps fairies, if they exist, would want to keep their existence a secret for a reason, given how we humans can be. Look at McCoy, Hatfield, and Jones! Would you want a fairy to be mistreated by those bullies?'

They sighed. 'I see your point,' Tiffany nodded.

'But you *did* see one?' Cece pressed. 'Tell me you've seen one.'

'Von Braun believes I have met one,' Mordecai said, 'I have a feeling he may try and ask you girls, too. He is obsessed with finding fairies, and if he finds one, I shudder to think.'

'So you *do* believe in fairies?' Cece asked.

'He seems sure of it, especially after he showed me a photo of the remains of one,' Mordecai said, 'I may be forced to agree that there *could* be fairies. Who can say for sure?'

Tiffany and Sharon looked at each other and said, 'He believes in fairies.'

Mordecai laughed. 'Come on, I only said there *could* be,' he insisted, 'I won't know for sure unless I see one for myself.' He did not mention that he had seen one, Raven, whom he was now thinking about.

He looked forward to returning home and returning to the woods. At least, he hoped Raven would be there despite the rain. It had stopped raining a couple of hours before but he wondered if fairies could fly in the rain. He decided to ask Raven the next time he saw her.

'I think Dr. Von Braun could be right about you,' Cece said.

'I think you could have seen one.'

Mordecai said not a word.

'Well, did you?' asked Cece, 'Did you see a fairy?'

Mordecai refused to talk. 'There was just me on that day, I did untie myself with no help, then made my way back to the main road where you found me.'

Sharon stared at him. 'You sure about that?' she asked.

'I'm sure,' Mordecai insisted.

Cece stared at Mordecai. 'If so, then where have you been going after school for the past three days?'

'Yeah, tell us,' Tiffany said.

After a moment of silence, he said, 'I can't tell you now.' He paused. 'It is personal. That is all I can say.'

Cece stared hard at Mordecai. 'Okay, okay, you can keep your secrets for now, but sooner or later, we will find out.'

'Perhaps when the time is right,' Mordecai said. He then figured that somehow, sooner or later, he would have to tell Cece, at least, about Raven. His thoughts once again dwelt on the young fairy whom he had fallen in love with. He hoped in his heart Raven somehow felt the same way.

Somehow, he was beginning to feel that Raven did feel the same way.

Raven hoped that Mordecai felt the same way about her and began to feel perhaps he did feel the same way.

Chapter Six

Two weeks had passed since Mordecai and Raven's first meeting. Mordecai had seen Raven every day since then, meeting her at the same place around the same time, even on weekends. They talked during that time about what they were going through in their lives. Mordecai was displeased that even with the evidence against the three bullies, they were not suspended or kicked off the football team. They had continued to bully Mordecai as well as the other kids they had been bullying, but Mordecai was the main person they picked on above all others, even Malik Johnson, who had filmed the bullying the week Mordecai and Raven had first met.

Despite the constant bullying, the love he had for Raven helped him endure the pain as well as the friendship that had developed with Cece's best friends, Tiffany and Sharon. Dr. Von Braun still hounded Mordecai about fairies, but Mordecai refused to tell him anything. He still did not tell his sister or their friends about Raven, but continued to keep it a secret, even as much as he wanted to. He felt more concerned about Raven's safety and was afraid of what would happen to Raven if Dr. Von Braun captured her, what he could possibly do to her. Her safety was his main concern. He was determined never to let anything bad happen to her.

Mordecai met Raven at the same place where they first met. He got off his ten-speed he rode and was welcomed by Raven with a warm embrace, holding each other longer than before. They had been growing closer and closer to each other with each meeting. Mordecai was sore from the beating he had received that day. 'I miss you so much, Mordecai,' Raven told him.

'I miss you so much too, Raven,' Mordecai smiled, 'I so looked forward to seeing you again.'

Raven saw him wincing in pain and stared at him. 'Are you okay?' she asked him, touching his face.

'The same guys again,' he frowned, 'They keep bullying me. I thought when they got caught that it would stop, but it seems those in charge are turning a deaf ear and refusing to punish them!'

'That's terrible,' exclaimed Raven, 'Are you okay?'

'I saw a bruise on my arm before I came here,' Mordecai told her, 'They never seem to stop bullying people like me!'

Raven shook her head. 'Why do they love to mistreat you so?' she sadly asked, 'I can't understand why they are allowed to do such things! If Queen Cymbaline was in charge, she would definitely not tolerate it! Kind of backs up what she believes humans are like, but I know that's not true. You are not like that.'

'I don't blame your Queen Cymbaline for believing such things,' replied Mordecai, 'and she would be right, I am forced to agree with her.'

'I know not all humans are like that,' said Raven, 'I have gotten to know you a lot better since we first met. Oh, if only Queen Cymbaline would know what you are like, how wonderful a person you are.' She stared into his blue eyes. 'So much pain in your beautiful blue eyes,' she sighed. 'It does not belong there.'

'It comes from being hurt a lot, mistreated, and bullied,' sighed Mordecai, 'I wish my parents understood what I've been going through. I am fortunate that Cece, my younger sister, has been the only one who's been supportive.'

'And me,' Raven added.

'Yes, Raven,' Mordecai smiled, staring deep into her eyes, 'and you. Your brown eyes are so beautiful.'

'I love looking into your beautiful blue eyes, as beautiful as the waters of the Silverstreams back home.' As they stared into each other's eyes, their lips drew close and then connected in a loving and tender kiss. Mordecai and Raven wrapped their arms around each other, Mordecai careful not to hurt Raven's wings, holding each other close. They became lost in the love they had for each other. Now they knew, beyond a shadow of a doubt, that they had the same feelings for each other. The wind was a little cold, but they did not seem to notice as their lips remained locked. Their lips separated after long moments. They stared into each other's eyes. 'Never before to my knowledge has a fairy ever fallen in love with a human,' Raven said softly. 'I fell in love with you the first day we met. I can no longer deny my feelings.'

Mordecai stared into her eyes. 'As have I,' he replied softly, 'I am glad what I have felt is true. I do feel the same way about you, Raven. I, too, fell in love with you, from the first day we met.' He touched the face of the black fairy. 'But would it be possible for a fairy and a human—'

'I believe in my heart it is possible,' nodded Raven, 'God did bring the two of us together. At night, I have such sweet dreams about you, about having a life together, being joined together, even about the children I would bear.'

'Would it be possible?' Mordecai asked. 'Would it be possible for a fairy and a human to have children together?'

'It has never happened before,' Raven said, looking to the ground, 'but I do believe it's possible. We are the same, you and I, despite the color of our skin and my wings.'

Mordecai then thought of the time Dr. Haman Von Braun had shown him the photo of the remains of a fairy and the words he had spoken: *I had studied the DNA and found it strangely similar to our own.*

Then it is possible, he thought to himself, for a fairy and a human to have children together.

'Yes, Raven,' he told her. 'I believe we are the same, you and I. I hope when the time is right, God willing, I will take you to be mine.'

'I so look forward to that day,' Raven smiled, 'I will be more than happy to be yours for life.'

'I love you, my sweet Raven.'

'I love you too, my sweet Mordecai,' Raven said as their lips touched again. They remained locked in a loving kiss as they held each other close, so happy their love for each other was no longer a secret, that each shared the same feelings for the other. Mordecai gently cradled Raven in his arms. He still couldn't believe he found a fairy and more so, that he and the fairy had fallen in love with each other. He was glad it was no dream.

Raven never thought in her wildest dreams that she would find love with a human. She felt blessed to find Mordecai, and Mordecai blessed to have found Raven. Their lips separated as they stared into each other's eyes. 'If only I could take you to Arundel Haven with me,' Raven sighed, 'but I know you would not be welcomed there by the other fairies, especially Queen Cymbaline. But I don't want to be without you, Mordecai!'

'Nor I you, my sweet Raven,' Mordecai replied, 'I have just found you, and I never want to let you go, I never want to lose you, ever! You have come to mean more to me than life itself! When I'm with you, I feel so happy and blessed. I forget all the cruel things that McCoy, Hatfield, and Jones have done to me, the rejection, the mistreatment. You are my emotional shelter from the storms of life. You're the only one, besides my sister Cece, who has shown me kindness. My parents don't know the pain I'm going through. Ever since I met you, Raven, it's just too wonderful to put into words. I feel so loved when I'm with you! I feel so happy when we're together!'

'I feel the same way, my Mordecai,' said Raven, 'My heart is bound unto you. I am yours and yours alone. I belong to you.'

'As well as my heart is bound unto you,' Mordecai replied. 'I belong to you and you alone, my Raven, my love, my life.'

As the lovers kissed, Seymour and Wilfred watched as Mordecai and Raven talked and kissed, taking photos of the lovers together. They had followed Mordecai after finding him, by chance, riding on his bike to the woods where he had his meetings with the ebony fairy. Wilfred had the camera and took photos. They made sure they weren't seen. 'This is interesting, indeed,' whispered Wilfred.

'Dr. Von Braun was right about the boy,' replied Seymour softly. 'Take a few more photos, then we can leave. We cannot let the boy know we are here.'

'A human in love with a fairy,' Wilfred mused, taking one more photo. 'Will wonders never cease! That ought to suffice for the doctor. Let's go!'

They left as quietly as they could as Mordecai and Raven continued to kiss, enraptured in the love they shared with each other. After a while, Mordecai knew he had to leave Raven. Both were unwilling to be apart, to be separated from each other, especially since they now knew their feelings for each other. 'I will be here tomorrow, like always, my love,' Raven said, 'I will miss you, my sweet Mordecai.'

Mordecai took Raven in his arms and kissed her. 'I will miss you too, my sweet Raven, my love, my life,' he said. They kissed and held each other close. They found it hard to separate, though Mordecai knew he had to head home. He unwillingly released Raven, grabbed his bike, got on it, and rode away.

Raven stood there until he was out of sight. Then she headed into the woods, stood under an open spot, and took to the air, rising above the clouds. She felt sorrow at being separated from her human lover as she vanished into the darkening sky.

It was when she had flown a short distance that she was approached by the familiar forms of Lavender and Laurelin. Both fairy women had sour looks upon their faces. 'So, this is where you go, Raven?' Lavender asked, 'This is your "secret place", in the human world?'

'What in the name of love is wrong with you, Raven?' Laurelin asked, 'You are sure to be spotted by the humans if you haven't been spotted already!'

Raven then stared hard at her friends, equally displeased. 'Have you two been following me?' she asked them.

'Don't think your visits to this part of the human world have gone unnoticed by Queen Cymbaline,' Laurelin retorted, 'In fact, it was Prince Avondale who had instructed us to follow you here the moment we saw you leave Arundel Haven to find out where you've been going.'

'Why are you risking being spotted by the humans, Raven?' Lavender asked, 'You know how many times Queen Cymbaline had warned us about the humans! What is wrong with you? Do you have a fascination with humans? By coming here, you risk revealing our existence to the humans, and heaven knows what would happen to us should that happen! Why has this part of the human world become your favorite haunt? What's so special about this place?'

Mordecai, Raven's thoughts replied, though she did not speak a word.

Lavender flew toward Raven. 'No way are you getting off that easy, Raven,' she said, 'How long have you been flying to this place?'

'Why do you ask? I like it here, and that's all you need to know. I don't really need to tell you my business here.'

Lavender stopped Raven from flying any further. 'Maybe not to us, but you will tell Queen Cymbaline and Prince Avondale about it. They will not be pleased when they hear you've been flying to this part of the human world!'

'You're not going to tell them, are you?' Raven asked.

'Raven, they already know something's up with you,' Laurelin told her, 'We have been commanded to find you, and if you should be in the human world, brought before them. You will have to tell the Queen and the Prince why you've been flying here. They will demand answers!'

'Raven, you know as well as all of us—humans are evil,' Lavender stated, 'You know that as well as any other fairy of Arundel Haven! Queen Cymbaline has warned us time after time about the wickedness of humans, how evil, violent, and corrupt they are: liars, thieves, murderers, animals! One of these days, Raven, your fascination with the human world will get us all in trouble! It needs to stop now!'

'Queen Cymbaline awaits us now,' Laurelin said. 'They are expecting us!'

Raven sighed, then followed them on the return flight to Arundel Haven.

In his office on the UCF campus, Dr. Von Braun waited impatiently, drinking a glass of bourbon. He had received a call from Seymour telling him that they have something they wanted to show him. He was tired and irritated. He tried, unsuccessfully, to obtain information from Mordecai about fairies when he had contact with the youth, but he told the geneticist nothing. He was starting to become frustrated with the search. He somehow knew Mordecai had an encounter with a fairy, but for some reason, refused to tell him.

At that moment, Seymour and Wilfred walked through the door. Wilfred gave the geneticist a couple of twelve packs of beer while Seymour hooked up his digital camera to the printer and started it up.

'This had better be good,' muttered Dr. Von Braun.

'I think you should see this for yourself, sir,' Seymour said as he loaded the photo paper into the printer and pushed the print button. It began to print out the photos that had been taken on the camera.

'You were supposed to be watching that Mordy Jefferson kid,' frowned Dr. Von Braun, 'It has been over two weeks now! Somehow, someway, he must have encountered a fairy! That's the only explanation of how he had been free of those ropes! I had offered him six million dollars for any info on fairies, but still, he will not tell me!'

'You may be interested to see why, Dr. Von Braun,' Wilfred said, smiling, 'Very interested indeed.'

'Show me.'

Three pictures were already printed. Seymour handed the pictures to Dr. Von Braun, who had poured himself a scotch. He stared at the pictures. His eyes opened wide, a smile slowly appearing on his face. He laughed softly. 'Interesting indeed.'.

'There are still more pictures coming, sir.'

Eight more pictures were printed and then stopped. Seymour gave the remaining pictures to Dr. Von Braun. 'That would explain things,' he smiled, 'How very interesting. Mordy has a fairy lover. Explains a lot to me.' To the men he asked, 'What do you know about this black fairy?'

'We weren't in close enough to find out her name or anything about her,' Seymour answered, 'We managed to take the pictures, but we could not hear them talking. We caught him riding away from the Southwood subdivision after school. We made sure he didn't see us. We followed him into the woods and found him with the fairy.'

Dr. Von Braun smiled and nodded. 'I knew it!' he exclaimed, 'This confirms everything! He and this fairy are in love and because of it, he refuses to reveal the truth of her existence. I cannot go public with this yet, but it only confirms what I have long believed. You have done very well, indeed!'

'What now?' Wilfred asked.

'We figure out a way to capture that fairy,' answered Dr. Von Braun, 'It will be the only acceptable proof of the existence of fairies. I will inquire of the boy one more time before I show President Farouk the photos. When I have captured the fairy, I will reveal their existence then. When I leave for Washington, keep a close eye on the boy, but keep your distance and be careful not to reveal yourselves to either of them.' He put down the scotch. 'But first, we celebrate. Surely this is just cause!'

When Raven, Lavender, and Laurelin returned to Arundel Haven, they were escorted to the castle by three of the guards. Raven sighed as they headed inside the castle. She said nothing for the rest of the trip. She did not want to reveal Mordecai's existence to the Queen if she could help it.

They were taken before Queen Cymbaline and Prince Avondale. As they stood before them, they bowed. Both Queen Cymbaline and Prince Avondale stared at Raven gravely, displeased of the news. 'We have heard about your journeys to the human world,' the Fairy Queen told Raven, 'This is ill news indeed.'

Raven sighed.

'Why have you been visiting to the human world despite our warnings?' Prince Avondale asked, 'Why do you fly to an area near the city they call Orlando, Florida?'

'I like the woods there, your highness,' Raven answered, 'I find it calming, helps bring peace to my mind.'

'Yet, you risk the humans spotting you,' frowned Queen Cymbaline, 'This is ill news, hearing of your journeys to this place. Sooner or later, you will be spotted by a human, no matter how careful you are! We cannot risk our existence being revealed to the humans! Why do you continually disregard the warnings I have given about contact with the humans? It is solely by the grace of God that Arundel Haven has remained a secret to the human world!'

'These visits to the human world must stop, Raven,' Prince Avondale demanded, 'Do you realize how much danger you put yourself in, not to mention all the fairies of Arundel Haven?' He paused and stared hard at Raven. 'There is something else, Raven,' he continued, 'There is more to your visit to that particular place than simply the woods itself. Tell us!'

Raven could not speak. After a long pause, she managed to say, 'Nothing. Th-there's nothing more. I will be careful, I promise.'

Queen Cymbaline stared hard at Raven with cold eyes. 'You are seeing a human, aren't you?' she asked. 'You know that contact with humans is strictly forbidden.'

Raven nodded. 'Yes, your majesty,' she said, gazing at the ground.

'Are you seeing a human?' asked the Fairy Queen, 'Have you met one?'

Raven shook her head. 'N-no, it's just me,' she insisted, determined not to reveal her meetings with Mordecai. She shuddered to think what Queen Cymbaline would do if she found out that she had indeed fallen in love with a human.

Queen Cymbaline gazed harder upon Raven but said nothing. Raven did her best to keep herself composed. Could she have guessed? Could she have somehow figured out that she had met and fallen in love with a human? She said nothing.

Finally, Queen Cymbaline dismissed them. As they were leaving, Lavender and Laurelin stared at Raven. 'Are you hiding something, Raven?' Laurelin asked as they left the throne room.

Raven shook her head. 'No, not at all,' she answered.

'Why do I have a feeling you're lying?' Lavender frowned. 'You are already in deep trouble as it is flying to the human world. What are you hiding?'

Raven remained silent.

'Raven,' Laurelin cried, 'The Queen will find out sooner or later. It will be better for you if you tell her—if you tell us, now.'

'I-I can't!' stuttered Raven.

As the three fairy maidens left, Queen Cymbaline turned to her brother with a sigh and said, 'There is more to this than Raven has revealed to us. I can feel it.'

Prince Avondale nodded. 'I can tell too,' he nodded, 'but what?'

'I have a feeling that despite my decree for any fairy not to journey to the human world, she will return,' said Queen Cymbaline, 'There is something there, perhaps someone, that compels Raven to return to that area.'

'Someone? A human, perhaps?'

'Maybe, maybe not,' frowned Queen Cymbaline, 'I only wish I could be certain. Only ill could come of it, whatever she is doing.'

'Perhaps, perhaps not,' stated Prince Avondale, 'but who can tell? Still, I believe you are right. There is more to this than Raven has revealed to us. Whatever secret she is keeping could bode ill for the fairies of Arundel Haven.'

Queen Cymbaline sighed. 'Maybe it could be nothing, but sometimes it is best to be overcautious in such matters.'

'We can have her friends, Lavender and Laurelin, keep a close eye on her,' Prince Avondale suggested, 'I would also suggest her older sister, Starla, as well, but she has her daughter, Twila, to look after, and it would not be a good idea at this point. She will return to the human world again.'

'I do have a feeling there is more to all this than the woods itself,' sighed the Fairy Prince, 'I can only hope our suspicions are wrong, however.'

Queen Cymbaline sighed. 'I hope so too, but Shadowfire is a different matter. It was fortunate that Raven did not meet the same fate as her parents. It could have been different than it actually was. Still…'

'What, sister?' Prince Avondale asked.

'Raven once told us there must be a way to end the threat of Shadowfire once and for all,' said Queen Cymbaline, 'and I have a feeling she could be right. But where does the answer lie?'

'If only we knew of such a way to destroy him once and for all,' Prince Avondale said. Though neither admitted it, they felt a peace about Raven if she returned to the woods, the good that would come of it, but they were unsure. They spoke not of it to each other.

Mordecai and Raven continued to meet as they had been doing. It was now two days later. Raven talked Mordecai into wanting to see his home. Mordecai warned her it would not be a good idea, but reluctantly agreed. He found some clothes for Raven to wear to hide her wings and allow her to show herself without revealing herself to be a fairy.

That day, he rode with Tiffany, Sharon, and Cece as he had been doing. Mordecai noticed when they pulled up into the employees' parking lot, the black limo parked on the other side of the street. 'We have company,' he told the girls. 'Either Dr. Von Braun is here or just his men. I recognize their car from when he had first stopped me weeks ago.'

'Still after knowledge of fairies?' Cece asked.

'No doubt,' Mordecai answered, 'They are beginning to get on my nerves.'

'Which do you think is worse, Von Braun and his men or the goon squad of McCoy, Hatfield, and Jones?' asked Tiffany.

'Both groups are bad news,' answered Mordecai as they stepped out of the car, 'I don't want to run into any of them, period!'

'Good luck with that,' replied Sharon, 'It's like bullying is one of the inescapable facts of life, along with death and taxes.'

Mordecai groaned. 'I wish I had the power to teach them a thing or two,' he ventured, 'but maybe it's just as well I can't do anything about it. What is it going to take to stop their bullying? The only thing left is to take it to the school board and show them the evidence.'

'You just may have something there, Mordy,' Sharon replied, 'We haven't tried that route. It's worth a shot.'

Mordecai headed to his locker while Cece and her friends headed for their first class. He opened his locker and grabbed the books he needed. He looked around and then headed to class.

During lunchtime, he noticed that Dr. Von Braun was again on campus. He groaned. 'Why does he keep showing up here?' he asked himself, 'This is ridiculous! He already has a teaching job at UCF. Is he that desperate to find out about Raven? I'm fortunate he doesn't know about her, and I am sure going to keep it that way!'

He felt the hard impact of his body being slammed into the steel lockers by Frank, who was passing by him. He dropped his books as he felt the pain from the collision. 'Oh, Dolly Parton me,' the bully said, 'I didn't see you there.'

'And Frank McCoy puts another big hit on the opponents' quarterback,' Chuck proclaimed.

'Good one, guys,' replied Stu, high-fiving both his friends.

Mordecai painfully stood up but was tripped by Stu, who swept his leg in his direction. He fell hard on the concrete floor. He heard the mocking laughter of his adversaries as they watched him rise up slowly. 'Had a nice trip?' Chuck laughed.

Mordecai made his way to his feet again. Chuck slammed into him with his shoulders, almost like Frank had done, laughing, 'And Chuck Jones scores from one yard out! Touchdown, Oak Ridge!'

Mordecai slumped to the ground as they laughed. Frank motioned to the others, laughing. 'Welcome to the school of hard knocks,' he said, 'The next lesson will be at lunchtime. Be sure to do your homework!' The bullies walked away as Mordecai sat there, wincing in pain.

While many around him laughed at him, three students stared in disgust at their fellow students as they walked away. One of them helped gather up Mordecai's books, while the other helped Mordecai to his feet. 'Why are they still up to their old tricks?' one of the students asked. 'I thought it had stopped a couple of weeks ago!'

'This can't keep going on,' the other one said, 'Why aren't the teachers and the principal doing anything about it?'

'Because they're three of the best players in the state,' Mordecai told them, wincing in pain, 'The principal, for some reason, won't do anything about their bullying. It needs to stop, but there seems to be no end.'

'How bad are you hurt?' the third student asked.

'Pain in my body, pain in my back,' answered Mordecai, retrieving his books, 'I think I can make it to my class.' He turned to the three. 'Thank you,' he said as he made his way to class.

Mordecai managed to avoid Dr. Von Braun, but did encounter the bullies one more time during lunch. As he left for lunch, Frank, Stu, and Chuck caught him and dragged him toward the dumpster, punching Mordecai when he resisted. 'What are you doing?' he cried. 'Let me go!'

'Time to take out the trash,' laughed Frank as Chuck and Stu tossed him into the dumpster. They laughed as they walked away. He smelled the foul stench of the garbage as he crawled out. He growled as he watched the bullies walk away.

As he crawled out, one of the staff members ran toward him, having witnessed the whole thing. The woman, who was in her early 40s, had an appalled look upon her face. 'Are you okay?' she asked.

Mordecai shook his head.

'What happened?'

'Why are they allowed to keep getting away with garbage like this?' Mordecai cried out in frustration and pain, 'They've been like this ever since I started attending this school! Constantly, they abuse me, physically, psychologically, and I'm not the only one they've been picking on. They keep getting away with it! When will it end?'

'Let's go to the office,' she told him, 'We'll try and talk to the principal.'

'Won't do any good,' Mordecai cried in frustration, 'He won't do anything about it because of them being all-state players! This is not right!'

'I agree with you,' the woman nodded, 'We can try. I had witnessed the whole thing.'

'Would Principal Spooney listen?' asked Mordecai. 'He didn't listen before. What makes you think he'll listen now?'

'Let's try,' urged the woman. 'If you need to go home, you can leave if you wish.'

'I don't have a car.'

'I can give you a ride if nothing else,' the woman said, 'You're right. This shouldn't be happening here in school.'

'Thank you,' Mordecai sighed.

Mordecai took a bath when he reached home. His body was still aching from the beating he had received from the bullies and from being thrown inside the dumpster. The woman who had helped him gave him a ride home while he told them about the bullies and how they've been bullying students like him ever since they started attending Oak Ridge. He had called Cece and told her he was being taken home. Cece was appalled when she was told what had happened. 'Mrs. Whitman said she's going to see what can be done,' he told Cece. 'She was witness to the whole thing with the dumpster.'

'It makes me so mad to hear that this is still going on,' Cece told him, 'We can talk when I get home.'

Mordecai got dressed and grabbed his bike. He got on and pedaled away from home.

He was in the woods where he and Raven first met. Raven saw him approach from the trees and flittered toward him. They ran into each other's arms, holding and kissing each other. Mordecai winced in pain. 'Baby, what happened?' the black fairy maiden asked.

'The bullies again,' groaned Mordecai, still in pain, 'I am bruised in my chest area as well as maybe my back.'

Raven shook her head, upset by what she heard had happened to him. 'This is not right, Mordecai,' she cried, 'How can they still be allowed to keep doing this to you?'

'I want to try and forget about them a while,' sighed Mordecai, 'I brought you some clothes to cover up your wings for when we walk to my house.'

He gave her the clothes. 'There is so much I want to show you, Raven. I still think it's risky. I hope the clothes can keep your wings covered. I will walk with you since you won't be able to fly.'

Raven embraced him and kissed him again. 'I am so excited, Mordecai,' she exclaimed, 'I can't wait to see where you live, all the wondrous things you humans have.'

Raven went behind the trees while Mordecai turned around, not looking while Raven put the clothes on. She did not take off her dress, but Mordecai would not look out of respect for the black fairy. The pants were dark blue, and shirt was light blue. Her wings were covered so that there seemed to be no trace of them. She told him to turn around. 'How do I look?'

Mordecai was awestruck by her appearance. 'You look beautiful, Raven,' he said.

Raven blushed. 'Thank you,' she smiled. She then stopped and asked, 'I mean, can you tell I have wings?'

'Not really,' answered Mordecai, 'You should be able to pass as human. I still don't feel good about this, since that madman Dr. Von Braun has been badgering me about you. He doesn't know for sure that I have met you. I'm afraid he won't give up until he finds and captures a fairy. He will try and question me again until he gets what he wants.'

'I am willing to venture it, my darling Mordecai,' replied Raven, 'I wish to go with you.'

Sighing, Mordecai grabbed his bike and waited for Raven to join him. Raven stood beside him and kissed him on the lips. 'I am ready, my love.'

With a sigh, Mordecai took Raven's hand and said, 'Here we go.' They walked out of the woods and walked adjacent to the highway. Raven stared at the cars passing by them as they walked. 'What are they?' the black fairy asked. 'How can they move without horses?'

'We call them cars, trucks, in general, we call them automobiles,' Mordecai answered, 'They run on electricity, kind of like lightning. They are fueled by what we call gasoline. They can only hold a certain amount, depending upon the vehicle. When they run out of gas, they cease to move. They need both electricity and gasoline to move.'

'So, you call what you ride a bicycle?' Raven asked.

'Yes,' Mordecai answered, 'As you can see, it is powered by pedaling. It doesn't take electricity or gasoline to run it. You just pedal it and it moves, but not as fast as a car, and as you can see, the cars go by fast.'

'And you said your parents won't let you drive?' Raven asked.

Mordecai sighed. 'They won't. You have to be a certain age to drive. I am old enough, but my parents will not allow me.'

'Why won't they?' Raven asked.

'I don't know,' Mordecai sighed, shaking his head. 'I am not sure myself. My older brother Randall had started driving when he was sixteen. I am seventeen years old but Cece, who is fifteen years old, is being taught how to drive, but not me. She was afraid I would wind up hating her, but I am glad that's not the case. She's the only other person other than you who has stood by me. It is unfair to me, but it's not Cece's fault.'

Raven touched his arm. 'I am sorry. You don't know why they're being unfair to you?'

'No,' answered Mordecai, 'but if you meet Cece, you will like her. She loves fairies and a part of her believes fairies are real. It hurts that my parents are doing me like that. It hurts me a lot.'

'How do you think your parents would feel about me?' Raven asked, 'minus the fact that I am a fairy?'

'I won't reveal that part to either Cece or my parents,' Mordecai told her, 'I will do my best to keep your existence as a fairy a secret. I hope my parents will see you as a wonderful person and not go by the color of your skin.'

'I hope so, too,' replied Raven.

'How old are you?' Mordecai asked her.

Raven giggled. 'It does seem strange that I am in love with a human younger than I am,' she replied, 'I will be twenty-two in a few weeks. It doesn't change the way I feel about you at all. I'm very much in love with you, my darling Mordecai, and I wish to stay with you.'

Mordecai stared into her brown eyes and smiled. 'I feel the same way about you, Raven my love,' he said, 'You are very much a blessing to me. I am so happy that we met.'

'So am I,' Raven smiled, kissing him on the lips.

They arrived at Mordecai's house. He entered through the garage door and locked it. He leaned his bike against the wall as he unlocked the door. Raven entered and looked around. 'Wow. This place is so big! So many things I have never seen before!'

Mordecai turned on the TV. Raven stared at it and asked, 'What is that?'

'We call that a television,' Mordecai answered, 'It shows pictures, moving pictures, videos as we call them.'

It was on a sports channel. Highlights of a football game were being shown. 'What are they doing?' Raven asked.

'They are playing football,' Mordecai answered, 'It's a game people play, which some do for a living. I love football, but I am not athletic enough to play.' As he spoke, he pulled two cans of soda from the fridge and returned, sitting down next to Raven and giving her one. 'We call this soda,' he told her, opening the can and drinking out of it. Raven did the same. She smiled. 'I like this,' she said. 'This has a great taste.'

'I'm glad you like it,' smiled Mordecai, 'I drink this because it has no alcohol. I don't like drinks like beer, wine, and other things with alcohol. Not good for you.'

'Have you ever drank anything with alcohol before?' Raven asked.

'No, and I never will,' answered Mordecai, 'Too many bad things can happen when a person drinks alcohol.'

'I am seeing so many things I have never seen before,' Raven marveled, 'The room is lit without candles. How is it that they could be lit without candles? How do such things work?'

'It's complicated,' the young man told her, 'I don't know how they make it so or how it works, but it's not magic. It is technology. I wouldn't know how to build any of those things or explain how they work, but all that I know is that they do work. I couldn't explain how electricity works to power things in this house or in places we humans live. We advance technologically, creating such wondrous devices: communication, entertainment, but sadly we wax worse and worse spiritually, becoming more and more depraved. I remember you said Queen Cymbaline thinks of us humans as evil, quicker to do evil than good, in which she is correct. I do agree with her on that. We are natural born sinners, born in sin and shaped in iniquity.'

'True,' the black fairy maiden replied, ''but I always believe there is good and bad in everybody. I believe there are good humans as well as bad, and I believe you are one of the good ones. I know not all humans are evil.'

'That is true,' Mordecai nodded, 'God looks at the heart of the person. He knows all hearts.'

'I pray Queen Cymbaline will see that there are good humans as well.' Raven sighed. 'I hope she will see that you are indeed one of the good ones.'

Mordecai exhaled slowly. 'She mistrusts my kind with good reason,' he said, 'We've all had a sin problem ever since Adam and Eve had disobeyed God and took the forbidden fruit. It is easier to do evil than it is to do good.'

'That does include fairies,' Raven replied, 'but I also believe that there are good humans, and you are one of them, like I said.'

'In a way, I don't blame your Queen Cymbaline in isolating Arundel Haven from the human world,' replied Mordecai, 'There are some horrible things going on, unspeakable and unnatural, things which they would find appalling, that should stay unknown to your people.'

They continued to talk. 'My parents are still working,' he told the black fairy, 'They will be home later on. My younger sister, Cece, should be home from school any time now. I have an older brother, Randall, who is attending a college in Louisiana and stays at a dorm there.'

'He doesn't live here?' Raven asked.

'Technically, no,' Mordecai answered. 'In a way, he still does, but he plans to move out once he graduates college.'

'And what are your plans?' Raven asked.

'Before I met you, I'd hoped to go to college,' answered Mordecai, 'but that has changed now that I have you. I don't know what kind of future we're going to have together, a fairy and a human, but somehow, I want to make it work for the both of us.'

Raven smiled, taking his hand. 'As do I.'

At that moment, they heard a car pull up. Mordecai rose from the sofa. 'That ought to be Cece being dropped off now,' he told Raven, 'I've already told her about what had happened.'

'I remember you told me she is into fairies,' Raven said. Mordecai nodded.

Cece opened the door and immediately headed toward Mordecai, weeping, and embracing him. 'I was so upset when you told me that McCoy, Hatfield, and Jones had been bullying you again,' she said amid her tears. 'How do you feel?'

'I'm still hurting,' Mordecai sighed.

'I can't believe they threw you into the dumpster,' Cece said angrily. 'How can the school allow this travesty to go on?'

'Cece, there's someone I want you to meet,' Mordecai said as he released Cece. He pointed at Raven. 'This is Raven.' To Raven, as she rose, he said, 'Raven, this is my sister, Cece.'

Cece stared at Raven. 'Your girlfriend?' she asked.

'Yes,' he answered, 'We've been seeing each other.'

Raven shook Cece's hand. 'Hi, Cece, I'm Raven,' she said.

Cece shook Raven's hand. 'Nice to meet you, Raven,' she replied.

'Mordecai has told me so much about you,' Raven said.

'Raven and I have been seeing each other for the past few weeks,' Mordecai told Cece.

Cece dried her eyes. 'So that would explain you leaving after school,' she said, 'I can't believe you found someone.'

'Mordecai is a wonderful young man,' replied Raven, 'He has told me about you. I am happy to meet you, Cece.'

'I am glad you found somebody, Mordy,' Cece told her brother, 'but I don't know if Mom and Dad will accept Raven. I doubt they will approve of you dating a black woman. I personally have no problem with her, as long as she treats you right.' She sighed. 'I need to talk to you, Mordy,' she continued. 'Something had happened at school.'

'What happened? Is it concerning Oscar?' Mordecai asked.

Cece shook her head. 'No, but it's something I need to speak to you about in private,' she told him.

Mordecai thought he knew what it was about.

'I can't talk to you about it in front of Raven,' Cece continued.

'Why do you say that?' Raven asked.

'It's about a certain man coming on campus who has been asking you about a certain thing,' Cece told Mordecai.

Mordecai nodded. 'I understand,' he frowned, 'We can go into the kitchen. I'll be right back, Raven.'

Raven nodded as the siblings headed into the kitchen. Mordecai grabbed another soda as Cece sat down. She asked for a soda. Mordecai gave her his unopened soda and grabbed another can for himself. Cece opened the can and started to drink. 'It's Von Braun again,' she said, 'This time, he had approached me. He asked me where you were. He was searching for you.'

'I'd seen him earlier today just before the bullies had thrown me into the dumpster,' he said, 'I knew he would be trying to see if I had found a fairy yet. He is insane like Hussein!'

'I don't understand why he is so obsessed with finding fairies?'

'I have a feeling it's not good,' sighed Mordecai, 'Even if I knew, I would not tell him anything. If fairies existed, I would keep the knowledge to myself. They deserve to live in peace.'

'I agree,' Cece nodded, 'I wouldn't tell Von Braun or his men anything about fairies even if I knew.'

'I am glad to hear that, Cece,' came Raven's voice. Both turned toward the entrance and stared at Raven in surprise as she entered the kitchen area. 'Raven,' Mordecai exclaimed.

'What-What did you hear?' Cece asked.

'I heard you mention that you would not tell this Von Braun anything about fairies even if you knew,' answered Raven, 'I am happy you feel that way.'

'Wait a minute,' exclaimed Cece, 'What do you mean?'

Raven sighed. 'Since your brother Mordecai knows,' she replied, 'I think you should know as well.'

'Mordecai, what does she mean?' Cece asked her brother.

Mordecai stared at Raven. 'Are you sure this is a good idea?' he asked. Raven took off the shirt and pants that had covered her wings, then began to flex and flutter slightly to bring circulation back to her wings. Cece stood with her mouth wide open, gasping in disbelief. 'You—you're a fairy,' Cece exclaimed.

Raven nodded. 'Yes, I am,' she nodded.

Cece turned to Mordecai, staring hard at him. 'Raven is a fairy, and you knew?' she asked him.

Mordecai nodded. 'I didn't want Von Braun to know I had actually met a fairy,' he told his sister, 'the day when those bullies had tied me up and taken me to the woods.'

'I remember,' Cece nodded, 'So, it was Raven who untied you?'

'He had untied himself just before I made myself known to him,' said Raven.

'I'm sorry I had to keep Raven a secret from you, Cece, but—'

'I understand,' Cece said, rising from her seat, 'With that madman Von Braun asking you about fairies.' Her voice rose in excitement. 'You're dating a real live fairy?!? I can't believe it!'

'Yes, you can say that.' Mordecai smiled, 'Raven and I fell in love the first day we met, but it was this past Monday it became clear that we both have the same feelings for each other.'

'That is so great to hear,' Cece exclaimed, 'but has there ever been a union between a fairy and a human before?'

'Not that I know of,' Raven answered, 'Mordecai and I would be the first of such a union.'

'But what will your leaders say about that, Raven?' Cece asked.

Raven sighed. 'I know Queen Cymbaline would not approve because of the way humans are,' she answered sadly, 'She is a good queen, a righteous and just ruler, but she does not trust humans.'

'Cece, we can't let anybody else know, not even Mom and Dad, that Raven is a fairy,' Mordecai told his sister, 'especially Dr. Von Braun.'

'What about Tiffany and Sharon?' Cece asked.

'Not even them,' Mordecai answered, 'The situation with Dr. Von Braun has gotten me very concerned and fearful for Raven's sake. So much is now at stake since Raven has chosen to reveal herself as a fairy to you.'

'Come to my room, Raven,' Cece told the black fairy maiden, 'I've got something I want to show you.'

Mordecai smiled. She knew what she was talking about.

Raven put the clothes back over her body to hide her wings and joined Cece upstairs. Mordecai was with them. Cece showed Raven the posters and figurines of fairies that she had. 'I even have a wallpaper on my laptop and a screensaver of a fairy,' she said.

'Wallpaper? Screensaver? Laptop?' Raven queried, confused. 'What are those?' She looked around the room. 'Wow, Mordecai told me you liked fairies, but I had no idea.'

'I never grew out of that phase,' replied Cece, 'Now I know that you are a fairy and fairies are real, I will do all I can to keep your existence as a fairy a secret. I am glad you trust me enough with your secret.'

'Raven, I don't want anything to happen to you,' Mordecai told Raven, taking her hands. 'I have just found you, and I don't ever want to lose you.'

'Since you trust me with your secret, Raven,' Cece said, 'I promise I will keep your existence as a fairy a secret as well. I still can't believe you are a real live fairy!'

'Thank you, both of you,' Raven smiled.

They walked back downstairs to talk. As they sat down, Raven leaned her head upon Mordecai's shoulders as Cece sat down on the easy chair. Cece gasped, then turned to Mordecai. 'Mordy, remember the dreams I had told you I had about you and a fairy?' she asked.

'Yes,' Mordecai nodded.

'It was Raven,' she exclaimed, 'I remember now! The fairy in the dream I had about you was Raven! I did not know her name, but I remember now it was Raven.'

'What were they about?' Raven asked.

'I had dreams on three different nights,' Cece answered, 'The first dream, you were singing a song of love to him. The second dream, you both were dancing together and singing love songs to each other.'

'Sounds beautiful,' Raven smiled, staring lovingly at Mordecai.

Mordecai returned her stare in like manner. 'I wish I had dreams about the both of us instead of about Shadowfire,' he said to her.

Raven nodded. 'Have those dreams about Shadowfire stopped?' she asked him.

'Yes, for now,' Mordecai answered, 'The last one was a few days after we first met. There were seven in all. I still don't understand what he meant by this prophecy?'

'It is a mystery to me too,' replied Raven.

'Wait, you mean to say that Shadowfire is real too?' Cece asked.

Raven nodded sadly. 'He killed my parents over a year ago,' she sighed, 'A few weeks ago, he came after me and my niece, Twila, but God rescued us.'

Cece sighed. 'Raven, I'm sorry to hear that. I'm sure you must still miss them.'

Raven nodded sadly. 'Very much.' After a pause she said, 'I have an older sister, Starla, who lives with her husband on a farm outside of the village. They have a daughter, Twila, who is two years old.'

Cece giggled. 'The terrible twos. Guess it's similar with fairy children as it is with human children.'

'Oh, you have no idea,' laughed Raven, 'One time, Twila, who discovered she could fly, flew away and into the castle where the Queen and her brother live. I thought I was in deep trouble when she made her way into the castle and into the arms of Prince Avondale. I was fortunate they were understanding, but they told me to keep a close watch on my niece. She is so lively. My sister says Twila reminds her of how I was when I was her age.'

'Were you?' laughed Cece.

Raven sighed. 'I guess I was.' She answered softly.

'Do you think you two can have children together?' Cece asked.

'I remember when Dr. Von Braun had shown me the remains of a fairy,' Mordecai said, 'he told me he had studied the DNA and said he had found it was similar to humans. I believe it is very much possible for such a union to happen.'

'Do you think your Queen Cymbaline would be willing to see that?' Cece asked.

Raven sighed. 'I don't know,' she answered, 'I hope so. I guess I'm more concerned about your parents, how they would react to me.'

Cece nodded. 'I hope they would accept you as a wonderful person, be you black or white, fairy or human. I, too, go by what a person is on the inside.' Her voice rose in excitement. 'It would be so neat to have a fairy as a sister-in-law!'

Raven and Mordecai smiled, staring into each other's eyes. 'I believe it will come true,' the young man said.

'So do I.' Raven smiled. Their lips came together as they kissed.

Cece smiled.

At that moment, there was a knock on the door. Mordecai and Raven separated. Cece rose from her seat, walked toward the door and opened it. She saw Tiffany and Sharon at the door. 'Hi, guys,' she said. 'Is there anything wrong?'

'Just wanted to check up on how your brother is,' Tiffany answered. 'Thinking about what those creeps had done to him. Did they really throw him in the dumpster?'

'*They* are the ones who need to be thrown in that dumpster,' Sharon replied as Cece invited them in. They saw Mordecai and then stared at Raven. 'Who's that?' Tiffany asked. 'I didn't know you had company.'

'This is Raven, Mordecai's girlfriend,' Cece told her friends, 'I just met her today. He's been seeing her for over two weeks now.'

'That would explain what he's been doing after school,' Sharon said.

Mordecai stood up, helping Raven up in return. 'Raven, these are Cece's best friends, Tiffany and Sharon.'

Raven smiled, shaking the hands of both Sharon and Tiffany. 'I am happy to meet you,' she said.

'You don't look like a student, unless you're in college,' Sharon said.

'How old are you, Raven?' Tiffany asked.

'I will be twenty-two in a few weeks,' Raven answered.

'You are seeing an older woman, Mordy?' Tiffany laughed. Mordecai nodded.

'Yes, I know he is seventeen,' Raven said slowly, 'but I don't care about age or skin color. It's the heart I look at.'

'Was it true you were thrown in the dumpster?' Sharon asked Mordecai.

Mordecai nodded. 'It was a horrible feeling,' he winced, remembering the incident, 'I had landed on something hard, but I didn't see what it was. I was too busy trying to get out, get away from the foul smell. It was good I was allowed to go home after that. I didn't want to go through the rest of the day smelling like trash or get into your car like that.'

'They are such wicked humans,' Raven frowned.

Sharon and Tiffany marked what Raven had said but said nothing.

'Where are you from, Raven?' Tiffany asked.

'You two want a soda?' Mordecai asked, making his way into the kitchen.

'If you have diet,' Tiffany answered.

'Yes, we do,' Mordecai nodded, 'I prefer to drink diet soda. What about you, sweetheart?' he asked, staring at Raven.

Raven smiled. 'I would like that very much, my love,' she nodded.

'You're going to need some help,' Cece said. She followed Mordecai in the kitchen. As Mordecai grabbed some sodas, he gave three cans to Cece. 'You don't think you should tell my friends that Raven is a fairy?' she asked.

Mordecai sighed. 'The two of us are enough, especially with Dr. Von Braun out there,' he answered, 'I'm very concerned about what would happen to Raven if that madman discovered her secret. I had warned Raven about Dr. Von Braun when we first met and told her he had suspected me somehow, I don't know how he could have known even before I had met Raven that I would come across a fairy, but now there is much more at stake than I could have ever thought. Raven and I have fallen in love with each other and want to spend our lives together. I am determined to never lose her, no matter what!'

'I think Raven got a little careless, talking about the bullies,' Cece said, 'I could tell Tiff and Sharon noticed it! She said, "They are such wicked humans!" She could have inadvertently revealed herself as being a fairy to them, especially with Dr. Von Braun on his quest to find a fairy! If she would have said "boys", it would be fine, since they do act like boys, but "humans", that's another story.'

'I'm sure they don't really think Raven is a fairy?' Mordecai protested.

'Can you be sure of that, Mordecai?' objected Cece, 'They will put two and two together and come up with, "Raven is a real live fairy". I trust them to keep that a secret if we tell them to.'

Mordecai thought for a moment. He was uneasy about the matter. He wanted so much to protect Raven and keep her from Dr. Von Braun. He was unsure what to do. Should he trust Tiffany and Sharon with Raven's secret? Her sister Cece trusted them. He let out a sigh and said, 'I will leave that up to Raven. I am still unsure about revealing her secret to anybody. Raven chose to reveal her secret to you.'

'Yes,' Cece replied, 'She felt she could trust me, and I won't betray that trust. Hey, she chose to reveal herself to you, and lo! You and her fell in love! Yes, Mordecai, leave the decision to Raven. You have to trust her, trust her to make the right decision, and you can trust me.'

Mordecai bowed, nodding his head.

They headed back in the living room and gave the drinks to Raven and Cece's friends. They sat down and continued to talk.

An hour later, Mordecai and Raven were in the backyard. Mordecai had his MP3 player hooked up to the radio. 'I am seeing so many things I never thought existed,' Raven said, 'Devices that play music.'

'Recorded music,' replied Mordecai, 'Different types, different genres of music, like rock, pop, country, R&B, classical, blues, jazz. Different styles.'

'I am confused,' said Raven.

'It's going to take a while for me to explain.' He put on a song; *I Will Be Here* by Steven Curtis Chapman. Raven drew close to him as they slow danced to the song. She stared into his eyes and smiled, giving him a gentle kiss on the cheeks. 'Sounds like a song of commitment,' she said.

'It is,' Mordecai nodded as they continued to slow dance. 'I dreamed when I listened to that song of having that special someone, being with that someone, and here you are! I never thought I would find someone.'

'I was wondering if I would find that someone myself,' Raven told him, 'I never thought in my wildest dreams I would fall in love with a human. I am glad I met you, Mordecai Jefferson.'

'And I you, Raven,' he smiled.

Raven leaned her head upon his shoulder as they danced. Cece, Tiffany, and Sharon caught a glimpse of them then stopped and watched as the lovers danced. Cece smiled, tears running down her eyes.

Tiffany stared at Cece and asked, 'Are you okay?'

'Mordecai deserves someone who loves him,' Cece said softly, 'He deserves to be happy. Raven is so right for him.'

Tiffany sighed. 'Strangely enough,' she replied, 'I believe they are right for each other.'

'They look so wonderful together,' Sharon smiled. She paused for a moment. 'Still, though…'

'What?' Cece turned to her.

'I sense there's something different about Raven,' Sharon ventured to say, 'I don't know what it is, but I feel it.'

'Now that you mention it,' Tiffany said, 'I sense the same thing. I can't put my finger on it. What about you, Cece?'

'Me?' Cece laughed, a bit uneasy, 'No, I sense nothing. All I know is that she is special.'

Both girls nodded. 'I think so too,' replied Tiffany.

The music continued to play, into *Cross My Heart* by Michael W. Smith and into *Faithfully* by Journey. Mordecai and Raven continued to dance in each other's arms, oblivious to the world around them. All that mattered to them was the love they had for each other: Mordecai, a young white teenage human and Raven, a black fairy in her early

20s. Nothing else mattered to them but the love they shared with each other, dreaming of a life together. They danced without a care in the world.

The song then went into *In My World* by the Moody Blues, the words echoing through their minds as they danced. In the middle of the song, they stopped dancing and held each other close, their lips drawing together and touching, engaging in a long, gentle loving kiss. They remained locked for long moments, standing still as statues as the air got a little colder and darker. When their lips disengaged, Mordecai caressed Raven's face and said, 'I feel blessed to have you in my life, my sweet Raven.'

Raven touched his face. 'Sweet darling Mordecai, my love, my life,' she smiled, 'I can't think of my life without you.'

'Nor I you, Raven. When the time is right, I wish to take you to be my wife.'

'Yes, Mordecai,' Raven answered, eyes swelling up with tears of joy, 'I do. I do agree to become your wife, to spend the rest of my life with you.'

'I wish I had a ring to give you,' said Mordecai.

'I do have something to give to you.' Raven disengaged from him and unfastened a necklace from around her neck. Upon the chain was a golden ring, with seven tiny diamond hearts embedded within. She took her hand and slipped it upon his finger. 'My mother had made this for me,' she said, 'to give to the fairyman who would be my husband as a betrothal gift. She had fashioned it for both Starla and me before she died, before Starla had married her husband, Roosevelt, four years ago. It turns out that my heart does not belong to a fairyman, but to a wonderful human whom now my life is interwoven with.'

Mordecai looked at the ring. 'It is beautiful,' he smiled, 'I gladly receive it, and you, Raven, my love, my life.'

'I am yours for life, Mordecai, my love, my life, my husband.'

'I am yours too, Raven, my love, my life, my wife,' he replied. They drew together in a loving tender embrace and kiss.

After he kissed her, he said, 'The skies have already darkened. I don't want you to leave.'

'I don't want to leave, at least, not yet,' replied Raven. 'I wish to meet your parents and see if they like me.'

'I hope so,' Mordecai sighed, releasing her, and taking her hand. They both walked away from the back door and continued to talk. 'I hope my parents can see what a wonderful person you are, how beautiful you are inside.'

'It may take some time, I guess,' said Raven, 'but I know eventually I'll have to reveal to them that I am a fairy. I will have to see first how they feel about the color of my skin. So such prejudice of skin color exists?'

Mordecai nodded sadly. 'Unfortunately. Some think their race is superior to another, but not so. God created people of all races. Jesus died for the Jew and the Gentile, the black and the white, Oriental, Latino, all races. The Word says, *Whosoever shall call on the name of the Lord shall be saved.* I believe that in my heart.'

'Be they human or fairy,' Raven added.

Mordecai nodded. 'I honestly believe that.'

'So do I,' replied Raven, 'No such prejudice exists among fairies. Only mistrust of humans. But here we are, you and me, together! God brought us together; I know that now beyond a shadow of a doubt. I pray that Queen Cymbaline will look at your heart and not the fact that you are a human.'

Mordecai and Raven stopped and stared into each other's eyes. Their hands came together and clasped.

They were about to kiss when there came a voice. 'Raven! Raven, what are you doing?'

Raven and Mordecai looked up toward the sound. Lavender and Laurelin hovered in the air along with three fairymen in strange attire.

Both lovers gasped. 'Let her go, human!' Laurelin cried to Mordecai.

'Lavender! Laurelin!' Raven cried, 'What's the meaning of this?'

The three fairymen landed and held their spears in Mordecai's direction. Raven turned to them and cried, 'Don't hurt him! Mordecai is with me!'

Lavender and Laurelin landed in front of the black fairy. Their faces showed that they were not pleased. 'So, this is your secret, isn't it, Raven?' Lavender cried, 'You want to explain this? Is this where you've been all this time? Why the human clothes?'

Raven slipped the clothes off her that hid her wings. 'Let me explain, Laurelin,' she told her.

'Are you in love with this human?' Laurelin asked, anger rising within her, 'Tell me that you are not in love with this human!'

Raven shook her head. 'I can't tell you that,' she sighed, 'I cannot deny I am in love with Mordecai.'

'You know that contact with humans is forbidden,' Lavender cried, 'and here you are in the arms of a human, a human, for crying out loud! You say you are in love with this human? This is wrong on all fronts, so wrong! Never before has a fairy and a human fallen in love! It should never be!'

'That's just your opinion,' shot back Raven, 'Originally, I did not come here to meet any humans, but God had arranged it so that I would meet Mordecai. Humans and fairies, we are both the same, save for the fact that we fairies have wings!'

'You can't be serious about this, Raven,' cried Laurelin,

shaking her head.

'I am,' Raven answered, 'I have pledged my love to a human, to Mordecai.'

Lavender and Laurelin shook their heads sadly. 'You've gone too far this time, Raven,' Lavender frowned, 'Again and again, you defy the decrees of Queen Cymbaline and once again, crossed the line where no fairy should have crossed!' She shook her head once more. 'Raven, I do not understand you. Why a human? Why him?'

'This is a matter of the heart, Lavender,' shot back Raven, 'Surely you would understand.'

'No, I don't,' retorted Lavender, 'This does not warrant giving your heart to a human! A human and a fairy should never be joined. You crossed the line, Raven, and crossed it once too often!'

Sharon was getting a soda from the refrigerator when she saw Mordecai, Raven and five fairies in the backyard. She rubbed her eyes. *Raven? Raven's a fairy?* She stood in disbelief.

She then heard Tiffany's voice cry out, 'Hey, Sharon, where's the soda?'

'You better come out here quick,' Sharon cried.

'Just leave Mordecai and Raven alone,' Cece cried, 'I'm sure they want their privacy.'

'You won't believe this,' Sharon said, stunned, 'but there are six fairies outside with Mordecai, and one of the fairies is Raven.'

'What?' came the surprised voices of Cece and Tiffany.

'Three of them have spears pointed toward Mordy!'

Cece and Tiffany raced into the kitchen and saw the gathering. Tiffany turned toward Cece and said, 'You didn't tell us that Raven is a fairy!'

'Never mind that,' Cece cried, 'Why do they have spears on my brother?'

They headed outside and approached them. Two of the fairymen turned around and pointed their spears at the girls. 'No, no,' Mordecai cried. 'Leave them alone!'

Cece cried out Mordecai's name.

'This is not my fault, Cece, I swear,' cried Raven, 'My friends, Lavender and Laurelin, they've been searching for me!'

'Why didn't you tell us Raven was a fairy?' Sharon asked Cece and Mordecai.

'For Raven's protection,' Mordecai cried as he was held at bay by the third fairyman. 'I wanted to keep her existence a secret to protect her from people like Dr. Von Braun.'

'I had chosen to reveal myself to both Mordecai and Cece,' Raven told her friends, 'My heart has led me to Mordecai, and I knew I could trust Cece as well.' She then turned toward Mordecai. 'These are my two friends, Lavender and Laurelin,' she said. To her friends she said, 'This is Mordecai Jefferson, the man I have pledged my heart to.'

'Are you out of your mind?' snapped Laurelin. 'You wish to become the wife of this human? This is an abomination! There has never been a union between a human and a fairy before, and such unions are forbidden! Raven, you know how wicked humans are, how violent and cruel they are! You want to join yourself with this human?'

'Beyond a shadow of a doubt,' shot back Raven without hesitation, 'I love him, and he loves me! He's a human and I'm a fairy, but we are both the same except for the wings!'

'You need to try and explain that to Queen Cymbaline,' cried Lavender. The two fairymen grabbed Mordecai and rose to the air.

Cece cried out her brother's name. 'Leave him alone!'

'Where are you taking him?' Sharon asked.

'Why should we tell you, human?' Laurelin snapped. She began to rise in the air.

'You're taking him to Arundel Haven?' Cece cried, 'Why? He has done nothing wrong!'

Lavender and Laurelin stopped in mid-flight, and each gave an angry glace at Raven. 'You told the humans about Arundel Haven?' Lavender asked her, 'You told them about our home?'

'I did,' Raven answered.

'Why? How could you tell them about our home?' Laurelin snapped. 'You are completely out of your mind, Raven! What other secrets have you told your human lover?'

'Arundel Haven was already known to a mad geneticist before I had met Raven,' Mordecai told Raven's friends, 'He already knows the existence of fairies even before Raven came here and eventually met me. I don't know how he could have known, but he had me under suspicion that I had knowledge about fairies even before my encounter with Raven. Even now, we are in danger of being spotted by that madman!'

The two fairymen who held Mordecai rose further into the air while Raven cried, 'Let him go! He's done nothing wrong!'

'Our orders come from Queen Cymbaline,' one of the guards proclaimed, 'You and the human shall be brought before the Queen. She will decide your fate!'

Raven flew toward Cece with tears in her eyes. 'I am sorry, Cece,' she wept. 'I did not mean for this to happen! I love Mordecai, I really do! I never wanted any of this to happen! Please believe me!'

Lavender and Laurelin pulled Raven away from Cece as she watched tearfully as her brother was being taken away. 'Mordecai!' she cried.

'Cece!' Mordecai cried as he was taken further into the air. Raven watched sorrowfully as her friends pulled her away from the grieving Cece, who had fallen to her knees, tended to by Tiffany and Sharon who gave equally unbelieving stares. 'I'm so sorry, Cece,' she wept.

'Come on, Raven,' Lavender said sternly. 'It's time to go home!'

Mordecai and the fairies were soon lost in the night sky. Cece wept bitterly, crying out her brother's name. Tiffany and Sharon did their best to comfort their friend. They continued to stare out into the night sky where the fairies with Mordecai had disappeared.

Amid her tears, Cece said to her friends, 'I'm sorry I didn't tell you about Raven. I just found out today myself.'

'And Mordy knew Raven was a fairy?' asked Tiffany.

Cece nodded. 'From the first time they met, they told me,' she answered, 'What will happen to my brother? Why are they taking him away?'

Tiffany and Sharon held their friend in an effort to comfort her. Cece wondered if she would ever see Mordecai again. She feared for his life.

Tiffany and Sharon helped Cece back inside the house. In the background was the sound of a car pulling up into the driveway.

Chapter Seven

From the arms of the two fairymen that supported him, Mordecai beheld the fairy home of Arundel Haven as they descended from the clouds. He felt the chill in the air and shivered from the cold. Raven flew close to his side but the third fairyman forbade her to speak. She wept off and on during the trip back home. She refused to speak to her friends Lavender and Laurelin. Mordecai glanced at Raven from time to time and let out a melancholy sigh. He wasn't sure what to expect from Queen Cymbaline since Raven had told her that she did not trust humans. He whispered a silent prayer as they headed into the castle.

When they landed, the two fairymen dropped Mordecai on the hard floor while the third pointed his spear at him. Raven rushed to Mordecai's side to the displeasure of her friends. 'Get away from the human, Raven,' Lavender cried.

'No,' cried Raven sharply, 'My place is by my beloved's side! I will not leave him!'

'Raven, you're crazy,' snapped Laurelin, 'Stop this foolishness! Get away from him.'

'You're not serious about this human, are you?' asked Lavender.

'I am,' answered Raven tearfully, 'I found the one person I love, and I am not about to let him go!'

Lavender and Laurelin shook their heads. Raven continued to weep. 'We'll see what Queen Cymbaline has to say about this,' Laurelin said.

'This way,' one of the guards commanded, leading Mordecai and the others to the throne room.

Mordecai looked around as he was led to where Queen Cymbaline and Prince Avondale awaited them. He, along with Raven, Lavender, and Laurelin, were escorted to the dais. Raven bowed along with Lavender and Laurelin. Mordecai did the same. He looked up and saw the grim visage on the faces of the two monarchs.

Queen Cymbaline stared grimly at Raven. She then turned to Lavender and Laurelin and asked, 'Where did you find Raven and this human?'

'At the house where this human lives,' Lavender answered, 'She indeed has been seeing this human.'

'You have been warned about venturing to the human world, Raven,' said Queen Cymbaline sternly, 'yet you disregarded my warnings and continued to see this human!' To Mordecai she asked, 'Who are you and what do you have to say?'

'My name is Mordecai, your majesty,' he answered, trembling. 'Mordecai Jefferson. Raven came to the house where I live along with my parents and sister at her request. Today was the first time she has been to the house. We have been seeing each other for over two weeks now. We had met in the woods where some bullies at school beat me up and bound me and had left me. Raven came down to me and helped me.'

'Disregarding my decree not to have any contact with the humans?' Queen Cymbaline frowned, staring hard at Raven.

'Forgive me, your majesty,' Raven said, 'I believe God had laid it on my heart to fly to that place and eventually brought Mordecai into my life.'

Queen Cymbaline shook her head. Prince Avondale stared grimly upon the young man.

'I had warned her of the danger of being spotted,' Mordecai told the monarchs, 'There is a madman who is obsessed with finding Arundel Haven, who had approached me even before I first met Raven. I sensed his intentions were evil toward your people.'

'How many know of your existence, Raven?' Prince Avondale asked.

'Just my sister, Cece,' Mordecai answered, 'and now her friends Tiffany and Sharon. I did not want anybody else to know about Raven. I wanted to keep her existence a secret from men like Dr. Von Braun.'

'Who exactly is he?' Lavender asked.

'A world-renowned geneticist,' Mordecai answered, 'He approached me about fairies and for some reason, thought I would have knowledge of having seen a fairy, even before I had met Raven. He had shown me a picture of the remains of a fairy and claimed that the DNA was similar to that of humans.'

'That's impossible,' Laurelin scoffed, 'Fairies and humans are not the same!'

'Enough, Laurelin,' cried Queen Cymbaline. She then stared hard at Mordecai.

'Dr. Von Braun kept asking me about fairies, but I refused to give it,' he continued. 'Something in my spirit said to me that his intentions were evil.'

'As with all humans,' retorted Queen Cymbaline suspiciously.

Mordecai sighed. 'It is true we were born in sin, shaped in iniquity,' he responded, 'A lot of my people have bad hearts. The Word of God backs up what you believe, your majesty, about humans. We were all born with sin, born into sin, shaped in iniquity. I know your decrees were made to protect fairies from humans, and I don't blame you, really. I see what humans can be like firsthand, having been bullied and picked on, beat up, abused physically and mentally by a lot of students, three people in particular.'

'Why did you make contact with this human, Raven?' Prince Avondale asked.

'God had laid it on my heart and led me to him, your majesty,' Raven answered, 'I believe that so strongly in my heart. Mordecai has shown me so much kindness since I've met him, both him and his sister, Cece. I believe that not all humans are evil.'

'It does not matter,' Queen Cymbaline proclaimed, 'You defied a decree I had made designed to protect all fairies. It displeases me greatly you have disregarded my warnings.' To Mordecai she asked, 'What makes you so special that Raven would come to you?'

Mordecai shook his head. 'I don't know, your majesty,' he answered sadly, 'I am not special at all, not even among my own people or my own house. I am a nobody really, but Raven believes otherwise.'

'I do, your majesty,' Raven said, staring at him, 'I do consider him special. I felt it in my spirit from the first moment I met him. When I asked him to take me to where he lives, he advised against it, to keep any of his people from finding out I was a fairy.'

'And yet you took her,' Prince Avondale frowned at the young man.

'I insisted,' Raven replied, 'His sister, Cece, is a wonderful person just like he is. Her friends only found out I was a fairy right before Mordecai was taken, when Lavender and Laurelin had led some of your soldiers to us.'

'Only then did you see the danger you have put yourself and all of us in, Raven,' Queen Cymbaline frowned, 'Four humans now know of your existence, including *this* human! Sooner or later, the humans may very well find out where Arundel Haven is! Why? Was it worth it to you?'

'That was not my intention, your majesty,' cried Raven.

'Be it your intention or no,' cried the Fairy Queen, 'you have compromised our existence to four humans! Why? Why did you continually return to the human world, to this human? Was it worth compromising our existence just for this worthless human?'

'I originally came to the woods in Orlando for peace,' Raven told her, 'Somehow, I felt peace there, calmness in my spirit. I later also found what I'd been searching for, which the others had, Lavender, Laurelin, Starla, something that I'd been looking for.'

'And what would that be?' Prince Avondale asked.

'She's in love with the human,' Lavender proclaimed.

Queen Cymbaline and Prince Avondale gasped in disbelief. They then gazed hard at Raven. 'Is this true, Raven?' Queen Cymbaline asked in disbelief.

Raven sighed. 'It is true,' she answered, 'I love him, and Mordecai feels the same way about me.'

'Is this true, human?' Prince Avondale asked, 'Is what Raven claims about you true? Do you feel the same way about her as she does you?'

Mordecai bowed again, nodding his head. 'It is true,' he answered softly, 'I gladly return her love.'

Queen Cymbaline stared hard at Raven, then Mordecai. Raven's eyes filled with tears. 'I have pledged my heart to him,' she said softly.

'This cannot be allowed,' Queen Cymbaline proclaimed sternly, 'No fairy should be permitted to be bound to a human! Such unions are forbidden! There has never been such a union and should never be! This is completely unacceptable, Raven! I will not allow or permit such a union!'

'But, your majesty,' Raven protested.

'You are forbidden from seeing this human, Raven,' Queen Cymbaline said in a firm voice, 'As for the human, he shall be kept in the dungeon until I decide his fate!'

Raven burst into tears, falling to her knees. 'Please, your majesty,' she cried, 'Please have mercy! I love him!'

'Take the human to the dungeons,' Queen Cymbaline commanded, 'The rest of you, you are dismissed! Raven is forbidden to visit the human! Keep her out of the castle and away from him! Now carry out my decree!'

The guards took Mordecai to the dungeons. Raven watched with tear-filled eyes as her human lover was taken away. Lavender tugged on Raven's arm and said, 'Let's go, Raven.'

Raven pulled away from Lavender. 'Don't touch me,' she snapped.

She quickly flew away from her friends.

'Raven, be reasonable,' Laurelin told Raven, flying after her, 'Do you think such a union would even work out anyway?'

'He may not have wings,' Raven snapped back, 'but other than that, there is no real difference. Why can't Queen Cymbaline see that? Why can't *you* see that? I do not repent of meeting Mordecai or of falling in love with him!'

'Open your eyes, Raven,' Lavender cried, 'You know this is wrong. This relationship has been wrong from the very beginning!'

'No!' snapped Raven, 'You are wrong, and as much as I love the Queen, she is wrong in this matter!' Tears rolled down her cheeks. 'I don't care what you think about me; think what you want! I love Mordecai, and when the time is right, we will be joined!'

Lavender and Laurelin shook their heads and departed from Raven as they flew away from the castle.

From their seats, Queen Cymbaline sighed and bowed her head. She had an uncomfortable feeling inside of her, something telling her what she had done was wrong. Prince Avondale gazed at his sister and asked, 'What's wrong, Cymbaline?'

Queen Cymbaline shook her head, rising from her throne. 'Nothing, dear brother,' she answered, 'nothing at all.' She headed away from the throne room, followed by Prince Avondale.

Prince Avondale stopped and thought about the human, Mordecai. He felt there was something about the human, he wasn't quite sure, but he felt there was something special about this human. He marked the countenance of Mordecai, how he had humbled himself before Queen Cymbaline, absent of haughtiness and pride, minding his attitude and words when he spoke. He was unsure what to think. He decided to keep an eye on the young human.

Mordecai was led to a dungeon and was pushed inside. The cell doors clanged shut. As the guards left, he took the blanket that was on the cot and wrapped it around his body to keep himself warm. He laid down on the cot, thinking about Raven, missing her. It was as Raven had expected: it was clear Queen Cymbaline had no love for humans, of that he understood. He then thought about the way he had been mistreated at school, how he was bullied. He wondered if he would ever see Cece again. He was glad their differences had been settled and grateful for her love and support. He wept softly, unsure of what his future would be.

Raven could not sleep at all that night. She wept, thinking about and missing Mordecai. She kind of expected Queen Cymbaline's reaction toward her relationship with Mordecai, a human, but the pain was still hard to bear. She wanted to be with Mordecai, to support him, to comfort him, to love him. *Father God, please open Queen Cymbaline's eyes that she will see that there are good humans,* she prayed in her heart.

When morning came, Starla dropped by and found Raven at the table drinking tea that she'd brewed. She had knocked on the door but there was no response. When Starla finally walked inside, that was where she had found Raven. Her eyes were red from so much weeping. Twila, who was in Starla's arms, noticed her aunt's countenance and asked, 'Aunt Raven sad?'

Raven nodded but said not a word.

'What happened?' Starla asked.

'Queen Cymbaline had thrown the man I love in the dungeon last night.'

'What do you mean by that?' Starla asked, confused.

'I was in the human world and had met Mordecai.'

'A human?' interrupted Starla, 'What in the world were you doing in the human world? You had met a human?'

Raven nodded.

'Raven, why did you make contact with a human when you know that it is forbidden? And what do you mean "Queen Cymbaline had thrown your true love in the dungeon"?' Starla gasped, realizing what her sister was talking about. 'A human? You're talking about a human?'

'Yes,' Raven answered. 'I had met him two weeks—'

'Raven, you had fallen in love with a human?' Starla gasped, the shock resonating across her face, unable to believe what her sister was telling her.

Raven nodded. 'I was led by God to the woods I'd been flying to and He eventually brought Mordecai into my life. Now he's in the dungeon inside the castle, no real crime against Arundel Haven has he committed!'

'Raven, this is totally unthinkable!' Starla exclaimed, 'This is crossing the line big time! No fairy should ever fall in love with a human! Queen Cymbaline has warned us so many times about how wicked and depraved humans are!'

'Not all humans are like that!' Raven snapped, 'A lot of them, yes, but not Mordecai! We both share the same beliefs, for one! He is so wonderful, if you only knew him. If only Queen Cymbaline would get to know him and see there are some good humans.'

'Raven, Queen Cymbaline's decrees are to protect us from the wicked influence of humans,' Starla proclaimed sternly, 'She knows how bad humans are.'

'Has she ever met one before she met Mordecai?' Raven shot back, 'Have you ever met one?'

'Raven, that is not the point. Time and time again, you have defied Queen Cymbaline's decrees and bans of visiting the human world, and with good reason! They fight amongst themselves over the stupidest of things, like status, race, creed, greed, and they kill each other for foolish reasons! They love riches over their fellow man, so low and depraved they are! Queen Cymbaline wants to protect us from their corrupt influences.'

Twila got down and started walking around while Starla and Raven debated. 'But we are no better than the humans,' Raven said, 'We fairies may not be as bad as humans, but we are not perfect.'

'Beside the point,' retorted Starla, 'Her decrees are for our protection! We don't want to learn the things that the humans have learned, the abominable and heinous things they practice, unnatural things they do, sins against nature. Do we really want their ways introduced into our ways? It would mean the downfall of fairykind as we know it!'

'Why are you against Mordecai, because he is a human and only because he is a human?' shot back Raven, tears in her eyes, 'I have gotten to know him and come to love him! He was protective of me and was unwilling to reveal the fact I was a fairy to anybody, even to his sister Cece, who loves fairies! I decided to let his sister know my secret and she is willing to keep it. She looked at me as the kind of person I was, not the fact that I am a fairy and had dark skin. That is how God looks at us, not at what we are on the outside, but what we are in our hearts, on the inside, where it counts!'

Starla shook her head. 'This is madness that you have fallen in love with this human,' she proclaimed, 'I don't know him, and I do not wish to know him! I'm sorry, Raven, but I cannot support you on this.'

'I have given him my word to be his,' Raven told her sister.

Starla stared hard at Raven. 'Raven, you didn't!'

'I did. I gave him the ring Mom made us to give to the one who would be ours before she died. Mordecai has it now,' Raven said defiantly.

'Mom and Dad would never approve of you being in love with a human or such a union, Raven,' Starla shot back, 'They would pitch a fit for sure if they were alive today! Take my advice, Raven, forget the human and find a good fairyman.'

'I have found someone, Starla,' Raven shot back, tears flowing from her eyes, 'My heart belongs to Mordecai! God has brought us together, that much I am sure of.'

'Not in that way,' protested Starla.

'Yes,' Raven insisted, 'I know beyond a shadow of a doubt. I will not abandon the man I love. My heart belongs to him, and his belongs to me. Nothing in this world is ever going to change that fact or change the way I feel about Mordecai!'

Starla picked up Twila and turned to go. 'I can't believe you, Raven,' she replied angrily, 'What will it take for you to come to your senses? Fairies and humans are not supposed to meet or be married.'

'Why, Mommy?' Twila asked.

'Hush, sweetie,' Starla told her daughter, 'You are too young to understand.' Without another word, Starla walked out the door. Raven wept when her sister had left.

Starla looked behind her at the closed door, a sad look upon her face. She sighed and started for home. Twila looked behind as her mother walked away from the cottage where Raven lived. 'Why Aunt Raven so sad, Mommy?' Twila asked.

'Now is not the time to talk about this, Twila,' her mother told her, 'It's time to go home now.'

'I don't like Aunt Raven be sad,' Twila said.

'I know, sweetie,' Starla sighed, 'but you aren't able to understand such things as yet. When you are older, you will.'

'Why, Mommy?' Twila asked.

Starla sighed. 'No more questions, dear.'

As Starla rounded a corner, Twila shot out of her arms and flew in the opposite direction. Her mother cried out her daughter's name and said, 'Not again! Not now!'

She flew after her daughter the best she could, slowed down by the child she was carrying inside of her. Her mind began to race, afraid of what trouble or harm Twila would get herself into. 'Twila, come back here,' she cried, 'Come back to Mommy!'

Twila rounded another corner, her mother flying after her, calling her name. 'Twila! Twila! Come back here!'

She made a grab for her daughter but missed.

Twila started giggling as she flew. The fairies in the way stared and some even laughed.

Starla had no time for games. She had to be careful since she was pregnant again. She tried as carefully as she could to try and catch Twila, but Twila only dodged her and giggled. 'You are in big trouble with Mommy, young fairy girl!' she cried.

To Starla's horror, Twila flew inside the castle, giggling as she went. She was doing the same thing she had done to Raven before. 'Twila, why are you doing this?' she cried. 'We are going to be in big trouble with Queen Cymbaline for sure!'

The guards only looked but did not hinder them. One of them laughed and thought of when Twila had done that to her Aunt Raven weeks before. 'Here we go again,' the first guard said to his companion.

'Maybe she should tie up her wings for a time,' the other laughed.

'Whatever it takes to slow that child down,' replied the first, 'I feel sorry for her mother, and for Raven as well.'

The second guard laughed. 'Have you ever heard of any toddler other than Starla's daughter that would fly out of the blue like that?'

'No, just this one,' the second guard answered, 'Makes me wonder if I would ever want kids of my own.'

The first guard nodded and laughed.

Starla was becoming frustrated. She dared not fly at full speed on account of the child she was carrying in her womb. Already, she was becoming winded, starting to slow down. She cried out her daughter's name, but Twila kept on flying. 'I know you love to fly, Twila,' she cried, 'but this is neither the time nor the place for it! Get over here right now! Listen to Mommy!'

Twila flew onward, flying around the corridors of the castle.

Mordecai sat on his cot, still cold. He was unsure what was going to happen to him. He laid his head upon his knees, tears flowing down his face. He missed Raven and longed to see her again. What would happen to her? How would Queen Cymbaline punish her for visiting the human world and for giving her love to him? He did not want anything bad to happen to Raven. He loved her very much. He then thought of Cece. He was sure she was distraught with him being taken to Arundel Haven by the fairies against his will. He hoped Cece would not blame Raven for all this, since it was not her fault. It was Lavender and Laurelin who had followed her and revealed themselves to Cece and her friends, Tiffany and Sharon. He knew Lavender and Laurelin did not like him because of the fact he was a human and were dead set against the relationship he and Raven had together.

He stared at the ring Raven had given him. He sighed. His heart ached to be with Raven, to hold her, to kiss her, to give her love and companionship, to encourage her, but he needed encouragement himself.

He did not notice a two-year-old black fairy toddler slipping between the bars of his cell and flittering toward him. When he felt the breath and heard the flittering of Twila's wings, he looked up and saw the toddler. 'Hello,' she said giggling.

Mordecai instinctively reached out his arms as Twila landed in his arms. 'Hello, little one,' he smiled, 'What are you doing here? A dungeon is no place for a little cutie like you to be in. You shouldn't be down here. I'm sure your mommy misses you very much.'

'Twila love flying,' she proclaimed as she touched his face.

'Twila?' Mordecai repeated. He then thought, *Raven's niece. I remember Raven telling me about her.* He found himself laughing softly, remembering what Raven had told her about Twila's escapade inside the castle. This is just another one of Twila's escapades, and he had just became a part of it.

'Why you no have wings?' Twila asked Mordecai, looking at his back.

'I am not a fairy, little one,' Mordecai answered, giving her a gentle kiss. Twila squealed in delight in response. 'I am human. Humans don't have wings. What are you doing away from your Mommy? Doesn't she miss you very much?'

Twila hugged his neck and gave him a kiss on the cheeks. 'I like you,' she proclaimed, 'You nice.'

Mordecai smiled. 'You are very sweet,' he smiled.

He suddenly heard a woman calling out Twila's name. Mordecai figured it was Starla Twila's mother searching for her daughter. He glanced at Twila and asked, 'Is that your Mommy calling for you?'

'Yes,' Twila answered, burying her head and giggling, 'That my mommy.'

'Did you fly away from your mommy again, Twila?' asked the young man.

Twila only giggled again.

Mordecai had his answer. 'She's very worried about you, little Twila,' he told the toddler, 'She loves you very much, do you know that?'

Starla reached the cell where Mordecai resided and was horrified when she saw her daughter in his arms. 'Twila, no!' she cried. To Mordecai she pleaded, 'My daughter! Let her go! Please don't hurt her!'

Mordecai stared sadly at Starla. 'You must be Starla. Raven has told me about you and Twila.'

Starla pleaded with Mordecai, not noticing that Twila had her arms around the young man's neck, interacting with the young man. 'Please don't harm my daughter, I beg of you!'

Mordecai turned his sad gaze toward Twila. 'I would never hurt her, Starla,' he said as tears flowed from his eyes. He slowly stood to his feet and headed toward Starla.

Twila looked at the tears flowing from Mordecai's eyes and wiped them from his face. 'Why you cry?' she asked.

'You are very precious to your mother, little Twila,' Mordecai said sadly, 'She is afraid I will hurt you, but I would never do such a thing, never to a child.' He held Twila and wept softly. 'You are a special little girl.'

'Please don't cry,' Twila said, placing her small hands on his face and wiping them.

'You are a very sweet little girl, Twila,' Mordecai managed a smile, giving her a gentle kiss. 'Your aunt Raven has told me so much about you, especially about your little unscheduled flights.'

Twila giggled in response.

Starla found herself doing the same as the young man tried to hand Twila back to her, but the black fairy toddler was unwilling to leave the young man. 'Why do you remain, little one?' Mordecai asked, 'Don't you want to return to your mommy?'

'Come to Mommy, Twila,' Starla told her daughter, tears filling her eyes. She was beginning to realize that Mordecai was no threat to her daughter, touched by the way Twila had wiped the tears from his eyes. Starla merely stared at Mordecai as Twila hugged the neck of the young human. 'I'm guessing you must be Mordecai,' Starla said, 'Raven has told me about you.'

'I am pleased to meet you and Twila, Starla,' Mordecai replied, 'Raven indeed has told me about you and Twila, especially Twila.' Twila gave him a kiss on the cheeks.

'I bet Raven had told you about her little flights,' said Starla.

Mordecai nodded as Twila giggled. Starla couldn't help but smile.

'Don't you want to return to your Mommy?' Mordecai asked Twila, 'A dungeon is not the place for a little cutie like you.'

'Twila like you,' Twila said, 'What your name?'

'Mordecai,' he answered.

'Morcai?' Twila said.

'Close enough,' Mordecai smiled, 'You can call me Morcai if you wish.'

'Morcai, Morcai,' Twila chimed.

Starla burst out laughing as a result. 'She sometimes has trouble saying people's names,' Starla found herself saying.

Mordecai stared gravely at Starla. 'I would never do anything to hurt your daughter or any child,' he replied sadly, 'All life is precious in the eyes of God. Your daughter is very beautiful. You should be proud of her.'

Starla gave a soft laugh. 'She seems to like you, Mordecai.' She then remembered the words she had spoken to Raven a short time before: *I do not know him and I do not wish to know him!* Inside, she began to feel the weight of her words, seeing how wrong she was. Tears continued to flow from her eyes as she stared at Mordecai and seeing Twila in her arms, beginning to accept the fact Twila was in no danger at all in the arms of the human Mordecai.

'Yes, Starla,' Mordecai answered, 'Your daughter is a little cutie, very precious. Raven had told me how you had lost both your parents to the dragon Shadowfire.'

'It was and is an evil time for us,' sighed Starla, 'May Shadowfire burn in the deepest pits of hell where he had been spawned! He had been afflicting my people for over one hundred fifty years!'

'Raven had told me that he wields sorcery and worships the goddess Ashtaroth, often sacrificing some of you people to her.'

'He would devour some of my people and sacrifice others to his pagan goddess,' Starla said grimly, 'No weapon our smithies can forge can bite him. His armor is invulnerable to our weapons. I fear he may never fall!'

'God must have a set time for his fall,' Mordecai replied as Twila touched his face, 'I am not sure how, but I feel his time of afflicting the fairies of Arundel Haven will soon come to an end. He shall not harm one hair from this precious little life.' He gave Twila a gentle kiss. She giggled. Raven had told me how lively Twila is.'

'Twila love flying,' Twila chimed. 'Can Morcai fly?'

Mordecai shook his head. 'I'm afraid not,' he answered. He sighed. 'It would be nice, though, if I could. You and your mother can fly. I can only dream of it, to soar through the clouds, to feel the breeze on my face, the world below, flying with the eagles.' He sighed. 'I can only dream of such things. How wonderful it must be to have the ability to fly without being in an airplane or such things.'

'What is airplane, Morcai?' Twila asked. Starla wanted to know the same thing.

'Humans use airplanes to fly from place to place,' Mordecai answered, 'We cannot fly on our own like you and your Mommy.'

Starla thought as Mordecai talked with her daughter. She saw how Twila took to him like she was her favorite uncle. She started to smile as she watched as Twila played with Mordecai. She sighed. *Perhaps you are right, Raven. Now that I have seen and met Mordecai for myself, how Twila has taken to him. Maybe fairies and humans are not so different as Queen Cymbaline or others like me would like to believe.*

One of the guards brought some food and drink to Mordecai's cell. He saw Starla and said, 'What are you doing here? You're not supposed to be here!'

My daughter had flown here after flying away from me,' answered Starla, 'She seems to like him.'

The guard saw the toddler in Mordecai's hand and quickly placed the tray down, reaching for his spear when Starla said, 'No, no, it's okay. He's not hurting her. My daughter had made her way here and came to his cell.'

The guard chuckled lightheartedly and said, 'I think she is in danger, in danger of being hugged and kissed to death. I have never seen anything like this before. I think she sees something in him we do not see.' He searched through his keys to the cell to unlock it. As he found the keys and unlocked the door, he said to Mordecai, 'How did this little one get inside your cell?'

'I'm guessing, Taris,' Mordecai answered as Twila touched his face, 'Twila may have slipped through the bars and had entered that way. I did not see her enter.'

'You must be special,' Taris ventured to say, 'for Twila to trust you and take to you. We can all learn from her.'

'I think it's time to return to your Mommy, little Twila,' Mordecai told the toddler.

'Twila no want bye-bye,' she said, 'Twila like Morcai.'

'I know, little Twila,' smiled Mordecai, 'but your Mommy loves you and misses you very much.'

Starla couldn't help but laugh as Mordecai handed Twila back to her. 'Now I see what Raven sees in you, Mordecai. Twila seems to have seen it, too.'

'Aunt Raven,' Twila chimed.

'Yes, Twila,' Mordecai responded, 'Your aunt Raven has told me about you and your little unscheduled flights.'

Starla and Taris laughed.

'You love my aunt Raven?' Twila asked.

'With all my heart I do,' Mordecai answered.

'And now mommy is approving of Mordecai,' Starla told her daughter, tears in her eyes, 'Your aunt Raven has indeed made the right choice. I know he loves her with all his heart.'

Twila let out a happy squeal and chimed, 'Yes!'

Mordecai, Starla and Taris laughed. 'The official squeal of approval,' laughed the young man before his smile disappeared, 'Could you please give a message to Raven?' he asked Starla, 'Tell her… so far I am okay, that I love her and miss her very much.'

'I will try, Mordecai,' sighed Starla, 'but I think she could be still mad at me, but I think this may change things now. I now wish you weren't imprisoned.'

'I have to respect Queen Cymbaline's decision,' Mordecai sighed, 'It was nice meeting you, though, Starla.'

Starla smiled. 'And I can honestly say the same thing,' she replied, 'even though it took a toddler who loves to fly to see that.' Both Starla and Mordecai laughed. 'You and your husband must be very proud of Twila,' Mordecai said. 'She indeed is a very special little girl.'

'Thank you, Mordecai,' Starla replied, 'Roosevelt and I are very proud of her, though she can… you see how she can be.'

'I understand, Starla,' smiled Mordecai.

'I miss you, Morcai,' Twila said.

Mordecai smiled. 'I will miss you too, little Twila,' he said, sitting back down on his cot. Taris grabbed the plate as Starla flew away with Twila in her arms. 'Thank you,' Mordecai said as he received the plate.

'Perhaps things will change,' Taris said, 'Maybe we could all take a lesson from little Twila. I'm still surprised how she has taken to you, and she had just first met you.'

'Indeed,' Mordecai nodded, 'God can use even the little ones to teach a thing to adults.'

In the distance, there was the faint sound of bells. Taris immediately ran out of the cell and grabbed his spear. 'What's going on?' Mordecai asked.

'Shadowfire!' Taris cried, 'Shadowfire is attacking!'

Mordecai headed to the door and closed it. He then thought about the dreams he'd had about dealing with the dragon. *Is he searching for me? Does he know I'm even here at Arundel Haven?*

He sat back down and tried to eat the food that had been given to him. When Taris saw that Mordecai had closed the door, he nodded grimly. 'If only there was a way to destroy the dragon,' he growled.

Mordecai sighed, thinking about some of the words the dragon had spoken to him in his dreams. *I can only hope he doesn't know I am here.* He was afraid but kept silent and watched as the guard looked through a nearby window. 'It doesn't look like he's flying close to the castle,' he heard the guard say. 'He seems to be making a random sweep around the village. Curse and crush Shadowfire! May he go back down to the pits of hell where he came from!'

Starla managed to reach Raven's cottage when the dragon appeared and attacked. She saw Shadowfire take two fairies and breathed out fire at various buildings. He laughed as he passed by. Three more fairies were engulfed in flames and were consumed. After a couple of more passes, he flew back to the Mountains of Shadow with the two fairies he had captured.

During the dragon's attack, Starla hurried inside, Twila crying and holding tightly to her mother. Raven had heard the screams and knew what was going on. She saw Starla inside with her and embraced her, weeping. 'I am so glad you're okay, Starla,' she said. 'I was afraid Shadowfire had taken you!'

'He came nowhere near me,' Starla replied, seeking to comfort Twila, 'He didn't spot me at least. He took two fairies, but I couldn't tell who they were.'

'I am so glad you are okay,' Raven wept, 'I feel so bad about the fight we had!'

'So do I, Raven,' Starla wept, 'I am so sorry, Raven! You were right! You were right about Mordecai!'

Raven stared into her sister's face. 'What?'

Twila began to calm down. She snuggled closer to her mother as she talked. 'You can thank Twila for that,' Starla told her sister.

'She had one of her flights again?' Raven asked.

'Into the castle like she did to you,' Starla laughed, 'This time, she had somehow made her way into the dungeons.'

Raven gasped. 'You have met Mordecai?' she cried, 'You had talked to him?'

'Twila had made her way inside the cell where he was,' Starla told Raven, 'I thought he was going to hurt her, but I saw how Twila took to him, like he was her favorite uncle. She seemed to hit it off with him right away, but I was too scared to see that at the time. I then saw Twila wipe tears from his eyes and said, "Don't cry, Morcai".'

' "Morcai?"' Raven smiled.

'Twila miss Morcai, Aunt Raven,' she said. 'I want go see Morcai again.'

Raven touched the toddler's face. 'Your aunt Raven misses Mordecai, too,' she replied sadly, 'Your aunt Raven loves him very much.'

'I like Morcai, Aunt Raven,' Twila said, 'Morcai nice.'

Both Raven and Starla smiled. 'Your Mommy now feels the same way about Morcai as well, Twila,' her mother said.

'Thank you, sis,' Raven said, 'That means a lot to me.'

Starla sighed. 'He doesn't deserve to be in prison,' she said, 'I wish there was something we could do, but I don't think Queen Cymbaline would listen to us.'

'If only she could see,' sighed Raven.

Starla embraced her younger sister. Neither of them said a word but wept softly together. Twila said, 'Don't cry, Mommy, Aunt Raven.' Starla merely kissed her daughter.

Prince Avondale looked out the window from one of the towers and saw the dragon attacking the village. He saw when two fairies were taken and three more were burned to death on the streets. He stared in anger at the dragon. He felt helpless to do anything about it. He wanted to do something but didn't know what to do. He could hear the mocking laughter of Shadowfire as he flew by the village a few times then flew back to his home.

Queen Cymbaline found her brother at the window, watching the carnage. She saw the dragon returning at last to the Mountains of Shadow. Both said not a word as they looked on at the fairies who tried to put out the fire that was set in his wake. They could only watch helplessly. Queen Cymbaline fell to her knees and wept. Prince Avondale followed suit. They earnestly prayed to God to provide a way to put an end to the dragon. 'I hate this helpless feeling,' wept Queen Cymbaline, 'We've done a poor job protecting the fairies of Arundel Haven against Shadowfire!'

'I know,' sighed Prince Avondale, weeping with her, 'How much longer, 'O Lord, must we suffer at the claws of the dragon? How long must You allow the dragon to continue to afflict our people? Please heed our cries for help, in the precious name of Your Son, Jesus Christ! Have mercy, we beg of you!'

Prince Avondale found himself heading down to the dungeon area to speak to Mordecai. He found him sitting on his cot, thinking and in prayer. He stared grimly at the young human. He commanded the cell door to be opened before entering the cell. 'I am here to see the human, Taris,' he told the guard.

'Mordecai Jefferson has behaved himself wisely, your highness,' Taris told the fairy prince, 'In fact, he has become a good companion, an almost fairy-like quality to him.'

Mordecai stared in his direction and when he saw the prince, he fell from his cot and bowed in respect before him. He then sat back down on the cot. 'The people at school could know that I'm missing,' he said, 'especially three bullies who love to pick on me. That I do not miss.'

'I do not understand why Raven would give her heart to you, human,' frowned Prince Avondale, 'She has crossed the line when she had met and given her heart to you.'

'I disagree, your highness,' he replied as respectfully as he could, 'I believe this is from God. However, I am nobody special, really. I still don't know why Raven would reach out to me like she did when those bullies left me in the woods.'

'Your name again,' Prince Avondale demanded.

'Mordecai Jefferson, your highness,' the young man answered, 'I have heard that there had been a dragon attacking earlier.'

'Our great enemy Shadowfire,' Prince Avondale replied grimly, 'He is a mortal enemy to all the fairies of Arundel Haven.'

'Raven has told me about Shadowfire, how he had killed her parents. How long has he been afflicting your people?'

'For 150 years, 150 years too long,' Prince Avondale answered grimly, 'Queen Cymbaline and I feel helpless to do anything about it. He is impervious to any weapon any fairy smithie could forge, more than likely because his side is protected by his magic. He is a wicked monster and great in sorcerous power.'

'He wields the black arts?' exclaimed Mordecai, 'Maybe that's how he has been able to enter my dreams for seven consecutive nights.'

Prince Avondale stared hard at him. 'Why would the dragon enter your dreams?' he asked skeptically, 'What do you have to do with him?'

'I don't know, your highness,' Mordecai answered, 'In the dreams, he seems to believe I am the one some ancient prophecy that foretells of his demise. He would tell me no more than that. I don't understand. The dreams frighten me all the same. I am nobody, really, the least in my father's house, nothing special at all. What could I do, anyhow?'

'The Prophecy of Queen Hephzibah,' Prince Avondale whispered almost involuntarily, remembering the old stories about how the ancestor of the royal family had foretold the death of the dragon. 'Could he be referring to the Prophecy of Queen Hephzibah?' *Could he be the one? Could this human Mordecai be the one spoken of in my foremother's prophecy she had given on her deathbed about the end of Shadowfire? Could indeed God has allowed this Mordecai to be brought to Arundel Haven? It has to be!* The fairy prince felt a touch in his spirit that it was so.

'Your highness?' Mordecai queried, marking the countenance of the fairy prince.

'I barely remember hearing about the prophecy of Queen Hephzibah,' Prince Avondale said, 'I had forgotten completely about it in these dark times.'

'I am unfamiliar with the Prophecy of Queen Hephzibah, your highness,' Taris said.

'I'm not surprised, good Taris,' Prince Avondale replied, 'Very few fairies even remember the old prophecy. They must be in one of the old books in the royal library.' He turned to go. 'I wonder if it could foretell the end of the dragon? I will get back to you.'

He walked out of the cell as Mordecai watched the door being closed. He thought about it. 'The Prophecy of Queen Hephzibah? Could it have anything to do with me? What is it actually?'

He remained seated as he thought of Prince Avondale's words. As Taris approached his cell, he told the young man, 'I'm afraid, Mordecai, that I don't know much about the Prophecy of Queen Hephzibah. The little I remember about it, I have since forgotten. I think Prince Avondale is going to find out about it. If indeed this has something to do with the destruction of Shadowfire, it is hope renewed.'

'From the dreams I had, Shadowfire referred to a prophecy dealing with his death and seems to think that I am the one,' Mordecai said, 'I can't see how that could be. I am no great warrior, no fighter. I am small and insignificant. I am the least among my people, even the least in my father's house.'

'Yet God has been known to use people like you for great things,' Taris stated. 'Who can say? Perhaps that is why you are here in Arundel Haven, a human who is the least of his people.'

'I know you are right, but I am afraid all the same,' sighed Mordecai, 'If I am the one, why me? There is nothing special about me.'

'In His eyes, Mordecai, all His saints are special, be they fairy or human,' replied Taris, 'All those in Christ are His saints according to His Word, and that, my friend, that is what makes you special. Please do not think yourself insignificant and worthless. Jesus showed that you are not by giving His life to redeem people like you and me and rescue us from hell when we put our faith and trust in Him.'

Mordecai returned to his cot and sat down again. He took Taris's words to his heart, knowing he was right. He prayed that God would provide a way to deliver the fairies of Arundel Haven from the claws of the dragon Shadowfire.

Raven tried to visit Mordecai, but the guards refused to allow her per orders from the Fairy Queen. Starla, Twila, Lavender, and Laurelin were with her. 'Queen Cymbaline has forbidden you to see the human, Raven,' the head guard told her. 'I'm sorry, but I cannot allow you to see him.'

'What about me?' Starla asked. 'She didn't mention anything about me.'

'Why do you want to see this human, Starla?' asked the head guard.

'I can at least deliver a message for Raven, if that is permissible,' Starla replied, 'Can that at least be permitted?'

'Twila want to see Morcai,' the toddler said.

'She's determined to see him,' Starla said, 'She is willing to fly into the palace and to the dungeons to see him if she deems it necessary.'

The head guard sighed and nodded his head. 'I guess that would be okay, then,' he told her, 'You can see the human.'

'We will come with you. Starla, Laurelin, and I,' Lavender said. 'Why?' Starla asked. 'Why do you wish to see him?'

'We have our reasons,' Lavender said, 'We want to see what makes this human so great that Raven would want to be with him.'

The head guard reluctantly agreed. They were led inside the castle, following one of the guards down the stairs. They at last came to the dungeons where Mordecai was being held. Taris had the guard dismissed as he unlocked the cell where Mordecai was being held. Twila immediately flew into the cell and into the arms of the young human. 'Morcai, Morcai,' she cried joyfully.

Mordecai laughed as he caught the toddler. 'I am happy to see you too, Twila,' he smiled, giving the toddler a kiss on the cheeks. He turned toward Starla and said, 'Thank you for visiting me, Starla.'

Starla smiled. 'Raven misses you very much, Mordecai,' she told him as Twila kissed the young man's cheeks, She has been forbidden by the Queen herself to see you, but we were allowed.'

Mordecai turned toward Lavender and Laurelin. 'You two are Raven's friends, aren't you?' he asked them.

'We consider ourselves her friends, but I don't know how she feels about us now that you are in prison,' Laurelin said.

'I understand you were doing this for the protection of your people, I know that,' Mordecai said as Twila leaned her head against his neck. 'I can't really blame you. The outside world is a dangerous place, the people cold and cruel, a lot of them. I've only had a taste of how bad they can be.'

'I thought you were against Raven being with this human,' Lavender said to Starla. She then stared in surprise at Mordecai and Twila, how the toddler had taken to the young man.

'I was at first,' Starla said as Twila laughed when Mordecai tickled her, 'but you can blame Twila for that. Just before the dragon came, Twila flew into the castle again in one of her flights.'

'Again?' Laurelin laughed, 'You've got to keep a hold on her.'

'Indeed,' replied Starla, 'Twila made her way here and somehow slipped inside Mordecai's cell. I feared at first that she would come to harm, but I was wrong. Twila seems to trust him, and now I am beginning to be of like mind. He thinks very highly of Twila.'

Lavender and Laurelin stared in astonishment at Twila playing with Mordecai. Mordecai held her and kissed her on the forehead. 'You are a special little girl, Twila,' he told her.

'I trust him now,' Starla told her sister's friends, 'Perhaps maybe fairies and humans are not as different as I once thought.'

'But will Queen Cymbaline see it that way?' Lavender asked, 'She has yet to decide his fate. Will he stay imprisoned be allowed to return to his home?'

'If he is allowed to leave,' Laurelin added, 'He knows how to get here now. He warns of a madman out there anxious to find Arundel Haven.'

'Dr. Von Braun must never find out,' Mordecai quickly stated as Twila yawned and leaned her head upon his shoulder. 'Twila is one reason to keep Arundel Haven a secret from my people. Little ones like Twila must never come to harm, from the dragon, from people like Von Braun. I will accept whatever fate Queen Cymbaline decides, even if it's to remain here at Arundel Haven.'

'How can we be certain you will accept her decision?' Laurelin asked skeptically, 'The Queen as well as us still don't trust you.'

Mordecai rocked the young fairy toddler gently. 'Some things are an act of faith, much like Twila has shown in finding me,' he told her, 'I will agree to abide by her decision. For Twila's sake, for Raven's sake. My people must never know!'

Starla drew near and watched as Twila closed her eyes. 'I will take her once she is sound asleep, Mordecai,' she said, 'I still can't believe she has grown so attached to you. I guess we can all learn from Twila.'

'I tend to agree,' Taris replied, smiling as he stared at the young man cradling the toddler in his arms. Lavender and Laurelin stared at the young guard. 'You trust this human?' Lavender asked.

Taris nodded. 'He is a brother in Christ,' he told them, 'He has acted honorably in my charge and has earned my respect and trust. Do not be surprised.'

'I'm beginning to see why Jesus said we must have the faith of a child,' Mordecai said, 'It's a lesson all of us must learn. I guess I still have to learn that lesson as well.' To Twila he said, 'Sleep well, little Twila. May there be a day when you and yours will never have to worry about Shadowfire or evil humans like Von Braun.'

When he was sure Twila was fast asleep, he handed the toddler to Starla. 'And I pray that day will come soon for Arundel Haven,' he added.

'You would make a great husband for Raven,' Starla smiled, embracing him, 'be you fairyman or human. Raven made the right choice in choosing you.'

'Thank you, Starla,' smiled Mordecai as Lavender and Laurelin stared in surprise and shock, 'That really means a lot to Raven and me.'

Lavender and Laurelin remained skeptical of Mordecai. They held their tongues, however. Mordecai somehow knew that Raven's friends did not trust him. He made no expression. To Starla he said, 'Tell Raven I am missing her so much, but I am fine, other than that. My jailor, Taris, has become a good companion.'

'I find no fault in Mordecai,' Taris said, 'I feel he does not deserve to be in prison. I see more and more why Raven has fallen in love with him.'

'She cares about him and misses him very much,' Starla said, 'Queen Cymbaline has forbidden her to see him. The guards would not allow her to pass.'

Taris sighed. 'At times, I hear Mordecai weep and pray for Raven as well,' he said, I wish Queen Cymbaline would reconsider. I, too, believe there are good humans in the world.'

Lavender and Laurelin shook their heads.

'Maybe you two will see,' Taris told Lavender and Laurelin, 'God looks at the heart, not what's on the outside. Like God had told Samuel in 1 Samuel 16:7: *For the LORD seeth not as man seeth; for man looketh at the outward appearance, but the LORD looketh at the heart.* I trust Mordecai since he is a brother as well.'

Starla turned to leave along with Raven's friends. 'I will deliver the message,' she told Mordecai ere she took her leave, 'We will return soon, Twila and me. She would say, "Bye bye, Morcai", but she's sound asleep.'

'Little girls need their rest,' smiled Mordecai, 'I look forward to seeing her again. Tell Raven I love her.'

Starla smiled. 'I will tell her that, Mordecai.' As she, Lavender and Laurelin took their leave, Mordecai sat back down on the cot.

Taris smiled on his friend.

Prince Avondale looked through the books in the library, thinking about the prophecy he had mentioned to Mordecai. He skimmed through different books, trying to find what he sought. He then found a book that mentioned Shadowfire.

He grabbed it and opened it. He then saw what he had been searching for. He took the book with him and left the library seeking out his sister to show her what he had found.

The next day, Mordecai was given soup and some bread and juice to drink by the guard Taris, whom he had become friends with. Taris saw how well Mordecai had conducted himself and had earned his respect. He marked the countenance of the young human. 'You're thinking about Raven, aren't you?' he asked.

'In part, yes,' Mordecai nodded, 'but the dreams of Shadowfire have returned, for the first time in over two weeks I've had a dream about him. Whatever this prophecy is, he seems to firmly believe I am the one the prophecy had spoken of.'

'I remember Prince Avondale talking about it with you,' Taris replied, 'I can't tell you much about the Prophecy of Queen Hepzibah. I'm guessing he is seeking a book concerning about it.'

'It's been on my mind since I first had the dreams just before I met Raven,' the young man sighed, 'I am frankly scared because of it.'

Taris bowed his head. He wished he knew what to say to encourage his new friend. 'It has become nothing more than a legend, though clearly Shadowfire is not,' he said, 'I know Queen Cymbaline and Prince Avondale are trying to do what they can, but what can they do? Every weapon the smithies had forged cannot bite his enchanted hide.'

'I think about little Twila,' Mordecai sighed, 'She shouldn't have to live with such danger. None of you should.'

'You miss your home?' Taris asked.

'In a way, yes,' Mordecai answered, 'My sister Cece I think about. She loves fairies and has a lot of fairy-related stuff, figurines, posters, in her room. She even found a fairy figurine that looks like her—red hair and all. What I don't miss are the three bullies at school.'

'What are they like, these bullies?' Taris asked.

'I wish I could put it in a way you can understand,' Mordecai frowned, remembering the evil they had committed against him, 'They play a game called football and are considered the best in the state, but they pick on and bully those who are weaker than them. They've been afflicting me ever since I started attending high school three years ago.'

'They have no right to pick on people weaker,' frowned Taris.

'The people in authority in my school ignore what they've been doing and take full advantage of it,' said Mordecai, 'I had been beaten up, tied up and left in the woods right when I had met Raven. I know the edicts from Queen Cymbaline are there to protect fairies, and frankly, I don't blame her, having been a victim myself. I don't want any of the fairies, especially not Raven or little Twila, to come to harm at the hands of evil humans like Dr. Von Braun. I would do anything in my power to protect them.'

'I have no doubt,' sighed Taris, 'To me, you seem more fairy than human, even though you have no wings.'

Mordecai smiled. 'I consider that a compliment,' he said.

At that moment, Prince Avondale appeared with three visitors, one of them a toddler in the arms of her mother, Starla, and another in a dark cloak. As Taris unlocked and opened the cell door, Twila flew out of her mother's arms and into the arms of Mordecai, who had risen to his feet. 'Morcai, Morcai,' she cried joyfully.

'Little Twila,' Mordecai cried, catching the young toddler, and kissing her on the cheeks. Twila giggled. 'I am so happy to see you, Twila.'

'Twila happy see you, Morcai,' she chimed.

'I see you know each other,' smiled Prince Avondale, 'I had heard Twila had ventured into the castle once again. I had no idea she had made her way to your cell.'

'It was an unexpected visit, but a welcomed one,' Mordecai smiled, 'She kind of took to me right way, like a favorite relative.'

Prince Avondale smiled as he nodded. 'She accepts you without prejudice,' he observed, 'There is someone here to misses you very much and is here to see you.'

Mordecai stared at the figure as the hood was removed and the face of Raven appeared. Twila flew out of Mordecai's arms as he and Raven embraced and kissed, weeping as they held each other. 'Mordecai, my love,' Raven wept. 'I missed you so much!'

'I missed you too, my sweet Raven,' he replied, tears flowing down his cheeks. They remained locked in a long embrace, kissing each other. Mordecai cradled her in his arms. Raven stroked his face. 'I was so worried about you,' Raven wept.

'Aunt Raven happy now?' Twila asked as she flew into Mordecai's arms. Mordecai released Raven and caught the young toddler.

'Yes, your aunt Raven is,' she answered, tears in her eyes. She wrapped her arms around Mordecai's left arm as Twila got comfortable in the young man's arms.

Starla smiled as she stared at the couple. She then turned toward Prince Avondale and said, 'I was afraid he would hurt her when I first saw her in there with him, but I am glad that wasn't the case. He had considered her life precious. I now see why Raven cares so much about him.'

Mordecai stared at Prince Avondale. 'Why did you allow Raven to come see me, your highness?' he asked him. 'Why have you shown me this kindness, totally unworthy that I am?'

'I do not see it that way now,' Prince Avondale replied gravely, 'Seeing how happy little Twila is to see you confirms that Raven had been right all along. You are a trustworthy human; I can see that now. God does look on the heart of a person, not at what they are on the outside. You will appear before Queen Cymbaline very soon. I had told her of a book I'd found of the Prophecy of Queen Hephzibah our foremother. She has begun to see now, as do I. We will tell you the tale when you are presented to her.'

'I don't understand,' Mordecai said humbly.

'My sister does not know yet that Raven has seen you,' Prince Avondale told him, 'I had her disguised and brought her here to you. It was the least I could do. Already, there is a bond between the both of you that not even my sister's decrees can defy.'

'I did not do it out of disrespect of your sister, your highness,' Raven said to the fairy prince, 'but because the bond of love is so strong between Mordecai and I.'

'I see that now,' nodded Prince Avondale. 'I sense no enmity from you toward my sister, but only a strong love that you have for Mordecai.'

'I gladly call Mordecai my friend as well, your highness,' proclaimed Taris, 'He has shown himself honorable in my eyes, never acting contrarily towards me in any means. He has behaved himself wisely. I have heard of the Prophecy of Queen Hephzibah in name only. What I had learned has been forgotten in my memory.'

'What does it have to do with Mordecai?' asked Starla, 'I am unfamiliar with the Prophecy.'

'Could this be the prophecy that Shadowfire has been referring to in my dreams?' Mordecai asked. 'It has weighed heavily on my mind from the first day the dragon had started invading my dreams. It has haunted my thoughts ever since.'

'It could very well be, Mordecai,' Prince Avondale replied, 'It could answer the questions we all have.'

'With the most important question being how to destroy Shadowfire,' Starla said.

'It could very well be,' replied Prince Avondale. He stared at Twila in Mordecai's arms. 'I'm still amazed how well she has taken to you, Mordecai.'

'So am I,' Raven said, 'I couldn't believe when I first heard from Twila. Lavender and Laurelin, however, still don't trust you, Mordecai.'

'I noticed,' Mordecai nodded as Twila kissed his cheek. 'You are very sweet, Twila.' He smiled.

Twila giggled. 'Twila love Morcai,' she said. Starla smiled.

'I wish to appear with Mordecai, your highness,' Raven said, 'when he appears before Queen Cymbaline. I feel my place is with him.'

'That is why I had brought you here to see your lover,' Prince Avondale told her, 'It would be wrong now to keep the two of you separate. I will request my sister Queen Cymbaline to release you.'

'I pray she would,' Taris replied, 'He does not deserve imprisonment. I will be sorry to see him go, however. He has proven himself a good friend.'

'Thank you, Taris,' Mordecai said.

Raven smiled as she saw her niece in the arms of Mordecai. 'Morcai love Aunt Raven?' Twila asked.

'With all my heart, little Twila, I do,' Mordecai answered.

'And your aunt Raven loves Mordecai very much,' Raven added, 'I am glad you like him.'

'Twila love Morcai,' the little girl chimed.

'I love you too, little Twila,' he replied, kissing her cheek.

Raven, Starla, and Prince Avondale smiled. They saw how unquestionably Twila had accepted Mordecai and loved him, even though he was a human. 'If only we could have Twila's innocence on such matters,' Prince Avondale said softly.

Twila gave Mordecai a kiss on the cheeks again. Mordecai kissed the toddler on the forehead. The toddler snuggled up into the young man's arms. She started to yawn. Mordecai rocked her gently as she yawned again. 'Somebody's getting sleepy,' Starla smiled.

'Does your husband, Roosevelt, know about me?' Mordecai asked.

'He was amazed when he first heard how Twila met you,' Starla said, 'He was concerned at first, but when he heard how much Twila had become attached to you, it was amusing to him. He was happy for Raven that she had found someone, even though you are a human. He says he wouldn't mind meeting you. He, too, looks at a person by what's in their heart. He also believes there are good humans, though I had disagreed with him before meeting you for the first time. You would be welcomed in our home should you have a chance.'

'I would love to come, Starla,' replied Mordecai as he heard Twila yawn again. Starla was still amazed by how attached her daughter was to the human. 'You tell her how special she is, Mordecai,' Starla said, 'You are very special as well, but of course, Raven has known that all along, though I was too blind to see it at the time.'

'He sure is,' replied Raven, kissing Mordecai on the lips. She looked down and caressed her niece gently as she slept in Mordecai's arms. 'Very soon, she will call you "uncle Morcai,"' she said to Mordecai.

'I would welcome it,' smiled Mordecai. Twila fell asleep peacefully in the arms of Mordecai. Starla took Twila back as she slept. Raven laid her head upon Mordecai's shoulders and kissed him on the lips.

Prince Avondale smiled.

Very soon, Mordecai was taken to the throne room by Taris. He was joined by Raven, Starla, and Twila, who was asleep in her mother's arms. Queen Cymbaline stared hard at Raven. 'She is with Mordecai by my leave, sister,' Prince Avondale said, 'Please allow her to remain.'

Queen Cymbaline nodded. 'Very well,' she replied, 'Prince Avondale has brought to my attention a book that had been forgotten for many years concerning what is known as the Prophecy of Queen Hephzibah. It tells of the first coming of the dragon Shadowfire to Arundel Haven.'

Mordecai bowed before the queen. 'It would perhaps answer the question why I've been having the dreams before I had first met Raven, your majesty, forgive me for speaking.'

'No, need to apologize, Mordecai Jefferson,' replied Queen Cymbaline, 'You may speak.'

'The dreams were relatively the same over the seven nights I had them, with some exceptions,' Mordecai continued. 'I dreamed I was in a dark valley. I felt death and darkness all around me as I walked. I saw a dragon, all black, very large, bat-like wings. Raven told me that it was Shadowfire.'

'It describes Shadowfire,' Prince Avondale nodded.

'He didn't know who I was or where I lived,' Mordecai continued, 'He asked me my name, but I refused to give it. He mentioned some prophecy, which he would tell me nothing about, but he seemed so convinced that I was the one this prophecy spoke of. I had told a little of it to Prince Avondale. It was then he had mentioned the Prophecy of Queen Hephzibah. I wonder if that was the prophecy that Shadowfire had spoken of? He insisted that I was, but I couldn't be. I am not a fighter or a great warrior. I am the least of my people and the least in my father's house, nothing special at all. What could I do as weak as I am against such a powerful dragon anyhow?'

'It would seem Raven would think differently when she had started seeing you, Mordecai,' Queen Cymbaline stated. 'This forgotten story would answer the questions we've all had, or at least most of them. Prince Avondale, my brother, had found it yesterday and brought it to my attention. Here is the tale:

'It was during the reign of the last king of Arundel Haven, King Zebulon, in the latter end of his reign. He had married a beautiful fairy, Beulah. They had a daughter together, Hephzibah. She would succeed Arundel Haven when her father's time was done. King Zebulon was beloved of the fairies of Arundel Haven. He ruled with strength and wisdom, kindness, and love, trying—though unsuccessfully—to rule like David and Solomon kings of Israel, to be a ruler after God's own heart. He was also humble and did his best to rule and serve the best interests of his subjects.

'But his rule was done too soon. In the last days of Zebulon's reign, Shadowfire arrived from the north. He started afflicting the fairies that lived here. What business brought him here was unknown to us. He started capturing fairies and was devouring some and sacrificing some to Ashtaroth.'

'The pagan goddess,' Mordecai said grimly, 'Tracing back to Nimrod and his wife, Semiramis.'

Queen Cymbaline nodded. 'You are correct, Mordecai. The worship of their virgin goddess reached down even unto today. Most humans in one way, shape, form, or another, worship the virgin goddess, going by different names.'

'It is manifest even unto today,' Mordecai added.

'Sadly, yes,' Queen Cymbaline said, 'You have knowledge of the Scriptures?'

'I do, but I am no scholar, your majesty,' Mordecai answered, 'I am just a simple man who believes in the authority of the sacred manuscripts of Antioch which came Textus Receptus, the pure infallible Word of God. I do not claim to be wise by any one's standards.'

Queen Cymbaline smiled. 'That is good to hear. From time to time, Shadowfire would offer sacrifice to the virgin goddess and even the devil. When Shadowfire had attacked the village, to the horror of the king, he captured his queen Beulah. He wanted to fly after them, but his advisors restrained him. "The dragon will have you too if you try and rescue your queen," they said.

'"I cannot leave her to the mercy of the dragon," King Zebulon replied.

' " You are throwing your life away if you attempt to rescue her, your majesty," they told him.

'"I cannot abandon Beulah," he insisted.

'Eventually, he did attempt to rescue his Queen. He was so distraught without her that he could no longer stay. He gave the crown to his daughter, Princess Hephzibah, who was stricken with grief with what her father was essaying to do. "I have lost my mother," she said, "I do not want to lose you, too!"

' "What is my kingdom without my beloved Beulah?" King Zebulon replied, "My heart aches for your mother. It would be better that I would lose my life trying to rescue her than to continue like this!"

' "Father, please don't do this," Princess Hephzibah begged.

' "I must do this, even though it would mean my death," King Zebulon insisted adamantly, "Unless by perchance I come back, you are the new Queen of Arundel Haven. Rule as I have ruled, my daughter."

' "I can't let you go," Princess Hephzibah wept, "Why are you doing this? The dragon has already taken my mother. I don't want to lose you as well! Already the pain is too great for me to bear!"

' "You are queen now, my beloved Hephzibah," he proclaimed, adamant in his decision, "Promise me you will never attempt to rescue me! Promise me that under your rule you will never attempt a foolish affront against the dragon. Promise me!"

' "I promise," Princess Hephzibah replied tearfully.

'That night, King Zebulon, along with three of the bravest fairies in Arundel Haven, journeyed to the Mountains of Shadow. Only one returned to bear the tale of the death of the king and his queen. Sorrowful at heart, Hephzibah was crowned the Queen of Arundel Haven. She kept the promise that her father had made her keep before he had flown to the Mountains of Shadow.

'In the fourth year of her reign, the dragon attacked again. He started ravaging the village as was his custom. She had seen a young fairyman rescue a fairy child and her mother from the claws of the dragon during one of his attacks. He managed to escape the dragon and kept the victims out of his claws. She inquired of him after Shadowfire had attacked, and it was he who had discovered the name of the dragon. Queen Hephzibah asked his name. "My name is Japheth, your majesty," he said.

' "It was foolish of you to take on the dragon alone, Japheth," Queen Hephzibah told him.

' "Maybe so," Japheth replied, "but my sister Dinah and her daughter Jocasta are the only family I have left. I could not let them die by Shadowfire's claws."

' "Shadowfire?" Queen Hephzibah exclaimed.

'"He had told me his name while we had fought," Japheth replied, "I could not let him take my sister away! I would have sacrificed my life if it would allow them to live."

'"You are fortunate, Japheth," Queen Hephzibah said, "that it did not come to that."

'"I lost my wife, who was pregnant at the time, a year ago to that monster," Japheth replied grimly, "I could not let the same thing happen to my sister. She, too, has lost her husband to Shadowfire!"

'Japheth would later become Queen Hephzibah's chosen king. They had two daughters together, Princess Bethany, who would later succeed her mother, and the younger Princess Madelyne. For a time, Queen Hephzibah was happy. From time to time the dragon would attack again. When Princess Bethany was ten and Princess Madelyne eight, the dragon attacked. King Japheth was one of the ones taken, much to the grief of the Queen and her daughter. She went into a state of mourning. She wanted to join her king but was restrained by the promise she had made to her father. She felt helpless to do anything about it.

'It was when Bethany had turned sixteen when Queen Hephzibah was stricken with a fatal illness. She had dreams before she died and told it to her two daughters. "You shall be queen now in my stead, Bethany," Queen Hephzibah told her elder daughter, "The terror of Shadowfire shall not afflict us forever. I've had dreams that in the future, a human shall come to Arundel Haven and with a fairy maiden, God shall use them to bring about the death of Shadowfire."

' "A human?" Princess Madelyne exclaimed, "No human has ever seen Arundel Haven, nor should there be, given the wickedness of the humans."

' "Indeed, Madelyne," Queen Hephzibah replied, "but God has revealed this to me. I don't know when or how, but when the time is right, this human will come, not great among his people, but someone small in their eyes, for such God has pleasure to use, and a fairy maiden will be used to bring about the death of the dragon."

' "Why can't God bring about the end of the dragon by raising up someone mighty?" asked Princess Bethany, "Why a human?"

' "Because God resists the proud but gives grave unto the humble," Queen Hephzibah answered, "It may not come, even in your lifetime, dear Bethany, but when the time is right, they will come."

'Princess Bethany and her sister found it hard to believe, though Bethany had written these words down. She was grieved when the next day, Queen Hephzibah died. In sorrow, she became the new Queen. She reported the words of the prophecy to her ministers, though they did not believe it any more than she or Princess Madelyne did. It became known as the Prophecy of Queen Hephzibah, though many in that generation did not believe it at that time. It became nothing more than a rumor after that, though the record of it my brother, Prince Avondale, had found yesterday. I was skeptical at first, but God rebuked me and told me that it was from Him.'

'God had directed me to the book,' Prince Avondale continued, 'I carefully read the words and the story it had told of the tale that Queen Cymbaline has just told you. I now believe that you, Mordecai Jefferson, are the one spoken of in this prophecy.'

Mordecai bowed his head. 'How could it be? How could I be the one? I know the dreams seem to confirm it, yet I am afraid all the same.'

Queen Cymbaline bade Mordecai to approach her. He fell to his knees directly in front of the Fairy Queen. With a grave look, Queen Cymbaline took the young man's hands. 'God chooses to use those who are small and insignificant in the eyes of the world and uses them to work His will,' she softly said, 'I ask your forgiveness for the harsh way I had treated you upon your arrival here. Prince Avondale told me of Starla's daughter, Twila, who came to you in the dungeon; unafraid, trusting, how she took to you right away.'

Mordecai nodded. 'Twila is a precious little girl,' he said, 'I personally don't understand the kindness that has been shown to me, despite the incarceration.'

'I decree that you are to be released from prison as of now,' Queen Cymbaline proclaimed, 'This night, you will no longer be a prisoner, but you shall be a guest. I know now this is from God, that Raven coming to you was by His design, despite my decrees.'

Mordecai kissed the hand of the Queen, who smiled. 'I do not deserve such kindness from you, your majesty.'

Queen Cymbaline bade him to rise. She sighed. 'Although you are the one the prophecy speaks of, which I am now convinced of, I will not force you to do this. This decision, I will leave up to you.' She touched Mordecai's face. 'I can only ask and implore you.'

Mordecai stared into the eyes of the Fairy Queen. He felt somehow that in his heart she was right, and that he was the one the prophecy had spoken of. He was scared inside and unsure. He thought of Raven, and then his thoughts went to Twila, the toddler who took to him right away. After a pause, he said with fear in his voice, 'I… I agree. I am scared about it, but I will help you however I can.'

'I know you are scared, dear Mordecai,' Queen Cymbaline replied gently, 'Shadowfire knows somehow it is you, but not your name nor where you live. Raven was right all along, only I was too overprotective to see it.'

'I knew you were doing it to protect your people, my Queen,' Mordecai replied. Queen Cymbaline seemed to smile when he had proclaimed her his Queen. Tears welled up in his eyes. 'I wouldn't want anything to happen to Raven, to Starla, or to Twila.' Raven and Starla approached him. 'I don't know how God can use a nobody like me to bring down the dragon, but if God wants to use me as such, as frightened as I am, I am willing.'

Queen Cymbaline kissed him on the forehead. 'It all starts with a willing heart, Mordecai,' she told him, 'We should all take a lesson from Twila, who accepted you without question, without reservation. When the time comes, God will use you, just be obedient to Him.' To Raven she said, 'I owe you an apology as well, Raven. Indeed, it was the will of God to allow this human, precious in His eyes, to find you and to be brought here. I see that now. Such a union has never happened before, but if you wish to be bound with him, Raven, I give you my blessing.'

'As do I,' Prince Avondale nodded.

Mordecai rose and faced Starla. He kissed the sleeping Twila and caressed the toddler gently. 'With your leave, Starla,' Mordecai said, 'I wish to take your younger sister, Raven, to be my wife when the time comes.'

Starla nodded with tears in her eyes. 'Yes, Mordecai. I give you both my blessing as well!' She kissed Mordecai on the cheeks. 'I'm sorry I had misjudged you because you are human. You and Raven are right! There is good and bad in both fairies and humans.'

'Thank you, Starla,' he smiled, giving her a kiss on the cheeks. 'It means a lot to me and Raven.'

Raven embraced her sister. 'Thank you, Starla!' she replied. She then bowed before the Queen and said, 'Thank you, your majesty!'

Queen Cymbaline smiled. 'Thank you, Raven, for bringing Mordecai here.'

Mordecai was led by Taris to one of the guest rooms in the castle. Queen Cymbaline had clothes made for him of fine satin, in light and dark blue with solid gold trimmings. Mordecai accepted them gladly. He put away the black clothes he had worn on his arrival here. He looked out the window of his room as his thoughts went to his sister, Cece. He longed to see her again. In the back of his mind was the Prophecy of Queen Hephzibah, which he now understood that it was himself whom the long dead queen was referring to. But who was the fairy maiden that would aid him in bringing about the death of the dragon? That puzzled him. He began to wonder if it was Raven. How exactly would they bring about the end of Shadowfire? How then could they slay the wicked beast? More questions filled his mind. He heard a voice inside saying, *In due time, I will guide and direct you. The time is not ripe yet, but it will be very soon. Fear not, Mordecai Jefferson, I am with you and the one I have chosen. Just trust Me. Through you, I will use the both of you to bring about the fall of the dragon. I will guide and direct you both. Even when things are darkest, know that I have overcome the world, and I will bring you and those you love through this. I will deliver you.*

Mordecai fell to his knees. 'I know You can do all things, Lord,' he replied. 'I cannot help but feel small and insignificant.'

Yet I choose to use people who are small in the eyes of the great. My hand will be upon you, and you shall not be afraid. The hour is approaching and will come soon. Just trust and obey Me, be not fearful or doubting. I used those small and insignificant like Moses and Gideon, raised David who was a shepherd and made him king over my people in Israel. Just trust Me, follow, and obey Me, and I will be with you.

'Use me according to Your will, Lord,' Mordecai said humbly, 'Be it unto your unprofitable servant according to Your word.' He worshipped the Lord in his heart.

At that moment, Queen Cymbaline entered his chambers and found him on his knees. She knelt by him and took his hand. 'You are worried?' she asked.

'I am,' the young man nodded, 'Now that I know I am the one your foremother had foretold, but what about the fairy maiden? The Lord spoke to me and told me not to worry and that He would reveal it to me in due time.'

'Take a lesson from Twila,' Queen Cymbaline smiled, 'We all can. We are to have the faith of a child. He shall use you and direct you and this fairy maiden, whoever it may be, when the time comes.'

'I miss my sister, Cece,' Mordecai sighed, 'I am happy here in Arundel Haven, but I think of my sister, who has supported me as of late when it seems the world was against me and even my own parents did not support me.' He sighed. 'I also know if I returned, Dr. Von Braun will be more determined to find out about Arundel Haven than before, especially since I've been missing for three days now.'

'I trust you with our secret,' Queen Cymbaline said, 'The Lord had spoken to me also. For a time, you must return to your home. I will give you a gift before you are to return.'

'My heart is torn, my Queen,' he told her, 'I want to return home because I miss my sister, Cece, but I will miss Raven so. I know Cece will be worried sick about me.'

'I'm sure she is,' Queen Cymbaline said, 'Perhaps she can be told about what you have found.'

'But your secret I will keep it a secret,' Mordecai proclaimed, 'I do not want you, or any fairy, especially Raven and Twila, to come to harm. They've become a part of my life, as have you and Prince Avondale. As the Lord lives, I will keep a tight hold on the secret and keep it from people like Dr. Von Braun.'

'I know you will,' smiled Queen Cymbaline, 'We will speak more in the morning. I am sure Raven wants to see you before you retire. And Twila, I imagine.'

'Is Raven here?' Mordecai asked.

'I am here, my love,' came Raven's voice. He looked up and saw Raven in a sky-blue dress. Her wings seemed to sparkle as the light hit them. Mordecai rose to his feet and took Raven in his arms as they kissed. Raven stared into his eyes. 'You look beautiful, Raven,' he said.

'As do you, my Mordecai,' Raven smiled, 'The clothes look better on you than your other clothes do.'

'I tend to agree,' nodded Mordecai, I like these better than my old clothes.'

'More appropriate on you,' replied Queen Cymbaline, rising to her feet. 'I thought you would want to see each other before you retire for the night.'

Mordecai walked over to the queen, embraced her and kissed her on the cheeks. Queen Cymbaline said smiling, 'How dare you kiss the Queen.'

'A kiss of gratitude, my Queen,' he said, 'You've done so much for me, much better than I feel I deserve. Thank you.'

Queen Cymbaline smiled again. 'You are a very special young man, Mordecai. You have those here who love you as well, including the prince and myself. You have found favor in my eyes, as well as Raven and Starla.'

'And Twila,' Mordecai added, 'I would do anything to protect her, though she is not my flesh and blood.'

'At least not yet,' Raven replied, falling into his arms, and kissing him. Their lips touched again as they wrapped their arms around each other.

Queen Cymbaline slipped out of the room to leave them alone.

Raven then took his hand and led him out of the room and took him to a parapet on the side of the castle where the moon was rising. It was a new moon. Raven leaned her head upon his shoulders, looking at the stars as well as the moon. The wind was cold, but they regarded it not, being enraptured by the love they had for each other. There seemed to be a soft romantic piece of music playing as they came together and started to dance to the music they heard. Where it came from they weren't sure, but it drew them on like a leaf in a gentle breeze, dancing on the wind. Mordecai cradled Raven in his arms, their lips touching as they danced. They forgot about the world around them as their hearts were set on each other.

Raven belonged to Mordecai. Mordecai belonged to Raven.

A human and a fairy maiden, bound together in love. Brought together by God. Blessed with love.

God had brought them together, and no man or fairy would tear them asunder.

They looked forward to the day when they took the vows.

Chapter Eight

'**W**hat do you mean, you can't find him?' Dr. Von Braun asked his two men. They were in the office of the geneticist on the UCF campus. It was Monday afternoon, over four days since Mordecai had been taken by the fairies to Arundel Haven.

'Not even his sister, Cece, knows,' Seymour told the geneticist, 'He's gone missing.'

'He couldn't have just vanished off the face of the earth,' Dr. Von Braun snapped. 'You searched everywhere on campus?'

'Some students have been talking about his disappearance, having missed two school days in a row,' replied Wilfred, 'His sister has been upset. When we asked her, she would tell us nothing!'

'And her friends?'

'Got nothing from them either,' Seymour answered, 'They've been silent on the matter.'

Dr. Von Braun thought for a moment. He had a grim look upon his face. 'I wonder,' he said softly. 'I have a feeling… That has to be it.'

'What?'

'That fairy woman,' replied Dr. Von Braun, 'She must have taken Mordy to Arundel Haven with her. In fact, I'm sure of it!' He rose from his seat. 'I think it's time to find that little sister of his and show her we know of his little secret. I'm sure she would break.'

'You think so?' Wilfred asked.

'If they are as close as I think they are,' Dr. Von Braun said, 'she will tell us for sure if this is so. I am certain he is in Arundel Haven.'

'What if Mordy Jefferson never comes back?' Seymour asked.

'Let me worry about that,' Dr. Von Braun said, grabbing the vanilla envelope that had the pictures of Mordecai and Raven together. He pushed a button on his cell phone. 'Hello, Sylvia? This is Dr. Von Braun. Have Dr. Thomas take over my classes for the rest of the day. I have something important I need to take care of. Thank you.' He hung up the phone and placed it in his pocket. He led the way as he left the office, followed by Seymour and Wilfred.

Cece sat down with Tiffany and Sharon, thinking about her brother, not knowing what was happening to him. It was now lunchtime. All she had was a can of soda. She had not eaten much for days ever since Mordecai had been taken away by the fairies. Even her parents were worried about where he was. However, Cece did not tell her parents it was fairies who had taken him, nor did she feel they would have believed her. She wept when she thought about him.

'I still can't believe all that had happened Thursday night,' Tiffany said, 'I still can't believe there are fairies. Do you think Raven had something to do with all this?'

'I have a feeling Raven wasn't at fault,' Sharon replied. 'Who were her friends? They seemed angry with her about something.'

'I caught their names: Lavender and Laurelin,' replied Cece amid her tears, 'How could they do that to my brother? Why did they take him away like that? Mordy never meant Raven any harm! He loves her! I don't understand why they would do this to him!'

Tiffany and Sharon shook their heads. 'I still can't believe all that happened that night,' Sharon said, 'It all seems so surreal!'

'The question is, is he gone for good, or will he come back?' asked Tiffany softly.

'How could Raven allow this to happen to my brother?' wept Cece, 'I trusted her! I believed she honestly loved Mordy! How could she allow them to take my brother? I don't understand!'

'Hold on, Cece,' Sharon exclaimed, 'It's not Raven's fault! She never intended for all that to happen! She really loves your brother. It was her friends, Lavender and Laurelin, who had led those other fairies here to take Mordecai away. I trust Raven.'

'So do I,' Tiffany proclaimed, 'I feel convinced now. I remember Raven had tried to talk her friends into not taking him. They seemed really upset with Raven. We have to believe we will see Mordy again!'

'I hope you're right,' Cece wept as tears continued to flow from her eyes. 'I miss him so much!'

'Cece, you need to eat something,' Sharon insisted, 'You need to keep your strength up for one. It won't do you any good if you don't at least eat something.'

'I can't help it,' Cece said sadly. 'I just don't feel like eating. I would feel a lot better if I knew my brother was okay. I am so worried about him.'

'Please eat a little something,' Tiffany begged softly, 'Sharon and I would feel better if you had at least a sandwich or something to eat.'

'I don't know if I can,' sighed Cece, 'I can't help but think about him.'

'I know, Cece,' replied Sharon, 'but you're not doing yourself or Mordy any good by refusing to eat. I know you're upset, but eventually your body's going to give out without something to eat.'

Cece only sighed.

Tiffany caught a glimpse of Dr. Von Braun, who was searching for Mordecai.. She gasped. She turned to Sharon and said, 'Looks like we've got some unwanted company, and it's not Hatfield, Jones, or McCoy.'

'What are you talking about?' Sharon asked, She then looked up and saw the reason. 'Judas Priest, not him! Not now! What the heck is he doing here? I declare, that jege needs to find a better hobby. Searching for fairies is not a good hobby at all.'

'What's going on?' Cece asked.

'Come on, Cece,' Sharon said as she and Tiffany rose to their feet. 'It's Mr. I'm-So-Obsessed-With-Finding-Fairies!'

'Von Braun?' Cece exclaimed as she wiped her tears away, 'I am so not in the mood to deal with him! Why doesn't he leave us alone? I lost my brother, for crying out loud! Hasn't he got something better to do?'

'Your brother is still alive, Cece,' Sharon told her, 'I'm sure they wouldn't kill him or anything like that. We have to believe he's still alive and that we will see him again. We have to believe the best.'

'We've got to get out of here before that nutcase Von Braun spots us,' Tiffany said.

They managed to make it to the side door before Dr. Von Braun could see them. Cece stumbled as they made it out the door. She was feeling lightheaded from not eating much in the past four days, ever since Mordecai had been taken to Arundel Haven. She was feeling the effects of lack of food. She sat down, weeping. 'Come on, Cece,' Sharon told her, 'We can't stop! You don't want Von Braun to find us and keep asking us about Mordy and Raven. We can't let him know about her!'

'I'm sorry, guys,' Cece wept, 'I just feel so weak. I just can't go on any further.'

'We can take you to the nurse's office,' Sharon suggested as she and Tiffany helped her up. 'I knew you should have eaten something while you could. This is not good for you to go without cating.'

They managed to reach the nurse's office, though Cece stumbled and fell to the floor a couple of times. When they reached the office, the nurse led her to the examining table and had her sit down. Cece could not sit up, so she laid down. 'She hasn't really eaten much in four days,' Tiffany told the nurse. 'She is so worried about her missing brother, who disappeared four days ago.'

'Missing?' the nurse exclaimed.

Cece wept.

'Do you need me to call your parents?' the nurse asked Cece.

Cece shook her head.

'Cece, you need to eat something,' Sharon said sternly. 'That's why your body is so weak. You're not helping yourself when you're worrying yourself to death. You need to keep up your strength.'

'I know,' wept Cece.

The nurse convinced Cece to eat two chicken sandwiches she had and gave her a soda to drink. Cece forced herself to eat the sandwiches. 'I will keep her here for at least one period,' the nurse told Cece's friends, 'I will contact her teacher and tell her the situation.'

'Are you sure you don't need to go home?' Tiffany asked. 'You're obviously not feeling too well. I think you do need to call your parents.'

'No, I'll be fine,' Cece insisted. 'I just need to lay down for a bit.

Perhaps the sandwiches will help me.'

'I hope so,' sighed Sharon, 'We're both worried about you. If you need to go home, I think you should call your parents.'

'No, I'll be fine,' reiterated Cece, 'I'm not going home.'

Both Tiffany and Sharon shook their heads. They did not want Cece to remain in school in the condition she was in, especially with Dr. Von Braun on campus, whom they were sure was going to seek them and interrogate them. They hoped the geneticist did not see them go into the nurse's office.

But the hope was all in vain. At that moment, Dr. Von Braun appeared through the door. Tiffany and Sharon groaned. Cece turned her head. 'How is the child?' he asked the nurse.

'She hasn't really eaten in four days,' the nurse answered. 'Her friends say that she is worried about her missing brother.'

'Is that so?' replied Dr. Von Braun, 'Would it all right if I speak to them alone? It is very important.'

'I suppose that would be all right, Dr. Von Braun,' the nurse answered. She walked out of the room and closed the door. Dr. Von Braun stared at Cece. 'Look, Doctor,' said Tiffany sternly, 'This is neither the time nor the place for your foolishness! Cece's brother has gone missing, and she doesn't know where he is.'

'So I have come to understand,' replied Dr. Von Braun, 'You know the reason why he is missing, do you not? And you also know where he had been taken and know who has taken him away!'

'Please leave me alone,' wept Cece.

'Not before you answer some of my questions,' insisted Dr. Von Braun sternly, 'You know the circumstances of your brother's disappearance, don't you? Do not lie to me, either! I want the truth!'

'What do you mean?' Sharon asked.

'He was taken by fairies, wasn't he?' replied Dr. Von Braun.

'What, are you crazy?' Tiffany exclaimed, 'What makes you think fairies took Cece's brother?'

'This,' replied Dr. Von Braun, pulling out the vanilla envelope containing photos of Mordecai and Raven together. Cece, against her will, grabbed the photos and glanced at them. She gasped when she saw them. Tiffany and Sharon then glimpsed at the photos. 'These are photos of your brother with a black fairy maiden,' proclimed Dr. Von Braun, 'taken last week, three days before his disappearance. It is clear to me that Mordy, your brother, is in a relationship with this fairy. Now, who is she? Do you know anything about her?'

Cece shook her head. 'This can't be Mordy,' she said simply, 'and she can't be a fairy.'

'I disagree, Miss Jefferson,' replied Dr. Von Braun, 'I surmise there were some fairies who did not approve of her relationship with a human and consequently had taken him away to be punished.'

'That's ridiculous,' laughed Tiffany.

'Do not deny or hide anything from me,' snapped Dr. Von Braun, 'Two of my men had followed Mordy Jefferson to the woods and took these photographs. Do you deny that this is your brother?'

Cece sighed. 'I do not deny it,' she answered tearfully.

'What do you know about this fairy?' asked Dr. Von Braun.

'Come on,' Sharon retorted,. 'How can you be sure that is a fairy?'

'Do not assume to play games with me,' replied Dr. Von Braun sharply, 'She is the key to Mordy's disappearance, is she not? His relationship with this fairy is the cause! Or maybe she had betrayed him somehow and set him up to be captured, perhaps?'

'No,' wept Cece. 'It can't be!'

'Oh, so you believe this fairy had betrayed your brother somehow? She was the cause of his disappearance, is that not so? She's to blame for why your brother is not here. He has been taken to Arundel Haven, their home.'

'Stop it!' shot back Sharon. 'It was never Raven's intention for him to be taken away! She defended him when—'

'Sharon, no!' Cece cried.

Dr. Von Braun smiled. 'Raven?' he repeated, 'The fairy in question's name is Raven. What do you know about this Raven?'

'Tell them nothing more,' Cece told her friends.

'Which direction did they fly when he was taken?' Dr. Von Braun asked, 'How many fairies were there?'

'Don't answer him,' cried Cece.

'Then you tell me, Miss Jefferson,' demanded Dr. Von Braun, 'After all, they took your brother, did they not? Raven betrayed your brother to her people. Or perhaps they were angry because Raven gave her heart and love to your brother. Which is the case, Miss Jefferson? Tell me now.'

'Raven would never betray my brother,' shot back Cece, 'She honestly loved Mordecai! I know she wasn't at fault that he was taken! She couldn't have been! Raven wasn't at fault for all this!'

'But what did she do to hinder your brother's capture?'

'That's not right for you to say,' snapped Sharon, 'She was outnumbered five to one. What could she do to hinder them?'

'Sharon!' cried Cece.

Sharon gasped. 'I'm sorry,' she cried, placing her hands over her mouth, 'I didn't mean to—'

'Five more fairies?' mused Dr. Von Braun.

'I'm so sorry, Cece,' Sharon quietly said.

Dr. Von Braun nodded his head. 'Very interesting. So your brother was taken away by five fairies not counting Raven?'

Cece nodded amid her tears. 'Please go away,' she wept. 'Don't ask us anything more! I miss my brother so much!'

'Please leave her be, Dr. Von Braun,' cried Tiffany. 'She's already in enough pain as it is! Have mercy on her, for crying out loud!'

Dr. Von Braun gathered up the photos and turned to go. 'Very well,' he said, 'but only because I have no more questions at this time. I will be in touch at another time.' Without another word, he left the room.

Cece stared at Sharon with tears in her eyes. 'I'm sorry, Cece,' Sharon said. 'I-I… I'm sorry for telling him!'

'Why did you tell him?' Cece wept, 'Raven trusted us with her secret!'

'It-it was like… it was like I couldn't keep from telling him,' Sharon replied regretfully, 'It just… it just came out of me.'

Cece wept on the bed as the nurse came back in the room. 'What happened?'

None of the girls would tell of the matter. The nurse turned toward Tiffany and Sharon and said, 'You two better head to your next class before you are late. I will take care of your friend for the time being. I need to tell her teacher that she is here with me, and I will keep her here during the last period if I deem it necessary. Go, before you are late.'

'I'll be okay, guys,' sighed Cece, wiping the tears from her face.

Tiffany and Sharon nodded as they headed to their respective classes. Cece laid there staring at the ceiling, wondering where her brother Mordecai was. She hoped and prayed he was okay. 'I miss you, Mordecai,' she wept. 'Please come back home!'

Raven led Mordecai to her cottage, where she had been living since the day she was born. She never moved out of the cottage but remained there even after her parents had been slain by Shadowfire.

'This is where I live,' Raven said. 'It's not like the home you live in, no electricity, no things that you humans have, but it is home.'

Mordecai looked around. He wasn't used to being in a place with no electricity, television, refrigerator, or any human necessities that his family had, but it was cozy and comfortable. 'I've lived here all my life,' Raven said, 'I never moved out, especially after what happened to my parents. One day, this will be your home as well here in Arundel Haven when our time comes to be wed.'

'It's a nice place, Raven,' Mordecai nodded, 'I know it must get pretty lonely here.'

'I do have Starla, Twila, Lavender, and Laurelin who come around and visit,' replied Raven, 'but what was missing, I have now found.'

Mordecai smiled. He caressed Raven's face and stared deep into her brown eyes. Raven did the same, touching his face, staring into his blue eyes. She smiled. 'I really missed you, my love,' she said.

'I really missed you too, Raven,' Mordecai replied smiling. Their lips met as their arms wrapped around each other. Their lips separated and came together again.

When they separated again, Mordecai said, 'Your place is nice, Raven.'

'I am glad you like it,' Raven smiled, 'We better head to my sister's place before it starts raining. I don't really like to get wet.'

'I know what you mean,' the young man nodded, 'I hate to ride in the rain, but in the past, until Tiffany invited me to ride with her, I had to. I did not want to ride the bus to school.'

'A bus?' asked Raven.

'Another human vehicle, like a car, but bigger and seats a lot of humans. I was picked on and bullied on the bus, too, by some other students besides the bullies I told you about.'

'Why weren't they stopped?' asked Raven.

'I don't know,' sighed Mordecai, 'The bus monitors would not do anything about it for some reason. Since they refused to, I made the decision to start riding my bike to school. I was tired of being picked on and bullied.'

'That should not have happened to you,' replied Raven as they walked out the door. 'Are they really that bad?'

'They are much worse than that,' answered Mordecai, 'capable of much worse things. But let us not talk about it. Let's talk about happier things, like us.'

'Yes,' nodded Raven, taking his hand. 'About us.'

It took them about a half hour to walk from Raven's cottage to the farm where Starla and her husband lived. In the fields, a muscular black fairyman close to thirty years old was out in the fields. He wore black slacks and a white shirt, which was covered in dirt and a little sweat. His sweater was hanging on the fence since he was getting hot from working. He was about six-four, 250 pounds, had long black hair, brown eyes. When he saw Raven and Mordecai approaching, he embedded his hoe into the ground, took to the air, and flew toward them, landing in front of them. 'Hello, Raven,' he said.

'Hello, Roosevelt,' Raven greeted him.

Roosevelt stared at Mordecai. 'And this must be Mordecai,' he smiled, shaking his hand. 'Welcome to Arundel Haven. Welcome to my home.'

'Thank you,' said Mordecai.

'Starla tells me my daughter has become quite attached to you.' He smiled. 'She kind of taught a lesson to the Queen and Prince, as well as to my wife. I've always believed there are some good humans in the world. I am happy to meet you.'

'Thank you,' said Mordecai. 'Twila is a very special little girl.

I'm sure you must be proud of her.'

'Yes, I am,' Roosevelt nodded, 'Very proud of her. Starla and Twila are in the house. Lunch should be ready soon.'

At that moment, they heard the Twila's voice cry out, 'Morcai, Morcai!' The toddler flew into the arms of Mordecai and kissed him on the cheeks.

He kissed her on the cheeks in return. 'I am happy to see you too, little Twila!' he said.

Twila then flew to her father and kissed him. 'Hi, Daddy!'

Roosevelt smiled. 'Mommy getting lunch ready?'

'Yes, Daddy,' Twila answered, flying into Mordecai's arms.

Raven smiled. 'We are heading to the house right now,' she said, 'I'm going to see if Starla needs any help with lunch. Mordecai can look after Twila for the time being.'

'I would be more than happy to look after her,' said Mordecai.

Twila leaned her head upon his shoulder.

Roosevelt smiled.

'I am glad Queen Cymbaline let you out of prison,' Starla said as they ate a little while later. 'I know Raven and Starla are glad, too.'

Mordecai nodded. 'So am I,' he said, 'Not the best place in the world to be for sure, but Taris has been kind to me. I still remember how Twila had slipped inside my cell, but I didn't see her until I felt the air from her flittering wings.'

'Why did Queen Cymbaline decide to let you go?' Roosevelt asked.

'I'm sure Twila had a small part of it,' answered Mordecai, 'but mainly on account of the Prophecy of Queen Hephzibah. I know now I am the one the prophecy spoke of in bringing down the dragon once and for all, but the fairy maiden I am not sure of. I am still scared about it.'

'Queen Cymbaline told us the tale yesterday,' Starla said, 'Mordecai agreed, but I could tell he was nervous about it.'

'I am no great person by any means, not even in the eyes of my people,' continued Mordecai, 'but I know God has chosen to use me when the time comes, but how, I am unsure. I could not say no since I met Twila. The dragon had been terrorizing your people for far too long.'

'I can imagine you were scared,' Roosevelt said.

'Very scared.' Mordecai nodded, 'I guess the future can be scary. I'm worrying about how the end of Shadowfire may be achieved, who is the fairy maiden is, things like that. I don't have any answers. I knew of Shadowfire even before I met Raven. He appeared for seven consecutive nights in my dreams and spoke of the prophecy, which at the time I did not know about. I had told the dreams to my sister.'

'What did he know about you?' asked Roosevelt.

'Only that I was the human spoken of in the prophecy,' answered the young man, 'He demanded to know my name, but I did not tell him who I was or where I lived. He did not reveal his name to me, but somehow knew I had contact with Raven, after Raven and I first met. It was just after one of the dreams that a name came to my mind: Shadowfire. I told it to Raven after she mentioned that she and Twila had been chased by the dragon, but God delivered them out of his claws. She confirmed to me that Shadowfire was indeed his name. He must have found out about me using the black arts, but I think God forbade the devils behind the magic from revealing my name or where I lived to the beast.'

Twila flew toward Mordecai and landed on his lap. The young human laughed as he kissed the toddler on the cheeks. 'You are something else, Twila,' he smiled.

'It's amazing how much Twila is taken with you, Mordecai,' Raven said, 'It's still hard to believe.'

'I know,' Starla interjected. 'I'm glad Twila did fly off to Mordecai.' To Mordecai she asked, 'Do you have any nephews and nieces?'

'Not at the moment.' Mordecai shook his head, 'My older brother, Randall, is still single and as far as I know is not dating anybody. My sister Cece is fifteen and still in high school like me.' He sighed. 'I miss her.'

'How close are you to her?' Roosevelt asked.

'For the past few weeks, we've become very close,' Mordecai amswered. 'Before then, we were typical brother and sister, fighting, not getting along, getting into arguments. As of late, before Raven came into my life, she started taking time to listen to me and supporting me. She thought because she is getting preferential treatment compared to me, being taught how to drive a car—I know you won't understand that. It's like a horseless carriage, but Raven has seen them—that I would hold it against her and hate her. I told her it was not. I love my sister and miss her, and I know she is worried sick about me.'

'She accepted me even after I had revealed to her that I was a fairy,' Raven continued, 'Mordecai was against it at first, concerned about the secret being exposed, almost like Queen Cymbaline was, but I felt in my heart I could trust her.'

'You are the first human to ever behold our home of Arundel Haven,' Starla said quietly, 'In so short of a time, you have earned the favor of Queen Cymbaline.'

'Would she have accepted me if I wasn't the one the Prophecy of Queen Hephzibah had spoken of?' Mordecai asked.

'I think so,' Starla answered, 'Twila had accepted you right away.'

Mordecai stared at Twila with a smile. He gently kissed the forehead of the fairy toddler. 'Twila love you, Morcai,' the toddler said.

'Morcai love Twila too, sweetie,' smiled Mordecai.

'Morcai stay here?' Twila asked, smiling sweetly with wide eyes.

Mordecai sighed. 'I would love to,' he said, 'to see you, play with you, but I have a sister who loves me too and is worried about me. I won't stay away, Twila. You will still see me.'

'Twila want Morcai to stay,' Twila said.

Raven and Starla smiled. 'As do I,' Mordecai nodded, 'I don't want to leave you or your aunt Raven.'

'Twila want Uncle Morcai stay,' she said, hugging his neck.

Mordecai held the young toddler. 'I will have to go away soon, Twila,' he said, 'but I will be back.'

'Promise, Uncle Morcai?' Twila asked, looking into his eyes.

Raven smiled when she heard what Twila called Mordecai.

'I promise, Twila,' smiled Mordecai.

'He will, sweetie,' replied Starla. 'He won't stay away from here.

He has Raven here who also loves him very much.'

After they had eaten, Mordecai, Raven, Twila, and Starla were outside while Roosevelt returned out into the fields to continue to work. Twila flew around. 'Stay close to Mommy, Twila,' called Starla.

'She may be close to taking a nap,' Raven said, 'Somehow, I

can feel it. How far along are you in your pregnancy?'

'Close to three months now,' Starla answered, 'Roosevelt was overjoyed when he heard the news.'

'Wow, I didn't know that Starla,' Mordecai said, surprised. 'Congratulations.'

'Thank you, Mordecai,' replied Starla, 'Twila is looking forward to having a brother or a sister. I'm sure you two will give her a cousin when the time comes?'

'Yes,' Raven answered, 'We do plan to. I know this has never happened before between a fairy and a human, but the child will have both parents who love them and love each other.'

'The most important thing,' Starla said, 'in any relationship.'

Twila flew into Mordecai's arms yawning. Mordecai laughed softly, knowing the toddler was getting tired. He allowed Twila to get comfortable and cradled her in his arms. 'At least this is practice for when you and Raven have one of your own,' Starla said.

Mordecai smiled. 'True,' he smiled, kissing the toddler, 'I'm still amazed how quickly she's become close to me in such a short time.' He rocked Twila gently as she yawned again and closed her eyes. 'Sweet dreams, little Twila,' he said softly.

Starla and Raven joined him. Raven kissed Twila and then Mordecai. It didn't take long for Twila to fall asleep. When she was fast asleep, Mordecai smiled. 'You are a blessed child and a blessing, Twila,' he said softly. 'A blessing to your parents who love you very much.'

Dark clouds began to gather up above. Raven smelled the air. 'It's rain, all right,' she said, 'No scent of the dragon in the air, thankfully. I remember when I was having a picnic with Lavender, Laurelin, and Twila at Rosemont Meadows when the dragon attacked. Before he attacked, there was a hot breeze, a foul reek of smoke and a foul stench. We heard a boom and knew the dragon was about to attack.'

'I am so thankful you got away, Raven,' Mordecai said, 'both you and Twila.'

'So am I,' Raven replied.

Two fairymen in the clothing of the palace guards arrived at the farm. They held their spears on their shoulders. One of them flittered toward Mordecai and said, 'Queen Cymbaline has summoned you, Mordecai Jefferson. She is waiting for you by the falls of the Silverstreams. We will take you to her.'

'Is all well?' Mordecai asked.

'It is well,' the second answered, 'She requires your presence immediately.'

'I wish to come,' Raven said.

'I'm afraid she requires Mordecai's presence only, Raven,' the first guard replied, 'but you may come if you wish.'

'I will come too,' Starla said, 'if that's okay.'

'We will carry you, Mordecai,' the first guard stated, 'It will be quicker.'

Mordecai nodded as they picked him up. Raven and Starla flew after them, following them to the falls of the Silverstreams.

Frank, Stu, and Chuck were becoming frustrated. They had been searching for Mordecai ever since Friday when he didn't appear in school. They had inquired of Cece, but she would only weep and turn away. 'Three school days, and still we haven't found that jege,' Stu said, 'Is he even in school?'

'He better be,' Frank frowned, 'It's been a long three days without any fun with him!'

'I hate going through days without our favorite victim,' Chuck said, 'Sure, there are other kids we can pick on, but it's not the same if it's not Jefferson.'

'Where could he be, anyway?' Stu asked, 'His sister says she is missing. Could she be right?'

Not another word was spoken as they searched for another kid they could pick on.

Cece was still in the nurse's office lying down on the bed, her eyes closed but tears still flowed from her eyes. As she rested, she felt a gentle comforting touch inside. She then found herself within a place she didn't recognize. She saw fairies of different ages and different skin colors, walking and flying through the town. She walked through, not being regarded by the fairies around her. She looked around awestruck at her surroundings, at what she had beheld.

Before her, she found a fairy woman in royal apparel of scarlet, purple and gold with a golden crown upon her head. She looked up at the fairy woman. 'Queen Cymbaline?' she managed to say.

'You miss your brother, Mordecai, Cece,' Queen Cymbaline said gently, 'I can tell. Mordecai had made mention of you to me. I see Raven had made mention of me to you.'

'Yes,' nodded Cece, 'It hurts not knowing if he is okay, how he is.'

'Do not fear, Cece Jefferson,' said Queen Cymbaline, 'Mordecai shall return to you very shortly. I am sending him back to you before he is needed. He will tell you the full tale upon his return.'

'When will he return?' asked Cece.

'Sooner than you expect,' answered Queen Cymbaline, 'Be comforted. He has now found favor in my eyes. Raven had chosen well when she found Mordecai.'

'Is this Arundel Haven?' Cece asked.

'You, too, shall behold Arundel Haven soon enough,' Queen Cymbaline smiled.

At that moment, Cece woke up. It was nearly time for school to end. 'It was only a dream,' she sighed, 'It seemed so real.' She felt a gentle touch in her spirit. 'Mordecai is okay,' she said softly. She wept anew. 'Mordecai is okay!'

The nurse appeared to check on her. When she saw she was awake, she asked, 'Feeling any better, Miss Jefferson?'

'A little bit,' Cece answered, 'The rest and the sandwiches seemed to help a lot. I still feel a little weak, but better than I did before.'

'You shouldn't go without eating for so long like that,' the nurse told her, 'I know you're worried about your missing brother, but you're not helping yourself when you don't eat anything.'

Cece nodded her head. 'How long did I sleep?' she asked.

'Close to the end of the school day,' the nurse answered, 'I already told your teachers where you were. They were concerned about you. You need to eat something when you go home.'

Cece nodded, wiping the tears from her eyes. 'I'll be okay, thank you.'

When the school bell rang for the end of the school day, Cece grabbed her books and waited for her friends to arrive. Minutes later, Sharon and Tiffany appeared. 'How are you feeling, Cece?' Tiffany asked.

'A little better,' Cece answered, 'A little better than before.'

'Remember to eat when you get home, Miss Jefferson,' the nurse told her, 'We don't want the same thing to happen to you again.'

Cece nodded. They walked out of the nurse's office and headed in the direction of the students' parking lot. When they were in the clear, Cece turned to her friends and said, 'He's okay. My brother is okay.'

'What makes you think that?' Tiffany asked.

'I had a dream,' Cece told them, 'I think I was in Arundel Haven because I could see fairies all around me as I walked. The next thing I knew, I was met by Queen Cymbaline.'

'Whoa, must have been some dream,' Sharon said, astounded.

'She told me she was going to send Mordy home very soon,' Cece continued, 'and told me he would explain when he returned. When I woke up, I felt a touch inside of me letting me know that my brother was okay and would be returning home soon.'

'How can you be sure?' Tiffany asked.

'I have that feeling,' insisted Cece, 'Somehow, I know now my brother is all right.'

'I hope you're right, Cece,' Sharon said, 'I honestly hope you're right.'

Mordecai was brought to a place where water flowed like a waterfall into the river, which was the beginning of the Silverstreams. The rain had started to fall when they had arrived, a light rain filling the area with the scent of rain. Mordecai looked up as he was placed down on the ground. There was a wall of solid rock running many miles, across that were the beginning of the borders of Arundel Haven. It stood just over 2,000 meters high. There was an opening where the waters poured from underground about two-thirds of the way up.

Queen Cymbaline awaited underneath a large tree as he bowed before her. Raven and Starla arrived as well, Twila sleeping in her mother's arms. They took shelter underneath another tree, which kept the rain off them. 'Thank goodness it's not raining too hard,' Starla said.

Queen Cymbaline dismissed the guards as she saw Raven and Starla huddle under a tree for protection from the rain. 'The beginning of the Silverstreams,' Raven said, 'I have never seen anything so beautiful.'

'The handiwork of God,' Mordecai replied softly, 'I am amazed by how wonderful He fashioned the Earth and all that is within it.'

'Is there a reason you brought Mordecai here, your majesty?' Starla asked.

'I originally asked for Mordecai to come, because this is his moment,' answered Queen Cymbaline, 'but since you are here, you will see the surprise. You must trust me in this, Mordecai. This gift is not given lightly nor has any human ever been given this before. To find out, you must do what I say.'

'I am listening,' Mordecai said.

'Inside the cave behind the waterfall, there is a loincloth upon a large stone,' Queen Cymbaline explained, 'It is required that you remove your clothes and put the loincloth on so you won't feel completely uncomfortable. Do you trust me?'

Mordecai took a deep breath. 'I do.'

'I know it sounds crazy, but you will see the end result when all is done.'

Mordecai headed into the cave and did what Queen Cymbaline had instructed him. While he changed, Raven and Starla heard Twila yawning, stirring but remaining sleep. Raven looked at Twila. 'How long do you think Twila will remain asleep?' she asked her sister.

'Hard to say,' Starla answered, 'Perhaps another thirty minutes, an hour. No telling with Twila.'

'Is she being kept dry?' Raven asked.

'So far, so good,' answered Starla, 'I feel some drops now and then but Twila is okay. She's still dry.'

'Wonder what Queen Cymbaline has in mind for Mordecai?' Raven asked.

'I don't know,' replied Starla, 'but I trust that it is good, whatever it is.'

'I trust our queen,' Raven said, 'I believe she wouldn't have Mordecai harmed in any way.'

After a minute, they heard Mordecai's voice. 'I am done, your majesty,' he shouted, 'Now what?'

'Head directly inside the waterfall, and let the streams pour over your body,' Queen Cymbaline answered, 'The water is very cold, but you must remain until I say it is time. Trust me on this.'

Taking a deep breath, Mordecai made his way into the flowing waters. He pulled back when he felt how cold it was. 'You're not kidding when you said it is cold,' he said.

'Do not give up, Mordecai,' replied Queen Cymbaline in a soothing voice, 'Take your time. Sometimes it takes courage and faith to do what you must do. When all is done, it will help you in your fight against the dragon.'

Mordecai took another deep breath. He tried again, but immediately pulled back again. He felt the water with his hand and pulled back again. He thought about the words Queen Cymbaline had spoken. *She must have a good reason for wanting me to do this, he thought, I trust you, my Queen. I will trust you on this.*

He forced himself full force into the waterfall, crying out from the freezing cold of the water. His senses screamed out to leave, but he held on. He took deep breaths as a result of the coldness of the cascading streams that poured all around his body. He felt like he was going to be frozen into a block of ice.

'Not yet,' Queen Cymbaline said. Mordecai felt the pain of the cold all over his body and felt his blood growing colder. Still, he held on. Queen Cymbaline would not tell him to do this for no reason at all. He knew there must be a reason for having him do what she had told him.

At that moment, he felt a warm feeling starting to surround his body. The water remained as cold as ever, but his body was beginning to feel warmer and warmer as if the temperature of the water had changed. Mordecai figured somehow his body was becoming used to the cold temperature of the water.

All of a sudden, he could not feel the ground underneath his feet. He looked down but saw only water. He could not see the ground or feel it. *What is going on? What is happening?* He didn't know what to think. All he could see was the rushing water all around him and nothing else. For a long minute, he remained as such, not knowing what was going on.

After another minute he heard Queen Cymbaline's voice again. 'Come out, Mordecai.'

He came out, but he was suspended in the air, about close to two hundred meters off the ground. He stared in shock. *Am I floating in the air?* He felt the wind blow and the rain falling gently on his body. He was too awestruck to worry about his appearance, at least not at the moment.

Raven flew toward Mordecai, equally as amazed, and took his hand. She giggled when she saw him only in a loincloth. 'I look ridiculous,' she heard Mordecai say.

Raven stared at Mordecai and then at Queen Cymbaline. She then took his hand and guided him around the area where Starla and Queen Cymbaline were standing. Mordecai had a shocked look on his face. *I'm flying? I'm actually flying?*

'Mordecai, you're flying!' Raven exclaimed.

Raven let go of Mordecai's hand as the young man circled around in the air. He concentrated and managed to learn to control where he flew. He then flew back into the cave and changed clothes.

Raven stared at Queen Cymbaline and bowed in gratitude. 'This is beyond my hopes,' she said to her, 'I could tell Mordecai is grateful for what you've done for him.'

'It is a gift given out of love,' replied Queen Cymbaline, 'and it will be much needed when the time comes. Indeed, he is a special young man, a very special human. You are blessed to have such a love, Raven.' Mordecai stepped out clothed again, his hair still wet. He stared at Queen Cymbaline in amazement. 'I was flying?' he said.

'Yes,' answered Queen Cymbaline. 'This is my gift to you.'

'I am unworthy of such a gift from a wonderful queen,' he replied, bowing before her, 'How long does it last?'

'It is permanent,' answered the Fairy Queen. 'It will last as long as you live.' Mordecai bowed before her, humbled by how much grace she had shown to him. Queen Cymbaline knelt with him and gently said, 'Do not bow to me, dear Mordecai. I am merely your fellow servant and a sister.'

'I don't deserve your loving kindness, my Queen,' he replied humbly.

'It is a gift given out of love,' Queen Cymbaline smiled, 'Now you can fly as fast and as well as any fairy in Arundel Haven. It was to be given to you before you battle the dragon, as well as the fairy maiden.'

'But who is the fairy maiden who will help me?' asked Mordecai.

'In time, she will be revealed,' Queen Cymbaline said, 'For now, the time is nigh for when you must return to your home. The dragon must not know who you are and that you are here at Arundel Haven. Let us return to the castle for now. There will be a feast before your departure.'

At that moment, Twila woke up. She yawned and opened her eyes. She looked up and asked Starla, 'Where's Uncle Morcai, Mommy?' she asked.

Starla laughed. *Your aunt Raven hasn't married Mordecai yet and already you're calling him uncle.* She kissed her daughter. 'He is here, Twila,' she answered.

Queen Cymbaline and Raven took to the air. Twila saw Mordecai as he, too, took to the air. Twila squealed in delight and flew toward Mordecai. 'Morcai fly, Morcai fly!' she cried in excitement.

Mordecai smiled. 'Yes, I can fly now,' he laughed, joining Raven, who took his hand. Starla joined them as well. They flew back to Arundel Haven and the castle. Mordecai was still amazed that now he now had the ability to fly, without an airplane, without wings. *Was it something in the water that gave me the ability to fly?* His thoughts quickly dwelt on his sister, Cece, whom he missed very much. He wondered how she was doing. *I will be home soon, dear Cece, your brother will be home soon.*

The rain had stopped by the time they arrived at the village area. Lavender and Laurelin caught a glimpse of the party. Their jaws opened in disbelief when they saw Mordecai flying with the Queen, Raven, and Starla. Twila was flying close to Mordecai. They shook their heads in disbelief. 'How can… Why is….' Lavender tried to finish her sentence but could not.

'Why is the human flying? This can't be,' Laurelin exclaimed.

'Isn't he supposed to be in the dungeon?' Lavender asked, 'He was the last time we saw him. Now he's flying like he is a fairyman.'

Laurelin flew toward them. Lavender followed her friend. They flew up to Raven as they entered the castle. 'What's going on here?' Lavender asked.

'Mordecai has been set free,' Raven told them.

'But why? Why is he flying?' asked Lavender, 'How can he be flying?'

Queen Cymbaline stopped and turned toward the two. 'Are either of you familiar with the Prophecy of Queen Hephzibah?' she asked.

Both fairies shook their heads.

Mordecai sighed as he flew in their direction. 'I still don't understand all of it when Queen Cymbaline relayed the tale to me,' he told them, 'It tells of how Shadowfire first came here to Arundel Haven and on her dying bed, Queen Hephzibah relayed to her daughters, Princess Bethany and Princess Madelyne, that a human would appear in Arundel Haven and along with a fairy maiden, God would use them to destroy the dragon once and for all.'

'It is true,' Queen Cymbaline nodded, 'Soon, I will be sending Mordecai back to his home to keep Shadowfire from learning that he is here. The dragon must not know, not yet.'

Lavender laughed. 'Him?' she exclaimed, 'What can he do against Shadowfire? Look at him! He's no mighty warrior! What can he do to even harm the dragon?'

'I'm forced to agree with Lavender,' replied Laurelin, 'The dragon has been afflicting us for 150 years now, and he has become stronger as the years have gone by. What can he do? What is so special about him?'

Raven was about to speak, angered by her friends' words when Mordecai stopped her. 'No, Raven,' he said, 'It's all right.' To Lavender and Laurelin he said, 'You are right. There is nothing special about me. I am no warrior, no fighter. From the dreams I've had recently and the Prophecy in which Queen Cymbaline had made known unto me, I know it is about me, though I'm scared to death about it. I don't know how it will come about or who the fairy maiden is who will be aiding me, but it is foretold that through us, God will bring down the dragon Shadowfire. Queen Cymbaline had implored me but did not demand or command me to help. Out of love, I said yes, out of love for the Queen as well as Raven and Twila, who has become very dear to me in such a short time. Am I scared? Yes. To say no would have been unthinkable, especially after meeting Twila. She should not have to live with the fear of the dragon in her life.

'I know you two still don't trust me, and that's okay. I love Raven with all my heart and have also come to love Twila, who has accepted me without question.' Twila flew into his arms and cuddled up to him. He kissed her forehead. 'I am still unsure about all of this, but I have to trust God in this. He said that He would reveal the fairy maiden who would aid me in the slaying of the dragon but…'

'It's me,' Raven said softly. She had been listening to Mordecai's words with her friends when she felt a touch in her spirit. She knew at that moment that she was the fairy maiden who would aid Mordecai in destroying the dragon, the love that they shared together.

Starla stared at Raven and said, 'What?'

'It's me,' repeated Raven, 'I am to be the one who aids Mordecai.' Mordecai turned to her in surprise. He felt inside at that moment that it was true, though he had found it hard to believe. 'Don't you see, Mordecai? That is the second reason God had brought us together. I am the one spoken of in Queen Hephzibah's Prophecy! I am certain of it now.'

'No, Raven, it can't be,' Starla exclaimed.

'God is going to use us and get us through it,' Raven said. 'I feel it in my spirit. I am scared all the same, but I know for certain that it is me.'

'Raven, this is ridiculous,' Lavender protested, 'You can't honestly believe that!'

'I do,' Raven professed, 'God has laid it on my heart. I believe that it is I who will aid Mordecai in destroying the dragon.'

Laurelin laughed. 'I'm sorry, Raven,' she replied, 'but I don't believe in God, and I don't believe that Jesus Christ is the Son of God.'

'But I pray both of you will see,' said Queen Cymbaline, 'I can only pray for you and tell you about the love of Jesus. Even though I am Queen, it is not a decree that all fairies of Arundel Haven accept

Jesus Christ as Lord and Savior. That would be wrong on my part had I done so. The gift of eternal life through Jesus Christ must be accepted willingly, acknowledging that we need Him, admit we are sinners and believing that Jesus would save us from hell. I will not force you to accept Him, but I pray that you would know of Christ's love for you. That decision you must make on your own. As for Mordecai, I had mistrusted him as well as all humans, but God showed me through Twila and the Prophecy that Raven had been right all along, that indeed there are good humans, though they are not many. There will be some exceptions, but the decree must stand.'

'I wish to return with him, your majesty,' Raven said.

Mordecai turned toward Raven as Twila touched his face. 'No, Raven,' he protested softly, 'It's too dangerous. Dr. Von Braun is already hell bent on finding out about Arundel Haven and the fairies here. I counsel you against this.'

'I cannot be parted from you,' Raven insisted.

'Nor can I you,' Mordecai sighed, 'I don't want you to be discovered by Dr. Von Braun or anybody else.' He touched Raven's face. 'We can meet in the same place we've been meeting at, I would have to ride my bike and try not to fly too much lest Von Braun or anybody else would figure out my connection with the fairies of Arundel Haven. I don't want anything to happen to you. I love you, Raven!'

'With all my heart, Mordecai, I love you too,' replied Raven, touching his face.

Twila looked up. 'I no want Uncle Morcai to go bye-bye,' she said.

Mordecai touched Twila's face. 'I don't want to go bye-bye either, little Twila,' he said softly, 'but I will return, though, I will return to see my little Twila.'

'Promise?' Twila asked with wide eyes.

Mordecai kissed Twila on the cheeks. 'I promise, little Twila. I will come back. I have you and Raven here.'

Raven smiled as she touched Mordecai's face. 'Your uncle Morcai will be back, Twila,' she said, 'We will be here for him, you and I.'

Starla took Twila from Mordecai's arms, though Twila was unwilling to go. 'Twila no want Uncle Morcai to go bye-bye,' she said.

'I know, honey,' Starla sighed, kissing her daughter.

They assembled in the throne room. Prince Avondale joined them as they sat in their respective seats. Mordecai, Raven, Starla, Lavender, and Laurelin stood before them. Twila watched from her mother's arms. 'I am grateful to you, my Queen, for what you've done for me,' Mordecai said gravely, 'for the kindness you've shown. The gift of flight is worth more than any amount of money in the world, but the greatest treasure that I have is Raven and the love we share, and little Twila.' He walked over to Twila and touched her face. Twila smiled. 'I will miss you, little Twila,' he said, 'but I will return as soon as possible to see you.'

'Twila love you, Uncle Morcai,' she proclaimed.

Mordecai kissed her on the cheeks. 'Uncle Morcai love you too, little Twila,' he smiled. He stared at Starla and said, 'Thank you for giving me your blessing to marry your sister. It is hard for me to leave her. I am glad to have gotten to know you.'

'And I you,' Starla smiled, 'You promise to take care of Raven, to stay with her and her alone, be faithful and true to her always?'

'I promise; that is what marriage is all about,' Mordecai answered. 'And I do not take the vows lightly. When we take the vows, it's for life.'

Raven approached him and wrapped her arms around him. 'I believe in my heart you will,' she smiled, 'And I will stay faithful and true to you alone as well.' Mordecai and Raven kissed each other and held each other close.

He gazed into her brown eyes. 'My sweet Raven, I don't want to leave you,' he said p0, 'but I know I must go, not only because of Shadowfire, but my sister, Cece, as well. I miss her very much.'

'And I am certain Cece misses you too,' Queen Cymbaline told him, 'I understand that she loves fairies, does she not?'

Mordecai turned to Queen Cymbaline. 'Yes, she does,' he answered, 'even from when she was a little girl.' He sighed. 'I remember I used to ridicule her for that but was rebuked by my older brother, Randall, but that was years ago. Things have changed and now we are close.'

'You are free to tell her about us,' Queen Cymbaline said, 'about all that you've been told during your stay.'

'I guess a part of me finds it hard to believe, especially the prophecy,' Mordecai replied, 'Now I know what Shadowfire has been talking about, what he was referring to in my dreams.'

'I think you must depart for your home soon,' Prince Avondale said, 'It may not be long ere Shadowfire finds out you are here. He must not know!'

'He will find out who he is and where he lives somehow,' sighed Queen Cymbaline, 'Not from Mordecai or Cece, but I fear by someone else.'

Dr. Von Braun? Mordecai thought. *It couldn't be Dr. Von Braun, or could it? I've seen so many unbelievable things lately that I must accept the possibility that he and Shadowfire know each other somehow. That would explain some things during my encounters with Von Braun.* 'I think I may know who, my Queen,' he told her softly, 'or at least, I must accept that possibility. There could very well be a connection between Shadowfire and Dr. Von Braun somehow, but I can't be sure.'

'We have to fear the worst,' sighed Queen Cymbaline, 'There could also be another involved in all this somehow, in some way or form. I fear it could very well be the case.'

'I will be wary, my Queen,' said Mordecai.

'I wish to fly with you when you leave, Mordecai,' Raven said, 'I wish to apologize to Cece and explain it was not my fault. I fear she may blame me for what had happened to you.'

Mordecai turned toward Queen Cymbaline. 'As much as I want her to accompany me, my Queen,' he said, 'I still think this is not a good idea.'

Queen Cymbaline sighed. 'Nor do I,' the Fairy Queen replied, 'but I fear Raven may go with you no matter what. She wishes not to be separated from you.'

'We will go with them,' Lavender interjected, 'Laurelin and I, just to keep Raven out of trouble. We still don't trust this human, but we are Raven's friends, no matter what, and we will stand by her.'

'Raven is blessed to have such friends as you two,' Mordecai told them. He sighed. He stared at Raven and said, 'I still don't like the idea. If it means a lot to you, with our Queen's blessing, you can come.'

'What do you mean "our Queen"?' Laurelin frowned, 'She's not your Queen!'

'I disagree,' Queen Cymbaline interjected, 'An honest heart should not be denied.' To Mordecai she said, 'I am honored you call me "my Queen", but more than that, we are brethren, you and I, since the bond of Christ we both share, and that we are both servants, as are Prince Avondale and Raven.'

Prince Avondale nodded. 'I am in total agreement with Cymbaline.'

Mordecai and Raven nodded as well.

'We shall have one last meal before you must depart for your home, Mordecai,' Queen Cymbaline told him, 'This must be kept a secret save to your sister. We know you will guard our secrets well. When the time has come to face the dragon, you will be summoned.'

Mordecai bowed.

The helicopter carrying President Farouk landed in a heavily wooded area, which he alone knew about. The President looked out the window waiting. In his hands were photos taken by Dr. Von Braun's men of Mordecai and Raven together, some of them in each other's arms. He looked at the photos carefully—they had been given to him two days prior from Dr. Von Braun—a copy of each picture made for him. He nodded as he looked at the pictures again. 'How very interesting that fairies are indeed real,' he said to himself, 'and this Mordy Jefferson has apparently fallen in love with one of them.'

He rose and poured himself a vodka. He noted how his aides were nervous and afraid about being at this particular spot. Two of the aides headed to the bar and made a martini. Another had a Jim Beam. 'I hate coming here,' one of the aides said.

'It's all part of the job,' President Farouk replied casually. He was the only one in the group who showed no fear. He drank his vodka. 'I assure you, none of you are in any danger unless you somehow choose to betray me. I must remind you that you are to keep this meeting a secret. Nobody must know about this, and I mean nobody!'

'Don't worry, Mr. President,' replied one of the aides, 'Nobody would believe us anyhow. They would think we have gone off the deep end.'

'Maybe so,' said President Farouk, 'but you know what will happen if you utter a word of this to anybody.'

'Yes, sir,' the aides said in unison.

At that moment, they heard an ungodly roar in the air. The aides shuddered and hid themselves. President Farouk merely smiled. 'Ah, he's here,' he said.

Shadowfire circled around for a few moments then landed two hundred meters from the helicopter. The door was opened. President Farouk walked out alone with the photos in his hands. Shadowfire bowed his head and smiled. 'Ah, Mr. President,' he smiled.

'Shadowfire,' the president said. 'Always a pleasure to see you.'

The dragon lowered his head and faced the president. 'It was hard to make time to meet with you given my hectic schedule,' the president continued.

'I can imagine, Ahmad,' replied Shadowfire, 'I trust my spells are working to perfection?'

'Like a charm,' smiled President Farouk, 'The media, as usual, are with me and keeping my opponents at bay. There are still those who stand against me, but they shall be dealt with in due time. I still have opponents in the House and the Senate who still try to thwart me. They are a nuisance, but they still have those who would give heed unto them.'

'A shame,' replied Shadowfire, 'I understand you have something to show me.'

'Indeed,' nodded President Farouk, 'but you may have to cast a spell for you to see them clearly.'

'Very well,' said Shadowfire. He chanted an incantation. The photos disappeared from President Farouk's hands. The first photo was projected in the air, larger than the helicopter that carried the President. The first one was of Mordecai and Raven together, holding hands. 'I know them,' Shadowfire proclaimed, 'both the human and the fairy! Yes, I know this fairy. I chased her and her child, but she somehow escaped me. I still do not understand how.'

'And the human?'

'He is the one the prophecy had spoken of to destroy me,' exclaimed Shadowfire, 'It is prophesied that he and a fairy maiden would be used to destroy me. I cannot allow that to happen! I had visited this human in his dreams, but his name and where he lives I do not know. By Ashtaroth, no matter how hard I tried, I cannot find out anything about him.'

'I can help you with that,' President Farouk said, 'An old friend of mine works in the Orlando area and has had contact with him. His name is Mordy Jefferson, and he lives in Orlando, Florida. He doesn't look like much.'

Shadowfire waved his hand, and another picture appeared, this one of Mordecai and Raven in each other's arms. He stared hard at the picture. 'A human and a fairy in love,' he said, 'My, my, what would Queen Cymbaline say about that? After all, she did forbid any fairy to venture into the human world, and yet, this fairy has done so. Could she be the one, too? I wonder. No, I cannot take any chances!'

'I do not know the fairy's name,' President Farouk replied, 'but it is obvious that she is in love with this Mordy Jefferson.'

'Mordy Jefferson, eh?' said Shadowfire. 'So that is the human's name. I know this Mordy Jefferson may not look like much, but I know that he is to be my bane along with perhaps this fairy maiden. I am not sure of the fairy maiden, but I know while Mordy Jefferson lives, he is a threat to my very life.'

President Farouk laughed. 'Him? That nobody?' he smirked.

'I would think so too,' replied Shadowfire, 'I would laugh too, but the danger to me is real. I must find him and put an end to the threat he poses to me once and for all! Tell me, Ahmad, how much does Dr. Von Braun know about this human?'

'Only with what contact he has had with him,' answered the President. 'I have personally never met Mordy Jefferson before.'

'I wish to speak to Dr. Von Braun the next time we meet,' Shadowfire proclaimed, 'I have spoken to him before in his dreams like I had done with Mordy Jefferson, revealing to him that there was somebody in Orlando who knew about fairies, but at the time, I did not know it would be Mordy Jefferson, the same human that is said to be my bane. He knows little about me, save what little I had revealed to him in his dreams, but I feel it is time he meets me face to face.'

'I will arrange for the both of us to meet with you tomorrow,' said President Farouk, 'I will talk to him when I leave here.'

Shadowfire nodded his head. He studied the rest of the pictures, staring closely at each one. After he had seen the last photo, he chanted a spell, and the photos appeared again in the hands of President Farouk. 'I am still amazed how powerful in magic you are, Shadowfire,' he said. 'I am grateful for your help in helping me get elected and re-elected.'

'I think this is just payment for the information you have given me, Ahmad,' Shadowfire replied, He growled. 'Now I know who you are, Mordy Jefferson. I will come for you.'

'I think it would be better,' he said to the dragon, 'that I send some of my men to keep a watch on him.'

'Dr. Von Braun has told me he already has two men keeping a watch on him,' replied Shadowfire, 'Very well, do so, then. But if worse comes to worst, I will be forced to reveal myself and take this boy. If this fairy is the one the prophecy speaks of, neither of them must be allowed to live. I will not let this prophecy be fulfilled!'

'What if the fairy was surrendered to Dr. Von Braun for research?' President Farouk suggested, 'If either one is killed, then there would be no chance for the prophecy to be fulfilled.'

'Perhaps you are right,' replied Shadowfire, 'but in this matter, I cannot afford to take any chances. I will be here tomorrow. I expect both you and Dr. Von Braun to be present.'

'We shall be,' replied President Farouk as Shadowfire spread his massive wings and took to the air. President Farouk walked back toward the helicopter and took out his cell phone. He entered inside and a short time later, the copter took to the air and headed back to the White House.

Mordecai was a bit sorrowful when he had walked out of the castle. Twila was in his arms one last time before he was about to leave. Twila was crying. 'Twila no want Uncle Morcai to leave,' she wept.

'I know, sweetie,' Mordecai nodded, tears in his eyes, 'I will miss you too.' He held her and cradled her in his arms as he, too, wept. 'I will be back soon, little Twila, I promise.'

Starla took Twila from Mordecai's arms. 'Mommy, I don't want Uncle Morcai to go,' she said, weeping.

Mordecai wiped the tears from his eyes. Raven kissed Twila. 'Uncle Morcai will return soon, Twila,' she told her.

The sun was beginning to set. Mordecai turned to the Queen. He embraced her and kissed her on the cheeks. Queen Cymbaline stared at Mordecai and said, 'Like Twila, it grieves me as well to see you leave. In the beginning, you were brought here as a stranger, but now you leave a dear brother, very much interwoven in our lives. We look forward to your return.'

'Thank you, my Queen, both to you and Prince Avondale, for being kind to this stranger,' he sighed, 'I am honored to have seen and to have come to know you.'

He released her and was embraced by her brother. 'Godspeed, dear brother,' Prince Avondale said, 'The end of the dragon is nigh, and God will bring you and us through this. Have courage and have faith.'

'I will miss you as well, your highness,' he replied. He then walked over and kissed Twila on the cheeks, wiping her tears. 'Uncle Morcai will return very soon,' he said. 'I love you, Twila.'

'I love you too, Uncle Morcai,' she replied, giving Mordecai a kiss on the cheeks.

Starla gave Mordecai an embrace and a kiss on the cheeks. 'Hurry back soon, my new brother,' she said. 'Hurry back. Roosevelt and I would welcome your return, as well as Twila.'

'I shall,' Mordecai nodded, kissing Starla on the cheeks. He turned to Raven and took to the air. Lavender and Laurelin followed them.

They reached the end of the village and soared higher into the air, making sure they were not spotted by the dragon. Mordecai and Raven held hands and flew close together while Lavender and Laurelin were at Raven's right-hand side.

Dr. Von Braun was in his office. It was now just past sunset when he received a call on his cell phone. He was gathering some material ready for the lessons the next day. He looked at the phone and simply nodded before answering it. 'Mr. President,' he said. 'So good to hear from you. What can I do for you?'

'Can you come to the White House?' President Farouk asked, 'I need to you to leave for Washington as soon as you can get here, by tomorrow at the latest.'

'Of course,' replied Dr. Von Braun, 'I can leave immediately. I will have to find out which planes leave. How soon do you want me to come?'

'By morning,' President Farouk answered, 'We are meeting near Mount Rushmore, so we need to leave in the morning. I will send a jet to pick you up at Orlando International. It is important that you be here. He requests your presence.'

'He?'

'An acquaintance of yours and mine,' replied President Farouk 'You know him and have spoken to him, but you may have never met him face to face in the flesh. He has a connection with the young man and the fairy.'

'Ah, Shadowfire,' Dr. Von Braun exclaimed, 'I look forward to finally meeting him. We have spoken in my dreams where he communicated with me about the young man and the fairy. I have found out the name of the fairy from Mordy's sister and her friends.'

'I am sure Shadowfire will be glad to hear it,' replied President Farouk, 'What about the young man, Mordy Jefferson?'

'He has been missing for five days now,' answered Dr. Von Braun grimly, 'His sister and her two friends had witnessed six fairies taking him away. I surmise that they have taken him to Arundel Haven. They have probably taken him, displeased with his love affair with the fairy, Raven.'

'So Raven is the fairy's name?' repeated President Farouk.

'Yes,' answered Dr. Von Braun, 'The names of the others are unknown to me. I plan to question them about the other fairies.'

'It looks like you're making progress,' replied President Farouk,

smiling to himself.

'If I could capture this Raven, then will I make known the fairies' existence,' proclaimed Dr. Von Braun. 'But Arundel Haven? That is another goal of mine, to find Arundel Haven.'

'I am sending a jet to pick you up and bring you to Washington,' President Farouk announced, 'After our meeting with Shadowfire, you can investigate the young ladies more and find out about Raven and her friends.'

'I will have Seymour and Wilfred continue to keep an eye on them while I'm gone,' said Dr. Von Braun, 'We will tell Shadowfire all we have found out. I'm sure he would find it interesting. I shall go home and begin packing immediately.'

After he hung up, he saw Seymour and Wilfred standing in front of his desk. 'I am on my way to Washington,' he told them. 'Cece and her friends, I want you to keep an eye on them like you did Mordy before he disappeared. Let me know anything unusual. Call me immediately. If I don't answer, I will return your call as soon as I can.'

'What is it about?' Seymour asked.

'A private matter,' Dr. Von Braun answered, 'dealing with Mordy and the fairy, Raven. Things are finally moving forward, my plan coming to fruition. We need Raven captured before I can reveal the existence of fairies. Finding Arundel Haven is my next goal, and Shadowfire knows where Arundel Haven is.'

'Shadowfire?' Wilfred asked.

'He is a dragon, great in sorcerous powers,' replied Dr. Von Braun, 'He has been communicating with me in my dreams, giving me information about Mordy Jefferson. Keep watching his sister and her friends while I'm away. Get some rest and first thing in the morning, find them and let me know what you can find.'

He grabbed his briefcase and left his office. Seymour and Wilfred followed him. The lights were turned off and the door was locked.

Chapter Nine

Cece was sitting in the kitchen with a can of soda in her hand. She wasn't able to get to sleep that night because of what had happened to her brother the previous week. She remembered the dream she had while she was in the nurse's office earlier in the day, but her heart ached for her brother. Her parents had retired for the night, but she could not sleep. She stared blankly at the can of soda she held in her hand. She occasionally took a drink, but she could not say a word. Tears flowed from her eyes as she sat. She sighed.

Just outside, Mordecai, Raven, Lavender, and Laurelin landed in the backyard. Both of Raven's friends did not like the idea of being among the habitation of humans and looked uncomfortable. 'The sooner we get out of here the better,' Lavender said.

Raven was still amazed by the way the neighborhood was lit up with lights coming from different houses. Mordecai gave a sigh. 'Home at last,' he said.

'Now that he's home, Raven,' Laurelin said, 'Can we just take to the air and leave?'

'Not yet,' Raven answered, 'I want to see Cece before we leave.'

'It's kind of a long flight back to Arundel Haven,' Mordecai told Raven's friends, 'I don't advise flying back right away. Already I could tell you are tired from the long trip here.'

'Now hold on,' Lavender objected, 'If you think we're going to spend the night here, you have got to be out of your mind!'

'I think we can still make it back to Arundel Haven by morning,' Laurelin insisted, 'No need to stop to rest.'

'I am not leaving,' Raven retorted, 'I will be glad to stay with Mordecai for the night at least. I will not make it back to Arundel Haven before I fall asleep.'

From inside, Cece stared out of the glass sliding door and saw three fairies in her backyard. She raised her head. One of them was Raven. Her eyes widened. She approached the door and then saw Mordecai. She burst into tears as she opened the door. Lavender and Laurelin glanced toward the door and found Cece running out, crying out her brother's name. Mordecai saw her and ran to her, embracing her as they both wept. Raven walked over to them as they held each other. 'Mordy, I thought I would never see you again,' she wept. 'I was so worried about you! I missed you so much!'

'I missed you so much too, Cece,' replied Mordecai amid his tears, 'I'm so happy to see my dear sweet sister again!'

Cece could say no more as she continued to weep in Mordecai's arms. Raven touched her shoulder and said, 'I'm sorry, Cece. I never meant for your brother to be taken.'

Cece turned toward Raven with tear-stained eyes. 'I know it wasn't your fault, Raven,' she sighed, 'Thank you and your friends for bringing him back.' She released Mordecai and embraced Raven. 'There was a time I thought you were to blame, but I knew it was not true.' She released Raven and stared at her friends. 'Why did you decide to bring him back home?' she asked them.

'Actually, that was Queen Cymbaline's idea,' answered Lavender softly.

Cece walked over to them. 'Lavender and Laurelin, if I remember correctly?' she inquired.

'You remember our names from when we had taken your brother away?' Laurelin asked, 'We must warn you, we do not feel the same about humans as Raven does.'

Cece turned toward Mordecai, staring at his clothes. She felt it and asked him, 'What is this? Where are your clothes?'

'We can talk more about this inside,' said Mordecai, 'and that includes you two, Lavender and Laurelin.'

Both fairies gave him a sour look. 'You've got to be kidding,' Lavender exclaimed, 'No way are we entering inside any human dwelling!'

'You risk being spotted out here,' replied Mordecai, 'especially with that madman, Dr. Von Braun, searching for fairies! You'll be safer inside.'

Grudgingly, Lavender and Laurelin obliged, entering the house. Cece shut the door and pulled the curtains shut. She turned to the two fairies and said, 'Welcome to our home. Would you like something to drink?'

'I definitely could use a soda after that long flight,' Mordecai

said. He turned to Raven and asked, 'Want one, my love?'

Raven nodded. 'Please, my darling Mordecai,' she smiled. Mordecai grabbed four cans and gave one to Raven. He headed to Lavender and Laurelin and said, 'Go ahead and drink it. It's not alcoholic or anything like that.'

'What is it?' Laurelin asked skeptically.

Lavender saw as Raven opened the can and began drinking from it.

'It's a soda,' Mordecai stated.

Both fairies decided to take the drinks. 'I've had it before,' Raven said, 'It's quite good.'

Laurelin opened the can and took a cautious sip. Once she'd tasted it, she drank a little more. Lavender stared at Laurelin and did the same. 'I must admit,' she said. 'It's not bad.'

'Who carried you home, Mordy?' asked Cece.

'Nobody,' he answered, as to Cece's surprise he rose into the air. He remained suspended in the air for a brief moment, then lowered himself to the floor. 'Were you… did you…'

'Yes,' Mordecai nodded, 'Right now, I have so much to tell you. It's going to take a while, but it can't wait until the morning. I will keep in mind we have school tomorrow.'

'I am glad the dream I had was right,' Cece sighed.

'What dream?' asked Mordecai.

'I had not eaten since you had been taken,' Cece replied, 'During school, I was weak from lack of food. Tiffany and Sharon took me to the nurse's office. I stayed there for the remainder of the school day. I had fallen asleep, and I had a dream that I was in what I thought was Arundel Haven. Fairies of different ages and colors, old and young, were in the village. I then met a fairy queen, with black hair, a crown upon her head, arrayed in a satin dress of scarlet, purple and gold. I assumed it was Queen Cymbaline.'

'Queen Cymbaline appeared in a dream to you?' Mordecai asked.

'It would seem,' Cece replied, 'She sensed I missed you very much. She said she would be sending you home soon until you were needed. She also told me that you have found favor in her eyes. "He will tell you the full tale upon his return," she told me.'

'Almost like when Shadowfire had appeared to me,' Mordecai said, 'but how?'

'Perhaps by a vision,' replied Cece, 'I'm not sure. What happened to you? What went on at Arundel Haven? How can you fly?'

'I was taken to the presence of Queen Cymbaline and her brother Prince Avondale,' Mordecai answered, 'She was angry that Raven had flown here and disapproved of her being in a relationship with me. I was taken to the dungeon until she decided my fate. Raven was right when she said the Queen mistrusted humans, but I didn't blame her. I know from what the Word says and especially from people like Hatfield, McCoy, and Jones how bad we humans can be, though they are mild compared to many others. I was very sad at being imprisoned, not knowing what was going to happen. I was missing Raven and was missing you.

'The day afterwards, I was in my cell feeling very sad. At the time I did not notice that I had a little visitor until I felt the breath of flittering wings. I saw a toddler flying in front of me. "Hi," she said.'

'Twila?' Cece asked.

'Twila,' answered Mordecai. Raven giggled thinking about the first time she heard of her lover's first encounter with Twila. 'She flew into my arms as if she knew me. "What are you doing here, little one?" I asked her.

' "Twila love flying," she told me. I then remembered Raven telling me about her, about her spontaneous flights. "Why don't you have wings?" she asked me.

' "I am not a fairy, little one," I told her, "I am a human. Humans don't have wings." Despite that, she accepted me as she hugged my neck and said, "I like you." I couldn't believe how she came to accept me right away. I then heard Starla call out for Twila from down the corridor.

'Twila told me it was her Mommy. "She's very worried about you," I told her, "She loves you very much, you know that?"

'When Starla first saw Twila in my arms, she thought I was going to hurt her. It moved me to tears. I wouldn't even think of hurting such an innocent child. She begged me not to harm her. I wept. Twila looked at me and asked, "Why you cry?"

' "Your mother is afraid that I might hurt you," I told her amid my tears, "but I would never do such a thing, not to a child."

'Twila wiped the tears from my face with her little hands and said, "Please don't cry." It melted my heart when she said that, as it did Starla's. I tried to give Twila back to Starla, but she was unwilling to leave me. "Why do you remain, little one?" I asked, "Don't you want to go to your Mommy? A dungeon is no place for a little girl,"'

'Twila sounds like she's a real sweetheart,' Cece smiled.

'She is,' Mordecai nodded, 'She asked me my name. I told her Mordecai. She could only say "Morcai."'

'I think that is so cute,' Raven said, 'She has trouble saying your name. I should have figured that out. I was surprised when Starla had told me of your first encounter with her.'

'I miss Twila already,' sighed Mordecai. 'She took to me at first sight, it would seem. Twila helped changed Starla's mind toward me when she went on one of her flights. Something good came out of all this.'

'That is what Starla had told me,' Raven said, 'Shadowfire had invaded the village at the time, but she and Twila managed not to be spotted. That's when I heard about her encounter with Mordecai. When she flew into the castle when I was watching her, she ran into Prince Avondale and Queen Cymbaline, who seemed amused with Twila's little trip. "You would have to keep a hold of your niece," the Queen smiled. I thought I was going to get into trouble.'

Lavender and Laurelin laughed. 'Starla says Twila reminds her of when Raven was her age,' Laurelin told Cece, who was too amused with the story to regard her mistrust toward her and Mordecai.

'So Starla says,' replied Raven, giving Laurelin a queer look, Lavender and Cece laughed. Lavender took another drink of the soda. 'I like this,' she said, 'We have nothing like it in Arundel Haven.'

'We are not perfect,' Cece said, 'and yes, there are a lot of bad humans out there, but I hope you two will see that there are some good humans as well.'

'So Raven believes,' replied Laurelin skeptically, 'I admit, your brother has won the heart of the Queen, but we still have doubts. I guess it's a start right there.'

'How did you earn the trust of Queen Cymbaline?' Cece asked.

'I think it started when I told Prince Avondale about the dreams

of Shadowfire I had,' answered Mordecai. 'I had mentioned the dragon kept telling me I was the one some prophecy had spoken of who would destroy him. That's the first time I heard of the Prophecy of Queen Hephzibah, which stated that a human and a fairy maiden would be used by God to destroy the dragon. He found the book dealing with it and delivered it to Queen Cymbaline. She then relayed the tale to me, on how the dragon first appeared 150 years ago and started terrorizing the fairies of Arundel Haven. The queen of the last ruling king, King Zebulon, who was called Beulah, had been taken by the dragon. He was so grief stricken that he tried to rescue her but he, himself, perished. Their daughter, Hephzibah, became Queen. Just before her death, she had a dream that a human would come to Arundel Haven and along with a fairy maiden, would be used by God to destroy Shadowfire. That was why I'd been having those dreams. I knew right then I am the one Queen Hephzibah's prophecy had spoken about. I am still scared about it, and I still don't understand how I could be the one. It was then Queen Cymbaline's heart and the heart of her brother changed concerning me. I agreed, though I was afraid of the affair, and I knew the prophecy was right about me. She did not force me, but said, "I can only ask and implore you." There was no way in my mind I could say no, especially concerning Raven and Twila, whom I have come to love dearly.'

'Then who is the fairy maiden that would aid you?'

'I realized just before we left that it was me,' Raven answered, 'I felt a touch in my spirit as Mordecai spoke to Queen Cymbaline. I'm just as afraid as he is.'

'I still don't agree that you are the one, Raven,' protested Lavender.

'It is me,' Raven insisted, 'The touch in my spirit confirms this. I don't know how it would come about, but Mordecai and I will be used to bring Shadowfire down once and for all.'

'How did you gain the ability to fly?' Cece asked.

'That I will not say at this point,' Mordecai said, remembering the freezing cold water of the falls that began the Silverstreams. 'Perhaps at a later time. I suppose I have told you enough for the time being. It is late, and we have school tomorrow.' To Lavender and Laurelin, he said, 'I suggest you two stay the night here. It is a long flight back to Arundel Haven, and you would probably fall asleep before you reach your home.'

'Not a chance,' Laurelin objected, 'We will not remain.'

'I will remain,' Raven said, yawning. 'I am too tired to make such a long flight.'

'If we were to stay, where would we sleep?' Lavender asked, 'Surely your parents will see us and know we exist.'

'You would be safer here than if you tried to return home,' Mordecai pointed out, 'I suggest for your safety—'

Before he could finish his sentence, his mother opened the door to the kitchen. When she saw Mordecai, she gasped, then cried out, embracing him. At first, she did not notice the fairies, being more concerned about her missing son returning home. She wept as she held her son. She cried out, 'Tony! Tony! Come down here!'

They heard the voice of their father. 'Molly, what's going on? Is somebody trying to break into the house?'

'Mordy's home, Tony,' she cried. 'Our son is home!'

'Mordy?' came his voice. They heard the footsteps from Tony descending from the stairs. Molly stared at her son and cried, 'Mordy, where have you been? We've been worried sick about you!'

Mordecai sighed but said not a word about what he was thinking. Tony opened the door and saw his son in his mother's arms and embraced him. He then gazed sternly at him and asked, 'Where have you been these past five days?'

Molly then caught a glimpse of Raven, Lavender, and Laurelin and gasped when she saw their wings. Lavender and Laurelin were about to exit when Raven told them, 'Stay right there, the both of you! Not another step!'

Molly walked over to Raven in amazement and in shock. She then remembered seeing different fairy figurines in Cece's room. She stared in disbelief. Tony released his son when he caught a glimpse of the three fairies. He, too, was dumbfounded by their appearance. 'This can't be,' Molly exclaimed, 'Tony, am I seeing things, or do they have wings?'

'We're both seeing the same thing,' gasped Tony. 'They can't be real! Who are you?'

'I'm Raven. I am so honored to meet you both.'

'Mordy, where have you been, and who are they?' asked Molly.

Mordecai sighed. 'It's going to take a while to explain,' he told them, 'I've just told Cece where I had been. You're going to find it hard to believe.'

'I think we ought to be going now,' Lavender told them, 'Let's go, Raven.'

Raven stood in front of the glass sliding door. 'You are not going anywhere, not yet,' she told them in a stern voice, 'Mordecai is right! It's too late to fly back to Arundel Haven. We would never make it without proper rest.'

'Arundel Haven?' Molly gasped, 'Then what I read is real?'

'Yes, Mom,' Mordecai nodded, 'I have been there for the past five days. It's kind of a long story, but we do have school tomorrow and we do need some rest.'

'Not before we get answers from you, young man,' Molly said sternly, Lavender and Laurelin started to chuckle softly. Raven gave them a stern look.

Mordecai sighed. 'It's a long story,' he sighed, 'It started when I first met Raven.'

'So, the black fairy is Raven?' Tony asked, 'What about these two?'

'Lavender and Laurelin, Raven's best friends,' Mordecai answered, 'like Tiffany and Sharon are best friends with Cece. They do not trust humans like Raven does.'

'You will explain where you'd been,' Tony said sternly.

'I was at Arundel Haven for the past five days,' Mordecai repeated, 'but I need to go back to when I had first met Raven before I get to when and why I was in Arundel Haven.'

Mordecai told them about how Frank, Stu, and Chuck had tied him up and left him in the woods, how he freed himself from the ropes up to when he met Raven. 'She was scared at first, but she did approach me and we talked for a bit,' Mordecai told them, 'She had been visiting the very woods I had been dropped off at against the decrees of her Queen not to fly to the human world.'

'Indeed,' Lavender replied, 'She would tell us very little about where she visited or your son. We spoke in protest against what she had been doing, but she insisted.'

'Why is that?' Molly asked, still in shock that they were fairies.

'Queen Cymbaline had warned us about how wicked you humans were,' Laurelin answered, 'Raven defied her decree and flew here anyway. When we questioned her, she refused to tell us and eventually, the Queen found out.'

Tony shook his head in disbelief. 'Why did you take my son to your home,' he asked, 'and why did your Queen release him?'

'He was taken because Raven had fallen in love with your son,' Lavender answered, 'It displeased the Queen when she first heard, when he appeared before her. She was unaware—'

Tony and Molly stood in shock when Lavender had proclaimed about Mordecai and Raven. They glanced sourly at Mordecai, then Raven, then Mordecai again. 'Is this true, Mordy?' he asked him sternly. 'Is what this fairy is saying true?'

Mordecai nodded. 'It is true,' he answered, 'Raven and I fell in love with each other from the first time we met, but it was not until two weeks later, when we were sure both of us felt the same way.'

Tony stared disapprovingly at Mordecai. He glanced at Raven and said to his son, 'I do not approve of this. The fact that she is black alone is reason enough. This is wrong, Mordy!' He scoffed. 'Add to the fact that she is a fairy and you are human. Mordy, what were you thinking?'

'You two are from different worlds, Mordy,' Molly admonished, 'What kind of life would the both of you have together? Would it work out? How would you be able to support her? What if others find out she is a fairy?'

'Raven was the only person besides Cece who has been there for me, even though you were not,' Mordecai explained, 'I mean you no disrespect, but there are matters where I feel you are being unfair to me!'

'Like what?' Tony asked sternly.

'Cece,' he replied, 'You are teaching her how to drive. You have never offered me to either drive or permit me to hold a job. I don't understand. Cece thought I would hate her for the favoritism, but this is not her doing. In fact, as of late, she has been emotionally supportive of me when I was being bullied by three jocks on the football team. They had tied me up and left me in the woods on one occasion, threw me in the dumpster on another, poured soda over me, for no reason at all but because they think I am a nobody. I am their main victim, as it were! The one good thing about being taken to Arundel Haven is that I wasn't bullied at all.'

Molly stared at his clothes. 'Where did you get them?' she asked, 'You have never worn those before.'

'From Queen Cymbaline herself,' Mordecai answered. 'She mistrusted me at first and had me thrown in the dungeon, but later set me free after I had earned her trust. She has shown great kindness to me, more than I deserve.'

'What about being thrown in the dungeon?' Molly scoffed, 'Was that kindness?'

'Queen Cymbaline only wanted to protect her people,' Mordecai replied, 'She learned a lesson from a particular toddler that not all humans are bad.'

Raven giggled when she thought about Twila and her first meeting with Mordecai. Lavender and Laurelin found themselves giggling as well. 'What's so funny about my son being imprisoned?' Tony asked sternly.

'They are laughing at my encounter with Twila,' smiled Mordecai. 'Twila is the two-year-old daughter of Raven's older sister, Starla. She had learned to fly and was flying a lot. She flew into the castle on one other occasion before she met me. She slipped into my cell and started talking to me. She took to me like I was her favorite relative.' He found himself laughing. 'She is a lively little girl.'

'You should have seen her,' laughed Lavender 'How she evaded Raven's grasp when she first entered the castle. Starla said that Raven was like that growing up.' Both fairies laughed.

Raven gave them a queer look and said, 'That's enough of that!'

Cece burst out laughing.

'She probably did the same to her mother the day she met Mordecai,' Raven said, 'as she did to me. It was then that Starla met Mordecai and found Twila in his arms. Twila had come to accept Mordecai, even though he was a human.'

'She did question why I didn't have wings but accepted me regardless,' added Mordecai, 'When Starla saw her in my arms, she thought I would harm her. It caused me to weep. I would never harm such an innocent life. Twila wiped the tears from my eyes with her little hand, which melted my heart as it melted Starla's. I tried to give Twila back to her mother, but she wanted to stay with me and would not leave.'

'She couldn't say his name but called him Morcai,' Raven giggled. Involuntarily, Molly smiled.

'I thought it was so cute,' continued Raven, 'She still has trouble saying some names. She is lively, though.'

Molly found herself laughing. 'The terrible twos,' she said, 'I remember when Cece was two.'

'Mom!' Cece exclaimed.

Tony found himself laughing as well.

'I wonder if Cece was like Raven?' Laurelin asked.

'She loved to run, I remember that,' Mordecai said, 'She had a long fascination with fairies growing up.'

'You should see her room,' Raven added, 'She even has one that looks like her. She showed it to me.'

'How long have you known Raven, Mordy?' Tony asked, his smile disappearing.

'For about three weeks,' Mordecai answered.

'And you kept that from us?'

'I had to,' explained Mordecai, 'I even had to keep it from Cece until Raven chose to reveal herself as a fairy to her. We believe fairies are a myth, that they don't exist. That belief, for the sake of the fairies of Arundel Haven, must remain. The fairies must be allowed to live in peace.'

'Why did Raven reveal herself to you?' Molly asked.

'I felt there was something different about him,' Raven replied, 'My heart had led me to him, my spirit was touched. There is a bond that was formed between us from the moment we first met.'

Tony and Molly shook their heads. They showed their disapproval of their relationship, and Mordecai and Raven could tell.

'Why keep their existence a secret?' Molly asked her son.

'Dr. Haman Von Braun,' Mordecai said darkly.

'The world-famous geneticist?' Molly asked, 'The one who is now teaching at UCF here in Orlando? What does he have to do with all of this?'

'Everything,' Mordecai answered, 'He is convinced fairies do exist. He had been interrogating me and Cece about fairies and if we have seen one.'

Molly laughed. 'You've got to be joking. This is all a rumor, a story to make him look bad somehow. I don't believe any of it.'

'It's true,' Mordecai insisted, 'He came to me at school on a few occasions. He showed me the remains of a female fairy who had died here, perhaps a year ago. He told me he had studied the DNA and found it similar to humans. He wants to find Arundel Haven for some purpose that I feel is evil toward the fairies there. He must not know about Raven.'

'He knows about Raven and your relationship with her,' Cece informed him, 'He showed me, Tiffany, and Sharon photos of you and Raven together. Sharon accidentally revealed Raven's name to him.'

Mordecai sighed. 'This is ill news,' he replied gravely, 'I was afraid that would happen!'

Lavender and Laurelin gave Raven stern looks. 'Now you see where this had gotten us, Raven?' Laurelin exclaimed, 'Our existence has been compromised! It will only be a matter of time before the human world at large knows of our existence, and it will be ill with our people when they find out where Arundel Haven is!'

'Was it worth it?' Lavender asked Raven.

'What about the prophecy?' Raven shot back. 'What about the Prophecy of Queen Hephzibah? Mordecai is the one who Queen Cymbaline's foremother had spoken of! It will be fulfilled soon!'

'What exactly is the Prophecy of Queen Hephzibah?' Tony asked harshly, 'What does it have to do with Mordy?'

Mordecai sighed. He had hoped to avoid that subject with his parents. He was still afraid of the matter, still unsure of himself.

'Do not tell me it is nothing, fairy,' Tony said sharply to Raven, 'I want to know about this prophecy, and what it has to do with my son!'

'I had hoped not to come to this matter,' sighed Mordecai, 'It all started when I had a similar dream for seven consecutive nights just before I met Raven. I dreamed I was in a valley where I had met a black dragon by the name of Shadowfire, who was also a sorcerer of great power. He entered my dreams and wanted to know who I was. He spoke of some prophecy, which spoke of his demise, and was convinced that I was the one this prophecy had spoken of. He would not answer any questions I had about the prophecy or how he knew, but he insisted I was the one who would destroy him.'

Tony laughed in incredulity. 'And this Prophecy of Queen Hephzibah was the prophecy this dragon was referring to?'

Mordecai nodded. 'It was later when I found this out to be the case,' he continued, 'When I told Prince Avondale, the younger brother of Queen Cymbaline, of the dreams about Shadowfire, he then mentioned the Prophecy of Queen Hephzibah and left my cell. He found a book and delivered it to his sister. When she told me the full tale, I knew then the Prophecy had spoken about me, that a fairy maiden and I would be used to bring down Shadowfire. Shadowfire fears me, and now I know why.'

'So, this Shadowfire exists?' Molly asked.

'He does,' Raven answered, 'He took my parents about two years ago and nearly took me and my little niece, Twila.'

'He tried to take us as well,' Lavender added, 'but we somehow escaped.'

'How?' Tony asked skeptically.

'A great wave along the Silverstreams,' Raven answered, 'It engulfed Shadowfire and caused him to release my friends. We flew away before the dragon could recover and recapture us.'

'Raven believes God had a hand in delivering us from the dragon,' Lavender added, 'but personally, I don't believe in God.'

'What about the other fairies in your home?' Tony asked.

'Very few of us believe that Jesus is Lord, including Queen Cymbaline and Prince Avondale, as well as myself,' Raven answered, 'Queen Cymbaline does not force her beliefs upon us but allows us to choose. That is one of the common bonds we share with Mordecai. He, too, is a brother of Christ, and it was that common belief that was part of the factor of Queen Cymbaline's heart turning toward Mordecai and caused her to set him free.'

'And who is this fairy woman who is supposed to be helping you?' Tony asked his son cynically.

'Raven believes it is her,' Lavender said.

'And how long have you known about this prophecy?'

'It is not well known in Arundel Haven,' Raven stated, 'I found out when Queen Cymbaline had told us the tale. I had not heard of it before, but after hearing the tale, I felt in my spirit that I was indeed the one who would help Mordecai bring an end to Shadowfire.'

Tony started yawning. He was starting to feel lightheaded. 'It is late,' he said, 'I will inquire more about this after school tomorrow. As for the fairies, I guess they can stay the night here, but I am still against your relationship with the black fairy Raven, Mordy. There are still questions I have, but they can wait until after you return home from school.'

Lavender and Laurelin stared at each other. Laurelin sighed. 'I guess we could stay the night at least,' she said, 'I still don't feel right about this—staying in a human house.'

'Better you stay here than out in the open where Dr. Von Braun can find you,' Mordecai told her, 'I suggest you two sleep down here. Raven can sleep in Cece's room.'

Tony nodded in agreement. 'Acceptable,' he said, 'but when I get home from work, I expect more answers.'

Mordecai nodded. 'Agreed.'

Molly brought blankets and pillows for each fairy: Lavender, Laurelin, and Raven. Raven's friends each took a couch to sleep on while Cece allowed Raven to sleep on her bed. Cece pulled out a sleeping bag and slept on the floor. Mordecai checked in on the fairies before he went to sleep.

After Tony and Molly entered their bedroom, Mordecai talked with Raven before heading to his bedroom. 'I don't regret ever meeting you, Mordecai,' she said, caressing his face. 'I hope your parents can see past my skin color and the fact I am a fairy. It's still a shock to me, the prejudice over skin color.'

'I know,' sighed Mordecai, 'It's not right. We will have to worry about that later. I hope they will accept you as a wonderful person, Raven. Sleep well, my love.'

'I hope I dream about you, sweet Mordecai,' Raven said. Their lips came together in a loving kiss. When their lips separated, they whispered, 'Good night!' to each other and headed to bed. Mordecai laid down and immediately went to sleep.

The next morning, Cece woke up and stretched. She found herself on the floor in her sleeping bag. At first, she was confused. 'What am I doing down here in my sleeping bag?' she asked herself.

She looked up and saw Raven, who was still asleep. She gasped. She then remembered last night. She quickly rose to her feet and raced out the room.

Mordecai was beginning to stir when his sister entered his room. She ran over and embraced him, so thankful it was not a dream. Mordecai opened his eyes. 'Cece,' he said sleepily.

'I thought it was a dream last night,' she said, 'I am so thankful that it's not! You are home!'

Mordecai stretched. 'Yes, I am,' he yawned, 'Guess I still have to wake up. You going to shower first?'

'Maybe you better go first,' Cece told him, 'It doesn't take you as long.'

Mordecai nodded. 'If I can force myself up. I don't look forward to seeing those bullies again.'

Cece frowned. 'Yeah, that is the bad thing,' she said, 'I bet they look forward to beating you up again. I can't stand them!'

'I know what you mean,' Mordecai yawned, 'They're not my only concern. I guess Raven and her friends will return to Arundel Haven once they wake up. I hate to see Raven go.'

'Who says I'm leaving?' Raven asked. She stood at the doorway and yawned. 'Lavender and Laurelin will leave, but I will not.'

Mordecai rose from the bed. He kissed Raven on the lips. 'Slept well, sweet Raven?' he asked.

Raven smiled. 'Yes, I did,' she answered, touching his face.

'I better go take a shower so Cece can take hers,' he said, grabbing the clothes Queen Cymbaline had given him. 'I'm not going to wear all black to school anymore. I like the clothes the Queen gave me.'

'I must admit,' Cece replied, 'they do look nice on you.'

Mordecai smiled.

He exited the bathroom a short time later. His hair was wet, and he was wearing the clothes he had received at Arundel Haven. Raven welcomed him with a kiss on the lips, holding him close. They walked together, their arms around each other, as they made their way down the stairs.

Lavender and Laurelin were waking up when Mordecai and Raven stepped downstairs. Laurelin yawned as she stood up and stretched her wings. 'I must admit,' she said to herself. 'I slept kind of well here.'

Lavender yawned. She stretched her body and then her wings. 'I hope Raven hasn't decided to fly to the human world,' she yawned.

'Lavender, we *are* in the human world,' she reminded her, yawning, 'Remember? We escorted the human back to his home, where we are now.'

Lavender stared at Laurelin in shock. 'What?' she cried. 'I hope Queen Cymbaline doesn't hear about this!'

'Who did you think sent you to escort me home?' Mordecai said, laughing from the doorway. 'Are you awake yet, Lavender?'

Lavender paused for a moment. 'Oh, yeah,' she said, 'Now I remember.'

'I want to come with you,' Raven told Mordecai, 'to see what this school of yours is like.'

Laurelin and Lavender stared at her and frowned. 'Are you crazy, Raven?' Laurelin exclaimed, 'to walk among the humans? Spending the night here is bad enough, but you're talking about heading to a human school! No way, Raven, out of the question!'

'I'm sure Cece will have something that could cover up our wings,' Raven suggested.

'Forget it, Raven,' Laurelin snapped, 'We are at risk of being discovered as it is, especially since this human—'

'The *human* has a name, Laurelin,' snapped Raven, 'and you and Lavender know it! His name is Mordecai! I would appreciate it if you would call him by his name!'

'It's okay, baby,' Mordecai said softly, caressing her face. 'I know it hurts you because you care so much about me. Perhaps there's a way I can earn their trust in the future. For now, I've got to get to school. I know I have a lot to catch up on.'

'You are not going to fly to school, are you?' Laurelin asked.

'Of course not, Laurelin,' Mordecai answered, 'I'm not going to fly anywhere while I am here. I am riding with Cece's friends once they arrive here. I can't fly as long as I'm outside of Arundel Haven. If people see me flying—'

'What do you mean by that, Mordy?' came Molly's voice. He looked up and saw his parents walking down the stairs. 'Are they saying you can fly?'

Mordecai sighed. 'Yes,' he answered. 'Queen Cymbaline gave me the gift of flight ere I left Arundel Haven. They flew with me here last night. If I started flying, it could arouse suspicion and is sure to draw the attention of Dr. Von Braun. Already, the situation is precarious as it is. Von Braun now knows of Raven and the relationship I have with her. He will search me out for sure for more information about Raven.'

'We still don't feel comfortable with Raven being here,' Tony said, 'but you are guests in this house after all. We can offer you breakfast if you wish.'

Lavender and Laurelin agreed.

Cece walked down a short time afterwards. Molly was in the middle of cooking grits and eggs. Lavender and Laurelin were on the couch talking. Raven and Mordecai sat together. 'I won't be flying with you right away when you leave after breakfast,' she told her friends, 'I want to stay here a while with Mordecai.'

Lavender shook her head. 'You always were stubborn, Raven,' she groaned, 'I know your boyfriend has favor with the Queen, but even he must agree that it's too dangerous.'

Mordecai nodded sadly. 'You are right,' he said, 'My heart doesn't want to be without her, but yes, Lavender, she is in danger, as well as you two, the longer you are here.'

Laurelin shook her head. 'It's no use trying to talk Raven out of it, Lavender,' she said to her friend, 'Raven is dead set on having her way. We both know her.'

'Is she always this way?' came Tony's voice. All were surprised when they heard him ask the question.

'Afraid so, Mr. Jefferson,' answered Laurelin, 'She had defied the decrees of Queen Cymbaline to fly to here, even before she met your son.'

Tony thought for a moment.

'You should have seen Twila,' laughed Lavender without realizing it, 'She is definitely another Raven: adventurous, headstrong. We can already tell.'

Tony laughed softly, then stared at Cece. Cece gave her father a sour look.

'What?' he asked.

'Not another word, Dad,' frowned Cece.

Lavender and Laurelin laughed.

At that moment, there was a knock on the door. 'That's got to be my friends,' Cece said, heading for the door, 'They already know about you two, Lavender, Laurelin, as well as Raven.'

'How many more people know about your fairy friends, Mordy?' Tony asked.

'Just Cece and her friends,' Mordecai answered, 'and unfortunately, Dr. Von Braun as well. I wanted to keep him from knowing of their existence.'

Cece opened the door and allowed Tiffany and Sharon to enter inside. Like her, they wore their cheerleading clothes. They stood in shock when they saw the fairies but were happy to see Mordecai again. They each embraced him and stood by him. 'Where did you go?' Sharon asked, 'and what are these clothes you have on?'

'It's a long story,' Mordecai replied. Turning to the fairies he said, 'These are Cece's friends, Tiffany and Sharon. They are to Cece what you two are to Raven.'

'I am so surprised to see you back,' Tiffany said. Both her and Sharon stared at Lavender and Laurelin as did Tiffany. 'Perhaps we are not as different as we would like to believe,' Lavender said.

'I am glad to meet you,' Laurelin said, shaking the hands of Tiffany first, then Sharon's. Lavender slowly did the same.

'When did Mordy get back?' Sharon asked Cece, 'and do your parents know?'

'We know,' Tony said, 'He returned home last night. We were introduced to Raven and her friends.'

'Why are you dressed like that?' Lavender asked Tiffany.

'It's our cheerleading clothes,' Tiffany answered, 'We are cheerleaders in our school. We have cheerleader practice today. Our team has a game on Friday against Apopka.'

'What are cheerleaders?' Laurelin asked.

'We have different sports in our high school,' Sharon told them, 'Teams for football, basketball, baseball. We cheer for them, like encouragement to the team to beat our opponents, in other words, win by scoring more points than the other team.'

'There is a lot I don't understand,' Laurelin replied curiously, 'So many strange but fascinating things here. So many things I have never seen before.'

'There's so much to show you,' Sharon said, 'but it would be a good idea to cover up your wings, so they don't see you are a fairy.'

'I advise against this,' Mordecai protested, 'It's too risky, and you know it. You see how Dr. Von Braun is obsessed with fairies and Arundel Haven, and from what you tell me, he already knows Raven by sight, recognizes her face. Besides, Lavender and Laurelin are anxious to return to their home.'

'Can't they stay a little longer?' came Molly's voice, 'I wish to know more about them. I have never told anybody before, but I was fascinated with fairies when I was Cece's age.' To Tony she said, 'I want them to stay, even Raven. I'm not that comfortable with blacks either, but I think there is something special about Raven . I think we should get to know her better before we rush to judgment.'

To Mordecai's surprise, his father sighed, saying, 'I have to agree with you.' To the fairies he said, 'I will allow you to stay as long as you wish. If you wish to return home, you are free to do so.'

Lavender and Laurelin gazed at Tony, then Raven, at Mordecai, then at Tiffany and Sharon. Lavender turned to Tony and said, 'We don't have to leave right away. I suppose we could stay a little longer.' She then turned toward Raven. 'Somebody's got to keep Raven out of trouble,' she added.

Raven was overjoyed to hear. She embraced her friends one at a time. 'Remember, Raven,' Laurelin added, 'We're here to keep you out of trouble.'

'Thank you, both of you,' replied Raven. Molly let them know that it was time for breakfast.

When Mordecai, Cece, Sharon and Tiffany arrived at school, Mordecai headed to his locker. He looked around, keeping a watch out for the bullies and in case Dr. Von Braun and his men were on campus. He grabbed the book he needed for his first class and headed to class as he had done before. He knew in the back of his mind that he would be tempted to use his newly given power of flight to evade the bullies and even Dr. Von Braun, but he knew it would be a bad idea if he wanted to protect Raven and the fairies of Arundel Haven, especially Twila, whom he had grown attached to. He had to use wisdom, restraint and discretion. He would only use it if extremely necessary. He would not take or use the gift that Queen Cymbaline had given him lightly.

As he walked away from his locker, he continued to look around, wary of his enemies. Around him, he saw the rest of his fellow students. He saw girls in cheerleaders' attire and boys that were members of the football team with the green and gold jerseys with the numbers on them. He didn't understand why the players were wearing their uniform tops. 'Maybe it's for a team picture?' he asked himself.

So far, he saw no sign of Hatfield, McCoy, or Jones—his adversaries. He headed toward his first class. His teacher inquired where he had been, but he would not say. He refused to reveal the fact he was at Arundel Haven, nor his involvement with the fairies there and all that dealt with him. 'It was circumstances beyond my control,' he could only say. The explanation did not satisfy any of the teachers at all. They let the matter go, however.

At lunchtime he, Cece, Sharon, and Tiffany were sitting together talking. From time to time those that barely knew Mordecai stared at the clothes given to him by Queen Cymbaline. He talked as discreetly as possible about his time in Arundel Haven. 'I can't speak much about it here,' he told the girls. 'Most of it I had already told Cece. It would be bad if I spoke anything more here, especially with Dr. Von Braun possibly on campus.'

Sharon looked apologetically. 'I'm sorry I mentioned Raven's name to him yesterday,' she sighed, 'I-I got careless. I didn't know what had gotten into me.'

'What's done is done,' replied Mordecai sadly, 'You have to be more careful about the secret, Sharon. There are lives at stake here. I don't know what I would do if harm came to Raven, Starla, Twila, or even Queen Cymbaline. They've become a second family to me, with all due respect to my sister.'

Cece nodded. 'I know, brother,' she said, 'I would love to see Arundel Haven myself. Queen Cymbaline herself in the dream had told me I would be there soon.'

Mordecai stared at her. 'She didn't mention anything of the kind to me,' he said.

'It was in the dream yesterday before you returned home,' explained Cece, 'I hope that somehow, I would be allowed to.'

'We should not speak of the matter anymore here,' said Mordecai. 'In public, we must guard our speech. Promise me you will keep that secret, the three of you?'

'We promise,' Cece, Tiffany and Sharon said together.

'What secret?' came a familiar voice. Mordecai's face turned hard, turning and beholding the forms of the three bullies behind them. 'Judas Priest, not you gorillas!' he said under his breath.

'Look who finally chooses to show up,' came Frank's voice again, 'and look at the duds he's wearing? Boring!'

Cece growled under her breath. Tiffany and Sharon gave them an angry look. 'What do you orcs want?'

'What secret are you talking about?' Chuck asked.

'Like we're going to tell you?' shot back Mordecai, 'If we told you, it wouldn't be a secret now, would it? None of your business, by the way.'

Frank pulled Mordecai out of the chair and slammed him against the wall. Cece, Tiffany, and Sharon immediately shot out of their seats. Stu and Chuck held them back. 'Let my brother go,' cried Cece.

'Stop it right this instant, McCoy,' cried Tiffany.

'Why do you defend the jege?' Frank frowned, 'You're too good to hang around this loser!'

'He is not a loser,' Sharon cried, 'The only losers I see are you and your gorilla friends!'

Frank threw Mordecai across the table. Mordecai landed on some of the students, knocking some of the plates of food to the floor. He rolled on the floor and quickly shot to his feet. He stared directly at his assailants. Frank charged toward him, but Mordecai rolled underneath the table and leapt to his feet.

'Where'd you get the new threads?' Frank asked, sliding over the tables after him.

'Like I would tell you, Azog,' snapped Mordecai, making a run for the door.

Frank turned to his friends and said, 'Forget the broads and get that jege!' They let Cece and her friends go and started after him.

Cece growled and grabbed her purse. 'Not this time, McCoy,' she cried.

'After them?' Tiffany asked, 'We can't keep up with them!' She grabbed her purse, as did Sharon, and raced after them.

When Mordecai ran out the door, he rounded the corner of the cafeteria, running as fast as he could. He knew with all the people around, he couldn't take to the air to escape his adversaries. He did not want to reveal that part if he could help it. He wanted to do it when nobody was watching. He had to rely on his feet and wits to keep from getting caught.

Frank, Stu, and Chuck kept on his trail. Mordecai ducked behind the wall of a building and leaned against it. He held his breath and waited. Soon, the three bullies dashed right past him and seemed not to notice him until they had passed and saw him run the other way.

'Stop, stop,' Frank cried. 'There he goes! The nobody is getting smart on us!'

'Time for another lesson?' Chuck asked as they hurried after him, breathing hard.

'Long overdue,' cried Stu as they chased after him.

Mordecai passed by Cece and her friends as he rounded the first corner of the cafeteria. The three girls watched as he dashed past them.

'We've got to slow them down,' Cece told her friends.

'How?' Tiffany asked.

The three bullies collided with the cheerleaders as they rounded the corner. They fell to the concrete, but it also tripped up all three bullies in the process. Frank had a furious look upon his face. 'Jefferson!' he screamed.

'Hey, you ran into us,' Tiffany shot back defiantly, 'What are you complaining about?'

'That's no way to treat a lady, I hope you know,' Sharon snapped.

'Who gives a foul about you wenches?' snapped Stu, 'Stay out of our way!'

'Or else what, you're going to beat us up too, like you do Mordy?' cried Cece, 'It's a sin that Principal Spooney lets you practically get away with murder, for beating up my brother and others like him!'

'Don't push it, Jefferson,' warned Frank.

'One of these days, McCoy,' replied Cece angrily, 'all of this is going to bite you and your friends in the butt with the teeth of a great white shark!'

'Ohh, I'm so scared,' mocked Frank.

'I hope you three get exactly what you deserve,' Cece snapped, 'Eventually you will reap exactly what you sow!'

'Forget the wench,' snapped Frank, 'We need to teach that loser Jefferson a lesson! We already wasted too much time dealing with them!' They shot to their feet and raced after Mordecai.

Mordecai rounded the corner of the cafeteria and headed to the middle of the campus. The temptation of taking to the air was so strong as he ran, but he did his best to fight it. If he took to the air, people would see him and possibly start linking him to fairies somehow, or at least talk about it, which would lead them to linking him to the existence of fairies. He did his best to keep from flying for the sake of Twila and Queen Cymbaline, to keep Arundel Haven a secret.

He stopped at the corner of the office. He took deep breaths as he leaned against the wall, trying to stay hidden from the bullies. He slumped to the ground, landing on his butt. He sat up and continued to take deep breaths. He staggered to his feet and prepared to run again.

At that moment, a woman in her mid-40s in a white blouse and green pants exited the office and saw Mordecai up against the wall. She gave him a hard look. 'Mr. Jefferson,' she said, 'What is the meaning of this? What are you doing?'

Amid his breaths he said, 'Hatfield, McCoy, and Jones are after me again! They've been harassing and assaulting me since I had started attending high school!'

'I find that hard to believe,' the woman frowned, 'Why would they want to do that?'

'You ask them,' Mordecai shouted, 'but they are after me!'

'I suggest you refrain from using that tone of voice with me, young man,' warned the woman, 'I could have you suspended for that!'

Mordecai groaned. It was clear he was getting nowhere. He shook his head and rounded the corner. He found the bullies had spotted him and were running in his direction. He stood there for a moment and walked back around the corner. He saw the woman still standing there, frowning at him. 'I suggest you get to your next class,' she told him.

Mordecai did not say a word but walked back around the corner and stopped as the three bullies stopped in front of him. 'Decided to take your medicine, did you, Jefferson?' Frank said.

'If I were you, McCoy,' Mordecai replied amid breaths, 'you and your ilk would just turn around and leave me alone.' The bullies continued walking toward him. 'Stay back,' cried Mordecai. 'Stay away from me!'

'You must be joking,' Stu laughed, 'It's been too long since we gave you a beating, and we're going to make up for lost time now.'

'Why do you afflict me so?' cried Mordecai. 'Why do you enjoy picking on people like me?'

'Like we need a reason?' Chuck taunted, 'It's obvious! You are a nobody, a loser! People like you deserve to be beaten up and picked on! You stay in line, you'll be fine. Give us slack, we'll pay you back. We hate you and others like you. You're here on this earth to be our personal punching bag, to be there for us to do what we want to do to you, and nobody will help you! The administration, the teachers, we've got them in our back pocket. They won't punish us, no matter what we do to you.'

'Should we throw him in the dumpster?' Stu asked.

'Tie him up and take him back to the woods and beat him up like we did last week?' Chuck suggested.

'Or be escorted to the office right now?' came the woman's voice. She appeared from around the corner after overhearing the conversation.

'Vice Principal Mallory,' Frank exclaimed, 'How… how long have you been there?'

'So, you have us in your back pocket, do you now?' Mallory replied sternly, 'What exactly do you mean by that?'

'No… nothing, really,' lied Stu, 'We were just playing with him.'

'I don't play your games, and I never will,' growled Mordecai.

He then saw Cece, Sharon, and Tiffany rounding the corner, winded after following the bullies.

'In this case, your games have gone on way too long, to me and people like me!' added Mordecai.

'I want the four of you in my office, now,' ordered Mallory.

'Wait,' Cece gasped, 'My brother… my brother was running from them! You… you can't punish him! Please, Vice Principal Mallory, hasn't… hasn't he suffered enough?'

'Get to your classes, the three of you,' warned Vice Principal Mallory, 'I have business with these boys!'

'We're coming too,' gasped Cece amid breaths, 'This travesty has gone on for far too long! Please, you must listen to us!'

'Very well,' replied Mallory sternly. They followed the vice principal into her office.

Dr. Von Braun and President Farouk were drinking while they sat in the presidential helicopter heading toward the spot near Mount Rushmore where the president had his meeting with the dragon. The president had a Jack Daniels, while Dr. Von Braun had a scotch. 'I am grateful you have scotch on board,' Dr. Von Braun said.

'I started buying it for you since I know you like scotch,' replied President Farouk, 'I somehow knew that sooner or later, you would have to know about Shadowfire.'

'I have already known about him for about two months now,' Dr. Von Braun said, 'The first time he spoke to me in my dreams, I was unsure what to think. He introduced himself to me right away. "This may be a dream," he told me, "but my communications to you, I assure you, are real."

' "How did you know about me?" I asked him.

' "I heard you are renowned in your field of study of genetics," Shadowfire said to me, "and I understand you have an obsession with finding fairies."

' "I don't know if you would call it an obsession," I replied, "though those who don't know me personally would think that I was. How did you find out about me?"

' "I wield great sorcerous powers," he told me, "Through divination I have come to have knowledge of you. I understand you wish to reveal the existence of fairies."

' "Indeed," I answered, "Do you know?"

' "Yes, fairies do exist," answered Shadowfire, "You have heard rumors of fairies that may be in a wooded area in the Orlando area. Sooner or later, you will come across a young man who will come across a fairy very soon."

' "That is what brought me to Orlando in the first place," I replied, "I have been searching for their hidden home as well, Arundel Haven." I told him how I found the book which told of the secret kingdom and all that was told in it. He told me of the remains of a fairy that had died about a year ago. I had told you about it, and it was from Shadowfire I had learned of the remains. I studied it and was astonished how similar to humans they were, practically the same identical DNA, but how they evolved wings still puzzles me. I asked him how I would know who this boy was, what his name was. "For some reason, I cannot find out his name or what he looks like," said Shadowfire, "though I enquired of the Holy Mother after offering Her a sacrifice. She said She was unclear, and something kept Her from finding out who he was. I was told of you and that soon, you would encounter him."

'I wasn't pleased that he wasn't clear on this boy, but eventually I found him, Mordy Jefferson. He overheard our conversation about fairies when I was buying a beer from a convenient store. Shadowfire proved to be right in this case about the boy.'

'I remember my first encounter with Shadowfire,' President Farouk said, 'He first spoke to me in a dream, telling me to come to an area near Mount Rushmore, where we meet now. I was scared when I first saw him. "I have noticed you for years," he told me, "My master had spoken about you, told me who you are. You wish to become president, do you not?"

' "Yes," I answered, still trembling.

' "Do not be afraid," Shadowfire told me, "I can help you win the election. That is why I'm here, to help you. I can invoke my master to influence the way the people think. It will not work on all Americans, but to those who are on the fence, the spell be the strongest. The media will help influence the voters, put many under a spell to support you."

' "What's in it for you?" I fearfully asked.

'"There is one thing, but it's minor," Shadowfire answered, "Somewhere in your country, there is a young man who is prophesied to be my bane. I have not found him yet. I had been searching for over a century but have not found him. I know now that my bane is alive and would be revealed. I know he lives here in the States, but which part has been hidden from me."

' "So you need to find this boy whom you believe to be the one some ancient prophecy says would destroy you?" I asked him.

' "It is all I ask of you," Shadowfire answered, "I know the time draws nigh when this boy will be revealed, but how soon, I do not know."

'I bowed. "I will help you," I replied, "If he is in the States, I will find him somehow."

'He let me go, and of course, I won the election in 2008. Last year before the election, I was compelled to return to the same spot where I had meetings with the dragon. "You will be re-elected," he said, "I will make sure of it. I have spells cast upon your opponent so that he will fail in his bid. I will make it seem like he may win, but it will only be for a time, it will seem like it until the election. No matter what happens, you shall win the election again."

' "I have heard nothing about the boy you speak of," I told him.

' "Not yet," replied Shadowfire, "but now I know the time draws nearer than I expected. I will continue to inquire my master. Let me know if you hear of anything."

'I nodded. And of course, the rest is history. For a while, I was worried, even though Shadowfire had told me it would be that way beforehand, that even the polls would be against me, but when election time came, I was re-elected. It was exactly what Shadowfire had said.'

Dr. Von Braun poured himself another scotch. 'How interesting,' he said, 'Somehow, Shadowfire knew you would win the election despite the polls and the plans of your opponents. I am glad things worked out the way it did. You were deserving of re-election for sure, and it turned out that way.'

'I had shown the pictures to Shadowfire,' said President Farouk, 'Using a spell, he projected the pictures as large as the helicopter so he could see. He knows now the boy's name, but not the fairy he's in love with.'

'We will talk more of this when we meet with Shadowfire,' Dr. Von Braun said, drinking his scotch. President Farouk had another glass of Jack Daniels. 'I never get tired of this stuff,' he sighed, 'My wife is concerned about how much of this I drink. "It would do the nation no good to have a president who drinks too much," Barbara told me, "Some are concerned about the example you're setting." '

'Barbara has good intentions,' replied Dr. Von Braun, 'She worries too much, but she can be right.'

'I have never seen you with your wife,' said President Farouk.

'I am not married,' Dr. Von Braun stated simply, 'I am married to my work, to my quest to find a fairy and reveal their existence to the world, to finding their hidden home, Arundel Haven. That has kept me going. I do not desire to have a wife.'

'A shame,' replied President Farouk, 'but to each their own. I thought with all the money you have, that you would have a wife and child.'

'When I am gone, I plan to leave the money to my niece Hazel Helmsley,' said Dr. Von Braun, 'She is twenty-three now, but she is the only one in my family who knows about my studies of fairies. "None of the family must know of this until I have proof," I told her. "I will not reveal what I have found until I find a real fairy."

' "How close are you to finding one, uncle?" she asked.

' "I have heard rumors of a possible fairy sighting in the United States," I answered, "in a wooded area in the city of Orlando, Florida." This was after I had seen a fairy firsthand but did not have a camera. Even if I had the fairy photographed, I would still need proof of a live fairy. If I can somehow capture this Raven, I will have the proof I need.'

'How often have you contacted your niece, Hazel?' President Farouk asked.

'About once every two weeks,' Dr. Von Braun answered, 'She knows about Mordy Jefferson and how I suspected he'd had an encounter with a fairy. Just yesterday, I had faxed the photos of young Mordy and Raven together. She is studying to follow in my footsteps as well.'

'That is great to hear,' nodded President Farouk, 'What are your plans if you were to capture Raven?'

'To study her, for one, and eventually,' the geneticist answered. 'to find out where Arundel Haven is. She may not talk, but now that she has a human lover, if I were to have both, I could convince her to tell me.'

'This is sounding like kidnapping,' chuckled President Farouk.

'I will do what must be done to find Arundel Haven,' replied Dr. Von Braun seriously, 'I will find it eventually. It's just a matter of time. I will reveal it to the world. And, of course, you could claim the land in the name of the United States.'

President Farouk smiled. 'I'm beginning to like the idea,' he said, 'Get whoever is the ruling power there to submit to U.S. control, make them submit to our laws and our rule.'

'Oh, you are sounding like an emperor, old friend,' chuckled Dr. Von Braun, 'Invade and conquer. My, my, what would your opponents say, as if you cared? It does not matter, though,' he added with a grim look upon his face. 'Whatever end justifies the means, and I mean to find Arundel Haven.'

The helicopter made a landing in the clearing. Both men heard the motor winding down and then become silent. Dr. Von Braun smiled. 'It is time,' he said as the door opened, and they disembarked from the helicopter.

From the skies, Shadowfire descended and landed in front of them. The aides refused to venture outside, but Dr. Von Braun and President Farouk walked toward the dragon without fear.

Shadowfire saw the two men approach and said, 'Welcome, my friends.' To Dr. Von Braun he said, 'It is a pleasure at last to see you face to face, Haman.'

'And to finally see you, 'O great Shadowfire,' he replied, 'I have been looking forward to this meeting for a long time.'

'I have seen the pictures of Mordy Jefferson you had given Ahmad,' said Shadowfire.

'I questioned his sister and her friends,' said Dr. Von Braun, 'She was clearly upset about his disappearance.'

'Disappearance?' Shadowfire exclaimed.

'From what I gathered from them, he was taken by fairies, perhaps taken to Arundel Haven,' replied Dr. Von Braun.

Shadowfire's face turned hard. 'He was in Arundel Haven?' he roared in surprise, 'He was there when I had last attacked its inhabitants? I am frustrated I could not find this out somehow. I do not understand.' He growled. 'So, he has met Queen Cymbaline.'

'Queen Cymbaline?' Dr. Von Braun asked, 'So, she's the one who rules Arundel Haven?'

'Shadowfire had mentioned her by name once at our last meeting,' explained President Farouk, 'I only heard her name, nothing more.'

'Yes,' nodded Shadowfire, 'by now, the boy has learned about the prophecy of Queen Hephzibah and that he is the one who will destroy me, along with the fairy maiden. I wonder if this fairy in the photo is the one as well?'

'Her name is Raven, I found out,' Dr. Von Braun proclaimed, 'One of the friends of his sister told me her name. She apparently knows her as well. I know the three of them had contact with Raven.'

'Raven,' mused Shadowfire. 'That child she had. It is not hers, then?'

'Shadowfire?' President Farouk asked, gazing at the dragon.

'When I was pursuing Raven, she had a child in her arms,' Shadowfire recalled, 'I thought it was hers, but apparently that is not the case. Who was that child? If it was not hers, then who does the child belong to?' He turned to Dr. Von Braun. 'You have done well, my friend,' he said, 'Now I know the name of the fairy as well as my bane.'

'So, you believe Mordy Jefferson is the one this prophecy says will destroy you?' Dr. Von Braun asked stoically, 'He is practically a nobody!'

'So I thought when I saw him in his dream,' replied Shadowfire, 'but I know beyond a shadow of a doubt that he is the one the Prophecy of Queen Hephzibah spoke of. I'm beginning to think that Raven is the fairy maiden as well. I can't take any chances!'

'I understand your concern, Shadowfire,' said Dr. Von Braun, 'I wish to take Raven to prove the fairies' existence to the world. I don't have sufficient proof without a live fairy, but with Raven, I can reveal my findings. Raven would be the final piece to the puzzle.'

Shadowfire chanted and raised his claws. Before them, a table with food and strong drink, vodka and scotch, appeared before them. Two chairs appeared at the table. 'Come, eat,' Shadowfire said.

Dr. Von Braun stared at a bottle. 'Ah, scotch,' he said, 'You know me too well, Shadowfire.'

Shadowfire chuckled. 'Of course,' he said, 'Only the best.'

'Indeed,' President Farouk said, 'We are grateful.'

'Only a small reward for your help,' Shadowfire replied, 'Now I know who the two are who are prophesied to destroy me.'

As they ate, Dr. Von Braun thought. 'Allow me to take care of Raven, Shadowfire,' he said, 'With her—'

'Of course,' nodded Shadowfire, 'I will allow you this. What could be worse for the fairies than the human world learning of their existence and have the humans invade their home?'

'Indeed,' replied President Farouk, drinking his vodka, 'or to have some form of human government take over their home? Of course, our enemies would protest and stand with them if they knew.'

'Perhaps that could be arranged,' Shadowfire said thoughtfully, 'I will leave Raven to you, Haman, but as for Mordy, I want him as a sacrifice to my master. I will deal with him myself.'

'I can send my men to take him if you wish,' suggested President Farouk.

'I would not advise that,' Shadowfire objected, 'If your enemies heard, it could give you bad press if you seize Mordy without just cause.'

'I could declare him as an enemy of the state,' the President said.

'Without just cause? Not a good idea politically, old friend,' replied Shadowfire, 'I will have to reveal myself after all to take Mordy and keep the prophecy from being fulfilled.'

'Then discretion must be used,' replied President Farouk, 'Such matters are delicate.'

Shadowfire nodded. 'I don't doubt you are right, but the time for the prophecy to be fulfilled is soon nigh, and I am becoming desperate. Your men can locate Mordy for me and aid in capturing his fairy lover, Raven. Haste in this matter has made it necessary for me to act.'

'If you believe it so, old friend,' President Farouk replied, 'then do what must be done. I will send my men to locate Mordy.'

'My men will help you in that,' added Dr. Von Braun. 'They know where he attends school and the area he lives.'

'I will access his address and give it to them,' President Farouk said as he drank his vodka.

Shadowfire nodded in affirmation.

'I do hope that is over,' Cece sighed as she, Mordecai, Sharon and Tiffany left the office, 'I hope this is finally it.'

'We thought so before when it seemed like it,' sighed Mordecai, 'but it turned out not to be the case. We can only wait and see.'

'Do you have any more clothes like the ones you're wearing, Mordy?' Sharon asked.

'No,' answered Mordecai, 'I will have to have the fairies ask Queen Cymbaline for more clothes like this. I like them.'

'It does look good on you, though,' Tiffany smiled, 'What happened to the other clothes you wore?'

'Back at Arundel Haven,' Mordecai answered, 'I had no need of them. I liked what Queen Cymbaline had given me.'

'You should have asked the Queen for more like this,' Sharon said.

'I am thankful for what she had already given me,' Mordecai replied, 'We can speak more about it after school is out. I look forward to seeing Raven again.'

Molly talked with Raven, Lavender, and Laurelin as they sat in the kitchen. The three fairies each had a can of soda in their hands. 'I'm beginning to like this,' Laurelin said. 'How do you make it?'

'I don't know,' Molly said, 'I buy them from the grocery store when I go shopping for food. We work to pay the bills, the mortgage and to buy food and our necessities. I know it's kind of complicated to you.'

'So many things we have never seen or known before,' Lavender said, 'I know the Queen would be mad if we ourselves came here without her leave, but we had gone with your son to make sure Raven stays out of trouble.'

'Is Raven always this adventurous?' Molly asked.

Raven gave Lavender and Laurelin a queer look. Molly laughed. 'I guess that answers my question,' she chuckled.

'Why are you uncomfortable with others with different skin colors, if I may ask?' Raven asked, 'No such prejudice exists among fairykind.'

'She's right,' Lavender replied, 'but we do have mistrust of humans. Somehow, Mordecai understands why.'

Molly sighed. 'I guess it's the way we were brought up as kids,' she attempted to explain, 'My parents did not like people with a different skin color when I was growing up, but I wasn't as against people of color as they once were. They had changed their views just after Tony and I got married, but I was still uncomfortable. Some of their friends are people of color and are close from what I now understand. Tony was brought up the same way I was.'

'What do you believe about those with dark skin?' Raven asked.

Molly sighed. 'I… I wish I could tell you, but since I got to know you, Raven, I see my misconceptions have been wrong. But then again, you're a fairy, not a human. But I think I see that perhaps we are not as different as I thought we would be.'

'Maybe you are right, Mrs. Jefferson,' Laurelin said softly, 'especially since we met Tiffany and Sharon. At least, that's how I feel.'

'No, no,' replied Lavender, 'you speak for the both of us. I'm beginning to see how Twila saw your son when she first met him.'

'Do all fairy toddlers fly off like that?' Molly asked giggling.

'Afraid so,' Raven answered, 'especially when they find out they can fly. Once they start, they don't want to stop.'

'So Twila wasn't afraid of Mordy when she first saw him?' Molly asked.

'Not at all from what Starla had told me,' Raven answered, 'She became attached to him the first time she met him. She did not see he was a human, not even when he told her so. All she saw was what a wonderful person he was.'

Molly smiled. 'I'm beginning to understand now,' she replied, touching Raven's hand. 'I am sorry I saw you as black and as a fairy instead of the person you are inside. I am glad Mordy met you, Raven.'

'Thank you, Mrs. Jefferson,' Raven smiled.

'What kind of life do you think you and my son would have together?' asked Molly.

Raven sighed. 'I know it will not be easy. He already has a place in Arundel Haven and is now in favor of Queen Cymbaline, but as for the human world, it would be harder. There has never been a union between a human and a fairy. We would be the first.'

'This is still a lot to take in,' Molly said, 'What about Shadowfire and the prophecy you had spoken of?'

'It is said that God will use Mordecai and me to bring an end to the dragon, but how, I do not know,' Raven said, 'Both of us are scared about it, but we both know in our hearts that it is true. He accepted it willingly, out of love, not of force, but for me, Twila, and the Queen herself. He has kept the secret to protect us.'

'But our presence here jeopardizes that secret,' Lavender stated, 'Don't get me wrong, I have come to accept that we are not as different as we would like to think, fairies and humans, but there are some ways…'

'No need to apologize, Lavender,' Molly said, 'Coming to think of it, my son was right in trying to protect your secret and your Queen in decreeing a ban on fairies coming here. There are so many bad things here that you should not be exposed to. I do not like the idea of the prophecy, though.'

'Because you love your son,' Raven nodded, 'I know. I love Mordecai with all my heart, which I pray you and your husband will understand. He would never do anything to hurt you, but what we do is out of love for each other, and the prophecy, out of love for those we love. We will prevail. God has promised that.'

Molly shook her head. 'But will that be enough, from what you told me of Shadowfire?'

At that moment, they heard the front door open and close. Raven rose out of her seat and when she saw Mordecai with Cece, Sharon, and Tiffany, she ran into his arms, holding and kissing him. They gazed into each other's eyes. 'I missed you, my sweet Raven,' he told her.

Raven kissed him, touching his face. 'I missed you as well, Mordecai, my love. I am glad you are home.'

Lavender, Laurelin, and Molly entered the room. Molly saw her son with Raven in his arms and was about to say something but stopped herself. She stared at the lovers. *Mordy, you seem so happy with Raven. Maybe your father and I were wrong for opposing your relationship with her. Now I have gotten to know her better, I see past her skin color and the fact she is a fairy. She smiled. Maybe I could get used to having a fairy, a black fairy, as a daughter-in-law. I hope Tony will see it that way, too.*

'I thought you had cheerleader practice today?' Molly asked.

'It got cancelled,' Cece said, 'The coach had an emergency she had to take care of right away. We came right home. Maybe they'll have practice tomorrow.'

Lavender and Laurelin greeted Cece, Tiffany, and Sharon. 'I hope you two will stick around for a while,' Tiffany said, 'I would like to know you two better.'

'So do I,' Sharon replied.

Laurelin nodded. 'I don't see why not,' she said, 'We're not in any hurry really.'

'Have you ever had pizza before?' Tiffany asked.

'What is pizza?' Laurelin asked.

'It's a long circle of dough, about 12 inches round,' Sharon explained, 'topped with tomato sauce and mozzarella cheese. You can have toppings like pepperoni, mushrooms, sausage, ham, chicken, onions, which is baked and eaten.'

'Sounds good,' Lavender replied, 'I have never had pizza before.'

'We can go to *Rossi's* on the Trail, the seven of us,' Tiffany said, 'and we can have pizza there.'

Mordecai released Raven and shook his head. 'I don't think that would be a good idea,' he objected, 'I don't want the other humans to know about them. Besides, Tiffany, the seven of us would not all fit into your car.'

'But the minivan is big enough,' Molly suggested.

'May be too risky, Mom,' Mordecai disagreed, 'If they had their wings covered, it could hide the fact that they are fairies, but things could go wrong.'

'Maybe so, Mordecai,' Laurelin told him, 'but I am curious about this pizza that your friend speaks about.'

Raven was surprised to hear Laurelin speak Mordecai's name.

'We're not in a hurry right now to go home,' Lavender added, 'I'm sure we could stay another night.'

Molly smiled.

Mordecai stared at Lavender and Laurelin. 'I thought you were not trusting of us humans—of me,' he said, 'I am still worried about having your existence exposed to the world. I do not want that to happen.'

'Oh, come on, Mordy,' Sharon said, 'It would give them a chance to know us better, to come and see that there are good humans. I think it's only right.'

'I think it's a good idea,' Molly told her son, 'I have errands to run, but you all can ride with me, and I can drop you off there. Cece and I can give Raven, Lavender, and Laurelin some clothes to cover up their wings, so they won't be exposed.'

Raven stared pleadingly at Mordecai. 'I am willing, my love,' she said, 'I think Lavender and Laurelin are beginning to see what I see. Let's do this.'

Mordecai sighed. 'I still don't think it's a good idea,' he sighed, 'but if that's what you want, Raven, okay, we can.'

'Then it's settled,' Molly said excitedly. Turning to Cece she said, 'Let's see what clothes we can gather for them.'

Tiffany and Sharon headed home to change their clothes and returned sometime later. By the time they returned, Raven, Lavender, and Laurelin wore human clothes that covered up their wings and their own clothes underneath. While they waited for Tiffany and Sharon to return, Mordecai and Raven were outside on the back porch dancing slowly, holding each other close. *Fields of Gold* by Sting was playing over the radio as they danced and kissed. Raven leaned her head upon his shoulders as they stared into each other's eyes.

From the door, Molly and Cece watched as the lovers danced. A tear started falling from her eye, seeing how happy they were together. Cece smiled. 'I can't remember seeing Mordy so happy before,' she told her mother.

'I know,' Molly sighed, 'I should have known there was something special about Raven. I now see how happy Raven has made him. He has indeed chosen well.'

Mordecai and Raven continued to dance as the song went to *Two Hearts as One* by Jesse Clemmons and Rosangela Ferreira as the words of the song echoed in their minds, binding their hearts closer and stronger than ever.

At that moment, they heard a cry in the air: *Morcai, Morcai!*

They looked up and saw Starla and Twila flying toward them. Starla carried in her hands a sack, while Twila had flown beside her. Twila flew into Mordecai's arms as she descended, laughing, and giggling and kissing him. 'Little Twila,' he cried, 'What are you doing here?'

'Twila miss Uncle Morcai,' Twila chimed, kissing him on the cheeks.

Raven and Starla embraced. Raven stared at her sister. 'What are you doing here?' she asked.

'I was sent by Queen Cymbaline,' Starla answered as an astonished Molly and Cece stepped outside. Starla was a bit afraid when they appeared. 'Don't be afraid,' Raven told her sister. 'This is Mordecai's mother, Molly, and his sister, Cece.'

Cece stared at Twila. 'So, you must be Twila,' she said.

'Twila love Uncle Morcai,' Twila told Cece.

Molly giggled as she shook Starla's hands. 'I've been told about your daughter, how lively she is,' she told Starla.

'I am Starla, Raven's sister. I am pleased to meet you, Molly.'

'I can't believe how attached your daughter is to my son,' Molly exclaimed, 'I know you must be proud of her.'

'I am,' Starla nodded.

Mordecai embraced Starla and said, 'I am happy to see you again, Starla, but what are you doing here? Is all well?'

'It is well,' Starla answered, 'For one, Twila wanted to see you again.'

'Wow, she is so cute, Starla,' Cece exclaimed, 'Raven told me she is two.'

'Twila two,' Twila stated proudly, holding up two little fingers.

Cece turned to Starla. 'I'm Mordecai's sister, Cece. He and Raven have told me about you.'

'And Mordecai has spoken about you, Cece,' replied Starla.

'I am happy to see you and Twila, Starla,' Mordecai said, 'but what are you doing here?'

'Queen Cymbaline had some clothes made for you much like the ones you are wearing,' proclaimed Starla, 'I volunteered to make the flight with Roosevelt's leave. Besides, if I didn't, Twila would have flown off again to see you.'

Mordecai took the bag, and with his free arm, looked through it. As he did, Lavender and Laurelin stepped outside and saw Starla with the others. Cece helped him with the clothes. 'Wow, she is really attached to you,' she told Mordecai.

Molly stared at Twila. Twila looked at her and said, 'Hi.'

Molly smiled. 'You are so cute. What's your name?'

'Twila,' the black fairy toddler chimed.

'Why are you dressed in human clothes?' Starla asked, 'I thought you didn't like humans.'

'We've gotten to know Mordecai and his family better,' Lavender explained, 'We are anxious to know Cece's friends, Tiffany and Sharon. They are taking us to a place to have pizza.'

'What is pizza, Uncle Morcai?' Twila asked Mordecai.

'It's almost like bread with tomato sauce and cheese on top,' Mordecai answered, 'Some meats and vegetables are put on top for toppings.'

'Twila have pizza?' Twila asked, her eyes sparkling.

Starla sighed. 'So that's why you're dressed in human clothes?' she asked.

'That too,' Lavender nodded.

Mordecai sighed. 'I still don't think this is a good idea.'

'Would you join us, Starla, you and your daughter?' Cece asked.

'I am curious about this pizza you speak of,' said Starla. She then paused. 'That reminds me,' she said, pulling three small bottles from the bag. 'Queen Cymbaline instructed me to give these to you, Cece. It will give you the ability to fly for a short period of time, unlike Mordecai, since his ability is permanent.'

'How long?' asked Cece. 'How long would it last?'

'About a week,' answered Starla. 'She gave me three to give to you, perhaps to share with two people close to you. Your brother is in high favor with the Queen.'

'Give her my thanks when you and Twila return to Arundel Haven,' Mordecai told Starla, 'You do need to rest after so long a journey, especially with the child you carry.'

'You're pregnant?' Molly asked, 'Congratulations, Starla! I am happy for you.'

'Thank you,' Starla replied.

'I don't think you should return right away, since you have just arrived here,' Mordecai said to Starla, 'You need sufficient time to rest, especially since you have a new life inside of you.'

'Little brother,' chimed Twila, pointing to Starla's stomach.

'Twila thinks it's a boy,' giggled Starla, 'I'm beginning to think so, too.'

'I agree with my son,' Molly said, 'You should give yourself ample time to rest. At least spend the night so you will be fresh for your return flight to Arundel Haven.'

'I will take you up on your kind offer, Molly,' said Starla, 'Thank you.'

Twila cheered as she hugged Mordecai's neck. Mordecai cradled the little fairy toddler in his arms. Molly smiled as she watched. 'Little Twila is a little sweetheart,' she said, 'If you come with me, Starla, I can find something for you to cover your wings.'

'I am grateful,' Starla smiled, 'Thank you.'

Cece stared at Mordecai and Twila. Raven wrapped her arms around him and kissed him on the cheeks.

Tiffany and Sharon arrived a short time later as Starla came downstairs. She did not recognize her but saw that she looked like Raven but was a little older. They saw the toddler in Mordecai's arms with a small shirt covering her wings. Twila laid contently in Mordecai's arms. They walked over to them as Sharon said, 'What a cute little girl!'

'Twila,' the toddler chimed, 'Twila love Uncle Morcai.'

'You're Twila?' Tiffany asked.

Sharon stared at Starla. 'Then you have to be Starla, Raven's sister.'

'I see that Raven has told you about me,' Starla replied.

'But what are you doing here?' Tiffany asked.

'Queen Cymbaline had sent her,' answered Mordecai. 'She gave me more of the clothes I wore on my return. I am glad they are here.'

'Twila miss Uncle Morcai,' she chimed.

'Starla and Twila are coming with us,' Mordecai said, 'but we'll have to take both vehicles as well. The minivan alone won't be enough for all of us, and none of us who can fly will fly in public. I still feel uneasy about his, but we must be mindful not to speak too much in public about Arundel Haven. It is not fit for public conversation since we do not wish for Raven and the others be revealed as fairies.'

'I will help keep it a secret,' Molly said, surprised how Mordecai was mature enough to handle the situation. She agreed, the fairies' existence must be kept a secret. She smiled as she saw Twila in Mordecai's arms, noticing how she called him *uncle Morcai*. 'You're not married to Raven yet,' she chuckled, 'and already, you have a little niece.'

Mordecai smiled as he cuddled Twila in his arms. 'She is a sweetheart,' he said.

'A lively one,' laughed Starla.

'I was told about her escapades into the castle of your Queen,' laughed Molly, 'Toddlers are a handful, whether they are human or fairy.' To Raven she said, 'Wait until you and Mordy have one of your own.'

Lavender, Laurelin, Cece, Tiffany, and Sharon gave out soft laughter. 'Look out!' laughed Sharon. 'You two sure you can handle children?'

'Let's not get too far ahead just yet,' Mordecai said, 'The time will come, but not yet.'

'At least Twila would be good practice for you,' Molly told him, 'Raven has some experience from what I'd been told.' To Starla she asked, 'How far along are you, Starla?'

'About three months,' answered Starla, 'For some reason, Twila thinks I'm having a boy.'

'So you're going to be an aunt again, eh, Raven?' Sharon smiled. Raven nodded her head.

'I guess we all are ready, aren't we?' Mordecai said, 'You comfortable in that, Starla?'

'I'm uncomfortable with my wings being covered up,' answered Starla, 'but I'll be fine. So long as we pass to other humans as human.'

Mordecai sighed. 'I still don't feel comfortable about doing this,' he said.

'They'll be fine, Mordy,' Molly said, 'We'll all be fine. You, Raven, Starla, and Twila will ride with me, and Lavender and Laurelin will ride with Tiffany, Cece, and Sharon.'

They headed out the door. Molly was the last one to leave the house. She closed and locked the door.

Mordecai had an uneasy feeling about bringing the fairies out in the open like this. He said no more of the matter as he and Raven slipped into the back seat, allowing Starla to sit in the front with his mother.

The cars drove out of the driveway and headed down the road.

Chapter Ten

They arrived at *Rossi's Pizzeria* on Orange Blossom Trail just off Oak Ridge Rd. They stepped out of the cars. Mordecai, still holding Twila, looked around. His mother noticed this and asked, 'Mordy, what are you doing?'

'Keeping a lookout for Dr. Von Braun or his men,' he answered grimly, 'He and his two men have been at my school on occasion and followed me when I was riding my bike to and from school. I fear they may be around.'

'Honey, aren't you being ridiculous?'

Mordecai shook his head. 'Not when it comes to Raven and the others,' he answered grimly, 'I'm nervous as it is having them out here.'

'Wow, there are so many things I have never seen before,' Starla said, looking around, 'I can't believe I rode in a human vehicle.' 'I like flying better,' Mordecai replied, 'only here, I have to refrain.'

Cece and the others joined them. Lavender and Laurelin were fascinated as well. 'I still can't believe I was in a horseless carriage,' she exclaimed, 'and how fast it goes.'

'I am amazed what you humans come up with here,' Laurelin said.

Molly prepared to slip back inside the minivan. 'I must take care of the errands I have,' she said, 'Call me when you are done, Mordy. And try not to look so tense. Raven and the others will be all right.'

Mordecai sighed. Raven kissed him on the lips. 'I'll look after Mordecai, Mrs. Jefferson,' she proclaimed.

Molly smiled as she sat back down inside the van. She drove off as Mordecai and the others entered the building.

The four fairies looked around. They saw the lights and heard the music in the background. Starla stared at Mordecai. 'Where is the music coming from?' she asked.

'From speakers, probably from a computer or radio, a human invention,' Mordecai answered, 'We can wait for someone to escort us to a table.'

Raven leaned her head upon Mordecai's shoulder. Starla took Twila from Mordecai as the toddler looked around. 'Pretty lights,' she said.

'Yes, they are, Twila,' Starla nodded.

It wasn't long until a waitress approached them. She looked at them and asked, 'You all together?'

'Yes, we are,' Mordecai answered, 'Nine of us, counting little Twila.'

The waitress smiled as she glanced at Twila. 'Oh, she's so cute,' she said.

'Twila two,' she told the waitress.

'Do you need a booster seat for your little one, miss?' she asked.

'Yes, she does,' Mordecai answered. 'Twila would want to sit up to the table.'

Starla nodded.

The waitress led them to a table in the corner. One side sat Lavender, Laurelin, Tiffany, and Sharon, while the other side sat Cece, Raven, Mordecai, and Starla with Twila at the end. Twila sat on Starla's lap while the waitress left to fetch a booster seat for the little fairy toddler. 'How many pizzas will we need, two or three?' Mordecai asked.

'We'll order three large pizzas,' Tiffany answered, 'One cheese, one pepperoni mushroom and sausage, and one with all meat.'

'Sounds good,' Cece nodded, 'We just need to find out what we want to drink.'

When the waitress returned with a booster seat, Starla set Twila down next to her. Tiffany gave the waitress the orders and asked for a sweet tea. Sharon, Lavender, and Laurelin asked for the same to drink. 'Give me a root beer,' Mordecai told the waitress.

'What is root beer?' Raven asked.

'It's not really beer, but it has a unique sweet taste,' Mordecai told her.

'I'll take a root beer as well,' Raven said.

Cece ordered a diet soda. 'Would you like to try one too?' she asked Starla.

'I will,' nodded Starla.

'What about Twila?' Raven asked.

'Give her what I'm having,' Starla answered.

The waitress nodded as she walked away to fill the orders. Twila and the other fairies looked around the room. 'This place has been around ever since my parents were children I was told,' Mordecai said. 'I remember times when my parents, Cece and I would come eat here. I love the pizza here.'

'Pizza,' Twila repeated, 'Twila get pizza?'

'Yes, Twila,' laughed Starla, 'We are all getting pizza.'

'I'm not sure what you girls wanted,' Tiffany told Lavender and Laurelin, 'so I ordered three different types of pizza.'

'We are fine with any of them,' Lavender said, 'I'm just undecided on what kind I want.'

'If three is not enough, I can have them make another one,' Tiffany said, 'I should be able to cover it.'

'Not without us chipping in,' Mordecai said, 'I can give you

at least a five.'

'Don't worry about it, Mordy,' Cece told him, 'I have some money to help out.'

'So do I,' Sharon replied, 'Between the three of us, we'll have enough to cover it.'

'We have nothing like this back home,' Laurelin said, looking around, 'We light our homes with candles. How can you light your buildings without candles?'

'With what we call electricity,' Tiffany answered, 'There are plants that bring power to the whole city. All of our cities are like that.'

'Being in what you call a car is nice,' Lavender said, 'but I prefer flying.'

'No arguments there,' Mordecai agreed, 'I never would imagine how wonderful it is to fly through the air.'

'Twila love to fly,' Twila chimed, 'Uncle Morcai love to fly as well?'

'Yes, sweetie, I do,' answered Mordecai.

'Wait a minute,' Sharon exclaimed, 'Mordy, you can fly? How? How is that possible?'

'Queen Cymbaline's doing,' Mordecai answered, 'There is a place where a river they call the Silverstreams begins, a waterfall flowing from the side of a cliff. The waters were freezing cold. She told me to immerse myself under the falling waters and warned me that it was ice cold, but I trusted her. I found it hard to do so but eventually I forced myself inside and allowed the cold waters to cover me. It was almost unbearable, but I endured it, trusting Queen Cymbaline. It was only a matter of time when I found myself rising from the ground, but I could not tell being covered by the icy cold water after my body started feeling warm. She told me to come out and I found myself floating in the air and soon, flying. She told me the effects were permanent on me. I'm guessing the water in those small bottles given to Cece come from the same water in the Silverstreams.'

'I will be careful with this to be sure,' Cece said, pulling out the bottles. She gave one to Sharon and then to Tiffany. 'They are not to be used lightly,' Mordecai told them, 'I am taking precautions in not flying with people around. They would become suspicious and would draw unwanted attention.'

The waitress returned and gave them each their drinks. Starla took a sip of her drink and nodded. The taste was pleasing to her. Twila had hers in a small cup with a straw. Mordecai took a straw and put it in his drink. 'This is how you can drink it, Twila,' he said as he put his mouth to the straw and sucked the root beer through the straw.

Twila did the same. As she did, a little bit of soda came up through the straw and into her mouth. She did it again, drinking more of the soda. 'I like it, Mommy,' she said as she licked her lips, the bubbles making them tingle.

Raven took a sip of root beer from her cup. She nodded. 'This is good, Mordecai,' she said, 'I wonder how it is made?'

'I have no idea myself,' Mordecai said, 'I just know they make it somehow, put them into cans or bottles, and we buy them at a market where they sell them. It would be interesting to find out how they make it.'

'How long will it take to cook the pizza?' asked Lavender.

'Perhaps ten to fifteen minutes,' Mordecai answered, 'It also depends on how many people the waitress is serving. I don't know the whole process.'

'So by drinking this, we can fly too?' asked Tiffany, holding a vial.

'Yes, but do not use it lightly,' Mordecai said, 'Be wise in when you use it and be careful never to be seen, especially by a certain geneticist who's been badgering us about a certain matter. I am more determined than ever to protect Raven, Starla, Twila, and the other fairies of Arundel Haven. I can't allow myself to be careless, and I pray you three, Cece, Tiffany, and Sharon, will do all you can to protect their secret as well.'

'You need to relax, baby,' Raven told him gently, 'We'll be fine. You worry too much.'

Mordecai stood silent. Starla touched his hand. 'Relax, Mordecai,' she said soothingly, 'Everything will be okay. We're fine.'

Minutes later, the waitress returned with the three pizzas they'd ordered. Twila pointed at the cheese. 'Want that one, Twila?' Starla asked.

'Yes, Mommy,' Twila answered.

Raven took a slice of all meat while Mordecai took the pepperoni, mushroom, and sausage. Lavender and Laurelin took the all meat as well while Cece, Sharon, and Tiffany took a cheese. The taste seemed pleasing to all five fairies, but Twila had trouble at first because it was hot. 'Be careful, Twila,' Starla told her. 'Let it cool down first.' Once it was cooled down enough for Twila, she ate it. She then took another bite. 'Twila like pizza?' Mordecai asked her.

'Yes, uncle Morcai,' answered Twila between bites, 'Pizza good.'

'Yes, I agree,' Laurelin nodded, 'I have never tasted anything like this before.'

'It's one of my favorite foods,' Mordecai said, 'I suppose it could be made in Arundel Haven.'

'You may have to show me, Mordecai,' Raven said, taking another bite of pizza.

'I will do my best, Raven,' replied Mordecai, 'I can cook a little bit, but not too well. I have cooked baked chicken before and made a green bean casserole, but I am still learning.'

'I'd be glad to show you upon your return,' Raven said.

'Have you had any of Mordecai's cooking before, Cece?' Laurelin asked.

'Yes, I have,' Cece answered, 'and he's not that bad really. The food was good. I did take some green bean casserole he cooked at one time. At first, I thought my mother had cooked it, but surprisingly she told me she didn't. Even she liked the way Mordy cooked it.'

'I think that is romantic,' Lavender said. 'I wonder if Derreck could learn to cook? I think it would be so romantic to have my fairyman cook for me.'

'Or Jax,' Laurelin added.

'Your respective boyfriends?' Mordecai asked, 'I have never seen them.'

'You hadn't had a chance to meet them since we didn't trust you at the time,' Lavender replied.

'How do you feel about me now?' the young man asked.

'Things are changing, but there's still some mistrust on my part,' Laurelin said honestly, 'but you're beginning to earn my trust. We have found a connection with Cece's friends, however.'

'I am glad you feel that way,' Tiffany said, 'We feel the same way as well. In a way, we thought Cece was crazy for having all those fairy figurines.'

Cece gazed at Tiffany with a sour look. 'Really?' she asked, 'You think my fascination with fairies is crazy?'

'Now we know it's not, since we met Raven and the others,' Tiffany replied, 'but at the time, we did think it unusual that you would still be into fairies at your age.'

'But there's nothing wrong with that,' Sharon added, 'There never was, even before last week. It was just your thing, and we respected it.'

Mordecai found it amusing. Raven leaned her head upon his shoulder. She had finished her root beer. Mordecai glanced at her glass and asked, 'Would you like some more, Raven?'

'Yes, please,' Raven answered, 'I like this root beer.'

'The only beer Mordy ever wants to drink,' Sharon broke in, 'He says he won't ever consider drinking real beer. He refuses to drink alcohol.'

'I don't blame him really,' Cece replied, 'hearing about what people do when they're intoxicated, especially when they're driving, how they get into accidents. It impairs judgment, and people do crazy things when they drink too much. I have heard such horrible stories.'

'That will never happen to me,' Mordecai said, 'I don't understand how they can drink such foul-tasting stuff. I remember the first time I met Dr. Von Braun, and he said after I refused to drink beer "You don't know what you're missing, boy." Oh yes, I do, more than he realizes.'

'So, I'm guessing he drinks,' Cece inquired.

'Yeah, but who knows what else besides beer?' replied Mordecai, 'I don't know, and I don't care. Whatever he drinks, he can have it, for all I care.'

Raven gently kissed him on the cheeks. Mordecai then turned and kissed Raven on the lips. Twila looked at them and said, 'Uncle Morcai kiss Aunt Raven.'

'Yes, because I love your aunt Raven, Twila,' smiled Mordecai, 'and your aunt Raven loves me too.'

Raven smiled as she nodded. 'Very much,' she added.

'Where will you stay should you and Raven wind up getting married?' Tiffany asked.

'Raven has a cottage in Arundel Haven,' Mordecai said, 'but it has none of the things we have, no electricity, no television or stuff like that, but I have seen it. It is a nice place.'

'But we would not be able to see you,' Cece exclaimed, 'I would miss you so.'

Mordecai nodded sadly. 'That would be our Arundel Haven home, but I would have to find a way to get a job to have a home in our world, and a good job, from the way this economy is, is very hard to find. We would find a way to adjust and figure out how before that day.'

'We'll take it one step at a time,' Raven replied, 'I am still waiting for Jax to propose to you, Laurelin.'

'Me too,' Laurelin sighed, 'I am becoming impatient. Lavender says she's still waiting for Derreck to propose as well.'

Lavender shook his head. 'No luck yet.'

'Could they be afraid of commitment?' Cece asked, 'It seems neither Mordecai nor Raven are.'

Mordecai and Raven stared at each other. 'No, I am not,' he said, 'We both agreed we want to spend our lives together.' His face turned grave. 'But there's the matter of Shadowfire to deal with.' His face softened. 'But this is neither the time nor the place to talk about the matter. Let's talk about better things.'

'I don't know if we'll have cheerleader practice tomorrow since it was cancelled today,' Sharon said, changing the subject, 'I am sure we'll be fine before our game on Friday.'

'I would like to see what one of your games is like,' Raven said.

Mordecai shook his head. 'I don't know if that would be a good idea. I'm sure they still have reservations about the human world.'

'We do,' Lavender said, 'and I am glad Mordecai is concerned about us. As curious as we are, I think he is right to be cautious.'

'But what game is it that you play?' Laurelin asked.

'It's not us,' Tiffany replied, 'Our football team. They play what we call football. The object is to score more points than the other team, and it can be scored by touchdowns, field goals or a safety.'

'I do not understand,' Lavender said.

'It would be interesting to see what you are talking about, Tiffany,' Laurelin said, 'What this football they play is like.'

Mordecai looked concerned. Raven glanced at him and kissed them. 'Baby, we'll be fine,' she said, 'Nothing will happen as long as we keep our wings covered.'

'I'm sorry,' Mordecai sighed, 'I can't help but worry. I don't want anything to happen to any one of you.'

Raven had her glass of root beer refilled by the waitress, as did Mordecai. The others got a refill of the drinks they had. Twila lifted her cup and asked, 'More, please?'

The waitress smiled as she took the cup and refilled it. 'She is so cute,' she said. 'What's her name?'

'Twila,' Twila chimed joyfully, 'Twila two.'

'Twila is my daughter,' Starla said.

'They're visiting from out of town,' Mordecai said, 'They're joining us for supper.'

'I remember seeing you two here,' the waitress told Sharon and Tiffany. 'Are you still dating the guys you ate with before?'

'They're both working now,' Tiffany answered, 'We plan to come dine here on the weekend, so you will be seeing us with them. We're here with our best friend Cece, her brother, and our friends.'

'I love pizza,' Twila chimed. She drank her soda.

The waitress smiled then left them again. Twila pointed at a slice with pepperoni, mushroom, and sausage. 'Mommy, pizza please?' she asked.

Starla grabbed a small slice for her daughter. Twila looked at the toppings and started picking them off the pizza and eating them. She then took the pizza and took a bite. Tomato sauce was starting to form around the toddler's mouth. 'Wow, Twila has really taken to pizza,' Sharon laughed.

'It would seem,' Starla replied, 'I like it, too.'

Raven took a slice of cheese pizza. 'Indeed, we need to learn how to make this back home,' she said, 'I have never tasted anything like this before.'

Lavender and Laurelin each took another piece. 'I am impressed,' Laurelin said. 'I would love to learn to make this myself.'

'So, I take it neither of your men proposed to either of you?' Starla asked, 'Why do you think that is?'

'Maybe afraid of commitment?' Tiffany suggested, 'Most men are. I guess it's like that to men here and fairymen as well, why, I don't know.'

'I remember my cousin Tommy,' Sharon recalled, 'He was in a relationship with this girl, Stacy, for almost ten years before he finally proposed. Even then, Stacy had to twist his arm to do it.'

'That must hurt,' Lavender replied, 'Is that the way you humans are in courtship?'

'No, no, Lavender,' Sharon answered, 'It's a figure of speech. Stacy had to convince him to propose to her, talked him into it. She didn't literally twist his arm, but it seems you may have to try that if you want your fairyman to propose to you.' She laughed.

'Not literally, Lavender,' Mordecai said, 'As for Raven and me, it didn't take much. We knew we were right for each other. Our hearts testified to that.'

'Yes,' Raven smiled, 'We knew right away from the moment we met. We felt a connection, but it took two weeks for each of us to have the courage to say it.'

'What we call love at first sight,' added Cece.

'Exactly,' Mordecai nodded, 'but neither of us were sure how the other felt. It was when we looked into each other's eyes deeply when we came together in a gentle kiss. That's when we were sure.'

'I'm sorry I had to keep it a secret from you two, Lavender and Laurelin,' Raven told them, 'but at the time, you wouldn't understand, and at the time, when you found me and Mordecai together confirmed why. But things worked out for the best.'

'But the dragon,' Laurelin said, 'Shadowfire. You still believe you are the one the Prophecy of Queen Hephzibah spoke of?'

'Without a doubt, yes,' Raven answered, 'but please, let us not speak of it here.'

'Twila no like Shadowfire,' Twila said, hiding her face, 'Shadowfire bad!'

'Yes, he is, Twila,' Mordecai nodded as Twila got up from her seat, crawled to Mordecai, and held him tight. 'I promise I will not let Shadowfire harm you.' He held Twila close for a moment and set her down on his lap. Starla took Twila's plate and set it near Mordecai. Mordecai took a napkin and wiped her face. 'You're starting to get tomato sauce on your face again, little Twila,' he laughed.

Twila giggled. Raven tickled Twila. 'No tickle, Aunt Raven,' she cried.

'I can see why you love to come here,' Laurelin said, taking another slice, 'I'm still amazed by the surroundings here.'

Cece caught a glimpse of a tall dark-haired teenager with his arms around a blonde-haired girl as they entered the restaurant. She gasped. Mordecai looked at her and asked, 'What's wrong, Cece?'

'Tess McElroy was right,' she exclaimed, clearly upset, 'There's Oscar with that Carol girl! How could he do this to me?' She started to weep.

Raven wrapped her arms around Cece. 'What happened?' she asked.

'She had been seeing this Oscar kid since earlier this year,' Mordecai told Raven, reaching over and taking his sister's hand, 'She stopped hearing from him back in mid-September when he didn't return her texts or calls. He must have started seeing this girl during that time. I plan to find out what's what.'

'Uncle Morcai don't leave,' Twila objected.

Mordecai sighed.

'Don't worry about it, Mordy,' Cece told him, 'Twila wants you to stay.'

'I just don't like what he had done to you,' Mordecai frowned.

'It kind of reminds me of a fairyman I had dated before we met,' sighed Raven, 'We had broken up two years ago after seeing each other for almost a year. He started some rumors afterwards that keep the other fairymen away from me.'

'What did he say and why did he say it?' Cece asked, wiping the tears from her eyes.

'Abin said that I had some fairymen on the side,' Raven answered sadly, 'which was not true. Because of his lies, I've been rejected time and again.'

'It doesn't matter now, though I know it hurts you,' Mordecai told her, kissing her.

Raven smiled as she glanced at him. 'No, it doesn't, not now,' she said, touching his face. Twila pulled her hand from Mordecai. Raven stared at her as the toddler giggled. 'You want me to tickle you, little girl?'

'Was this Abin seeing another fairywoman on the side, do you think, Raven?' Cece asked.

'I'm not sure, Cece,' sighed Raven. 'I can't say for sure.'

'Sure sounds like it,' Laurelin frowned, 'When some men can't get what they want, they usually start seeing somebody else and tell vicious lies. I'm sure it happens here in the human world, too'

'Does that happen here, too?' Raven asked.

'As you can see, it had just happened to Cece,' answered Tiffany, 'with that Oscar guy. What is wrong with that boy, besides the obvious?'

'I'm just angry the way he did my sister,' Mordecai growled, 'I don't like to see Cece get hurt like that. It makes me angry all the same. I'll wait till school tomorrow to have a talk with him.'

'Let us come, too,' Sharon suggested, 'I don't want you to do anything you'll regret.'

Mordecai nodded. 'I think I see what you mean. Right now would not be a good time anyhow. I just don't like for Cece to be hurt like that!' He took an all-meat pizza slice. 'I better cool down some. Calm down some.'

'Then think about us, Mordecai,' insisted Raven, kissing him.

Twila pushed Raven away. Raven looked at Twila and asked, 'What do you think you're doing, Twila?'

'Aunt Raven don't kiss Uncle Morcai,' Twila giggled. The others laughed.

'And why not?' Raven asked her.

Twila just giggled.

'I can kiss your uncle Morcai if I want,' retorted Raven as she kissed Mordecai again.

Twila pushed Raven away again as she giggled.

'Twila,' Starla exclaimed, trying to keep from laughing.

Mordecai looked down at Twila and kissed her on the cheeks. 'Come on, Twila,' he smiled, 'Your aunt Raven can kiss me. She loves me very much. I love her very much, as I do you.'

'I love you, Uncle Morcai,' Twila said as she stood up and hugged his neck.

She sat back down on his lap as he asked, 'You want to eat some more pizza?'

He was about to grab it when Twila pushed his hand back. 'I do it, Uncle Morcai,' she told him.

'Okay, sweetie,' chuckled Mordecai. Twila took another bite of her pizza and took another drink of her soda.

They continued to eat as they talked. Every slice of pizza was gone save the little bit Twila had on her plate. 'Is anybody still hungry?' asked Tiffany.

'I'm fine,' Mordecai answered.

'I'm okay,' Raven said.

The waitress had the bill in her hand. Tiffany took the check and glanced at it. Cece and Sharon gave a 20-dollar bill each to Tiffany. Mordecai was about to pull out his wallet when Tiffany said, 'I've got this. We have enough.'

'You sure?' Mordecai asked.

'Once you get a job, you can treat us,' Tiffany said. 'We've got enough to cover this.'

'Fair enough,' Mordecai nodded.

When Tiffany paid the check, the waitress asked if any wanted refills. 'I could take another root beer,' Mordecai said. 'We're in no hurry right now.'

'At least not yet,' Sharon added, 'Keeping in mind we do have school tomorrow. I'm just glad I don't have any homework tonight.'

'I hate homework,' Tiffany grumbled, 'There're three things that are constant in life when you're in school: homework, tests, and curfews. Fortunately, mine is not until nine since it's a school night.'

'What's a curfew?' Laurelin asked her.

'Parents set a set time for their children who are in high school to be home by,' Sharon explained, 'Otherwise, they are going to get mad and pitch a fit.'

'I am still in trouble as it is for that accident a few weeks back,' Tiffany frowned, 'I am almost done paying for it, but I'll be glad when it's out of the way. It's been frustrating.'

'I can't wait until I finally get my license to drive,' Sharon stated, 'My father already has a car, but it's got to be fixed first, and the money I'm earning is helping to pay for the parts and repairs the car needs.'

'You have to have a license to drive?' Raven asked.

'It's the law here,' Tiffany answered, 'And insurance as well.'

'Sounds complicated,' Raven frowned.

'Unfortunately, we tend to make things more complicated than they're supposed to be,' Mordecai sighed, 'It seems to be human nature. From laws to religion, man makes difficult what God has made simple. It seems we humans are good at that, sadly. It seems your home, Raven, lacks the complexity that the human world is full of. That is one advantage your people have, which I appreciate.'

'There is nothing complicated about Queen Cymbaline's rule,' Starla replied, 'The laws are simple and easy to understand, though it had not kept Raven from seeing you, Mordecai.' To Twila she said, 'You full, sweetie?'

'Yes, Mommy,' Twila answered, 'I love pizza.'

'I'm glad you enjoyed it, Twila,' Tiffany said.

Raven gave Twila a little tickle, causing her to giggle.

'When I return, I need to take a look at what the laws are in your home,' Mordecai said to Raven, 'I'm sure it won't be complicated like it is here. Oh, you have no idea, and I don't think you want to hear. A lot of us don't understand it either.' He pulled out his cell phone and pushed a button.

'What is that?' Starla asked.

'Humans use it to communicate with each other,' Raven answered, 'They call it a cell phone.'

'These days,' Cece said, 'they add so many things to cell phones, which I find confusing: access to the internet, music applications. I'm sure it's confusing to you and yours, Raven.'

They heard Mordecai speaking on the phone. 'Hi, Mom. We have just finished eating and we're ready to be picked up.'

'I wonder what it'd be like to have such devices at home?' Raven wondered.

'Well, it would be easier to keep track of you, for one,' laughed Laurelin, 'I wonder how it works?'

'How is it possible that Mordecai can speak to his mother when she's somewhere else?' Starla asked. 'How does it work?'

'It's kind of complicated to explain,' Sharon said, 'So many things involved that are hard to explain. All I know is that it works, but magic has nothing to do with it, though it may seem like it to you.'

'Indeed it does,' Raven nodded, 'I remember I found it just before we saw each other the second time. When it started making noises, I jumped. It had startled me when I first heard it. He told me what it was as I gave it back to him.'

'McCoy must have thrown it away along with my wallet before they left me in the woods,' Mordecai said, 'I figured he would take all the money I had in the wallet, but that was of no surprise, given the type of person he is.'

'I wish I could have given him a piece of my mind and then some,' Raven said in a bitter voice. 'I still remember what they did to you when we first met. I would have helped him get out of it, but he had already gotten himself loose.'

'I can only hope after today that my brother and others like him will have no more problems with them,' Cece said, 'but right now, I don't feel that confident that they have been properly punished.'

Mordecai felt the same way. He figured that somehow, someway, they would again get away with murder and get nothing more than a slap on the wrist if they even get that. He wondered if it would truly be over dealing with the bullies. Raven gazed at Mordecai and caressed his face.

Twila looked at Mordecai as well. 'Why Uncle Morcai sad?'

'You okay, baby?' Raven asked.

Mordecai shook his head. 'Uncle Morcai okay, sweetie,' he sighed, kissing the toddler on the cheeks. He kissed Raven's hand and said to her, 'I'm sorry, Raven, I was just thinking about those bullies. Before, we thought their bullying would stop, but it turned out not to be the case. They continued their antics. I'm not convinced they will stop what they are doing.'

'I'm beginning to agree with you,' Cece sighed, 'but let that be a problem for another time. How long will it take for Mom to get here?'

'In a few minutes,' Mordecai answered, 'I want to finish my drink before we go.' He sighed. 'I still have the talk with Dad to deal with. I am glad Mom has accepted Raven, but I don't know about Dad. Perhaps his heart will change like Mom's has.'

'Your mom just needed to get to know us better,' Starla said, 'Who knows? Maybe your father will be the same way.'

'He's always been uncomfortable with people with black skin,' Mordecai said, 'He and my paternal grandparents have always been like that. He's not as uncomfortable with them as his parents were.'

'Are your grandparents still living?' Raven asked. 'Will they hate me because I'm black?'

'I believe so,' Mordecai sighed, 'My father compared to them is more tolerable, though like I said, still uncomfortable. They live in the northern part of Orlando in the Lockhart area.'

'I guess they would feel even more against me if they found out I was a fairy?' she said quietly.

'I believe so,' Mordecai nodded sadly, 'I haven't seen them in months. My grandfather has been in and out of the hospital for the past nine months because of his heart condition. They are close to seventy years old.'

'But I think our grandparents on our mom's side could be accepting of Raven,' Cece said, 'They don't share the same prejudice as our grandparents on Dad's side.'

'Our school is close by their house,' Mordecai said, 'They've been there for close to forty years. I hope for an opportunity to introduce you to them. They are strong in their faith, and it was them who had led me to Christ.'

'How often do you see them?' Lavender asked.

'Not very often,' Mordecai answered, 'They are usually at their church helping out others. They've been that way since they both retired.

'Since they retired, they remain active, going out visiting and doing what they can. I am so thankful for them. I do need to introduce you to them, Raven. They believe in looking at the heart of a person.' He stared at Starla and Twila. 'And you, too, my future sister-in-law and niece.'

Starla held Mordecai's hand. 'Perhaps we can meet them before we leave for home,' she suggested, 'but I hope for any opportunity to meet them. They sound like good people.'

'They are,' Mordecai nodded, 'If not this time, then I hope you will return so you can meet them the next time you visit here.'

'Yes, I would like that,' Starla replied.

Raven sighed. 'I hope God will change your father's heart toward me the way He changed your mother's, Mordecai,' she said, 'I pray he looks at my heart.'

'It's going to take some time,' Mordecai gently said, 'Sometimes, it's got to take time to change a person's heart. We can only hope so, but there was some promise.' He thought about this morning. 'We just have to take it slow in this case.'

'I think I will return here,' Laurelin said, 'to come to this place. On our return home, I can try to learn how to make pizza.'

'It will probably be trial and error,' Mordecai said, 'I have never made pizza from scratch before, pizza dough and all. I have seen it done, but that's not the same as actually making the pizza itself.'

The waitress returned. She checked on them to ask if any of them wanted a refill before they left.

'I will take a refill,' Tiffany said, 'Go ahead and put it in a cup to take with me.'

'Same here,' Sharon said.

Starla looked at Twila. 'Do you want any more to drink, Twila?'

'Yes, Mommy,' Twila answered.

The waitress took the cups and left to refill them for the group. Raven leaned her head upon Mordecai's shoulder. She kissed him. 'I really enjoyed myself, Mordecai,' she said to him. 'Thank you for bringing me here.'

'I am glad we came here too, Raven,' Mordecai smiled, 'I enjoyed myself here, too. We can make it a point to come back…'

At that moment, he saw two men walk through the door, dressed in black suits. At first, he thought it was Dr. Von Braun's two men, Wilfred and Seymour, but was relieved that they were not. However, he still felt a sense of danger. The men were led by a waitress to a table on the opposite side of the restaurant. Something told Mordecai to get the fairies out of there. 'What's wrong, Mordy?' Cece asked.

'Maybe it's nothing,' Mordecai replied, 'but I saw two men I thought were Dr. Von Braun's men, but I can't shake the feeling of danger. It is very strong.'

The waitress returned with the sodas and gave them to Twila, who took the cup, and to Tiffany and Sharon. 'We better get out of here while we can,' Mordecai insisted.

Sharon laughed. 'What makes you think we're in danger?'

'Not you, Tiffany or Cece,' Mordecai replied as they rose out of their seats. 'Let's just move out of here casually, like there is nothing wrong.'

They made their way toward the exit. Starla took Twila in her arms. They were about twenty feet before they reached the exit when Twila dropped her drink and gave out a cry. The others, startled, stared at the toddler. 'Twila,' Starla said irritably.

Twila started crying. 'Shadowfire, Shadowfire,' she cried, burying her head into her mother's shoulders.

'Impossible,' Starla exclaimed, 'Shadowfire can't be here.'

Mordecai rushed out the door followed by Raven. In the distance, they heard the crashing of cars. Raven smelled the air and gave out a cry. 'No, it can't be,' she cried, 'It is Shadowfire! Twila was right!'

'Shadowfire? Here?' Mordecai cried, 'How could he have found out where I live? How could he have found out where I am?'

Mordecai looked in the air as he heard screams in the distance. He saw a black shape descending from the air. The dragon let out a mighty roar as he landed. Mordecai and Raven tried to head back inside but were tripped up by the mighty claws of the monster. 'Mordy Jefferson,' the dragon boomed. 'Where do you think you're going? We have business together, you and I!'

Mordecai and Raven dodged another swipe from the claws. 'How do you know my name?' he cried. 'How did you know where I live? How did you find me?'

'At last, we meet face to face, Mordy Jefferson,' the dragon boomed, 'I have longed for this meeting since I heard of you and the prophecy. I know you have been in Arundel Haven until last night, haven't you?'

'None of your business, monster,' cried Mordecai defiantly.

'Do not lie to me and do not deny it,' boomed Shadowfire, 'I smell the scent of fairy all around you! How long have you been there? I know you were there when I had last attacked the city!'

Mordecai refused to answer.

The dragon was infuriated. 'You *have* been there,' he bellowed, 'It is useless to deny it! You *have* been to Arundel Haven somehow! No doubt you know more about the Prophecy of my demise, don't you?'

Once again Mordecai refused to answer.

'By all that's unholy,' roared the dragon, enraged by Mordecai's refusal to answer, 'it shall not come to pass! I will do everything in my power to keep the Prophecy from being fulfilled!'

'You think you can stop the Prophecy from coming to pass?' retorted Mordecai, 'You must be desperate if you think so!'

'So you acknowledge the Prophecy at last,' cried the dragon, 'You have learned more about it during your visit to Arundel Haven! Did Raven bring you there?'

'You must be desperate to come looking for me,' Mordecai cried out, 'You fear the Prophecy being fulfilled, fear me as a result. What makes you think you can defy the words that the LORD Himself spoke unto Queen Hephzibah on her deathbed? Whatever He says will come to pass!'

Shadowfire growled. 'I will show you the meaning of the word fear when all is said and done,' he roared, 'and the Prophecy shall come to naught!'

'Leave us alone!' Raven cried.

Shadowfire gazed at Raven. 'Ah, Raven, is it?' the dragon said, 'What is a fairy doing in the human world in human's attire of all things? Are you trying to pass as human? Does Queen Cymbaline know about this? Who do you think you're fooling?'

'What's it to you?' Raven shot back, 'That is none of your concern.'

'The Prophecy concerns me greatly, Raven,' growled Shadowfire, 'Be careful, lest you meet your lover's fate!'

'How did you know about us?' Mordecai asked. 'How can you be sure we are involved in such a relationship?'

'Do not presume to lie to me, Mordy Jefferson,' snapped Shadowfirem 'I know you two are involved, and now I know more than romantically! I am beginning to believe that you, Raven, are the fairy maiden spoken of in the prophecy much as I know Mordy Jefferson is the one spoken of! However, your fate shall be sundered from his!'

'What do you mean?' cried Mordecai, 'If you even dare to lay a claw on her—'

Shadowfire laughed. 'As if you can do anything about it, Mordy Jefferson,' he scoffed, 'What can you do to defend her from me? Tell me that, human! If not for the Prophecy, I would laugh at you, seeing that you are a worthless nobody! But as long as you live, you pose a real danger to me, both you and Raven!'

Cece, Tiffany, and Sharon stepped outside and stared in awe and fright at the size of Shadowfire. He stared at Mordecai and said, 'You need not worry about your fairy girlfriend, Mordy Jefferson. It is only you I am after. Make any attempt to escape, and I will start killing humans!'

Tiffany and Sharon stepped back and screamed. Cece turned to her friends and cried, 'Back inside! Back inside! Tell the others to stay inside!' To Shadowfire she cried, 'Stop!'

The dragon gazed at Cece, smoke billowing out of his nostrils.

'Ah yes, the sister,' he sneered, 'Cece, is it? I have heard about you, yes indeed.'

Cece jumped. 'How do you know my name?'

'So many questions, but no answers will I give you,' replied Shadowfire.

Mordecai stared sternly at the dragon. 'Like you had told me when you had invaded my dreams,' he said grimly. 'I remember. You refuse to reveal the Prophecy to me, you thought I was the one involved. Now I know the tale! I know now how you invaded Arundel Haven 150 years ago and oppressed the fairies living there, how Queen Hephzibah on her deathbed told the dream to her daughter how God was going to use a human and a fairy maiden to bring about your demise!'

'So you finally admit you have been in Arundel Haven,' growled the dragon, 'How did you arrive there? Did Raven carry you there?'

Mordecai refused to answer.

'I will not allow that Prophecy to be fulfilled, human,' cried Shadowfire. His claws made a swipe for Raven's clothes, ripping them to shreds, though not doing her harm. 'You think you could walk among humans like you're trying to do, fairy? Let the world see the truth!'

The clothing fell from Raven's body and her wings were exposed, though the clothes she had worn underneath remained. 'Such a shame you would fly to the human world, Raven,' he told her. 'Let the world know who you are, who you really are: a fairy of Arundel Haven! This is Queen Cymbaline's worst nightmare: to have the existence of her people revealed to the human world, the secret of Arundel Haven uncovered! What would she say now?'

Mordecai turned to Raven. 'Fly, Raven, fly!' he cried.

When Raven tried to fly away, Shadowfire swatted her to the ground. She fell hard. 'I do not want you, Raven,' Shadowfire told her, 'but somebody else does.' To Mordecai he said, 'An acquaintance of yours requires her presence, and you know well who I am talking about.'

'Dr. Von Braun,' Mordecai cried, 'Dr. Von Braun, isn't it? He's the one who told you my name when the devils that serve you couldn't!'

'My plans for you, Mordy Jefferson, you will find out when I take you to my home, to the Mountains of Shadow,' declared Shadowfire, 'Such shall be your fate, like the fate that awaited King Zebulon when he tried to rescue his beloved Queen Beulah from my claws.'

Shadowfire grabbed Mordecai before he tried to escape. Two men immediately appeared out of the pizzeria and grabbed Raven before she could rise from the ground. 'Let me go!' the black fairy cried, 'Take your hands off me!'

'Raven!' Mordecai cried.

Cece tried to help her but was knocked down. 'Get out of here, girl,' one of them warned, 'This does not concern you!'

'Let Raven go,' cried Cece. 'Let go of my friend!'

'Better stay out of the way if you know what's good for you,' the other man warned.

'Raven!' Mordecai cried, struggling to free himself from the dragon. 'Let Raven go!'

'Mordecai!' Raven cried.

'Send her to Dr. Von Braun with my compliments,' Shadowfire said to the men, taking to the air. Cece cried out her brother's name as Shadowfire disappeared with her brother in his claws. As the men took Raven to the black car that was parked nearby, Lavender, Laurelin, Tiffany, and Sharon rushed out and knocked the men down. Raven managed to take to the air before the men recovered. Lavender and Laurelin took off the shirts that covered their wings and took to the air as well. Starla took Twila's off as she ascended before she did the same. Tiffany and Sharon watched as the fairies suspended themselves in the air.

At that moment, the familiar minivan of their mother pulled up and parked. She stepped out and saw the fairies in the air. She looked around. 'What happened? Where's Mordy?' she cried.

Raven lowered herself. 'Shadowfire took Mordecai,' she cried, 'He somehow found out where he was and flew here to take him captive! He left me with those men!'

'The men are working with Dr. Von Braun,' Cece cried, 'Shadowfire and Dr. Von Braun are in league together. Von Braun's men tried to take Raven!'

'Mordecai, my son,' Molly cried. 'He's going to kill my son!'

Cece pulled out the vial of the water from the Silverstreams.

'Tiffany, Sharon,' she cried, 'the vials of the waters from the Silverstreams! Drink the water! We've got to help Mordy!'

'Where is he taking him?' Molly cried.

'To his home in the Mountains of Shadow,' Lavender answered, To Raven she said, 'It's too dangerous to fly there!'

'I don't care,' Raven protested, shaking her head. 'We've got to do something! I'm going after him.'

'Raven, that's crazy,' Laurelin cried, 'It's suicide if you attempt to rescue him! He will kill you too!'

'I won't abandon Mordecai,' insisted Raven grimly. 'We are the ones the Prophecy of Queen Hephzibah had spoken of to destroy him, and God will use us to do so! I have to go!'

'Raven, that's crazy talk,' cried Lavender. 'Remember what happened to King Zebulon when he tried to rescue his queen when Shadowfire first encroached upon Arundel Haven to afflict us? The same thing will happen to you, too!

'No, it will not,' Raven protested, 'The time is very near when the Prophecy will be fulfilled. I am not sure how, but the Words are true! I feel it in my spirit! I know this beyond a shadow of a doubt.' To Molly she said, 'I will find my love and your son, Molly. I love him more than life itself! I can't leave him! I won't leave him! Thank you for accepting me.'

'Please bring back home my son, Raven,' Molly cried, tears flowing from her eyes, 'Promise you will return him safe and sound.'

'I promise,' Raven vowed. Without another word, she flew in the direction that Shadowfire had gone. The two men were about to pull their guns when Cece, Sharon, and Tiffany aimed kicks at them from the sky. The three women had drunk the water from the Silverstreams in the bottles. Twila looked around. 'Where Uncle Morcai?' she asked, 'Where Aunt Raven?' Her lower lip trembled.

Molly turned toward Starla. 'You must deliver a message to your Queen,' she said. 'Tell her what happened! Can you see if you can save my son?'

'We will do what we can, Molly,' replied Starla, 'Try to make your way back home. Tell Tony what has transpired.'

'I wish to come with you, Starla,' Cece told her. 'Tiffany, Sharon, go with my mother and tell my father what happened!'

'Why are you flying to Arundel Haven?' asked Sharon.

'Mordecai is my brother,' Cece cried, 'I have to do something.

If I can!'

'Then go quickly, Cece,' cried Molly, 'Please bring your brother back.'

'You can come with us,' Starla told Cece. 'We must make haste!

Every second counts!'

'Lavender and I will stay with Molly,' Laurelin said, 'We will return to Arundel Haven as soon as we can. Go!'

Cece took Twila, who allowed herself to be held by her, and followed Starla away from the restaurant and into the skies. 'Laurelin and I will meet you at your house, Molly,' Lavender said.

She sighed. 'Raven, I hope you know what you are doing,' she then said quietly.

Laurelin thought the same as they quickly rose into the air.

Tony pulled the car he was driving into the driveway of his home. He had received the message from Molly about what had happened to their son. As he stepped out of the car, his cell phone rang. Checking the number, it was Cece. He pushed a button. 'Cece, where are you?

'I'm flying with Starla and Twila to Arundel Haven,' Cece answered hurriedly.

'Flying?' Tony exclaimed, 'What do you mean you are flying? How can you be? Are Lavender and Laurelin with you?'

'No,' Cece answered, 'They're on their way to our home. Shadowfire had arrived and captured Mordecai, and Raven has gone after them.'

'Alone?' Tony exclaimed, 'What can she do alone?'

'She's determined not to abandon Mordecai but to rescue him somehow.'

'She can't do it alone,' Tony declared, 'What is she thinking? She could wind up dead if she thinks she can take on the dragon!'

'She is willing to do just that if there is any hope of rescuing him,' Cece replied, 'She cares nothing about her own life at this point.'

Tony thought about what Cece had said. He still had doubts about Raven, still felt uncomfortable about the color of her skin. He then saw that Raven would even risk death if she thought it would save the life of her lover. His heart started to soften toward her. He sighed.

'Dad? Dad?' he heard the voice of his daughter.

'I'm okay,' Tony replied quietly, 'But did you say you were flying?'

'Yes,' Cece said, exasperated. 'The small bottle Queen Cymbaline had given me has allowed me to fly for a short period of time while Mordecai's ability is pretty much permanent.'

'You mean to say that Mordy will always have the ability to fly?'

'Mordy told me how he obtained it when we were at Rossi's,' Cece explained, 'from the falls that begins a river, which the fairies call the Silverstreams. The water I was given came from the same falls. I had three, and I gave one to Sharon and one to Tiffany.'

'This is a lot to take in,' Tony said, 'I need you to come home.'

'I can't. I'm en flight to Arundel Haven with Starla and Twila.'

'You're *what*?'

'We have to tell Queen Cymbaline what had happened… and warn…'

'Cece? Cece? You're breaking up! What's going on?'

As Cece flew beside Starla and Twila, she heard only static and lost contact with her father. She put the cell phone back in her pocket.

'I lost reception,' she told Starla. 'I think we must be moving out of range or network problems.'

'I still don't understand how you can communicate with your father from such a long distance,' Starla puzzled, 'You humans have a lot of fascinating things.'

'Not compared to flying,' Cece said, feeling the wind whip through her hair, 'Wow! This is amazing! I have flown in a plane before, but not like this! I love it!'

'Remember it only lasts a week,' Starla warned, 'You must be mindful of that.'

Cece nodded. 'I only hope there's something we can do to help my brother.'

'It may be up to Raven,' Starla said gently, 'I can't help but fear the worst.'

When Molly's minivan pulled into the driveway, she looked to find her husband standing by his car with his cellphone in his hand. He had been trying to get back in contact with Cece since the call went dead but was unsuccessful.

A minute later, Tiffany's car pulled behind Tony's. As they slipped out, they headed to where Tony was standing. 'What went on?' Tony asked.

'Did Cece try and get in touch with you?' Molly asked as they headed to the door.

'I've been trying to get her back for about a minute now,' Tony replied as they were joined by Lavender and Laurelin. He saw the fairies land and made a motion to make their way inside the house as quickly as possible. Tony unlocked the door and opened it. 'Why did Raven try and take on the dragon herself?' he asked.

'Raven's always been strong willed,' Lavender told him, 'I'm afraid that this time, it's going to get her killed.'

'I hope not,' Molly sighed, 'I have gotten to know her, Lavender, and Laurelin while Cece and Mordy were in school today and met her sister, Starla, who was here.'

'Starla?'

'Raven's sister,' Molly explained, 'She had her daughter Twila, who is very attached to Mordy. She brought some things for Mordecai and even the bottle of, I think water…'

'It is,' Sharon said, 'but it allowed Cece to fly. She also gave a flask to me and Tiffany. We were told it would only last a week.'

'Dr. Von Braun told Shadowfire who Mordy was, where he lives, and I don't know how he found out he would be at *Rossi's* with us,' Tiffany said.

'He probably used divination to ascertain where Mordecai was once he knew who he was and where he lives,' Laurelin replied, 'Two men tried to take Raven, but Cece and her friends stopped them. I think they may be on their way here.'

'Then it's not safe for you here if they followed us,' Molly told the fairies, 'They may try to take either you or Lavender, Laurelin. They must not take either one of you.'

'I agree,' Tony sighed, 'You both will have to fly home, lest they find you.'

'But what will happen to you and Molly?' asked Lavender.

'We'll be fine, Lavender,' replied Molly, 'I'm afraid since Shadowfire has shown himself and the witnesses who saw Raven and the both of you that the secret is out.'

Lavender sighed. 'When we flew here, we hated being here,' she said, 'We had mistrusted humans because of the wickedness in their hearts. Now we've met you, and Laurelin, I don't know about you, but I have come to know that Raven has been right all along.'

Tony sighed. 'You taught us roughly the same thing,' he said, 'I mistrusted even humans with black skin and was taught that when I was growing up, but now hearing how Raven is putting her own life on the line for my son for the fact that she loves him, it has caused me to rethink what I have thought about those, even fairies, with darker skin. If Raven succeeds in rescuing Mordy and this prophecy of yours comes true, I will welcome her as family. I would approve of Mordy taking Raven's hand. If you should see either Raven or Mordy again, you can tell them I said so.'

Molly smiled, kissing her husband. 'I am so happy to hear you say that, Tony,' she said, 'When I saw little Twila, I remembered she accepted our son without reservation and came to love him. I can only hope and pray they both survive.'

At that moment, they heard a car pull up. Tiffany looked out the window and saw the car the two men tried to pull Raven inside of, seeing the door open and two men stepping out. 'They're here,' she cried. 'Lavender, Laurelin, you have to fly, now! The men that tried to take Raven are here!'

'The back door, quick,' Tony cried frantically, 'Hurry, girls!'

They headed to the glass sliding door and Tony opened it. Lavender and Laurelin took to the air. Tiffany and Sharon jumped and rose from the ground. They joined Lavender and Laurelin in the air.

'We wish to come with you,' Sharon told the fairies.

'Just go,' Tony cried. 'Quickly!'

Lavender and Laurelin flew higher into the air. Tiffany and Sharon joined them.

As they rose into the clouds, Laurelin said, 'I don't think it's a good idea for you to come, but since you are friends of Cece and Mordecai, and considering the danger Mordecai is in, we will allow it.'

'I just hope Queen Cymbaline won't be too upset with us bringing you with us,' Lavender said.

'I'm sorry for all that happened,' Tiffany said, 'I feel bad about—'

'No apologies needed, Tiffany,' Lavender interrupted, 'None of us knew about Shadowfire's arrival and how he knew about Mordecai or his involvement with this Dr. Von Braun. We can only tell Queen Cymbaline what transpired and what we can do.'

'This shouldn't happen to Mordy,' Sharon said, 'We found him to be a great guy. Raven thinks so, too.'

'And we agree with Raven now,' Laurelin sighed, 'He was still concerned about our secret and keeping it that way to those around him. I can only hope they can escape the dragon.'

'We'll have to see what Queen Cymbaline suggests when we arrive at Arundel Haven,' Lavender said.

'What about Cece?' Sharon asked, 'Would she welcome Cece?'

'I believe so, since she specifically gave the water to her and she to you two,' Lavender replied, 'We shall see when we get there.'

They flew on into the night sky.

Eventually, Starla, Twila, and Cece arrived at Arundel Haven. Cece looked around and remembered the dream she had the day before. It was like she had seen in her dream. Fairies who saw them stared at Cece and many frowned. When they arrived at the entrance of the castle, the guards bade them to halt. They saw Cece and frowned. 'Why have you brought this human here?' the first one asked.

'This is Cece, Mordecai's sister,' Starla told them, 'I need to see the Queen immediately. Something bad has happened that I must tell her!'

'Very well,' nodded the first guard. He blew a horn. Before them appeared Taris, the fairy guard whom Mordecai had befriended during the human's time in prison. He gazed at Cece and then to Starla. 'Why have you brought this human here, Starla?' he asked.

'This is Mordecai's sister, Cece,' Starla told him, 'I nccd to scc Queen Cymbaline. Something bad happened to Mordecai!'

'What happened?' he asked as he motioned to them to follow him.

'Shadowfire,' Cece cried, 'He flew to our world and captured Mordecai!'

Taris's face turned pale with horror. 'This is ill news indeed. I will take you to Queen Cymbaline.'

He took them to the throne room and the Queen was summoned. They had not waited long until Queen Cymbaline and Prince Avondale appeared. The Queen stared at Cece. The young girl bowed before her. 'It is a pleasure to meet you at last, Cece Jefferson,' Queen Cymbaline said, 'Your brother is an exceptional young man.'

'I only wish the news was better, your majesty,' Cece said, 'Shadowfire appeared in Orlando and kidnapped my brother! He is taking him to his home in the Mountains of Shadow!'

Both monarchs bowed their heads. 'This is ill news indeed,' Prince Avondale declared gravely, 'How did he come to know where the both of you live?'

'Dr. Von Braun told him his name,' Starla answered, 'He and the dragon are in league with each other!'

'How can this be?' Queen Cymbaline exclaimed, 'How did this human come to have contact with Shadowfire?'

'He never told us when he questioned me and my friends,' Cece replied, 'Shadowfire also knows about Raven and that she is the fairy maiden spoken of in the Prophecy. I do not understand it myself. One of my friends accidentally mentioned Raven's name to Dr. Von Braun. I feel responsible for that. Mordecai was determined to keep Raven's existence a secret, but we have done poorly.'

'What do you mean?' Queen Cymbaline asked.

'We were curious about the food they call pizza,' Starla said quietly, 'Mordecai counseled against this, but we wanted to try it, Raven, Lavender, Laurelin, Starla, and I. We had covered our wings to walk among humans.'

Queen Cymbaline frowned. 'Mordecai was right to be concerned,' she stated, 'Now ill has come of it.'

'I know now,' Starla replied, 'We were about to leave when Shadowfire appeared and pretty much revealed Raven's existence. He captured Mordecai but left Raven to be taken by some humans to

Dr. Von Braun.'

'Raven? Where is she?' Queen Cymbaline asked.

'She flew after Mordecai,' Cece answered, 'My friends and I kept the men from taking Raven. I feel responsible for all this.'

Queen Cymbaline sighed. 'This is not your doing, Cece. What is done is done. How did you help Raven?'

'We used the gift you gave me,' Cece answered, 'They were about to put Raven into their car when we stopped them from the air. Raven flew out of their grasp and out of their reach. I'm very worried about my brother! Isn't there something we can do?'

Queen Cymbaline bowed her head. 'I wish there was,' she said quietly, 'There is nothing we can do. We have no weapon that would even hurt Shadowfire.'

'No, I can't accept that,' cried Cece. 'There's got to be a way!'

'If we sent out a rescue party,' stated Prince Avondale, 'they would meet the same fate as our King Zebulon 150 years ago. We dare not attempt a rescue.'

'Are you just going to leave him to die, then?' Cece cried, tears flowing down her cheeks. 'Are you going to let Shadowfire do what he will with Mordecai and even Raven? I can't believe what I am hearing!'

'Cece, please,' Starla said, trying to calm her.

'This is my brother we're talking about,' cried Cece, angrily, 'How can you turn your back on him like that? He is one of the few good people in this world! He did all he could to keep your secret safe, and for his part, he did, though Raven chose to reveal herself to me! Even when we were out at a restaurant, he was very careful and concerned about the secret! Why have you turned your back on him?'

Prince Avondale's face tightened. He was about to say something when Queen Cymbaline restrained him. 'No, Avondale,' she told him sadly, 'I understand her pain.' To Cece she said, 'We must trust in the LORD in this, Cece. We have no weapons that can hurt Shadowfire. Without the means to hurt him, we are helpless to do anything.'

'No,' wept Cece, dropping to her knees, 'I can't accept that! I can't!'

Queen Cymbaline bowed her head sadly. At that moment, they were joined by two guards escorting Lavender, Laurelin, Sharon, and Tiffany. The four headed toward Cece, who was kneeling and weeping. Queen Cymbaline stared at the two human girls. 'You are friends of Cece, are you not?' she asked.

Tiffany and Sharon turned toward Queen Cymbaline and bowed before her. 'Forgive our intrusion into your kingdom, your majesty,' Tiffany said.

'We are Cece's friends,' Sharon replied, 'She is very worried about her brother.'

'I would bid you welcome,' said Queen Cymbaline, 'but as you may know, Mordecai had been captured by Shadowfire.'

'Yes,' Sharon nodded 'and we saw Raven fly after him. We are very worried about them.'

'We can do nothing since we do not have the weapons to even harm Shadowfire,' Prince Avondale said, 'How can we mount a rescue if we don't have anything that can bite the dragon's enchanted hide?'

Twila flew from Starla's arms and toward Cece. She wiped the tears from her eyes. 'Why so sad, Cece?' she asked.

Cece could not talk but only wept.

'She misses her brother,' Starla told her, 'Shadowfire has your uncle Morcai.'

Twila looked at Cece and dried her eyes. She then said, 'God will help Uncle Morcai and Aunt Raven. Shadowfire go bye-bye for good.'

Cece smiled. She touched the face of the fairy toddler. 'I hope you're right, little Twila,' she said.

'God promise, and God keeps His promises,' Twila added, 'God is good!'

Cece hugged the little toddler and wept. Queen Cymbaline placed her hands on Cece's shoulders. 'We must trust God in this,' she said softly, 'We will fast and pray for him immediately. I will have rooms prepared for you and your friends.'

'Forgive me, your majesty,' Cece said amid her tears.

'I understand your pain,' Queen Cymbaline said softly, 'Both Avondale and I understand. We had a sister years ago, who was twenty-four. Our sister, Felicia, was the youngest of us. She had rescued two fairy children from the claws of the dragon but wound up being taken and slain as well. We still miss her. We had tried to create weapons strong enough to even penetrate his armor to no avail. No sword would bite him, no spear could pierce his defenses. Our only hope now is that the Prophecy will be fulfilled.'

'God promise,' Twila repeated, 'and He always keeps His promises. Uncle Morcai and Aunt Raven beat Shadowfire.'

'The faith of a child,' Cece found herself whispering.

Queen Cymbaline heard and agreed, 'The faith of a child.'

Immediately, Queen Cymbaline and Prince Avondale fell to their knees. She turned to one of the guards and said, 'Spread the word throughout Arundel Haven. Let all those who are saints of God fast and pray for Mordecai and Raven, that God deliver them out of Shadowfire's claws. There is not much time!'

Taris stepped forward. 'I will spread the word, your majesty,' he said, taking to the air.

Queen Cymbaline turned to another guard and said, 'Take Cece and her friends to the guest chambers. Have food prepared for them.'

'I wish to stay with you and pray with you,' Cece told the Queen earnestly, 'I am too distressed to eat. I am much too worried about my brother.'

Queen Cymbaline nodded as Cece knelt beside the monarchs as they began to pray. Starla joined them as well as Tiffany and Sharon. Lavender and Laurelin were compelled to do the same, though they did not believe. There, they joined Queen Cymbaline and Prince Avondale as they prayed and wept, praying that God would intervene and deliver Mordecai and Raven from the dragon and for the Prophecy that He spoke of to their foremother Hephzibah would be fulfilled and that the death of the dragon would come to pass.

Twila knelt by her mother and bowed but said not a word.

The monarchs felt the Spirit in the room, telling them the time of the Prophecy's fulfillment was at hand as they prayed.

Chapter Eleven

What do you mean she got away?' Dr. Von Braun said over the phone. He was talking to one of his men, Wilfred from the guest room in the White House where he was staying during his visit to his friend, President Farouk.

'That's what Garfield and Terrell told me,' Wilfred replied over the phone, 'They said they had Raven, but Cece and her friends attacked from the air.'

'From the air, did you say?' exclaimed Dr. Von Braun, 'Are you saying they were flying, too? Are you sure about that, Wilfred?'

'That's what they said,' Wilfred answered, 'I don't know how that is possible, but—'

'I will have President Farouk send them here to Washington immediately,' interjected Dr. Von Braun, 'I want to know everything they have to say! What about the other fairies?'

'They got away,' Wilfred said quietly, 'They followed them to the house where Mordy stays and found they were gone, the fairies.'

'How many were there?' demanded the geneticist.

'Two I believe, not counting Raven,' Wilfred answered, 'Shadowfire had already taken Mordy Jefferson, and they said Raven had flown after them.'

'A foolish gesture on her part,' scoffed Dr. Von Braun, 'Unless they plan to fulfill this prophecy that Shadowfire had spoken of. I am disappointed to say the least, hearing of Raven's escape.'

'What shall we do, boss?' asked Wilfred.

'I will let you know soon,' replied Dr. Von Braun, 'Be ready to act when I call you. I must consort with the president.'

He got off the line and frowned. 'I have gone too far and I'm too close to be foiled now,' he fumed, 'Nothing's going to stop me from capturing a fairy and finding Arundel Haven!'

He dialed a series of numbers on his cell phone and sat on the bed.

Mordecai watched the surrounding area from the claws of the dragon as Shadowfire flew toward his home. The valley below was much like in his dream: desolate, barren. He could feel death all around him. He struggled to break free, but he could not. He kept his eyes on the ground as the dragon flew over the valley.

Before him, he saw three large mountains, standing close to 100,000 meters tall, but the tallest peak rose to 125,000 meters. At the side of the largest mountain was an opening nearly sixty meters round, more than large enough for Shadowfire to enter and exit the mountain. Neither he nor Shadowfire had spoken during the flight. It was very dark around him, but Shadowfire had no problems seeing in the dark. On top of the mountain, he noticed a symbol of an upside down cross with the short ends broken and pointing downward, the symbol of rejecting Jesus Christ, Mordecai noted. He face was grim as the dragon entered inside his lair.

Inside, there was a large tunnel heading upward. It connected to various caves Shadowfire had dug out when he first arrived here, 150 years before. The cave that Shadowfire brought Mordecai to was large, three times as large as the New Orleans Superdome. The young man saw an altar with an upside-down star with a large figure of a goat's head within. Next to it was a sixty-meter-tall stone image of a woman with a baby in her arms. He then thought of how many countless millions bow down and worship this idol and what different names they give to Semiramus and Tammuz, the divine Mother and Child. He should have known Shadowfire would worship them as well as the devil. He merely shook his head.

He continued to look around as he was shoved inside a cage, which hung from the roof of the cave. It was like a large bird cage but was about thirty square feet in diameter and about twenty feet from roof to ceiling.

Mordecai looked around. The air was foul and smelled of death. Bones were scattered about, remains of fairies, Mordecai guessed. He felt the bars of his prison. It felt hard and cold. The door was locked by an incantation.

'Tomorrow, there will be a full moon,' Shadowfire told him, 'You will be sacrificed at its height. You have less than a full day to think about your fate.'

Mordecai did not speak as he sat down inside the giant cage.

'You will not be able to escape,' the dragon continued. 'No key can unlock the door bound by magic, no matter what kind.'

'All magic is controlled by devils,' Mordecai replied, 'Sooner or later, the devils behind the magic will betray its users in one form or another. I know of no magic, nor do I wish to.'

The dragon gave Mordecai an angry look but said nothing. He knelt in front of the Mother and Child idol and spoke in a language Mordecai had never heard before. As he continued, the air seemed to grow hotter and hotter, almost stifling and unbearable to the young man. Eerie sounds were heard all around, which chilled Mordecai to the bone. Mordecai thought they came from the devils behind the idols. He prayed softly, almost inaudibly, as the noise continued. He then felt a hot wind blowing and intensifying in strength, reaching hurricane strengths. Through the mists that developed, he saw a woman, very beautiful to look upon, dressed in scarlet and gold appearing before the dragon. Shadowfire bowed low to her.

Mordecai turned away, knowing the evil hiding behind such beauty, though he found it hard to drag his eyes from her beauty. She spoke to the dragon in an unknown tongue. Shadowfire spoke in the language and then pointed at Mordecai.

The image nodded and spoke again. Mordecai did not reply, not understanding what she had spoken to him. Shadowfire then returned speaking to her in the same tongue. What language were they speaking? Was it some kind of devil language? He was unsure of the speech. For long minutes, they continued their dialog in the same language. Once again, Shadowfire bowed before the effigy and spoke in the same speech as the effigy placed its hand upon the shoulder of the beast. She made the sign of an upside down cross and then disappeared in the gathering of black clouds. Without a word, Shadowfire turned to leave his lair and took to the air.

Mordecai tried the doors again. It did not budge. He shook harder, but again, the door did not open. He sat down with his back to the door and stared at the floor. *I hope Raven is safe,* he thought, *I should have figured somehow that Shadowfire and Von Braun were working together, but I have a feeling somebody else is involved, but who?* At that moment, he involuntarily thought of President Farouk. *It can't be President Farouk, could it? He espouses policies that are unconstitutional and immoral, but in league with Shadowfire? Is that even possible?* He put the thought out of his mind. *I'm probably a fool for even thinking it.*

'There is a way out,' came a voice. He turned toward the voice and saw the figure Shadowfire was talking to earlier. 'There is a way to escape your fate.'

'Who are you?' Mordecai asked, 'and why are you telling me this?'

'I am known as many things,' the image said, 'called by many things. Even in the unlikeliest of places, I am worshipped and prayed to.'

Mordecai knew what she meant.

'I offer you this chance before you are to be sacrificed,' she continued, 'Many fairies have been sacrificed on the altar you see before you, including some of the royal house of Isachar, the rulers of Arundel Haven.'

'Like King Zebulon of old,' Mordecai mused.

'You have been told the tale?' the image queried.

'Yes, by Queen Cymbaline herself,' Mordecai answered, 'She says that—'

'She says that you are the one the Prophecy of Queen Hephzibah had spoken of to destroy the dragon Shadowfire,' interrupted the image, 'Shadowfire has been afraid of the Prophecy since he first heard of it over one hundred years ago. It is well known unto him.'

'Shadowfire mentioned this prophecy before I heard it from Queen Cymbaline,' Mordecai said, 'but he told me nothing about it, not even what it was about.'

'You are afraid, I can tell. I sense it.'

Mordecai sighed. 'Yes, I am,' he admitted.

'You can escape your fate,' the image said, 'escape being sacrificed by the dragon. I can convince Shadowfire to spare your life.'

Mordecai stared at the image. 'What do you mean?' he asked skeptically, 'Why would you want to convince him to do that?'

'I know many things,' continued the image, 'I am the Holy Mother. I know all. Countless of millions worship and trust in me, and I have given them peace and they are safe within my everlasting arms. I grant them entrance into Paradise and spare them from their enemies.'

Mordecai did not feel right about her words. He knew she was an evil spirit, a devil in disguise. He knew she was giving him promises that only God could give and fulfill. He knew, even when he first saw her speaking to the dragon, that she was a devil. 'How do I know what you're saying is true?' he asked.

'You doubt me?'

'To say the least,' the young man implied.

'I can save you from the dragon,' the image said, 'The Prophecy is nothing but a sham, a lie for the fairies to get you to throw away your life so meaninglessly. Queen Cymbaline doesn't even trust humans.'

'With good reason' replied Mordecai, 'We are born into sin, shaped in iniquity. We are all born with a sinful nature.'

'That is not what the world believes or is taught,' the image retorted, 'Man is naturally good. They were taught they were born sinners. Do not believe what you have been taught. Do you think God loves you? What about the bullies at school and the fact that Shadowfire is about to sacrifice you to the devil?'

'And to you,' added Mordecai.

'I can save you,' the image claimed, 'I can save you from being sacrificed. I can spare your life. All you have to do is bow down to me.'

'Now why would I want to do that?' asked Mordecai skeptically.

'You are afraid of the Prophecy, it's easy to tell,' insisted the image, 'There is no way to defeat Shadowfire. No spear or arrow could bite him, no sword in the world can penetrate his defenses. He is invulnerable, indestructible, invincible. What hopes do you and the fairy maiden have to defeat him?'

'With men, it is impossible,' Mordecai said, 'but with God, all things are possible.'

The image laughed. 'Do you honestly believe that?' it scoffed, 'I sense you do not. I smell the fear you feel inside of you. You are insignificant and worthless. What makes you think God would waste time on a nobody like you?'

'I don't know, but He does,' insisted Mordecai, 'That is how I felt in dealing with the Queen. I do not consider myself anybody special—that we both can agree on—but I know His words are true despite my doubts and fears.'

'The Prophecy will not come to pass, Mordy Jefferson,' the image replied, 'There is no escape for you. You will be sacrificed tomorrow night when the full moon is at its peak. Your only hope is to trust me, to bow down to me.'

Mordecai thought for a moment, feeling a struggle inside. He felt the fear growing stronger, his doubts gnawing at his being. The image sensed this and spoke of it. 'Do not deny it, the fears, and doubts. Perhaps you know the Prophecy is not true and that you and the fairy maiden will die in the attempt. What hope do you have of victory against the dragon? To beg for mercy is your only option.'

'The tender mercies of the wicked are cruel,' Mordecai said, 'I will still be sacrificed no matter what. I do not trust Shadowfire. I trust in the Word that God has spoken.'

'Then you are a fool, Mordy Jefferson,' the image sneered, 'If you don't bow down and surrender to me, you will die as a sacrifice.'

'Then so be it,' Mordecai replied defiantly, 'Jesus made the promise, *I will never leave you nor forsake you. Lo, I am with you always, even unto the end of the world,* and He never fails in His promises. I believe God gave the prophecy to Queen Hephzibah on her deathbed, and though as scared as I am, I am the one the Prophecy has spoken of. He has used people like me in the past, and even though I don't know why or how He would use me, He will use me and the fairy maiden to bring down the dragon.'

The beautiful form of the image slowly and gradually turned hideous and ghastly, deathly. In a demonic voice it said, 'Then you shall die in hell! I gave you a chance to save yourself, but you refused me! You turned me down. Die then, Mordy Jefferson!'

'Depart from me, devil,' proclaimed Mordecai, 'The blood of Jesus Christ is against you and your master! Go back to hell where you came from! The Lord rebuke you, devil!'

With a cry, the image disappeared. Mordecai fell to his knees, exhausted and feeling dehydrated as the air around him began to grow colder. He sat down on the cell floor and bowed his head, whispering a silent prayer, praying for help and strength.

Cece sat in her room in the castle looking out the window, thinking about her brother. She knelt and prayed, weeping that he would be delivered from the claws of Shadowfire. She could not eat or sleep. Taris, one of the guards, entered the room and found Cece on her knees. He sighed, knowing the reason. He leaned his spear against the wall and knelt by her. 'Would you like some company, Cece?' the fairyman asked.

Cece shook his head. 'I'm afraid I would not be good company right now,' she wept as he placed his arms around her in an effort to comfort her.

'I was the guard watching over your when he was imprisoned,' said Taris, 'He gave me no problems but acted virtuously and showed no disrespect. We developed a friendship during that time, before Queen Cymbaline released him. I was told you are his sister.'

'Yes,' Cece nodded.

'You two are very close, from what I was told.'

'We are now,' nodded Cece, 'Before, we were typical brother/sister, arguing, bickering. He went through some difficulties in school, where even our parents did not stand by him. I was favored above him, given things and opportunities which he never got. I thought he would hate me, but I found out it was not so. I was the only one who had stood by him when he needed someone to talk to. We put away our differences and have been close since. Raven had chosen to reveal herself to me when she asked Mordy to let her join him to the house where we lived.'

'I only wish we had some kind of weapon sharp enough to penetrate that seemingly impenetrable hide of his,' sighed Taris as she leaned her head upon his shoulder. 'We have tried ever since he started afflicting us to no avail. Many of us forgot the Prophecy of Queen Hephzibah and those that heard, did not believe it.'

'I feel like a bad guest,' wept Cece. 'I was summoned to dinner by Queen Cymbaline, but—'

'Queen Cymbaline understands, Cece,' said Taris gently as she wept upon his shoulders. 'She sent me here to check up on you and your friends. She sent Lavender and Laurelin to your parents with the same water she gave you that allowed you to fly. They will use it as well, and they will be brought here.'

Cece stared in surprise at Taris. 'Queen Cymbaline is sending for my parents?' she exclaimed.

'Yes,' Taris answered, 'They, too, are in danger from this Dr. Von Braun. From what Lavender and Laurelin told the Queen, two men arrived for both fairies when Raven escaped.'

Cece sighed. 'Queen Cymbaline has been very kind to me, my friends, and my parents as well, though we don't deserve it,' she wept,

'I was too worried about my brother to see how wonderful it was to be flying like I'd been doing. I'm only sorry I got angry with Queen Cymbaline for not trying to rescue Mordecai.'

'She has forgiven you, and she understands.' Taris was anxious to comfort her. 'Like she said, we have no weapons that would even faze Shadowfire or hurt him. We tried for over a century but were unable to form a weapon against him. Our only hope is fulfilling the Prophecy of Queen Hephzibah, and Shadowfire is desperate to keep it from coming to pass.'

'So my parents are being brought here by Lavender and Laurelin with the Queen's leave?'

'That is true,' Taris answered, 'They had left nearly an hour ago.'

'Surely they must be tired from the long trip,' Cece sighed.

'They had volunteered to go,' Taris said, 'They are flying with all haste. Queen Cymbaline believes the time has almost come for the Prophecy to be fulfilled and the dragon will die.'

'I hope so,' wept Cece, 'I am afraid. I fear the worst has happened to my brother.'

Taris sighed as he held her and allowed her to weep on his shoulder. He, too, was worried about Mordecai. He prayed silently as Cece continued to weep.

***

Raven watched from a distance as Shadowfire left his lair and headed into the air. She breathed a sigh of relief when he did not head for Arundel Haven. She waited long minutes before she headed toward the entrance. She took a deep breath and began flying in the direction of the entrance.

She reached the entrance and stopped. She looked back in the direction of where the dragon was heading but did not see him. She took another deep breath and entered.

She looked around. Inside, it was larger than she could ever have imagined. She glanced above and saw many caves, many entrances. Raven smelt a foul odor all around. *This is a dragon's lair all right, she thought, It reeks of Shadowfire. Which cave is Mordecai in, though?*

She flew upward and into the first cave. It was large to human and fairy standards. She saw the remains of fairies that had been captured by Shadowfire over the years. She looked around and saw only more bones. She flew out of the first cave and headed to the nearest cave.

When she entered the second cave, she found more of the same: more bones, some burned. She continued to look around. She suddenly found a pair of bones with familiar clothes. She gasped as tears filled her eyes. 'Mom, Dad!' she whispered. There were the remains of her parents. She recognized the clothes they wore the last time she had seen them. She wept there for long minutes. 'I still miss you so much,' she said amid her tears. She saw the necklaces around their necks and the wedding bands that hung from their skeletal fingers. With tears in her eyes, she took the necklaces and the wedding bands and put them in her pocket. She continued to weep as she stared at them. She then rose up and flew away.

She then flew to the next cave. Various jewels and gold coins and things of value were scattered round about the floor inside, some in piles. There were no remains in that chamber from what she had seen. She stood there for a long time staring at it until she heard a roar from below. She gasped and searched for a place to hide.

Shadowfire flew through the gap which connected to the caves and chambers he had dug out of the mountain upon his arrival. He stopped midway, sniffed the air and growled. 'Fairy,' he muttered. 'A fairy would dare enter my home? How unfortunate for them!' He then gave out a roar. 'I know you are here, fairy,' he cried, 'I can smell you! What reason, besides your demise, do you dare to enter my lair unbidden?'

He checked the first chamber closest to the entrance. He smelled the air and looked around. Raven heard the rumble of his movement as she hid in a corner behind a big boulder.

'Where are you, fairy?' he roared.

'Like I would ever tell you, monster,' whispered Raven softly in defiance.

'Do not bother to hide from me, fairy,' boomed the dragon's voice again, 'Rest assured; I will find you! You would make a great sacrifice to my master when I catch you! You should have never entered my lair!'

Shadowfire slammed his massive claw into the wall of the cave when he couldn't find anything. He growled and flew out of the second chamber.

He then flew inside the chamber where Raven was hiding. Raven gasped silently as her body started to tremble. She moved as close to the boulder as she cold in hopes that Shadowfire would not spot her.

Shadowfire sniffed the air. 'You are here, aren't you, fairy?' he boomed, 'Are you after my treasure, perhaps? Answer me now!'

Raven remained silent as Shadowfire searched. He growled softly but menacingly as he searched through the gold, jewelry, and gems upon the floor. 'Where are you, fairy?' he growled. 'I will find you sooner or later!'

Shadowfire drew near the boulder Raven was hiding behind and walked past her. He slammed the wall and roared. He swiped the boulder where Raven was hiding, and it flew toward the entrance. Raven adjusted her flight as to not have the boulder land on her and crush her as she fought to remain hidden from Shadowfire's sight.

He gave out a roar of frustration. It was at that time Raven made a bee line out of the cave, hoping Shadowfire would not spot her. Shadowfire looked back but saw nothing.

He sniffed the room again and growled. 'You're making this hard on yourself, fairy,' he cried, 'You're only delaying the inevitable!'

Raven ducked inside the second cave she was in before, hoping Shadowfire would not have seen her flying into this chamber. She peeked from behind the entrance but heard only the dragon letting out his frustration. Shadowfire finally flew of the chamber and flew upward.

She flew up after him but did her best to stay hidden and out of sight of Shadowfire. She heard roaring and Shadowfire shouting in frustration. Raven hid behind the entrance of a nearby chamber while Shadowfire rose to another chamber.

Mordecai heard the roars and shouts of the dragon from his prison. He stood up and walked up to the door again. *What is going on to cause Shadowfire to throw a tantrum like that?* He then tried to listen to what Shadowfire was saying. He caught the words of the dragon, 'Where are you, fairy?'

A fairy is here? But who? He then thought of Raven. *But Raven was captured by two flunkies working for Dr. Von Braun, or did she escape? If it is Raven, she's putting her life in danger!* He wasn't sure what to think, or to hope it was Raven. Either way, she was in danger, but he wasn't sure which danger was the lesser of the two.

It sounds like whoever this fairy is, they're really frustrating the tar out of Shadowfire, or at least I hope so. It sure sounds like it, though.

He heard more roars and the angry, frustrated voice of Shadowfire. He found himself laughing softly. He then moved from the door and sat down again on the cold, hard floor of the cage. He sighed. He bowed his head and prayed silently for his deliverance from the dragon.

It was a few minutes later when he heard the footsteps of the dragon and the movement of his wings. He glanced up and saw Shadowfire staring at him. 'I see you are making peace to the God you believe will save you,' he said, 'He will not deliver you out of my claws.'

'How can you be sure of that, dragon?' Mordecai challenged.

'I have captured many fairies who dared to believe that their God, their Saviour, would save them from me, but it never happened. Some wound up being sacrificed, while others I devoured. You see around you the remains of those who had been sacrificed. You shall be no different.'

Mordecai said not a word.

'This is your fate after the full moon tomorrow night,' Shadowfire continued, 'Your blood shall be shed in honor of my god.'

'To the devil, that should be obvious,' Mordecai sneered, 'God allows some bad things to happen for a reason.'

'You don't know how many times I have heard that from others who became sacrifices to my master,' Shadowfire scoffed, 'It shows one of two things: your God don't exist, or your God doesn't really care about you at all. Why else was I allowed to sacrifice so many fairies to my master over the years?'

'Because the Prophecy has yet to be fulfilled,' Mordecai shot back.

'But you are scared of it,' retorted Shadowfire. 'Afraid, perhaps, of the fact that it will not be fulfilled. You don't believe it will come to pass, do you? Your doubts and fears are plain for me to see. What makes you think your God will deliver you out of my claws and bring about my demise? My armor is impenetrable, invulnerable! No weapons the fairies have formed against me can bite me or harm me in any way! They have tried for 150 years but they cannot make anything that can even wound me! What makes you think this Prophecy can succeed where the best efforts of fairy smithies could not?'

Mordecai stared in defiance at Shadowfire. 'Your fear is proof enough,' he replied, 'If you honestly didn't believe the Prophecy would come to pass, then why capture me? Why even appear in my dreams? Why all this effort to keep this Prophecy from coming to pass?'

'It is irrelevant,' roared the dragon, baring his teeth.

'You do not think so,' replied Mordecai sternly, 'Your expression and how you still consider me a threat speaks volumes. Yes, I am scared, I will not deny that, but the LORD has spoken to me, and in the past has used others like me, small and insignificant in the sight of the world, to work His will.'

Shadowfire laughed. 'You say that to encourage yourself,' he mocked, 'Your trust in your God is nothing but a farce, a sham! God doesn't care for people like you! If He did, why did He allow me to capture and imprison you? Why did He not protect you from me when I came for you? Why did He leave you to die? Why did He abandon you?'

'He has not,' Mordecai said simply, 'He is with me even in the worst of my circumstances, even here in the dragon's lair, your lair! Do not deny that you fear the Prophecy, and the time is at hand when it shall finally be fulfilled, and your end shall be achieved!'

Shadowfire growled. 'By your sacrifice, the Prophecy shall come to naught,' he insisted, 'I will live on while any threat against me will be removed, and I never need to fear the Prophecy ever again! You will burn in hell, along with all those who falsely believed that God would save them.'

Mordecai shook his head. Inside, he felt a gentle touch, a strengthening in his soul. The fear he'd had was subsiding and he felt renewed and refreshed in his confidence in the LORD. He merely sat down again and spoke not a word.

'When you are sacrificed, you will know the truth at last,' continued Shadowfire, 'that your faith in your God is in vain! When you die, you will open your eyes in hell, where my master awaits you! Your soul belongs to him, and he will ravage your soul for all of eternity! You will find out too late how wrong you are!'

Mordecai refused to speak. He merely stared at the floor of his prison with a grim look upon his face. Shadowfire laughed wickedly as he turned to leave. 'I have business I need to take care of,' he said as he turned to go, 'Enjoy your last day of life, Mordy Jefferson! When the full moon is at its peak, you will be sacrificed and be cast into hell. There is no hope and no escape for you at all.'

He flew out of the chambers, leaving Mordecai alone. The young man rose to his feet and walked over to the bars again. He bowed his head and prayed inaudibly, falling to his knees.

Inside, he felt his soul refreshed, being strengthened by the touch of the LORD. He continued to pray as he remained like that for a long time.

Tiffany and Sharon were with Starla and Twila in the cottage where Raven stayed. They were drinking juice Raven had given them. Starla, like Cece, could not eat because she was worried about her sister. Tiffany held Twila in her arms while Sharon sat by Starla, anxious to comfort her. 'Raven has always been headstrong and stubborn,' Starla said amid her tears, 'but this time, she's sure to get herself killed by trying to rescue Mordecai.'

'What about the Prophecy?' Sharon asked, 'I still don't understand much about it. Mordy said he was the one spoken of to destroy the dragon.'

Starla shook her head. 'I don't know,' she sobbed, 'I don't know what to think! Raven said that she was the one spoken of, too, but I don't see how they could bring about the end of the dragon!'

Twila flew toward her mother and wiped the tears from her eyes. 'Please no cry, Mommy,' she said.

Starla took her daughter in her arms and wept. Tiffany stared at her and said, 'Starla, you need to be strong for the sake of the child you're carrying.'

'I know,' Starla wept, 'but I miss Raven so much! I fear for her, and for Mordecai as well! I had just gotten to know him and found out how wonderful he is! Both Raven and Twila were right about him.'

'I miss Uncle Morcai, Mommy,' said Twila sadly, 'and Aunt Raven.'

'We know, sweetie,' Tiffany replied softly, 'We all do.'

'Cece's really taking it hard as well,' sighed Sharon, 'I'm worried about her. She refuses to eat anything since Mordy had been captured by Shadowfire.'

'No, Morcai,' corrected Twila, 'His name Morcai.'

The three girls laughed.

'Uncle Morcai,' repeated Twila.

Starla took Twila in her arms and kissed her, laughing amid her tears. 'Okay, Twila, you win,' she said, wiping her tears away, 'We all miss your uncle Morcai and aunt Raven.'

'Maybe you should tell your husband you have retlurned,' Tiffany said.

Starla sighed. 'We can head for our farm when the sun comes up. We do need to tell him about Shadowfire taking Mordecai prisoner. I wish there was something we could do to help him and Raven! Why did she have to fly off after Shadowfire like that?' She wept anew.

'What do you know about the prophecy?' asked Sharon.

'Only what I have heard from Queen Cymbaline,' Starla answered, 'what she told us.'

'Did it mention how Shadowfire would fall?' Tiffany asked.

'No,' answered Starla. 'Only that a human would come to Arundel Haven and that God would use him and a fairy maiden to bring about the death of the dragon. It doesn't give anything more specific than that. It hurts not knowing whether they're still alive or if they are dead.'

'We have to believe the Prophecy will come true, if nothing else,' Tiffany proclaimed, 'and hope that both Mordy and Raven will survive somehow.'

Twila began to yawn as she settled into her mother's arms.

'Looks like somebody is getting sleepy,' Tiffany said. 'I am getting a little tired as well, but I don't know if I will be able to get any sleep.'

'I know I can't,' Starla sighed, 'You can sleep in our old bedrooms. Raven keeps the bed in case Twila and I want to spend the night with her, just to keep her company. Raven has taken the master bedroom as her own since our parents' passing.'

Tiffany and Sharon stared at Starla sadly. 'I can't forget how Raven first told us how the both of you had lost your parents, Starla,' Sharon said quietly, 'It's terrible hearing what had happened. Have the smithies tried everything to forge something that could harm the dragon?'

'Ever since the dragon first appeared here,' sighed Starla, 'but unsuccessful. His armor is too strong for anything they could contrive to forge that could even penetrate his armor. Nothing has worked, and we have lost so many of my people as a result.'

'Do you think bullets may penetrate his armor?' Tiffany asked.

'Bullets?' Starla repeated, confused, 'What are bullets?'

'They don't know anything about guns, Tiffany,' Sharon reminded her.

'What's a gun?' asked Starla.

'A gun is a weapon,' Sharon answered, 'They shoot what we call bullets. They can kill, though, but from what you are telling me, I don't think bullets would work on Shadowfire.'

'Do you think something like rockets or heavy military weapons would?' Tiffany asked.

'Probably not, if he is strong in sorcery as we have heard,' Sharon surmised, 'Perhaps the combination of his armor and his magic make him safe from even our modern weaponry.'

'Then how are Mordy and Raven supposed to bring about the death of Shadowfire?' Tiffany asked.

'I'm guessing they have to trust God in that,' Starla stated, 'Trust Him that He will provide a way to destroy him.'

Tiffany and Sharon shook their heads but said nothing. Starla noticed that both girls were yawning. 'You two try and get some rest,' she told them, 'Take either of the guest rooms. I can at least lay Twila down on Raven's bed since I won't be able to sleep.'

Both girls nodded as Starla showed them the rooms. Tiffany chose Raven's old room while Sharon took Starla's old room. Starla headed into the master bedroom, which Raven had made her room, and laid Twila down. Twila stirred and opened her eyes. 'Mommy no leave Twila,' she said sleepily.

Starla smiled as she laid down beside her. 'No, Twila,' she replied, kissing her, 'Mommy's not going anywhere. Mommy's right here.' She caressed her daughter's face. 'Mommy misses your uncle Morcai and aunt Raven very much.'

'I miss Uncle Morcai and Aunt Raven, too, Mommy,' yawned Twila.

Starla laid down on the bed and wept softly, holding Twila close. Twila said nothing as she touched the tears that fell from her mother's eyes. She yawned and snuggled up to her mother. Starla whispered a silent prayer, barely audible to Twila. Very soon, Twila fell asleep amidst her mother's prayers.

Soon afterwards, Starla found herself falling asleep.

Hours later, she was awakened by Roosevelt, who kissed her on the cheeks. He smiled as he saw Twila fast asleep. Starla saw the familiar face of her husband and embraced him, weeping. Roosevelt kissed her as he held and caressed her. 'What's wrong, Starla?' he asked her. 'When did you get back?'

'We had arrived overnight,' Starla answered, weeping, 'Shadowfire came to the human world and seized Mordecai.'

'Shadowfire?' the black fairyman gasped, When was this?'

'Just last night,' Starla answered, 'Raven had escaped from the humans who had tried to capture her and had flown off to try and rescue Mordecai.'

Roosevelt sighed, shaking his head. 'Tis sad news indeed,' he said, 'It was foolish for Raven to go after him like that.'

'Raven has always been headstrong,' Starla said, 'I'm just afraid that we will lose her.'

'Who had returned with you?'

'Mordecai's sister, Cece, is a guest in the palace,' Starla answered, 'Her friends, Sharon and Tiffany, are both asleep in the guest rooms here.'

'I caught a glimpse of them,' Roosevelt said, 'Does Queen Cymbaline—'

'She knows about Tiffany and Sharon' Starla continued, 'They wanted to stay with me to keep me company.'

'Where are Lavender and Laurelin?'

'Queen Cymbaline had sent them to bring Mordecai's parents here,' Starla answered, 'They may be on their way here now. What time is it?'

'It is about two hours after sunrise,' Roosevelt answered, 'I didn't know you were here, but something told me to come here first, and here you and Twila are.'

At that moment, Twila stirred and opened her eyes. She saw her father and flew into his arms. 'Daddy's here,' she cried.

'Yes, Twila, Daddy's here,' Roosevelt smiled, kissing her on the cheeks.

'I miss Uncle Morcai and Aunt Raven,' the toddler added.

Roosevelt nodded his head sadly. 'I know, Twila.'

'God bring Uncle Morcai and Aunt Raven soon?' Twila asked.

'I wish I knew,' Roosevelt said, shaking his head.

'Yes, Daddy,' Twila said, nodding, 'God bring back Uncle Morcai and Aunt Raven back to Twila soon.'

'And how do you know, young lady?' asked Starla.

'God never lies, Mommy,' Twila answered.

The faith of a child, thought Roosevelt. *Perhaps you are right, my daughter. We should trust the LORD in this. I will believe His word as well.*

He held his wife and daughter close to him, kissing them. 'I choose to believe God, then,' he said softly.

Starla only wept as she held Roosevelt tightly.

Raven waited a long time before she attempted to fly inside the chamber where she had heard Shadowfire talking, to Mordecai, she hoped. She sighed as she carefully made her way toward the chamber.

She moved cautiously through the opening. She found it to be large, seeing the idol of the Mother and Child and not too far from it, an altar underneath an upside-down star with a figure of a goat's head within.

She then saw the remains of past victims scattered around the room, victims who had been sacrificed to Shadowfire's unholy master. She bowed her head sadly in respect to the victims, remembering that her parents had been sacrificed in the same way.

She heard a rumble from not too far away and quickly hid herself and waited for signs of the dragon. She cautiously stepped out from behind a boulder and looked around. She sighed. She hoped that Shadowfire was asleep and just talking in his sleep or whatever dragons do.

She then looked up. She saw a cage suspended by a chain that was attached to a ceiling. She flew toward the cage and gasped. Mordecai was asleep in the middle of the cage, trying to keep himself warm. Raven hovered at the cell door and tried to open it, but it would not budge. As the cage rattled, Mordecai stirred and looked up. He saw Raven at the door. He immediately rose to his feet and ran toward her, saying her name. 'Raven!'

Both lovers touched each other's face through the bars.

'My darling Mordecai,' Raven said, tears filling her eyes, 'I am so glad you're alive! I miss you so much!'

'You shouldn't have come, Raven,' Mordecai warned, 'Shadowfire plans to sacrifice me tonight when the full moon is at its peak.'

'I had to come, Mordecai, my love,' Raven said, 'I would not abandon you! We're both in this together, for better or for worse.'

Mordecai sighed as kissed Raven's hand. 'For better or for worse, then,' he agreed, He then thought of the Word when Ruth, a Moabitess, refused to leave her Hebrew mother-in-law, Naomi, even after her husband had passed away. *Where you lodge, I shall lodge. Where you go, I will go. Your people shall be my people, and your God my God, and may God deal with me severely if anything, but death separates me and you.*

He had seen that in Raven. He sighed. 'Together, then,' he repeated, 'The two of us; human and fairy. God brought us together, and not even Shadowfire will tear us apart.'

'God will deal with me severely if anything short of death separates the both of us, Mordecai, my love, my life,' Raven whispered.

Raven tried the door again. The door remained locked and did not open. 'I tried it before, Raven,' Mordecai said quietly, 'but Shadowfire says that magic binds the door shut.'

'What if we both tried it together, pray God would open it?' suggested Raven, 'No magic, no matter how powerful, is any match for the power of our God. The devil's power is but a flyspeck compared to our LORD. Yahweh is the Creator, while Satan is just a creation, a fallen angel, who was cast out of heaven along with a third of all the angels, those that had sided with him.'

Mordecai nodded.

Both placed their hands on the door of Mordecai's cage. As they touched it and a silent prayer was said, they heard a clicking sound. The door moved and opened. Mordecai immediately flew out of the cage as Raven flew into his arms, holding each other, weeping, and kissing each other on the lips. They remained that way for long moments, holding each other and weeping. 'You are intelligent as well as beautiful, my love,' Mordecai told her.

'I had feared the worst,' Raven said, wiping the tears from his eyes as Mordecai wiped hers away, 'I am so thankful to God that you are alive!'

'Hey, there's still the Prophecy to be fulfilled,' Mordecai replied, 'I missed you so much, Raven!'

Raven sighed. 'I found my parents,' she said sadly, 'or what's left of them.'

'Where did you find them?' Mordecai asked.

'In one of the chambers,' Raven sighed.

Raven took him to the place where she found the remains of her parents. Mordecai bowed sadly as she showed him where their remains laid. He knelt in front of them. Raven wept as she knelt beside him. 'I only wish they could have seen you for real,' she said amid her tears. 'This is exactly what they wore when they were taken by Shadowfire.'

'What were their names, Raven?' asked Mordecai.

'My father's name was Japeth and my mother Jochabed,' Raven answered, 'They only knew their granddaughter Twila for a short time. I'm not sure if Twila even remembers her grandparents.'

'Would they have accepted me, Raven, if they were alive?' Mordecai asked.

'I wish I could say,' sighed Raven, 'I honestly wish I knew.'

She leaned her head upon his shoulder and wept. Mordecai held her as she wept. 'I still miss them, Mordecai!'

Mordecai kissed her. 'I know, sweetheart,' he sighed, 'When we beat Shadowfire, we will return and bury them properly and not leave their remains here in Shadowfire's lair.'

Mordecai then stood up and lifted Raven to her feet. 'We better get out of here,' he said. 'No telling what Shadowfire is doing or how long it will be until he finds out that I have escaped.'

They then heard a mighty roar from above, startling both lovers. 'I think he might have just found out,' Raven said grimly, 'We better hide!'

'I wonder how far this chamber goes?' wondered Mordecai, 'We have to make our way out carefully, lest he sees us!'

They heard the rumble of the dragon's approach coming closer. They decided to head up toward the roof and hoped there was a space for them to hide.

They heard the dragon cry out, 'I know you're here somewhere, Mordy Jefferson! You will not escape me, so help me Ashtaroth!'

They rose to the roof. 'Shadowfire doesn't know I can fly yet,' Mordecai whispered to Raven, holding her close as they hid within a crevice.

'I just hope that remains unknown to him,' Raven replied softly. Shadowfire flew inside the chamber where they were hiding. Both Mordecai and Raven huddled close together as they heard the footsteps of the dragon enter and walking below them. He smelled the air. 'You are here, Mordy Jefferson,' he growled, 'You and the fairy! What fairy would dare…'

He paused.

Mordecai and Raven held their breaths collectively.

'Raven!' came the voice of the dragon, 'It was you, Raven! You dare to invade my chambers and somehow freed Mordy Jefferson from his cell? By Semiramus, how is this possible?'

Mordecai and Raven heard the dragon pass by and were compelled to fly from their hiding place. They flew as fast as they could out of the chambers.

But Shadowfire turned around and happened to spot them flying. He gave out a roar. 'No,' he cried, 'By Ashtaroth, you will not escape me!'

Mordecai and Raven flew into another chamber, flying deeper and deeper inside the cave. Shadowfire followed them but could not see them.

'There is nowhere you can hide, Mordy Jefferson,' he cried, 'nor you, Raven! I don't know how you had gained the ability to fly, boy, but neither of you shall outfly me!'

He belched forth fire, which briefly lit up part of the chambers. Mordecai and Raven were fortunately out of range. They looked around as best they could for a place to hide, or better yet, a way out. They heard the footsteps of the dragon approaching, belching forth fire as he stepped deeper inside. 'Nowhere to fly to, nowhere you can hide,' cried Shadowfire, 'Where can the two of you fly? There's no way out of here!'

Raven happened to spot an opening small enough for them both to enter. She pulled on Mordecai's arm and pointed at it. 'Over here,' Raven said softly.

'Are you sure?' Mordecai asked, 'How far will it go? Shadowfire may spot it and figure out we are inside.'

'We may not have a choice,' Raven whispered.

Mordecai nodded. Out of caution he entered inside first, followed by Raven. They made their way deeper into the tunnel. They saw the light from behind from the flames spewed out by the dragon. Mordecai noticed an adjoining tunnel and with Raven, ducked behind the wall.

It was after Raven had followed Mordecai and hid behind the corridor that the eye of Shadowfire peeked inside the hole. He had never noticed the hole before when he was digging out the chambers but he grew suspicious. He had no idea how it got there or where it led. He spewed out flames, engulfing the small cave. Mordecai and Raven scurried further down the corridor to avoid the flames, the small space filling with intense heat.

Mordecai moved down further into the corridor. He felt a slight breeze blowing from deeper down. He turned to Raven and asked, 'You feel that?'

Raven paused for a moment. 'A way out?' she asked him hopefully.

'Only one way to find out, love.'

'Guess we don't have much of a choice, do we?' replied Raven.

They made their way down the corridor as the flames stopped from behind them. They felt the walls shake as they walked further down the winding cave. 'This looks like it had been made some time ago,' said Mordecai, 'but who made it? Were there some fairies who had survived and had made it, using it to escape or found it?'

'I don't know, Mordecai,' replied Raven, 'I have never heard of any fairy successfully escaping Shadowfire after being taken to this ungodly place.'

'I wish there was a way to find out,' said Mordecai.

'Maybe it has been here even before Shadowfire arrived to this mountain to dwell in?' mused Raven. 'I'm just thankful that it is here. But where does it lead?'

'Raven, listen,' Mordecai said as he bade her to halt.

There was no sound.

'I don't hear anything,' said Raven.

'Shadowfire has stopped,' Mordecai said tentatively, 'I have a feeling he may have guessed that this tunnel leads to an exit. If there is one, we must be cautious in case he suspects this cave does connect to a way out.'

They continued further down the tunnel. A short time later, they felt the breeze blowing stronger and saw the morning light at the end. They breathed a sigh of relief. 'At least it leads to a way out,' Mordecai said, 'One question is solved.'

'Now the next question needs to be answered,' replied Raven, 'is Shadowfire out there waiting for us?'

'I think we can count on that,' sighed Mordecai, 'It's going to be difficult to return to Arundel Haven without being pursued by the dragon. He may even figure out where we will be heading.'

'So what do we do?' Raven asked.

'We may have no choice but to return to Arundel Haven,' frowned Mordecai, 'I have a feeling the time of the fulfillment of the Prophecy of Queen Hephzibah is at hand.' He took Raven's hand. 'We will have to figure out where it leads and go from there, flying low to the ground,' he said, 'We may have a better chance then. We would be hard for Shadowfire to spot if we're as low to the ground as possible, at least I think so. You are more familiar with Shadowfire than I am.'

Raven agreed, squeezing his hand. 'No matter what, my love,' she sighed, 'we are in this together.'

'Either we both escape or neither of us,' sighed Mordecai.

They walked up toward the opening. They carefully looked out into the open air. Mordecai suddenly heard rushing wings and pulled Raven deep into the cave again. They saw the shadow of the dragon fly past the cave and disappear. They waited there for long moments. Then, they heard the dragon's wings two minutes later and saw his shadow. 'The next time he passes by,' Mordecai said to Raven, 'we must make a break for it. We must stay as low as possible in hopes he doesn't spot us.'

Raven nodded. She kissed him on the lips. 'Kiss for luck,' she said.

'We don't believe in luck, sweet Raven,' the young man replied, 'We believe in God and His divine design. He's going to bring us through this.'

Raven nodded, kissing him again. Letting out a deep breath, she said, 'Let's do this!'

They once again heard the wings of the dragon approaching. Mordecai held Raven's hand. 'Get ready to fly,' he told her.

'I am ready,' Raven replied.

They saw the shadow of the dragon pass by, then disappear. When he had passed, Mordecai cried out, 'Now!'

They made a dash toward the opening and jumped, soaring downward and as close to the mountain as they could. They kept falling like that until they nearly reached the bottom before leveling off and flying as low to the ground as possible, flying hand in hand. They briefly stared at each other then looked ahead. Mordecai looked back briefly. 'So far so good,' he said. 'Shadowfire hasn't spotted us yet.'

'Not yet, at any rate,' Raven said, her heart thundering.

When Shadowfire circled toward the cave the lovers had been, he stopped and spotted the opening. He growled as he hovered and stared into it, seeing nothing but darkness. He took a sniff around the area. He caught the scent of both the human and the fairy. He growled. He then looked around before letting out a mighty roar, which caused the lovers to turn around.

'He noticed where we were,' Raven said.

'We need to stay low,' cried Mordecai. 'Perhaps he hasn't spotted us yet. We can fly into the woods up ahead. The trees should cover us.'

'I had tried that before,' Raven cried. 'He set out enchanted flames to encircle me and to drive me out when he was sure where I was. Twila and I were nearly caught.'

'Right now, it may be our best bet,' Mordecai shouted over the wind blasting past his ears, 'Once we evade him, we can find our way back to Arundel Haven and tell Queen Cymbaline what had happened.'

Shadowfire spotted the woods and growled. He figured they would be flying there to try and elude him. 'Fools,' he scoffed. 'If you think you could hide yourself there you are sadly mistaken. Have you forgotten, Raven, what had happened the last time you did so?' He soared toward the woods Mordecai and Raven had entered where they had to land. It was too narrow for them to fly. They ran as fast as they could through the woods, hoping Shadowfire had not spotted them, hoping he would search somewhere else for them.

But Shadowfire had already figured out their plan. When he reached the wooded area, he made a guess where they could be. He made an incantation, then spewed out blue flames as he flew around. He made a circle about five kilometers around.

Mordecai and Raven noticed the dragon had trapped them within a ring of fire and thought he had spotted them. 'I should have listened to you, Raven,' he told her. 'I'm sorry!'

They searched for a way out, running in different directions until they found blue flames drawing closer to them. They ran the opposite way and found the same thing.

'I know you two are in here somewhere,' they heard the dragon bellowing, 'I thought you would have learned from our first encounter, Raven! You should have never listened to the human!'

'We can't give up, Raven,' Mordecai shouted, leading Raven away from the flames. Every direction they turned, they found blue flames closing in on them.

'You have two choices,' the dragon roared, 'You can either burn to death or escape the flames only to be caught by me.' They heard the wicked laughter growing louder.

'We're not finished yet, pet of *Loserfer*,' Mordecai said in soft defiance. Heading north, they kept running until they ran into an approaching wall of flames. 'We're running out of options, Mordecai,' Raven cried.

'We can't give up, Raven,' Mordecai said simply. They then headed south but found the same thing. They turned around and headed north again. They frantically looked around for a possible way out.

'Decide quickly,' mocked the dragon. 'You are running out of time!'

They were at the point now where they could see the wall of flames closing in all around them. Raven was in a panic. Suddenly, amidst the mocking laughter, Mordecai felt a calmness in his spirit as he looked. He saw an opening form within a part of the wall. He pulled on Raven's arms and pointed at the opening. 'We must hurry,' he softly told her.

Raven followed Mordecai through the opening as they both ran as fast as they could. When they had passed through, the wall of flames closed up again, but they did not look back. They tried to put as much distance as possible between them and the dragon.

'If you two wish to burn to death,' they heard the dragon's angry voice boom, 'then so be it! So long as the Prophecy does not come to pass. I will have to find another sacrifice for my master.'

Raven pulled on Mordecai's arm as they reached a large boulder. 'This way,' she said.

Mordecai followed her.

They soon came to a part of the woods where the gap was large enough to fly through yet was still covered by the large branches. 'How long is the gap?' Mordecai asked. 'How far does it go?'

'About five kilometers at least,' answered Raven, 'If we stay close to the trees, we shouldn't be spotted by the dragon. We must make as much distance between us and Shadowfire as we can!'

As they took to the air, they stayed as close to the large branches as they could without being in the line of Shadowfire's vision should he be searching in their direction. They then heard an angry roar from behind them and curses coming from the dragon. 'How could this be?' he cried angrily. 'How could they have escaped? No remains, no sign of them! What trickery is this?' He growled. 'No, no,' he snarled, 'You've got to be here somewhere! I know you can't be far!'

Mordecai and Raven continued to fly close to the overhanging branches as possible. They heard the roar of the dragon as he approached and hid themselves underneath a large oak branch. They heard the dragon pass by with a growl. He then circled around and returned the way he came. From time to time, he sniffed the air but found nothing. He growled softly and menacingly. 'You couldn't have gotten far,' Shadowfire snarled as he continued his search.

They continued on as he flew back the way he came. They stayed close to the branches in hopes that Shadowfire would not spot them should he search their way again. 'Is there somewhere we could hide until he decides to give it up?' Mordecai asked.

'Not around here,' Raven answered, 'There is a hill with a small cave, hidden even from Shadowfire's eyes. It's about ten kilometers away, but too far for us to fly with Shadowfire so close.'

'We have to do something,' Mordecai said desperately.

Again, they heard the rush of the approaching wings of the dragon. They managed to find another large oak branch to hide behind. Shadowfire hovered in the area and sniffed the air. 'They're here somewhere,' he muttered, 'I can feel it!' He hovered there for a long moment without a word.

Mordecai and Raven huddled as close to the branch as possible, holding their collective breaths, afraid to do anything. They remained there, unsure of what was going to happen.

The hearts of both Mordecai and Raven were racing wildly with fear. Mordecai stared at Raven and touched her cheek.

Raven did the same thing to Mordecai.

Mordecai held Raven close to him protectively. 'Why doesn't he do anything?' whispered Mordecai as he fought to keep control.

Raven buried her head in Mordecai's shoulder as she held him tight.

Mordecai held Raven as close to him as possible, gazing in the direction of the dragon.

Once again, the dragon sniffed the air. A cold breeze blew from the direction of the dragon, which frustrated the monster. The scent he had caught was gone. He let out a heavy sigh. 'Perhaps it is time,' the dragon mused, 'time for me to reveal the location of Arundel Haven to President Farouk.'

Mordecai gave out a barely audible gasp, though not loud enough for Shadowfire to hear it.

They heard Shadowfire laugh. 'Maybe I should have told Dr. Von Braun a long time ago,' he said to himself, 'I'm sure President Farouk would want to claim Arundel Haven for his country.'

'No,' whispered Mordecai fearfully.

'Yes, make Queen Cymbaline's worst nightmare come true,' he laughed softly, 'to have the humans know the existence of Arundel Haven and who knows what they will do to the fairies. That would make Dr. Von Braun happy for sure. Why did I not think of this before?' He laughed as he flew away, heading back to his home.

Mordecai gasped as he and Raven flew away from the branch. 'So, it is true,' the human gasped, 'I had always known President Farouk supports unconstitutional policies and immoral agendas, but I guess I should have known he would have an alliance with Shadowfire.'

'Your president?' Raven asked.

'He's an elected leader of our country, Raven,' Mordecai explained, Every four years, the people in the United States elect a president, someone to be the head of our country. Last year, President Farouk was re-elected by receiving the most votes. I suppose many have been duped into buying into his agenda. He has told lies, broken promises, supporting ungodly agendas, ignoring the will of the people, going against our Constitution. We're in a bad mess because of it. I had no idea he would be in league with Shadowfire.'

'I guess this President Farouk is a bad man,' Raven replied.

'To many he is,' the young man nodded, 'He has given money to terrorists, stood against Israel, forced his personal beliefs upon us.'

'How could he stand against Israel?' Raven exclaimed, 'How could he stand against God's chosen people?'

'Unfortunately, there are a lot of humans who hate Israel without a just cause,' he replied, 'I, too, believe that Israel are God's chosen people. God tells us to *Pray for the peace of Jerusalem.'*

'Queen Cymbaline, though she mistrusted humans before you came, also believes the same about Israel that *God will bless them that bless thee, and curse them that curseth thee, and through thee all families of the world shall be blessed.'*

'I would have loved to visit Jerusalem someday,' Mordecai said, 'if God is willing. Since President Farouk is in league with Shadowfire, we must tell Queen Cymbaline right away!'

They took to the air and headed back to Arundel Haven.

Shadowfire returned to his home. He knelt before the idol of the Mother and Child and began to chant. As he chanted, he slowly went into a trance, speaking in a strange tongue. There he remained for long moments as he continued his chanting.

President Farouk was having breakfast in the White House with Dr. Von Braun. They talked as they ate. 'I am sorry my men have failed you,' he said, 'I thought they had been trained better than that!'

'Perhaps they underestimated those that defend the fairies,' Dr. Von Braun replied. He had a bottle of scotch he was drinking as he ate. 'I am not very pleased with the results, of course. Raven got away and their effort to capture at least one of her friends is most disappointing.'

'I assumed they had flown to the place where Mordy Jefferson lives,' President Farouk replied, 'His parents were most uncooperative.'

'How did they find the house?' asked Dr. Von Braun.

'They had followed one of his classmates who were dining at a local pizza parlor with the fairies,' President Farouk explained, 'They had their wings covered up, according to my agents. They were able to keep from being detected until Shadowfire arrived and ripped the clothing off Raven's body to expose her wings.'

'How interesting,' mused Dr. Von Braun.

'She had clothes on underneath,' President Farouk continued, 'The others did as well. They had put enough clothing on to cover their wings. There was reportedly a small fairy child there as well.'

'Whose child?'

'I'm guessing one of the other fairies, but not Raven,' President Farouk answered, 'I have not heard whose child it was.'

At that moment, President Farouk's body stiffened, dropping the glass of vodka he held in his hand. 'Ahmad?' exclaimed Dr. Von Braun. 'Ahmad, are you okay?'

President Farouk did not respond immediately. He remained in a trance for a long minute while Dr. Von Braun continued to call his name.

Then a thought came to him. *Shadowfire, perhaps? Heck of a way to communicate, my friend.*

He waited for a long minute until President Farouk came out of his trance. He then took his cell phone and dialed some numbers. 'Are you okay, Ahmad?' the geneticist asked.

After a few seconds, President Farouk spoke. 'Holder, this is the President. Have my private chopper ready immediately. Dr. Von Braun and I have something to take care of. We will finish our breakfast and be ready to depart at once. Thank you.' He hung up the phone.

'Shadowfire?' asked Dr. Von Braun.

President Farouk nodded. 'Shadowfire,' he answered, 'I had just finished speaking to him. He wishes to speak with us right away. I will not talk about it until we are on board the chopper.'

'About a certain subject we're both familiar with?'

President Farouk nodded. 'He will tell us more when we reach the rendezvous point,' he said, 'Our usual spot. He would tell me nothing more than that, but he says he will explain things when we reach our meeting place.'

Dr. Von Braun laughed. 'Of course,' he nodded, 'Got to keep all this hush-hush. I'm sure he has his reasons. I am curious what he has to say. What do you think it could be, Ahmad?'

'Who knows, Haman?' replied President Farouk, 'but I hope it is what I think it is, though.'

'Well, we'll just have to find out when we meet him there,' Dr. Von Braun replied, taking another drink of his scotch.

President Farouk drained his cup and poured himself another glass of vodka.

Mordecai and Raven flew to her cottage first for something to drink. They landed at the front door, which Raven opened. 'I should still have some juice stored up,' she said, 'We can get a drink before we meet with Queen Cymbaline.'

'I thought I was going to die from dehydration inside Shadowfire's lair,' Mordecai said, 'I kind of wished we had stopped by the Silverstreams so I could properly rehydrate.'

Suddenly, they heard voices from one of the rooms. 'Who's there?' came Starla's voice.

'Uncle Morcai? Aunt Raven?' came Twila's voice as she flew from the master bedroom. She cried out when she saw the young human, flying into his arms. 'Uncle Morcai, uncle Morcai,' she chimed happily.

'Twila,' Mordecai exclaimed, catching her and kissing her on the cheeks.

'Mordecai?' came Starla's voice. She and Roosevelt stepped out into the living room where they embraced each of them, Starla bursting into tears as she embraced her sister. 'Thank God you're alive, both of you!' she wept.

Raven was in tears as well. 'I'm so happy to see you again too, Starla. I was afraid I had lost Mordecai!'

Roosevelt stared at Mordecai and Raven. 'How did you escape the dragon?' he asked, 'I thought you two would end up like countless others!'

'He had stopped his pursuit of us,' Mordecai stated, 'but I need a drink first. I feel dehydrated right now.'

Starla released Raven and headed to the kitchen to fetch Mordecai some juice.

'We overheard him talking,' Mordecai continued. 'It seems he is also in league with the President—the leader of our country. Raven and I had flown here so I could get rehydrated before we tell Queen Cymbaline what we had overheard from the dragon.'

At that moment, Tiffany appeared out of one of the guest rooms and saw Mordecai and Raven talking with Roosevelt. She ran over to Mordecai and embraced him. 'Is it really you, Mordy?' she asked. She then called out, 'Sharon, Sharon, Mordy is back, and so is Raven!'

Mordecai was surprised to see Tiffany in Arundel Haven. 'Tiffany? What are you doing in Arundel Haven?'

'We had flown here with Lavender and Laurelin,' Tiffany replied as Starla gave Mordecai the cup of juice.

He drank it and sighed. 'Much better.'

Sharon appeared in the room and gave Mordecai an embrace. 'It is you, Mordy,' she exclaimed, 'How did you and Raven escape from the dragon?'

'He was chasing us for a while,' Mordecai sighed, 'but such news I must deliver to Queen Cymbaline. It's become worse than I thought!'

'Cece will be relieved to hear you are okay,' Tiffany said. 'She is in the castle now.'

'Wait a minute,' Mordecai exclaimed, 'You're saying that Cece is here, too?'

'Yes,' Sharon answered, 'and she's worried sick about you. She fears the worst.'

Mordecai sighed. 'How did she get here?'

'Cece had flown with me after she and her friends had drunk the vial of the water from the Silverstreams,' Starla clarified, 'We had flown to Arundel Haven just after you had been captured by Shadowfire and Raven had flown after you. It seems her rescue was successful.'

'Indeed, it was,' Mordecai smiled, turning toward Raven. He kissed her on the lips and said, 'Thank you, sweet Raven, for coming after me.'

Raven grinned. 'I was more afraid of losing you than losing my own life,' she proclaimed, 'I couldn't bear to live without you now that we have found each other.'

'Your mother will be relieved that you are safe again,' Starla told Mordecai as Twila laid her head upon the young man's shoulder. He kissed the ebony fairy toddler and smiled at her. 'She and your father are being brought to Arundel Haven just after you were taken by Shadowfire. She will be happy to see you when she gets here.'

'Wait a minute,' Mordecai exclaimed, 'My parents are being brought here?'

'With Queen Cymbaline's leave,' Sharon answered, 'They may be here by now. Lavender and Laurelin had left to bring them here, and I imagine they will be given the water that Queen Cymbaline had given to Cece.'

'We better fly to the castle immediately,' Mordecai declared, 'I wish to see my sister and to let her know that I am all right. I have news the Queen must hear.'

When they arrived at the castle, they met Taris, who was relieved to see his friends return, giving Mordecai a brotherly hug. As they talked, Taris said, 'We thought we would never see you again.'

'God had delivered us out of the claws of the dragon,' Mordecai said gravely, 'but there is news Queen Cymbaline needs to hear.'

'I am thankful you are safe,' Taris sighed, 'and your sister will be relieved to hear as well.'

'Yes, I understand that she is here in Arundel Haven,' said Mordecai.

'Your parents had arrived not too long ago,' Taris said, 'Lavender and Laurelin have returned to their homes to rest after the trip.'

'I only wish this news could wait, Taris,' sighed Mordecai, 'The dragon had stopped searching for us, but we overheard him say something that Queen Cymbaline needs to hear. Things are worse than we first thought.'

'I will take you to the throne room and summon Queen Cymbaline and Prince Avondale,' Taris said, 'I will let your sister and your parents know that you are here and you are safe.'

'Mordy, what are you talking about?' Tiffany asked.

'It's our president, Ahmad Farouk,' explained Mordecai as they followed Taris.

'What does President Farouk have to do with this?' Sharon asked.

'I will explain things when we meet with Queen Cymbaline,' replied Mordecai, 'I must tell her directly. I'm not even sure that I believe it myself, but I can't take chances when it comes to the fairies of Arundel Haven.'

They were led into the throne room where they awaited Queen Cymbaline and Prince Avondale. Water was fetched for Mordecai, who was still feeling dehydrated from being imprisoned inside the lair of the dragon.

He sat down on a chair, still holding Twila, who refused to leave her uncle Morcai. Starla was about to take her, but Mordecai said, 'It's okay, Starla. With your permission, she can remain.'

Tiffany and Sharon stared at Mordecai and Twila and couldn't help but smile. Raven kissed Mordecai as she placed her arm around him. Mordecai looked at her and said, 'You are such a blessing to me, my sweet Raven. Thank you for coming after me.'

'What you did was foolish,' Starla told Raven, 'You were fortunate you and Mordecai had escaped Shadowfire, but what if you hadn't?'

'Do not be too hard on Raven, Starla,' Roosevelt told his wife, 'Raven did what she thought was right. She listened to her heart, and it has not failed her. God had delivered them out of Shadowfire's claws, and He shall deliver the dragon into their hands and will bring him down.'

Cece ran into the throne room and headed toward Mordecai. She wept as she embraced her brother, thankful and relieved that he was alive. Twila flew toward her mother and was received into her arms. Mordecai wept as well, as Raven wrapped her arms around the both of them. Cece could not say a word as she wept upon his shoulders. Mordecai gently kissed Cece's forehead. 'I'm surprised to see you here, Cece,' he said.

'I was so afraid I wouldn't see you again,' Cece wept, 'Mom and Dad are here as well.'

'I was surprised when I had first heard they were here,' Mordecai said, 'when I was told Lavender and Laurelin had returned to our home and had brought them here. I was told it was by Queen Cymbaline's leave.'

'She was the one who had sent for them,' Cece nodded.

Mordecai sighed.

'Baby, are you okay?' Raven asked him.

'You know that my mother is accepting of you,' Mordecai told her, 'but my father is another story. He may not be accepting of our relationship.'

'It was not the case when we had flown with Lavender and Laurelin to Arundel Haven,' Tiffany said, 'He was impressed when he had heard Raven had put her own life on the line to rescue you, and he says he would welcome her as family and give you his blessing to take Raven's hand.'

Mordecai nodded as he released Cece, who turned toward Tiffany and asked, 'He really said that?'

'Yes, he did,' Sharon answered, 'You can ask him yourself when he wakes up.'

At that moment, Queen Cymbaline and Prince Avondale entered the room. Mordecai approached them as the Queen embraced him with tears in her eyes. 'I thank God you are still alive, both you and Raven,' she told Mordecai, 'Avondale and I had feared the worst.'

'For a while, I thought I wouldn't make it,' Mordecai said quietly, 'I still feel dehydrated from being incarcerated.' He released Queen Cymbaline. 'Things are worse than I anticipated. Shadowfire had stopped pursuing us. Raven and I overheard him say that he would tell our president, Ahmad Farouk, the location of Arundel Haven. They have an alliance together, President Farouk, Dr. Von Braun and Shadowfire. He departed for the human world and plans to tell both of them about Arundel Haven, where it is.' He fell to his knees. 'I feared this would happen, that somehow my people would know of this and try to invade and take Arundel Haven.'

Queen Cymbaline sighed as she knelt by him. 'Do not feel this is your fault, dear Mordecai,' she said gravely, 'I know it is not. I know you have done all you could to protect our secret, and we trust you.'

'There must be a way to keep them from setting foot within Arundel Haven,' Cece exclaimed, 'I still can't believe that President Farouk would be in league with the dragon, *our own president!* This is insanity!'

'I counsel that we must meet them before they even reach the Mountains of Shadow,' Prince Avondale told his sister, 'I will have our army assembled and ready to fly to Nebechadrezzar Valley. It may be the only way to keep the other humans from reaching Arundel Haven.'

'I am willing to help out, my Queen,' Mordecai told Queen Cymbaline.

'Nay,' replied Queen Cymbaline, 'You and Raven must concentrate on Shadowfire as the Prophecy states. My heart tells me that the time is nearly nigh.'

Mordecai nodded. 'I sense it, too.'

'As do I,' Raven sighed, kneeling by Mordecai, and taking his hand, 'I'm still scared, Mordecai, but I am with you however it ends.'

'As am I, Raven,' Mordecai nodded, 'I am just as scared as you are, but we will trust God in this. He will bring us through this, the both of us.'

'All of us, dear Mordecai,' the Fairy Queen said, touching his shoulder, then Raven's. 'I believe God will bring us through this no matter what.'

'I only wish the secret of Arundel Haven would remain a secret from my people,' sighed Mordecai. 'I feared this would happen. I don't want anything bad to happen to you, to Twila, to Raven, Starla or Roosevelt.'

'We all must trust God in this,' Queen Cymbaline stated.

Prince Avondale nodded and left.

'Prince Avondale has gone to assemble our army to face and repel our enemies,' she told Mordecai. 'They will fight to the death to defend us, no matter what weapons they may possess.'

'I will do my part, my Queen,' Mordecai replied, touching her face. 'I promise.'

Queen Cymbaline nodded. 'I believe you,' she smiled, 'We are together in this, you, Raven, all of us. God shall bring us all through this.'

Mordecai sighed. 'Whatever happens, I will stand by Arundel Haven, by you, my Queen, all the way, no matter what happens. By you, by Raven, Starla and Twila and the ones I love, as the LORD lives, I will stand by you and by all in Arundel Haven.'

Queen Cymbaline smiled and gave him a gentle kiss on the forehead.

Inside, Mordecai was scared for what will soon come, but he confirmed his commitment in his heart and was determined to keep the promise he had made.

He felt Raven giving him a gentle kiss on the cheeks. Cece leaned her head on Mordecai's shoulders as they knelt together, praying, and thanking God for His mercy and grace, praying for victory and deliverance from their enemies and for the fall of the dragon, Shadowfire.

Chapter Twelve

The helicopter carrying President Farouk and Dr. Von Braun landed at the rendezvous point where the two of them were to meet with Shadowfire. When it landed, only President Farouk and Dr. Von Braun walked out into the open while his aides remained inside, too scared to face the dragon. Dr. Von Braun shook his head. 'Some people fear what they don't understand,' he said.

'My aides have been with me countless times to meet with Shadowfire,' replied President Farouk, 'but they are still afraid for their lives.'

'They do not trust the dragon as we do,' stated Dr. Von Braun, 'I wonder why Shadowfire had requested the both of us?'

'He said he will explain when he arrives,' replied President Farouk, 'I have a feeling it must be important if he has summoned the both of us.'

'I should have had another drink of scotch before we left the chopper,' frowned Dr. Von Braun.

'Perhaps I can arrange that, old friend,' boomed a voice. Both men looked up and the familiar form of Shadowfire appeared, landing one hundred meters in front of them. 'I am glad the both of you are here,' he continued, chanting an incantation. A bar appeared in front of them with different alcoholic drinks, including vodka and scotch. Both men poured a glass of their preference.

'I had captured Mordy Jefferson last night, but with the help of Raven, he had escaped my clutches,' the dragon said grimly, 'Apparently, your men were not good enough to keep a hold of Raven, Ahmad.'

'She had help,' President Farouk replied, 'My men had told me three girls had helped free Raven. They told me they could fly, but they were not fairies—they did not have wings.'

'So they do know more about fairies than I thought,' Dr. Von Braun said, 'That would explain why they could fly.'

'So there are others?' asked Shadowfire. 'Mordy has the power of flight. He must have received it from Queen Cymbaline for sure. I imagine that he and Raven have returned to Arundel Haven.'

'How many know the secret of Arundel Haven?' Dr. Von Braun asked, 'Apparently, those girls, including Mordy's sister, know more than they care to tell.'

'His parents do, too,' President Farouk mused, 'My men had questioned his parents, but they would reveal nothing. I wonder if they could have the power of flight too?'

'I will have my men sent over there and question them,' Dr. Von Braun said, grabbing his cell phone, 'I will find the address from Rodham and Clinton since they know the way. I will personally go over there—'

'No, Haman,' Shadowfire interrupted, 'There is no need to head over there yourself. I should have mentioned this sooner, but I can take you to Arundel Haven. Both you, and Ahmad.'

Dr. Von Braun smiled.

'You can claim Arundel Haven for your country, Ahmad,' Shadowfire told the President, 'Three thousand men would only be needed for this operation, I believe, but they must be men whom you can trust, men who have no regards for your Constitution, those who are totally loyal to you.'

He chanted and spoke in a strange language, lasting for almost a minute.

He then stopped.

'Too many of your military personnel still hold to your Constitution,' he told the president. 'The spell I have put on you will direct you to choosing only those soldiers who will assist you in taking Arundel Haven. They will be more than a match for the armies of the fairies. Their weapons consist of only swords, spears, and arrows, but no weapon they formed can hurt me. I am immune, but your men are not. I give you three days to gather your forces for the invasion.'

'We will be ready by then,' President Farouk nodded, 'I will get started right away when we return to the White House. We will be ready in three days.'

'Very good,' Shadowfire nodded, 'You shall be with them, Haman. What better evidence to show that fairies exist than to show them the Queen of the Fairies herself? It would be her worst nightmare come true.'

'Yes indeed,' replied Dr. Von Braun, 'I like it. I will have my men, Seymour and Wilfred, with me to find and extract the Queen.'

They heard Shadowfire growl in anger. 'By Ashtaroth, I will not let the Prophecy come to pass! Mordy Jefferson and Raven will die, and I shall live on, no longer living in fear of the Prophecy ever being fulfilled!' Looking down at the two men he said, 'You must return to Washington now. There is much preparation to do before the invasion of Arundel Haven.'

He waved his hands as the two men put their glasses down. As soon as they did, the bar, along with everything on it, disappeared. 'This is only a small sample of my power,' Shadowfire told them, 'The human and his fairy lover will see the full extent when I face them. In three days, Arundel Haven shall fall.'

'And I shall claim it for myself,' boasted President Farouk.

Shadowfire simply nodded as the two men boarded the plane. The engines started and soon took to the air. The dragon watched as the helicopter rose and headed eastward and then disappeared. He spread his wings and rose from the ground, flying in another direction.

Mordecai and Raven headed for the dining hall with Tiffany, Sharon, Cece, Starla, and Twila. Twila was in Mordecai's arms, touching his face. 'I hope Mom and Dad were able to get some sleep,' he said, 'I know they must be worried about me.'

'I hope so too,' Cece replied as she tickled Twila. She smiled at the toddler.

'Cece no tickle me,' Twila giggled.

'How about your aunt Raven?' Raven replied, tickling the toddler.

'No, no,' laughed Twila, 'No tickle me, Aunt Raven!'

Mordecai kissed the toddler. 'They will be relieved when they see that Raven and I have returned,' he said, 'I can't believe they are here in Arundel Haven. I still don't understand why Queen Cymbaline had sent for them and brought them here? I'm still surprised to see you, Tiffany, and Sharon here.'

'I still can't believe that Arundel Haven exists,' Tiffany exclaimed, 'It is so wonderful here!'

'I guess Cece was right all along in believing in fairies,' Sharon added.

'I had no idea fairies were real and how much like us they were,' Cece said.

'Why did Queen Cymbaline bring our parents here?' Mordecai asked.

'She felt they were in danger, so she had them brought here,' Starla answered, 'I was worried about Cece when she refused to eat when you had been captured by Shadowfire, but I am relieved that the both of you had escaped.'

'I think he only decided to let us go because he had a change in plans,' replied Mordecai, 'I have no choice but to remain here when Shadowfire attacks and brings government soldiers. The time is nigh, but I am still frightened all the same.'

'I am happy you are okay, Mordy,' Cece replied, 'I was so worried about you.'

'All of us were,' Sharon said, 'I feared for Raven's life as well when she had flown after you.'

'It was a foolish move, I know,' Raven said softly, 'but I had to do something. I could not bear to be without Mordecai.'

Mordecai touched Cece's face. 'I am thankful that you care, Cece, my sister,' he said, 'I am glad you, Mom and Dad are here.'

At that moment, Taris joined them as well as both of Mordecai's parents. Both were dressed in similar clothing to Mordecai. His mother embraced him weeping. 'Mordy, I was so worried about you,' she said, 'I am glad you are okay.'

'How did you and Raven escape from Shadowfire?' Tony asked.

'More like he had a change in plans,' Mordecai told them, 'He's gone to tell President Farouk where Arundel Haven is. I told Queen Cymbaline about the matter. I have a feeling he may try and take it as his own.'

'He can't,' Tony exclaimed, 'He must not! What would the House and the Senate say?'

'He may not care about what they say,' Mordecai said gravely, 'I have that feeling. No doubt when the troops reach here, Dr. Von Braun will be there as well. We have to expect the worst.'

'No doubt you are right, Mordecai,' replied Taris, 'Already, Prince Avondale is gathering a host to repel the invaders and to camp in Nebechadrezzar Valley in expectation of their arrival. He will lead the fight while you and Raven engage the dragon.'

'You don't mean that my son and Raven will fight the dragon by themselves?' Tony protested.

'That is what the Prophecy states,' Mordecai replied, 'Both of us are scared, but we know we are the ones God has chosen to bring the dragon down.'

'But how can you two defeat Shadowfire when the hosts of Arundel Haven have no swords, arrows or spears that can even hurt him?' Tony asked.

'God has already provided a way that we know not of,' Raven answered, 'We trust him to reveal it to us when the time comes. The dragon will fall.'

'How can you be sure, Raven?' Molly asked.

'God had spoken to the both of us,' Mordecai answered, 'I was told, *When the time comes, I will guide and direct you. Through you, I will use the both of you to bring about the fall of the dragon. I will guide and direct you both.* This was just after Queen Cymbaline had told me the tale of the Prophecy of Queen Hephzibah.'

'What is this prophecy?' Tony asked.

'God had revealed to Queen Hephzibah ere she died through a dream,' Mordecai answered, 'She had told it to her daughters, Princess Bethany and her younger sister Princess Madelyne, on her deathbed, revealing to them that a human shall appear in Arundel Haven and God will use that human and a fairy maiden to bring about the death of Shadowfire. It was mostly forgotten because very few believed the Prophecy. Shadowfire fears the Prophecy and knows I am the one and has found out Raven is the fairy maiden that will bring about his demise. Not even Bethany, who became Queen after her mother's death shortly afterwards, or her younger sister Princess Madelyne, believed the Prophecy. It was mostly forgotten by the fairies here.'

'Because they didn't believe it?' Tony asked.

'It has been forgotten save for very few here,' Raven explained, 'Price Avondale must have remembered it somehow the first time he had visited Mordecai in prison. He found the book and told Queen Cymbaline, his sister.'

Tony stared at Raven, a grave look upon his face. 'I am amazed how you put your life on the line for my son,' he told her, 'I am thankful you and Mordy were able to escape the dragon.'

Raven sighed. 'I even found the remains of my parents in one of the chambers inside the Mountain,' she said sadly.

'Mom and Dad?' cried Starla. 'What happened?'

'More than likely they had been both sacrificed and their remains taken to where I found them,' Raven answered sadly, pulling out the rings and the necklaces, 'They still wore the clothes from the day they had been taken. That was how I knew it was them.' She burst into tears.

Molly placed her arms around Raven. 'I am so sorry, Raven,' she said softly, 'You and Starla must still miss them.'

'That is so sad to hear,' Tiffany said, 'I don't know what I would do if it was my parents lying there.'

'They hardly got to know Twila before Shadowfire had seized them,' Starla sighed, tears filling her eyes, 'I'm sure they would be amused if they heard about Twila's escapades.'

'Why so sad, Mommy?' Twila asked.

'Your mommy and aunt Raven miss their mommy and daddy,' sighed Mordecai, holding Twila close, 'Your grandparents, they were, Japeth and Jochabed were their names.' To Starla he asked, 'What about Roosevelt's parents? Are they still alive?'

'Alas, no,' Starla answered, 'Shadowfire had seized them just days after we were married. This was about five years ago. Twila has no living grandparents.'

Mordecai kissed Twila's forehead. 'Shadowfire had deprived Twila of both her grandparents,' he said quietly, tears filling his eyes, 'This is not the way she should have to live.' To Twila he said, 'Your uncle Morcai and aunt Raven will make sure you never have to fear Shadowfire anymore, little Twila. Soon, Shadowfire will be no more.'

'Shadowfire bad,' Twila said, 'Uncle Morcai and Aunt Raven make Shadowfire go bye-bye forever?'

'Rather, God will make Shadowfire go bye-bye forever, little Twila,' Mordecai replied.

Tony and Molly smiled, staring at Mordecai and Twila. 'She is one special little girl you have, Starla,' Tony said, 'I have never seen Mordy like this, but I must admit, I do like what I see about him.' To Raven he said, 'I was wrong about you, Raven. I ask for your forgiveness. I am grateful you came into Mordy's life.'

'Morcai,' corrected Twila, 'Uncle Morcai.'

The others laughed.

'He is a blessing to me, Mr. Jefferson,' Raven told him, 'I believe God has chosen him for me and me for him. He has a wonderful heart, and that is what I see: the person he is inside.'

'As I should have done,' Tony replied gravely, 'You had risked your life to save my son, and you and your people have shown me and my family great kindness.' To Mordecai he said, 'I give you my blessing to take Raven to be your wife.'

Mordecai bowed his head. 'Thank you, Dad,' he replied softly, 'It really means a lot to me to hear you say that.'

Raven gave Tony a kiss on the cheeks. 'Thank you,' she said as he smiled.

They joined Queen Cymbaline and Prince Avondale in the dining hall. Mordecai and Raven sat beside the Queen while Mordecai's parents sat on Prince Avondale's side. As they ate, they talked. 'I am honored, your majesty, that you allowed us entrance into your kingdom,' Tony said to Queen Cymbaline.

'I hope you were able to sleep well,' replied Queen Cymbaline, 'though I imagine it was difficult given Mordecai's predicament.'

'Where's Roosevelt, Starla?' Mordecai asked Starla.

'He said he could not stay,' Starla answered, 'He flew back home to work in the fields. He says he still has work to do. He offers his apologies to the Queen.'

'I understand,' Queen Cymbaline said, 'but it would help him if he had something to eat first.'

'He said he wasn't hungry,' replied Starla, 'He told me when he gets hungry, he still has something to eat at the house. He is expecting us afterwards. He looks forward to meeting Mordecai's parents.'

Molly turned toward Queen Cymbaline. 'I am grateful for the kindness you have shown to my son,' she said, 'I was told that you distrust humans.'

'I did,' replied Queen Cymbaline sadly. 'In general, I still do, but Mordecai had earned my trust. That was why I had him imprisoned in the first place, which was my mistake, although he had fully understood why.' She then smiled. 'You can blame that on Twila, for one.'

Twila leaned her head upon Mordecai's shoulders. 'Twila love Uncle Morcai,' she said, giving Mordecai a kiss on the cheeks.

'That we can see, little Twila,' smiled Molly. She and Tony laughed.

'God showed me through Twila that there are some humans that can be trusted, though they are few and far between, it would seem,' said Queen Cymbaline, 'Mordecai told me of Dr. Von Braun when he was first brought here. I felt led to invite you and Cece here, especially since I felt you, too, were in danger.'

'We were all relieved when we found out you and Raven had escaped Shadowfire,' Prince Avondale told Mordecai, 'but very disturbed by what you told us. Our weapons may not be any match for theirs, but we have to do what we can to protect our home.'

'I guess we have to place it in God's hands,' Mordecai said, 'I still don't see how He will use Raven and me to destroy the dragon, hearing how impenetrable his armor is.'

'You say that Shadowfire has been afflicting your people for over a century and a half?' Tony asked the Queen, 'Sounds almost unbelievable.'

'No one knows how long Shadowfire has been alive,' Prince Avondale replied, 'Perhaps two hundred years, maybe more. We can only guess at this point.'

'But for the sake of the fairies of Arundel Haven, it must end,' Starla said boldly, 'I've had friends and family who had fallen victim, including our parents Japeth and Jochabed, whether through sacrifice or being devoured. Raven told me she had found their remains within his lair.'

'There are a number of chambers,' Raven explained, 'Some with remains, one with gold coins and precious jewels. The only thing I took were the rings and the necklace that our parents wore.' She pulled them out of her pocket. She sighed. 'I took Mordecai to where I found their remains.'

'It didn't take long until he found out that I had been freed,' Mordecai said, 'The locks were secured by magic, but it was broken by God's power when we both touched the lock. We managed to find a tunnel in one of the chambers that led to a way out. We're not sure how long it had been there.'

'But we were thankful that it was there,' added Raven, 'It led to a way out, but Shadowfire took up the chase and guessed we would be hiding in the nearby woods. He sent his enchanted fire to try and flush us out, but an opening had appeared, which we ran through. For some reason, shortly after that, he had stopped his pursuit, and we overheard him talking about revealing our home to the President.'

'I feared sooner or later that would happen,' Queen Cymbaline said solemnly, 'that Shadowfire would decide to reveal our home to the humans, those who wish to do us evil.'

'The problem is when will he return?' Mordecai said, 'How long it would take him to get here and how many the President may bring with him to try and take your kingdom? I feared this would happen.'

'Do not think you are at fault in this, Mordecai Jefferson,' Prince Avondale replied, 'Neither my sister nor I consider you at fault. We know you have done what you can to protect our secret. Our main concern is beating them back, no matter how many may come against us. You and Raven will have your hands full with Shadowfire.'

Tony sighed. 'I still don't like the idea of Mordy and Raven going against the dragon, no matter what the Prophecy says. I mean no disrespect, your majesty, but—'

'None taken,' Queen Cymbaline replied, 'I understand as a father you are concerned for the safety of your son.'

Tony nodded. 'Yes,' he said softly, 'but I fear for his life and Raven's as well. Surely, they deserve a life together and not to throw it away in a battle with Shadowfire.'

'Yes, I am scared, Dad,' Mordecai told him. 'I still am, but I am being reassured that both Raven and I will come through all right, and that Shadowfire will fall.'

'But how will you both do it?' Molly asked.

'I do not know,' Mordecai answered, 'but God has a way to provide when all seems impossible. With men, it is impossible, but with God all things are possible.'

Queen Cymbaline turned toward Mordecai's parents. 'When we have finished dining, Tony and Molly,' she told them, 'I wish to speak with you two in private. There are some things I need to discuss with you both.'

'I would love to see the farm where you and your husband live, Starla,' Tiffany said, 'I am very curious to see it. It's a shame he could not stay to join us.'

'I would be more than happy to have you over, both Roosevelt and I,' Starla replied, 'He still has to meet Cece and Mordecai's parents as well.'

'I would be glad to come,' Cece said, 'I hope when Lavender and Laurelin wake up, they can bring my parents over as well.'

Minutes later, they had finished eating and Mordecai, Raven, Starla, Cece, Twila, Sharon, and Tiffany took leave of the Fairy Queen. They followed Starla out of the city and to the farm where she and her family lived. Cece was starting to fully enjoy her gift of flight now she knew that her brother was safe. Sharon and Tiffany were still amazed that they could fly. 'Too bad it lasts only a week,' Tiffany sighed.

'It is wonderful, isn't it?' Mordecai smiled as Twila giggled as she flew close to him.

'Twila happy Uncle Morcai can fly,' she said.

'So am I, Twila,' Mordecai replied.

'I like it, too,' said Cece.

'Cece fly with Uncle Morcai and Twila,' the toddler chimed.

'Hey,' Raven retorted. 'What about your aunt Raven?'

Twila giggled.

Raven grabbed her and tickled her. Starla laughed as she saw the joy on the young fairy's face.

'It shouldn't take us long to fly to Roosevelt's farm,' Raven told Mordecai, 'since we are flying. Walking does take longer.'

Mordecai nodded. 'I guess it shouldn't be too much longer, then. I'm enjoying the view here from the sky.'

'So am I,' nodded Cece. 'I still can't believe I am actually flying!'

'If this is a dream,' Tiffany said, 'please don't wake me up.'

'No dream, Tiffany,' Mordecai replied as they reached the farm.

Roosevelt saw them from the ground. He put down his hoe and joined them in the air. Twila flew into her daddy's arms. 'Hi, Daddy,' she said, kissing him on the cheeks.

'Hello, Twila,' smiled Roosevelt. He glanced at Cece. 'You must be Mordecai's sister, Cece,' he said, 'I am pleased to meet you.' He shook her hand.

'And you, Roosevelt,' replied Cece, 'I feel much better now that Mordecai is safe again.'

'I am happy to hear,' Roosevelt replied, 'Your friends were worried about you, and understandably so. We thought Raven would be lost to us, too, when she had flown off to try and rescue Mordecai.'

'I hope to see Lavender and Laurelin again,' Cece said, 'I know they must be tired from all the flying they've done.'

'They will fly over when they've rested up,' Starla said, 'They've had a long night to be sure. We all have.'

Roosevelt showed Mordecai, Cece, Tiffany, and Sharon around the farm. They had different vegetables growing; grains like wheat, corn and oats; livestock like cattle, sheep, horses and chickens. Mordecai was amazed how big the farm was. He had never been on a farm in his life before he had visited Roosevelt and Starla. Twila was in Mordecai's arms and cuddling up to him. 'How long have you had this farm, Roosevelt?' he asked.

'My parents had passed it on to me before Shadowfire took them,' Roosevelt answered, 'For some reason, Shadowfire won't touch any of the livestock here or on any other farm in Arundel Haven. He only takes fairies away.'

'How many farms are there?' Cece asked.

'At least a dozen,' Roosevelt answered, 'The largest of the farms is on the other side of the village owned by Derreck's family, which has been in his family for over 100 years. My farm has been around for 75 years. It had originally belonged to my great grandfather Manassah. I'm the fourth generation in my family. It will belong to Twila when she comes of age, and she finds a husband.'

'That is good to hear,' Mordecai nodded.

'From time-to-time, Starla would help me out, so she has Raven babysit Twila,' Roosevelt said, 'It has been a big help. We are almost ready for the coming winter.'

They landed on the path near where the cattle were grazing on the other side of the fence. Mordecai felt the wind growing colder.

'Feels like we may get some snow soon,' Roosevelt said. 'Temperature's definitely dropping.'

'Do fairies have problems flying in the snow?' Mordecai asked.

'Sometimes,' Starla answered as Twila sought for warmth in Mordecai's arms. 'We do not like to fly in the snow. The cold does cause problems with our wings.'

'I guess there are some fairies who love to fly when it's cold,' Raven replied, 'I personally do not. We fly in the snow if we have to, but when it's raining it's hard for us to fly at times.'

Mordecai nodded.

'It's a big farm all right,' Cece said, 'I'm impressed.'

'Maybe we should head inside,' Starla suggested, 'We can start a fire in the fireplace and have some hot tea.'

'That would be nice, thank you,' Cece nodded.

Roosevelt gathered some firewood and proceeded to start a fire in the fireplace inside. Mordecai, Raven, Cece, Sharon, and Tiffany sat down as the fire was started. Starla came out minutes later with some hot tea. 'I will have to purchase some cocoa sometime before it gets any colder,' she said, 'Twila loves to drink hot cocoa, though at times it's too hot for her to drink.'

'I remember drinking it when I was young when the weather was cold,' Cece smiled at the memory, 'when our mom made hot cocoa, brownies, and cookies. Those were good times growing up.'

Mordecai nodded.

'Do you have any other siblings, Mordecai?' Starla asked.

'Our oldest brother, Randall, is attending college out of state,' Mordecai answered, 'He is not married yet.'

'Does he know about Raven or Arundel Haven?' asked Roosevelt.

'No,' Mordecai answered, 'He knows nothing about this whole affair. Sooner or later, he will probably have to be told, at least about Raven.' To Raven he said, 'I should have shown you a photo of Randall.'

'What's a photo?' Raven asked.

'A picture,' Mordecai answered, 'It's not something that's painted. I don't know how to describe it, but a moment captured in time. I wish I could describe it to you better.'

'This is what it looks like,' Tiffany said, pulling out her small purse and pulling out a photo of herself, Sharon, and Cece. Raven, Starla, and Roosevelt gazed at the photo and were amazed how it looked.

'I have never seen anything like this before,' Roosevelt said in awe.

Tiffany put the photo back in her small purse and put it away. 'That's what a photo looks like,' she told them.

'Wow, I'm amazed by the things you humans come up with,' Raven exclaimed.

'Indeed,' Roosevelt replied.

Mordecai drank some of his hot tea. Twila looked at Mordecai and said, 'Tea hot, Uncle Morcai.'

Mordecai nodded and gazed at Twila. 'Yes, it is, sweetie,' he smiled.

'It is good, though,' Cece said as she drank hers.

'We need to find something warm to wear once we return to the village,' Mordecai said, 'I can't believe how much the temperature is dropping.'

'Nor can I,' Cece replied, 'I wish I had known so I could have brought something warm.'

'We were in haste,' Starla said, 'I'm sure we can find something warm for you to wear before we return. I do have some things to give you and the others. I have some old warm clothes to keep you warm.'

'Thank you, Starla,' Cece said gratefully.

'I'm sure I still have something I left over here from last winter,' Raven added, 'I don't know what Starla did with it, though.'

Twila sat up and had a sip of Mordecai's tea, which was a little bit on the hot side. She drew back a little bit. 'You should have been careful, Twila,' Mordecai told her gently.

'I will look for it,' Starla said, 'I should have it stored somewhere.'

Raven nodded. 'I know I will need it,' she said, 'The only problem is getting my wings through the openings in the back. One reason I don't like winter.'

'Must be a problem with all fairies,' Mordecai observed.

'You guessed it,' Roosevelt said, 'Because of how heavy some of our winter clothes are, it's hard to slip our wings through. Twila has a fit when we try to put something warm over her body.'

'Because of trying to slip her wings through the opening?' Mordecai asked.

'She doesn't like wearing them,' Starla told him, 'Not just for the problems of getting her wings through.'

'But we've got to keep you warm when it's cold, honey,' Mordecai told Twila, kissing her.

'Twila don't like the cold,' Twila said, looking up at Mordecai.

'Your uncle Morcai don't like it either,' said Mordecai, taking a drink of his tea. Twila reached out to the cup to drink it. It had cooled down enough for the toddler now. She drank a little and looked at Mordecai. 'Don't drink all my tea, Twila,' he told her.

Twila just giggled and hid her face.

They continued to talk for two hours. When the flames were about to die, Roosevelt put two more logs into the fire and fanned the flames. It wasn't long until the logs began to catch fire. Raven saw that Twila was asleep in Mordecai's arms, resting peacefully. Starla rose and took her daughter into her arms, kissing her on the cheeks. Raven leaned her head upon Mordecai's shoulder as he kissed her and wrapped his arm around her. 'This is what I've been missing all this time,' Raven said as she caressed his face and kissed him on the lips.

At that moment, there was a knock on the door. Starla cradled Twila in her arms and headed for the door. When she opened it, she saw Lavender and Laurelin, along with Jax and Derreck. As they entered, they walked over to Mordecai and Raven. 'This is my boyfriend, Derreck,' Lavender told Mordecai, 'and Laurelin's boyfriend, Jax.' To the boys she said, 'This is Mordecai, Raven's boyfriend.'

'Lavender and Laurelin have told us about you,' Jax told Mordecai as they shook hands. Derreck did the same. 'So, you are human from what I understand.'

'Yes,' Mordecai nodded, 'This is my sister, Cece, over there and her two friends, Sharon and Tiffany.'

'Pleased to meet you two,' Cece smiled brightly at them.

'You too,' Jax replied, 'and Queen Cymbaline knows about you four?'

'Yes, she does,' answered Laurelin. 'The parents of Mordecai and Cece have been personally invited by Queen Cymbaline. Cece is here, but her parents are with the Queen in the castle. I don't know why she wanted them to remain with her for a while.'

'Must be something special,' Roosevelt replied.

'You want some tea?' Starla asked.

'Yes, please,' Laurelin nodded. Lavender, Jax, and Derreck all said yes as well.

Roosevelt took Twila and sat down with her in his arms as she slept.

'What made Queen Cymbaline change her mind about the humans, especially Mordecai and Cece?' asked Jax.

'Believe it or not, Jax,' Laurelin replied, 'it was Twila.'

'One of her unscheduled flights again?' laughed Derreck.

'Yes,' Mordecai answered, 'I was in the dungeon at the time. Twila made her way into where I was being held and she had slipped inside my cell. She took to me right away. Starla thought I was going to harm her but found out that I meant her no harm.'

'She refused to return to me at the time,' Starla recounted as she returned with four cups of tea. Each fairy took a saucer from the platter. 'I was so afraid at first, but then I saw how she wiped the tears from his eyes. He would not think of hurting her. He considered her life precious. She's become so attached to him.'

'So, Twila was the reason Queen Cymbaline changed her mind?' asked Derreck in disbelief.

'I believe it was,' answered Mordecai, 'Prince Avondale had come to my cell and spoke to me. I told him about the dreams I had about Shadowfire, how the dragon had claimed I was the one some prophecy spoke of. Prince Avondale then mentioned the Prophecy of Queen Hephzibah. He then left and later that day, I was presented to Queen Cymbaline again, where she relayed the tale to me. I knew right then I was the one the Prophecy spoke of, that a human would appear in Arundel Haven and along with a fairy maiden, God would use us to destroy Shadowfire. I am still scared about it, but I knew in my heart that I was indeed the one to fulfill the Prophecy. Shadowfire was so desperate that he had captured me and tried to sacrifice me to his master, but Raven flew after us and freed me, and we escaped, but Shadowfire had stopped pursuing us and headed for our world. We then told Queen Cymbaline about what happened.'

'You and Raven had escaped Shadowfire?' Jax asked, stunned.

'Yes, we did,' Raven answered.

'You flew inside Shadowfire's lair in the Mountains of Shadow and escaped?' Derreck asked Raven.

'He stopped his pursuit solely because of a change in his personal plans,' Mordecai explained, 'He is in allegiance with some evil humans I know of—Dr. Von Braun and the president of the country where I live, the United States—who are obsessed with finding Arundel Haven. I have a bad feeling President Farouk will be led here to conquer Arundel Haven and claim it for himself. That must not happen!'

'So that's why Prince Avondale is having the army assembled,' Derreck responded, 'Jax and I have been summoned as well.'

'I wish it didn't have to come to this,' Mordecai sighed, 'The time for the Prophecy to be fulfilled is now at hand. God has yet to reveal to Raven and me how Shadowfire will meet his end, especially since hearing that no weapon the fairy smithies have ever forged can penetrate his armor.'

'Wait, you said that the Prophecy states a human, and a fairy maiden will be used to bring down the dragon,' Derreck said slowly, 'And Raven is the fairy maiden?'

'Yes, it is I,' Raven nodded, 'I am the fairy maiden that was prophesied.'

'How can you be sure?' asked Jax, 'How do you know you are the one?'

'The LORD had touched my heart and told me,' Raven answered, 'Both of us know that we are the ones. We are scared about it, yes, but we know that it is the both of us.'

'I still can't bring myself to believe it,' Lavender frowned.

'I believe it to be true,' Starla sighed as she sat down, 'but something tells me they will fulfill the Prophecy and will survive. I'm not crazy about it either, but I, too, have come to believe that they are the ones, but I fear for their lives all the same. I have come to love Mordecai like he was my own brother now that I have gotten to know him.' She sighed. 'Before Twila arrived at his cell, I remember telling Raven "I don't know him, and I do not wish to know him!" I felt the weight of my own words when I saw how precious Twila was in Mordecai's sight.'

'You know better now, Starla,' replied Raven, 'You now know how wonderful he is, so forget about what you thought of him before.'

'We were convinced when we got to know Mordecai's mother better,' Lavender said, 'I began to see that Raven was right: there are so many similarities between fairies and humans. We ate at a human restaurant in disguise. Mordecai was against it, not wanting to put us in danger. We ate what they call pizza.'

'Pizza?' Roosevelt asked, perplexed.

'Yes, and Twila likes it too,' Starla told her husband, 'I was told it was described as dough with tomato sauce and shredded cheese on top, and they put things on top like meat and vegetables.'

'Sounds good,' Roosevelt nodded, a slight smile on his face.

'I've got to learn how to make it,' Raven said, 'When Mordecai and I get settled together, he's going to help me.'

'Oh, yes,' Laurelin said, recalling what she had been told, 'Mordecai can cook from what I was told.'

'Yes, but not as well as a lot of people,' Mordecai said, 'but I can cook certain things.'

'I look forward to trying some of your cooking,' Raven smiled.

'As well as Twila, I imagine,' replied Starla, 'I'm sure she wants to try some of Uncle Morcai's cooking.'

'We'll see what we can do,' nodded Mordecai.

Lavender turned toward Derreck. 'Perhaps you can learn how to cook?' she told him. 'I do think it'd be romantic if you did.'

'Sorry, Lavender,' Derreck laughed nervously, 'I'm not that good as a cook.'

'What about you, Jax?' Laurelin asked him.

Jax shook his head. 'Not a chance,' he answered.

'Why not?' frowned Laurelin.

'I'm not a cook,' he answered.

'Don't be too hard on them,' Mordecai told Lavender and Laurelin, 'Some guys can cook, and some can't. I happen to be one who can cook, though I feel not very well.'

'Are you kidding, Mordy?' exclaimed Cece. 'When I tried your green bean casserole, I first thought Mom had made it. Even both Mom and Dad liked it. You are a great cook.'

'But not as good as Mom or a lot of people,' replied Mordecai, 'I won't even compare my cooking to Mom's.'

Twila was laid down on a small bed not too far from the fireplace while they continued to talk. Raven snuggled up to Mordecai as she laid her head upon his shoulder while he caressed her face. She closed her eyes as they continued to talk. Mordecai turned his attention to Raven as he gently kissed her. He pulled her close as they both drifted off to sleep. Starla noticed this and was about to say something when Roosevelt said quietly, 'They both must be tired from their ordeal. Let them rest.'

Starla smiled as she then turned and talked to the others, allowing Mordecai and Raven to sleep.

Cece smiled at them both. 'Sweet dreams, the both of you,' she whispered.

Over an hour later, they were awakened by Tony and Molly. They looked around and the others were gone. 'Where is everybody?' Mordecai asked.

'They have been summoned to the castle by Queen Cymbaline,' Tony answered, 'You both have been summoned as well.'

'Is all well?' Raven asked.

'It is well,' Molly nodded, 'You and I will meet up with Starla while Mordy will go with Tony and meet up with Prince Avondale and Roosevelt.'

'What's going on?' Mordecai asked.

'You will find out when we reach the castle,' Tony said, 'Roosevelt and Prince Avondale are waiting for us.'

'As well as Starla and Cece for us, Raven,' Molly explained, 'Starla has already laid out warm clothes for you in the corner.'

'How are you feeling?' Tony asked.

'Still tired, I'm afraid,' sighed Mordecai, 'I had a long night with the dragon. I am still concerned about what he is up to.'

'You got my curiosity,' said Raven, 'I would love to know what's going on.'

'I think both of you will like it and agree,' Molly said, 'Now, come, both of you. Our parties are waiting for you.'

Mordecai and Raven changed into the clothing laid out by Starla. Raven had taken time to slip her wings through the openings of her coat. 'This is why Twila hates coats,' she explained, 'Be glad you don't have that problem, Mordecai.'

'Need any help?' asked Mordecai as he slipped into his coat.

'I've got it,' Molly told her son, helping Raven slip her wings through the opening. Raven flittered her wings. 'Still feels uncomfortable,' she said, 'but I should still be able to fly.' She flittered her wings again.

'I still can't believe how low the temperature is dropping,' Molly said, 'It seems like it won't be much longer until it starts snowing.'

'How do you like flying?' Mordecai asked his parents.

'It still feels weird,' Tony said, 'It takes some getting used to. How long does it last?'

'One week, from what I understand,' Molly answered, 'I do find it both frightening and exciting at the same time.'

'I couldn't believe I was flying the first time,' Mordecai said, 'I was a bit scared when I came out of the cold waterfalls that begins the Silverstreams and found that I was off the ground, about 100 feet at least, I wasn't sure. Raven helped me fly around.'

Raven giggled.

'What are you laughing about?' Molly asked.

'Oh, nothing,' Raven replied, smiling.

'I was clothed only in a loin cloth,' Mordecai said, remembering the time, 'The waters surrounded me. I had trouble submerging inside because it was ice cold. By Queen Cymbaline's urging, I entered the falls. She said it would help me in the battle with Shadowfire. I endured the freezing cold, and after a time, my body started feeling warm. When Queen Cymbaline told me to come out, that's when I saw I was in the air. The effects are permanent she told me, that I would have the ability to fly for the rest of my life. It would be nice to fly from place to place, but in Orlando, it would be unwise for me to fly as it would draw too much attention.'

Tony and Molly nodded in agreement.

'It was embarrassing being in only a loin cloth,' Mordecai continued, 'I was glad to put the clothes back onto me.'

Molly laughed. 'I can see why Raven was laughing, but we must fly to the castle now. We are expected.'

Mordecai nodded. They stepped out of the house and took to the air. Mordecai could tell in his parents' faces that they were beginning to enjoy the feeling of flying. He did his best to disregard the cold and focus on the feeling as well. 'I think of when I was young when your grandparents and I lived in Philadelphia,' Molly told Mordecai, 'The snow, the cold air. I enjoyed the weather because I knew we were not so far from Christmas.'

'I spent my childhood in Georgia, and we had snow, but not as much as your mother's family,' Tony added, 'I didn't like the snow or cold, but I tolerate it. I wish it was springtime instead of the fall. I could enjoy this more in the warm weather.'

'I know what you mean,' Mordecai concurred.

'Only you can enjoy it in the springtime,' Molly told him sadly, 'since your gift of flight is permanent. We kind of envy you on that, Mordy, but you have won the favor of Queen Cymbaline. I still don't like the idea of the Prophecy, however.'

Mordecai nodded his head. 'I know,' he said gravely, 'but we are the ones, Raven and I. We have reassurance that God will bring us through this.'

Raven nodded.

When they reached the castle, Molly took Raven down a corridor while Tony led Mordecai to another room. He was about to ask where his mother and Raven were going, but Tony would not tell. 'You will find out soon,' he told his son. 'Prince Avondale awaits us.'

Mordecai simply nodded.

Raven was taken by Molly to a room where Queen Cymbaline, Starla, Twila, Lavender, Laurelin, Tiffany, and Sharon awaited them. Hanging on a wooden mannequin was a white dress of silk with gold trimmings. She walked toward the dress and touched it. She looked at Queen Cymbaline and said, 'This is beautiful!'

'It is a wedding dress,' Queen Cymbaline told her.

'But I didn't know you were getting married, your highness.'

'It is not my wedding dress, Raven,' the Queen replied, 'It is yours.'

Raven stood in surprise. 'M-mine?' she stuttered.

'Yes,' Molly smiled, 'That is what Queen Cymbaline had been talking to Tony and me about, and we agreed. We talked about it at lengths, and even though Mordy is not of legal age in the human world, no such law exists here. At first, we felt the time would not be right, but given the circumstances, Tony and I agreed that we could have the marriage here. We wanted to surprise the both of you. We know you are of age, Raven.'

Raven said without hesitation, 'Yes, yes!' Tears of joy fell from her eyes as Starla embraced her. 'I want that so much!'

'We can't wait to see you try it on,' Laurelin said excitedly, 'I'm sure Mordecai would love to see you in that.'

'That I can be certain,' Cece agreed.

'Does Mordecai know?' Raven asked hesitantly.

'He will be told once he meets with Prince Avondale and the boys,' answered Queen Cymbaline, 'We have all wedding attire waiting for us and we need to prepare for the wedding.'

'Wow, I never thought you would be getting married before Laurelin and me,' Lavender exclaimed as the women received their wedding attire from the handmaidens.

Tiffany felt the material. 'Wow… pure silk.'

'From the finest materials in Arundel Haven,' Queen Cymbaline said, 'Some of the dresses were made years ago. My handmaidens happened to find the appropriate clothing at my request for all of you. They have been delivered to the men as well.'

Molly wept. 'I can't believe my little boy is getting married,' she said, 'and I never thought in my wildest dreams it would be this way.'

'I am glad you came into Mordecai's life as well as ours, Raven,' Cece told Raven.

Mordecai and Tony entered the chambers where Prince Avondale awaited along with Taris, Roosevelt, Jax, and Derreck. Hanging in a corner was a white cloak of satin and silk with golden lining. 'You are a very lucky man,' Jax told Mordecai.

Mordecai stared at the clothes. 'Who are these for?' he asked.

'They are yours, Mordecai,' Prince Avondale answered.

Mordecai took the clothes in his hands. He felt them. 'It looks like something you would wear, your highness,' he told the Prince.

'They are wedding attire,' Tony explained, 'There are clothes made for all of us as well, but this is your time and Raven's as well.'

Wedding? Raven and me? Now? He stared at the clothing as he thought. 'For Raven and me?' he asked Tony, astonished, 'Was that what Queen Cymbaline was talking to you about?'

'Indeed,' Prince Avondale nodded.

Mordecai again stared at the clothing. He thought about it and smiled. *This is my heart's desire. I never dreamed it would come this soon.* He turned to Tony and asked, 'Are you sure about this?'

Tony nodded. 'I know we haven't been as supportive of you in the past, Mordy, your mother and I,' he told his son, 'It is true that we were against Raven at first, looking at her skin color and the fact that she is a fairy, but we all agreed that it is the heart that is important. We figured since we all are here, now would be a good time for you and Raven to be married.'

Mordecai gave a nod. 'When will the wedding be held?' he asked.

'Right now, Raven is getting ready,' Prince Avondale said, 'As soon as the both of you are ready, we will gather in the throne room and have the wedding there. Already, rings are being forged for the both of you, but the rings that Raven had retrieved from her parents' remains are being cleansed and used as surrogate rings.'

'Once the rings are made,' Mordecai said slowly, 'we will take the rings used in the wedding and they will be kept in a place of honor in memory of her parents, and we will wear our own in their place.'

Nearly an hour later, they were assembled in the throne room. Queen Cymbaline and Prince Avondale sat on their thrones. Before them, Mordecai and Tony stood at the front. Roosevelt, Jax, and Derreck stood on the opposite side of the aisle, standing behind a long red carpet, which made an aisleway leading to the throne. Mordecai sighed. Tony looked at his son. 'Nervous?' he asked.

Mordecai nodded. 'My heart desires it, Dad, but I can't help but be a little nervous. I never expected to get married while still in high school. I will need to return to Orlando and finish my education, if nothing else.'

'Would you still want to learn how to drive, even though you can fly?' his father asked.

Mordecai nodded. 'I can't fly while I am in Orlando,' he explained, 'I will have to learn to drive sooner or later. I feel content, however, especially with Raven in my life.'

The royal musicians began to play a tune as the women, both human and fairy, entered through the doorway. First was Cece, Tiffany, and Sharon, then Lavender and Laurelin. Twila flew low to the ground with flowers in her hands. Lastly, Starla and Raven entered. Starla led Raven to the dais, where Mordecai and the others waited. Mordecai turned around and saw Raven, who had her face veiled. The sight of her took his breath away. He found himself falling in love with Raven all over again. *Raven, you are so beautiful!*

Starla and Raven reached the dais, standing beside Mordecai as they faced each other. Starla placed the left hand of her younger sister into Mordecai's left hand. Behind her veil, Raven's eyes flowed with tears of joy as she stared lovingly into Mordecai's eyes.

Mordecai smiled at his bride.

Queen Cymbaline rose up and stood in front of Mordecai and Raven, a long, thin, white satin strip laced with gold in her hands. 'The institute of marriage was first started in the Garden of Eden with Adam and Eve and blessed the union of one man and one woman for life. The Word says that a man shall leave his father and mother and shall be cleaved unto his wife, and the two shall become one flesh. It is my pleasure to join these two in holy matrimony. Never before has a human and a fairy ever been joined in such a union until this time. We are gathered here to join Mordecai Jefferson and Raven daughter of Japeth in marriage. Both are willing to be joined and to be husband and wife. Is there any just cause that these two should not be joined in marriage? Let them speak now or forever hold their peace.'

There was a pause. Nobody spoke.

Queen Cymbaline stared at Mordecai. 'Mordecai Jefferson, do you wish to take Raven to be your wife?'

Mordecai nodded. 'I do,' he answered solemnly.

Queen Cymbaline then gazed at Raven. 'Raven, do you wish to take Mordecai Jefferson to be your husband?'

With tears in her eyes, Raven said, 'I do.'

Queen Cymbaline turned to Mordecai and said, 'Go ahead, Mordecai.'

Mordecai knew what she meant. Staring at Raven he said, 'I, Mordecai Jefferson, do take you, Raven, to be my wife, to have and to hold, forsaking all others, to love, honor and cherish, through good times and bad, for richer or for poorer, in sickness and in health, till death do us part.'

'Now you, Raven,' said the Queen.

'I, Raven, do take you, Mordecai Jefferson, to be my husband, to have and to hold, forsaking all others, to love, honor, cherish and obey, through good times and bad, for richer or for poorer, in sickness and in health, till death do us part.'

She then paused a moment and continued. 'Where you will go, I will go. Where you will stay, I will stay. Your people shall be my people and your God, my God. May God deal with me severely if anything but death separates me from you.'

Queen Cymbaline took the strip and started wrapping it around Mordecai's outstretched arm and extending to Raven's outstretched arm. 'This strip symbolizes the joining of these two souls before the LORD our God,' she pronounced, 'two hearts joining together and becoming one, becoming one flesh.'

Roosevelt then took out the rings and presented one of them to Mordecai, who took the smaller ring with his free hand. He then slipped the ring upon Raven's finger, saying, 'With this ring, Raven daughter of Japeth, I thee wed.'

Raven did the same, taking the other ring and slipping it upon his finger. 'With this ring, Mordecai Jefferson, I thee wed.'

Queen Cymbaline smiled. Molly, Cece, and Starla were weeping with joy. Raven wept as well. Tears were flowing down Mordecai's eyes as he smiled. 'It is my pleasure to pronounce you husband and wife,' the Fairy Queen proclaimed, tears filling her eyes. At her signal, Mordecai removed the veil from Raven's face as they kissed. Both wept for joy as they held each other. They were now husband and wife.

The first union between a human and a fairy.

After the wedding, they had a wedding feast for the newly married couple. Mordecai and Raven sat together with his family on Mordecai's side and Raven's sister, husband, and friends to Raven's side. Music played as they ate and talked. Raven leaned her head on Mordecai's shoulder and kissed him on the lips. 'We'll have to make extra room for Raven in your room, Mordy,' Tony told her son, 'We'll have to get you a larger bed.'

'Thank you, Dad,' Mordecai smiled, 'I will have to finish school, of course. Raven and I have a place here already, but for sure I want to graduate high school. It's going to be hard to explain my absence to my teachers and the principal. My marriage, I will tell them , but nothing about Raven being a fairy or Arundel Haven.'

'We will continue to keep it a secret,' Cece agreed.

'But what about the men who came for Raven?' Molly asked, 'They know where we live.'

'I had almost forgot,' sighed Tony, 'They may return sooner or later.'

Mordccai sighed. 'I have to try and finish my education, at least,' he repeated, 'I know I should not return at all, but I would miss Cece and all of you too much.' He paused. 'It's no use trying to convince Raven to stay, and I can't do that, since I don't want to be without her.'

'You must decide for yourself what you and Raven will do, Mordy,' Tony told his son, 'What do you feel is best for the two of you?'

'I think we must return, Mordecai,' Raven told him, 'I know it's dangerous, but we're both in this together. You say you need to return to finish your education. We can't stay away forever since we are family now.'

Mordecai thought for a moment. 'My heart tells me to return to Orlando,' he stated, 'I want Grandmom and Grandad Eppright to meet you, for one. I'm sure they'll want to meet you.'

'I still can't believe the change in my parents after all this time,' Molly said, 'They were prejudiced toward blacks when I was growing up.'

'I didn't know that,' Mordecai said, surprised, 'That's news to me. They would have their friends and church members, most of them black, to visit when I was young. They told me so much about Jesus and were used by God to lead me to Christ.'

'I look forward to meeting them,' Raven said.

'What are their names?' Queen Cymbaline asked.

'Gabriel and Naomi,' Mordecai answered, 'I didn't know that they were prejudiced before. I always knew them to be Godfearing, loving everybody. They are such wonderful grandparents.'

'I know my parents will not like their grandson being married to a black woman,' sighed Tony, 'much less a fairy. I hope they can see what I have seen, what your mother and I have seen.'

'My parents changed just after we got married, Tony,' Molly reminded him, 'Maybe there is still hope that they will change in that regard.'

'I hope so,' Mordecai said, 'Raven means the world to me.'

A large cake with white frosting was brought out. From time-to-time during the night, Tony, Molly, and Cece would take pictures from their cell phones, which had cameras. Queen Cymbaline gave them leave to do so. Mordecai and Raven cut the cake together. Those around them applauded and cheered as Raven kissed Mordecai.

Twila flew toward them. 'I want cake,' she demanded.

Mordecai and Raven laughed. They cut a small slice for Twila and put it on a plate. Raven handed it to the toddler. 'Thank you, Aunt Raven,' she said sweetly.

They cut pieces for all those in the room. At last, they each had a piece for themselves on separate plates. They cut a piece and fed each other.

'I can't wait to see the pictures,' Tiffany said.

'I hope I have a wedding this beautiful,' Sharon said.

When the feast was over, Mordecai and Raven headed to the cottage where Raven stayed. Raven lit the candles in the room. They held each other close as they stared into each other's eyes.

They spoke not a word but stared into each other's eyes. Their lips came together as they stood there, enjoying the closeness of one another. They felt so much love for each other, happy that they were married, joined together in holy matrimony.

They stood there for long moments in each other's arms. Though they could feel the cold, their hearts were glowing with the warmth of their love. They did not take thought of how cold it was as they held and kissed each other. Their thoughts were on each other. Raven then started singing a love song to him. Mordecai listened, marking each word that was sung. After Raven had finished, Mordecai then sang for her, taking joy in the love they both shared. After he had finished, Raven said, 'I love it.'

'You have a beautiful singing voice, Raven,' Mordecai told her.

'That song came from my heart.'

'As did the song I sang,' Mordecai replied, 'I am glad we are married now, though I did not expect it this soon.'

'Neither did I,' Raven replied, 'but I am glad it happened.'

'So am I,' Mordecai smiled.

Their lips came together and remained locked in a loving kiss as they stood there in each other's arms. It is there they remained for long moments, still as statues and enraptured by the love they had for each other.

Mordecai loved Raven. Raven loved Mordecai.

They were committed to each other. For life.

Chapter Thirteen

The next day, Mordecai and Raven sat together talking in Raven's cottage, which now belonged to Mordecai as well.

They had grits and eggs as their first meal together as husband and wife. They spent most of the night talking before falling asleep a short time later. They had woken up around nine in the morning. Raven cooked, but Mordecai helped her. 'I'm not used to cooking without electricity,' he said, 'but it will be something I have to get used to. I like it here.'

'It's our home now, Mordecai my husband,' Raven smiled, kissing him on the lips.

'Very simplistic,' replied Mordecai. 'There are times that our technology can be a burden. It's sad that we depart from what is simple.'

'How much longer will you have to be in school, Mordecai?' Raven asked.

'This will be my final year,' Mordecai answered, 'It will be hard to explain to my teachers where I've been and that I am married now. Even if I told them, they might find it hard to believe.'

'I remember you telling me about your grandparents on your mother's side,' said Raven as Mordecai set the table. 'I look forward to meeting them.'

'When my parents told me they were prejudiced against people of color before, I couldn't believe it,' Mordecai said, 'at least they were before I was born. I had always known them to be strong in their Christian faith. I would go to their church from time-to-time when I spent the nights there. I was baptized there.'

'They sound like wonderful people,' Raven said, 'I look forward to meeting them when we return to Orlando.'

Raven prepared the plates and served the grits and eggs. They both drank cups of juice that Raven had purchased the week before. They continued to talk as they ate.

After they had finished eating, Mordecai helped Raven clean up. While the dishes were being washed, there was a knock on the door. Mordecai headed to the door and opened it. His parents and Cece appeared in the doorway. Twila, who was in Cece's arms, flew into the arms of her new uncle. 'Uncle Morcai, Uncle Morcai,' she chimed, kissing him on the cheeks.

'Hello, little Twila,' Mordecai smiled, kissing the toddler. He then embraced and kissed his sister and his parents. 'Come in,' he told them.

They entered the cottage as the three looked around. 'This is a nice cottage,' Molly said, taking in her surroundings, 'So, this is your Arundel Haven home now.'

Mordecai nodded as Raven entered the room and embraced her new in-laws. 'I like your place, Raven,' Tony said, 'So, you've lived here in this cottage all your life?'

'Yes, I grew up here,' Raven answered, 'It became mine when my parents had been taken by Shadowfire. I take it that my sister is helping Roosevelt out in the fields?'

'Yes, she is,' answered Molly, 'We agreed to watch over Twila for a while. Of course, she wanted to see her uncle Morcai.'

Twila giggled.

'Have you eaten anything yet?' Raven asked, 'Mordecai and I have just finished breakfast. He was helping me out in the kitchen, even with cooking.'

'We had breakfast with Starla and Roosevelt,' Tony replied, 'We pretty much had the same thing you had. It's kind of hard getting used to having no electricity. I do like how simplistic life is here, though.'

'As do I,' Mordecai nodded, 'I know when I have problems with a radio, music player or computer, it gets frustrating. Things go wrong. Arundel Haven doesn't have those things, but sometimes, the simplest of things make the biggest differences in the world. I still miss those things, though.'

'Yet you have so many wondrous things,' Raven replied. As Mordecai cradled Twila in his arms, Raven put another log in the fireplace. 'I don't like this time of year,' she continued, 'About this time of year, the snows will start to come. I tolerate it the best I can, but I don't like it.'

'I don't like the cold, Aunt Raven,' said Twila.

'It's okay,' Cece said, 'I don't mind it much. What do you do in celebration of Christmas?'

'I don't understand,' Raven said, confused.

'I guess you're not familiar with Christmas,' Cece said, 'We celebrate the birth of Christ.'

'Though December 25 is not the correct day He was born,' Mordecai continued, 'Nobody knows the exact day, but the important thing is that He was born. I guess we just chose that day.'

'We call it Saviour's Day,' Raven said, 'though many fairies do not acknowledge that Jesus Christ is Lord. It was instituted by King Zedekiah almost two hundred years ago and has been observed since. Queen Cymbaline would read the holy scriptures of when Jesus was born every Saviour's Day, stressing that it is not the day when He was born in the form of His creation.'

'Do you exchange gifts?' Tony asked.

'Yes,' Raven answered, 'We do give each other gifts.'

'We put them under a tree and open them on Christmas day,' Cece said.

'We don't put them under a tree,' Raven said, 'We, however, do light special candles and sing songs in praise to the Lord, though many do not believe. Queen Cymbaline would sing a song for the holidays. You should hear her! She has a wonderful singing voice. The best part is that she sings from her heart.'

'I like that,' Mordecai smiled, 'Saviour's Day.'

'What about Easter?' Tony asked.

'We do not celebrate that,' Raven answered, 'We celebrate Passover and the Day of Firstfruits, celebrating the resurrection of Christ, starting on Saturday night on the fourth week of March. It never changes.'

'Like we celebrate Thanksgiving on the fourth Thursday of November,' Mordecai said, 'Celebrating when our forefathers came to Amcrica to escape religious persecution by the Church. Our nation was founded on Biblical principles, but today, you cannot tell so. We have departed from the foundations of our nation, rejecting God, and embracing things that are evil in the eyes of God. It is a sad state to be sure.'

'That is terrible,' Raven said woefully.

'There are so many bad things going on that I feel the hand of God has turned against us,' Mordecai continued as Twila touched his face, 'The Word of God taken out of our schools and the government has become hostile toward those who are Christians. It grieves me the way things are going. Queen Cymbaline was correct to forbid contact with my people, given how wicked we are.'

'Not all humans thankfully,' Raven reminded him, 'God looks at the heart of a person. You and I are the first union of a human and a fairy. God brought us together not just to be used by Him to bring about the end of Shadowfire. Our children will be special, resulting from the love that you and I share, born from the union and love of a human and a fairy.'

'The best of both worlds,' Cece smiled.

Mordecai nodded.

Twila got comfortable in Mordecai's arms. Tony and Molly smiled as they stared at them. Cece smiled as well. 'I still can't believe how attached she is to you, Mordy,' his sister said.

Mordecai smiled as he kissed the toddler. 'She's a very special little girl.'

'But lively,' added Raven, tickling her niece.

Twila burst out laughing. 'No, no tickle me, Aunt Raven.'

'Roosevelt said that he and Starla are finishing preparations for winter,' Tony said, 'They should be finished today, I was told. Roosevelt said the snow will come very soon.'

'How soon?' Mordecai asked.

'Could be anytime from what he told me,' Tony answered, 'The temperature is dropping from what I could feel in the air. If it snows, it could be hard to defend Arundel Haven and make the battle more difficult. Prince Avondale is assembling the army and encamping in Nebechadrezzar Valley beyond the Mountains of Shadow. It's kind of risky with Shadowfire so close.'

'We can only hope he is not there,' Mordecai replied, 'especially since they have no weapon that can pierce his armor. If only there was. Arundel Haven's armies are vulnerable.'

'I do not doubt you're right,' Tony replied, 'The soldiers are being supplied with swords, armor, shields, and arrows. I don't know how we can prevail against the troops President Farouk will bring with guns, and who knows what other weapons. Queen Cymbaline has proclaimed a fast throughout her kingdom. Personally, I don't hold any hope of victory.'

'The dragon will fall, though I don't know how,' Mordecai said with conviction, 'All I have is His word, and that will have to be enough.'

Tony shook his head. 'I'm afraid I am not convinced. I don't understand how you can believe that. I still believe you and Raven may be going to your own demise.'

'How can you be so certain that you and Raven will slay the dragon?' Molly asked, 'All you have is a prophecy spoken by a former queen, long dead.'

'Shadowfire fears the Prophecy,' Mordecai told her, 'He was desperate when he had appeared in Orlando and carried me away. I could also detect a trace of fear in his voice when he spoke to me, though he did his best to hide it.'

'I still fear for your life,' Molly told her son, 'I am not certain that we will survive this.'

'God promised,' Twila said, 'and God never lies. He always keeps His promises.'

Tony and Molly stared at Twila, not speaking a word. They could not respond at that moment. Cece stared at Twila. She sighed.

'I choose to believe God,' Mordecai repeated, 'though I am scared. I have known Raven, Twila, Starla, Queen Cymbaline, and Prince Avondale for a short time, yet they have become just as much as family as you, Mom, and Cece are. I was not forced to do this, but though scared I was, I was compelled out of love to agree, believing God and His word He spoke to me. It was later when Raven realized she was the fairy maiden spoken of in the Prophecy.'

Raven nodded. Looking Tony and Molly in the eyes, she said, 'We will get through this. Shadowfire will perish and God will preserve us and deliver us out of the hands of our enemies. I choose to believe God's word, both Mordecai and me.'

'Yes, both of us,' Mordecai nodded, 'God will bring us through this, wait and see.'

Tony and Molly said nothing, though they doubted their words and their faith.

Cece stared at Mordecai and said, 'I choose to believe as well.'

Mordecai and Raven smiled. Twila looked at Tony and Molly and said, 'God make Shadowfire go bye-bye for good.'

After noon, they flew toward Roosevelt's farm. They wore clothing to keep themselves warm from the cold in the air. The temperature had dropped to close to freezing. Twila was in Mordecai's arms, trying to keep herself warm as they flew. 'I don't like the cold,' she said to Mordecai.

Mordecai kissed the toddler as he held her close. Cece took a glance at Mordecai. 'I don't think I like to fly either when it's this cold,' she said.

'I don't think there is a fairy in Arundel Haven to my knowledge that likes to fly in the cold,' Raven told them, 'I certainly don't. I like the warmer weather better.'

'I would like so much to be able to fly when it's warmer,' Cece said, 'not when it's this cold.'

When they arrived, they immediately headed inside. Roosevelt had a fire burning in the fireplace. They were glad to be out of the cold, especially Twila, though she remained in Mordecai's arms. Starla tried to take Twila from Mordecai, but the toddler refused to leave. 'My, aren't you attached to your new uncle?' she said.

Roosevelt laughed as did Tony, Molly, and Cece. Raven tickled her little niece. 'Stop,' Twila cried out laughing.

'I can't believe how much the temperature is dropping,' Mordecai said.

Roosevelt sighed. 'It must be rough for Prince Avondale and the armies at Nebechadrezzar Valley,' he said, 'The cold would be the least of our worries. I am supposed to join them later once things are squared away. I am no fighter, but I will do the best I can.'

Starla embraced her husband. 'I pray nothing happens to you, Roosevelt,' she sighed, 'I will be worried about you.'

Mordecai bowed his head. 'This is a messy business. I wish it did not come to this, but I know what's at stake here. President Farouk and Dr. Von Braun must not come near Arundel Haven!'

'I still don't know how we're supposed to bring about the death of Shadowfire,' Raven replied, 'What kind of weapons would even penetrate his armor? It's going to take something supernatural to do so.'

'I don't know either, Raven,' Mordecai said quietly, 'It still scares me all the same. Right now, only God knows how it's going to be done.'

'When are you supposed to leave, Roosevelt?' Tony asked.

'When Taris arrives,' Roosevelt answered, 'He should be here soon. He said he would come for me, and we would fly together.'

'We can stay with Starla if you wish, Roosevelt,' Tony told him.

'Please do,' Roosevelt replied, 'I would appreciate you watching over her. I can only pray we return safely, though I fear the worst.'

At that moment, there was a knock on the door. Roosevelt opened the door as Taris appeared. His face was grave. 'Come in, Taris,' the farmer said.

Taris entered as he greeted Mordecai, Raven, and the others.

Cece embraced him. 'I fear for your life, Taris,' she said.

Taris nodded. 'I fear for all our lives,' he said quietly, releasing her, 'I have received word that we who remain must join the others at Nebcchadrezzar Valley. I was sent to fetch you.'

'We have just finished preparing for the winter,' replied Roosevelt, 'I have no sword.'

'Weapons will be supplied,' Taris told him, 'They were taken to the encampment when the first wave of troops left Arundel Haven.'

'What good will it be against their weapons?' Tony asked, 'They have guns and other weapons that are more effective than bows and arrows.'

'It is all we have,' Taris replied, 'We will have to make do with what we have and pray the hand of the LORD will guide us to victory.'

'I still can't believe our president would be in alliance with an evil dragon,' Molly said, astonished, 'How did they come to an alliance in the first place? I still don't understand all this.'

'It's all hard to believe, I know,' Mordecai frowned, 'I still can't believe about Dr. Von Braun.'

'How did you meet him in the first place?' Molly asked.

'It was weeks ago before I had met Raven,' Mordecai answered, 'the day that Tiffany got into a minor accident. It was after school, and it was on a day it had been raining. I stopped at a convenience store to purchase a soda. While I was choosing, I overheard Dr. Von Braun and his men talking about fairies. I disregarded it, but somehow, he sensed that I had overheard their conversation. He followed me all the way to the Southwood subdivision and stopped me. He claimed that I had seen a fairy before. The night before, I did see something, or I thought I had seen something flying through the air. I still wasn't sure what it was to this day. Maybe it was a fairy.'

'Raven?' Cece asked.

'No,' answered Raven, 'I can honestly say it wasn't me. I had not been anywhere in that area before you took me to your home at my request.'

'Dr. Von Braun was convinced I had seen a fairy,' Mordecai contined, 'but if it was a fairy or not, I am not certain. He inquired a few more times at school about fairies and on one occasion, had shown me a photo of remains of a fairy who had died some time before. He then told me the DNA in humans and fairies were the same, save for the fact that fairies had wings.'

'Wait, are you saying Dr. Von Braun had visited Oak Ridge just to inquire about fairies?' Tony asked.

'He told me he had been a guest speaker on some of his visits,' Mordecai replied, 'He even stopped Hatfield, McCoy, and Jones from beating me up on one occasion. He kept hounding me about fairies. I sense his intentions toward fairies are evil. I felt that the first time I saw him. I tried to keep Raven's existence as a fairy a secret, but Raven chose to reveal herself to Cece.'

'Because I felt I could trust her,' Raven continued, 'I felt led in my heart to do so, since Mordecai and Cece were very close.'

'We had started becoming very close shortly before you and Mordecai met,' Cece told Raven, 'I was the only one he could talk to at the time and he had nobody to turn to when he was being bullied by the three jocks.'

'And now I feel bad about us not being supportive of Mordy,' Tony said quietly, 'We had dismissed it as a result of his depression—'

'Morcai,' corrected Twila. 'His name is Morcai.'

Tony and Molly burst out laughing. Mordecai kissed the toddler. 'Uncle Morcai loves you, Twila.'

Twila kissed him on the cheeks. 'I love you, Uncle Morcai,' she chimed.

Raven smiled.

'I feel bad as well,' Molly added, 'We didn't quite understand what Mordy was going through. I only wish we could have really listened to him and not dismissed it as we had done.'

Mordecai stared at his parents. 'Let the past go. I do not hold it against you. I believe in forgiveness. At least all this is bringing us closer together as a family, and our family has expanded.' He kissed Twila and then Raven.

Raven smiled. 'I feel blessed to be part of the family,' she said, 'Mordecai is such a blessing to me. I love him with all my heart.'

'We see that now, especially since you had put your life on the line to rescue Mordecai,' Tony told her, 'It got me to thinking that Mordy had been right all along. We had been wrong for looking at Raven as having black skin and being a fairy. So little Twila here was a factor in changing the hearts of Queen Cymbaline and Prince Avondale?'

'And me as well,' laughed Starla, 'I remember when Twila broke away from me after Mordecai had been taken to prison. I had been in a disagreement with Raven for even giving her heart to a human. I was heading home when she broke away from me. She made her way into the castle and found Mordecai. She took to him right away, but I was afraid at the time that he would harm her, but my fears were needless. She was and is precious in his eyes.'

'I remember when we were first told of Mordy's encounter with Twila,' Molly reminisced, 'Although we were disapproving at first toward Raven, I found it amusing how he had encountered her. It made me think how Cece was, with her running around when she was Twila's age. It's kind of funny to hear how fairy toddlers are.'

'Yes,' Starla said, 'Once they find out they can fly, they don't want to stop. Twila, however, is so attached to Mordecai.'

'It is easy to see,' Cece said, 'I remember when you and Twila visited our home to deliver clothes for Mordy.'

'Morcai, Cece,' Twila interrupted. Cece laughed as did the others.

'I was surprised when they first appeared in the human world,' Mordecai said, 'even more surprised when she had a gift for Cece as well. I was also happy to see Twila again.'

Roosevelt smiled as he gathered warm clothes. 'Twila is indeed a blessing,' he said. 'She has taught us more than we realize.' He sighed as Starla kissed him. 'I will miss you, Starla.'

'Please come back to me and Twila safe, Roosevelt,' she told him, holding him close.

'I will return, Starla,' Roosevelt vowed.

Twila flew from Mordecai's arms and into the arms of her father. 'Daddy no go bye-bye,' she cried.

'I wish I didn't have to, Twila,' Roosevelt said sadly, 'I will miss you.'

'Daddy and Uncle Morcai stay here,' Twila said.

'I will hurry home as soon as I can, Twila,' Roosevelt told his daughter, embracing and kissing her.

Mordecai hung his head. 'I pray you come through this all right too, Roosevelt,' he said, 'My family will look after Starla and Twila while we're gone.'

Roosevelt embraced his family and left with Taris to Nebechadrezzar Valley. Starla wept as she watched her husband leave. Twila flew into her mother's arms and leaned her head upon her shoulders. 'Twila miss Daddy, Mommy,' she said softly.

'We all do, Twila,' Starla said.

The next day, Mordecai and Raven were all alone in their cottage. Raven had brewed some tea the night before and were drinking it as they talked. Snow had started to fall overnight and had covered the land and unto Nebechadrezzar Valley. 'I imagine it must be tough for Roosevelt, Taris, and the soldiers out there awaiting the invaders,' Mordecai said, 'I can't help but worry about them.'

'It's going to make it tougher to fight Shadowfire without knowing how to take him down,' Raven said, clearly worried.

'You're scared too,' Mordecai observed.

Raven nodded.

Mordecai took Raven's hands. Neither of them spoke a word as they looked into each other's eyes. Their thoughts were on the dragon, uncertain of how they were supposed to take him down and bring about his demise. After long moments of silence, Mordecai started praying silently, Raven bowing her head as he began praying. Mordecai prayed to reveal to them the way to slay the dragon, for a way to penetrate the thick and seemingly invulnerable armor that covered his body.

They also prayed for God to deliver the armies of Arundel Haven from President Farouk's soldiers and beat them back. They prayed for nearly twenty minutes, praying for His intervention. 'Please protect Your servants: Prince Avondale, Taris, Roosevelt, and those fairymen fighting to defend their home,' Mordecai prayed, 'Give them Your divine protection in Jesus' name.'

In the valley of Nebechadrezzar, Prince Avondale had the men set up tents despite the falling snow. Those who had already pitched their tents started fires to keep themselves warm. A large tent was set up for the prince, where he met with his captains. He had a watch set up a few kilometers from where the encampment was. Food was delivered to the soldiers from Arundel Haven as they awaited the invading armies.

Prince Avondale took counsel in his tent with his captains. Queen Cymbaline was present as well. 'From what Mordecai and his family have told us,' Prince Avondale began, 'their weapons are superior to our swords, arrows, and spears. We will be hard put to counteract the humans' devices.'

'Nevertheless,' added Queen Cymbaline, 'we cannot simply give up. If we can keep them away from Arundel Haven, there may be a chance they will not find our home.'

'How can we counteract and overcome our disadvantage?' a captain named Toran asked.

'One way is to set up an ambush somewhere,' another captain, Shinar, suggested. 'We could have some of our soldiers lead them to the hills of Moran and surprise them there.'

Prince Avondale nodded. 'We can set it up there,' he agreed, 'Mordecai also mentioned they may be coming in steel flying machines he calls planes or helicopters. We must find a way to draw them out and somehow stop them from landing.'

'I can have our fastest flyers overtake them and try to find a way to disable them,' another captain named Chebar said, 'It could create confusion with them. From what we understand, none of our weapons will be able to penetrate their machines. Bringing them down will be, perhaps, impossible.'

'Indeed,' Prince Avondale said. 'We go into this battle with little or no hope.'

'If little hope,' Queen Cymbaline said, 'then it is better than none at all. Mordecai and Raven will be busy engaging Shadowfire.'

'But how will they be able to destroy Shadowfire as the Prophecy states?' asked Captain Toran, 'No weapon we have can penetrate or even mar his armor.'

'Mordecai and Raven will have to find out,' Queen Cymbaline replied, 'The LORD will have to reveal it to them. God made a promise, and if I remember what a certain toddler said, God never breaks a promise. God never lies.'

'We will be hard pressed for sure,' Captain Shinar replied, 'There is no telling how many of their soldiers they will bring with them. We are dealing with unknown factors and possibly outnumbered.'

'Nevertheless, we will meet them,' Prince Avondale said, 'We have to. We are fighting for our freedom and our home. We must not lose!'

'I agree,' Captain Toran said, 'We are with you to the end, your majesties.'

Queen Cymbaline and Prince Avondale fell to their knees. The three captains did the same as the Fairy Queen led them in prayer, praying for deliverance from their enemies. They prayed for guidance and direction and for the strength to defend their home.

After Queen Cymbaline finished, she told the captains, 'Tell those who know Jesus Christ to pray for deliverance as well, implore God for help and deliverance.'

The three captains bowed and carried out the Queen's command. Both her and her brother remained on their knees, bowing, and praying silently.

Captain Shinar gathered his battalion and told them of the plans for ambush. 'When the watchman sounds,' he said, 'be ready to move out to the hills of Moran quickly. We will have very little time to prepare.'

'How many of the human soldiers will we have to face?' one fairyman asked.

'We do not know,' replied Captain Shinar, 'We have no idea at this point in time, but we must be prepared for anything.'

'But are the humans' weapons superior?' another fairyman asked.

'We can expect so,' frowned Captain Shinar, 'We must use our abilities to fly as an advantage, hit them from the skies if need be. I am ready to defend Arundel Haven to the death.'

Captain Shinar led his soldiers to a cave close to the hills of Moran and encamped there. Messengers were sent to the different camps, to the captains and to the Queen and Prince.

Taris was the second in command in his battalion under Captain Tebar, who had his group camp not too far from the main camp. Roosevelt was with him. He had one of the soldiers set up watch upon Tarragon Hill, which stood six kilometers from the hills of Moran. There was a cave where Captain Tebar had his troops take shelter from the snow and the cold. Taris stared out into the distance watching the snow fall. 'We will be hard pressed for sure,' he told the 45-year-old dark-skinned fairyman.

'I know,' sighed Captain Tebar, 'The odds are definitely against us. Not quite knowing how many humans are invading and dealing with the dragon.'

'We should not worry about the dragon, captain,' replied Taris.

'Yes, the Prophecy of Queen Hephzibah,' stated Captain Tebar, 'I hold no hope in it coming true. What can this Raven and this human do to even hurt Shadowfire?'

'I do not know how they will bring about the end of Shadowfire,' Taris replied, 'but I believe the Prophecy will be fulfilled.'

'I wish I had your confidence, Taris,' sighed Captain Tebar, 'Every circumstance says that we will lose, that Arundel Haven shall fall.'

'We cannot give in to despair, old friend,' replied Taris, 'I will not give up. If I die, I will die fighting. I believe there is hope, and I personally will hold onto that hope with my last breath.'

Captain Tebar nodded. 'We shall fight because we have no choice, though no hope do I see. Perhaps you are right, Taris.' He paused. 'I understand that you know the human Mordecai personally.'

'I was his jailor when he was in prison,' Taris said, 'He showed himself to be honorable. He quickly earned my respect and my friendship. Prince Avondale found the book relating the Prophecy and told it to Queen Cymbaline. They then knew that Mordecai Jefferson is the one the Prophecy had spoken of. Yet Mordecai accepted it willingly, though he feared it, he was compelled out of love for Queen Cymbaline as well as for Raven, the fairy maiden he has fallen in love with.'

'So, is it true what I heard—that Queen Cymbaline allowed Raven to marry this human?' asked Captain Tebar.

'She, herself, had performed the ceremony,' Taris answered, 'I was there, as were his parents, his sister, Cece, and her friends, Tiffany and Sharon.'

'So, there are six humans in Arundel Haven?'

'By Queen Cymbaline's leave,' Taris answered, 'She had allowed Cece, Sharon, and Tiffany to enter Arundel Haven and a short time later, summoned his parents here. They are with Starla Roosevelt's wife to look after her and Twila.'

'Against her own decrees?' exclaimed Captain Tebar.

'She had deemed it necessary,' Taris said, 'They are trustworthy, especially Mordecai. I have gotten to know Cece, as well as her parents, when they stayed at the castle.'

'But how did they managed to arrive here?'

'Water from the Silverstreams, which Queen Cymbaline herself had given them,' Taris answered, 'For Cece and the others, it is only temporary, but Mordecai's ability is permanent.'

'This human must have found so much favor in the eyes of our Queen to warrant her kindness,' Captain Tebar stated, 'I can only hope the Prophecy is correct.'

'I believe so,' Taris nodded, 'I believe it in my heart. I will not doubt the word of God.'

'If only we shared your beliefs, Taris,' sighed Captain Tebar.

Starla did her best to prepare dinner, but her mind was on her husband Roosevelt, her sister Raven, and Mordecai. Molly volunteered to help Starla out. 'We are all worried, Starla,' she said.

'I have fears that the Prophecy will not come true and that I will lose Roosevelt, Raven, and Mordecai,' sighed Starla, doing her best to keep herself composed, 'I wish I could just let it go, but I am worried.'

'You've got to keep it together for the sake of Twila and your unborn child,' Molly told her gently, 'As hard as it is to do so, you've got to be strong.'

Tony and Cece watched over Twila. The toddler was in Cece's arms as she gazed at Tony. 'You Morcai's Daddy?' she asked.

Tony smiled. 'Yes, I am, little one,' he said.

'Twila love Uncle Morcai.'

Cece held Twila close. 'We all love him, Twila,' she sighed.

'Cece sad?' Twila asked, staring at her.

'Yes,' answered Cece, 'I miss your uncle.'

'You Uncle Morcai's sister?'

Cece gave out a soft chuckle. 'Yes,' she answered.

'Uncle Morcai and Aunt Raven come back,' Twila assured her, 'make Shadowfire go bye-bye.'

'I wish I believed that,' sighed Tony.

'God promised,' Twila chimed, 'and God never lies. He always keeps His promises.'

Cece smiled.

'You are right, Twila,' Starla said, walking into the room. She wiped the tears from her eyes. Twila saw her mother and flew toward her. 'I choose to believe God,' Twila told her.

Starla let out a heavy sigh. 'The faith of a child.'

'You believe that, Twila?' Molly asked as she entered the room.

'Yes, Morcai's Mommy,' Twila answered, 'God never breaks His promises.'

'Are you okay, Starla?' Molly asked. 'Do you need to sit down for a moment?'

Starla shook her head as she held Twila. 'I'll be okay,' she said as she sighed, 'I wish Mordecai and Raven were with us.'

'I don't know if they would venture out of their home in this snow,' Cece replied, 'It would be nice, however, if they were here. It would help to have them here.'

'Where are Tiffany and Sharon?' Tony asked.

'With Lavender and Laurelin, I imagine,' answered Cece. 'I'm not sure if they are over with Mordy and Raven or not. Both Lavender and Laurelin are worried about their fairymen, Jax and Derreck.'

'If you need to sit down, Starla, I can continue with the cooking,' Molly offered, 'You can relax and give your body some rest.'

'Thank you, Molly, but I will be fine,' Starla assured her, handing Twila to Cece, 'You will need my help.'

Both Starla and Molly returned to the kitchen.

Twila touched Cece's hair. Cece sat back down on the couch as she allowed Twila to touch her hair and her face. 'Twila two,' she told Cece, holding two fingers in front of her face.

'Yes, you are,' nodded Cece, trying to smile, 'You are two.'

'How old Cece?' the toddler asked.

'Fifteen,' Cece answered.

'How old Uncle Morcai?'

'Seventeen.'

'You are sure full of questions, aren't you, Twila?' Tony laughed.

'Do you know how old your aunt Raven is?' Cece asked.

Twila merely hid her face and giggled. Tony laughed.

Cece tickled the toddler. 'No tickle,' the toddler laughed, 'No tickle Twila!'

At that moment, there was a knock on the door. Cece rose and walked toward the door. Opening it, she saw her friends, Tiffany and Sharon along with Lavender and Laurelin, who immediately entered inside. They had snowflakes on their body, which melted when they entered the warm room. 'I can't believe how cold it is,' Sharon said. 'I am not used to the snow.'

'This is the first time I have ever been in the snow,' Tiffany admitted, 'and flying, no less. I wish I would have saved the water for when it's warmer. I think I would prefer Arundel Haven when it's warmer.'

They warmed themselves beside the fire. Tony put another log in the fireplace. 'It's been years since I've experienced snow,' he said. 'Starla and Molly are making dinner.'

'I don't know if I'll be able to eat,' Laurelin sighed, 'I miss Jax already. It's frustrating not knowing if he'll even survive the battle.'

'War is a terrible business altogether,' Molly said grimly, walking into the room. Starla joined her. 'There is way too much of it going on. Many lives sacrificed oft times for nothing. I don't understand.'

'Humans can be hard to figure out sometimes,' Starla said.

'I don't doubt you're right,' Tony replied, 'We can be very hard to understand, some of the things some people tend to do. I fully understand why Queen Cymbaline wanted to do all she could to protect the fairies of Arundel Haven. But Raven coming into Mordy's life was the best thing to happen to them both.'

'Not to mention Twila and the inhabitants of Arundel Haven,' Starla added, 'but I am referring to outside of the Prophecy. Raven knew, as well as Twila, how special Mordecai is, even at the risk of facing criticism and harsh words.'

'So both of them are at Raven's house?' Laurelin asked.

'It's *Mordecai and Raven's house* now,' Starla said, 'I'm not sure, but I'm guessing that's where they are now.'

'Can I see Uncle Morcai and Aunt Raven, Mommy?' Twila asked.

'It's snowing outside, dear,' replied Starla, 'It's very cold. You don't like the cold.'

'I miss Uncle Morcai and Aunt Raven,' said Twila.

'I know you do, sweetie,' replied Starla, 'but your uncle Morcai and aunt Raven need some time alone together because they love each other very much.'

'Twila like pizza,' the toddler said, 'Twila want to eat pizza.'

'I have to learn how to make it,' Starla told her.

'So, you like pizza, don't you, Twila?' Tony asked.

Twila looked at Tony and smiled. 'Morcai's daddy,' she said.

The others laughed.

'Yes, he is,' Molly said.

'Morcai's mommy,' said Twila, pointing at Molly.

Molly laughed.

'And who am I?' Cece asked, looking at her.

Twila merely giggled and hid her face. Cece tickled her. Molly and Starla returned to the kitchen to continue cooking.

Fairy soldiers were set up in various places to keep a constant lookout for the approach of their enemies. One took up watch upon a hilltop within a tall solitary tree hidden behind a branch thick with leaves. He continued to keep watch as he battled the cold and the snow. He kept himself warm as best he could. He sighed.

At that moment, he felt a breeze, warm and bitter. He sniffed the air. He knew Shadowfire was nearby. He took his horn and winded it.

Another soldier raced up toward the tree and called out to him. The soldier in the trees looked down and cried, 'Shadowfire! Shadowfire is near!'

The soldier on the ground took to the air and flew back toward the main camp.

The sound of horns echoed through the air. From within the large tent, Prince Avondale heard the horns in the distance. He raced out and was met by a soldier landing in front of him. 'Your highness,' he said breathlessly, 'Shadowfire approaches! Shadowfire is here!'

The dragon appeared in the air and began to descend, swooping down upon the soldiers and scattering them. They heard the wicked dragon laugh as he swooped down. Many dived into the snow as Shadowfire ascended in the air again. He smiled before swooping down again, scattering another group, but he did not attempt to seize any of the fairymen. He was content to play his little game and to instill fear into their hearts. Many cursed the dragon.

'The fires of hell will take you, Shadowfire,' one fairy shouted into the sky.

Shadowfire just laughed as he swooped down upon the camp. Prince Avondale stood motionless as the dragon made his pass. Again, Shadowfire made no attempt to capture any fairyman. Prince Avondale had a grim look upon his face.

Shadowfire made another pass but this time, landed in the midst of the camp. Many fairy soldiers pointed their spears at the dragon. He only laughed. 'You know you have nothing that can hurt me,' he boasted. He walked toward Prince Avondale, who stood there motionless with a grave look upon his face. 'Prince Avondale, I presume,' the dragon said with a flourish and a mock bow.

'Why are you here?' asked Prince Avondale sternly.

'Merely a parley, nothing more,' replied Shadowfire, humor dancing in his voice, 'I prefer to speak with your misbegotten sister, but she is not here.'

'You will speak to me,' insisted Prince Avondale.

'While your sister is safe within the castle, you and your troops are in the cold waiting for your deaths,' replied Shadowfire, 'Where is Mordy Jefferson and Raven?'

'They are not here,' answered Prince Avondale, 'Where they are, I cannot say.'

'Or won't.'

'Even if I knew, why should I tell you?' asked the Prince.

'Such arrogance,' sneered the dragon, 'I could take you and devour you right now if I wished.'

'I do not fear you, dragon,' Prince Avondale replied defiantly.

'That would be the easy way out for you and for your sister, if she was here. I will fly to your town and force her to come to me.'

'There is no need, dragon,' came the voice of Queen Cymbaline, stepping out of the tent, 'I am here.'

The dragon laughed. 'How surprising it is to find you here, Fairy Queen,' replied the dragon, 'No doubt you have Mordy Jefferson and Raven in Arundel Haven. I come only as a messenger for now.'

'What do you want?' asked Queen Cymbaline.

'The ruler of Mordy Jefferson's people is on his way here with an army to take your Arundel Haven,' said the dragon, 'Raven's relationship with Mordy Jefferson has brought this upon you. You have the human to blame for this.'

'We had been warned by Mordecai of your involvements with Dr. Von Braun and President Farouk,' Queen Cymbaline said grimly, 'I do not blame him for this. He had done his best to keep the secret that Raven is a fairy from others. I know you were the one who had revealed it.'

'And how do you know that?' Shadowfire quipped, 'Did the human tell you?'

'The time of the fulfillment of the Prophecy of Queen Hephzibah, my foremother, is at hand,' said Queen Cymbaline. 'I am out here with my brother of my own choosing to bring courage to our troops.'

'I could devour the both of you and leave Arundel Haven without a monarch,' Shadowfire growled, 'but I have my own reasons to spare you. I will leave the both of you in the hands of my allies. Do not tempt me to destroy you!'

'Why are you telling us this?' Prince Avondale asked.

'I have my own reasons and purposes,' replied Shadowfire, 'Your fear of the humans discovering the secret of Arundel Haven shall come to pass, and there's not a thing you can do about it. Your worst nightmare will come true, Cymbaline! You can blame that on the human, Mordy Jefferson, all because Raven met him!'

Queen Cymbaline sighed. She thought about Shadowfire's words. She remembered when Mordecai was first brought to Arundel Haven, how she had him imprisoned upon his arrival. She then thought of all that had happened afterwards: Twila entering the castle and visiting Mordecai and how she had accepted him on sight; the Prophecy of Queen Hephzibah; the dreams that Mordecai had; how he had humbled himself before them upon his arrival, never speaking haughty but minded himself wisely. When she had told Mordecai the tale of the Prophecy, he accepted it, though fearful he was of it, agreeing to it of his own free will, out of love for Raven, Twila, and of the Queen herself. She narrowed her eyes at the dragon. 'It was the will of God that Raven had met Mordecai,' she told the dragon, 'I refuse to blame him for all of this!'

Shadowfire growled. 'So, you believe the Prophecy will come to pass? You are a fool, Cymbaline, you and Avondale! My presence here serves a purpose that you may see you have no hope at all! Humans are on their way here to take Arundel Haven as their own! If you were wise, Cymbaline, you would surrender right now! They will be here very soon, but I will not tell you when! I want you all to know fear, for you to see that there is no hope at all! The Prophecy shall fail, and I shall live on! Mordy and Raven shall die, and all hopes of the Prophecy being fulfilled shall die as well! What makes you think Mordy and

Raven have any chance of defeating me? No weapon you have can even bite me, not even the sharpest spear, arrow, or sword! What hope do you have?'

'We believe the word of God,' Prince Avondale shot back, 'and God never lies!'

'You don't know how many times I have heard that from the victims I have sacrificed to my master,' laughed Shadowfire, 'My victims would tell me that God allows bad things to happen for a reason, and each one of them were sacrificed to my master!'

'Save one,' retorted Queen Cymbaline, 'Mordecai Jefferson.'

'I let Mordy and Raven go only because I had a change in plans, nothing more,' snapped Shadowfire, 'I had decided right then and there to bring the leader of the most powerful nation on earth to Arundel Haven along with someone who has an interest in the existence of fairies! Your people shall be revealed to the human world at large! There is nothing you can do to stop it!'

'We will try, nonetheless,' cried Prince Avondale, sheathing his sword, 'My blade cannot bite you, but in the name of our Lord and Saviour Jesus Christ, we will defend our home with our lives!'

The dragon laughed. 'Then you will see your faith is in vain, is sorely misplaced. Your God, whom you serve, has abandoned you, left you at the mercy of your enemies!'

'You fear the Prophecy,' Queen Cymbaline said sternly, 'You were desperate to keep the Prophecy of my foremother from being fulfilled. That's why you flew to where Mordecai lived in Orlando, Florida to take him.'

'I fear nothing!' growled Shadowfire, beating his wings.

Queen Cymbaline stared hard upon the dragon. 'You lie,' she proclaimed, 'I can tell in my spirit that you do fear it coming to pass. It was a desperate move on your part because you know your time is at hand.'

'Mordy is *nothing*!' stormed Shadowfire, his voice booming around the entire camp.

'But you fear him and the Prophecy nonetheless,' snapped Queen Cymbaline, 'Why else would you bother to invade his dreams and reveal the Prophecy though in small parts? He does not deny the fear he has, but he knows that he is the one. I gave him a choice and he was free to choose not to help, but despite his fear, he did, out of love! Out of free will, out of love, he chose to adhere to the Prophecy!'

Shadowfire scoffed. 'You are a fool, Cymbaline,' he growled, 'You, your brother, Mordy, Raven! What will happen to you will make you beg me to devour you or sacrifice you to my master!'

He spread his massive wings and took to the air, hovering about a thousand meters from the ground and remained suspended. Many of the soldiers stood there and stared, wondering what the dragon was going to do. After long minutes, he made several passes, swooping down on certain soldiers without an attempt to seize them and made one last swoop, flying very low toward Queen Cymbaline and Prince Avondale. They were knocked down into the snow as the dragon ripped their tent, made one last dive, and flew into the clouds and disappeared. Soldiers rushed to the aid of their monarchs, helping them to their feet.

'Avondale?' Queen Cymbaline said to her brother.

'I am okay, Cymbaline,' he assured her, 'What about you?'

'I am unhurt,' Queen Cymbaline answered.

A dozen soldiers made their way to repair the damaged tent where Queen Cymbaline and Prince Avondale had been staying. They brushed the snow from their bodies. 'What if the dragon is right?' one of the soldiers asked.

'No, we cannot give in to fear, despair and doubt,' Prince Avondale quickly told him, 'His presence here was clearly meant to instill fear in our hearts, but we must not let him succeed! We must be strong!'

Roosevelt stared in the direction where Shadowfire had taken flight and disappeared. He had an angry look upon his face. 'It has only served to anger me,' he said grimly, 'I do not fear Shadowfire! I know that my family is safe. When he would come near my farm, I feared he would take Starla and Twila, but since they are safe, I will not fear.'

'We must all be strong,' Queen Cymbaline cried, 'To give into fear would not only serve Shadowfire's purpose but would give an advantage to our enemies. We will not have to worry about Shadowfire. The time of the Prophecy's fulfillment is almost here. I can feel it!'

'And I am certain Mordecai and Raven can sense it as well,' Prince Avondale added.

'But how?' another soldier asked, 'How can they even harm Shadowfire when none of our weapons can harm him?'

'Leave that to God,' Queen Cymbaline said, 'He will reveal the way to Mordecai and Raven. I remember the words of a certain toddler, Twila, daughter of Roosevelt: "God promised, and God never lies. He always keeps His promises."'

Roosevelt smiled, thinking about Twila. 'For someone so young, it is she who has taught us.'

Prince Avondale nodded. 'Indeed. God uses the small and insignificant in the eyes of the world to work His will. I, too, will believe what God says.'

'As do I,' replied Queen Cymbaline.

One of the captains in the camp unsheathed his sword and raised it in the air. With a clear voice he said, 'No matter what happens, your majesties, we are with you all the way!'

Prince Avondale raised his sword in the air. 'For Arundel Haven!'

'For Arundel Haven!' came the cries of the soldiers in the camp.

The next morning, Mordecai was up and about. He had a glass of tea. He was in deep thought. He drank sporadically out of his cup. He felt a touch in his spirit, hearing the Spirit speaking to him. He bowed his head and whispered a silent prayer, his voice barely audible. He continued to pray silently for long minutes.

As he prayed, he did not notice Raven walking into the room. She found her human husband with his head bowed. She felt a gentle touch on his shoulder. He stopped praying, raised his head, and rose slowly to his feet. He turned toward Raven and said, 'It is time.'

Raven nodded, understanding what he meant. 'I felt it in my spirit too,' she said quietly, 'but how are we going to slay Shadowfire?'

'Get some warm clothing on,' Mordecai told her, 'I know where we must go.'

'But where?'

'To the beginning of the Silverstreams,' he answered, 'where I had received the power of flight. We must move quickly! Already, Dr. Von Braun and President Farouk's troops are on their way here.'

'Why the Silverstreams?'

'You will see when we reach there,' Mordecai said quickly, 'The LORD had told me to return to the falls of the Silverstreams. You will see when we get there, but time is short! The hour of the Prophecy is at hand!'

Raven nodded. She rushed to put on warm clothing for her and Mordecai. They slipped them on and flew out of their home in the direction of the Silverstreams. The snow continued to fall as they took to the air. Mordecai held Raven's hand to help her fly through the snow. They flew together hand in hand as they left the town. 'Can you fly all right, Raven?' he asked.

'It is difficult, but I can still fly,' answered Raven. 'I don't know of any fairy that likes to fly in the snow. I sure don't.'

'Just keep a hold of my hand, Raven,' Mordecai told her.

'I am never letting go of you, my husband,' Raven replied as she smiled. Mordecai stared at her and smiled back. He squeezed her hand as she squeezed his. They flew hand in hand all the way to their destination.

When they arrived at the waterfall and the beginning of the Silverstreams, Mordecai led Raven behind the waterfall inside the cave.

'I imagine the water is colder than before, especially with the snow,' Mordecai said, stalling a little. He saw the loincloth lying on a boulder. Raven giggled. 'It did look cute on you,' the black fairy said.

Mordecai merely smiled.

'But why are we here?'

'The Spirit told me to come here,' answered Mordecai, 'but I don't know why.'

He looked around. He stared at the wall for a long moment. He then felt compelled to touch a small stone that was affixed to the wall. He stared at it. *Why didn't I notice this before?*

'What's wrong, Mordecai?' Raven asked, noticing him staring at

the wall.

'I don't remember seeing that stone before, the stone on the wall,' replied Mordecai. He pushed it. They heard a click, and a hidden door appeared and opened from the inside.

'A secret passage,' Raven exclaimed.

Mordecai nodded as both he and Raven entered. Upon the wall, they saw written on the wall these words:

Put on the whole armor of God, that ye may be able to stand against the wiles of the devil.

For we wrestle, not against flesh and blood, but against principalities, against powers, against the rulers of the darkness of this world, against spiritual wickedness in high places.

Wherefore take unto you the whole armor of God, that ye may be able to withstand in the evil day, and having done all, to stand.

Stand, therefore, having your loins girt about with truth, and having the breastplate of righteousness,

And your feet shod with the preparation of the gospel of peace.

Above all, taking the shield of faith, wherewith ye shall be able to quench all the fiery darts of the wicked.

And take the helmet of salvation, and the sword of the Spirit, which is the Word of God.

Praying always with all prayer and supplication in the Spirit and watching thereunto with all perseverance and supplication for all saints.

'Ephesians 6:11-18,' Mordecai said quietly. 'Wonder why those scriptures are engraved on the wall?'

'How does it apply to us slaying Shadowfire?' asked Raven, 'Those verses apply to spiritual warfare, against Satan and his devils, against his minions, the rulers of the darkness of this world and spiritual wickedness in high places as the Word states.'

'There's got to be a reason for this,' Mordecai said, examining the words.

'Maybe this is the reason, Mordecai,' Raven said. 'Look over there!'

Mordecai looked in the direction Raven was pointing. Hanging on the wall, they saw two sets of armor, almost like what the scriptures they read was describing. Two shields, seemingly of solid gold were hanging on the wall. It bore no jewels, but upon each shield was the Star of David.

Two sets of breastplates hung beside them, both with the image of a lion and a lamb lying down together. Two sets of loin plates of pure silver hung underneath. Below were plated shoes of silver, light but strong.

Above the breastplates were helmets of silver with gold plating with twelve diamonds in a circle. Separating the armor were two swords in a sheath with twelve stones of different colors set upon them.

Mordecai and Raven stared at the armor and the gears of war. Mordecai took the sword and unsheathed it. The sword was smooth and sharp. Upon the hilt were the words: *The battle belongs to the LORD.* The sword Raven took in her hands had the same inscription.

'Mine has words on it, Mordecai,' Raven told him.

'Mine has: *The battle belongs to the LORD,'* Mordecai informed her.

'So does this one,' replied Raven. She stared at the armor. 'This one looks like it could fit me,' she said.

'I imagine this one could fit me as well,' replied Mordecai, taking the breastplate. Raven took the other set as they placed them upon their bodies.

'This seems to fit me perfectly,' Raven told Mordecai.

'And mine as well,' Mordecai nodded.

They slid the shoes on and the belts, securing the sheaths around their waists. Raven unsheathed her sword. 'These are supposed to pierce through Shadowfire's armor?' she asked.

'We have to believe God in this,' Mordecai told her, 'Like the inscriptions say, the battle belongs to the LORD.'

He then remembered reading: *It is not my might, nor by power, but by my Spirit, saith the LORD.*

Raven felt a touch in her heart. There came a voice like the sound of rushing waters, clear and pure: *Through the both of you, I will bring about the end of the dragon, as I had revealed to My servant, Hephzibah. I have brought the two of you together. Be strong and courageous! I will deliver Shadowfire into your hands. I will go before you. Through this, I shall be glorified, and they shall know that I am. The time is now here. Go forth, fear not, doubt not, for I shall be with you. I will guide you and through you two, I shall bring about the end of the dragon as I had spoken 150 years ago. I am with you now and forever. Only trust and obey Me.*

Mordecai and Raven fell to their knees and worshipped the Lord. 'We shall,' Mordecai said. 'We trust You and we thank You for the victory and the deliverance You will accomplish against our enemies.' As they rose to their feet, Mordecai turned toward Raven and said, 'It is time.'

Raven nodded as they each took a shield. They sheathed their swords and headed out of the cave. When they reached the open air, they took to the air and flew away to face Shadowfire.

The snow fell harder as they flew.

One of the watchmen stood within one of the trees furthest from the encampment keeping a lookout. He divided his time between trying to keep warm and keeping watch. He saw only snow and now and then birds flying through the air. He sighed. He saw no sign of anything else. He did his best to protect himself from the chill in the air, blowing warm air into his cupped hands.

Within the camp, Prince Avondale looked out into the distant sky. He wore a heavy cloak over his armor-covered body. He spoke not a word as he continued to stare out into the distance. One of the captains walked over to him. He, too, had a heavy cloak over his body. 'I hate all this waiting,' he said.

Prince Avondale simply nodded. 'They are coming,' he said, staring into the distance. 'I can feel it.' He gripped the hilt of his sword. 'It is only a matter of time.'

'If you don't mind me saying, your highness,' the captain said, 'but I do not feel we have any hope against the humans, especially with what advanced weapons they have.'

Prince Avondale nodded in response. 'I know this may seem like a hopeless battle, Haggai,' he said, 'but we cannot give in to despair. We have no choice but to fight and try and keep the evil humans from reaching our home!'

'We are all with you and Queen Cymbaline,' said Captain Haggai, 'but I fear we don't stand a chance in this battle.'

'I sense that in a lot of our fairymen,' sighed Prince Avondale. 'I have no doubt that every single one of you is with me, but you are afraid we may not survive. I believe there is hope, and I personally shall hold on to it with all my might and trust in God to deliver us.'

'The weather is colder than it is normally this time of year,' said Captain Haggai, 'or am I just imagining it?'

'No, Captain Haggai, I feel it too,' replied Prince Avondale, 'It could be that Shadowfire has cast some kind of spell to make it colder than usual. I wouldn't doubt it.'

'What are your orders, your highness?'

'Be ready when the watchmen give the signal,' Prince Avondale said, 'Keep warm the best you can but be at the ready for when our enemies arrive.'

Captain Haggai bowed and departed. Prince Avondale sighed as he watched the captain walk away. He then headed back inside his tent.

Queen Cymbaline sat down on the ground, bundled up in a blanket. Her younger brother stared at her. 'You shouldn't be here, Cymbaline,' he admonished her, 'I counsel you against being here.'

'Maybe so,' Queen Cymbaline replied, 'but I feel this is where I needed to be. I cannot bear being in the castle and knowing so many fairymen are putting their lives on the line to defend my kingdom from the humans.'

'I still don't feel right about you being here, sister,' repeated Prince Avondale, 'You are the Queen of Arundel Haven. If I fall, you still have a chance to produce an heir. Being here puts you in danger. I do not desire to be king. I am content with you as Queen. You have ruled Arundel Haven well, with justice, mercy, righteousness. I do not wish to succeed you but to have you and your heir's rule.'

'I have no doubt you are right,' replied Queen Cymbaline, 'but my heart tells me my place is here, even if it is to bring encouragement to our people. They are disheartened, but I pray my presence here may encourage and inspire them.'

'They are discouraged, Cymbaline,' agreed Prince Avondale, 'but you are putting yourself in danger. It is dangerous for you here.'

'No less than my people, whom I love with all my heart,' Queen Cymbaline said, 'If there is something more I can do, I will do it.'

'But you are no warrior,' objected Prince Avondale.

'Mordecai is not, either, yet he and Raven are willing to put their lives on the line to fight Shadowfire,' Queen Cymbaline said, her voice rising slightly, 'Afraid though he was, he accepted the Prophecy out of love for me and our people, as well as for Raven. I pray I could do much more somehow.'

Prince Avondale shook his head. 'I still don't feel right about you being here, sister,' he repeated.

Queen Cymbaline rose and placed her hands upon her brother's shoulders. 'In all my years of ruling Arundel Haven,' she said, 'I have done my best to serve and govern our people well. In dealing with Shadowfire, I feel I have failed in my duties.'

'You have ruled us well, Cymbaline,' Prince Avondale replied.

'If my presence here encourages our soldiers, then it will be worth it,' Queen Cymbaline said, 'I will be offering prayer and supplication while the battle is going on.' She stared into the eyes of her younger brother. 'We shall get through this, Avondale. The LORD of Sabaoth is with us. I feel His reassurance in my spirit. We will survive.'

Prince Avondale thought for a moment. He thought about what Queen Cymbaline had told him. He was still uncomfortable with his sister being in danger, facing death in battle, but he then knew that the soldiers needed encouragement and a reason to fight and not give up. He bowed his head and sighed. 'I still don't like the idea of you putting yourself in danger.'

'I know, but I believe my place is here. Suffer my presence here. It is needed.'

Prince Avondale sighed. 'I still don't feel right about this,' he said once more before turning and leaving the tent.

Queen Cymbaline knelt and began to pray.

When the prince exited the tent, he headed to the fire that three of the captains had built. Roosevelt was among them. 'I can't remember it being so cold this time of year,' he said, 'Maybe in the beginning of wintertime, but not now.'

'May be Shadowfire's doing,' replied Prince Avondale, 'but we are not certain. He could have cast a spell to slow us down, knowing the snow has an adverse effect on fairies. We cannot let that slow us down!'

'So we've heard nothing yet?' a captain asked.

Prince Avondale shook his head. 'We will know when the watchman sounds,' he said, 'That is why we must stay ready!'

'What bothers me,' said the captain, 'is not knowing how many humans we must face, what their capabilities are. It's the unknown that bothers me.'

'I know,' Prince Avondale nodded, 'but we cannot worry about that. We will find out when they arrive.'

'I never thought we'd be involved in a war in our lifetime,' Roosevelt said sadly, 'I can't remember a time, if any, that we've been in a war with humans.'

'It has been close to 700 years, I think,' Prince Avondale replied, 'when a human army, led by religious men in black and some in brown robes in the name of their goddess tried to take Arundel Haven during the reign of King Manasseh. It lasted a week, but in the end, they were beaten back, and King Manasseh destroyed the image of their Holy Mother, which they brought to set up in the square of our city. We lost many good fairymen at the time, including his younger brother, Prince Hosea. Now it could be worse than back then.'

'I have not heard that before, I'm sorry to say,' replied Roosevelt.

'I remembered reading about it in the archives before Mordecai was brought here,' said Prince Avondale, 'In the enemy camp, the books we found were burned and their images destroyed. None of the humans who had invaded had survived from what I understand, none to return to where they came from to relay the tale of their loss.'

Overhead, they saw groups of birds, some small and others large, flying. They looked up. A flock of ravens circled around an area outside the camp while a flock of vultures flew to the opposite side. 'This is a bad sign indeed,' the captain sighed.

'I do not like their presence either, Captain Shem,' replied Prince Avondale, 'It is as if they have heard rumors of a battle and are awaiting their feast.'

'Carrion birds,' growled Roosevelt. 'How I hate them!'

They heard the ravens crying out to each other. Most of the soldiers gazed at them and some were disheartened. One of the fairymen pulled out an arrow and prepared to shoot.

'Put down your arrow, Saul,' Captain Shem told him, 'Do not waste your arrows on them! You will need all the arrows you have against our enemies.'

Saul did as he was told, though he growled at the birds.

'Pay the birds no mind,' Prince Avondale said, 'We have more important things to worry about. The enemy will be here soon, and we must concentrate on beating them back.'

Roosevelt grabbed more faggots that laid nearby and threw them into the fire. The branches began to burn as the flames covered them and rose about a half a meter.

Prince Avondale's thoughts were on his sister. He was still disturbed about her presence in the camp, fearing for her life. He knew it was a risk for his sister to be there. He stared grimly into the fire as it burned, the wood popping and crackling. His hand instinctively touched the hilt of his sword. He, too, was growing anxious from the waiting. He hid the frustration that was building inside of him and kept it shut. He kept himself composed and focused on the upcoming battle.

Around the camp, many of the fairymen were gathered around open fires, throwing bundles of faggots that they had found near dead trees nearby. Some of them still had dead leaves attached. Many were growing anxious from the waiting like Prince Avondale was, not knowing how many humans would be in the fight and not knowing when they would arrive. Some decided to walk away from the fire and unsheathed their swords, swinging them around, parrying and thrusting at the air. Prince Avondale saw this and unsheathed his sword as well. He saw the light from the flames reflecting off the blade. He swung his sword away from the fire, getting the feel of the sword and its weight. He swung it a few times more, then stilled. He again stared at the blade.

At that moment, they heard a horn being sounded in the distance. The fairyman in the camp with the horn blew his as well. 'They are here,' whispered Prince Avondale. He then said in a loud voice, 'The enemy is here!' He took up his horn and blew it.

Six large helicopters, led by Shadowfire, made their way to the valley. From the cockpit, President Farouk and Dr. Von Braun watched as a fairy flew from a nearby tree and shot away. 'Follow him,' the President said.

Shadowfire rose to the air and disappeared into the clouds. A dozen fairymen appeared in the air before them, hovering, then flying away. One of the helicopters gave chase, while the other five kept on their course. 'At last,' Dr. Von Braun proclaimed, 'Arundel Haven! I have dreamed for many years of finding it, and now soon, I shall behold it for myself.'

'We will head to Arundel Haven and find Queen Cymbaline,' President Farouk stated, 'After we capture her, I will claim her kingdom in the name of the United States. We will bring her to the White House and reveal the existence of her people.'

The helicopter that pursued the dozen fairies kept up the chase. When they reached the hills of Moran, Captain Shinar winded his horn. The battalion of fairies under his command flew out of hiding and gathered toward the helicopter, surrounding it. Some of them flew right into the windshield and obstructed the views of the pilots. Some pounded on the door to try and break inside, but it was too hard.

Suddenly, the door opened, and two soldiers started firing. Two fairies were hit and fell to the ground, while others flew to try and dodge the bullets. Two with bows and arrows shot and hit one soldier. The arrow hit him in the chest, causing him to fall from the helicopter. Others began shooting.

Three fairymen who were close by grabbed two of the men and pulled them out of the helicopter. They engaged the men and slew them before being shot down by another soldier.

The pilot did his best to keep the helicopter in the air despite his vision being obstructed, but was unable to do so. The fairies suddenly flew from the windshield and seconds later, the helicopter crashed into the hillside. Soldiers raced out of the plane and started firing. Two fairies were hit before the men were cut down.

Fairies flew around to evade the oncoming bullets and some eventually were able to land and engage their enemies. The soldiers were not used to fighting fairies with swords and arrows. Some fought in hand-to-hand combat, some pulling out army knives. The snow was being covered by the blood of humans and fairies that had fallen.

Another helicopter followed another dozen fairies and was led to another ambush at Tarragon Hill.

Captain Chebar winded his horn as the fairies under his command took to the air and began their attack. The side door of the large helicopter opened as it made its descent, revealing four armed soldiers who opened fire. They hit three fairies before one was cut down by a spear thrown by Taris. He managed to avoid a shot as the helicopter buckled from the impact of the landing.

Once they had landed, soldiers started pouring out of the helicopter, firing as they went.

From on top of the hill, archer fairies let loose their arrows. Five humans fell while some returned fire. One fairy was shot, but the others had taken to the air.

Another group of hidden archers let loose their arrows. Three humans fell dead while others were wounded. Those that were wounded returned fire. Two fairies fell while the rest raced for cover. The leader of the group urged his men to pursue the fairies.

The other four had almost reached the camp when Prince Avondale blew his horn the moment they saw the helicopters. Fairies took to the air as they flew toward the human devices. Three helicopters landed and soldiers opened fire as they raced out.

Arrows flew and struck the soldiers while the return fire from the humans caught a dozen fairies. From the skies, fairies dived and kicked some of the soldiers down, slaying some of them. The fairies fought with desperation and determination, relentless in their attacks. They had everything to lose and were determined to fight to the death for their home.

The helicopter with President Farouk and Dr. Von Braun landed in the middle of the camp. When the door opened, the fairies within the camp let their arrows fly. Two soldiers fell dead while the others avoided the arrows and returned fire. Three fairies fell dead as a result.

Prince Avondale blew his horn and gathered the fairies beside him. When a group of soldiers charged them, they took to the air, dodging the bullets that were shot their way. Prince Avondale slew two of the soldiers and avoided a strike by another. He was joined by other fairies who came to his aid and started beating back their assailants.

Two fairies fell but four soldiers fell as well. When half of his party fell, Prince Avondale took to the air, as did the survivors.

As the battle raged, bodies of humans and fairies alike stained the snow with the blood of the fallen.

From the helicopter, President Farouk and Dr. Von Braun watched as the battle raged. The fairies fought with such ferocity and desperation, refusing to back down from the onslaught of Farouk's men. President Farouk had a stern look upon his face. 'They are showing more fight than I expected,' he frowned, 'Major Moore assured me that they were the best in his regiment! We are losing too many men for my liking!'

'I am disappointed to say the least,' Dr. Von Braun replied, 'I cannot accept defeat, especially since we are so close!'

They saw Prince Avondale cut down three of the soldiers as the troops charged forward. Fairies from the sky soared toward their attackers and tackled them to the snow-covered ground. One soldier struck a fairy with the butt of his gun and shot him down before Prince Avondale ran him through with the sword. He blew his horn as more soldiers charged, firing. 'Stand your ground,' the prince cried. 'Protect Queen Cymbaline!'

Captain Shem ordered his archers to open fire.

Invading troops let loose a hailstorm of bullets, which cut down five fairies before the survivors let loose their arrows. Three soldiers fell and four more wounded. The fairies did not back down, though more fell by the bullets.

Arrows flew from above and started striking down soldiers. A group of fairies had taken to the sky led by Roosevelt and fired from above. They scattered when the soldiers returned fire. One of the archers was cut down as a result. They dodged the bullets that were fired, trying to make it harder for the gunners to get a bead on the fairies.

Prince Avondale had gathered a group of fairies and charged the ranks from the air, dodging bullets as they flew. Archers bent their bows and let loose their arrows. When five of the soldiers were felled, they scattered again. For the time, it seemed the armies of Arundel Haven were winning the battle.

But the tide turned. From the sky, Shadowfire descended, spewing fire upon the fairies. Six were overtaken and consumed by the flames.

Soldiers at first shrunk back in fear of the dragon, but Shadowfire turned to them and cried, 'Stand and fight, you fools! Forget about me and kill the fairies!'

Many fairies cursed when they saw the dragon. Prince Avondale hovered in the air and stared at the dragon.

'You are not thinking of striking me with your sword, fairy,' Shadowfire laughed, 'You know full well that it has no effect on me!'

'We will not surrender, Shadowfire,' Prince Avondale gritted his teeth in defiance, 'no matter how much the odds are against us!'

'You will die, you and your people,' cried Shadowfire, 'Your faith in your God is all in vain! This day, the fairies of Arundel Haven shall be no more!'

'You forget the Prophecy of Queen Hephzibah,' cried Prince Avondale.

'Damn the Prophecy,' cried Shadowfire, belching forth fire in Prince Avondale's direction. Prince Avondale avoided the blast, but two fairies were caught and consumed.

Instinctively, the prince swung his sword. The armor repelled the blow as Shadowfire laughed. The dragon belched forth fire again.

Prince Avondale managed to fly out of the way of the blast. Three soldiers fired at Prince Avondale. He managed to avoid the gunfire. Some of them hit Shadowfire and bounced off his thick hide.

Shadowfire growled at the soldiers but said nothing. Three fairies fired at the dragon, but Prince Avondale cried, 'Stop! Focus on the humans! Our weapons cannot penetrate his hide, or have you forgotten?'

Shadowfire laughed. 'Where are Mordy and Raven, 'O Prince of the fairies?' the dragon mocked, 'Where are the ones that are supposed to slay me? I do not see them! They have fled because they know they cannot find any weapon that would harm me!'

Prince Avondale said nothing as he concentrated on fighting the invading humans. Shadowfire belched forth more fire. The fairies scattered and flew to avoid the blasts. Two were cut down by gunfire as a result. Prince Avondale winded his horn to reassemble his fairymen. Many that had survived joined him, dodging the gunfire. 'Fall back,' he cried. 'Fall back!'

The fairies joined him, trying to lead the humans away from camp and in the opposite direction of their home. The human army followed them, firing as they went. Three more humans fell by the bows of the fairy archers.

From the direction of the hills of Moran, Captain Shinar led the remnants of his warriors into the battle. From the air, the archers let their arrows fly as they went. In the process, three fairy archers were hit and fell hard to the ground. Captain Shinar winded his horn and the fairies scattered and flew into different directions. Unfortunately for Captain Shinar, he flew into the blast of Shadowfire and was consumed. The fairies under his command watched in horror at the death of their captain. They heard a horn being winded and turned toward the direction of the blast. Prince Avondale began to gather more fairies to him.

The surviving troops from the hills of Moran joined in the battle and began to fire upon the fairies again. The remnant of Captain Shinar's troop engaged them, diving toward them with swords drawn. Three fairies were cut down before they reached their enemies. When the fairies got the upper hand, Shadowfire intervened, belching forth fire. Half of the surviving fairies were caught in the inferno and perished. He laughed.

Suddenly, they heard a horn sound, different from the horns used by Prince Avondale and the others. Prince Avondale turned and looked. He smiled as he winded his horn. 'The time for the Prophecy of Queen Hephzibah to be fulfilled is here,' he cried.

Shadowfire growled and turned to look.

Hovering in the air in full armor were Mordecai and Raven, swords drawn. Mordecai winded his horn again. 'I was wondering where you and Raven were, human,' the dragon said grimly, 'Both of you should have stayed away! No sword can bite me, you both know that! You shall die, I swear it this day!'

Mordecai and Raven took up their shields.

Shadowfire let out a loud roar and took to the air. 'I will not let the Prophecy be fulfilled,' he bellowed.

Mordecai and Raven glanced at each other and nodded. They flew toward Shadowfire; swords raised in the air. No quarter asked, no quarter given.

To the death.

Chapter Fourteen

Shadowfire unleashed a blast in the direction of Mordecai and Raven as they approached, scattering as they saw the flames approaching. They circled behind the dragon and slammed the shield against his face as he turned his head, Mordecai first, then Raven.

With his massive claws he made a swipe at each but missed. He scoffed. 'Is that the best you can do?' he cried.

Neither Mordecai nor Raven responded.

'You are fighting a battle you cannot win,' boasted Shadowfire, making another swipe as Mordecai and Raven flew further away. Occasionally, missed shots from the human soldiers would hit and bounce off the thick hide of the dragon, but he did not notice. His attention was solely focused on Mordecai and Raven.

A few soldiers looked up and stared at Mordecai and saw he was no fairy. 'Who is he?' one of them asked. 'How on earth can he fly if he is no fairy?'

They were then attacked by five fairymen who dived from the sky and tackled them to the ground.

'Forget about this human,' boomed Shadowfire. 'Mordy and Raven are mine! Concentrate on fighting the fairies!'

Mordecai slammed his shield into the face of Shadowfire again. The dragon made a vain attempt to take the young man down with his claws as he flew out of range. 'You expect to slay me doing this?' scoffed the dragon.

'Keep it up, Raven,' Mordecai cried, 'Let's make sure that it is us he's going after.'

Raven nodded as she did the same thing. It did not hurt Shadowfire, but it made him angry. He took another swipe at the ebony fairy but missed. 'All you are doing is incurring my wrath, fools,' he cried, 'I will catch you and destroy you both, I swear by Ashtaroth!'

Raven glanced at Mordecai. 'We can lead Shadowfire to the hills of Moran,' she said to him, 'There, the fairies will not have to worry about him, just the humans. They would stand a better chance if we took Shadowfire out of the battle.'

Mordecai nodded. 'We will make our stand there, then,' he replied, 'It would be one less thing for Queen Cymbaline and Prince Avondale and the others to worry about.'

Mordecai slammed his shield again into Shadowfire's face and flew away. The dragon let out an angry roar and exhaled fire in their direction. Raven led the way as Mordecai followed, making sure Shadowfire was following them. The dragon took to the air and headed after them, roaring as he went.

'Here he comes,' Mordecai cried. 'It's working!'

'I knew he'd be focused on us,' cried Raven. 'I just hate dealing with this cold and the snow!'

'Hold on, Raven,' Mordecai cried.

Shadowfire scoffed as they flew away. 'Is this a part of the Prophecy?' he cried, 'the both of you fleeing in terror? Flying for your lives?'

Mordecai said nothing, but as he looked back, gave a simple nod. *Go ahead and think what you will. You're doing exactly what we want you to do.*

'How much further?' he asked Raven.

'We're almost there,' Raven answered, her face tight with concentration.

They arrived at a group of large hills where the dead and dying of both humans and fairies stained the snow with their blood. They reached the largest of the hills and stopped. Shadowfire hovered in the air. 'Nowhere to fly,' he cried. 'Nowhere to hide!'

Mordecai and Raven held their swords at the ready, facing the dragon. Shadowfire scoffed. 'You ought to know by now no weapon can bite me, none forged can penetrate my hide,' he laughed, 'So many years, the fairy smithies have tried but failed. Not even the advanced weapons of the humans can harm me!'

'Time we put that to the test,' Mordecai cried confidently. With a nod he and Raven scattered, flying in different directions, avoiding the claws and flames from Shadowfire.

He turned and spewed fire in Mordecai's direction. The young man instinctively grabbed his shield and withstood the blast. The shield managed to protect Mordecai from the heat of the flames. When the flames died down, Shadowfire swatted the young man from the air, sending him falling into the cold icy ground.

Mordecai held on to his shield and sword as he hit the ground. Stunned from the impact, he got on his knees and tried to rise from the ground. He saw that Shadowfire was about to land a blow his way.

But Raven had seen this. She flew toward the dragon and struck a blow to the outstretched foreleg of the dragon. The blade cut deep, penetrating his thick armor. Shadowfire roared in pain. He then stared at the wound, seeing his black blood flowing from the cut. He had a look of shock on his face. 'How… how can this be?' he cried. 'This is… this is impossible! No blade has ever harmed me before! What devilry is this?'

He unleashed fire in Raven's direction. She flew out of range of the blast while Mordecai stood his ground. When Shadowfire sent flames his way, the young human blocked them with his shield. He saw when Raven had drawn blood from the dragon with her sword. He stared at his and smiled, nodding his head. *These seem to be no ordinary blades, but where did they come from? Who forged them? If Raven's sword can cut through his thick armor, then mine can, too.*

Shadowfire let out a mighty roar. When Raven tried to attack again, he swatted her away with his left foreleg as his claws scraped the armor that the black fairy wore. Although it left a telltale mark, it did not penetrate. Raven glanced at the claw marks. She was glad the armor had protected her, that she was unharmed, at least from the claws, although her side was hurting from the impact with the ground.

Shadowfire approached the fallen Raven, who managed to rise to her feet. He raised his left claws to strike her again, but Mordecai flew toward the beast and connected a blow to his left foreleg. The blade cut deep, allowing the black blood of the dragon to flow out of the cut. The dragon roared and stared in disbelief at the wound. 'How can these blades harm me?' he roared. This had never happened before in the long life of the dragon. 'This is unthinkable!' He saw his blood flowing from the wound and let out a mighty roar, of disbelief and of anger.

Mordecai landed by Raven's side, seeing the blow she had received. 'Are you okay, Raven?' he asked.

Raven nodded. 'I am unhurt by the blow,' she answered, 'Somehow, the breastplate shielded me from his claws. I still can't believe my blade had cut through his hide.'

Mordecai nodded. 'We can't give him a chance to recover,' he said quickly, 'This is the time the Prophecy is to be fulfilled. Shadowfire shall fall.'

'No,' they heard the reply of the dragon, 'The Prophecy shall not come to pass! It cannot come to pass! I don't know how your blades could hurt me when others forged by the fairy smithies of old could not, but I will not let insignificant nobodies like you undo me!' The dragon approached them as the wounds to his legs stung and dripped black blood that hissed on the snow as it fell, melting through it.

Mordecai raised his blade. He readied his shield as Raven stood by his side and did the same. 'We can take him,' Raven told him, 'God gave us a way to destroy him.'

'For the LORD and for Arundel Haven,' Mordecai shouted.

Shadowfire unleashed his flames, as hot as he could summon.

Mordecai and Raven blocked the flames with their shields, kneeling behind them and withstanding his attack. 'I am thankful we have these shields,' Raven said, panting with the effort of the battle.

'The scriptures on the cave refer to the spiritual,' Mordecai replied, 'We must realize that it is through His might that we will overcome the dragon.'

'He can't keep this up forever,' replied Raven, a grim look of determination painting across her fair face.

The flames stopped. Once they stopped, Mordecai and Raven took to the air. Mordecai flew for the front. Shadowfire swatted the young man away before he could reach the dragon. From behind, Raven thrust her sword into the back of the monster. She was knocked off his back by the reflex of the dragon's massive wings.

Her sword remained impaled in the back of the dragon. She saw the blood flowing freely from the wound. She headed back toward him to retrieve her sword, but Shadowfire knocked her down. 'No,' cried the dragon. 'I won't let you recover your sword!'

Raven rolled to her feet and took to the air before Shadowfire unleashed another blast her way. Mordecai struggled to his feet and took to the air. Shadowfire saw his foe approach and unleashed another blast. Mordecai managed to raise his shield in time to deflect the blast, though the impact drove him back to the ground. Somehow, Mordecai kept the shield in front of him and continued to shield himself from the blast.

Raven landed on the back of the dragon and tried to recover her sword again. As she grabbed it, she, in turn, was grabbed by the vice-like grip of Shadowfire. When he did, Mordecai took to the air and slashed at his claw. It was not deep, but it was enough to make the dragon release the ebony fa*iry and roar in pain.

Mordecai was knocked down in return. He lost the grip of his sword as it fell out of his reach. Raven fell to the ground while Shadowfire focused his attack on Mordecai, trying to keep him away from his sword. Shadowfire roared. 'I will make you pay for the wounds you've inflicted upon me,' he cried, 'You will not have another opportunity to use it, I swear it!'

Shadowfire used his clinched claws to keep Mordecai away from his sword, slamming it down to the ground like a hammer. Mordecai was forced away, rolling to avoid the strikes. He did not have time to return to his feet to take to the air again. Shadowfire kept up his attack to keep his foe unbalanced. 'Raven, are you okay?' Mordecai cried.

'Forget about your worthless girlfriend,' cried Shadowfire, unleashing a blast from his jaws. Mordecai stood behind his shield to withstand the blast.

Raven rose to her feet. She saw the dragon keeping up his attack and keeping her husband from returning to his feet. 'Mordecai,' she cried.

'I've lost my sword,' Mordecai cried, 'I can't get to it!'

'Hold on, Mordecai,' Raven cried, taking to the air.

Shadowfire turned and saw Raven swooping upward. He swiped at her the best he could despite his wounds, but the fairy avoided his attacks, but it kept Raven from retrieving her sword. He felt the pain in his back from the embedded blade, still in disbelief that he could be hurt. He wasn't about to let her retrieve her sword.

It was just enough time for Mordecai to leap and recover his sword. Shadowfire saw him in time for the young man to arm himself again. 'No,' he cried, unleashing a blast in his direction, 'This cannot be happening! This can't happen!' He was still in disbelief that the blades could hurt him. He felt the blood flowing from his wounds, Raven's sword embedded in his back. When Mordecai had the dragon occupied, Raven made an effort to remove her sword from the beast's back.

With a mighty effort, she managed to dislodge it. She fell to the ground, her hands firmly holding her sword, blood gushing from the dragon's wound.

Shadowfire roared as he turned around and saw Raven with the sword in her hands. He let out another mighty roar and cried, 'This travesty has gone on long enough!'

He cried out, chanting in an unknown tongue. He started growing, his wounds healing in the process. His claws grew longer and sharper. His wings grew larger and wider, with claws protruding from the tips of his wings. He stood over fifty meters tall now, his teeth sharper. 'You managed to hurt me before, but not even your blades can hurt me now! All the powers of hell now stand behind me! What hope do you have now?'

'Even with all the powers of hell behind you, pet of Loserfer,' cried Mordecai in return, 'do not expect to prevail! The battle belongs to the LORD! The Prophecy shall come true, and you will be cast into the pits of hell where you belong!'

'You speak as a fool, Mordy Jefferson,' cried Shadowfire, 'You are a nobody, and I shall show you that you are indeed a nobody! It is you and Raven that shall fall before me!'

Mordecai turned to Raven. 'God didn't say it would be easy,' he told her, 'but our trust shall be in Him nonetheless.'

'I am with you, my husband,' panted Raven, 'no matter what!' 'And I with you, Raven my darling wife,' he said between

breaths, his chest heaving.

Shadowfire overheard their words. 'Husband and wife? You two?' he laughed, 'A human and a fairy, husband and wife?' He scoffed. 'Never before have I heard of a union between a human and a fairy but enjoy the last moments of your married lives together, short that they are! They shall end now!'

Mordecai and Raven raised their swords and shields, ready to continue to fight. 'We are in this together,' Mordecai told Raven.

'Yes,' replied Raven, 'For better or for worse, we are in this together.'

Shadowfire let out a mighty roar as Mordecai and Raven took to the air.

Prince Avondale noticed that Mordecai and Raven had led Shadowfire away. He sighed. 'We don't have to worry about Shadowfire now,' he told a captain near him. 'He is following Mordecai and Raven.'

'Are you sure they are the ones to fulfill the Prophecy?' asked the captain.

'I believe it in my heart,' he nodded, 'Now we must focus on beating back these humans and keep them from reaching Arundel Haven!'

Prince Avondale winded his horn. Fairies were seen diving from the air, avoiding gunfire, and diving toward the soldiers. Swords drawn, they attacked the soldiers, who used their weapons to deflect the blows. A few fairymen were shot in the back by other soldiers before the rest retreated.

From the chopper, President Farouk and Dr. Von Braun watched as the battle raged. Neither of them smiled as they saw the battle. 'They are more formidable than I thought,' Dr. Von Braun said grimly, 'I thought your troops would be able to handle them.'

'Apparently, Major Moore didn't take into account the capability of flight that the fairies have,' frowned President Farouk, 'He told me that his men were the best in the military.'

'Perhaps we have underestimated them,' replied Dr. Von Braun scowling, 'We need to find Arundel Haven and capture the Queen. Once we do, I can expose and reveal the existence of fairies.'

'I did not expect it to be this difficult,' groaned President Farouk.

'I do not see Shadowfire,' Dr. Von Braun observed.

'I thought I saw the boy and the fairy Raven earlier,' replied President Farouk, 'It looks like they were wearing armor, had a sword and shield in their hands.'

'Ha! Little good that would do them,' laughed Dr. Von Braun, 'Shadowfire told us that no sword, spear, or arrow can bite him. What hope do these fools have against him?'

'He still fears the Prophecy he told us about,' President Farouk replied, 'I cannot help but wonder what if this prophecy does come true?'

'I think we should worry about finding Queen Cymbaline,' Dr. Von Braun said, 'Make our way to Arundel Haven and find her. The four men we have still on board should suffice.'

President Farouk stared and saw one of the fairies enter a large tent. He turned to Dr. Von Braun and pointed at the tent. 'One of the fairy soldiers went inside of there,' he said. 'It can't be the Prince in there since I saw him in the battle.'

'And you think Queen Cymbaline is inside?'

'Only one way to find out,' President Farouk mused.

"There are too many fairies in the area,' replied Dr. Von Braun, 'but still…'

President Farouk walked to the passenger area where four soldiers were awaiting his orders. 'Commander Rodham,' he told the highest-ranking officer there, 'I want you and your men to check out the largest of the tents in the area. Take whoever is inside there as prisoners and bring them back here.'

Commander Rodham saluted. 'As you wish, Mr. President,' he replied. They headed out of the helicopter as both President Farouk and Dr. Von Braun returned to the cockpit and watched the battle.

Prince Avondale and his army were driven back by the approach of the armies. The fairies who had spent their arrows drew their swords and prepared for the advancement. Those still with arrows continued to shoot until some of them had spent theirs. 'We don't have many arrows left, your highness,' Captain Shem cried, 'We're at a disadvantage now with the weapons they have.'

'And they're driving us away from the camp and Queen Cymbaline,' frowned Prince Avondale, 'I don't want to take any chances, whether they know she is there or not! Their projectiles from their weapons are small, but they seem to be deadly.'

'If we can, we can retrieve what arrows we can if we have an opportunity and reuse them.'

'Just be careful,' said Prince Avondale, 'We can't leave Queen Cymbaline defenseless, whether they know if she's there or not.'

'I will take eight fairymen and fly over to the camp and try and keep the humans from finding her,' said Captain Shem.

Prince Avondale nodded. 'Just be careful,' he reiterated, 'I will join you as soon as I am able.'

Captain Shem took eight of his fairymen and took to the trees. Jax, Derreck, and Captain Haggai joined Prince Avondale. Derreck let loose an arrow and managed to hit one of the soldiers in the throat. 'I'm worried about the Queen, your highness,' Derreck said.

'I know,' Prince Avondale replied, 'I have sent Captain Shem and eight of his solders back to camp to try and protect her.'

'We can't do much against their weapons except to dodge them,' Captain Haggai said grimly, 'They come in faster than we can fly!'

'I know,' replied Prince Avondale, 'but flight is the only advantage we have over them, and we must try and use it if we can.'

'We can try and lead them away from the camp,' Captain Haggai suggested, 'keep their focus on us so they won't have time to search for the Queen.'

'We must lead them to Tarragon Hill,' cried Prince Avondale, 'We must send word to the other captains that we are to assemble at Tarragon Hill. Captain Tebar will need to be reinforced. We can make our stand there.'

'I will send word,' Jax said.

'I'm coming with you,' Derreck said. Both fairies took to the air and headed toward Tarragon Hill. As they flew, some of the soldiers aimed their guns at the two fairies. One of the bullets struck Derreck in the right shoulder. He spun out of control. Jax heard his cry and shouted, 'Derreck!'

He dived toward his friend as he hit the ground. Derreck was crying out in pain. Jax took his right arm and draped it over his shoulder. 'Can you get up?' he asked.

'My shoulder is badly hurt,' Derreck cried.

'Can you fly?' asked Jax.

'I think so,' Derreck answered, gritting his teeth in pain.

Soldiers continued to fire. Jax helped Derreck as both took to the air. Derreck did his best to stay in the air as shots were being fired. Prince Avondale and those who still had arrows fired at the soldiers in retaliation. Two humans fell. Those without arrows attacked with their swords drawn, trying to buy the two fairies time to reach the others as they drew back.

Two fairies beside Prince Avondale fell as they drew back. He winded his horn as many of the fairymen that remained took to the air while the others that remained on the ground continued to shoot their bows.

Captain Haggai remained on the ground, shooting what arrows he had to cover Prince Avondale. One of the soldiers threw a grenade in his direction and caught him in the blast. The captain fell dead in the snow.

'What devilry is this?' one of the fairies cried. 'A ball that explodes?'

'Fall back,' another fairy cried, 'We must warn Prince Avondale that Captain Haggai has fallen!'

'No,' another cried as the first fairyman was cut down, 'We must buy a little more time for Prince Avondale!'

He was then cut down by another grenade that was tossed his way. The rest of the fairies took to the air before another grenade was thrown.

Prince Avondale and the fairies with him retreated and joined the other fairies who had beaten back the group that had assailed them. Captain Tebar, Taris, and Roosevelt flew toward him. 'We just got word from Jax and Derreck,' Captain Tebar said, 'Derreck was struck in the shoulder from one of the shots the humans had taken. Jax is tending to him.'

'The humans are on their way here,' Prince Avondale cried, 'I hope our foes will follow us and leave Queen Cymbaline.'

'She's not left unprotected, is she?' Captain Tebar gasped.

'No,' answered Prince Avondale, 'I have sent nine fairymen to watch over her and protect her if need be. I knew it wasn't a good idea for her to join us. I had counseled her against this.'

'Maybe so,' Taris replied, 'but I think she still feels bad about letting us down when it comes to Shadowfire. Where is the dragon?'

'Mordecai and Raven have led Shadowfire away from us,' Prince Avondale answered, 'That's one less problem for us to worry about. My concern is to protect my sister and beat back the evil humans.'

'I'm ready for them, your highness,' Roosevelt said with determination, 'I want so much to see Starla and Twila again that I will do whatever it takes to see that it happens.'

'And I plan to make sure you do, and the others in my charge,' Prince Avondale replied grimly, 'We fight for your family, Roosevelt, and we fight for my sister, and for all of Arundel Haven! Here, we shall make our stand! The humans have gotten this far, but they shall come no further! They shall regret ever trying to find Arundel Haven!'

They heard a horn being sounded. 'They're coming,' cried Captain Tebar, 'The humans are here! Get ready!'

'Take cover,' cried Prince Avondale. 'Our only hope may be quick strikes from the air for those who don't have arrows! Those with arrows, stay hidden until the humans appear! The rest of you, fly! We'll attack from the air!' He and many of the fairies took to the air.

Taris stared at Roosevelt and gave him the arrows he had left. 'You are a better shot than I am, Roosevelt,' he told him, drawing his sword, 'I am a better with a sword and a spear than arrows. I will go with Prince Avondale.'

'God guide you, my friend,' replied Roosevelt, placing his hand on his shoulder before Taris took to the air, knowing it may be the last time he may see him.

As Taris flew, his thoughts went to Mordecai's sister, Cece. He couldn't explain why, but since her arrival in Arundel Haven he had grown close to her. He sighed. He determined somehow, someway that he would see her again.

It gave him another reason to fight, not just for his Queen and prince, but for Cece as well.

The snow began to fall harder as they flew. As Taris joined the others, they fought to remain in the air despite the falling snow. Prince Avondale and Captain Tebar led the charge as they circled around and then descended upon the oncoming hosts, penetrating their ranks with swords drawn, pressing their attack.

The humans used the butts of their large guns as weapons once they had a fairy close at hand. Some who were not in close hand-to-hand combat shot at whatever fairies they could fire at until they were engaged close up.

Prince Avondale was in close combat with a heavily-built human, who was trying to disarm him. When Prince Avondale was knocked to the ground, the man pointed his gun at him and was about to shoot when Taris ran him through with his blade. The man dropped his gun and fell lifeless to the ground. Prince Avondale sighed. 'Thank you, Taris,' he said.

'We can't afford to lose you, your highness,' Taris said, panting.

Human blood speckled both his clothes and his face.

Prince Avondale rose to his feet. 'We've still got a long way to go,' he replied.

Captain Shem led the eight fairies back to camp where the helicopters stood. They saw four men heading for the tent where Queen Cymbaline was. Two of the fairies took arrows and bent their bows. They let their arrows fly.

One of them was struck by the two arrows. Seymour was struck in the throat by another. As he fell dead, his companion Wilfred cried out his name. He and the three turned their guns toward the approaching fairies and opened fire. Two fairies were struck and fell from the sky. The rest scattered. Commander Rodham turned to the other two and said, 'Go inside the tent and capture whatever fairy is in there. Hurry!'

'But what about the other fairies?' one of them asked.

'I will take care of them,' replied Commander Rodham, 'Now go, hurry!'

The two men did as they were told. Commander Rodham fired at the remaining fairies, hitting two of them. Captain Shem dived toward Commander Rodham and knocked him down. They wrestled in the snow, each trying to get the advantage over the other. The man who had been struck by two arrows managed to get to his knees and began to fire at the other fairies in the air. He managed to hit two more before he succumbed to his injuries.

Commander Rodham knocked Captain Shem off him and grabbed his gun. He hit him with the butt of his weapon and fired a fatal shot at the fairyman. He fell dead in the snow. The remaining four tried to draw closer, but the human continued to fire. One more was hit.

At that moment, the two soldiers stepped out with Queen Cymbaline bound. The remaining three cried out and to the horror of the Queen, two of them were shot down by one of her captors. When the last one flew out of sight, Commander Rodham gazed at the Queen. 'You must be the ruler of Arundel Haven,' he said, a smile lighting his face.

'Let me go,' cried Queen Cymbaline, 'You have no right to be here!'

'You have a date with President Farouk,' said Commander Rodham, 'and a certain person who has been seeking your kind for a long time.'

Queen Cymbaline's face turned hard. 'So, Dr. Von Braun is here too,' she said, her face hard, 'Mordecai has warned me about him.'

'Who the blazes is this Mordecai?' asked Commander Rodham.

'He is not of your concern,' Queen Cymbaline snapped.

'Take her to the President,' Commander Rodham told them.

The two men were about to force Queen Cymbaline forward when she tried to take to the air. The two soldiers immediately grabbed her and threw her to the ground pointing their guns at her. 'I wouldn't suggest you try that again, queenie,' Commander Rodham warned, 'You see what these babies can do, they can and will kill!'

Queen Cymbaline stared with anger at her captors but said nothing. They grabbed her arms and headed back to the helicopter where President Farouk and Dr. Von Braun awaited them.

Prince Avondale took to the air and retreated to the other side of the hill as they fought the humans. Others with him retreated as well but were shot down. On the ground, Derreck watched as the battle raged. He had trouble moving his left arm because of the bullet in his shoulder. 'I wish it didn't hurt so bad,' he told his friend, Jax.

'The others are retreating,' Jax replied, He saw that Roosevelt and the others who had arrows had not taken to the air and had drawn their own swords. 'They must have spent their arrows,' Jax said, 'but how do these humans seem to have an endless supply?'

'I don't know,' frowned Derreck, shaking his head, 'but I think we better get out of here while we still can.'

Jax took to the air, as did Derreck, but before they could fly any higher, one of the men shot Jax in the head and in his back. He fell to the ground in a lifeless heap.

Derreck cried out when he saw this. He cried out his friend's name and landed beside him. 'Jax! Jax!' he cried, trying to shake the fairy.

Jax did not respond. He laid motionless on the ground, his eyes glazed.

Derreck cried out in despair and anger. Raising his sword with his good arm, he flew toward the approaching group of men. He swung his sword with all his rage and strength, cutting down two of the men. 'Shoot him,' cried one of the soldiers. 'This fairy is mad!'

'You will pay for killing my friend,' cried Derreck, dodging the blows from his enemies. His mind was clouded by the death of his friend, overcome by rage and grief. Two more fell by his blade as he continued to fight.

One of the soldiers caught Derreck in the face with the butt of his weapon. Two more fired their weapons, aiming for the chest of the fairyman. The shots pushed him back, he clutched his chest before falling to the ground.

Derreck laid lifeless and bloodied on the snow-covered ground, a pool of blood seeping around him, turning the snow a deep red.

At that moment, Taris, with six other fairymen, dived from the sky and caught the human soldiers off-balance. Taris had seen the fall of Derreck and had his spear in his hand. He thrust it through the man who shot Derreck in the head. The other fairymen took care of the soldiers around them. Taris knelt at the lifeless form of Derreck. He sighed, shaking his head. 'Poor Lavender will grieve when she hears of your fall, my friend,' he said sadly, 'Rest in peace, Derreck,' he whispered as he closed the fallen fairy's eyes.

'We found Jax, Commander Taris,' one of the fairies said.

'Is he still alive?' asked Taris.

'No, sir,' answered the fairy soldier. 'He is dead.'

Taris flew toward the lifeless body of Jax. He saw the blood stains in the snow from the wounds. He knelt there motionless in memory of his fallen comrade.

A bullet whizzed by and hit a nearby tree. Taris quickly jumped to his feet and signaled for the other fairies to take to the air. As they obeyed the command, the thirteen soldiers that had appeared continued to fire at them.

But a group of fairies led by Roosevelt with swords drawn dived from the sky and attacked them. Two humans fell by Roosevelt's swords. Though caught by surprise, they retaliated enough to kill three fairymen before Roosevelt killed the last of the thirteen. He sighed. 'I hate war,' he said softly, 'Why does it have to come down to this?'

He looked down at Jax's lifeless body. He sighed. 'Much blood was spilled to defend Arundel Haven,' he lamented, 'I pray that the sacrifice will not be in vain.' His face turned hard. 'Not if I can help it!' he cried out in a mighty voice. 'The humans shall proceed no further! No quarter asked, no quarter given! For Queen Cymbaline and for Arundel Haven!'

The fairies led the human soldiers to a heavily wooded area where they would have somewhat better protection from the bullets. Prince Avondale had his back against a great oak as he kept a lookout for the approach of human soldiers. Some took to the treetops of some evergreens, hiding themselves amid the branches and the foliage. Prince Avondale had no more arrows in his quiver as he looked at his sword. He and the others waited for the approach of the humans.

At that moment, there was an explosion not too far away from the fairy prince. The fairy behind it was knocked down, blood covering his body. More grenades were thrown at the trees. The explosion blew the fairies hiding nearby from their hiding place. Some of the fairies hiding took to the air. Some of them were shot down as a result. Those fairies who remained hidden like Prince Avondale waited until the humans were close enough before they made their move.

When a bullet hit the tree that Prince Avondale was hiding behind, he blew his horn and flew from his hiding place. The other fairies rushed from their hiding places and began their attack.

Some soldiers fired wildly but missed the oncoming fairy army and were slain. Prince Avondale, with Taris by his side, fought their way through the ranks of their enemies and were quickly joined by other fairies. The humans began to retreat and to regroup.

Somehow, Prince Avondale figured they would do that. He blew his horn and commanded to press their advantage. 'Don't give the humans a chance to regroup,' he cried, 'Keep them off balance!'

Fairies scattered when the soldiers fired their guns. Some remained to try and buy time for the others, trying to delay the fairy advance. Two fairymen were shot down.

'Keep away from the fire of their thunder sticks,' cried Prince Avondale, 'Keep flying!'

At that moment, Prince Avondale saw a single fairyman flying toward him. As he descended, a bullet caught him in the upper chest area as he fell to the ground. Instinctively, Prince Avondale ran toward him. He recognized the fairy as one from the company of Captain Shem who were commanded to protect Queen Cymbaline. He suddenly feared the worst. He knelt beside him.

'Forgive me, your highness,' he said in a weak voice, 'We have failed.'

'Where's your company?' asked Prince Avondale, 'Why aren't you protecting Queen Cymbaline?'

'She had been captured by the humans,' he rasped, 'Captain Shem is dead, and I was the only one to survive. I have failed you, failed my Queen!'

Prince Avondale looked up grimly. He sounded his horn again. He immediately took to the air. Roosevelt joined him. 'Keep fighting,' he told Roosevelt, 'Queen Cymbaline has been taken by the humans!'

'You will need help, your highness,' Roosevelt replied as Taris joined them.

'What happened?' asked Taris.

'The humans have your Queen,' Prince Avondale answered, 'I am going to rescue her. Go lead our troops!'

'But surely you won't face the humans alone,' Taris gasped.

'I will have to,' replied Prince Avondale, 'I need you two to stay here and keep the humans from finding Arundel Haven.'

'I must counsel you against this, your highness,' Taris objected. 'You can't face the humans alone. Let us go with you.'

'No,' replied Prince Avondale sharply. He then flew back toward the camp. Before Taris and Roosevelt could start off after him, bullets whizzed past their heads. They flew in different directions and with a group of fairy warriors who had joined them, charged the ranks as they dodged the bullets.

Commander Moore and his two men took Queen Cymbaline inside the helicopter. As they stepped inside, Moore headed toward the cockpit and told the men, 'Don't let her get away! Keep a close watch and hold on her.'

He headed into the cockpit.

Seconds later, President Farouk and Dr. Von Braun appeared, followed by Commander Moore. Dr. Von Braun had a smile on his face, a smile of satisfaction. He then turned toward Wilfred and noticed that Seymour was missing. 'Where is Seymour?' he asked Wilfred.

'Seymour is dead, Doctor,' Wilfred answered, 'He had been struck down by a fairy arrow. I hope this is all worth it!'

'Indeed it is,' answered Dr. Von Braun. He stood face to face with the Fairy Queen. 'After all these years,' the geneticist said. 'I have looked forward to seeing a fairy with my own eyes.'

'Dr. Von Braun, I presume,' Queen Cymbaline said as she frowned.

'Oh, so you have heard of me?' Dr. Von Braun smiled, 'So, you are the ruler of Arundel Haven, are you not? Queen Cymbaline, I believe.'

'No doubt Shadowfire told you my name and about me,' said Queen Cymbaline grimly, 'Mordecai had told me of your association with the dragon.'

'And no doubt Mordy told you about me as well,' replied Dr. Von Braun, 'I have dreamed of this for so many years since I had read of your home of Arundel Haven.'

'How could you have known?'

'A book I had found in my days at Oxford,' explained Dr. Von Braun, 'Even before I met Shadowfire and Mordy. I have kept this a secret until I have found empiric proof of your people's existence, and now that I have found it, I plan to go public with it, and you, my dear Queen, shall be the evidence.'

'I have worked hard for many years to keep the existence of my people a secret,' replied Queen Cymbaline, 'This is a great evil to my people. We will never have peace again if you expose us.'

'All I care about is money and fame,' said Dr. Von Braun apathetically, 'I had offered Mordy Jefferson six million dollars to even tell me even news of the existence of fairies, but what does he do? He turns me down flat! I found out why when my men caught him and the fairy maiden, Raven, in the woods in each other's arms. Such a union is forbidden, is it not?'

'Why should I tell you?' snapped Queen Cymbaline.

'It is too bad, however, that both Mordy and Raven will fall before Shadowfire,' said Dr. Von Braun, 'Shadowfire has told me about some prophecy that states they are the ones who are supposed to be the end of Shadowfire. It's a fool's hope.'

'Believe that if you must,' shot back Queen Cymbaline, 'God made a promise he told to my foremother, Queen Hephzibah, and this is the day that it is to be fulfilled.'

President Farouk laughed. 'So you foolishly believe.'

Queen Cymbaline narrowed her eyes at the president. 'And you must be the President of the United States, am I right?'

'So, the boy has told you, I presume,' replied President Farouk.

'Would your people not be ashamed to hear what you are doing?' asked the Fairy Queen, 'or do you only care about money and power?'

'They would think Arundel Haven as a myth,' replied President

Farouk, 'I plan to claim your kingdom as a part of the United States. You will be subject to the laws of my people and override your laws.'

'No,' cried Queen Cymbaline, 'My people will not submit!'

'Your worst nightmare come true, from what Shadowfire has told us,' Dr. Von Braun sneered, 'that your people be exposed, and your land taken in the name of the President.'

'We are a sovereign people,' shot back Queen Cymbaline, 'You cannot do this! Mordecai told me that your House, Senate, and Congress would not approve of this.'

'It shows him what he knows,' laughed President Farouk in contempt, 'One, they will not know about this, and two, if they did, I have more people who follow what I say than those who don't. They would be overridden.'

'My people will not submit,' reiterated Queen Cymbaline, 'We will not submit to your authority. The fairies of Arundel Haven are loyal to me and my house!'

'We shall see,' smiled President Farouk.

At that moment, two soldiers brought Prince Avondale into the helicopter. He had a gash on his head and some blood from the wound that was inflicted by one of the soldiers. He saw his sister and ran to her, embracing her. The two solders kept their guns on them both.

'Bind this fairy,' President Farouk told them. To Prince Avondale he said, 'Apparently, you are part of the royal house. Husband, perhaps?'

'I am her brother, human,' growled Prince Avondale, 'I command you to let us go.'

'Not a chance, fairy,' laughed Dr. Von Braun, 'You both have saved us the trouble of finding you. We were to fly out to Arundel Haven and capture your Queen, but since you are both here, there is no need as of yet. Once this battle is over and we have won, we will take you to our world and your existence will be revealed to the public.'

'We will not surrender, human,' protested Prince Avondale defiantly, 'We will take care of your army, and Mordecai and Raven will slay Shadowfire as the Prophecy states.'

'The prophecy?' laughed Dr. Von Braun, 'The prophecy, you say? How? Shadowfire told me that no weapon your fairy smithies have forged could penetrate his armor. How long have you tried, 150 years? Oh, yes! That is what Shadowfire has told us. What makes you think that Mordy and Raven will prevail?'

'God made a promise, and He never breaks His promises,' retorted Prince Avondale, 'None of His promises have ever failed, and He never fails to keep a promise that He made!'

'What makes you think your God can deliver you or would deliver Shadowfire into the hands of two nobodies?' retorted President Farouk.

'Mordecai Jefferson is no nobody,' shot back Queen Cymbaline, 'though I distrusted him when he was first brought to Arundel Haven.'

'When Raven's friends had him taken away, I remember,' replied Dr. Von Braun, 'when Cece's friends told me. He did not keep your secret well, did he?'

'It was not Mordecai's fault,' shot back Queen Cymbaline, eager to defend the human, 'He was careful with our secret, though Cece's friends weren't at that instant. Mordecai was a stranger when he first came to me, but now he is a dear brother, precious in my eyes! He accepted, though scared he was, that he was the one the Prophecy had spoken of, out of love he took it upon himself. Soon, you shall see the fulfillment of what God promised so long ago!'

Both Queen Cymbaline and Prince Avondale were bound and held fast to one of the seats. Their arms and legs were chained to the posts of the seat to prevent their escape. They watched as President Farouk and Dr. Von Braun drank their beverages from their bar, Von Braun a scotch and President Farouk a whiskey.

Queen Cymbaline and Prince Avondale remained silent, a grim look upon their faces.

Shadowfire let loose his flames as Mordecai and Raven scattered. He let out a mighty roar and swatted at the two with his massive claws. Mordecai was nearly engulfed in the gaping jaws of the dragon. 'This may be harder than ever to bring him down,' he said quietly.

'Don't expect us to give up, dragon, even though you are bigger than before,' cried Raven, avoiding another swipe.

'Beg for mercy, and I may spare the both of you,' cried Shadowfire.

'Not an option,' cried Mordecai, avoiding another swipe, 'We know the tender mercies of the wicked are cruel, and there is none in you. We know you will destroy us no matter what!'

'And how would you know that?' retorted Shadowfire.

Without another word, Mordecai delivered a blow to the back of the dragon. Though the hide of Shadowfire was thicker than before, the blade still cut through, but not as deep; still, a little blood was drawn. Shadowfire grabbed a large tree, uprooted it and used it to try and strike down his foes.

Mordecai and Raven continued to dodge the blows as best they could. Raven swung her sword at the hind leg of the dragon, driving as deep as she could. Shadowfire roared out in pain, but Raven managed to pull out her sword. 'We know our blades can cut him,' she cried, 'but not deep enough!'

'I kind of found that out, Raven,' Mordecai cried as he dodged another blow. Out of frustration, Shadowfire caught Mordecai with a blast of flames. Although the shield protected him from the flames, the impact caused him to fall to the ground. As he fell, Shadowfire continued his assault. The force of the blast was like a giant wielding a sledgehammer, swinging it with all his might with each crushing blow.

Raven drove her sword on the top of the dragon's head. The blade bit deep. Shadowfire bellowed in pain. As he tossed his head, Raven fell away and toward the ground. She managed to keep flittering her wings as her descent was slowed and she remained suspended in the air.

Her sword remained embedded on top of Shadowfire's head. With his massive claws, he pulled the sword out and chanted in an unknown tongue.

To the dragon's dismay, the sword just glowed brightly in response but nothing else.

Again Shadowfire chanted a spell. Again nothing. Brightly the sword glowed brighter.

He lost his grip on the sword as it tumbled down to the ground. Shadowfire cried out in pain as if the sword had burned his claws. Mordecai tried to retrieve his sword, which stopped glowing, but a blow from the dragon caught him. As he was struck, he found himself falling to the ground. His body hit hard as he landed, knocking the wind out of him for a moment.

Shadowfire stared at the wound in his paw and growled. He stared in disbelief. *How? How could this be possible? Even in my most powerful form, they can still hurt me?* His thoughts went to the Prophecy itself. Even though he hid it, fear continued to grow strong in his heart. He gnashed his teeth and stared at Mordecai. He let out a mighty roar, if only for the sole effort of hiding the fear in his heart. He let loose another blast of flames.

Mordecai had the presence of mind to curl himself underneath the shield as the flames engulfed him. The young teenager could feel the intense heat and despite the cold, he was sweating profusely. Around the flames, the ice began to melt as the dragon continued to spew flames at Mordecai.

'Mordecai!' Raven cried. She grabbed her sword from the ground and flew toward the face of the dragon. She slashed at his face, causing Shadowfire to cease his attack as he covered his wounded face. He felt the blood flowing from the strike as he turned toward Raven. He let out a roar as he missed with a swipe.

That gave Mordecai the opportunity to roll to his feet. He rose from the ground as quickly as he could and grabbed his sword. He took to the air and joined Raven. Without a word, they flew high into the air.

Shadowfire followed them, spreading his massive wings.

He overtook the couple and tried to catch them, but they managed to elude his grasp. They flew down toward the ground and headed to a wooded area.

'He's faster than before,' Mordecai said to Raven, 'No use outflying him.'

'Why are we heading into the woods?' Raven asked, 'He is sure to use enchanted flames to flush us out.'

'I know,' nodded Mordecai, 'It's safe to assume that. We do need a little bit of time.'

Shadowfire pursued them as they flew into the woods. He laughed briefly before his face turned hard. *Fools. Do you not know that it failed you the last time? You have only sealed your doom; I shall make sure of that!*

Inside the woods, Mordecai and Raven landed as they saw the enchanted flames appearing around them. 'His armor is too thick to do any real damage,' Mordecai said, 'We can hurt him, but not fatally I'm afraid.'

Raven looked around at the flames. 'How then, can we slay him?' she asked, disregarding the enchanted flames.

'Maybe one of two ways,' answered Mordecai, 'We can go for his throat and hope we can cut him deep enough to incapacitate him, or else we have to go down the very throat of the dragon.'

Raven sighed. 'I am not thrilled about the latter choice,' she groaned, 'I don't have the desire to be devoured.'

'That's not my plan,' Mordecai replied, 'but he is vulnerable on the inside. We can decapitate him from the inside if we have to. I am willing to go with plan A for the time being, but if we have to, we'll take the matter down his throat!'

Raven sighed. 'If that's the only way,' she sighed as the flames closed in, 'I guess I'm with you on this.'

'Our shields will protect us from the flames when we break through,' Mordecai said, 'but we need to mark where he is, surprise him if we can. Remember, Raven, the LORD is with us. Like Twila said, "God promised, and God always keeps His promises."'

Raven raised her sword. Mordecai did the same. As they came together, both swords glowed together with a bright light, growing brighter. It lit up the area, drowning out the light of the enchanted flames. 'For the LORD, for Queen Cymbaline and Arundel Haven,' she cried.

'For the LORD, Queen Cymbaline and Arundel Haven,' Mordecai echoed.

They heard the mocking voice of the dragon. 'Fools,' he roared. 'Your God shall not deliver you out of my hands! Both of you shall die by my claws, so I swear to Ashtaroth!'

Mordecai pointed in the direction of where the dragon's voice came from. They readied their shields, holding it in front of them. Mordecai pointed at the direction he wanted to go. 'Now, Raven,' he cried. Both ran and took to the air, flying low. They crashed through the enchanted flames, their shields in front of them and darted out of the woods and into the air.

Shadowfire turned around in time to find Mordecai and Raven turning around and flying toward him. He let loose another barrage of flames. Although their shields protected them, the force of the blast knocked them out of the air as they both fell to the ground.

Raven growled. 'This is getting real old, real quick,' she said, exasperated.

'I couldn't agree more,' frowned Mordecai, quickly rising to his feet, 'I hate it myself!'

Shadowfire grabbed Mordecai as he rose to his feet. Raven cried out as she saw her husband in the vice-like grip of the dragon. She took to the air and thrust her sword into his claw. Shadowfire cried out and released his hold on the young human. She then flew toward the throat of the dragon and tried to deliver a blow, but she was knocked to the ground.

Mordecai flew toward Raven to aid her, but he was knocked down from behind by the mighty claws of the dragon. He found himself rolling to the ground again. He kept rolling for a couple of seconds before jumping to his feet. He quickly took back to the air just before incoming flames could reach him.

Raven managed to roll to her feet and took to the air again. She joined Mordecai as they avoided the blast. 'He's not going to allow us to get close to his throat,' she told him.

'Obvious to see,' groaned Mordecai, 'Well, there's always plan B.'

'Not my choice, sweetheart,' frowned the ebony fairy.

'Believe me, darling,' Mordecai replied, 'Not one of my favorites, either, but it may be the best chance to destroy him.'

'Would our shields be able to handle the blast?' asked Raven.

Shadowfire interrupted their conversation with a blast of flames. He then lifted his forelegs and chanted in an unknown tongue. As he chanted, the winds began to pick up and the snow turned into a blizzard, a snowstorm. The winds picked up to hurricane strength, which made it hard for Mordecai and Raven to stay in the air. 'Now I definitely do not like winter,' she grumbled.

'Being a Florida boy,' replied Mordecai, 'I'm not that thrilled with it either!'

Raven was knocked out of the sky as he winds drove her to the ground. Mordecai found himself doing the same. He was sent into a nearby tree. He cried out in pain. 'Mordecai,' Raven cried.

Mordecai struggled to get a grip on the tree, but the ice covering made it impossible to do so. He fell to the ground near Raven, who was trying to keep on her feet. 'Never has there been a snowstorm like this,' Raven cried.

'It's not natural,' Mordecai shouted as he tried to mark where Shadowfire was. 'Shadowfire summoned it with his sorcery! We can't and we won't give up!'

'We can try flying with the wind,' Raven cried, 'Glide like the eagles do, ride with the currents of the wind!'

Mordecai nodded. 'Even with the wind at our backs, I don't think we could outfly the dragon, but still, we could try to use it to our advantage. It's time we take this battle down his throat!'

Raven sighed. 'Baby, I was afraid you were going to say that,' she grimaced.

Mordecai and Raven took to the air, letting the winds carry them. Shadowfire saw them and took to the air. He opened his jaws seeking to devour them but missed when an updraft caught the two and lifted them high into the air. He growled.

Raven felt cold all over. The combination of the wind and the temperature caused her body to shake. Mordecai's body did the same. 'Temperatures are dropping, Mordecai,' she cried.

'I can feel it, too,' Mordecai exclaimed, 'We can't give up now!'

'I'm not talking about giving up,' Raven frowned as they avoided the jaws of the dragon.

'Maybe you should, the both of you,' cried Shadowfire, making an attempt to grab Mordecai, 'I grow tired of this!'

Mordecai turned around, taking a swipe at Shadowfire's throat. Unfortunately, his blow was not deep enough, although it hurt the dragon. The young man growled and allowed an updraft to carry him away. 'I grow tired of these games,' the dragon snarled.

'You're not the only one, pet of *Loserfer*,' cried Mordecai.

'Funny, doesn't seem like a game to me,' shouted Raven.

'I'm not crazy about it either, dear,' Mordecai frowned.

Mordecai and Raven were carried further up by a draft while another one caused Shadowfire to descend. They heard the dragon curse. 'What devilry is this?' they heard the dragon cry.

Mordecai and Raven saw the dragon struggle to recover and then saw him stare up at them. Shadowfire spread his massive wings and with great difficulty flew after them. One gust managed to blow the dragon off balance. 'Seems his magic is working against him now,' Mordecai said, 'or else the LORD is sending a blast to knock him off balance.'

'Or both,' Raven grinned grimly.

Mordecai nodded. They saw a blast of flames being sent their way, but another gust blew the young couple out of the way of the blast. They allowed the gusts to carry them wheresoever it blew. Again, Shadowfire sent another blast, but again, Mordecai and Raven were helped out by the gusts, carrying them out of danger.

Another gust carried Mordecai and Raven higher and higher into the clouds. They heard the curses of the dragon as another gust blew him off balance. 'I am glad we are being helped out here,' Raven said, 'but for how long?'

'Shadowfire is not going to give up, that's for sure,' Mordecai replied, 'It's a safe bet to assume that.'

Just then, another gust blew them downward, falling close to the dragon. They struggled to stay in control, to try and ride with the gusts, but another gust came from the opposite direction and were driving them down. It wasn't long until they were too close to the dragon, who tried to grab them, but another gust had pushed the couple away. As another gust carried them up again, Raven gave out a sigh of relief. 'That was too close,' she said.

'I feel like a yo-yo,' Mordecai frowned, 'and I don't like it.'

'A yo-yo?' Raven asked.

'I'll tell you what it is when we survive this,' Mordecai told her, 'but first, we've got to take care of Shadowfire.'

A series of gusts carried them up again, high into the clouds. Suddenly, the breezes stopped. The swords started to glow. A bright light increased and expanded, surrounding and covering the forms of Mordecai and Raven. They heard the roars of Shadowfire as they looked down. They slowly brought their swords together as the light covered their bodies, their forms lost amid the light.

Shadowfire roared and belched forth more fire. Mordecai and Raven faced the dragon and, without a word, flew straight into the flames, becoming engulfed. The flames grew more intense, but it did not stop Mordecai and Raven. With full speed, they continued toward the mouth of the dragon.

They entered amid the inferno. Once they entered, the flames stopped. Shadowfire cried out in pain. He fell from the sky, spiraling down toward the ground.

Before he struck the ground, an intense light exploded from the dragon's chest. The light faded, and Mordecai and Raven emerged, unscathed by the flames. The earth shook as Shadowfire fell lifeless to the ground. His head landed with a thud as his body shrunk down to his original size.

The winds died down, the snow decreased and fell at a steady pace. The air did not feel as cold as it did before. Mordecai and Raven landed and stared at the dragon's lifeless form. They dropped their sword and shield and embraced each other while kissing. 'We did it,' Raven cried, 'Baby, we did it!'

Mordecai kissed Raven. 'God did it,' he cried, 'He did what He said He promised he would do. The Prophecy of Queen Hephzibah has finally been fulfilled!'

Raven laughed as Mordecai kissed her. 'I can't believe that after all these years, Shadowfire is dead! God has delivered Shadowfire into our hands!'

Suddenly, Mordecai's face hardened as he released Raven. 'Baby, what's wrong?' she asked.

'Queen Cymbaline,' he cried, 'She's in trouble! I can feel it!' He picked up his sword and shield. 'I feel it in my spirit!'

Raven's face hardened as well. 'Dr. Von Braun has found her?' she asked.

'I sense it,' Mordecai cried, 'Somehow, I can feel it.'

Raven picked up her sword and shield and took to the air. Mordecai joined her as they flew back in the direction of camp.

At that moment, the battlefield was hit by a blizzard, with winds reaching hurricane speed. Fairies in the air were caught and were tossed about, some landing on the ground. The humans were also adversely affected. They fought to keep on their feet as they tried to keep sight of the fairies. Taris was knocked to the ground. 'A snowstorm?' he cried.

'Shadowfire's doing,' Roosevelt cried, trying to remain on his feet, 'It has to be! This is not natural!'

'No use trying to take to the air,' cried Taris, 'It would be almost impossible for us to fly.'

'Get behind one of the bigger trees,' cried Roosevelt.

They struggled to find a tree to shield themselves from the hurricane force winds. One soldier took a shot at Taris, but his aim was affected by the winds, and the bullet struck twenty meters in front of him. Taris managed to scramble to his feet and duck behind a big tree beside where Roosevelt was behind for cover. 'Arrows will do us no good, even if I had any left,' he cried out, 'We have to either wait until the winds die down or the humans draw close. Either way, we are at a disadvantage.'

'I wonder if Prince Avondale managed to rescue Queen Cymbaline?'

'I hope so,' Roosevelt sighed, 'I remember Mordecai telling me some bad things about Dr. Von Braun and the President running his country.'

Two tried to throw grenades, but the winds caught them and blew them away from their targets. They struck harmlessly and detonated where no fairy was. 'At least the wind is affecting the way they throw their thunderballs,' Taris shouted over the roaring winds.

'But they will adjust, I'm sure,' cried Roosevelt, 'We can't stay here.'

'We have no choice,' cried Taris, 'To take to the air is out of the question as long as the wind blows at this strength.'

'Any suggestions, my friend?' Roosevelt asked.

'I wish I had one,' Taris said grimly.

A handful of human soldiers managed to rise to their feet and press forward despite the winds. One of them took a grenade and tossed it. The wind carried it to one of the nearby trees and exploded. The fairyman hiding behind it was caught in the blast and perished.

Roosevelt growled. 'I was afraid of that. There are times I wish I wasn't right, and this is one of them.'

The winds shifted. Now it was blowing in the opposite direction, pushing the two fairymen against the trees. Taris sighed. 'This is bad.'

The advancing humans fell into the snow as they tried to advance forward. One had thrown a grenade foolishly, but the winds blew it back and it exploded in the area of five soldiers, who died as a result. Roosevelt and Taris saw this. 'I bet they won't try that again,' Taris said.

'I hate to be the one who threw that thunderball,' replied Roosevelt.

'If only the winds would die down,' Taris frowned.

It wasn't too long afterwards when the winds suddenly stopped and the amount of snow falling decreased. Taris marked this and sounded his horn.

Fairymen sprang from their hiding places and took to the air. Roosevelt and Taris led a charge of the fairies on the ground against the nearby humans and engaged them. Fairies dove from the skies and penetrated the ranks. The soldiers were caught off balance from the onslaught. Most of the survivors retreated while the others engaged the charging fairies. Roosevelt and Taris led the charge as human soldiers fell before them. Taris saw the ones retreating and sounded his horn. 'After them, but be careful of their thundersticks and thunderballs,' he cried.

The rest retreated with their fellows as they fired at the fairymen to cover their escape. Five fairies fell while the others continued their pursuit. Some of the fairies who had gathered up the fallen arrows began to shoot at the humans. The gunners who were trying to cover their escape were cut down. The fairies on the ground took to the air and continued their pursuit. When more with guns moved to the rear to fire, they were cut down by arrows.

The leader of the armed forces cried out. The soldiers stopped their retreat and pointed their guns at the fairies. They opened fire, seeking to hit as many fairies as they could. One fairyman tried to aim his arrow at one of them but was cut down by bullets.

'Keep flying,' cried Taris, 'Keep flying! Don't give the humans a chance to fire!'

From the rear, a group of fairies charged and knocked them off balance. Many were knocked down and slain. Some retaliated, gunning down five fairies, but the ferocity of their attack set the humans in disarray.

When the leader of the company was slain, the twenty who remained dropped their guns, fell to their knees and surrendered. Eighty fairies remained of Taris' company, including Taris and Roosevelt. Swords were held in the face of those who surrendered. One fairy said, 'We should kill these humans. They are too close to Arundel Haven, and they could very well find it.'

'No,' Taris cried, 'They have surrendered. We shall leave their fate to Queen Cymbaline and Prince Avondale. I choose to show mercy. To kill them when they have surrendered to us shows that we are no better than they are.'

The leader of the survivors looked up at Taris. The fairyman sensed remorse in the face of his enemy. 'All of this is unbelievable,' he told Taris. 'I thought President Farouk was crazy when he said we would be heading to Arundel Haven. I thought it was a myth.'

'It is not, human,' said Roosevelt grimly. The fairymen relieved the humans of all their weapons.

'Your fate I shall leave in the hands of our rulers,' Taris added.

'Then you must know,' the leader said, 'President Farouk and Dr. Von Braun are after your Queen. He wants to make Arundel Haven a territory of the United States under his rule.' He sighed. 'I am ashamed to be a part of this. This is not what our founding fathers had wanted us to do. We have betrayed our country in attacking your sovereignty.'

'Why should we believe this human?' another fairy asked.

'Enough, Armas,' Taris cried, 'Their fate should be decided by Queen Cymbaline, but if what he said is true, then we should find and protect her.'

'What about Prince Avondale?' Armas asked, 'He has flown off to protect her. Perhaps he is in danger as well?'

'I believe so,' frowned Taris, 'We must assume so, since we have not heard from him.'

The leader of the human troop stared at him and said, 'Our surrender is unconditional. Do with us as you see fit.'

Taris nodded. Turning to Armas he said, 'Take the men back to camp, march with them. Roosevelt and I will take ten fairymen to fly ahead and try and rescue Queen Cymbaline if she has been captured, and we fear Prince Avondale may have been captured as well. We don't know how many human soldiers we will have to deal with.'

He and Roosevelt chose ten fairymen to accompany them as they flew ahead to rescue Queen Cymbaline if need be. The rest of the fairies marched with their prisoners in the snow.

The helicopter stopped shaking as the winds died down. The hurricane force winds had buffeted the machine where Dr. Von Braun, President Farouk and their royal prisoners were inside. Dr. Von Braun and President Farouk were in the cockpit and had watched for the short time the blizzard started and stopped. Just before the blizzard stopped, they felt a tremor, almost like an earthquake. After it stopped, Dr. Von Braun frowned. 'I do not like this sign,' he said.

'What do you mean?' asked President Farouk.

'Little is known about this area,' replied Dr. Von Braun, 'For all we know, we could be sitting on a fault line.'

As the blizzard died down and snow slowed its fall, they looked out. President Farouk turned to Commander Moore. 'Get me Sergeant Pelosi and tell him to give me a progress report,' he said.

'Commander Moore to Sergeant Pelosi, report!'

Nothing but static came back.

'Come in, Sergeant Pelosi!'

Still no answer.

'Sergeant Lerner, report!'

No answer.

'Anybody, this is Commander Moore, report! President Farouk demands a report!'

Again, no answer.

'What the devil's going on?' growled President Farouk.

'No, it can't be possible,' Dr. Von Braun exclaimed, 'They couldn't have beaten us, could they?'

'Sergeant Reid, Sergeant Lerner, Sergeant Pelosi, report!'

'Commander Moore, get this bird in the air, now!' cried President Farouk.

'What about our men?'

'They have the other choppers to use, now get this chopper in the air!' the President cried.

Commander Moore sat down at the pilot's chair and turned the engines on. President Farouk and Dr. Von Braun headed to the seats near where Queen Cymbaline and Prince Avondale were bound. Prince Avondale stared at Dr. Von Braun grimly. 'I'm afraid your human friend and his fairy lover has lost,' Dr. Von Braun said.

Queen Cymbaline managed a whisper, 'No! It can't be!'

'Shadowfire has prevailed against them,' said Dr. Von Braun callously, 'Now we are flying to Washington and your existence shall be revealed.'

'You lie, Von Braun,' replied Prince Avondale softly.

'You are calling me a liar?' asked Dr. Von Braun.

'I do not trust you,' growled Prince Avondale.

Queen Cymbaline wept softly.

'The prophecy of old has failed, and Shadowfire shall live on,' stated President Farouk, 'After my term, I shall nullify the Constitution and I shall become Emperor of the United States for life. The bothersome parchment that the forefathers had written shall be null and void. Arundel Haven shall swear allegiance to the Farouk Empire.'

'Never,' whispered Queen Cymbaline amid her tears, 'My people will never bow to you!'

'Oh, I think otherwise, *your highness,*' mocked President Farouk,

Mordecai and Raven arrived just as the helicopter was taking off. Taris and Roosevelt arrived at the same time. They embraced both of them. 'Thank God you're alive,' Taris said.

'The dragon?' Roosevelt asked hurriedly, 'What about Shadowfire?'

'The Prophecy of Queen Hephzibah has been fulfilled, God has kept His promise,' Mordecai said, 'Shadowfire is dead.'

'That is great news to hear,' Taris said, 'but we think—'

'Queen Cymbaline has been taken?' Mordecai asked, 'I fear it is so.'

'Mordecai, look!' cried Raven.

The helicopter rose to the air. 'Farouk and Von Braun,' growled Mordecai.

He, Raven, Roosevelt, and Taris flew toward the helicopter as it began to slowly move away. They easily overtook it as Mordecai opened the hatch. He found Dr. Von Braun and President Farouk staring at them and found Queen Cymbaline and Prince Avondale bound to a chair. Dr. Von Braun stared in surprise. 'Mordy Jefferson,' he snarled, 'You and your fairy lover are alive?'

'Mordecai,' Queen Cymbaline cried. She was happy to see him alive.

'Your majesties, are you okay?' Mordecai asked.

'Where is Shadowfire?' President Farouk demanded.

'Shadowfire is dead, and the Prophecy fulfilled,' answered Mordecai, 'We've come for Queen Cymbaline and Prince Avondale. Let them go!'

Dr. Von Braun laughed. Wilfred and the two soldiers appeared with their guns readied and shot at the intruders. Roosevelt and Taris dodged the fire and slew both men, throwing them out of the helicopter. Wilfred fired and missed with his shot but wound up slain by Roosevelt and thrown out the copter door into the snow.

'You expect us to let them go just because you asked, Mordy Jefferson?' snarled Dr. Von Braun, 'I have come too far in my quest to have you stop me!'

'I am not asking you, Von Braun,' said Mordecai grimly, 'I am *telling* you!'

'Go to hell, boy,' snapped President Farouk, 'I don't know how you and that worthless fairy lover of yours managed to escape Shadowfire, but when he comes—'

'You must have trouble hearing,' Mordecai snarled, 'You and your party seem to have hearing problems! You show it when it comes to the will of the people. Shadowfire is dead! Raven and I slew him, and the Prophecy has been fulfilled! We've come here for Queen Cymbaline and Prince Avondale. Now let them go!'

'And you didn't hear me, traitor, *go to hell!*' snapped President Farouk, 'You either leave now, or you will be arrested as a traitor!'

'I don't care what you call me, *your Imperial majesty,*' he said in a strong voice, 'I am here for my Queen and her brother, and we are not leaving without them!'

Dr. Von Braun charged at Mordecai. He dropped his sword as he was wrestled to the ground. Taris and Roosevelt held President Farouk at bay while Raven freed Queen Cymbaline and Prince Avondale. They embraced the ebony fairy maiden. 'Praise God you two are okay,' wept Queen Cymbaline, 'I can't believe after all these years that Arundel Haven is finally free from the terror of Shadowfire.'

'Get Queen Cymbaline and Prince Avondale out of here,' cried Mordecai, kicking Dr. Von Braun off him.

President Farouk managed to pull out his gun. He pointed it at the two fairies with the sword. 'Not another step, fairies,' he told Roosevelt and Taris, 'I'm sure you know what these can do now. That is why I've been trying to ban guns and nullify the second amendment: to keep our political enemies and Constitution loving Americans from possessing them, to take away their means of self defense, but I keep one for protection. Now back away!'

Mordecai and Dr. Von Braun slammed into President Farouk. While the fight continued, Roosevelt and Taris managed to lead Queen Cymbaline and Prince Avondale off the helicopter. Raven remained, not willing to leave Mordecai. President Farouk pointed his gun at Raven. 'You are a fool to stay,' he told her.

'I will not leave my husband,' replied Raven grimly.

Dr. Von Braun overheard what Raven said. 'Did she just call you her husband?' he said, throwing him against the wall, 'I'm very surprised. You are not much of a fighter, are you, Mordy?'

'The dragon is dead, isn't he?' retorted Mordecai.

'Slaying a dragon and winning a hand-to-hand combat is not the same thing, boy,' snapped Dr. Von Braun, 'I have been trained in over twenty forms of combat. You are no match for me.'

Raven charged toward President Farouk, trying to disarm him. During their struggle, the gun was accidently set off, firing twice. One bullet hit Commander Moore in the head, while the other hit the control panel.

Sparks flew and a small explosion came as a result.

The President managed to knock Raven away. He struck her in the face with the butt of the gun. Mordecai saw this and cried, 'Raven!' To President Farouk he cried, 'Son of a vulture!'

'Forget the worthless wench, boy,' growled Dr. Von Braun, 'You've got me to worry about!'

Mordecai gave Dr. Von Braun a head butt and grabbed his fallen sword. He pointed it at his foe. President Farouk fired at Mordecai. The bullet struck him in the shoulder, causing the young man to roll out the open door.

Another explosion rocked the helicopter. President Farouk and Dr. Von Braun were knocked off their feet as the helicopter started spinning out of control. Raven managed to roll out of the helicopter and fell to the ground. She rose up and immediately flew toward Mordecai, who laid on the ground. 'Mordecai,' she cried, 'My Mordecai!'

Mordecai rolled to his feet. The bullet remained stuck in his breastplate but did not penetrate it. She ran into his arms, holding and kissing him. 'Are you okay, my love?' she asked.

Mordecai took off his helmet and breastplate. He checked his shoulder. 'I am unhurt,' he answered, staring at the area struck by the bullet. Raven took hers off as well. They held and kissed each other.

Suddenly, they heard a loud explosion from over a kilometer away. President Farouk and Dr. Von Braun's helicopter had crashed, so Mordecai surmised. He and Raven took to the air and flew to the crash site. Before they could proceed any further, the helicopter exploded again, louder than ever. They managed to stay out of range of the blast.

Mordecai sighed. 'Nobody could have survived that blast,' he said, 'I didn't want this fate even unto the likes of them.'

'At least Arundel Haven is safe,' sighed Raven, leaning her head upon his shoulders.

They were joined by Queen Cymbaline, Prince Avondale , Taris, and Roosevelt. They embraced and cheered, praising God for delivering them, for the victory He had given them.

They flew back to camp. Mordecai saw twenty men kneeling in the snow surrounded by armed fairymen. He sighed. 'Is that all the fairymen left?' he asked.

'I'm afraid so,' Taris answered, 'Lavender and Laurelin will be grieved to hear that their men, Jax and Derreck, are among the casualties.'

Mordecai and Raven bowed their heads sadly. 'We are checking among the fallen for those who may have survived,' Taris added gravely, 'I am glad, Mordecai, that you and Raven have slain Shadowfire.'

'He will terrorize Arundel Haven no more,' said Mordecai,

'Twila and others like her will no longer have to live in fear of him.'

Queen Cymbaline turned her attention toward the prisoners. She glared at them one by one. She said nothing as she stared at them. The leader glanced at the queen. He said nothing as well, though he struggled for the words.

'What shall be done with these humans?' Prince Avondale asked.

'Some think they do not deserve mercy,' Taris said, 'They are too close to Arundel Haven for my liking.'

Mordecai and Raven appeared by the side of Queen Cymbaline. One of the soldiers stared in disbelief. 'Is he human?' one of them asked.

Mordecai nodded. 'I am,' he answered, 'I, along with Raven, my wife, have slain the dragon, Shadowfire. He is no longer a threat to the fairies of Arundel Haven or to any of us.'

'Your wife?' another exclaimed, 'You have a fairy as your wife?'

'Is there a problem with that?' growled Prince Avondale.

'That is why Mordecai Jefferson was allowed here, to fulfill the prophecy of the death of the dragon, which has been fulfilled,' stated Queen Cymbaline, 'However, your fate is in my hands.'

'Please let us return to our home,' the leader begged, 'We were only following orders.'

'Maybe so,' replied Prince Avondale, 'but now your President cannot help you. You are at our mercy now, and we must decide what will be done to you.'

Mordecai sighed. 'I can't help feel this is my fault, my Queen,' he said. 'I tried so hard to keep your existence a secret.'

Queen Cymbaline shook her head. 'No, no, Mordecai,' she said earnestly, 'You have no control over some things in this matter. Shadowfire had revealed the location to your President and Dr. Von Braun. I know you did all you could to protect us. You are one of the very few humans who are good, and you have earned my trust and love. None of this is your fault.'

'But what will become of the humans?' Taris asked.

Queen Cymbaline stared hard at the prisoners. The leader bowed his head before her and said, 'Please let us go. We will reveal this to nobody, I swear it!'

'And the rest of you?' asked the Fairy Queen, 'If I let you go, will you keep our existence a secret?'

'We promise,' answered the leader.

'Swear by the LORD,' demanded Queen Cymbaline.

'We swear,' the leader responded.

'Swear as the LORD lives, you will not reveal our existence to the public!'

They took the oath.

'May the LORD deal with you severely if you in anyway break this oath,' Queen Cymbaline said.

They were allowed to board one of the helicopters, but their weapons were not returned to them. Mordecai sighed as he watched the helicopter rise from the ground and head back the way it originally came. Raven leaned her head upon Mordecai's shoulders and wrapped her arms around him.

The fairymen managed to find close to eighty survivors who had been wounded in battle. They had the wounded tended to while others spent the time gathering their dead and burying them at Tarragon Hill.

The human dead they buried close to the body of the dragon laid at the hills of Moran. They burned Shadowfire's lifeless body where he had been slain. The wounded were taken to Arundel Haven and tended to, though removing bullets was new to them.

Mordecai and Raven stared sadly at the bodies of the fairymen who had lost their lives in the battle. Raven wept in his arms, as did Mordecai.

Mordecai hated to bring the news to Lavender and Laurelin. 'I feel so sad about their loss,' she told Mordecai.

'I know,' nodded Mordecai, 'They did not sacrifice their lives in vain. Arundel Haven is safe; the dragon is dead.'

'Do you think President Farouk and Dr. Von Braun are dead as well?' asked Raven.

'I can't help but wonder,' Mordecai replied.

They returned to the site of the crash. They found the remains of the pilot but not of President Farouk or Dr. Von Braun. 'They must have survived somehow,' Mordecai said coldly, 'I don't see their bodies, just the pilot.'

They returned to Queen Cymbaline and told her about what they had found. Immediately, she had fairy scouts fly around Nebechadrezzar Valley searching for President Farouk and Dr. Von Braun. While they did, the rest prepared for the return to Arundel Haven. Mordecai and Raven returned with Queen Cymbaline and Prince Avondale while Taris and Roosevelt volunteered to remain to help with the wounded and the dead. During their flight back to Arundel Haven, Mordecai couldn't help but wonder what had happened to Dr. Von Braun and President Farouk. He spoke nothing of it, but it remained in the back of his mind. He somehow had the feeling that he may have not seen the last of either of them.

Chapter Fifteen

Starla wept on the couch, worried about her husband, her sister, and Mordecai. Molly sat down beside her, holding her hand, anxious to comfort her. Lavender and Laurelin each thought about their boyfriends. They wondered if they would ever see them again. Cece, thinking about Mordecai, held Twila in her arms. She was asleep in the human's arms. Tony looked on in sadness as he put another log on the fire. Sharon walked over to Cece. 'Do you want me to take Twila, Cece?' she asked.

Cece nodded, her thoughts on Mordecai.

Tiffany stared at her. 'We all miss Mordy and Raven,' she said softly, 'I never thought in my wildest dreams that we would see all this.'

'It does seem pretty wild, doesn't it?' Cece replied as Sharon took Twila.

Starla approached Sharon. 'You can lay Twila down in that small sleeper,' she said, wiping the tears from her eyes.

Sharon nodded. She laid Twila down gently on the small bed.

Tiffany walked into the kitchen to fetch some water. Starla stared up at the ceiling. She sighed, trying to compose herself. She turned to Molly and asked, 'You told me you have another son?'

'Yes,' Molly answered, 'I had talked about him before.'

'Randall, wasn't it?'

'It is Randall,' said Tony, 'and he is not going to believe all of this, about Arundel Haven, about fairies, that Mordy has a fairy wife now.' He gave out a small laugh. 'I think I have a hard time believing it myself, but I know it is true.' He sighed. 'I can't help but think about Mordy and Raven.'

'I don't know how we're going to explain our absence from school,' Cece sighed.

'I know,' Sharon replied as Tiffany returned to the room. 'I can see my father now: "You better have a good explanation for this, young lady." I'm not sure if he'll even believe the truth.'

'We can vouch for you and Tiffany, Sharon,' Molly said, 'though how to do it without revealing the existence of fairies is going to be the hard part. I will do all I can to keep Arundel Haven a secret, though I will miss it here when I leave.'

'Is Mordy going to return home to finish school?' Tiffany asked.

'This is Mordy's home now,' Cece said, 'but if you're talking about our home—'

'He says he will return,' Tony said, 'Mordy now has two homes, here in Arundel Haven and Orlando, Florida as well.'

'I know Twila will be sad when Mordecai leaves,' Starla said, 'when he returns to finish his education. That is, if he and Raven survive.'

'Little Twila believes he will survive,' Molly replied, 'and from what I've heard, she hasn't been wrong.'

Starla gave out a faint laugh. 'Like when she had met Mordecai for the first time,' she said, wiping the tears from her eyes, 'The faith of a child. Her faith has been rewarded. Raven was right as well in choosing Mordecai. Taught me, taught Queen Cymbaline and Prince Avondale as well.'

'And us as well,' Laurelin stated, 'or at least partially. Tiffany and Sharon kind of helped as well. It took us a while, but you two, Tiffany and Sharon, convinced us.'

'I hope Jax and Derreck do propose to you two,' Tiffany said, 'We would love to be at the wedding. You're going to have to convince them somehow to pop the question.'

As they talked, Twila stirred in her little bed and woke up. She yawned and opened her eyes, rising to her feet, staring at the door and cried, 'Uncle Morcai! Aunt Raven!'

Starla turned toward Twila. 'Twila, Uncle Morcai and Aunt Raven are not here.'

'No, Mommy,' Twila objected, 'Uncle Morcai and Aunt Raven are home!' She took to the air and flew toward the door.

As she did, the door opened. Mordecai and Raven, to everyone's delight, walked through the door. The armor they wore was gone, their swords and shields gone. They had left them at their house to give them to Queen Cymbaline to keep under her care afterwards. Twila cried out with joy and embraced her uncle, kissing him on the cheeks. 'Twila miss Uncle Morcai and Aunt Raven,' she said.

Mordecai kissed the toddler as he was embraced by his mother, then his sister. They were welcomed with embraces and kisses. Molly kissed her son with tears in her eyes. 'Oh, Mordy,' she cried. 'I thought I would never see you again!'

Cece embraced and kissed him on the cheeks. 'I am so happy to see you again.'

'And I all of you,' replied Mordecai as Tiffany and Sharon embraced him.

Starla gasped. 'Where is Roosevelt?' she asked.

'He is fine,' Mordecai answered. Starla let out a sigh of relief and wept happily that he was still alive. 'He and Taris are helping out with the wounded.'

'The dragon,' Tony said, 'What about the dragon?'

'Shadowfire go bye-bye for good,' Twila chimed.

Mordecai kissed her and smiled. 'Twila, I couldn't have put it better myself,' he laughed.

'The dragon is dead?' Lavender cried.

'The Prophecy of Queen Hephzibah has been fulfilled,' Mordecai answered gravely, 'Indeed, Shadowfire is dead.'

The others cheered when they heard the news. 'God delivered Shadowfire into our hands,' Raven stated, 'Our ancient enemy is no more. God has kept His word.'

'Are Jax and Derreck helping out with the wounded, too?' Laurelin asked.

Mordecai had a sad look upon his face. Both Lavender and Laurelin gasped. 'I-I'm sorry,' he said, tears in his eyes, 'We were told by Taris.'

'I'm sorry, Lavender, Laurelin,' Raven said with tears in her eyes.

Lavender leaned her head upon Mordecai's shoulder and wept.

Raven held Laurelin to comfort her.

Sharon and Tiffany stood by their friends, bowing their heads in sorrow.

'We had lost so many,' Mordecai said sadly as Lavender wept.

'Daddy, okay?' Twila asked.

'Your daddy will return as soon as he can,' Mordecai answered, kissing Twila, 'He is helping Taris and the other survivors. He will come home as soon as he can.'

'I miss you, Uncle Morcai,' she said, kissing him on the cheeks, 'and Aunt Raven.'

'We missed you too, sweetie,' smiled Mordecai.

'We did not find President Farouk or Dr. Von Braun,' Raven said gravely.

'So, the president was there?' Tony asked.

'Yes, he was,' Raven answered, 'He and President Farouk had kidnapped Queen Cymbaline and Prince Avondale and were going to expose their existence and force Arundel Haven to comply to his laws. We had stopped him from succeeding, Roosevelt, Taris, Mordecai, and I.'

'We couldn't find them,' Mordecai said dejectedly, shaking his head, 'I have a feeling they may have survived the crash. Queen Cymbaline has scouts looking for them.'

The scouts never found any sign of Dr. Von Braun nor of President Farouk, neither alive nor dead. Mordecai assumed that somehow, they had both survived the crash but wished he was certain.

Queen Cymbaline held a feast celebrating the victory God had given them over the dragon and over the human invaders. She made a proclamation that Mordecai and Raven would be a part of the royal house, the Jefferson royal house, naming them Lord Mordecai and Lady Raven. His parents were surprised and overjoyed, happy for their son. She also named Cece a member as well, giving her the title Lady Cece. Cece was speechless at the proclamation. She bowed low to her. 'Thank you, your majesty,' she said.

Queen Cymbaline had Tony and Molly stand before her. 'Blessed you two are for bringing forth Lord Mordecai,' she said. 'You two will always have a place here as well. I am proud to have known your son and to know you and your family. You shall have a place of honor here.'

They both bowed. 'So much kindness you have shown to our son and our daughter,' Tony said, 'and to us, for bringing us here.'

'I am glad to have gotten to know Raven, Lavender, and Laurelin as well,' Molly replied, 'I grieve for the loss of their boyfriends.'

'I like it here, your majesty,' Tony sighed, 'but I kind of long for home. Yet, I find it hard to leave.'

'I know you miss your home,' Queen Cymbaline said, 'Before you return, I shall give you the water to allow you to return here. In the spring, if you and yours desire, I will make the gift of flight permanent.'

'Us too?' cried out Sharon and Tiffany.

Queen Cymbaline laughed. 'Yes, the both of you too,' she answered, 'I'm sure Lavender and Laurelin would want you to return, too.'

They had another feast before Lord Mordecai and Lady Raven, along with the Jeffersons and Lady Cece's friends, Tiffany and Sharon, returned to Orlando. Gifts were given to them, including the water to allow them to fly. Lord Mordecai and Lady Raven received the wedding bands that were made for them. The wedding bands they used in their wedding were placed in a solid gold box and were given into the keeping of Lady Raven's sister, Starla.

The parting was hard. Twila did not want to see her uncle Morcai leave or her aunt Raven. She wept as she hugged him one last time. 'Your aunt Raven and uncle Morcai will return soon, sweetie,' Lord Mordecai told her, 'This is not goodbye for good.'

'No go bye-bye, Uncle Morcai,' Twila wept, 'No go bye-bye, Aunt Raven!'

Lady Raven kissed Twila. 'We will miss you too, sweetie,' she said, 'We will return as soon as we can.'

Lord Mordecai bowed before Queen Cymbaline, but the Fairy Queen forbade him to bow anymore as she embraced and kissed him. 'It is hard to see the both of you go,' she said, tears flowing from her eyes.

Lord Mordecai wept. 'You have shown me much more kindness than I deserve, my Queen,' he said. 'Thank you for everything.'

'No, sweet brother,' she said, 'Thank you. Out of love, against your fears, you accepted the Prophecy, and God had used you and Lady Raven to bring about the end of the dragon. To me, you do deserve this, out of love it was given.'

'And out of love received,' replied Lord Mordecai, 'I cannot and will not stay away from here. This is my home as well, and I promise I will return as soon as I am able.'

Lady Raven bowed before Queen Cymbaline. 'Bow not before me, Lady Raven, my dear sister,' she said amid her tears, 'for we are fellow servants.' They embraced and wept.

Prince Avondale embraced them both. 'Farewell, Lord Mordecai and Lady Raven, dear brother and sister,' he said. 'May your return to Arundel Haven be soon.'

'We shall return,' declared Lord Mordecai.

He and the others took to the air and disappeared into the skies. They did not fear passing by the Mountains of Shadow, knowing now that the dragon was dead and gone. They passed Nebechadrezzar Valley and flew back home to Orlando.

It was a week after Lady Raven turned 22 years old. They stepped off the bus that ran past the street where Lord Mordecai's grandparents lived. Lady Raven had her wings covered while in the human world.

As they walked, they talked about their time in Arundel Haven. 'I am getting kind of homesick,' Lady Raven told her husband, 'and I miss Twila.'

'So do I,' Lord Mordecai nodded, 'but I wanted you to meet my grandparents on my mother's side, the Epprights.'

'Yes, the ones you had told me led you to Christ,' Raven replied, 'I've been so looking forward to meeting them.'

'How are your wings?' asked Lord Mordecai.

'Still not used to being covered up,' Lady Raven answered, 'I love the bed that your parents had bought for us.'

'Sooner or later, we will have to find a place of our own, especially for whenever you become pregnant,' said Lord Mordecai.

Lady Raven nodded. 'I am looking forward to that time,' she smiled.

They reached the door of a one-story house. Upon the door was a small Israeli flag above two small flags, one a US flag and the other a flag of Ireland.

Lady Raven found it curious.

'The flag of Israel they have because they know that Israel is God's chosen people,' Lord Mordecai told her, 'The flag other than the U.S. flag is one of Ireland, since my mother's side is Irish.'

He knocked on the door. Opening the door was a man in his early 70s. He was just over six feet tall, about 180-pounds. In his blue eyes was a light shining like a star. He wore a red flannel shirt and dark blue pants. He had a mixture of dark and gray hair. He smiled as he saw Lord Mordecai. 'Naomi,' he cried. 'Mordecai's here!' To his grandson he said, 'Come on in, the both of you.'

Lord Mordecai and Lady Raven stepped inside. The old man embraced Lord Mordecai and then Lady Raven. 'You must be Raven,' he said, 'I am so happy to meet you at last!'

'And you, Mr. Eppright,' Lady Raven replied, 'Mordecai and his parents have told me so much about you!'

From the kitchen, a 70-year-old red-haired woman with touches of grey entered the room. She wore an emerald-green dress and glasses in front of her green eyes. She was a few inches shorter than her husband but, in her eyes, shone the same light. 'Mordecai,' she cried, embracing him.

'Hi, Grandmom,' Lord Mordecai said, 'I want to introduce Raven to you and granddad.'

Lady Raven was embraced by his grandmother. 'I am so happy to meet you, Raven!'

'And you too,' Lady Raven replied.

'Where are you originally from, dear?' Naomi asked.

'It's kind of a long story, and I don't know if you're going to believe us,' Lord Mordecai laughed, 'but Mom and Dad can back it up as well as Cece.'

'I can't believe your parents are accepting of her,' Naomi said, 'I hope you know Jesus, Raven.'

'I do, Mrs. Eppright,' Lady Raven nodded, 'I was glad when I heard Mordecai was saved as well. He told me you were the ones who helped lead him to Christ.'

'Yes,' Gabriel nodded, 'but his cousin Amelia the niece of my son-in-law had planted the seed. I still pray for our daughter and her husband that they would accept Jesus. I hope that this Sunday you would both come to church with us.'

'We would love to,' Lord Mordecai nodded, 'Raven and I look forward to it.'

They sat down at the table drinking sodas. 'How are things at school?' Gabriel asked, 'Are those bullies still bothering you?'

'I am thankful to say not anymore,' Lord Mordecai answered, 'The principal finally did something about it, and now they're minding themselves, lest they get kicked off the team. Some of the other students are helping to make sure they keep in line. I have to do some catching up still.'

'I heard that you and Cece had missed some days,' Naomi said. 'What happened?'

'It's a long story,' Lord Mordecai said, 'but there are things you may find unbelievable that you deserve to know. Mom and Dad and Cece already know, so I think you deserve to know.'

Raven took off her sweater. Gabriel and Naomi looked on in amazement when they saw Raven flittering her wings to bring back circulation. 'Is she… a fairy?' Naomi whispered.

'Raven is a fairy,' Lord Mordecai answered, 'and there's something else.' He showed them the ring upon his finger.

'Mordecai, what does this mean?' Gabriel asked, perplexed.

'Mom and Dad will verify this, but Raven and I are married,' Lord Mordecai answered, 'She is my wife now.'

Gabriel and Naomi stared at him in disbelief.

'Have you ever heard of a hidden fairy kingdom of Arundel Haven?' Lord Mordecai asked.

Naomi's eyes widened. 'You mean Arundel Haven is real?' she asked. She felt Raven's wings and found that they were real. 'They are real,' she exclaimed, 'I can't believe, Raven, that you are a fairy.'

'It's a long story,' Lady Raven said, 'I think Mordecai and I must start from the beginning.'

They spent over three hours telling the tale of their adventures, from when they first met, to Lord Mordecai being taken to Arundel Haven, to the Prophecy, to the marriage and to the death of Shadowfire. Gabriel and Naomi still found it hard to believe.

After Lord Mordecai finished the tale, Gabriel said, 'I knew President Farouk was capable of horrible things, but this?' He sighed. 'And Dr. Von Braun. I can't believe he was obsessed with trying to find fairies.'

'They are real,' Lord Mordecai nodded, 'and Lady Raven is living proof of that. At first, Queen Cymbaline was against me and against our marriage, but as I told you, God had used little Twila to open their eyes. She was attached to me the moment she met me.' He sighed. 'I still miss Twila, and Starla, Taris, Roosevelt, Queen Cymbaline, and Prince Avondale.'

'This Twila must be a lively little girl,' laughed Naomi.

'Indeed, Mrs. Eppright,' smiled Lady Raven, 'She—'

'No, Lady Raven,' interrupted Gabriel, 'You will refer to us as your grandparents. You are our granddaughter by marriage.'

Lady Raven bowed. 'I am honored,' she smiled.

Naomi took Lady Raven's hands. 'I bless the day you came into Mordecai's life, Raven,' she said, 'I rejoice that you are washed in the blood as well. Mordecai is blessed to have you as his wife.'

Lord Mordecai nodded, kissing Lady Raven. 'Yes, I am,' he nodded.

At that moment, the door opened and closed. They looked over to see who it was.

A familiar toddler cried out, 'Uncle Morcai, Uncle Morcai!' and flew into his arms. Lord Mordecai's parents were there, as well as his sister, Lady Cece. With them were Starla and her husband, Roosevelt.

Lady Raven embraced her sister and her brother-in-law. 'I am so happy to see you,' she said.

Gabriel and Naomi gazed at Twila, who snuggled up into the arms of Lord Mordecai. 'So, this is Twila,' Naomi said. She kissed her. 'You are a real sweetheart.'

'Twila love Uncle Morcai,' she chimed.

Gabriel and Naomi laughed. 'You know,' Gabriel told the toddler, 'your uncle Morcai has told us so much about you.'

'Hi,' Twila said.

'Twila, Starla, Roosevelt,' Lord Mordecai said to them, 'these are my grandparents, Gabriel and Naomi Eppright, my mother's parents.'

Starla and Roosevelt shook their hands. 'Welcome to our house, Starla, Roosevelt,' Gabriel said.

'These are your uncle Morcai's grandparents, Twila,' Lord Mordecai told the toddler, 'Morcai's Mommy's Mommy and Daddy.'

'Twila two,' she said, hiding her face and giggling.

'You and Starla have a beautiful daughter, Roosevelt,' Gabriel told him, 'She is a sweetheart and a blessing.'

'But lively, Mrs. Eppright,' Starla laughed.

'Does Randall know about Raven and her marriage to Mordecai?' Gabriel asked Tony.

'We told him about Raven,' answered Tony, 'but nothing more than that. We prefer to tell him face to face when he returns from Baton Rouge.'

'So did I hear correctly that Mordecai can fly?' Naomi asked Molly.

'If we weren't in Arundel Haven ourselves,' Molly told her mother, 'we wouldn't have believed it ourselves. Only thing, Mordy's powers of flight are permanent. He chooses not to fly here in our world.'

'It would not be a wise thing to do,' replied Lord Mordecai, 'I mean to keep Arundel Haven and the existence of fairies a secret as long as I live, and I take it very seriously.' He paused. 'Oh, if only I could show you Arundel Haven. It is such a wondrous place, especially since Shadowfire is dead.'

Twila yawned and snuggled up to her uncle Morcai. Lord Mordecai sat down on the rocking chair and gently rocked in it, kissing the toddler. Lady Raven kissed both her husband and her niece.

'Wait until you two have one of your own,' Naomi told Lady Raven. 'So, there has never been a union between a human and a fairy before you two?'

'No, Grandmom,' Lady Raven answered, 'Mordecai and I

are the first. I kind of look forward to it.'

'I have a feeling that your little one will become another you or another Twila,' laughed Starla.

The others laughed.

Lady Raven smiled, as did Lord Mordecai. 'I look forward to it,' Lord Mordecai said, kissing Lady Raven. He then kissed Twila as the toddler drifted off to sleep in the arms of her uncle.

'Sleep well, little Twila,' he whispered, kissing her.

Chapter Sixteen

ARUNDEL HAVEN: SAVIOUR'S DAY STORY

Cece, Sharon, and Tiffany ran out to Tiffany's car cheering after the final period bell at Oak Ridge High School. It was the last day of school before the Christmas break. The temperature was about 53-degrees outside, colder than they would have liked it to be. Mordecai was not with them since he and Raven had been staying with the young man's grandparents for a while at their request, agreeing to spend some time with them, especially since Mordecai had figured Dr. Von Braun could have survived the crash and was searching for him and Raven again. It was now two months after the Battle of Nebechadrezzar Valley and the death of Shadowfire, the dragon. Mordecai found out that at least President Farouk had survived, but he surmised that somehow Dr. Von Braun had survived as well. Strangely, Tony and Molly had not been bothered by President Farouk's men or from Dr. Von Braun for that matter since the young couple had started staying with the Epprights. 'Maybe Dr. Von Braun is dead,' Molly suggested.

Mordecai disagreed. 'I think he may still be alive,' he told them, 'I mean to stay and complete my education before deciding on my future. I know I have a home in Arundel Haven and that there, I am Lord Mordecai of the house of Jefferson, but here, I am just ordinary Mordecai Jefferson, just another nobody.'

Molly disagreed. 'That you are not,' she told him, 'Raven and Queen Cymbaline do not think so, neither does Twila. That should be proof enough that you are not a nobody.'

Although Mordecai and Raven had been staying with his grandparents since late October, there were times when the both of them would spend a little time with his own parents. Raven learned about Halloween, which displeased her because it seemed to give honor to the devil. 'It's sad many people celebrate this,' Mordecai said, 'but I prefer to celebrate Reformation Day.'

'What's that?' Raven asked.

'October thirty-first came from the Church of Rome, from All Hallows Eve, thus Halloween,' he told her, 'It is a big day for devil worshippers, originating from the Druids. Rome celebrates November 1 and calls it All Saints Day. October 31 was the date in 1517 when Martin Luther had nailed the 95 theses against the selling of indulgences upon the door of Whittenburg Cathedral in Germany, thus sparking the Reformation. The Reformation urges the saints to get back to the Bible, to sound Biblical doctrine, to cast away doctrines of devils and get back to the simplicity of the Gospel. It is sad that Martin Luther had still retained Rome's views about the Jews, refusing to accept them as God's chosen, but he wasn't perfect. We both know better, know that the Jews are indeed God's chosen people, never rescinding His promises to Israel. My grandparents know the truth as well.'

Gabriel and Naomi loved having Mordecai and Raven stay with them. Although Raven had cooked twice for them, it was Mordecai who had done the majority of the cooking and wound up being the main cook since his grandparents loved the way he cooked. They were surprised when they first tried Mordecai's cooking. 'I can't believe how well you can cook,' Naomi told Mordecai.

'I am happy you and Granddad enjoy it,' replied Mordecai, 'I love doing the cooking.'

'And we can tell in the foods you've cooked,' Gabriel said, 'How did you learn to cook so well?'

'I was self-taught,' answered Mordecai, 'I guess it just comes naturally.'

The wedding pictures taken at Arundel Haven were brought together and put on a disk for the young couple. Copies of all the pictures were given to the family members as well as Tiffany and Sharon.

Raven learned about the Christmas traditions from Mordecai and his family. Gabriel had helped, putting up lights from the fairy maiden, though she did not expose her wings or use her powers of flight. Neither Mordecai nor Raven flew as long they were away from Arundel Haven and among other humans.

Raven loved the Thanksgiving traditions but was told by Mordecai, 'The real reasons we celebrate Thanksgiving the God haters are trying to make America forget. Our forefathers came to this land to flee religious persecution by Rome, for the freedom to worship God. America was founded on Christian principles, which the God haters are trying to remove.'

'That's terrible,' Raven exclaimed, 'Why are they doing this? Don't they know that it's God who causes this nation to prosper?'

'They do not want to acknowledge that,' Mordecai sighed, 'They hate God with a passion. They prefer to use God and Jesus Christ as a cuss word, profaning it at every turn.'

Mordecai was met by Raven as he got out of school the last day before Christmas vacation. The wings of the black fairy maiden were covered up so that nobody knew she was a fairy. Raven greeted him with a kiss. 'It seems so strange for me to be in high school still and be a married man,' he said.

Raven smiled, wrapping her arms around him. 'And married to a fairy maiden, on top of that,' she said. She kissed him on the lips. They walked away from the campus of Oak Ridge High School.

As they were about to cross the street, they were nearly hit by a Cadillac familiar to Mordecai. Raven barely remembered seeing it before when she had first met Mordecai, how he had been taken to the woods by three bullies, beaten up, and then tied up and left in the woods. Their meeting was the only good thing that came out of the unpleasant affair for the young man. They dove out of the way. Mordecai looked up. 'Jones,' he growled.

'I thought they were supposed to mind themselves,' Raven exclaimed, 'I thought they would stop bullying you and others like you. I don't understand!'

'That was during football season,' frowned Mordecai, helping Raven to her feet, 'They have been back to their old tricks ever since we won the state title late last month. They started up again earlier this week. They never change!' He gave Raven a gentle kiss. 'Are you okay?'

Raven sighed. 'I'll be fine,' she answered, angered by the incicdent, 'I just hate it that they continue to bully you and others like you. I would like to give those evil humans a piece of my mind! Why do those in charge of your school allow this travesty to go on? There are times I don't understand you humans.'

Mordecai sighed. 'I guess we can be hard to understand,' he sighed, 'I don't blame you really for feeling that way.'

Raven kissed him as she stared into his eyes. 'I still don't regret meeting and marrying you, sweet Mordecai,' she said, 'You truly are one of the good humans. Your family are good humans, too. I am proud to be a part of your family.'

'If only your parents were alive,' said Mordecai.

'Your parents cannot replace my real parents,' Raven sighed, 'but they love and accept me, which is important. I am happy and thankful for that. Shadowfire has finally paid for his iniquities against my people since God had used us to destroy him.'

They walked down the sidewalks adjacent to Winegard Rd., then turning and walking adjacent Lancaster Rd. and finally walking aside Lee Lan Dr. to his grandparents' house where they stayed. 'I like staying with my grandparents,' Mordecai said, 'though I do miss my parents. I hope things will remain calm enough so we could stay with them again.'

'You still think Dr. Von Braun is still alive?' Raven asked.

'I'm certain of it, though I've heard nothing about him lately,' answered Mordecai, 'If he is dead, no remains were found in the wreckage of the helicopter they were in. Since President Farouk had survived somehow, it's safe to assume that Von Braun must have survived as well, though I think he may be laying low.'

Raven laid her head on his shoulder as they walked. Mordecai caressed her face and kissed her. 'I am so glad I have you as my wife, Raven,' he said.

'And I am so blessed to have you as my husband, my sweet Mordecai,' she smiled, kissing him.

As they headed toward Mordecai's grandparents' house, two of the kids who lived next door to them ran over to them and greeted them. The boy was ten years old, standing at almost five feet tall, had dirty blonde hair and green eyes. He wore a blue sweater and blue pants. The girl, who was eight years old, wore black pants and a hot pink sweater. She was just a few inches shorter than the boy. They welcomed the couple. 'Hi, Mr. Mordecai, Ms. Raven!' they said.

Mordecai and Raven recognized the two kids. 'Hi, Steve! Hi, Robin!' Mordecai said as he smiled, 'You looking forward to Christmas?'

'Yes, Mr. Mordecai,' Steve answered, 'I am so excited!'

'As am I,' Robin chimed.

Raven just smiled.

'Will you come play with us?' asked Steve, 'I love it when you come throw the football with me.'

'I will in a few minutes,' Mordecai said, 'I just got out of school. I need to go change clothes first.'

'Okay,' replied Steve and Robin. They ran back into their yard while Mordecai and Raven walked inside the house. Gabriel was watching a preacher named Leslie Hale, known as the Irish Preacher, talking on the television. 'I like him,' Mordecai said. 'He believes in sound doctrine.'

Gabriel smiled. 'How was your day at school, Mordecai?' he asked.

'I had another run-in with those bullies,' Mordecai sighed, 'They've started up again. They nearly ran over me and Raven as we were leaving the school grounds.'

'I thought their bullying had stopped last month,' Gabriel said, 'I'm sad to hear you're still having trouble with them. The principal needs to do something about that! This can't continue!'

'I hate it when they pick on Mordecai,' Raven frowned, 'It hurts me when they hurt him. I feel like giving them a piece of my mind and then some!'

'I have to go get changed,' Mordecai said, 'I told Steve and Robin that I would play with them.'

'And so will I,' Raven replied.

'It seems that the Thompson kids are attached to you and Raven,' Gabriel said in observation, 'I am sorry to hear that their parents are having problems. It's good that they have you and Raven to look up to. They need some stability in their lives.'

'I don't understand why they're having problems, why they argue constantly,' said Raven, 'I've been living here for two months and still don't understand the ways of you humans.'

Gabriel sighed. 'It may well have to do with their situation,' he replied, 'Robert had lost his job when the company he was with went out of business and he couldn't find anything. Margaret has not been supportive of him, and it's created a strain on their marriage. It's helped Steve and Robin so much when you started staying with us, both of you. It's kind of like when you told me about Twila, how she became attached to you. I saw how lively she is when Tony and Molly brought her and her parents over here.'

Mordecai sighed. 'I do miss Twila,' he said, 'It's very sad to hear about the Thompsons, though. I hope Robert does find something.'

'I only wish there was something more we could do,' Raven replied sadly, 'Why hasn't Margaret been supportive of her husband? I don't understand.'

'I'm afraid we humans can be hard to understand, Raven,' Naomi replied, 'Sometimes, we tend to make things more difficult than they should be. Is there divorce among fairies?'

Raven shook her head. 'It's a rarity,' she said, 'but I was shocked how much divorce there is in the human world. I remember Jesus said that Moses had allowed divorce for the children of Israel out of the hardness of their hearts. That I understand from the scriptures, but it seems we fairies value marriage much more than you humans do. God did not intend for couples to divorce.'

Gabriel nodded. 'We can learn a lot from your people, Raven,' the elderly man said, 'in a lot of ways. God Himself instituted marriage in the garden of Eden between one man and one woman, but unfortunately, divorce is so high even among professing Christian families. Satan is an expert in destroying marriages and families and has been doing it for thousands of years.'

'It is very sad,' Raven sighed, 'I am going to make sure divorce is never a part of our vocabulary.'

'Amen to that, Raven,' Mordecai smiled at his black fairy wife, taking her hands.

There was a knock on the door. Raven looked out and saw the two children standing behind. 'It's Steve and Robin,' she said.

Mordecai headed into their room to change clothes. Raven allowed Steve and Robin to enter the house. 'Thank you, Miss Raven,' Robin said.

Raven smiled. 'We haven't forgotten about you,' she said, 'Mordecai is getting changed now.'

'Would you two like some hot chocolate and brownies?' Naomi asked the children, 'Mordecai made the brownies.'

'Yes, please,' Steve and Robin both chimed. They had tried Mordecai's brownies before and loved them. They sat up to the table while Naomi gave them hot chocolate and brownies.

While Mordecai got changed into the clothes given to him by Queen Cymbaline, Raven entered the room. She had a sad look upon her face. Mordecai turned and faced the ebony fairy. 'You okay, Raven?' he asked.

'My heart is grieved dealing with Robert and Margaret,' she said, placing her arms around him, 'the problems they are having. I still don't understand.'

'To tell you the truth, Raven,' sighed Mordecai, 'I don't understand either. It's very sad that Steve and Robin are caught in the middle. I'm sure it hurts them, the way their parents are arguing.'

Raven leaned her head upon his shoulders. Mordecai held her close and gently kissed her. 'We can do what we can to help Steve and Robin by spending time with them. That would help somewhat, but I hope and pray that things would get better for Robert and Margaret.'

After Steve and Robin had hot chocolate and brownies, Mordecai and Raven went outside with the two children. Mordecai threw the football with Steve while Raven played with Robin and the dolls she had. 'We never had dolls like this when I was growing up,' Raven said.

'Where did you grow up?' Robin asked.

'I grew up out of state,' Raven answered, 'I am not originally from here.'

'Did your Mommy name you after a bird as well?' Robin asked.

Raven laughed. 'I don't think so,' she answered, 'I guess they loved the name, so they named me Raven. It does happen to be the name of a bird, but I'm kind of used to it.'

'Do you love Mr. Mordecai, Miss Raven?'

'With all my heart,' Raven smiled.

Raven noticed Robin had a doll with the wings of a fairy. Robin showed it to her. 'This is my favorite, Miss Raven,' she said. 'I call her Sunshine.'

'That's a beautiful name, Robin,' Raven smiled.

'I named her myself,' Robin replied, 'My Mommy doesn't believe it, but I think there are fairies in the world.'

'Really?' Raven exclaimed, 'Believe it or not, I believe so, too.'

'I think fairies are small like this doll,' Robin whispered.

'I believe fairies are the size of humans,' Raven whispered back, 'They live in a kingdom called Arundel Haven ruled by a wise and virtuous queen, Queen Cymbaline, and her brother, Prince Avondale.'

'Wow, really?' cried Robin in surprise.

Raven giggled. 'Yes,' she nodded, 'However, fairies can be mistrusting of humans.'

'Why is that?' asked Robin, her eyes wide.

Raven sighed. 'The heart of man has the natural tendencies to do evil, to hurt, cheat, lie, steal, to do such wicked things. That is why Queen Cymbaline does not trust humans and has forbidden the fairies there to fly to the human world.'

'How do you know this, Miss Raven?' Robin asked quietly.

'I'll tell you a secret,' Raven told her, 'but you mustn't tell anybody. Mordecai knows, as do his grandparents.'

'What?' Robin asked.

Raven told her in a low voice, 'I am a fairy.'

Robin gasped. 'You are?'

'Yes,' Raven whispered, 'I will show you my wings.'

Raven looked around to make sure nobody else was present. She then took off her sweater and showed Robin her wings, flittering them briefly. Steve caught a glimpse and stared at Raven's wings. Mordecai stared at Raven and sighed. *Baby, are you sure this is the right thing to do?*

He was concerned about who else may have seen her.

Robin gasped. 'Wow, Miss Raven,' she cried, 'you are a real live fairy!'

'Yes, I am, Robin,' Raven nodded, 'I hope you will keep that a secret.'

'Is Mr. Mordecai a fairy as well?' she asked.

'No, I am not, Robin,' Mordecai answered as he and Steve approached, 'I am human like you and your brother.'

Raven slipped the sweater back over her body, covering up her wings.

'Do your granny and grandpa know?' asked Steve.

'Yes, they do,' Mordecai answered, 'as well as my mom and dad and sister, Cece. You've got to keep Raven's existence a secret for the protection of her people. Nobody must know that Raven is a fairy.'

'Is Arundel Haven real, Mr. Mordecai?' asked Robin.

Mordecai nodded. 'Raven herself is from Arundel Haven,' he told them, 'I have seen what no human has seen before: the hidden fairy kingdom, which is Raven's home. I am doing all I can to protect the fairies there to keep their existence a secret.'

'Promise you can keep that a secret?' Raven asked them.

'We promise, Miss Raven,' they said quietly.

Mordecai turned toward Raven gravely. She could tell her husband was displeased for revealing her wings to Robin. He sighed. 'I'm not sure it was the right thing for you to do, my love,' he said, 'revealing yourself to Robin. Steve now knows, too.'

'I know how you feel, baby,' Raven replied, wrapping her arms around him, 'but I felt led to do so. I did not mean to make you upset with me.'

'Maybe I'm just being overprotective like Queen Cymbaline,' he told her, 'I just don't want anything bad to happen to you or your people. Raven, I love you and care about you very much, and I want to keep you and your people safe.'

Raven smiled, kissing him. 'I know, my love,' she replied, 'but sometimes God wants us to take a leap of faith in certain matters.'

Mordecai sighed. 'I trust you, my sweet Raven,' he said. Raven kissed him on the lips. 'I'll trust you.'

'I love you, sweet Mordecai,' Raven replied softly, 'and I am glad to have you in my life, my lover, my best friend, my husband.

Mordecai smiled.

'You are married to Miss Raven?' Robin asked Mordecai, having overheard their conversation.

Mordecai and Raven turned toward them and nodded. 'Yes, I am,' answered Mordecai, 'She is my wife, I am proud to say. My parents, sister and my grandparents know about it, too. We were married in Arundel Haven.'

'Has a human and a fairy ever been married before?' Steve asked.

'Not before us,' Mordecai replied. 'We are the first, Raven and I.'

'I wish I could see Arundel Haven,' Robin said.

Mordecai and Raven stared at the children, then at each other again.

At that moment, a green car pulled up into the driveway. A tall man with black hair and a moustache, wearing a brown coat and black slacks stepped out of the car. He was 32 years old, over six feet tall, had green eyes, and wore black glasses. He sighed as he stepped out. The children ran up to greet him. 'Hi, Daddy,' they both cried.

The man picked up Robin as he kissed her. 'Had a good day at school, Robin?' he asked.

'They let us out early,' Robin said, 'We got home before Mr. Mordecai and Miss Raven returned.'

The man turned toward the couple. 'I appreciate you two spending time with my children,' he sighed, 'I only wish there was a way to show my appreciation.'

'Don't worry about it, Mr. Thompson,' Mordecai replied, 'Raven and I enjoy spending time with them.'

'You okay?' Raven asked.

Robert shook his head. 'Maggie's not going to be happy that they did not hire me,' he said, 'They chose somebody else over me. I was hoping to find something soon. It's not going to be much of a Christmas this year.'

Mordecai sighed as he glanced at Raven. 'Jobs are so hard to come by these days, especially with the government healthcare plan that President Farouk has passed,' Robert continued, 'There are not many full-time jobs, people losing their jobs.' He sighed. 'I'm sorry. I did not mean to burden you with my problems.'

'Don't think that way,' Mordecai told him, 'It is no burden. I should know what it's like to be hurting and struggling and needing someone to turn to. Steve and Robin are no burden at all.'

'Times are tough,' sighed Robert, 'Those of us without jobs can't get jobs because there is no full-time work out there, more part-time than full-time, and even those jobs are hard to find. There are some companies who are firing even long-time workers and hiring illegal immigrants in some cases. This is not right!'

Mordecai thought about President Farouk and what he was about to do when he and his men had sought to take Arundel Haven and wanted Arundel Haven to be subject unto the laws of the United States. Yet despite that, he was still in office and still president and had gone unpunished for his crimes. He also wondered about Dr. Von Braun, where he was, if he had indeed survived. Nothing had been heard about him since the Battle of Nebechadrezzar Valley. He somehow figured that Von Braun was indeed still alive and laying low for a time. President Farouk was leading America into ruin, yet the mainstream media still defended him and treated him like he was a savior. He shook his head sadly. 'I am sad that all this is going on.'

Robert walked inside. Steve did not enter inside. He stared at Mordecai and Raven and said, 'I hate it when Mommy and Daddy argue. It makes me so sad.'

'We know,' nodded Mordecai sadly. 'Raven and I will be here, as well as my grandparents. We will pray for your Mommy and Daddy.'

'I don't understand,' Steve shook his head, sitting down on the steps, 'If God loves us, why are my parents having problems?'

Mordecai and Raven sat down beside him. 'I wish I could tell you,' he replied sadly, 'I don't have all the answers, nor do I claim to have them. There are times when God allows the devil to do whatsoever he will but ultimately, he will bring good things out of the devil's bad things. I know it is of no comfort to you, Steve. It hurts us to see your parents like this.'

At that moment, they heard arguing inside. Robin ran outside in tears. She couldn't bear to see her parents arguing. She ran into Mordecai's arms. 'I'm so sorry, Robin,' Mordecai said softly.

Raven noticed Steve was starting to weep as well. She held the young boy as he wept. Raven couldn't help but start to weep herself. 'This shouldn't be,' she said amid her tears.

'Come with us, you two,' Mordecai told them, wiping the tears from his eyes, 'Neither of you should have to be exposed to this. We can only hope that this will pass very soon.' They led Steve and Robin into his grandparents' house.

That night, Mordecai and Raven were having dinner with Gabriel and Naomi. Mordecai had cooked baked chicken, green bean casserole and salad, and Raven had made homemade biscuits. They also had some tea that Raven had brewed earlier. 'What is your secret, Raven?' Naomi asked. 'I love how you make it.'

'I add some pure vanilla extract and the no calorie sugar you have,' Raven answered, 'Mordecai introduced me to it.'

I still can't believe how well Mordecai can cook,' Gabriel replied, taking a chicken leg and thigh.

Mordecai sighed. Raven turned toward him and placed her hand upon his shoulder. 'Thinking about Steve and Robin?' she asked.

'It's been weighing heavily on my heart,' Mordecai said sadly, 'I can't help but think about their situation. Robert is very discouraged about not finding a job, and Margaret is not helping matters, for sure.'

Both of Mordecai's grandparents nodded. 'It's so hard to see such a young couple going through such a tough time,' Gabriel sighed, 'especially when Margaret does nothing but criticize and chide him. It's affecting the kids in an adverse way.'

'Maybe we can invite them to dinner?' Raven asked, 'Do you think that would be a good idea? Mordecai and I can cook.'

'It's worth a shot,' Naomi nodded, 'but I don't know if that would help.'

'It would let them know that they have people who love and care for them,' Gabriel replied, 'I'm for it.'

Mordecai and Raven were washing dishes while Gabriel and Naomi were sitting in the living room watching television. Mordecai washed while Raven dried and put away the dishes. 'I'm still amazed, even after being here for nearly two months of the things here,' she said, 'The refrigerator, the television, radio.'

'We don't have a dishwasher here like at my parents' house,' Mordecai replied, 'but my grandparents are content, however. I don't mind cooking and cleaning, knowing that I have you here with me, Raven.'

Raven kissed him on the lips. 'Mordecai, I am so much in love with you,' she said.

Mordecai placed her arms, wet though they were, around her. Raven drew back briefly, flittering her wings to shake the water off them. 'Sorry,' he said.

Raven giggled. 'It is kind of cold,' she replied as she drew close again. Mordecai shook the excess water off his hands and pulled Raven closer. 'I love you so much, Raven,' he said.

Raven touched his face. 'I love you so much, too, my darling Mordecai,' she replied. Their lips came together in a gentle kiss as they wrapped their arms around each other. As they returned to washing the dishes, they heard some chatter in the living room and the door opening and closing. There were cries of joy and laughter. 'Wonder what's going on?' Mordecai asked.

Cece appeared from the living room and embraced both her brother and her sister-in-law. 'Hey, Cece,' Mordecai said.

'Come into the living room,' Cece said, pulling on his arm. Mordecai put the plate he was washing down and followed Cece. In the living room, he saw his parents and the familiar face of a six-three tall 22-year-old young man with an LSU purple and gold jacket over his 225-pound frame. He had long black hair and blue eyes, a moustache upon his face. Mordecai ran up to the young man and embraced him. 'Randy,' he cried. 'When did you get home?'

'It's good to see you, Mordy,' Randall replied, 'I heard you and sis have been getting along now from what Mom and Dad have told me.'

'You heard right,' Mordecai nodded as he embraced his parents.

'Cece told me she still believes in fairies,' Randall said, 'I hope you haven't been teasing her like you did when you were young.'

'No, not anymore,' Mordecai answered, 'My word, it's so good to see you again! How was your trip?'

'The flight was nice,' answered Randall. 'However, I was hoping to get away from the cold when I left Baton Rouge but it seems like it has followed me here. It's as if I'm being followed by the Snow Queen like the old tales.' To Cece he asked, 'Has Mordy been treating you good?'

Cece nodded. 'As a matter of fact, yes he has,' she answered, 'He had stopped teasing me months ago. The both of us, I am proud to say, are very close, almost like he is close to our cousin, Amy. It hasn't been the same since she had left for Gainesville last year to attend college. I'm sure she was just as upset that she had to leave.' To Mordecai she said, 'You know, you will have to introduce Raven to Amy. I am sure she would want to meet her.'

Mordecai sighed. 'I do miss Amelia so much,' he said, 'I can't wait to see her again and have her meet Raven.'

'I thought he would be mad at me,' Cece said, turning back to Randall, 'because Dad was teaching me how to drive and wasn't teaching him, but he never blamed me. I was the only one who had supported him emotionally in his bout with depression, listening to him, being there for him. We have been close ever since.' She paused. 'Wait until you meet—'

Mordecai interrupted her. 'Allow me, sis,' he started. To Randall he said, 'Randy, there is someone I want you to meet.'

Tony and Molly smiled.

'Mom, Dad and Cece have met her,' Mordecai continued, 'but...'

'Raven?' Randall asked.

'Yes, Raven,' Mordecai said.

He led his older brother into the kitchen. When Randall saw Raven, he gasped. His mouth opened in disbelief as he stared at her wings. 'Is she... Are those...'

'They are wings, Randy,' Mordecai laughed, 'Your eyes are not playing tricks on you. Yes, she is a fairy, a real fairy.' He paused. 'She is also my wife.'

'Your wife?!?' exclaimed Randall. 'You... you're kidding, aren't you?'

'No, he's not, son' Tony said, 'Your brother is telling the truth. Meet your new sister-in-law.'

'But I thought—' Randall stuttered.

'We were against Raven before because she was black,' Molly explained, 'but after getting to know her and her friends Lavender and Laurelin, I came to accept her as a person, and I am glad I did. Raven has shown herself to be a virtuous and wonderful young fairy woman. I am proud to have her in the family.'

'As am I,' Tony nodded, 'Raven is indeed a blessing; I am not ashamed to say.'

'Then that means… Arundel Haven—' Randall said.

'Is real,' Mordecai finished for him, 'We have been there before, me being the first human.'

Raven approached Randall and shook his hand. 'You must be Randall, Mordecai's brother,' she told him, 'I am so happy to meet you.'

Randall gave out a nervous laugh. 'I can't believe this,' he said, 'You, Mordy, had made fun of Cece growing up because of her belief in fairies, and now here you are married to a fairy, a black fairy on top of that.'

'She had risked her life to save Mordy from the dragon Shadowfire when the dragon had captured him,' Tony said, 'That convinced me to look at her in a favorable light. It also showed me that she loves him very much.'

'Dragon? Shadowfire?' exclaimed Randall, 'This is all a bit much to take in.'

Mordecai and Raven sat down. Randall did the same. 'I think it's time to tell you everything, the whole story,' Mordecai told his older brother.

He relayed the tale of his adventures to his brother, how he had met Raven, of the Prophecy of Queen Hephzibah, the marriage ceremony, and the death of the dragon.

Tony broke in when his son was in the middle of the story. 'We had been invited to Arundel Haven by Queen Cymbaline herself,' he added, 'after Mordy had been taken by Shadowfire. After Raven had rescued Mordy, the dragon wanted to lead President Farouk and Dr. Von Braun to Arundel Haven, but the fairy soldiers met them at Nebechadrezzar Valley to keep them away from their home. Many fairy lives had been lost in that battle, but President Farouk's men lost. At the time, your mother, sister, and I had agreed to look after Raven's sister Starla while they had kept Farouk's soldiers from reaching Arundel Haven.'

Randall sighed. 'I can't believe what I heard about Von Braun is true,' he exclaimed, 'Why did he believe you knew something about fairies, Mordy?'

'Shadowfire had feared the Prophecy,' he continued to explain, 'Somehow, he had contact with Dr. Von Braun, perhaps through his dreams like he had entered mine. I first met Dr. Von Braun at a convenience store on my way home from school just before I had met Raven. I had accidently overheard his conversation with his men working with him at the time asking the students about fairies. He followed me to the Southwood subdivision and was convinced I knew something about fairies. At the time, I thought he was totally insane.

'The dragon did not know my name at the time or where I lived until Dr. Von Braun told him, I'm sure of it. He had flown to our world and captured me while we were leaving *Rossi's* and took me to the Mountains of Shadow, which was called the Rundle Mountains before the dragon came and is called the Rundle Mountains once again. There, Raven had rescued me.'

'Who else knows about this?' asked Randall as Naomi pulled out a small album with the photos of the wedding of Mordecai and Raven.

'Sharon and Tiffany, Cece's friends,' Mordecai answered, 'They, too, had flown to Arundel Haven with Lavender and Laurelin. Cece had flown with Starla and Twila after Raven flew off to rescue me.'

Randall looked at the pictures. He was amazed by what he saw. 'That's Queen Cymbaline?' he asked, pointing at the figure of the Fairy Queen.

'Yes,' Mordecai answered, 'and that's her brother, Prince Avondale.'

'And I bet that toddler is Twila,' he laughed.

'I still find it amazing how quickly she became attached to Mordecai when she first met him,' Raven told Randall, 'She couldn't say his name, so she called him *uncle Morcai.*'

' "Uncle Morcai?"' laughed Randall.

'You remember how I told you Twila came to my cell after one of her flying escapades,' said Mordecai as he smiled. Raven smiled with him.

Randall laughed. 'Yes, I remember.'

'Roosevelt, Starla, and Twila had visited us not too long ago,' Tony said, 'At the time, they had spent a few nights with us, especially since Twila wanted to spend time with her new uncle.'

Mordecai smiled.

'And you were flying? Through the air?' asked Randall.

'Their powers of flight were only temporary while mine is permanent,' Mordecai explained, 'It has long since worn off on them, but they do have water from the beginning of the Silverstreams—as the fairies of Arundel Haven call it—so they can return there in the spring.'

'You are returning to Arundel Haven?' Randall asked.

'We plan to,' answered Cece, 'Queen Cymbaline has offered to give us the gift of flight that would be permanent like Mordy's ability.'

Randall gazed at the rest of the photos. He was still in awe by what he saw. Mordecai turned to Randall as he said, 'Since I have met Raven, I have worked hard to keep her existence as a fairy and Arundel Haven a secret. We have told you since you are family and there should be no secrets, but we all must keep it that way. Nobody else should know about Raven or her people.'

Randall stared at Mordecai. 'So, nobody else knows?'

'Dr. Von Braun knows about fairies, but he is one of the people who intend evil upon them,' he replied, 'He and President Farouk came too close to Arundel Haven when they invaded their lands.'

'Has there ever been such a union before?' Randall asked.

'No,' Raven answered, 'Mordecai and I are the first. Queen Cymbaline herself, as you can see from the photos, performed the ceremony herself, though she was against our relationship at first.'

'What changed her mind?' asked Randall.

'You can thank Twila for that,' Mordecai answered, 'Starla was against it as well, but when Twila came to my cell and what went on caused her heart to change. Twila accepted me without question or reservation.'

Randall stared at Mordecai. 'You sure don't act like *Lord Mordecai of the royal house of Jefferson.*'

'It is a title only recognizable in Arundel Haven,' Mordecai told his brother, 'The title is meaningless here. Here, I am just plain old Mordecai Jefferson husband of Raven.'

Randall shook his head. 'This is a lot to take in for sure. I have a fairy as a sister-in-law, my brother, a lord of Arundel Haven and has the ability to fly.'

'I know this is a lot to take in, Randall,' Molly said, 'If we hadn't met Raven and been to Arundel Haven, we would have a hard time believing it ourselves, although it was fun to fly.'

'But not in the snow,' Cece said, making a face.

Randall laughed. 'It would be nice to know how it feels to fly without being in an airplane,' he said, 'but how old are you, Raven? You look to be my age.'

'I am twenty-two,' Raven answered.

'Judas Priest, you are my age,' Randall exclaimed, 'You know how old—'

'Yes, I know Mordecai is seventeen,' Raven replied, 'God had brought us together regardless. I did not look at age or skin color or that he is a human and I a fairy. It's what's in the heart that counts.'

'And I am surprised that Mom and Dad are okay with Raven.'

'Of course, we weren't at first, neither of us,' Tony told his eldest son, 'but we did get to know them better and saw past Raven's skin color and that she was a fairy. I am personally glad now that Raven came into our lives as well as Mordy's.'

'And you say that both Mordy and Raven slew this Shadowfire?' asked Randall, still in awe from the story he was being told.

'That's what the Prophecy had stated,' Mordecai replied, 'God used us to slay Shadowfire and to end his reign of terror upon the fairies of Arundel Haven. Believe me, it wasn't easy.'

'What about Grandfather Geoff and Grandmother Connie, Dad?' Randall asked, 'Do they know about Raven?'

Tony shook his head and sighed. 'I know they must know sooner or later, but they will not accept Raven at all. Their prejudice is too deep in their hearts. Somehow, your mother's parents had lost that before you all were born.'

'And I am still kind of surprised,' Molly said.

'But don't give up on your parents, Tony,' Gabriel told his son-in-law, 'God had changed our hearts; He can do the same for Geoff and Connie.'

'Those are your grandparents' names?' Raven asked.

Mordecai nodded. 'I hope their hearts will change,' he sighed, 'I hope they will see what my parents saw in you, Raven, but I am afraid they would only look at your skin color and chide me for even seeing you. From what I was told, I guess my grandfather's still having heart problems.'

'Is he doing any better?' Randall asked, 'I was concerned when I heard he had to have a triple bypass.'

'He was better the last time I spoke to my mother,' Tony answered, 'He is supposed to be back home by now.'

'We will continue to pray for him,' said Gabriel, 'but Mordecai, I think you do need to tell him about Raven. They do have a right to know.'

Mordecai nodded. 'I know,' he said softly, 'but I am scared.'

'Remember what Queen Cymbaline had said to you when you were to enter the freezing waters of the Silverstreams falls when you had received your power of flight?' Raven told her human husband, *Sometimes, it takes courage and faith to do what you must do.* I still remember that day.'

'So *that's* how you gained your powers of flight,' Randall said, 'You did not tell me that.'

'I did forget that part, didn't I?' replied Mordecai. He sighed. 'You are right, Granddad, Grandfather Geoff and Grandmother Connie have that right to know.'

'Sometimes, my grandson,' Gabriel replied, 'the right thing to do is often the hardest. It's not too hard to think of what he and your grandmother would think of Raven. But they must know.'

Mordecai nodded. Raven gave him a gentle kiss.

When it turned dark, Gabriel turned on the Christmas lights that were hung above . The lights flashed different colors: red, blue, green, yellow, orange, purple. Raven looked around at the Christmas lights that others in the neighborhood had hung up. 'Wow,' she said, 'It is so beautiful! Like on the tree!'

'I always loved the lights this time of year,' Mordecai told her.

'I love it too,' Raven replied, 'We have nothing like this back in Arundel Haven.'

Molly smiled. 'Wait until you see the lights in our neighborhood, Raven,' she told the ebony fairy, 'You will love how our neighbors decorate their yards. To me, that's the best part about this time of year. Mordy always loves to see the lights.'

Mordecai nodded. 'Mom pinned me, Raven,' he told her, 'I've always loved seeing them since I was young.'

In the other yard, Steve and Robin looked at the lights. Behind them, their parents stood, not speaking to each other. Margaret was 30 years old, had short brown hair, blue eyes, and stood about a few inches shorter than her husband. She wore a long yellow and blue dress with a heavy brown sweater over her slim frame. They heard Robin say, 'I love looking at the lights.'

'I know you do,' her mother said.

Steve saw Mordecai, Raven and the others and ran over to them. Robin followed close behind. Somehow, both of their parents seemed to smile as they stopped near the young lovers. 'Hi, Steve and Robin,' Raven said. 'You watching the lights?'

'Do they have lights like this in Arundel Haven, Miss Raven?' Robin asked quietly.

'No, we don't,' Raven answered, 'We do have candles, but they are nothing like this, I must admit.'

'They know about Raven?' Randall asked Mordecai, 'They know she is a fairy?'

'Yes, the children do, but not their parents,' Mordecai answered, 'Raven had chosen to reveal herself to the children.'

'I wonder what Arundel Haven is like?' Randall asked.

'It is beautiful,' Mordecai answered, 'There is no electricity or modern things like we have here, it's a simple life there, a wondrous place nonetheless.'

'I wish I could visit Arundel Haven,' Robin said wistfully.

Tony and Molly nodded. Gabriel turned toward them. 'I am curious about Arundel Haven myself,' he told him, 'but that would have to be up to Queen Cymbaline, of course.'

'We can ask her for you, Granddad,' Mordecai replied, 'both Raven and I.'

Raven nodded.

Steve and Robin heard their parents call their names. Steve sighed. 'I hope they don't end up fighting again,' he said, 'I hate it when they fight.'

'Hold on,' Mordecai said to them. He walked with the two kids to their parents. Raven was quick to join them. 'How are you two doing?' the young man asked.

'Seen better days,' Margaret sighed, 'I want to thank you, Mordecai and Raven, and your grandparents for looking after Steve and Robin for us.'

'No problem,' Raven replied, 'We're more than happy to.'

'I still can't believe how much kindness you and your grandparents have shown us,' Robert said.

'We're only more than happy to,' Mordecai said, 'I talked it over with my grandparents, and we would like to know if you would like to come over and have dinner with us tomorrow night.'

At first, Robert and Margaret did not respond.

'Please?' Steve and Robin implored them, 'Mr. Mordecai is a great cook. He makes a great veal parmesan and green bean casserole.'

'I didn't know you could cook, Mordecai,' Margaret said.

'He sure can,' Raven replied, 'He's been doing most of the cooking lately. Even his grandparents love his cooking. He also baked the brownies that your children had.'

'You baked some brownies, the ones Steve and Robin brought to me yesterday?' Margaret asked, 'I thought it was your grandmother who made them.'

'No, it was Mordecai,' Raven said proudly, 'We had baked chicken tonight and I brewed the tea as well. Please, come and have supper with us.'

With a sigh, both parents agreed.

'Tomorrow night would be fine?' Mordecai asked.

'Okay, tomorrow night, then,' Robert nodded.

The next night, Mordecai and Raven made preparations. Raven had her wings covered with a blue blouse. Mordecai did most of the cooking, but Raven made the tossed salad, the biscuits, and the tea. She also set the plates while Mordecai concentrated on the cooking. 'I have never made food for this many people before,' he said.

'Nor have I,' Raven replied, rejoining him in the kitchen.

While they cooked, Robert, Margaret, and their two children arrived from next door. They could smell the cooking. They sat down on the couch. 'So, Mordecai is supposed to be a great cook?' Margaret said, 'Steve and Robin seem to think so.'

'He's been doing most of the cooking since he started staying here,' Naomi replied, 'He is a great cook, believe me.'

Steve and Robin headed into the kitchen, but Margaret called out to them. 'Steve, Robin, get back in here,' she said.

Mordecai and Raven saw the two kids in the kitchen with them. Mordecai called out, 'It's okay, Mrs. Thompson. It's okay for them to join us if it's okay with you.'

Margaret sighed, nodding her head.

Raven brought in two chairs for them, and the kids sat down. 'Smells good, Mr. Mordecai,' Steve said.

'I hope your parents will like it,' Mordecai said, 'I've got steak, sautéed mushrooms, mashed potatoes, spinach and green beans, and Raven's got a salad, biscuits, and tea made.'

'The vanilla tea?' Robin asked.

'Yes, and I have regular tea as well,' answered Raven as she smiled.

When supper was served, they gathered at the table. Mordecai led the prayer, giving thanks to God. Then the meal was served. Robert and Margaret each took a bite. Margaret smiled. 'I can't believe you cooked this, Mordecai,' she said. 'This is great!'

Robert nodded. 'I am impressed,' he replied, 'How long have you been cooking?'

'For about five years, I think,' answered Mordecai, 'When I stayed with my parents, they enjoyed the cooking. Even before I met Raven, I was cooking.'

'I am sure impressed,' Margaret said, smiling.

'Why did you start staying with your grandparents?' Robert asked Mordecai, 'Did you have problems with your parents?'

'No, not really,' Mordecai answered, 'There were no problems between me and my parents to speak of. We just wanted to stay with my grandparents for a while.'

' "We?"' Margaret asked.

'It was closer to Oak Ridge, so I decided to stay here for a while,' Mordecai continued, 'Besides, my grandparents needed our company.'

'You mean to tell me that you and Raven stay here?' Robert asked.

'Yes,' Mordecai answered, 'Raven and I got married a couple of months ago.'

'Married and still in high school?' laughed Margaret.

'I know it sounds unusual,' Mordecai said, 'but both my parents approved of the wedding.'

'I can't believe that you're married and still in high school,' replied Robert, taking another bite, 'Still, I have to admit, this is good.'

'How do your parents feel about this?' Margaret asked Raven.

Raven sighed. 'I had lost my parents over a year ago,' she said, hanging her head, 'They were killed by a wicked beast.'

Robert and Margaret sighed. 'I'm very sorry to hear,' Robert said softly, 'You must miss them very much.'

Raven nodded sadly. 'My older sister, Starla, gave me away at the wedding,' she said, 'since my parents weren't alive. I'm sure they would like Mordecai the way he is.'

'It's been a long time since we sat down together for a dinner,' replied Robert, 'It is good to have a nice quiet dinner.'

'I just don't like it when you and Mommy argue,' Robin said quietly.

'Robin, that's enough!' snapped Margaret. She turned to Gabriel and said, 'I'm sorry about that.'

'It's okay,' Gabriel replied, 'Don't worry about it.'

'What do you plan to do after you graduate high school, if I may ask?' Robert asked Mordecai.

'I will eventually have to find a job,' Mordecai answered, 'Raven and I plan on raising a family.'

'That's going to be tough to do with the way this economy is,' Robert said.

'I understand that,' Mordecai nodded sadly.

'The job market is tough,' he continued, 'I should know.' 'Robert!' shot in Margaret.

'Well, Mordecai has a right to know,' replied Robert irritably, 'He's too young to be married. He needs a way to support his children if they decide to have them.'

'We do,' nodded Raven.

'What kind of future is there if there are no jobs?' added Robert, 'Are you going to stay with your parents or stay here?'

'No, sir,' answered Mordecai, drinking his tea, 'Raven and I plan to have a place of our own.'

'Will you be able to find work too, Raven, if need be?' Robert asked the fairy.

'I'm sure I will,' answered Raven.

'I don't have confidence that there are jobs for people like us,' replied Robert irritably, 'Most of the jobs have been taken by and given to illegal immigrants thanks to President Farouk's open border policies. President Farouk made a bad decision, taking jobs away from U.S citizens, even those immigrants who came here legally are thrown under the bus in favor of illegals. It's not right!'

'Robert, will you stop?' cried Margaret, 'We are guests here!'

Mordecai bowed his head low as they argued. 'Do you even realize how hard the job market is, do you?' Robert asked Mordecai.

Mordecai nodded his head sadly. 'I know it's difficult.'

'That's enough, Robert,' snapped Margaret, 'They were kind enough to invite us to dinner fixed by Mordecai himself—which is surprisingly great, by the way—but this is how you thank him?'

'I'm just telling him the way things are, Margaret,' replied Robert angrily, 'Life and marriage are no fairytale, no "happily ever after!" Life is full of pitfalls and difficulties where you have to fight to survive! Nobody's going to come to him and offer him a job!'

Steve and Robin began to cry as they started to move away from the table. 'No, you two stay right there,' Margaret told them, 'You finish your meal right now.'

'It's not the food,' Raven told her, 'Can't you see how much your arguing and fights are upsetting them? It's really affecting them. I understand and realize that a marriage is hard work, but a marriage worth fighting for is a marriage worth keeping! Your children love you and care about you both! It hurts them badly when you two argue! Can't you see that?'

'And what would you suggest, young lady?' snapped Margaret.

'I know Mordecai and I are new to the marriage thing,' replied Raven, 'and our marriage is yet to be tested, but all we have is the love we have for each other. Where I come from, divorce is an extreme rarity.'

'And where did you come from?' retorted Margaret.

'Please, please settle down,' cried Mordecai, standing up, 'Can't we all take some time and cool down? It's hurting Steve and Robin with all this arguing going on! I can't imagine what you are going through, and I know things are tougher than I could ever imagine, I admit that, but all this strife, this fighting, is bad for the both of them! Please, I beg of you, work it out!'

'And who are you to say?' Robert snapped.

Mordecai bowed his head and sat down.

'One of these days, boy, you and your loving wife will come to the same place that we are, and you will know how rough life can be! It may be fine right now since you're still in high school, but once you get out into the real world you might understand!'

'Please, Mr. Thompson, please be calm!' Raven begged, 'I know how bad humans can be. I have seen only a brief taste while I've been here. I know all marriages take a lot of work, including ours. We will definitely have ups and downs, but Mordecai and I are together in this. Divorce will never be a part of our vocabulary.'

'Wait till you been married for ten years,' Margaret snapped, 'You will see that marriage is not all rainbows and yellow brick roads! The cruel reality of life will sooner or later catch up with you both and shatter your fairytale world, and you will see that divorce will become a stark raving reality! And besides, where do you come from that you say divorce is an extreme rarity?'

'Arundel Haven,' snapped Raven.

'Raven!' Mordecai cried.

Gabriel and Naomi gasped.

'Raven, why?' Naomi said softly.

'Arundel Haven?' scoffed Margaret, 'You've got to be joking!'

'No joke, mommy,' wept Robin, 'Miss Raven is a real live fairy!'

'Robin, no!' cried Mordecai.

'I'm sorry, Mr. Mordecai,' wept Robin, walking over and weeping on his shoulder.

Mordecai sighed, holding the little girl. 'I know,' he replied softly.

'You can't be serious,' Robert laughed. 'You, Raven, a real live fairy?'

Raven sighed. As she was about to pull her blouse off that covered her wings, Gabriel asked, 'Raven, are you sure this is a good idea?'

Raven pulled her blouse off. She wore another blouse underneath. She revealed to the children's parents her wings, flittering them a little. 'It is true, Mr. Thompson,' she said softly, 'I am a fairy. I am originally from Arundel Haven. It hurts me so much to see Steve and Robin hurt by your arguing.' She started to weep as she tried to talk. 'Both Mordecai and I know that marriage is not an easy road, but we know that the love we have for each other is worth fighting for, no matter what the devil throws at us.'

Both Robert and Margaret rose from their seats and stared at Raven's wings. Each one felt them as they stared at them. 'They are real,' Margaret exclaimed, 'The wings *are* real, but how….?'

'Long story,' Raven replied amid her tears, 'It just hurts me the way your children are hurt with the arguing. Isn't the love you have worth fighting for? No, things are not easy, not even in Arundel Haven. We fairies and humans have more in common than either of our respective peoples realize. We hurt, we love, we feel pain, heartache. I can't imagine what problems and pain the both of you are going through, but you need each other. Your children need the both of you, together. Aren't your children worth fighting to keep your marriage for?'

Without another word, Robert and Margaret took their children, who were weeping, and headed out the door. Raven wept as Mordecai wrapped his arms around her. Gabriel and Naomi walked up to them and engaged in a group hug. 'It was risky what you did, Raven,' Gabriel said softly, 'but I think I understand why.'

Mordecai wept. 'I know what they say about marriage is true,' he said, 'but it still hurts to see both Steve and Robin suffering like this.'

Naomi kissed her grandson. 'I know, sweetie,' she replied, 'My heart goes out to them as well. Yet both sides are right. Marriage is hard, but a marriage worth keeping is a marriage worth fighting for. You two go ahead to your room if you wish. We'll clean up. You are a great person, Mordecai, and a great cook as well. Thank you.'

Mordecai kissed his grandmother. 'You are welcome, Grandmom,' he replied amid his tears.

'All we can do is keep praying for them,' Gabriel said, 'God can change their hearts and heal their marriage.'

'I hope so,' wept Raven. 'I hate to see Steve and Robin like this!'

'Me too, Raven,' sighed Gabriel, kissing the ebony fairy on the cheeks. 'Me too.'

After church the next day, Cece, Sharon, and Tiffany drove over to a two-story house in the Lockhart area. Mordecai and Raven were with them. Mordecai seemed apprehensive and worried, and Cece and the others could tell. Raven was worried as well. 'I know they must know about me,' she said, 'but I am scared. I'm not sure what to expect.'

Mordecai took her hand. 'Me too,' he replied softly.

'Why do your grandparents have a problem with people of Raven's skin color?' Tiffany asked, 'I don't understand.'

'They have always been like that,' Cece responded, 'I couldn't believe to hear that my mother's parents were like that one time, at least before I was born.'

'Your grandparents on your mother's side are nice, Cece,' Sharon said, 'I can't believe they used to be prejudiced like your paternal grandparents are. I didn't know about Mordy, though! It's still hard to believe how great a cook he is.' To Mordecai she asked, 'How often do your grandparents allow you to cook?'

'I've been doing all the cooking for the past two weeks now since they love it,' Mordecai answered, 'but Raven has helped too. She's done salads, made homemade biscuits,'

'But Mordecai has made such wonderful brownies,' Raven added, 'The two Thompson children love his brownies.'

'Wow, that good, huh?' Sharon asked.

They pulled into the driveway of a two-story house. They walked over to the front door. Cece rang the doorbell. A woman wearing a light blue dress opened the door. She was 71 years old, slim, short, with black and grey hair. She looked at and embraced Cece. 'Hello, Cece,' she said.

'Grandma, you know Sharon and Tiffany,' she told her.

'I sure do,' she nodded, 'Hello.'

'Hello, Mrs. Jefferson,' Tiffany said.

Then she glanced at Mordecai and Raven. Her smile disappeared when she saw the black fairy. Mordecai sighed. 'Hi, Grandma,' he said.

'Mordy,' she simply said as she frowned.

Mordecai turned toward Raven and gave out a nervous sigh. Raven could not speak a word.

In a low voice, she told them, 'Come in.' She allowed them to enter, though she frowned at Raven. Raven could tell her dislike, felt it in her spirit. She sighed. 'I'm guessing, Mordy, this is your girlfriend your father has been telling me about? I am disappointed in you.'

'This is Raven,' Mordecai introduced her.

'You know how your grandfather and I feel about black people,' she frowned, 'Why have you brought her here? You know her people are not welcomed here.'

'I want there to be no secrets,' Mordecai answered. 'I do know of your feelings toward people of color, but—'

'I thought we had taught Tony better than that,' he heard his grandmother say. 'Has he lost his mind in allowing you to date her? Don't expect us to give her a warm welcome.'

On the rocking chair sat Geoff, the grandfather of Mordecai and Cece. He was 73 years old, wore a long flannel shirt and blue jeans, had short gray hair with a receding hair line. He had glasses upon his face. He turned around and smiled when he saw Cece, then frowned when he saw Raven. He slowly rose from the chair. 'It's good to see you, Cece,' he said.

'And you too, Grandpa,' Cece replied.

Geoff then stared frowning at Mordecai and Raven. 'So, this is what your father said that you were going to tell me, wasn't it, Mordy?' he said in a low voice, 'You wanted to tell me that you are dating a black woman? You know how your grandmother and I feel about her people! I am very disappointed in you.'

Mordecai hung his head.

'You ought to be ashamed of yourself,' he continued angrily, 'Why did you bother to bring her over here given our feelings toward her kind? You know our feelings all too well!'

'There is more to her than just appearance, Grandpa,' replied Mordecai softly, 'My parents saw this, though they rejected her at first. They eventually saw what was in her heart.'

Geoff was not convinced, nor was Connie. 'Why did you start dating her in the first place?' the old man asked, 'How could you shame this family by choosing to date a black woman? This is completely unacceptable!'

'Because she took the time to listen to me,' Mordecai answered softly, 'She was there at the lowest point in my life. She is a special young lady, and that is what I saw.'

'So you say,' Connie frowned, 'Don't you know that this is wrong on all fronts, Mordy? Mixed marriages should never be allowed or recognized. It is wrong for anybody to date outside of their race! What were you thinking? You have done ill in bringing her here!'

'With all due respect, why do you hate people of color?' Raven asked.

'Blacks are violent, thieves, so foul mouthed,' Geoff replied, 'They will do anything to get what they want.'

'Doesn't that describe all humans?' Raven asked, 'Don't all humans fit that category?'

'That's not the point,' Connie said quickly.

'Why do you choose to hate people of different skin color?' Raven asked, 'I just don't understand you humans . Are we not all the same? All of us were created in the image of God.'

'Raven,' Cece warned her.

'Aren't we all the same, no matter what skin color?' Raven continued, 'Have the same color blood, hurt the same, feel the same, suffer hunger and thirst the same? Didn't God create people of all races? Why are you so intolerant of all those who do not have your skin color? I just don't understand.'

'I don't get your point,' Geoff replied grimly.

'If you only knew,' sighed Raven. 'God looks at the heart of a person, looks on the outside, not the inside . Why do you hate those who have darker skin than yours?'

Both Geoff and Connie stared at Mordecai and Raven grimly. Mordecai knew visiting his paternal grandparents was a mistake.

'Why have you chosen her?' Geoff asked Mordecai, 'Why are you going out with her? I do not see why you would shame the family with such a thing as this! Our feelings on this matter have not changed! What good reason do you have in justifying your relationship with her?'

'Because I love her,' Mordecai answered, 'and Raven loves me. That is good enough for us.'

'No! No, it is not!' snapped Geoff, stamping his foot once on the floor, 'This is not a good reason!'

'Not to us it's not,' Connie replied sternly, 'We will never approve of this relationship. You have brought shame to this family by choosing her. This is wrong on all fronts! You would do well in breaking up with her and finding a girl with the same skin color! We will not accept her!'

'Know this, Mordy,' growled Geoff, 'Neither you nor your girlfriend are welcome in this house, do you understand? I do not want you or her to show yourselves around here ever again, unless you stop going out with her! She is not welcome, nor will she ever be welcome in this house! As long as you are with her, you will never come around here again, do I make myself clear?'

'Clearly,' Mordecai answered, 'That is not the only reason we came here, though. You would like the two reasons even less, or at least one of them.'

'What do you mean?' Connie asked with a sour look upon her face.

'Explain yourself,' Geoff commanded.

'Go ahead, Raven,' sighed Mordecai.

Raven took her sweater off and revealed to Geoff and Connie her wings. They gasped when they saw her flittering them. 'What the devil is this?' Geoff cried. 'What is she?'

'Have you ever heard of a place called Arundel Haven?' Mordecai asked.

'Wait a minute,' Connie exclaimed, 'are you saying that the old tales are true, that Arundel Haven is real, and that your girlfriend is a real fairy? I have read that Dr. Von Braun believed that fairies exist, but I did not believe in the things I heard and read. This can't be real!'

'I am a fairy,' Raven said quietly, 'I am from Arundel Haven.'

'Are all fairies black?' Geoff asked skeptically.

'No, not all,' Raven answered, 'There are fairies of different colors, only skin color prejudice does not exist among my people.' She flittered her wings enough to allow her to rise off the ground to the surprise of Geoff and Connie. 'We have no such prejudice, but we do not trust humans because of their nature.'

Connie could hardly speak. Geoff stared hard at the fairy and asked, 'Why him? Why Mordy? Why did you choose to come into his life and fall in love with him? This is preposterous! If your kind don't trust humans, then why are you in a relationship with him? This makes no sense at all!'

'Because God had led me to him,' Raven answered, 'We were the ones who were used by God to destroy the dragon Shadowfire, who had been afflicting my people for 150 years.'

Geoff staed at Mordecai sternly. The young man could feel the hate toward people of Raven's skin color coming from his grandfather. 'Please don't see Raven as black or as a fairy, Mr. Jefferson,' Sharon said. 'Your son and his wife saw how wonderful she is, how she proved her love for Mordy when she risked her life—'

'I will never approve of you having this black fairy as your girlfriend, nor will your grandmother,' replied Geoff sharply, 'If you seek our approval of your relationship with this… Raven, then you are sorely mistaken! It is wrong for the both of you to be together! We will never accept her as your girlfriend, as long as you choose to be with her!'

'I am not Mordecai's girlfriend,' shot back Raven, 'I am his *wife*!'

Geoff and Connie recoiled when Raven made that proclamation. After a moment, his expression turned into anger as he told Mordecai in a soft, angry voice, 'Get out of my house, both you and your black fairy!'

'Please, Grandpa, no,' Cece cried.

'I want them out of my house *now*!' he hissed.

Raven burst into tears. Mordecai was equally as upset as Geoff chased them out of the house with the others behind. As they ran, they both took to the air, too upset to be cautious. As Geoff chased them out of the door, he stopped and stared in shock to see them flying, particularly Mordecai, out of sight. When the others caught up to him, Connie stood with the same shock. 'Mordy can fly?' she whispered.

'That's not possible,' Geoff uttered, 'How could this be? How can it be possible for Mordy to fly?'

Without another word, Cece, Sharon, and Tiffany headed into the car and drove off . Geoff and Connie stared at the open space where Mordecai and Raven had disappeared for a long moment.

Minutes later, Mordecai and Raven landed in the backyard and hurried inside the house of their grandparents. Gabriel was at the table having a cup of coffee. He was surprised to see them come in from the backyard. 'Mordecai? Raven?' he said, rising from his chair. 'You flew here?' He then saw the tears in their eyes and sighed. 'I think I know what happened.'

Raven nodded amid her tears. She wept on Mordecai's shoulders as he held her, tears streaming down his face. 'I knew they had to be told,' said Mordecai amid his tears, 'I knew they would respond the way they did, but it hurt.'

'Did you tell them everything?' Gabriel asked as Naomi walked into the dining room.

'We told them what we could,' wept Raven, 'The fact that I was a fairy and that Mordecai and I are married. I don't understand such hate!'

Naomi embraced them both and kissed them. 'I know, sweetie,' she replied, 'I can imagine the pain you two are feeling. Unfortunately, all we can do is leave them in the Lord's hands.'

'Cece just called from her cell phone just before you arrived,' Gabriel said, 'we told them that you two hadn't made it back yet. They're just as upset.'

Mordecai and Raven sat down. Naomi poured for them each a glass of tea that Raven had brewed the night before. 'Thank you, Grandmom,' Mordecai and Raven said.

'They did not hear the tale of what happened between you two and all in Arundel Haven?' Gabriel asked.

Mordecai shook his head. 'We never had the chance to tell them,' he wept as Raven wept upon his shoulders, 'I couldn't imagine the extent of their hatred toward blacks. I had known about it but seeing it firsthand. Facing Shadowfire was easier than facing Grandma and Grandpa, knowing of their bigotry. I knew it was to be expected, but it hurts all the same.'

At that moment, there was a ringing from Mordecai's cell phone. He pulled it out of his pocket and spoke into it. 'Hello?'

'Hi, Mordy.' It was the voice of his father. 'Your grandfather told me what had happened. I know you and Raven must be very upset right now.'

'It needed to be done, I know,' replied Mordecai amid his tears as he struggled to compose himself, 'As I was telling Granddad, facing Shadowfire was easier than facing them.'

'He chewed me out for allowing you and Raven to get married, and for you marrying a fairy on top of that,' sighed Tony, 'I would have reacted the same way had I not gotten to know her and her friends. I don't regret having Raven as a daughter-in-law seeing the kind of person she is. She is a true blessing indeed. How is Raven taking it?'

'She is also taking it hard,' answered Mordecai as Raven continued to weep, holding Mordecai close, 'I knew it was to be expected, but it doesn't make the pain any less.'

Raven indicated to Mordecai that she wanted to speak. 'It's my father,' he told her.

Raven nodded as she took it. She struggled to say, 'Hi, Daddy.'

'I know it's a foolish question to ask, Raven,' Tony replied, 'but are you okay?'

'It's unbelievable how much hate there is in your parents' hearts,' wept Raven, 'We weren't even given the chance to tell them all that happened in Arundel Haven. They have closed their hearts to me since I am black. I cannot understand their hate.'

'We're on our way over,' Tony said, 'your mom and I. We have visitors who wish to see you very much. We're not telling you or Mordy yet.'

'I'm not sure if we can see anybody right now,' Raven wept, 'Mordecai and I would not be good hosts now, but—'

'I'm sure you want to see them, Raven,' said Tony, 'We're on our way now.'

Raven nodded. 'Okay,' she nodded, then gave the phone back to Mordecai. 'You still there, Dad?' he asked.

'I just told Raven we're on our way there,' Tony replied, 'We have a surprise for you and Raven. See you when we get there.'

'Okay,' sighed Mordecai as he hung up. He turned to his grandparents. Wiping the tears from his eyes he said, 'Mom and Dad are on their way here, with guests, they tell me.'

'Did he say who?' Naomi asked.

'No, he didn't,' answered Mordecai, 'He didn't tell me.' 'Nor me,' sighed Raven.

'I'm sure we have enough tea, if need be,' Naomi said, 'the regular and Raven's vanilla tea.'

About twenty minutes later, Mordecai and Raven sat down at the dining room table drinking tea. Raven's head was leaning upon Mordecai's shoulders as he caressed and kissed her. 'I'm still upset about your father's parents, Mordecai,' she told him.

Mordecai kissed her. 'I know,' he sighed, 'I know I expected their response, but it doesn't make the pain any easier to bear. I still love them, but rejecting you really cuts me to the core.'

'I wish they could see what you and your parents see in me,' Raven said sadly, 'It still comes as a shock, such prejudice, and it hurts worse seeing it for myself.'

Mordecai caressed her face and kissed her. He wished he knew the right words to say to encourage her. It hurt him deeper that Raven was hurt, even moreso than his grandparents had hurt him. 'We will honor their wishes, and not go there again,' he sighed, 'It's no use going where we are not wanted. They reject you; they then reject me.'

'I don't regret meeting you and falling in love with you, Mordecai,' Raven replied, touching her husband's face, wiping the tears from his eyes. Mordecai did the same with Raven. 'I know God brought us together, and that is what makes our love right.'

Mordecai nodded. 'It still hurts my grandparents' response to you,' he sighed, 'It hurt me when he hurt you. I wish they could see how happy you make me, and how happy I make you.'

'I am thankful that your parents had accepted me, even though they were against me at first,' sighed Raven, 'They have become just as much as my parents as my own when they were still alive.'

'I keep wondering how your parents would react to me if they knew about me?'

Raven shook her head. 'I keep wondering that myself,' she said, 'There are times I do miss them.'

Mordecai nodded. 'I know,' he replied, 'I hope they would see how happy I make you and how happy you make me.'

Raven kissed Mordecai gently on the cheeks. 'I feel blessed to have you, Mordecai, my love, my life,' she said, 'I love you with all my heart and bless the days that we are together.'

'I love you too, my sweet Raven,' replied Mordecai, 'with all my heart; my best friend, my lover, my wife.'

'I am blessed that you are my husband, sweet Mordecai,' Raven said as tears continued to flow down her cheeks.

At that moment, they heard the front door open and close. As they talked, a familiar fairy toddler appeared flying toward them, crying, 'Uncle Morcai, Uncle Morcai!'

Both of their faces lit up as Mordecai stood, moving away from the table, receiving Twila into his arms. Twila kissed him. 'I miss you, Uncle Morcai,' she said.

'I miss you too, Twila,' Mordecai replied as he held her close.

Raven saw Starla and Roosevelt entering the kitchen area. She ran over and embraced them. 'Starla! Roosevelt!' she cried. 'I am so happy to see you!'

'How are you both doing?' Roosevelt asked as he and Starla embraced Mordecai.

'We told my father's parents,' Mordecai replied in a soft voice, 'but they rejected Raven, going by her skin color.'

'Your father told us about your grandparents,' Starla said sadly, 'Both his parents were very mad at him for allowing you to marry Raven. How are the both of you?'

'We're still grieved by it,' Mordecai sighed, 'It was expected, but it still hurts, nonetheless. We are so happy to see you.'

'We do have others who wish to see you,' Roosevelt said, 'We're not the only ones anxious to see you.'

'Yes, yes, Uncle Morcai,' Twila chimed as she kissed him on the cheeks.

The familiar forms of Lavender and Laurelin appeared in the kitchen. Raven embraced both friends. 'I am so happy to see you!' she told them.

'It's been a long time,' Laurelin said, 'Mordecai's parents told us of what happened to you two while telling his grandparents about you.'

'Both of us are grieved by the whole thing,' Raven sighed, 'It was to be expected, though, but it still hurts nonetheless.'

'There is someone else who wants to see you as well,' Lavender added.

Mordecai and Raven looked and saw a familiar form in a dark robe laced with gold enter the kitchen. They saw the familiar dark hair, fair features, and the golden tiara of the ruler of Arundel Haven. 'Queen Cymbaline!' Mordecai cried.

Queen Cymbaline embraced and kissed Mordecai, stared at him. 'It's been too long since we've seen you, Lord Mordecai,' she said, 'My heart rejoices to see you again.'

Raven embraced her. 'Your majesty,' she cried. 'What are you doing here?'

'For one,' Queen Cymbaline said, 'I wished to see Lord Mordecai and Lady Raven of the house of Jefferson again. Also, I wish for your presence at the Saviour's Day celebration this Tuesday night in Arundel Haven.'

'Of course, my Queen,' nodded Mordecai, 'We would be more than happy to come!'

Raven sighed.

'What is wrong, Lady Raven?' Queen Cymbaline asked, marking her countenance.

'Apart from Mordecai's grandparents on his father's side,' sighed Raven, 'two kids living next door have been on our hearts.'

Lavender and Laurelin groaned. 'Here we go again,' muttered Lavender.

'That's enough,' Queen Cymbaline told them sharply. To Raven she said, 'Go ahead.'

Raven took a deep breath. 'Their names are Steve and Robin Thompson,' she said softly, 'Mordecai and I have spent a lot of time with them. Their parents are constantly arguing because Robert, their father, lost his job and is trying to find work but he can't. His wife, Margaret, hasn't been supportive of him. She constantly argues with him for not being able to find work. They are bitter about their situation and it's having an ill effect upon the kids.'

Queen Cymbaline bowed her head. She sighed, thinking about what Raven had told her. They were soon joined by Tony, Molly, Randall, Gabriel, and Naomi. She turned to Gabriel and asked, 'How long has this been going on, Gabriel?'

'For three months, I'm afraid,' Gabriel answered, 'When Mordecai and Raven came to stay with us, Steve and Robin had been spending a lot of time with them and took to them right away. It seemed to help both children. Robert and Margaret are a good couple all in all. They have been going through some tough times, with the loss of Robert's job. They've been living next door since they got married. Things were fine until the arguments started—for what reasons I don't know—but they got worse since Robert lost his job.'

Raven sighed. 'They know I am a fairy,' she told the Queen.

'They what?!?' exclaimed Lavender and Laurelin.

'Raven, have you lost your mind?' Laurelin added.

'Enough, both of you,' Queen Cymbaline said sternly to the two fairies. To Raven she said, 'Explain.'

'Friday, I told Robin since she believes in fairies,' Raven said, 'Steve saw as well when I showed Robin my wings. I had felt led to do so. When we had them over to dinner last night, Robin did tell her parents about me.'

'Raven, what is wrong with you?' Lavender exclaimed, 'Why did you reveal yourself to them?'

'She must have had her reasons,' Mordecai answered quietly.

'I thought you cared about our secret, Mordecai,' Laurelin replied sharply.

'I do,' answered Mordecai, 'She told Robin before I could realize it. I'm sure she had her reasons to do so. I don't like it, but what's done is done.'

'And that's all you're going to say about it?' Lavender asked harshly.

'Lavender, Laurelin, that's enough!' snapped Queen Cymbaline.

'Forgive me, your majesty,' Raven said softly.

Queen Cymbaline stood silent for a long moment. Afterwards, she turned to Gabriel. 'I would like to personally meet them,' she said to him, 'I feel led in my heart to do so.'

'Your majesty, do you think that's wise, exposing yourself to more humans?' Lavender asked.

'I know,' Queen Cymbaline replied, 'but God has laid it on my heart to see them. Raven may have been right to reveal herself to them.'

Mordecai and Raven headed next door and knocked on the door. Margaret opened the door. 'Mordecai,' she said. 'What are you doing here?'

'There is someone I know who wants to meet you,' Mordecai said, 'She cannot come here but has requested your presence nevertheless.'

Margaret shook her head. 'This is not such a good time,' she frowned.

At that moment, Steve and Robin appeared at the door. They smiled when they saw him. Then Robert walked to the door, catching a glimpse of Mordecai and Raven. 'I am sorry about last night,' he sighed.

'Please come with us, Mr. Thompson, all of you,' Raven told them, 'There's someone who wants to meet you. She can't come over to you, but—'

'Please, Mommy?' cried Steve and Robin.

Robert shook his head. 'Very well,' he sighed. Margaret reluctantly agreed. They stepped out of the house and followed Mordecai and Raven. As they did, the others walked out of the Epprights' house, since it was too crowded inside for everybody. The fairies had their wings covered with sweaters. Twila did not like the idea of having a sweater. 'Twila no like sweaters, Mommy,' she told Starla.

'Sweetie, we have to keep our wings covered,' Starla told her daughter as she got down and walked toward Mordecai. She told him, 'Twila wants to fly, Uncle Morcai.'

Mordecai picked her up. 'I know, sweetie,' he said, kissing her, 'but here, it's not safe for you to fly. We can't let anyone else know you're a fairy.'

'Why, Uncle Morcai?' Twila asked.

'It would be bad for fairies if any more of my people found out,' answered Mordecai, 'There are bad humans out there who want to hurt you, your mommy, your daddy, your aunt Raven. I don't want anything bad to happen to any of you.'

Steve and Robin stared at Twila. 'Is she a fairy, too, Mr. Mordecai?' asked Robin.

'Not just Twila, but also her mommy, Starla, and daddy, Roosevelt,' Mordecai answered. As Queen Cymbaline approached, he said, 'This is Cymbaline, Queen of the Fairies of Arundel Haven. She has asked to meet with you.'

'Yes,' nodded Queen Cymbaline.

Robin stared at Queen Cymbaline. 'Wow, you are the queen?' she asked.

Queen Cymbaline laughed. 'Yes, I am, little one,' she smiled.

'Why did you come to our world?' asked Robert.

'I came with Roosevelt and Starla and Lavender and Laurelin to see Lord Mordecai and Lady Raven again,' she answered, 'I have asked them to fly back to Arundel Haven for Saviour's Day.'

'Is it anything like Christmas, Queen Cymbaline?' Steve asked. 'Are there gifts?'

'Yes, little one,' Queen Cymbaline answered, 'It is a little. We do not have lights like you humans have. We light special candles as well as give gifts. I have seen the trees decorated and lit, but we have no such custom in Arundel Haven.' She looked around at the houses lit up with Christmas lights. 'I must admit,' she said, 'I am amazed at the different color lights you have. You have them every day?'

'No, your majesty,' Gabriel answered, 'Just this time of year. It's a tradition this time of year to have houses decorated with lights and ornaments. There are even lights we put on our Christmas trees.'

'A very unusual practice,' replied Queen Cymbaline.

'Indeed,' Raven agreed.

Lavender and Laurelin gazed at the lights as well. 'I'm still amazed the things you humans come up with,' Lavender said.

'It's been going on for years before I was born,' Randall replied.

Laurelin stared at Randall. 'I'm amazed how much you look like Mordecai,' she said, 'but of course, I know that you and he are brothers.'

'Do you have anybody in your life, Randall?' Lavender asked.

Randall shook his head. 'Not now,' he answered, 'Ever since Roxanne and I broke up, I've been too busy with my studies to look, well at least, not much looking.'

'Yeah, I forgot,' Tony exclaimed, 'you two broke up last year. What a shame, and she seemed like a nice girl as well.'

Randall sighed. 'Maybe it's just as well. She began to have a crush on the quarterback in college.'

'"Have a crush?"' Laurelin repeated. 'What does that mean?'

'Become interested in, fall in love with, attracted to,' Randall told the fairy.

'Tyler Banks?' Molly replied. 'She dumped you for him?'

Randall nodded sadly. 'I can't understand why she did that to me,' he said sadly, 'The only thing I have against him is his attitude.'

'Not because he's black?' Tony asked. 'Raven has taught us better now. We now go by what the person is like on the inside. If only my parents would do the same instead of judging by the color of one's skin.'

'I feel sad for Mordy and Raven about Grandma and Grandpa,' Randall sighed, 'I had almost forgotten the prejudice they hold.' To Mordecai and Raven, he asked, 'How are you two feeling?'

'It still hurts us,' Raven answered, 'Both Mordecai and I are still hurt by your grandfather's heartless words. I'm glad Mordecai never held such feelings.'

'Maybe a part of me does,' admitted Randall, 'but I fight against that part. I choose to go by what a person is like inside, not skin color, like you just said. Raven, however, I find her to have a sweet spirit about her. Mordy chose well. I'm very surprised that you accepted Raven.'

'Morcai,' burst in Twila. 'Uncle Morcai.'

Mordecai and Raven laughed as Mordecai kissed the toddler. The others laughed as well.

With a look of mock anger in his face, Randall got into the toddler's face. She giggled as she pushed him away, causing Randall, as well as the others to burst into laughter. He got close and asked, 'Do you know who I am?'

'Uncle Morcai's brother,' Twila answered.

'Do you know my name?'

Twila just giggled and hid her face. Randall tickled her in response. She burst into laughter.

'I wish to come to Arundel Haven,' Robin said.

'Robin!' cried Margaret, staring hard at Robin and apologetically at the Queen. 'I am sorry, your majesty, but—'

Queen Cymbaline stared thoughtfully at them. 'Perhaps that can be arranged,' she said, 'but first, I wish only to talk. Gabriel and Naomi have told me of your situation, how you, Robert, lost your job, and how you, Margaret, have not supported him. I don't know of the complete circumstances, nor do I seek to judge. I have no authority here, and there are a lot of things about the human world that I don't understand.'

Robert and Margaret frowned.

'It is clear that Lord Mordecai and his grandparents and Lady Raven care very much about you and your children,' the Queen continued, 'I know you will not consider my words. However, I would like to offer you an invitation to come with us to Arundel Haven for Saviour's Day.'

Steve and Robin cheered. They begged their parents, 'Please say yes! Please say yes!'

Margaret stared at Queen Cymbaline and said, 'We don't want to impose upon you.'

'You can stay with me and Roosevelt,' Starla said, 'on our farm, if you wish.'

Robert and Margaret thought for a moment. After being urged by their children, Robert asked, 'How will we get there?'

'We will fly there,' Tony answered, 'all of us.'

'On what?' Margaret asked. 'I don't think there are any flights available for Arundel Haven.'

'No, we don't fly in a plane or anything like that,' Molly replied, 'At home, we have a special water that allows us the capability of flight for a week. Only Mordy's ability to fly is permanent.'

'Wow, you can fly, Mr. Mordecai?' Steve asked in wonderment.

Mordecai nodded. 'I sure can,' he answered, 'but I take care not to fly here in the human world. I seek to keep fairies and Arundel Haven a secret.'

'Uncle Morcai fly,' Twila chimed, kissing him.

Margaret smiled. 'Oh, you are so cute,' she said.

Twila hid her face, causing both Robert and Margaret to laugh.

'We have plenty of the water at home to give to you and the others so we can fly to Arundel Haven,' Tony said, 'given to us before we returned to our home. We have enough to give to you and your family as well as Randall and my parents. We can go back home and get them and we can leave tonight.'

Margaret stared at Robert and sighed. Robert let out a sigh and said, 'Okay, your majesty, we'll take you up on your kind offer.'

The children cheered.

'I can't believe we're going to Arundel Haven,' Robin cried.

Mordecai smiled as Twila leaned her head against his shoulders.

Margaret found herself smiling. 'I can see that you're no stranger to children, Mordecai,' she said.

'No,' Twila corrected, 'Uncle Morcai.'

Both Robert and Margaret laughed.

It was at that moment when Cece, Tiffany, and Sharon arrived and saw the gathering. They slipped out of the car and saw that Queen Cymbaline and her party were in the yard. There were embraces of greetings and laughter. Cece saw Twila and tickled her. 'No,' giggled Twila. 'No tickle me!'

Cece embraced Queen Cymbaline as well as Lavender and Laurelin. 'I'm surprised to see you here, your majesty,' Cece said, 'How long have you been here?'

'They arrived minutes after you had left to pick up Mordy,' Tony answered, 'We have been invited by the Queen to Arundel Haven, all of us, to celebrate Saviour's Day.' To Randall he said, 'You will see Mordy and Raven's home in Arundel Haven.'

'Will you have enough water for everybody, Dad?' Mordecai asked.

'We have brought some extra vials, if need be,' Roosevelt answered, 'enough for all those who cannot fly.'

'I so look forward to returning back to Arundel Haven,' chimed Sharon excitedly.

'It's best if you bring some warm clothes,' Laurelin told them, 'It's snowing now back home. I hate flying in the snow.'

'I no like it either, Laury,' Twila said.

'Your aunt Raven doesn't either,' frowned Raven.

'Raven and I can show you our home,' Mordecai told Randall, Gabriel, and Naomi. 'It's small, but it's cozy. We can have you two stay with us, Grandmom and Granddad since you allowed us to stay with you. It's the least we can do.'

'We will take you up on your kind offer, Mordecai,' smiled Gabriel.

It was about midnight when they left for Arundel Haven, arriving hours later. The snow was falling at a steady pace. Mordecai and Raven immediately headed for their cottage, joined by Twila, Gabriel, Naomi, and Randall. They looked around in amazement at the city. Roosevelt and Starla led the Thompsons to their farm, but Steve and Robin wanted to see where Mordecai and Raven lived. At the cottage, Mordecai got a fire going in the fireplace. Raven showed the others around. 'You can take the master bedroom,' Mordecai told his grandparents.

'No, we couldn't,' Gabriel replied, 'This is your house.'

'We insist,' Raven said, 'Mordecai and I will take my old room and if you wish to stay here, Randall, you can take Starla's old room.'

Gabriel and Naomi conceded to their hosts' request. Raven brewed some tea while they talked. 'We'll rest a bit before we take you to the castle,' Mordecai said, 'Raven and I will fix dinner later. We can get some food from the market here.'

'I'm not used to being in a place without electricity,' Randall said.

'It was tough the first time I came here after I was released from prison,' Mordecai replied as Twila got comfortable in his arms, 'but I love the simplicity of life here. It did take some time to get used to, but I kind of like it.'

Randall stared at Twila in Mordecai's arms. 'This is amazing, seeing how much Twila is attached to you,' he laughed softly, 'It would be interesting to see what your children would be like, the child of a human and a fairy.'

'Our child would be the first of such a union,' Raven said, 'At least Twila will be good practice for us both.'

'You having a baby, Aunt Raven,' Twila asked, 'like Mommy?'

'Not yet,' Raven giggled to the toddler, 'but I will someday. My baby will be your cousin.'

'Mommy give me a brother,' said Twila, her eyes shining.

'How far along is Starla?' Randall asked.

'About five months,' Raven answered, 'Twila, as you can see, thinks the child may be a boy.' She giggled. 'I think Starla believes the same thing as well.'

'We shall see, I guess,' replied Mordecai.

Raven turned to Mordecai. 'If I was pregnant right now,' she said, 'Which do you hope we have first, a boy or a girl?'

Mordecai did not answer right away, thinking about the question. Randall stared at his younger brother and asked, 'Well, what do you think?'

Mordecai shook his head. 'I have not thought about that before,' he said, 'I'm not sure really, so long as the child is healthy. That child will have both parents who love them and who love each other as well.'

'Aunt Raven have a girl,' chimed in Twila.

They all laughed as Mordecai tickled the toddler.

Later, they headed to the castle where Queen Cymbaline and Prince Avondale awaited them. The prince welcomed both Mordecai and Raven with an embrace. Mordecai stared at Prince Avondale. 'I am happy to see you again, dear brother,' the prince said, 'both you and Lady Raven. Welcome back to Arundel Haven!'

'Thank you, your highness,' Mordecai replied. He pointed as his grandparents and his brother Randall. 'These are my grandparents, Gabriel and Naomi Eppright, my mother's parents,' he told Prince Avondale. 'This is my older brother, Randall.'

Randall bowed before him. Prince Avondale smiled. 'So, you are the brother of Lord Mordecai I hear,' he said.

'I am honored to be acknowledged by you and your sister, your highness,' replied Randall.

'And who are these little ones?' Prince Avondale asked.

'These are guests of the house of Jefferson,' Queen Cymbaline answered, 'I have given their family leave to spend Saviour's Day here with us. Their parents, as well as the parents of Lord Mordecai and Lady Cece, are at Roosevelt's farm.'

Steve and Robin looked at Prince Avondale with wonder. The children bowed in respect before him. The prince smiled. 'Welcome to Arundel Haven, young ones,' he said.

Queen Cymbaline stood by Mordecai's grandparents. She turned to her brother and said, 'The grandparents of Lord Mordecai have also been invited here to spend Saviour's Day with us.'

Gabriel and Naomi bowed low.

Prince Avondale forbade them. 'You do not need to bow,' he said, 'We are brethren here. Besides, you are honored guests being the grandparents of our Lord Mordecai and Lady Cece. My sister has told me about you, how God had used you both to lead Lord Mordecai to Christ.'

'We are honored to meet you and to be here, brother,' replied Gabriel as the prince embraced them both. 'Indeed, Mordecai has told us so much about you, as did your sister.'

'Where are you staying?' Prince Avondale asked.

'We are staying with our grandson and his wife,' Naomi answered.

Queen Cymbaline turned toward Mordecai. 'By your leave, Lord Mordecai,' she said. 'I would like for your grandparents to stay in the castle with us, and we wish for you two, as well as your brother to stay here, too.'

Mordecai nodded. 'In my eyes, they deserve to be honored,' he said humbly, 'They have been a blessing in my life. I humbly grant it, and we accept your invitation.'

Taris showed the Epprights to their chambers. As he led them, Naomi said, 'My grandson told me how you and he became friends while in prison.'

Taris nodded. 'We became friends shortly after his incarceration,' he said, 'He acted with honor and respect and quickly earned my respect and friendship in the process. He never behaved unbecomingly but was humble and contrite, even when he was first brought here. Of course, God had used Twila to change our hearts.'

Both Gabriel and Naomi laughed. 'She is a blessed little girl,' Naomi replied, 'Having seen her for myself, we know why. She is so attached to my grandson.'

'She had accepted him from the start,' Taris said, 'At first, I, like Starla, thought Mordecai would do her harm, but when I saw him weep and Twila wiping the tears from his eyes, my heart toward him changed as well, and he has shown himself to be a good, faithful friend.'

Later, Mordecai and Raven led them to where Roosevelt and Starla stayed. Raven frowned as they flew. 'You okay, Raven?' asked Naomi.

'Aunt Raven no like the cold,' said Twila. 'Twila no like the cold.'

Mordecai nodded, kissing the toddler. 'I know, sweetie,' he said, 'Once we are inside Mommy and Daddy's house, we'll be warm. Your daddy should have the fire going.'

'I'm kind of used to it,' Randall replied, 'It does snow from time to time in Baton Rouge. I'm thinking about just moving there, though it would be far away from the family.'

'You like Baton Rouge that much?' asked Mordecai.

'Oh, yes,' Randall answered, 'I may wind up getting a job on campus after I graduate. I still have another year to go, so I have time to think about it.'

'It took me some time to get used to being in Orlando,' Raven said, 'I still miss Arundel Haven, but I wanted to be with Mordecai. He said he wanted to finish his education at Oak Ridge.'

'What then, Mordy?' Randall asked his brother.

'I'm not sure,' Mordecai replied, 'Raven and I may wind up alternating between Orlando and Arundel Haven. I would still have to see.'

'Wouldn't that be hard, Mr. Mordecai?' asked Steve.

Mordecai nodded. 'Yes, it would be. What's harder is not knowing for sure about Dr. Von Braun, if he had survived the crash at the battle of Nebechadrezzar Valley or not. President Farouk did, so I think it's a safe bet to say that Dr. Von Braun did survive.'

When they arrived at the farm, they entered the house. Mordecai's parents and the Thompsons were sitting down with Starla and Roosevelt. Raven sighed. 'I am glad to get out of the cold,' she said, shivering.

'Come on, Raven,' chuckled Randall. 'It wasn't that bad.'

Raven turned toward Randall. 'You try being a fairy and having to fly in the snow,' she told him, 'You try having the snow fall on your wings. You have it made not having to worry about having wings in the wintertime.'

Mordecai chucked to himself. 'Some things never change,' he said, 'Better watch yourself, Randy! I have a wife now, and we will stick up for each other!'

Cece laughed. Raven kissed Mordecai on the lips.

'Come on, Mordy, Raven,' Randall said, 'you know I meant her no harm.'

Tony and Molly found it amusing. 'You are right, Mordy,' laughed Tony. 'Some things never do change.'

Mordecai's parents gave up their seat so that his grandparents could sit down, though at first, they refused. 'Please, Dad,' Molly begged him.

Finally, Gabriel and Naomi agreed as they sat down. Mordecai and Raven sat on a large rug on the floor. 'I am sorry,' Roosevelt said. 'I never expected to have so many visitors here.'

'That is okay, Roosevelt,' Tony replied, 'We are still grateful to be your guests.'

Twila sat down upon Mordecai's lap as Raven kissed him. The fairy toddler pushed her aunt away. 'Aunt Raven no kiss Uncle Morcai,' she said.

The others laughed.

'And why not, little girl?' retorted Raven.

Twila giggled.

Both Mordecai and Raven tickled her in response.

'What you two have to deal with when you start having children,' Starla told the young couple as Twila laughed.

Mordecai and Raven laughed. Starla brought to them cups of hot tea for the newcomers as some of them sat down. 'Don't you put up a tree on Christmas?' Steve asked.

Starla looked questionably at the boy. 'Christmas?'

'They celebrate Saviour's Day here, Steve,' Mordecai explained, 'It is almost like our Christmas, only they don't put up trees. I do love the lights this time of year.' He thought for a moment. 'I wonder if we put candles in lamps of different colors, like the lights we have back home? I wonder if that is doable?'

'I think I know what you mean, Mordecai,' Raven said, 'Light candles and have it surrounded by glass of different colors.'

'Yes,' Mordecai nodded, 'We are thinking alike, Raven.'

'Hey, baby,' Raven replied, kissing him, 'I am your wife.'

'True,' smiled Mordecai, 'Smart and beautiful.'

Starla laughed. Twila pushed Raven away from Mordecai. 'Twila,' cried Raven.

The others laughed as she said, 'Aunt Raven no kiss Uncle Morcai!'

Raven tickled Twila. 'Stop,' the toddler cried amid her laughter.

That night, Steve and Robin were outside the house building a snowman. It was the first time in their lives they had experienced snow. Mordecai and Raven, along with his family, had left just before sundown for the castle. Twila, along with her mother, were outside as well. Twila watched as the two siblings built a snowman. 'What is that?' Twila asked them.

'A snowman,' Robin answered, 'I have always dreamed of building one. I can't believe I am actually doing it.'

'Snowman,' Twila repeated.

'Yes, Twila,' Steve said, 'We have never had an opportunity to build a snowman before.'

'This is new to me,' said Starla. 'I have never heard of building a snowman before.'

'It's fun, Miss Starla,' Robin told her, 'only it doesn't snow where we live. I have always seen snow on TV, but never experienced it before. I am glad it's snowing.'

'Twila no like snow,' said Twila.

'Why not, Twila?' Robin asked.

'It's hard for fairies to fly in the snow,' Starla explained, 'but we can fly in it with difficulty, as you can see.'

Twila walked over to the snowman while the two human siblings were building it. 'Twila help,' she insisted. She patted the large snowball on the bottom.

Steve and Robin smiled.

In the castle, Mordecai and Raven were in their chambers. They had wanted to stay in their cottage, but they had agreed at the Queen's request to stay in the castle instead. They had checked on Mordecai's parents and grandparents before they retired for the night. They were sitting down on the bed they were sleeping in. 'I am glad we are back in Arundel Haven,' she said.

'So am I,' Mordecai nodded, 'I know you are happy to be back here. I noticed you were becoming homesick.'

'True,' Raven replied, 'but there is nowhere I would rather be than with you.' She caressed his face. 'I was thinking about what Twila had said earlier today when we were in the cottage.'

'What did she say?'

'Remember when she said that I was having a girl?'

Mordecai nodded.

'I also thought about what you said,' said Raven, 'that you didn't care if our first child was a boy or girl as long as the child is healthy.'

'Did I say anything wrong?' asked Mordecai.

'No, no,' Raven said quickly, 'I'm not saying that you did. I was just thinking, that's all.'

'About what?'

Raven took Mordecai's hands and stared into his eyes. 'Mordecai, I love you with all my heart, and I bless the day God brought us together.'

'As do I, Raven,' Mordecai smiled lovingly.

'I don't know if I am pregnant or not, and I think it is too soon for me to tell,' Raven started, 'but… but…'

Mordecai stared at Raven. 'Raven?'

Raven squeezed his hands. 'I want to have a baby, Mordecai,' she told him. 'I feel I am ready to become a mother. I don't know how you feel, but—'

'I know there is that possibility,' Mordecai said, 'I will do my best to make you happy, to please you, and for you to conceive. I am with you on this, Raven.'

Raven embraced and kissed her husband. 'I am so happy to hear that, Mordecai,' she exclaimed, kissing him again. 'Our child will be so beautiful!'

'Just like the mother.' Mordecai smiled, kissing her. Raven leaned her head upon his shoulder as she kissed him. 'I love you, dear Mordecai.'

'I love you too, my sweet Raven,' Mordecai replied. They laid back on the bed as they remained in a loving, warm embrace and a loving kiss.

The night drew on.

The snow continued to fall the next day. Mordecai and Raven flew over to Roosevelt's farm. There, they were building snowmen with Steve and Robin. 'I have never built a snowman before,' Mordecai told Raven, 'I have seen it, but since it practically never snows where we live, it is impossible to do so.'

'It's all new to me, too,' replied Raven, 'I have never seen a such a thing in my life. Why do they build a snowman?'

'I guess because it's fun,' replied Mordecai.

'It is, Mr. Mordecai,' Steve told him, working on the bottom of the snowman he and Robin were building. Mordecai and Raven were working on the bottom part of theirs. 'I have to admit,' Raven said, 'it is kind of fun. This is new to us fairies.'

At that moment, Twila flew toward them. She flew into the arms of Mordecai, kissing him on the cheeks and hugging his neck. 'Can Twila help, Uncle Morcai?' she asked.

Mordecai nodded as he kissed her. 'Of course you can, Twila,' he laughed.

Raven giggled. 'Can you build a snowman, Twila?' she asked.

'Yes, Aunt Raven,' Twila answered, 'Steve and Robin show Twila. Twila show Uncle Morcai and Aunt Raven.'

Mordecai laughed. 'Good deal, sweetie.'

Starla and Roosevelt watched as Mordecai, Raven and Twila built snowmen along with Steve and Robin. Starla found herself smiling. 'I must admit, it looks like fun.'

Roosevelt nodded. 'This is all new to me,' he said, 'It must be a human thing to build a man made of snow. I have never heard of fairies building something like this before in the snow.'

Suddenly, Robin threw herself to the ground as she laughed, moving her arms and legs against the snow.

'What are you doing?' Starla asked, alarmed.

'Making a snow angel,' Robin answered as Steve did the same.

Twila fell on her back in the snow and did the same thing as she giggled. Mordecai looked at her and laughed. 'You're really enjoying this, aren't you, little fairy girl?'

'Look, Uncle Morcai,' Twila chimed, 'Twila make a snow angel, too!'

Roosevelt and Starla laughed. 'I have never seen Twila have so much fun in the snow,' Roosevelt said, 'It is good to see she is having a good time.'

'Especially since her uncle Morcai is with her,' laughed Starla, 'She loves her uncle!'

'Yes, Mommy,' chimed Twila, rising up from the snow. She flittered her wings to remove the excess snow. 'I having fun, Mommy!'

Starla giggled. 'Mommy can see that, dear.'

From the doorway, Robert and Margaret watched as their children built a snowman. To their surprise, they saw Mordecai and Raven doing the same thing, joined by Twila, who was helping her uncle and aunt. They smiled when they saw the trio. Robert laughed. 'It's so cute the way Twila is helping,' he said.

Margaret laughed. 'I can't believe that Steve and Robin are having so much fun in the snow.'

Robert sighed. 'This is my favorite time of the year. I'm only sorry it won't be as great a Christmas as I had hoped.'

Margaret frowned at Robert. 'I'm very disappointed that you haven't found a good job by now,' she said in a voice that showed her displeasure, 'Maybe if you would have found something—'

'Do you think I haven't been trying?' retorted Robert irritably, 'I was hoping to have found something by now, but with this bad economy and the way Faroukcare—'

'Is that an excuse?' Margaret shot back.

'Do you know how hard it is to find a good job these days?' snapped back Robert, 'I'm not using that as an excuse, but it hasn't been from lack of trying! I don't like this any more than you do!'

'You're right, I don't!' retorted Margaret, 'Very soon your unemployment benefits are going to run out, and where will we be then? What will we do then? No job, no money, no way to pay the bills!'

'You don't think I know that already, Margaret?' shot back Robert.

At that moment, Mordecai and Raven stared back toward Robert and Margaret as they continued to argue. Twila looked at them as well. 'Why they argue, Uncle Morcai?' she asked.

Mordecai shook his head sadly. 'It's very difficult for you to understand, Twila,' he sighed.

Raven sighed.

Steve and Robin stopped and looked back. To their dismay, they saw that their parents were having another one of their arguments. Without a word, they took to the air and flew away from the farm as Roosevelt and Starla looked back. 'What's going on with them?' asked Roosevelt.

Mordecai sighed. 'Not again,' he groaned. He looked toward the other snowman and found that Steve and Robin were gone. 'Steve! Robin!' he cried.

Raven looked toward where Mordecai was looking. 'Where'd they go?' she cried.

'Where Steve and Robin, Uncle Morcai?' asked Twila.

'They're upset about their parents' arguments,' answered Mordecai, 'They must have overheard and gotten upset! Can you fly, Raven?'

'I should be able to, baby,' answered Raven, flittering her wings.

Margaret happened to glance toward where Steve and Robin had been and found them gone. She cried out, 'My babies! Steve and Robin!'

Robert stared in the direction of where his children were. 'Where'd they go?' he cried. They ran toward the group. 'Why did they run off like that?'

'Because of your arguing,' Mordecai answered, 'Don't you understand? Your constant arguing has affected them in such an adverse way. They hate it when you two argue!'

'Then what are we supposed to do about this situation?' retorted Robert.

'For one thing,' Raven started, 'stop arguing and come to some kind of agreement, be supportive of each other for their sake! They love you two very much, but they hate it when you two argue.'

'For now,' Mordecai said, 'we've got to find them! I wonder which way they could have gone?'

'That way, Uncle Morcai,' said Twila, pointing in the direction of the woods.

'Raven and I will take that direction then,' Mordecai said, 'I'm sure they couldn't have gotten far.' He and Raven took to the air. Twila was in Mordecai's arms as they took off.

Roosevelt and Starla took to the air as well. As they did, the snow began to fall harder, and the winds began to pick up. Roosevelt sighed. 'Not good,' he said, 'It's going to make our search for the kids that much harder.'

'Steve! Robin!' cried Margaret.

'I think it's best you stay here,' Roosevelt told them. 'You do not know Arundel Haven like we do. You would get lost, and who knows what would happen to you.'

'We can't,' Robert objected, 'They are our children. We must find them no matter what!'

'I understand,' replied Roosevelt, 'You will have to stay with us, though. Mordecai and Raven are fine. Hopefully, one of us will find the kids.'

Starla lowered herself to the ground as the winds picked up and the snow fell down harder. 'Are you okay, Starla?' asked Roosevelt.

'We can't fly in the snow,' Starla told him, 'The wind's too rough for me to remain in the air. We'll have to stay on foot until the winds die down.'

Without another word, Roosevelt and Starla headed in the direction that Mordecai and Raven had gone, followed by Robert and Margaret, who were worried about their children.

As the winds picked up and the snow fell harder, Steve and Robin, still grieved by the argument that their parents had, continued onward. Further, they headed into the woods, running away from the direction of the farm of Roosevelt and Starla. They stopped underneath a tree and huddled together to keep each other warm. 'Why do Mommy and Daddy argue so much?' wept Robin.

Steve shook his head. 'I wish I knew,' he said sadly as the snow continued to fall.

'What will we do now?' Robin asked. 'I don't want to stay with Mommy and Daddy who are always arguing!'

'I don't like it either,' replied Steve, 'It's driving me crazy every time they argue! I don't hear Mr. Mordecai and Miss Raven arguing nor Mr. Mordecai's grandparents. Why can't Mom and Dad be like them?'

They sat down against the tree as they continued to try and keep warm.

Mordecai and Raven continued to search for Steve and Robin. They were now on foot since the winds had picked up, preventing them from taking to the air. Twila was in Mordecai's arms trying to keep warm. 'I no like it Steve and Robin run away, Uncle Morcai,' the toddler told him.

'I know, sweetie,' sighed Mordecai, kissing his fairy niece, 'I don't like it either.'

'Why they run away, Uncle Morcai?' asked Twila, 'They no like Twila?'

'It's not you, sweetie,' Raven told her niece, 'It's their mommy and daddy. They argue and fuss at each other, which makes them so sad.'

'I no like their mommy and daddy to fight,' said Twila sadly. 'I no like Steve and Robin to run away.'

'We'll find them, Twila,' Mordecai said, kissing her on the forehead.

Twila huddled as close to her uncle as she could, trying to keep warm. 'Twila cold,' she said.

'I know, sweetheart,' Mordecai said, holding the toddler closer to him.

'Where could they have gone?' asked Raven, 'I wonder if they tried to take to the air? It's too rough for me to fly.'

'I will stay with you,' said Mordecai, 'I don't want to lose you.'

They called out the names of the children as they made their way through the snow, making it harder for them to move, being driven back by the winds. 'It's as if Shadowfire is still alive and afflicting us,' cried Raven.

'I am thankful he is dead,' replied Mordecai, 'but I see what you mean. The storm he had summoned was worse than this. We can't place the blame on the dragon.'

'Where are they?' asked Raven as she called out the names of the children.

It was now an hour before sunset. The search continued for the children. As Roosevelt, Starla, Robert, and Margaret called out the names of the children, Margaret stared sadly at her husband. 'I still don't understand why they would run away,' she said.

Robert sighed. 'I do,' he said, hanging his head, 'Ever since I lost my job, we've not been on agreeable terms, to say the least. I can remember when we were having dinner at the grandparents of Mordecai that Raven told us they have been upset by our arguments. What happened to us?'

Margaret sighed. 'We have somehow drifted apart. I am still angry about how you lost your job.'

'But it wasn't my fault,' replied Robert, 'I can't help it that I was one of the ones they laid off.'

Margaret sighed, hanging her head. 'Things for us have been worse since you lost your job,' she said, 'Raven was right, though. Our arguments are tearing this family apart.' Tears welled up in her eyes. 'Now I understand why they ran away! I would do anything to see them back home safe with us again!' She stopped. 'I'm sorry, Robert!' She burst into tears as she fell into her husband's arms.

Robert wrapped his arms around her. 'Me too,' he nodded.

'I know I should have been more supportive of you rather than critical,' said Margaret, 'I just want to see my babies back safe with us again!'

'We will find them, Margaret,' Robert assured her, 'both Steve and Robin.'

'I pray to God so,' wept Margaret.

Steve and Robin continued to huddle close together as the snow continued to fall. They were feeling hungry as well but were frightened to go back to the farm and their arguing parents, yet they thought about going back. 'What do we do?' Robin asked her older brother. 'I don't want to hear Mommy and Daddy arguing again.'

'What choice do we have?' Steve asked, 'We have to go back, Robin. We have no way of getting food, and we are sure to freeze to death if we remain out here.'

'But which way back to the farm?' asked Robin.

Steve stood up. 'I don't know,' he said, looking around, 'I don't remember which way we came.'

'We're lost?'

Steve nodded.

'Do you think Mommy and Daddy are looking for us?' asked Robin.

'I hope so,' replied Steve, 'I wish we could stay in Arundel Haven instead of returning home, but I don't think Queen Cymbaline would allow us to remain.'

'I don't want to go back to Mommy and Daddy and all their arguing,' Robin wept, 'I hate it when they keep arguing!'

Steve sat back down as he and Robin continued to huddle close together. It wasn't very long when they saw something moving in the distance. Steve sat up. 'What is it, Steve?' Robin asked.

'I see something, but I can't tell with all the snow falling,' Steve replied.

The figure drew closer, though it was difficult for Steve to see.

'Mr. Mordecai? Miss Raven?' Steve cried.

The figure drew closer, but Steve could tell it was neither Mordecai, Raven, nor their parents. Steve gasped. He saw a white lion with a heavy white mane approaching them. His mane fluttered with the wind as he approached. Both children screamed, huddling up to each other for protection.

The lion made no sudden moves as he walked closer toward the children in a nonchalant manner, making no noise. He merely stared at the children. He cautiously moved slowly toward them.

'Go away!' cried Robin.

The lion reached them, getting close enough to sniff them. Both children were too frightened to move, in fear that he would devour them. But the lion made no such move. He merely sniffed them again.

'Please leave us alone,' wept Robin, 'We're lost and hungry and ran away from our Mommy and Daddy because they argue too much, and it frightens us!'

'Please don't eat us,' begged Steve.

The lion closed his eyes and bowed his head as if in sadness.

Almost unwittingly, Robin disengaged from her brother's arms and reached her hand out to touch the nose of the lion. As she touched it, the lion merely looked at the children and rubbed affectionately against the young girl's arm. Steve and Robin realized that somehow, the lion had no intentions of devouring them or doing them any kind of harm. Steve stood up as the lion allowed the boy to touch his face. 'I don't think he's going to hurt us,' Robin said quietly.

The lion reached out his paw and gently touched the face of the girl, keeping his claws sheathed.

'I wish you could help us,' Steve told the lion.

The lion seemed to nod in affirmation, as if he understood.

'Are our parents or anybody else looking for us?' Robin asked.

The lion nodded in affirmation. He backed up, gave out a soft roar, then headed back into the woods. 'Where is he going?' Robin asked.

'I don't know,' Steve replied, perplexed.

Mordecai and Raven continued to search. Twila held Mordecai close as she tried to keep warm. She missed Steve and Robin and was just as worried about them as the others. They continued to call out the names of the children as the snow continued to fall. The wind was still blowing as they made their way through the woods.

'Where Steve and Robin?' asked Twila, worried about them.

'Do you hear anything besides the wind, Mordecai?' asked Raven, trying to keep herself warm.

Mordecai paused and called out the children's names again. 'Not so far,' said Mordecai disappointedly, 'I am beginning to become very discouraged. I hope there are others searching for them as well.'

'I am sure my sister, Roosevelt, and their parents are doing so as well,' Raven replied, 'I am sure we are not the only ones. I only wish we could take to the air, but the wind doesn't seem to be dying down at all.'

'I could,' Mordecai said, 'but it would not be a good idea for us to be separate, the way this weather is. I am beginning to feel a little numb from the cold.'

'So am I,' Raven replied. 'How is Twila?'

'Twila very cold, Aunt Raven,' Twila told them, holding Mordecai closer, her teeth chattering, 'but Twila want to find Steve and Robin.'

'Don't worry, little Twila,' Mordecai told her, 'We'll find them.

We're not giving up until we find them.'

At that moment, Mordecai caught a glimpse of something in the distance amid the flurries of snow. He noticed a figure was approaching them. Raven caught a glimpse of it too. 'It doesn't look like Steve or Robin,' the black fairy said.

'No,' replied Mordecai, 'I wish I could tell what it is, though. I was hoping it would be the children.'

They saw a white lion approaching them, stopping just about fifty meters in front of them. Raven gasped. Only Twila did not appear to be startled or frightened. Mordecai stepped backwards as the lion approached them. 'I didn't know there were lions in Arundel Haven,' he told Raven.

'To my knowledge, no,' replied Raven, drawing close to him.

The lion approached without a growl or any kind of noise.

Suddenly, Mordecai stopped. The lion continued to approach in a non-threatening manner. Mordecai stared closely at the lion. 'Lion no hurt us, Uncle Morcai,' Twila told him.

Mordecai felt it in his spirit that Twila had spoken the truth. Raven stared at him. 'Mordecai, what are you doing?' she cried.

'Twila's right,' Mordecai said, slowly approaching the lion.

The lion bowed his head briefly.

Twila got down from Mordecai's arms and flew toward the lion. He scooped the toddler gently in his paws and allowed her to get cozy and warm herself against his warm coat. Raven stood in amazement. 'Steve and Robin!' she cried. 'We have to find them!'

The lion glanced at them and pointed his right forepaw in the direction he came from.

'Have you found them?' Mordecai asked. 'Do you know where they are?'

The lion nodded his head.

'Can you take us to them?' asked Raven.

The lion gave out a soft roar, allowing Mordecai to take Twila, and indicated to them that he wanted them to follow him.

Mordecai nodded, holding Twila close to him again. The lion led the way, making sure Mordecai and Raven were following him.

It wasn't long until the lion led Mordecai and Raven to where Steve and Robin were. They were surprised to see the lion returning with the young couple. Twila flew out of Mordecai's arms and hugged both children. 'Steve! Robin!' Twila cried, 'Twila happy see you!'

Steve and Robin stared in amazement at the lion and the young couple. 'We are so glad you could find us,' Steve said.

'Can you move?' asked Raven.

'I feel too cold to move,' Robin answered, shivering, 'Are Mommy and Daddy searching for us?'

The lion nodded, then turned away from them, giving out a mighty roar. At first, the children were frightened.

'No worry,' Twila said. 'The lion helping.'

Mordecai stared at the lion. He pointed his paw at the children, indicating that he would bear both Steve and Robin.

Mordecai understood. He picked up Steve and Robin and placed them on the back of the lion. 'We need to find the others,' Mordecai said.

The lion grunted, indicating that he wanted them to follow him. Mordecai nodded as he carried Twila in his arms.

It wasn't long until the lion led them to the others, who were resting before they continued their search. At first, they were frightened of the lion but were astonished to see Steve and Robin riding him, as well as Mordecai, Raven, and Twila behind them.

Robert and Margaret picked up their children from the back of the lion, hugging and kissing their children, weeping. 'We are so happy you are safe,' wept Margaret, 'We were so worried about you!'

'We were scared, Mommy,' wept Robin, 'not from the lion, but—'

'I know now, sweetie,' wept Margaret, 'Both your father and I know now. We are so sorry!'

'We're just thankful the both of you are all right,' Robert replied, tears in his eyes. He knelt by the lion and said, 'Thank you! Thank you for finding our children.'

The lion purred in response.

Both Steve and Robin embraced the lion, who held them gently with his paws. He seemed to smile as he gazed at them.

Mordecai marked this and smiled.

They returned to the farm where Steve and Robin sat near the fire as the snow continued to fall outside. Starla made them some broth for them to drink. Twila was still in Mordecai's arms, hugging and kissing him on the cheeks. 'You feeling better, sweetie?' Mordecai asked her.

'Twila feel better, Uncle Morcai,' Twila answered, 'Twila still cold, but Twila happy now that we found Steve and Robin.'

'So am I, Twila,' Raven replied.

Robert and Margaret sat down next to their children. Steve looked at his father and said, 'We ran away—'

'Your mother and I know why you two ran away,' Robert replied softly, 'We both owe you two an apology. We allowed the situation to make us forget that we do love each other. We're sorry, children.'

Robert embraced Steve while Margaret embraced Robin as the four of them wept. 'We're so sorry, Robin, Steve, the both of us!' she said amid her tears. 'Your mommy and daddy do love you very much!'

'We love you too,' Robin replied amid her tears.

Mordecai and Raven smiled. They were happy it was all over, and that Steve and Robin were safe again. They were also happy that Robert and Margaret had put away their quarrels for the sake of their children.

They hoped and prayed for the best for them.

On the night before Saviour's Day, at Raven's suggestion, the fairies of Arundel Haven had lit candles and put them in lanterns with different colors. Mordecai and his family also participated as well. He saw the many different colored lanterns and said, 'It is almost like the Christmas lights we have at home. It's beautiful!'

'I like it too, Uncle Morcai,' Twila chimed, smiling.

They gathered at the castle where Queen Cymbaline and Prince Avondale each had a lantern as well, the Queen with a blue and the Prince with a red. There were lanterns of different colors and different shades of red, blue, green, violet, orange, yellow.

Mordecai and his family stood with the royal siblings. Queen Cymbaline sang a song before the fairies that had gathered, singing a song of praise and thanksgiving unto the LORD.

After she had sung, she spoke to the fairies. 'Fairies of Arundel Haven,' she told them. 'This Saviour's Day Eve is very special! Two months ago, God had given to us a great deliverance when He brought into our lives His servant, Lord Mordecai, and used him and Lady Raven to strike down the dragon, Shadowfire, according to the word He had spoken unto my foremother, Queen Hephzibah. Although this is not the exact day or season that Jesus came down in the form of His creation, we choose this day to celebrate the greatest gift that could ever be given: Himself, of eternal life through His blood, which He sacrificed on Calvary. It is my honor and pleasure to welcome to this Saviour's Day the young man whom God used to deliver us from the claws of the dragon, Lord Mordecai of the House of Jefferson.' The crowd cheered as Mordecai bowed.

Queen Cymbaline introduced the crowd to Mordecai's family, mentioning each by name. She then sang a hymn of praise and thanksgiving, lifting and magnifying the LORD.

In the morning, though the snow was falling, the fairies gathered again around the castle. There, Queen Cymbaline read to them from the second chapter of the Gospel of Luke beginning with the fourth verse: *And Joseph also went up from Galilee, out of the city of Nazareth, into Judaea, unto the city of David, which is called Bethlehem (because he was of the house and lineage of David): to be taxed with Mary, his espoused wife, being great with child. And so it was, that, while they were there, the days were accomplished that she should be delivered. And she brought forth her firstborn son, and wrapped him in swaddling clothes, and she laid him in a manger, because there was no room for them in the inn.*

'And they were in the same country as shepherds abiding in the field, keeping watch over their flock by night. And lo, the angel of the Lord came upon them, and the glory of the Lord shone round about them: and they were sore afraid. And the angel said unto them, Fear not: for I bring you good tidings of great joy, which shall be to all people. For unto you is born this day in the city of David, a Saviour, which is Christ, the Lord. And this shall be a sign unto you; Ye shall find the babe wrapped in swaddling clothes, lying in a manger. And suddenly, there was with the angel a multitude of the heavenly host praising God and saying, Glory to God in the highest and on Earth, peace and good will toward men.

'And it came to pass, as the angels were gone away from them into heaven, the shepherds said one to another, let us now go even unto Bethlehem, and see this thing which is come to pass, which the Lord hath made known unto us. And they came with haste, and found Mary, and Joseph, and the babe lying in the manger. And when they had seen it, they made known abroad the saying, which was told them concerning this child. And all they who heard it wondered at those things, which were told them by the shepherds. But Mary kept all these things and pondered them in her heart. And the shepherds returned, glorifying, and praising God for all the things they had heard and seen, as it was told unto them.

'The second chapter of the Gospel of Matthew tells of the caravan of wise men who came from the east, following a star when Jesus was born. When they arrived at the palace where King Herod lived, they inquired of him, "Where is he that is born King of the Jews?" Now when Jesus was born in Bethlehem of Judea in the days of Herod the king, behold, there came wise men from the east to Jerusalem, saying, Where is he that is born King of the Jews? For we have seen his star in the east and have come to worship him. When Herod the king had heard these things, he was troubled, and all Jerusalem with him. And when he had gathered all the chief priests and scribes of the people together, he demanded of them where Christ should be born. And they said unto him, In Bethlehem of Judaea: for thus, it is written by the prophet, And thou Bethlehem, in the land of Juda, art not the least among the princes of Juda: for out of thee shall come a Governor,

'Three gifts, in particular the wise men, gave unto Jesus on that day: gold, which symbolizes His royalty; frankincense, that He is God Almighty; and myrrh for His burial, for He would be sacrificed and have His pure holy blood shed for our sins, but He would show that not even death could hold Him. We celebrate this day for the ultimate gift He has given us: Himself, His love, the gift of eternal life to all those who would receive it. As for me and my house, we will serve our Lord Jesus Christ, as do Lord Mordecai and his house.'

She then sang a hymn of praise, of thanksgiving and of love for the Lord Jesus Christ.

Afterwards, gifts were given among the people and the royal house. There was great rejoicing throughout the kingdom. Randall looked out at the crowd. 'Looks like Baton Rouge on gameday,' he said, 'before we play one of our rivals.'

'Why do you say that?' Mordecai asked.

'It almost like tailgating before a game,' Randall answered.

'What is tailgating?' asked Queen Cymbaline.

'It's a human thing,' Randall told the Queen. 'Before we play a football game, there is a large gathering to barbecue things like hot dogs, hamburgers, chicken, steak.'

'But we are celebrating something greater,' Mordecai replied, 'which I hope and pray you would understand.'

Even though the snow continued to fall, it did not faze the celebration, the joy felt by all those within the fairy kingdom. When Mordecai and his party left, they found it hard to leave, especially Twila, who hated to be apart from her uncle and from Steve and Robin.

One good thing came out of the time there: Robert and Margaret had reconciled, for the sake of each other and for their children. They knew that family was the best gift of them all outside of our Saviour.

www.ingramcontent.com/pod-product-compliance
Lightning Source LLC
Chambersburg PA
CBHW062059290726
48975CB00001B/43